Runestone

Other Bantam Books by Don Coldsmith

Runestone

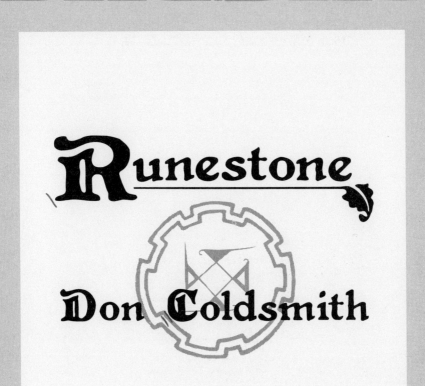

Don Coldsmith

BANTAM BOOKS

New York Toronto
London Sydney Auckland

RUNESTONE

A Bantam Book / March 1995

Library of Congress Cataloging-in-Publication Data

Coldsmith, Don, 1926-
    Runestone / Don Coldsmith.
        p.   cm.
    ISBN 0-553-09643-5
        1. America—Discovery and exploration—Norse—Fiction.   2. Indians of North
America—First contact with Europeans—Fiction.   3. Explorers—America—
Fiction.   4. Northmen—America—Fiction.
    I. Title.
PS3553.O445R8   1995
813'.54—dc20

                                                                94-12779
                                                                    CIP

Published simultaneously in the United States and Canada

Bantam Books are published by Bantam Books, a division of Bantam Doubleday Dell Publishing Group, Inc. Its
trademark, consisting of the words "Bantam Books" and the portrayal of a rooster, is Registered in U.S. Patent and
Trademark Office and in other countries. Marca Registrada. Bantam Books, 1540 Broadway, New York, New
York 10036.

PRINTED   IN   THE   UNITED   STATES   OF   AMERICA

BVG   0 9 8 7 6 5 4 3 2 1

To Greg Tobin, editor and friend,
without whose encouragement, interest, and confidence
this project might never have become a reality.

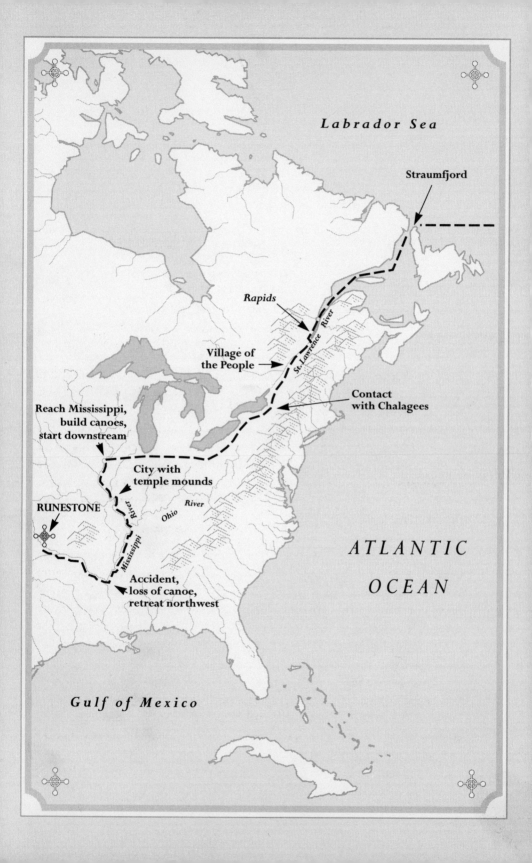

Labrador Sea

Straumfjord

Rapids

St. Lawrence River

Village of the People

Contact with Chalagees

Reach Mississippi, build canoes, start downstream

City with temple mounds

Ohio River

Mississippi River

RUNESTONE

Accident, loss of canoe, retreat northwest

ATLANTIC OCEAN

Gulf of Mexico

Prologue

I

Elk Woman reached the top of the rise and paused to catch her breath. She turned to see how her young son was faring. He had done quite well, she thought, for a child of seven summers. It was too bad. One of the worst things about watching her world fall apart was the thought that she would never see Deer Mouse grow to manhood. He might survive this tragedy, though she doubted that any of them would. If he did, though, he would be raised as a captive foster child by strange warlike Shaved-heads. He would never know the joy of the Sacred Hills and Tallgrass prairie, the thrill of the great hunts astride a fine buffalo horse.

She did not feel the tragedy so deeply for herself. Her life was already over. It had ended three days ago when the Shaved-heads struck their party. Her husband, Shoots Far, was one of the first to fall. There had not even been time to mourn his passing, or to prepare his body. She regretted that; she would mourn for him later. If, of course, she lived long enough. She would try to protect Deer Mouse as long as she could. At the end, if there was time, she would mourn her husband. If not . . . well, she would join him instead. She smiled grimly at the irony in such a thought.

Deer Mouse now came struggling up the slope, carrying his small pack bravely. He looked tired. *We are all tired,* she thought. *If only we could rest.* But Tracker had kept them moving, at a punishing pace. There had been times when she hated Tracker, these past three days. But, in her more rational moments, she knew that they were alive only because of his skills.

They were the only survivors. At least, she thought so. The Shaved-heads

had been merciless in their slaughter and mutilation. The entire party of the
People, some eleven families, had been destroyed in the massacre. They should
never have come so far from their own Tallgrass country, she thought. But what
else could they have done? A bad season, no buffalo . . . at least the hunt into
the semiwooded country to the southeast had been moderately successful. There
had been deer and elk, enough to store winter supplies.

They had discussed whether to winter here, in the shelter of the scrub
oaks, or to move back into more familiar country and try to rejoin the rest of
the band. No matter, now. The attack had come, and the Shaved-heads had
seemed to strive for total annihilation. Even young women, younger and prettier
than she, had been struck down and scalped. That was why she had little hope
that she would be spared, even for a slave-wife. She hoped now only for the
opportunity to take one or two Shaved-heads with her when she crossed over.
That would help to avenge her husband.

Spirit Walker now struggled up the trail toward them, bringing up the rear.
The old holy man was the fourth survivor. His medicine was said to be of great
strength. Greater, possibly, than that of any holy man of the People since Red
Horse recovered the white buffalo cape, several generations ago. It was said that
Spirit Walker could walk on water. Elk Woman had never quite believed that. In
his youth, maybe, but that was long ago. Now the snows of many winters shone
white upon his head, and their chill was seen in the hesitancy of his stride. Spirit
Walker was slowing their flight, perhaps more than young Deer Mouse, even. He
had urged them to leave him behind.

"My medicine will protect me."

"No, Uncle," Tracker insisted, with his quiet smile. "We may need your
medicine to save *us*."

It was a noble thing for the young man to do, Elk Woman thought, even
though not too wise.

"You should save yourself," she had told Tracker, aside, on that first terrible night, hidden in the rocky cleft.

"No, the People must stay together," he had stated flatly. There had been
no room for compromise.

So they had stayed together, four people, fugitives in a strange land.

"I am sorry about your wife and children," she told him.

"And I, for you. Shoots Far was my friend."

"I know. We must mourn them."

"Yes . . . later."

Tracker had hidden them, cleverly concealing their hiding place with
branches from the oaks.

"We will go south a little way to confuse the Shaved-heads," he explained. "Then, turn west, and back toward our own country."

"It is good," agreed Spirit Walker.

But it was not good. Somehow, the Shaved-heads had realized the next day that some had survived. Wilted oak leaves on the brush that had screened their hiding place, perhaps. Since then they had been hotly pursued. By using all his skills, Tracker had kept them alive, so far. They had waded in the icy water of a stream for a long time, to conceal their tracks. Spirit Walker waded, too, confirming the suspicion of Elk Woman regarding his diminishing powers. The stream took them farther in the wrong direction, farther southeast.

When they finally emerged from the water on a rocky ledge, Tracker was confident that they had eluded pursuit. But he was mistaken. After he scouted the back trail that afternoon, he came hurrying to rejoin the others.

"They come," he announced grimly. "Their tracker is good . . . better than I thought."

"*Aiee!*" exclaimed Elk Woman softly. "It is over!"

"We are not dead yet," assured Tracker. "Come!"

They moved on, tired and hungry, still farther in the wrong direction. There were times when Elk Woman wished that she could stop and rest to gain strength for the final death struggle. Yet Tracker's calm confidence did not seem to permit such an outcome. *He expects to escape this!* she finally told herself with some degree of surprise. With such a man leading the retreat, she could do no less than follow, both for herself and for her son. So, she struggled on, every muscle crying out for a respite from the punishment. And, if her younger body cried in protest, how much more difficult it must be for old Spirit Walker.

"How is it with you, Uncle?" she asked as he came up beside her, breathing heavily. "Uncle" was the term of respect used by the People for any adult male older than oneself.

He smiled ruefully.

"I am here," he said. "Not much more."

Tracker was pointing ahead. There was a level, grassy valley before them, and a range of wooded hills to the southeast, beyond. Tracker glanced at the sun.

"We can cross this valley before night," he announced. "There will be places to hide in the hills, there. We can rest tonight."

And then, what? thought Elk Woman, but she said nothing.

"I will scout the back trail," Tracker said. "Go on ahead, and I will catch up." He pointed at the distant ridge. "Head toward that notch." He turned away, down the trail they had just ascended, shifting his flintlock rifle to the crook of his arm.

At least, the going was easier on the level plain. She found a game trail that wandered in the general direction of their travel, and followed it. The *wrong* direction, she noted to herself. And into the hills? Would it not be better to make the last stand in the open, like people of the prairie? The People did not cower in the trees among rocks. But, she had to admit, they were still alive. Tracker's skills had proven effective so far. The People were survivors, willing to do what they must to survive. And Tracker was a very remarkable man. She had known of her husband's respect for this friend, and was just beginning to see . . . but no matter, now. She led the way through the grasses toward the distant hills.

Shadows were beginning to lengthen when Tracker rejoined them. Elk Woman's heart was not quite so heavy now, and she wondered at this. Their plight was no less hopeless, but she received strength and courage, somehow, from his presence.

"Come," he said simply, leading the way up the slope on the faint trail leading into the hills.

"Do they still follow?" she asked, though she knew the answer.

Tracker nodded, but made no comment.

It was somewhat cooler in the shade of the trees. They were making their way upward along the edge of a ravine when Tracker suddenly stopped with an exclamation.

"What is it?" she asked.

"I do not know," he said slowly. "Something . . ." He began to peer among the sassafras bushes.

"Danger?" she asked impatiently.

"No, no. Something else. A different spirit, somehow. Wait here."

He parted the bushes and was gone. They waited impatiently. In the distance somewhere, Elk Woman heard the trickle of water . . . not a large stream . . . a spring, maybe. Its song was inviting.

The bushes parted again, and Tracker stepped out, a pleased expression on his face.

"It is good!" he stated. "An old trail, a cave, water. Come." He held the branches aside. "Follow the path," he said. "I will cover our tracks. Try not to disturb anything."

Elk Woman led the way down the steep rocky slope. It was like another world, damp and mossy. Ferns sprouted from crevices and lichens adorned the gray stone that formed the walls of the canyon. There were oaks and nut trees, and plants she did not recognize. Birds sang in the shrubbery, and she heard again the song of the water somewhere below. The path was steep, twisting back on itself repeatedly.

Then she saw the cave. A heavy shelf of stone spanned a space between the shoulders of the rift, and beneath it was a concavity. A person could stand almost upright under this roof, it appeared. The floor was several paces across, and she could see the back wall of the shelter. She fought down the trapped feeling that assails a child of the open prairie in such a place. It would furnish shelter and protection, for now. She led the way toward the cave. Maybe Tracker would have some plan as to what they would do next. At least, tonight they could find rest. Let tomorrow take care of itself.

She dropped her pack and sank to the sandy floor of the cave. Deer Mouse crept into her arms and she rocked him gently.

II

Some distance on the back trail, the war party waited for the return of the scout. Fifteen warriors with shaved heads squatted on their heels, joking and visiting to pass the time.

"Their tracker must be good," observed one.

"So says ours," joked another.

It was a wry twist to their war party that four had escaped the destruction when they attacked the camp of the trespassers. Even worse, Sees All, their own tracker, had told them that three of the four were an old man, a woman, and a child.

Usually, it was just as well to let a survivor or two escape to tell the tale. It was a deterrent to further incursion into their territory. But in this case, it had become a matter of principle. It would be a loss of face to be outwitted by a woman, a child, and an old man. And for three days! They could not let this go, now. The tracker of the group they followed was, of course, a special quarry. A slow death would be reserved for that one. Release one of the others, maybe the woman, to carry the warning, perhaps. Or, maybe not.

Somebody grunted and pointed to the returning scout. "Sees All comes!"

"Yes! Ho, Sees All! Do we attack now, or in the morning?"

The scout made his way back down the slope, a serious look on his face.

"My friends," he began, "this is a different thing, now. They have gone into Madman's Canyon."

There was a mutter of astonishment. Did the fugitives not *know*? Of course, they were strangers to the area, and might not. . . . Black Bear, leader of the war party, spoke.

"We must consider this, my brothers. We will camp here, and hold a council tonight. Maybe they will come out in the morning."

III

Elk Woman picked up an empty waterskin.

"I will go and fill the skins before dark," she suggested, picking up the other one, also.

Deer Mouse was asleep, the deep sleep of the innocent, lying on his mother's robe.

"I will go with you," Tracker offered, rising. "It may not be safe."

Nowhere is safe, she thought. But it was a thoughtful gesture. He must be hurting as much as she. More, maybe . . . Tracker's whole family was gone.

"Thank you," she murmured.

She headed down an obscure trail in the direction of the water's song. There was a seep spring at the cave, but she was seeking a deep, clear pool to fill the skins. Ah, yes, there! A wide spot in the trickle that wound along the canyon floor. The pool was scarcely two paces across, but cold and inviting. They drank from cupped palms, and then filled the waterskins. Elk Woman cupped more water to splash on her face and neck.

She raised her head, feeling somewhat better. She looked up the slope, and gasped in surprise.

"Look!" she pointed.

Tracker had instantly dropped to his fighting crouch, and his belt ax was in his hand. But this was unnecessary. Elk Woman was pointing at a massive slab of stone. It appeared to have fallen from a higher position on the canyon wall. It must have been long ago, because a sizable tree had grown up around its flank. It was a squarish shape, maybe three paces wide and two high, propped on edge. Even its thickness was massive, as thick as the length of a man's arm.

Its flat face was nearly straight up and down. There were other, similar stones along the canyon, but this one was different. A series of lines was carved in its face. Not the deeply scored scratches that were seen on some of the other stones from the shifting and grinding of past ages, but marks chiseled there by some intelligent being. Yet different there, also, Elk Woman realized. These were not the rock carvings of the Ancient Ones. Not pictographs of animals and hunters and Sun and Moon. The People were familiar with those, in their own territory.

These were straight lines, in a uniform row, but in different arrangements. The two climbed the few steps up to approach the stone, and to touch the characters. Each was about a hand's span in height, carved deeply in straight grooves.

"Look," Elk Woman pointed. "It is very old. Lichens grow in the bottom of the groove."

Tracker nodded. He had, of course, noted the same thing.

Elk Woman was still staring in awe. "Can you feel its spirit?" she whispered. "It is very strange."

"Yes. Go and bring Spirit Walker, Elk Woman. He must see this before it grows dark."

She hurried away, her head whirling. It was ridiculous, she told herself, to attach so much importance to this chance find. Somehow, it seemed more significant than their impending deaths. She shook her head, confused.

Spirit Walker was not very interested at first, but quickly sensed her urgency. He rose and followed her. Elk Woman had gathered up her child, unwilling to leave him alone, even the short distance away. The four gathered in front of the stone.

"Tell us, Uncle," Tracker said reverently. *"What is it?"*

Spirit Walker reached cautiously to run his fingers over the surface, but quickly drew back, as if the stone were hot.

"Aiee," he muttered to himself. He touched the grooves again, drew back again.

"The spirit here is very strong," he said, to no one in particular.

"Yes," agreed Tracker. "I felt it up there, on the trail. Could it be the Old Ones?"

Spirit Walker was slow to answer, but finally shook his head. "No, not them."

"An older tribe, even?" Tracker persisted.

"No, no. Not *older.* Well, maybe. But *different.* I have never met this spirit before."

The old man turned to look at them, and his eyes were wide. They were like those of a child who sees a wondrous sight for the first time.

"This is a powerful spirit," he told them. "I do not know it. But, someone, long ago . . . he who carved this, maybe . . . This place was very important to someone."

"Who, Uncle?" Elk Woman asked.

"I do not know. This is completely foreign to me."

The others were astonished. Spirit Walker was said to know all things. *Aiee*, if even *he* was completely puzzled . . . Who was it, then, who stood here long ago in this very spot and struck the rock to make these marks of great importance? Why was the spirit that lingered here one of such power? What was its nature?

Somehow, Elk Woman felt that if she could answer these questions, she would also have beaten the disaster that would soon face them.

"What should we do, Uncle?" she asked Spirit Walker.

The holy man shook his head. In all her life, she had never seen him look so tired and defeated.

"I do not know," he said. "But, let me pray and ask my guides. Maybe I can learn of this foreign spirit." He seemed to straighten and become taller, regaining some of his dignity. "It must have been long ago. . . ." he mused.

Walker feels it too, she thought. *If we knew more of this carver of the stone . . .*

IV

They huddled together in the little cave that night. The three of them, that is. Tracker seemed not to sleep at all. Each time that Elk Woman dozed from sheer exhaustion, she would rouse with a start, feeling guilty for her negligence. And each time, young Deer Mouse was sleeping soundly, his face peaceful in the dim moonlight that filtered into the canyon.

Each time, she looked around for the others. The holy man was beside her, his knees drawn up to his stomach in the fetal position. She wondered if his dreams told him anything that would bring comfort in this hopeless situation.

Once she rose to exercise her stiffening limbs. They had not risked a fire, and there was a chill to the night, even though it was late summer. It would soon be the Moon of Falling Leaves, one of her favorite times of the year. She had been married in that season. *Aiee*, so much had happened since then. She and her husband, Shoots Far, had each season relished the remembrance of the establishment of their lodge. It had been good. Now, it was over. . . .

She moved stiffly, feeling her way along the path, flexing her knees to restore the circulation. Something moved ahead, and she crouched, reaching for the knife at her waist.

"Sh . . . sh . . ." A whisper, from a pace or two away. "It is I, Tracker. Is something wrong?"

"No, no," she protested quietly. Then the ridiculous nature of both the question and the answer seemed to strike them both.

"What could be wrong?" she asked with a wry chuckle.

"Ah, I cannot imagine," Tracker rejoined.

He was sitting on a large block of the grayish stone. She wondered if he had been there all night, or if he had been prowling. She approached and sat down on another rock, close to Tracker's.

"Tell me, Tracker," she asked, serious now, "is there any chance at all?"

He was silent for a little while. *He has always been quick to show hope before,* she thought. But now, it was time for reality. She realized that he had not wished to cause useless pain to young Deer Mouse. She appreciated that.

"I thank you that we are still alive," she said, choosing her words carefully.

"It is nothing," Tracker said quickly. "We do what we must."

"So, about—"

"Yes," he interrupted, "I did not answer yet, your question."

He lapsed into silence again, and she waited, becoming a little impatient.

"Elk Woman, wife of my friend," he began seriously, "you see how it is. I cannot deceive you, and I *would* not. But yes, while we are alive, there is always the chance to stay that way. The only thing that can take that chance from us is our death, and that has not happened yet. Now, how we use this chance . . . that is what keeps us alive."

He paused, and somehow Elk Woman felt reprimanded for her lack of hope. *He is not talking of whether there is a chance, but of how to use it,* she thought.

"It is not yet time to sing the Death Song," he said bluntly. "If the time comes, we will sing it proudly. But not yet."

She thought of the words of the Death Song, used many times as a vow to die fighting when the odds were hopeless.

> *The earth and the sky go on forever,*
> *But today is a good day to die.*

Yet Tracker seemed to have a genuine feeling of hope in this hopeless situation. Well, so far he *had* kept them alive. And what he said was true. The chance is always there until death actually occurs.

No, she told herself irritably, *it is stupid to think such thoughts. In the morning, it will be over, when the Shaved-heads attack.*

Tracker interrupted her morose thoughts.

"You felt it, did you not," he asked, "the strange spirit of this place?"

She was startled at his question, yet she understood it. She had lain there in the cave for a long time, in wonder at the carving on the stone slab in the canyon. Here they were, facing certain death (well, *almost* certain), and the scratches on an ancient rock seemed somehow more important. *Why?* What was there about the carvings, about the place, that had seized the attention of them all?

"We all did," she said quietly. "Did you see how the holy man touched the stone, as if it were hot? What is it here, Tracker?"

"I do not know. The spirit of the place reached out to me today. It must be a powerful spirit, Elk Woman. The holy man feels it, too."

"Yes. But does it have meaning for us?" she asked.

Even as she spoke, she realized that it seemed so to her. Again, she was struck by the strange spirit-power that they were all feeling here. The *importance* of the place and the carvings.

"I am made to think so," Tracker said thoughtfully. "If it does not have meaning for us, at least, it had for the one who carved the marks in the stone. Now, go and get some more sleep. Tomorrow is a big day."

Yes, she thought, *a "good day to die."*

Aloud, she said, "I will keep watch for a while. You need sleep, too."

Tracker chuckled softly.

"No, you join your son. I am awake."

Elk Woman realized that it was useless to argue. She rose and made her way back to the cave. Her son appeared not to have moved. Old Spirit Walker muttered a little in his sleep, and she hoped that his night-visions were good. (*Aiee,* how could they be *good?*)

She lay down next to her child, and drew her robe around them. Deer Mouse stirred but did not wake. Elk Woman doubted that she could sleep, but hoped to rest. She would need her strength when morning came. She hoped to cross over taking with her the spirits of enough Shaved-heads to make her husband proud. Already, Tracker's assurance that there *was* a chance of escape was fading in the cold darkness of reason.

Elk Woman wondered, though, about the carver of the stone. What had been his situation, to leave so powerful a spirit behind, to survive through many lifetimes? Was he happy? Sad? Desperate? *Maybe,* she thought as sleep was about to overcome her, *maybe he died here, and crossed over.*

No matter . . . Her thoughts became confused, heavy. Maybe she would learn more when they too crossed to the Other Side. Maybe she could talk to him, and discover why the spirit presence was so strong here. She began to dream.

Strange, frightening dreams they were, linked maybe to the mystery of the place. Dreams of great canoes that held many people, men whose appearance was strange to her. One figure kept turning up in her visions, a tall warrior with white hair like that of an old man. Yet he did not seem old, but young and strong. She knew that it was a dream, even as she watched it, but could not escape it. It was frightening, this night-vision. Especially when the old-young warrior, before her eyes, seemed to change into a wolf who howled as he leaped into a battle to the death with countless enemies.

She woke, startled. Spirit Walker was mumbling again, and she wondered if the holy man was having a similar dream. Maybe Walker would be able to make more sense of it.

Part I

I

ils Thorsson stood in the foredecks, watching the other ship cleave her way through gray-green water. A white curl of foam spewed out on each side of the prow as she ran before the wind. Running with a bone in her teeth, the old men called it. It was a glorious feeling, the free-flying run of a well-built ship, looking alive as a bird in flight.

It was easy, as he watched the *Norsemaiden's* trim lines and the nodding of the tall dragon's head on her prow, to see her as a living thing. The red-and-white sail bulged full-curving, filled with the wind's push.

The two sister ships raced forward, running parallel courses. The *Snowbird*, on whose deck he now stood, was slightly ahead.

It had been a good voyage so far. Only once since they left Greenland's south coast had the men been forced to turn to the oars. Even then, Nils thought, it might have been unnecessary. He suspected that the commander, Helge Landsverk, had ordered the stint at rowing only to test the mettle of his crews. Thirty-two oarsmen the ships each boasted, all handpicked for the voyage. They had done well, and soon a freshening breeze had made it possible to unfurl the sails again to run with the wind.

He could sense the shudder of resilient timbers under his feet when they struck a slightly larger wave. The ship seemed to raise her head for a moment, and then plunged back to her task. Again he felt the life within her sleek hull. She was a living, breathing creature with a spirit of her own that seemed to communicate with his. Nils wondered if everyone felt this affinity for a good

ship. Probably not. Some did, though. He could tell by the glow in the eyes of
the old men when they told their sea tales of long ago.

Why, too, did one ship have a different spirit, somehow, than another?
These two, for instance. The *Snowbird* and the *Norsemaiden* were as nearly alike as
the shipbuilder's skills could make them, yet everyone knew they were different.
Neither was better or worse than the other, only different. As two women may
be different, perhaps, he thought. Both beautiful and desirable, yet different.

The *Snowbird* always breasted the swells as if she challenged the sea, asking
for the contest, daring the legions of the sea-god Aegir to do their worst. She
savagely reveled in the struggle. Perhaps it was only something in the painted eye
of the dragon's head above the prow. There was definitely a proud, aloof expression. But no, it was more than that. She *did* have such a spirit.

Norsemaiden, on the other hand, was more sedate. Perhaps her responsibility
as the flagship of the commander gave her a more mature dignity.

Nils could see the arrow-straight figure of Helge standing in the bows. He
had known Landsverk since they were boys. It was because of this friendship, in
fact, that Nils now commanded the *Snowbird*.

It was a great adventure that his friend had sketched out for him. Helge
Landsverk, skilled as he was at navigation, had been eclipsed by the dazzling
exploits of an older relative, Leif Ericson. Leif had already led an expedition on
the course they were now following, and had founded a colony on the new land.
Vinland, Leif had called it, for the myriad of grapevines he found growing there.

There were some who thought it a new continent, as large as Europe,
perhaps. It was on this precept that Helge based his ambition. Let Leif explore
the seas, establish colonies in the islands and extend the new religion that so
obsessed him. He, Helge Landsverk, would push into the western continent
itself, this Vinland that seemed so exciting. If grapes could grow, so could other
crops. He spoke with admiration of Thorwald Ericson, Leif's younger brother,
who espoused similar ideas.

Nils had once met the young Ericson, a bombastic, hard-driving youth of
about his own age. It was easy to see, in the enthusiastic demeanor of Thorwald
Ericson, the influence of the old Viking blood that coursed in his veins. It was
said, Nils recalled, that Thorwald was much like his father, the irrepressible Eric
the Red. Perhaps even *old* Thorwald, Eric's father, who had fled to Iceland to
escape prosecution for murder.

Yes, there was little doubt that a generation or two ago, young Thorwald
Ericson would have been the forefront of those who went a-viking, raiding and
pillaging mercilessly along the coast and into the Isles.

It was exciting to hear Helge's stories of the sea, to see his eyes glitter in the light of the smoky oil lamp on the table.

"Thorwald is somewhere over there now," Helge had told him.

"Where? Vinland?"

"Yes!"

Landsverk's face was ruddy with excitement and wine as he described the deep fjords and clean cold water of the coasts. Nils was confused.

"You have been there?" he asked.

"No, no. Only as far as Greenland. But, Nils, Vinland is better. I have talked to Thorwald. There are bold headlands, sheltered harbors, all just waiting for settlement."

"There are no people there?"

"No. None civilized. A few Skraelings."

"Skraelings?"

"Yes. Primitives. Barbarians. They are no problem against civilized weapons."

Nils ignored the faint warning deep in his consciousness, the hint that his friend was actually anticipating such an opportunity for combat. He was excited at the possibilities, too.

He became more so as Helge unfolded the plan, an exploring expedition paid for by Helge's father. It was hoped to establish trade. In his semi-inebriated condition, it did not occur to Nils that the goal of trade was moderately incompatible with that of invasion and combat, leading to colonization.

After much further drinking of wine and recalling of childhood memories, Nils had accepted Landsverk's offer to command the *Snowbird.* He did protest, though not too strenuously, that he was not skilled in navigation. It was no matter, Helge had insisted; "I will be navigating anyway, and you will have a skilled crew."

They had embarked from Stadt in late May. Now, here he was, far from Norway, gaining experience as sailor and navigator, setting forth on another leg of their journey. And he had found it good.

Thus far, they had made brief stops at Iceland and again on the southern tip of Greenland, where a vigorous colony flourished. Each time, the sailors spent a few days recovering from the pitching roll of the Atlantic and loading supplies for the next leg of the journey. To be light and fast, yet sturdy, a ship had little room for supplies and cargo. The crew was cramped for space. Even the larger ships, such as these two, carried little beyond necessities and a few items for trading.

Water, of course, was one of the biggest problems on a long sea voyage. Casks were stowed amidships and refilled at every opportunity.

Across the waves, Landsverk waved and pointed ahead. A waterspout spewed into the air as a whale breached the surface and rolled. The creature was close enough for the men to see the great eye, fixed for a moment on the intruders before the monster slipped beneath the sea again.

They had seen whales before, east of Greenland. It was a frightening thing, a feeling of vulnerability, to watch the creatures calmly approach. There had been a moment of terror while the mind tried to comprehend the enormity of the creatures. Longer than the ship, they could have destroyed the entire expedition with a flick of the tail. It was only slight consolation to recall that there had never been an instance of one of these giants attacking a ship.

The shiny gray bulk slipped out of sight and they were alone on the sea again. Svenson, the steersman, had relinquished his task to a relief man and was making his way forward.

"You see him?" Nils asked.

"Aye, a big one!" Svenson grinned.

"It always surprises me. I'm never expecting it."

"Right. Ye never get used to it."

The men stood at the prow, studying the sea, but the whale did not reappear. Svenson was pulling his cloak around him more snugly.

"By the hammer of Thor, there's a bite to the wind. It will be a cold one tonight."

Nils nodded, amused. Svenson wore a crucifix around his neck, symbol of his conversion. Still, in matters like the sea and the weather, he swore on the names of the old gods. Such habits die hard.

"Sven," he asked, "you have been to Vinland before?"

"Yes, of course."

"How many days yet?"

The old sailor chuckled.

"You grow impatient, lad."

He looked at the sky, the horizon, and the gently nodding sea, as if for a sign.

"Maybe two, three days."

Nils nodded again.

"There is a harbor?"

"Yes. It is much like the coast at home. Fjords, deep inlets. They were building a dock when I was there."

"That is good."

"Yes. It will be much easier."

Abruptly, Svenson turned and made his way back to the stern to take the steering oar again. Only for a short while was he ever willing to relinquish the responsibility. That, Nils supposed, was one of the qualities that made Sven a good steersman.

Nils shivered a little against the wind, and pulled his wolfskin cloak up around his ears. Even the setting sun looked cold and watery. Svenson was right. This would be a chill night.

2

The colony nestled in a meadow that sloped down to the sea on the north shore. Nils wondered at the exposed location, but soon realized its advantages. The little harbor opened on a deep channel, with plenty of room for maneuvering. In the distance to the north lay a massive headland, tall enough, it appeared, to provide some degree of shelter from the winter's blasts.

The land mass where the colony stood stretched southward as far as eye could see, green with vegetation during this summer season. There were trees and meadows and rolling hills, much more hospitable in appearance than the barren slopes of Iceland, or even Greenland.

Of course, they were now farther south. For the past several days, it had been apparent that the Polestar was lower in the sky at night than in the more northern regions. Svenson had demonstrated an old sailors' method of reckoning position. He lay on his back on the deck with his head pointing south, knees raised and feet near his rump. Then he placed a fist on his right knee with the thumb sticking straight up.

"See?" he invited. "When ye're this far south, the Polestar is not far from the thumb. Farther north, she's farther away, higher in the sky."

It was reasonable, and so simple that Nils was surprised that he had never heard of this trick. Of course, he had never had to reckon his position north and south to any extent. Most of his sailing experience had been along the coast, seldom out of sight of land.

More important in the open sea was identification of direction, rather than position. In clear weather it was no problem, by the position of the sun. At noon a shadow, cast by a stick, pointed due north. At night, the Polestar provided orientation. It was more difficult in overcast weather, especially in the absence of prevailing wind. Then the whole world became a faceless, unfeeling gray. Nils could well remember the first time he had felt the terror of the *hafvilla*, the panicky feel of being lost at sea. It was all he could do to maintain his composure until the sky cleared enough for him to see the red stripe of the sunset far to the west along the horizon.

On this expedition, however, they had been relatively free of such difficulty. The weather had been cooperative, and except for a chilly night or two, it had been a comfortable crossing. Nils was gaining confidence, aided by the sage advice of Svenson, who had taken a liking to the young shipmaster.

They steered into the channel from the northeast under full sail, tacked toward the distant harbor, and then furled the sails to approach the dock with the oars.

Three cargo ships wallowed at anchor near the docks, potbellied *knarrs*, heavy and slow compared to the trim dragon ships. They reminded Nils of three fat sows nosing around a trough. He looked again with a seaman's eye. They were well built, their massive holds designed to carry livestock and cargo amidships. Fore and aft there would be living quarters. Thorfinn Karlsefni had brought his settlers in these ships, some hundred and sixty men and women, to sink their roots into the soil that Leif Ericson had called Vinland.

At the dock rode a sleek ship with slender lines. It was a thrill to look at her, bright paint glistening in the sunlight. Men moved along her decks, performing the constant tasks required for the maintenance of an ocean-going ship. Nils turned to ask Svenson about her, but the old sailor anticipated his question.

"Ericson's here," he grunted.

"Leif Ericson?"

It would be an honor to meet the famous explorer.

"No, Thorwald. You know him?"

"Not really. I met him once."

"A little crazy," Svenson commented as he turned his attention to the steering oar.

Crazy or not, Nils told himself, the man is exciting. The very thought of charting unknown coasts made his heart race, and sent a tingle up his spine to prickle the hairs at the back of his neck.

Ahead of them, *Norsemaiden* completed her turn and headed for an area near the landing. Svenson heaved on his oar and *Snowbird* followed. People were coming down to the docks, to stand waving as the ships approached. The arrival of ships from home would be a major event for people in such isolation.

Beyond the landing area, he could see the several buildings of the village of Straumfjord. Three of them appeared to be of the common Norse longhouse style, dwellings for a number of families each. These would be temporary, until the colony became better established, he knew. Then each couple would be drawing apart to build their own houses. He wondered in passing if living with fifty or more people in one house inhibited romance. He could hardly imagine making love with the knowledge that dozens of other couples were listening in the darkness. Of course, they would have the same problem.

A familiar sound struck his ears, the ring of a smith's hammer on an anvil. He spotted the smith's forge, to one side of the settlement, by the occasional puff of smoke and sparks that rose when someone pumped the bellows. He wondered if they were mining iron here, or bringing it from home. Well, he would find out later.

Sheep grazed on the meadow behind the village, in the care of a handful of young men. Nils noted that they seemed to be herding rather closely. Somewhat more than would be expected, he thought. He wondered if this was because of fear of attack, or threat of wild animals. He knew nothing of what sort of beasts might be found here. Wolves? Probably. Perhaps bears, even some type of the great cats reported elsewhere. Very little was actually known about this new land.

Possibly, even, there was a threat from the natives. What had Helge called them? Skraelings, that was it. Helge had referred to them as barbarians. Further suggestive evidence was seen in a high palisade of poles that encircled the compound. Nils wondered how they compared to the natives in southern Europe, or in the islands of Britannia. Some of them could be quite formidable. Would there be different tribes, as the Scots seemed to have? Ah, well, that too could wait.

Norsemaiden slid smoothly alongside the dock, her sails now furled. Men standing there caught thrown lines fore and aft, dallying expertly around the pilings that formed the support of the structure. There was a cheer from the shore as the ship settled to, rocking slightly and tugging gently at her tethers.

Nils saw that there was no room for the *Snowbird* at the dock. He turned to call to the steersman, but once more Svenson anticipated him. A pull on the steering oar, and the ship responded eagerly with a slight change in direction. Nils had his doubts about this maneuver, but Sven had, after all, been here before. He should know . . . ah, yes, there on shore were pillars made of stones piled carefully to indicate the landing area. They must have used this stretch of shore before the dock was built.

Knowing what was needed, Svenson altered his stroke and *Snowbird* curved forward, running at an angle toward the sandy beach. She turned, easing in parallel to the shore. There was a sliding sound, then a soft hiss as the underbelly of the hull gently brushed on the sandy bottom. The incessant rocking of the sea had ceased, and the heaving deck was still. Nils stood, still swaying. It would take a little while to regain his land legs.

Nils jumped down and splashed ashore, helping drag the bowline, and ran up the beach to a piling to secure the ship. He looked back to check the *Snowbird*'s position. Yes, good, his eye quickly estimated. Secure now, but at high tide she'd be afloat. He dreaded this maneuver on a strange beach. A hidden rock, even a relatively small one, could disembowel the light dragon ship, ripping the thin shell of her belly from stem to stern. There had probably been no cause for concern. This landing had been used by Karlsefni's ships since they arrived. The colonists would know every stone. Still, he was glad the mooring was over.

People from the colony swarmed down to the beach, laughing, jostling, and shouting. Nils turned and waved to the crowd. Strange, the affinity of these people for adventure. He had thought of *them* as the adventurers, carving a colony out of the rugged wilderness. They, in turn, regarded him, as master of an exploring ship, a person of excitement and daring.

Men waded into the surf to examine the lines of the *Snowbird*, and run hands along the planks of her sleek hull. There was something about a ship or boat that stirred Norse blood. Maybe that was it. He remembered his grandfather, who had told him endless stories of the sea.

As a small child, Nils had been fascinated by his grandfather's stories. The old man had been well educated, and had contributed much to Nils's general knowledge. His lifetime had spanned many changes. The new religion, the change from the old runic alphabet to the new . . . he had attempted to teach both to Nils . . . and the change in philosophy from Viking raiding and plunder to exploration, settlement, and trade. But most of all, his love of the sea came through to the eager ears of his young listener.

"A man without a boat is a man in chains," the old man had once said.

Nils recalled his grandfather for a moment as he saw the light of excitement in the eyes of the men who affectionately caressed the flanks of the *Snowbird*.

He was jolted back to reality by a pair of blue eyes. The girl was standing quietly on the beach, not running excitedly or shouting with the others. She only stood and looked at him, coolly and confidently. She was tall and well formed, almost manly in appearance. There was a suggestion of motion, however, in the way she stood. It was like the energy one feels in a cat, waiting tensely to spring at any moment. The girl moved a step or two, out of the way of someone carrying a burden. Her willowy motion extended his impression of latent agility. He could visualize the lithe body, now concealed by the rough cloak that hung from her well-formed shoulders. Her hair, the color of ripe wheat, curled around her neck and fell across those shoulders in a shining sheaf.

The strongest impression of all, however, was that of her spirit. It reached out to him, through the sky blue of those striking eyes. It was easy for him to believe, at least for the moment, that this woman had come to the beach for the sole purpose of welcoming him, Nils Thorsson.

He pulled his gaze away, realizing that he had been ogling the girl. *Thorsson,* he told himself, *you have been at sea too long.*

Still, he answered his own thought, the girl did not seem to object. Perhaps he would encounter her later.

3

There was a celebration that night, with feasting and revelry. The feasting was necessarily restrained because of the obvious shortage of supplies, but the spirit of merriment was apparent. A moderate quantity of wine was consumed, partly from the stores of the travelers. The wine that the colony had fermented from wild grapes harvested the first season was appreciated, even though young. The newcomers pronounced it a success, and admired the musty, robust flavor of the native fruit, not quite like any European grapes.

Dancing continued until far into the night. The women were eager to dance with the visitors, to entertain them royally, and sailors were not hesitant in their participation. Nils noted a few jealous stares from husbands. Even so, there was so little opportunity to stray, in the close confines of the colony, that there seemed to be little danger. Everyone was having a good time, dancing until physically exhausted, which would itself help to preclude any unacceptable trysts.

Additionally, Nils was sure that such a colony would contain mostly, if not entirely, married couples. At least, if he planned it, he would declare it so. It would avoid much trouble. It seemed he had heard, back in Stadt, of two women who had returned with Leif Ericson's ship. Their husbands had been killed in a fight with the natives, as he recalled.

He finished a dance with a toothsome redheaded wench, who then moved on to another partner. He sat on a bench, breathing hard, warm from the wine and the exertion, and sexually aroused from the fleeting touch of the girl's soft body. His thoughts and his vision were a trifle blurred, dreamlike, when he saw the blue-eyed girl. She was whirling in the arms of one of the sailors, laughing and showing even white teeth. She tossed her head and the sheen of her hair in the flickering firelight was a glimpse of loveliness.

His first thought was one of jealousy toward the man who held her. The next was that she must have a husband here in the colony, and close on the heels of that, resentment that *anyone* should share the bed of this beautiful creature. It was a strange emotion, that of resentment and jealousy toward a man he had never seen. To make matters even more confusing, that jealous feeling was over a woman he had never met, with whom he had never even spoken. Ridiculous, he told himself.

Still, as he watched the whirl of the dancers, he could not control his fantasies. He kept visualizing the motion of that lithe young creature in bed. He shook his head to clear it of thoughts that might lead him into trouble. They *had* been a long time at sea. Human nature could sometimes become quite animal. Some of the sailors would manage a romantic interlude with some of the colonists' wives, unless Nils missed his estimate of men and women.

What was he thinking? A little disgusted with himself, and more than a little frustrated, he rose to leave the party. He was a bit unsteady on his feet, tired and pleasantly drunk, and went to seek his blankets. Nils had always been something of a loner, and periodically found it pleasant to be alone to think. He took his blankets and his wolfskin cloak, and sought a secluded spot near the log palisade.

Nils was almost asleep, dimly aware of the distant sounds of revelry, when he heard someone approaching. Some other sailor was searching for a place to spread his robes, and he resented the intrusion on his privacy. He turned his back, and drew his cloak up around his ears.

Almost immediately, however, he felt the warming touch of a soft body, as someone lay down next to him. Startled, he turned to face the newcomer. The starlight was dim, but he could see, as well as feel, that it was a woman. Then realization dawned. Not only a woman, but the incredibly beautiful blue-eyed woman he had seen at the shore and again at the dancing. Smoothly, she lifted the edge of his blanket and slid in beside him. Almost simultaneously, she bestowed a kiss squarely on his lips.

Perhaps it was the surprise, the wine, or the long weeks at sea, but this was a kiss like no other. It was warm, moist, urgent yet yielding, lingering on his lips, with just a tantalizing hint of an exploring tongue before she pulled away.

"Nils Thorsson," she said.

It was not a question, merely a statement of fact. Her voice was deep and seductively husky.

"Yes," he blurted, his breath coming in excited gasps. "What?"

"Would you do something for me?" she whispered in his ear.

He wanted to shout "Anything!" but managed to control himself.

"What is it?"

She snuggled against him, rubbing her knee against his thighs, encircling his chest with her arm. She breathed tantalizingly into his ear.

"Will you take me with you?"

She kissed him again, before he could answer. A longer, deeper kiss, filled with promise of things to come. His hands were caressing her body, pulling her closer to him, but she gently pushed him away.

"Will you?"

He paused, confused. The girl was giving him mixed messages, enticing him while she held him off. This helped to bring him back to reality.

"You have no husband?" he asked pointedly.

The girl shrugged.

"He is nothing. As interesting as a sack of flour."

She snuggled closer to him again.

"He does not know how to treat a woman."

Resentment flared in Nils. He could not imagine a man who would fail to treat this woman like a goddess. He cradled her in his arms and rocked her gently.

"I would leave him for you!" she whispered.

Tears were wet on her cheeks.

"But," Nils protested, "I am just starting on this exploration."

"Then take me with you!"

"No, no, it would not be possible."

"You do not like me," she pouted, pretending to turn away from him. "If you really loved me, you would take me away."

"But I hardly know you!"

She cuddled closer and kissed him again, making his heart race and his breath come in short, excited gasps once more. This girl could turn hot and cold as quickly as . . . She was nibbling on his earlobe now, driving him crazy with desire.

"You *could* know me better," she whispered. "Better than my clod of a husband. Please help me."

Nils was beside himself with a mixture of sympathy and desire. He genuinely wanted to help this desperate young woman, who appeared to be trapped in an unfortunate marriage. Why did she not simply leave her husband, he wondered. It was quite permissible under Norse custom.

Except, he reminded himself, there would be nowhere for her to go, unless she left the colony. And, of course, there was no way to do that, except on one of the infrequent ships that stopped at Straumfjord. And what could she offer in exchange for help? She had nothing. Nothing, that is, except herself. Her body. The exquisite, desirable body that now snuggled against him under the wolfskin cloak.

Nils was of a sympathetic nature anyway, and the plight of this woman tugged at his heartstrings. Of all the men here at Straumfjord tonight, she had chosen him to ask for assistance. It was a tremendously uplifting, flattering thing to be the one she felt she could approach. He felt that he *must* help her. Besides, the promised rewards were so desirable. He gathered her to him and kissed her, trying hard to control his breathing.

"I cannot take you with me now," he whispered, "but when I come back—"

She pushed him away.

"You will never come back!" she sobbed, tears starting again.

"Yes, yes, I will. When we finish the exploration, we will stop here on the way home."

"Really? You will come for me?"

She was happy in an instant.

"Yes," Nils promised.

He was trying to ignore the faint warnings in the back of his mind, to go slow, be careful. He kissed her again, long and passionately, and she responded with equal fervor. Gently, he stroked her body, reaching down for the hem of her skirt. He had just succeeded in touching the smooth skin of a shapely leg when she suddenly pushed his hand away and sat up.

"No!" she said huskily. "Not now. The risk is too great. Later, it will be better."

She kissed him, warmly but briefly, and sprang to her feet, smoothing her skirt as she turned.

"Later," she promised.

She blew him a kiss and was gone.

Nils lay in the dim starlight, staring after her gracefully retreating figure. He was completely frustrated, still breathing heavily, and with the dull ache of unfulfilled desire in his groin. An even worse ache was that of doubt. Had she been only toying with him? Was it a game with her, to see how far she could go with her torment and then give nothing? He was angry, disappointed.

As his anger cooled, he began to rationalize. He wanted badly to justify the girl's behavior. She was desperate, he assumed, or she would never have approached a stranger with this sort of proposition. And, since she had only one thing to offer, it must be held in reserve until she was certain of the bargain. Seen in this light, her behavior was at least understandable, if not totally acceptable to him. His sympathy for her plight began to return. He hoped he could prove worthy of her trust.

The ache of frustrated desire still remained, and he thought for some time of her promise. "Later." How much later, and under what circumstances, he wondered. There were many unanswered questions here. He thought again of the warmth of her kiss, the feel of her body against his, and the seductive thrill of her breath in his ear.

Restless, he rose and went back to the area near the fires, where the thinning crowd still laughed and sang, and wine still flowed. He did not see the girl, and the revelry was not the same. Even the wine had lost its savor. Disappointed, he turned away.

Back in his blankets, he was almost asleep when an odd thought struck him. He did not even know her name, the name of the blue-eyed goddess who had offered to share his bed.

4

"What about the Skraelings?" Helge asked.

Ericson and Karlsefni nodded and exchanged serious glances.

"Yes, they can be a problem," admitted the colonist. "We have been attacked."

Thorwald Ericson was more direct.

"You have to fight them!" he stated positively. "Show them a taste of steel! Any Norseman is worth a dozen of these barbarians."

"But there are different kinds of Skraelings, different tribes," protested Karlsefni. "Some are timid, and they run and hide. Some fight. Fierce fighters. You can't lump them all together, Thorwald."

"They all bleed and die," Thorwald retorted. "They must be taught that."

Karlsefni appeared to have doubts about this approach. He diplomatically changed the subject.

"Where will you go from here?" he asked Ericson.

"South, I think, along the coast. And you, Helge?"

"We had not decided," Landsverk answered. "What do you think, Nils?"

Nils was looking at a rough map on the table.

"Is this a bay or gulf?" he asked, pointing with a finger.

"Yes," Karlsefni told him. "The headland across the channel runs southwest. We do not know how far. It may be a large island, but it goes on for as far as we have explored. Odin says it leads to freshwater."

"Odin?" asked Nils, puzzled.

Karlsefni chuckled.

"Yes, an old Skraeling. He came crawling in last year, half-starved. It seems the other Skraelings were after him. Different tribe, or something. He's helpful. Has a fair use of our tongue."

"He speaks Norse?"

"Yes, some. Probably understands more."

"Why is he called Odin?" Helge wanted to know.

"Oh. Someone called him that because he has only one eye. Like the god Odin, you know? The name stuck."

"But what is this about freshwater?" Thorwald asked.

"Oh, that. Yes, Odin says this gulf leads to freshwater. A big river, apparently."

"You see?" exclaimed Thorwald. "A new continent!"

"Have you been to this river, Thorwald?" Helge asked.

"No. I've sailed down the west coast of this land, where we are now. But I think that's the continent, over there. I'm going to see."

"Then you'll go south?"

"Yes. And then, west. You might want to look at this river the Skraeling tells about."

"Perhaps we will," Helge pondered. "What do you think, Nils?"

"It would help finish this map," Nils agreed, pointing to vast white areas of unexplored territory on the chart. "Karlsefni, may we take this Skraeling, Odin, with us?"

"No!" snapped the colonist. "I may need him as an interpreter."

They quickly abandoned that idea. There was some further discussion, of routine sailing plans, supplies, and water. Thorwald Ericson stated his intention to depart on tomorrow's high tide.

As the meeting broke up, an idea occurred to Nils.

"Karlsefni," he asked, "who is the tall woman with blue eyes and blond hair?"

The colonist chuckled.

"Ah, you have met Ingrid!"

"Ingrid?"

"Yes. You can take her with you, instead of Odin."

The others laughed, and Nils felt himself beginning to redden. He wished he had not inquired. The woman was apparently well known. But, he decided, since he had begun this, he might as well play it out to the end.

"But who is she? Does she have a husband?"

"Of course. Olaf, the cooper, poor bastard. A good, hard-working lad, to be treated so."

"Treated how?"

"Like she treats him. Like dirt. She's like a bitch in heat. Wanted you to take her away? I thought so. The woman is constant trouble. After a man like a dog on a bone."

Nils was embarrassed and a bit angry that he had been taken in by this wench. But no, there were two sides to any story. He thought of the tears, the pleading, and the warmth and feeling of those kisses. The girl really did have a problem, and he had promised to help her. He would do so, when the time came. On their return, when they sailed for Norway again, he would keep that promise. He would like to see her again, to talk to her and assure her that he planned to take her away. He would attempt to contact her before their departure. But meanwhile, he must think of other things.

Thorwald and Helge were discussing navigation as Nils turned his attention back toward them. Helge was examining a small object that Thorwald had just handed him.

"It can find north even in an overcast," Thorwald insisted.

"But how? How does it work?" asked the puzzled Helge.

The object, which Thorwald had just taken from a soft leather pouch, was a flat stone, oval in shape and very thin. Its color was a dull gray, but it was almost translucent as Helge held it up to the light between thumb and forefinger.

"What is it? I do not understand," Nils asked, puzzled.

"A *solarstein*," Thorwald explained. "It sees the sun when we cannot. Come, I will show you."

The four men trooped outside.

"Now," announced Ericson, "it is easier to show with clouds overhead, but watch the sun-stone."

He held the stone above his face at arm's length, the flat surface exposed to the sun's rays. There was nothing special in evidence, except that it was apparent that the translucent stone allowed some of those rays to pass through. Then Thorwald began to rotate the disc slowly, the flat surface still facing upward. As the long axis of the oval began to approach the north-south position, Thorwald spoke again, his voice eager with excitement.

"Now watch!"

There was a subtle change in the color of the stone, a bluish tint that seemed to grow in intensity as he continued to rotate it, ever so slowly. When the stone pointed due north, the blue color had actually become a glow, an exciting, living thing that caused Nils to gasp in astonishment. Karlsefni crossed himself.

"Magic!" he muttered.

"No," insisted Thorwald Ericson, "not magic. The stone is aligned to the north, just as the Polestar is. The sun tells when it is right. When it is not, the stone is gray."

"But it works even in cloudy weather?" Helge asked.

"Yes. It is better then, because there are no shadows. It takes only enough daylight to light the stone."

Thorwald was elated at the success of his demonstration.

"See how this will aid navigation?"

Helge, too, was becoming enthusiastic.

"Where can I get one?" he demanded.

Thorwald chuckled.

"Helge, I give you this one, in honor of your first voyage to the continent of Vinland. Use it well!"

Helge was overcome by the generosity of the gift.

"But, I . . . you . . ." he stammered.

Thorwald waved him aside.

"No, no, this is yours. I have another."

Nils, too, was impressed by the gift. He resolved that on his return to Stadt he would investigate the possibilities of acquiring such a sun-stone for his own use.

Helge carefully replaced the stone in its leather pouch, and the four men parted to attend to various tasks. Nils called after Karlsefni.

"Could I talk to this Odin of yours?" he asked.

The colonist looked at him suspiciously for a moment, and then smiled.

"Of course. Come."

He led the way around and between the longhouses, and pointed to a rude hut, not large enough for a man to stand upright. It huddled against the outside wall of a sheepfold. Nils did not see how a man could survive the winter there.

"Go ahead, talk to him," Karlsefni offered. "But you can't take him."

Nils walked over, to find the Skraeling sitting on the sunny side of the structure with his back to the wall. He was carving on a piece of bone or ivory with a small pointed knife. He looked up.

Odin was not really old, Nils saw in a moment. He was leathery and wrinkled from a hard life of exposure to the elements. But his one eye held a gleam, an interest in his surroundings, and a curiosity. More than that, the gaze of the Skraeling bored right into his very soul. Nils was caught off guard, not expecting so powerful a spirit in this beggarly fugitive. Here was a man of some intelligence and insight, despite his ragged appearance and strange garments of ill-fitted skins.

"You are Odin?" Nils asked.

There was a long silence, and finally the barbarian nodded.

"So they call me. How are you called?"

"I am Nils Thorsson. I would ask you about the bay, the other end."

"Yes?" the one-eyed man asked, rather patiently.

"Well, I . . . you have been there?"

"Of course. That is my home."

"Not here?"

"No. I was captured and brought here, many winters ago. I escaped."

"These Skraelings, here, are your enemies?"

Odin spread his palms in unresolved question.

"What is an enemy? Maybe a friend you have never met. There are many tribes."

"But, they held you captive?"

"Yes, and gouged out my eye. But sometimes they were good to me, too."

Nils was finding the easygoing philosophy hard to understand, so he changed the subject.

"I am told that there is freshwater, a river, maybe, at the head of this inlet."

"Yes."

"How many days there, to the river's mouth?"

"How fast do you travel?"

Nils's anger flared at the impertinent remark. Then he cooled a bit, realizing that the other man had asked a legitimate question. He smiled.

"I do not know how to tell you. Faster than some boats."

The Skraeling nodded, understanding.

"Maybe this many sleeps," he said, holding up his hands with fingers extended.

Ten days, thought Nils. A very deep gulf.

"Is it a big river?" he asked.

The man nodded slowly, seemingly in deep thought. Finally he spoke.

"It flows out of the freshwater sea."

Nils was startled. Karlsefni had said nothing about such a sea. Surely he had misunderstood the meaning of the man's remark. A large body of freshwater? Big enough to be called a sea? A lake, maybe? Interested, he asked more questions, but gained little information. The Skraeling persisted in referring to an inland sea, and repeatedly insisted that it was freshwater. Nils disregarded as a language problem the distinction between lake and sea, and as exaggeration one statement that this inland sea was only one of several.

"You go there?" Odin asked, his one eye bright with interest.

Nils shrugged.

"Maybe. Who knows?"

He had seated himself during the conversation, but now he rose to depart.

"Thank you," he said uncertainly.

Odin only nodded.

Nils turned away, uncomfortable over the conversation. He had been seeking information, and had learned much. Or had he? A crazy legend about two seas, one fresh and one salt, connected by a river? Probably a native myth, he decided.

But the encounter with the Skraeling had affected him deeply. He had been so impressed by the spirit of this man, and the uneasy feeling that Odin could tell what he was thinking. The feeling became stronger the more he thought about it. Before long he was convinced that of the two, the Skraeling had learned far more from the conversation than he had.

5

ils had met Olaf Knutson, the cooper, on their second day in Straum-fjord. The *Snowbird* needed another cask or two for water, and he had gone to make the purchase. Partly, he had to admit, he was curious about the girl's husband. His first impression was one of wonder that such a man could ever have acquired such a woman as the blue-eyed Ingrid. The man's nondescript reddish hair and beard stood out in all directions, brushy and matted, like the hair of an ungroomed horse in winter. Somehow, his thin body, his clothing, all reflected the same impression. There were even flecks and chips of sawdust in his hair and beard, as well as on his tunic and trousers. Of course, the man was working at his trade. Yet, Nils had the strong feeling that some of the larger chips in his hair and beard had resided there for some time. It was doubtful if there had ever been a time when Olaf the cooper had not appeared disheveled. Again, the jealous resentment surfaced, resentment that such a man would be permitted to share the bed of such a woman of quality.

The other emotion that Nils felt, though more slowly, was an appreciation for the artistry of the cooper's work. He watched the shavings of oak curl from the knife's keen edge like living creatures, to drop to the ground in a fragrant-scented pile around Olaf's feet. He watched the staves fitted together, the hoops hammered into place, skillfully and accurately. There was no doubt, the man was an artisan at his craft.

By the time he had finished his business with the cooper, Nils saw him in a new light. There was respect for his skills, yet pity for the man. Undoubtedly Olaf knew that everyone laughed at him because of his wife's promiscuous ways. He did not look like a man who would beat her because of it. No, he had instead withdrawn into his work.

This meeting had entirely changed Nils's attitude toward the cooper. Previously, he had envied the man whose bed Ingrid shared. Now he pitied him. There could be nothing but frustration in the life of this unkempt, hardworking man of great skill. His bed, far from being the paradise Nils had first imagined, was undoubtedly as cold and frustrating as any man's bed had ever been. Worse, most likely. To have that magnificent body within reach yet unattainable would be torture beyond belief.

He saw the girl, Ingrid, occasionally during the remaining days at Straumfjord. Usually it was at a distance. He could not help but admire the movement of her body, the swing of her hips as she walked. He resented her, because it seemed certain that she had attempted to use him. Perhaps the resentment was directed more toward himself. If truth were known, he was embarrassed that he had been so completely fooled by this woman whose reputation was legend in the colony.

That was most of the time. But sometimes their eyes met, and he experienced emotions of an entirely different sort. The blue eyes looked deep into his, wordlessly pleading for help. At these times, he could not believe that there was any truth in the rumors of her indiscretion. As he looked into that angelic face, he saw only a frightened, helpless child, of unquestionable purity, who needed help badly. It was only a short step to the conclusion that he, Nils Thorsson, was the only one who could help her. And he had promised to do so. The memory of the implied reward was still strong. He recalled vividly the feel of her warm body and long legs against him in his bed.

His frustration continued, however. Only once was there an opportunity to speak to her. It was after dark when he encountered her as he walked around the corner of a longhouse. She had apparently planned it. She stepped out of the shadows and into his arms, softly yet with a certain urgency. There was no one else in sight. He kissed her warmly, and she returned his eagerness, then pushed him away in the frustrating manner he remembered.

"You have heard bad things of me," she suggested sadly.

"No, I . . . it does not matter," he stammered.

"You will still take me away? Now, when you go?"

"Not now."

Their departure would be two days hence, at high tide. Thorwald Ericson's ship had departed already, and the *Snowbird* had been moved to its place at the dock for easier loading.

"Not this trip," Nils repeated. "We will sail up the headland there, explore this bay, and return here. I will come for you then."

"But I can cook for you," she pleaded, pressing against him enticingly.

It was plain that she offered more than a cook's services. With difficulty, he reminded himself of the old seaman's adage, that a woman on board ship brings bad luck.

"No," he said firmly. "I have said I will come for you."

She kissed him again before she faded into the darkness, and it was as exciting as before. Even so, he sensed that she was irked at him for postponing her promised release.

"Until later," she whispered, her hands caressing him even as she turned away.

He wondered how long Helge Landsverk wished to explore.

When the longships prepared to leave with the tide two days later, a large proportion of the colony turned out to bid farewell. The sun was just emerging from the sea on the eastern horizon when the *Norsemaiden* cast loose her moorings and the oarsmen maneuvered out into the channel. The sail was unfurled and she began to run before the wind, cleaving the water and leaving a wisp of foam in her wake. The crowd cheered from shore.

Nils allowed the other ship to clear the mouth of the cove and begin to run before he cast off. He was searching the faces of the people on shore, searching for a pair of clear blue eyes. Somehow he expected that Ingrid would manage to give him a meaningful look, perhaps even blow him an unseen kiss as he headed off into the unknown. Instead, she had not even seen fit to come to the dock. Even though he realized that this was quite sensible, it rankled him. He was irritated again when it dawned on him that he was actually expecting, perhaps hoping, that she would behave irrationally. Could it be that part of her attraction was the thrill of danger in her behavior?

He tried to put the girl out of his mind. The ship swung out of the cove and into the channel, with Svenson skillfully bearing on the steering oar. The bright red-and-white sail was unfurled and the canvas filled with a loud snap. The *Snowbird* seemed to leap forward. There was a slight shudder in the timbers, as if she were awakening and ready for the run.

Nils looked back at Svenson, smiling broadly as he plied the steering oar. He was glad to be afloat again.

Landsverk set his course to follow the coast, but far enough out in the bay to avoid shallow water. The two dragon ships settled into the day's run. The shore slid past on their right, rocky palisades and level beaches, forested slopes and meadows. Twice, in the distance, Nils thought he saw a plume of smoke. Each time it quickly vanished, but it was enough to indicate human presence. He could not help but think of the Skraelings, and wonder whether they would encounter any.

"If you don't see any Skraelings," Karlsefni had advised, "that is when they are watching."

The thought made Nils a little uneasy. Were there dark eyes even now, peering from hiding, watching the dragon ships race up the bay?

They made fast time, an excellent day's travel on a good sea. Late in the afternoon, the wind began to moderate. It was time to look for a place to stop for the night, so Helge pulled closer to land, slowing speed as he evaluated the shoreline. Finally he signaled and pointed to a sheltered cove with rock formations that hinted of deep water. There they would spend the night.

The longships were of shallow draught, requiring much less depth than the potbellied *knarrs*, but it was wise to be cautious. With sails furled, they carefully rowed into the cove, watching for submerged rocks and sounding depth occasionally.

"Are we going ashore?" someone asked.

"I think not," Nils answered. "We do not know the area. But we will see what the commander decides."

There was no further mention of going ashore. Another time, maybe, but this run was to cover distance, chart the shoreline, not to explore the land mass. They had been traveling only one day. This would be merely a stop for the night.

When the ships had been moored, the sailors began to haul out their blankets and sleeping gear, to be settled before darkness fell. A few hardy souls were swimming in the chilly water, and Nils was watching their antics with amusement.

"Captain!" a sailor called from the storage area, where he had been retrieving his blankets. "Here is a stowaway!"

Anger flooded over Nils. He whirled and made his way forward, muttering to himself as he did so. Now he knew why the girl had not turned out at dawn to see the ships off. She had been already on board. He could not forgive her for this. The men would think he had encouraged her to do so. Worse, he must protect and support her, and this would result in unrest and damage to discipline. It could threaten the entire expedition. Damn her, how could she expect him to tolerate such a stupid move? A woman . . . bad luck!

He swung down from the walkway into the hold, ready to loose a tirade at the girl. Several men stood staring in the fading light at the huddled figure, half hiding among the supplies. Crouching, fearful, half expecting a blow, the stowaway peered anxiously from one to another, seeming to be searching for a friendly face.

Nils's jaw dropped in astonishment. The stowaway, huddled behind a water cask, was not Ingrid. It was not even a woman at all. It was Odin, the one-eyed Skraeling.

6

ils Thorsson was furious.

"Why? What in the name of Odin . . ." he yelled at the man.

He paused, trying to control his temper. He realized the ridiculous contradiction in the question he had started. Still tight with emotion, he tried to steady his voice.

"What in God's name are you doing here?" he demanded.

There was no answer. The Skraeling simply sat and stared at him with the one baleful eye. He seemed to have no fear, only resignation.

"Is there any reason," Nils shouted, "why I should not cut your throat and feed you to the fishes?"

A couple of sailors laid hands on the Skraeling to drag him out of the hold, but Nils stopped them.

"Is there?" he demanded.

"Yes," Odin stated calmly.

"Then what is it? Your time is short, Skraeling, damn your soul!"

The man spread his hands in his characteristic gesture of resignation.

"If I am dead, I cannot help you."

Nils began to calm now.

"How can you help me?"

"I can take you where you wish to go. I can speak the tongues of many tribes."

Yes. Nils had all but forgotten that he had previously tried to borrow the Skraeling to use as a guide. But, worse luck, now Karlsefni would think that they had stolen the man. Why, Nils wondered, why had he been so stupid as to request the loan of the Skraeling, thus calling attention to his disappearance? Would Karlsefni ever believe on their return that Odin had stowed away? Well, that was in the future. For now, it would be enough just to keep the man out of harm's way. It was only that a stowaway represented an intrusion, a violation of ship's security. It could be a serious breach.

"Let him go," he said more calmly. "Find him some food and a place to sleep."

"I have my own," Odin said simply.

Damn, it was difficult to stay angry at this man!

"Tell me," Nils asked, "you said you speak several tongues?"

"Yes."

So, Nils told himself, *I was right. This is no ignorant savage.* One other thing bothered him. Now that the exchange had calmed a little, he repeated a previous question.

"But why, Odin? Why choose my ship? What do you have to gain?"

Odin stared for a moment.

"I wished to go home. You were the first to understand."

"Understand what?"

Again came the quizzical palm-spread gesture.

"That I am a man."

Nils was embarrassed. In truth he had not understood. He had thought of this Skraeling as lesser, a savage, nonhuman. He had been kind, perhaps, but only to gain more and better information. His actions had been misinterpreted. Well, he saw no need to correct that misunderstanding. One caught more flies with honey than with vinegar. He turned away.

The next time he saw the Skraeling, Odin was squatting and visiting comfortably with Svenson. In a way, those two reminded Nils of each other. Good. He would ask Sven later about his impressions.

Helge Landsverk was angry, of course. At first he blamed Nils for the security breach. He ranted and yelled and made threats, but soon realized the potential benefits of the Skraeling's presence. Helge subsided into withdrawn muttering.

"Remember, he is your responsibility," Helge called across the water, to indicate that he reserved the right to the last word.

Nils nodded and waved. By this time he was beginning to feel that this could be a fortunate situation.

By the next morning, Odin was moving unobtrusively about the ship, showing intelligent interest in its operation. He watched, fascinated, as the oarsmen maneuvered the ships out of the cove. He peered closely at the oarlocks, seeming to try to understand the leverage gained by such an arrangement. When the great sail was unfurled in its red and white glory, the Skraeling was enthralled. He grinned broadly and nodded to Svenson as the *Snowbird* settled forward into her run.

Odin went aft and watched the steersman at his oar for a while, until Nils finally beckoned him forward. They stood in the bows, watching the shore on the right slip past.

"What is ahead?" Nils asked.

The Skraeling shrugged.

"More like this. Five, six sleeps."

"And then what?"

"The river."

"Yes, you told me of that. It runs into this sea?"

Odin nodded.

"You can sail up the river."

"Sail? The dragon ships? The river is big, then?"

"Yes. You could go five, six more sleeps."

"*After* we reach the river?"

The Skraeling nodded again.

"As far as Talking Water."

Nils missed the implication of that name.

"Is that where your people are?"

"I do not know. Somewhere. It has been many winters."

"Your people are hunters? Fishers? What?"

"Both. We grow some pumpkins, beans."

"They use boats?"

"Yes. Not like this. Skin boats. Two, three men."

Nils nodded, and fell silent. There was so much he wished to know, and he did not know where to begin.

Odin watched the shoreline, occasionally pointing out a geographic feature. Again they saw smoke in the distance two or three times, which sparked great interest on the part of the Skraeling. Then, midway through the afternoon, they sighted a village on the shore. Everyone who was not otherwise occupied stood staring with interest.

The structures appeared to be of logs with thatched roofs, little different from the familiar Norse longhouse. Even at this great a distance, they could see people moving excitedly and gathering to watch the ships pass. Nils wondered if Helge Landsverk would put in to contact the natives, but there was no change in the smooth run of the *Norsemaiden.* The village slipped behind with the rest of the scenery. Odin had said nothing, but had only stood and stared.

"Your people?" asked Nils.

Odin seemed to emerge from his reverie.

"No. We are kin to them, but different."

An opportunity lost, thought Nils. He was becoming a trifle concerned about Helge's approach to the whole expedition. There seemed to be a driving urgency in the man, an urge to explore and conquer. Nils was afraid that it was not balanced with caution and reason. This village, for instance. It might have been a great advantage in the future to have a port on this coast, a place to stop and trade as allies. It would have cost them less than a half-day's travel, and provided a place to moor for the night. Especially when they had an interpreter on board the *Snowbird.*

It was the next day that the fog bank rolled in. Until now, they had seen only favorable weather. The fog was thick and lay close to the water, making progress impossible. The wind was light and changeable, and in a very short while they had completely lost sense of direction.

By shouting, they maintained contact between the two ships long enough to furl the sails and use the oars to come closer together. Here, they would ride out the overcast before proceeding. It would be too risky to move into uncharted waters with poor visibility. They would wait for the fog to lift.

The *Norsemaiden* came alongside, and a sailor tossed a line to the *Snowbird.* This would eliminate the risk of drifting apart. There were old seamen's tales of ships losing each other in a fog at sea, with one missing when the fog lifted, never to be seen again. This, with the threat of the *hafvilla,* made the company of the other ship a reassuring thing. The men joked and called across to the other ship, while they rocked gently on the waves. Nils wanted to ask Helge about the village, and whether it might be good to stop if another opportunity offered. It seemed inappropriate, however, to shout such a conversation, in the hearing of the crews. Instead, they made small talk, and tried to estimate when the fog would lift. Probably not until morning, they agreed.

"The sun-stone!" said Helge suddenly. "We can try it!"

He fumbled in his pouch and drew out the stone. There was much interest as the sailors gathered to watch. Nils could not see the stone itself, but there was no question about when it indicated north. There was an audible gasp from the cluster of men on deck.

"It works!" Helge chortled, pointing. "That is north. The land is there." He indicated a slightly different direction.

Nils was delighted. This would be a great step forward for the oceangoing ships.

"What is it?" asked the puzzled Skraeling.

"Nothing," Nils brushed the question aside.

Then he reconsidered.

"It is a stone," he explained. "A sun-stone. It can tell north."

The one eye widened considerably.

"How?"

"I do not know," answered Nils irritably. "It turns blue when pointed north."

"Magic?"

"Maybe."

That was an answer close enough for an uneducated savage, he decided. However, he saw that Odin realized the importance of the sun-stone. He would have reason to appreciate that understanding in the weeks to come.

7

he Talking Water," said Odin simply.

Nils listened, and in the silence of the wilderness came the whisper of sound. Water, tumbling and murmuring over the rocks as the river sought a lower level. It was still wide and deep, but at this point it spread out to find its way over a rocky slope. Only now did he understand Odin's reference. They could sail, the Skraeling had said, as far as the Talking Water. Here, the ships could go no farther.

They had been on the river for several days, a fine, majestic stream. The bay had narrowed, and one morning they were surprised to find that they were sailing on the fresh water of a deep, clear river. They had explored it to the point of these rapids. Now, it appeared, they would have to turn back. The ships lay at rest, sails furled, while they tried to plan their next move. Nils had a thought.

"Odin," he asked, "you know this place?"

"Yes."

"Your people travel this river in skin boats, you said?"

The Skraeling nodded.

"How do they get across the rapids, the Talking Water?"

"Go around."

"Carry their boats?"

"Yes. That way."

He pointed to a well-used trail that led away from the water and into the woods. It would be worth a half-day's effort to send a party around the rapids for a look. Odin had been lavish in his praise of the upper river, and the country of his people.

Nils called across the water and drew closer to the *Norsemaiden* to discuss it with Helge.

"Yes, of course!" Landsverk called excitedly.

His enthusiasm had grown daily. Sometimes Nils was just a trifle concerned about his friend's exuberance. There was a point somewhere, a circumstance that might result in a wrong decision, when emotion would override calm judgment. Still, Nils was glad for the opportunity to explore a little farther.

Preparations were brief. It was possible to draw near enough to shore to lay the planks across. Both Nils and Helge would go, accompanied by Odin and a dozen well-armed men. The main force would stay with the ships.

The path around the rapids was easy and plain. Centuries of use by men carrying boats had resulted in the best and easiest route, the path of least resistance. The slopes were gentle, the way between the pines wide and open. Nils was surprised that the trail was no longer than it was. They came into the open above the rapids within two or three bowshots.

Here the river widened into a lake, cool and clear, stretching into the distance upstream. Odin was as pleased as if he had created it himself.

"You see? It is as I said!"

"Your people live here?" Nils asked.

"Farther upstream. They come this far, sometimes."

"And this river goes on like this, like a lake?" Landsverk demanded.

Nils became uneasy. He hated to see such a driving emotion in his friend as he saw now reflected in Helge's eyes.

"Yes," the Skraeling was answering. "Many sleeps."

Many days' travel. This was surely a remarkable country, Nils thought. An unusual land formation, with a great river flowing to the sea.

"We can do it!" Helge Landsverk announced suddenly.

"Do what?"

"Explore the river!"

"Helge, we have no boats."

"We will bring one of the ships around."

"Have you gone mad?" Nils blurted.

"No! Look. A wide path, easy slopes. We cut a tree there, another where the path turns, use them for rollers. We have enough men to move a ship with ropes and levers."

Landsverk's face was shining, his eyes glittering with excitement. The faint warning sounded again in the dim recesses of Nils's consciousness. Still, how exciting, if they could manage to launch a ship on this beautiful expanse of water.

"Maybe," he said cautiously, "it could be done."

"We will do it!" Helge announced positively.

He immediately started back down the trail, pausing to mark a tree here and there for cutting, to straighten the path. It was easy to be caught up in Helge's exuberance. The men were already beginning to chop trees, their axes ringing through forests where such a sound was never heard before. At least, not with modern tools, Nils thought to himself. From what he had heard, the Skraelings had only primitive stone implements. He glanced over at Odin, who seemed as excited as anyone over this project. That, Nils reflected, was what made a good leader of men. Helge could inspire men to do their best, accomplish more than could be expected. Helge was much like Thorwald Ericson, or Thorwald's brother Leif, who could do great things. Nils did not understand what it was, that driving force that could make men undertake the impossible, and *do* it, but his friend Helge Landsverk possessed it.

By evening, the trees were felled and trimmed, the trunks cut into short sections for rollers. The *Norsemaiden* was gently nosed up on the shore, but left there for the night, resting mostly in the water. She was emptied of all cargo to lighten the pull. Water casks would be unnecessary, so they would be left behind on the shore near the *Snowbird*. Other supplies would be carried around the trail and reloaded. Ropes and pulleys were put in place and readied for the task that would begin as soon as it became light enough in the morning.

Nils slept little that night. Aside from the excitement of the coming day, he had much to think about. He had now overcome his doubts about the beautiful Ingrid. He managed to rationalize her treatment of her husband, and to dismiss her reputation as mere gossip. Her failure to come to the dock to see him off was, after all, only good judgment. He thought with longing of her warmth pressed against him in his blankets, and the soft urgency of her kisses. Again he wondered how long it would be before they would return to Straum-fjord and he could fulfill his promise to help her, to take her away, out of her intolerable situation. Finally, he fell asleep, out of sheer physical exhaustion.

Some distance away, a runner trotted into a village and made his way to a longhouse where three elders of the tribe waited. He paused to catch his breath, while the elders, after nodding in greeting, sat and smoked and waited.

"We have watched them," Gray Owl announced finally. "They are camped below the Talking Water."

"They are in two boats, we are told?" one of the chiefs inquired.

"Yes. Great boats, longer than this lodge. They carry many warriors, maybe seventy."

"Who are these men? What is their purpose?"

"We do not know. Today they cut down trees."

"Cut trees?"

There was a murmur of nonunderstanding.

"Yes. Along the path around the Talking Water," Gray Owl reported.

He paused self-consciously.

"Blackbird and I think they will take the great boats around."

"But how?"

The scout shrugged.

"Sometimes these boats, long and narrow, seem to have many legs, like a caterpillar. Maybe they will crawl around."

There was a chuckle of disbelief, and Gray Owl was embarrassed. The presiding elder looked at the others.

"What shall be done?" he asked. "Shall we meet these outsiders and talk to them?"

There was quiet around the fire for a moment.

"They have shown no hint of purpose?" one asked.

"No, they just travel," Gray Owl answered. "Yesterday they killed a deer for meat."

"How? How was it killed?"

"With an arrow," Gray Owl answered.

"Then their weapons are like ours?"

"Maybe. Their axes cut fast."

"Let us watch them a little longer," one suggested. "Let us see if they can bring these great boats around the Talking Water."

"It is good," said the elder chief. "Then we are agreed?"

The others nodded.

"Continue to watch, then," he instructed Gray Owl, "until we see what they mean to do. But first, get some food and sleep."

Tired and hungry, Gray Owl turned away and headed for his own lodge.

8

opes stretched and pulleys creaked as the *Norsemaiden* seemed to haul herself out of the water like some gigantic sea dragon, to crawl upon the land. The seamen hauled and strained, chanting in unison to coordinate each effort. Rivulets of sweat trickled from brawny arms and shoulders.

Helge Landsverk was everywhere, pacing from the bow to the stern and back, helping to call the cadence, assisting with a shoulder to the hull. Some men worked with short poles used as levers, while others hauled on the ropes. The improvised tree-trunk rollers turned slowly, and the dragon ship crept forward, up the slope and through the trees.

In some places, it was necessary to cut overhanging branches to allow the tip of the mast to clear. The ship's progress was so slow, however, that it was possible to continue motion forward, even while the axmen cleared the way ahead.

The pulley blocks were fastened to trees along the trail ahead. When all the slack was utilized and the ship neared such an anchor point, the pulley could be quickly removed and placed farther up the trail, even while the ship continued to creep forward.

It was nearly noon when the *Norsemaiden* reached a level spot, and Landsverk called a halt. Spirits were high. There may have been some doubt initially about the possibility of actually hauling the ship around the rapids, though doubters had remained silent. Now, there was confident exuberance. It could be seen that it *was* possible, this scheme of Landsverk's. Had they not already come nearly a third the distance?

In the afternoon, the terrain was more difficult. The trail was rocky and uneven. Some rocks could be removed, but others were too large. It was constantly necessary to reposition the rollers, while men strained at the ropes and pry poles to hold the ship steady. There were also the stumps of the trees that had been cut, jutting out of the ground like jagged teeth, ready to tear the underside of the *Norsemaiden*.

Crossing one small ravine, it was necessary to bridge across with two tree trunks, and use the rollers to support the ship's belly. At the deepest point, the hull was a man's height above the floor of the gully. It was a bit frightening to stand below and see the ship towering above, where a ship should not be. Nils wondered how they could possibly handle the ship if she started to roll.

No sooner had the thought crossed his mind than there was a creaking sound of protest from deep within the *Norsemaiden*'s belly.

"She's slipping sideways!" someone yelled.

Men rushed to support the hull as a rope snapped and the severed end came whistling through the party like a cracking whip. A couple of men were slashed cruelly by the whipping rope's end, but scrambled back to their positions, oblivious of their bleeding welts. Svenson thrust his pry pole between a roller and the shifting hull. This seemed to slow the movement, and someone else followed suit. It seemed an eternity before the motion was completely controlled. Someone retrieved the broken rope to use for a temporary lashing while the pulleys were readjusted and the ship steadied. Men began to relax as the crisis appeared past.

There was a cry of pain now from underneath the ship's hull. Kyrre Rafn was trapped in a half-standing position, his hand crushed between the hull and one of the rollers. Unfeeling at first because of the rapidity of the accident, now the pain flowed back into the injured member. Rafn screamed, and then again as he looked and realized that his hand was crushed and held. He could not stand up under the hull, but neither could he sit or lie down. He remained, half hanging by the trapped hand while he screamed in pain and terror.

Nils squatted to evaluate the situation. To move the ship at all would be risky. She still balanced precariously, creaking unsteadily against her fetters. She could still slip or roll with disastrous results. It might take some time to be sure that they were ready to proceed. Even then, they could not roll the vessel forward. That would draw Rafn's arm farther into the roller, crushing the forearm and elbow. No, they would have to reverse direction, give up the last hour of progress, to roll the ship backward. It was the only way to free the crippled hand.

"We'll get you out, Kyrre," Nils encouraged the young man.

He turned to report the situation to Landsverk, who was elbowing his way forward. Landsverk stepped down and squatted, evaluating the scene quickly.

"We'll have to roll it backward," Nils spoke.

Helge Landsverk did not answer. He stood and looked quickly around the circle of onlookers. Then he stepped over and grasped an ax from the hand of one of the woodcutters.

"No!" cried Kyrre Rafn.

The ax swung, its powerful arc flashing in the mottled sunlight of the clearing, Rafn screamed at the top of his lungs, muffling the sodden thud of the ax into the log roller. He dropped free, grasping at the stump of his wrist, frantically trying to stop the pulsing blood.

"Get him out of there," snapped Helge. "You two, Knutsen and Ingstadt, take him back to the other ship. Sear the stump, bind it up. Then come back. We need you."

He turned away, handing the ax back to the stunned woodcutter. There was a low mutter around the circle as the two sailors jumped down to assist the injured man. Helge glanced back, appearing irritated, then turned again to walk on up the trail ahead. Nils followed.

"My God in heaven, Helge! Why did you do that?"

Helge turned on him.

"Do what?" he challenged.

"The hand," Nils sputtered. "We could have rolled the ship back."

"And lose half a day!"

"But Helge, the man . . ."

"Look, Thorsson, the hand was crushed. No use to him. I helped him get it over with. The incident is finished, and we can move on. Now, I want to get this far tonight."

Nils did not even see, as Helge pointed around a level clearing where he hoped to rest the *Norsemaiden* for the night. He was thinking of the scene back at the other ship. They would bind the wrist to control bleeding, while an ax head was heated in the fire. The flat side of the heated steel would sear the stump to close the severed ends of the blood vessels.

He looked at Helge as if he had never seen him before. Could this be the man with whom he had grown up, his childhood friend? Here was a side of Helge Landsverk that he had never seen. Cruel, practical, almost sadistic. Had his friend gone mad? Maybe it was the influence of this strange wild country. But no, he thought not. It seemed more like . . . Was Helge reverting back to the violence of the old Viking days? A generation or two ago, the Norse raiders had had a well-deserved reputation for cruelty. Nils recalled now that Helge had once related a humorous incident about his grandfather's experiences. It involved the torture of captured enemies, flaying alive, and dismemberment, while wagering over how long the victim would live. It had seemed far away, impersonal.

Now it had become real. Nils could easily believe that his friend had related the torture story with a spirit of admiration. *My God,* he thought, *how did I get into this?* He found himself a little bit afraid of his friend. *What if it had been my hand?* Nils thought. *Would my friend have been so quick with the ax?*

"What are you staring at?" Landsverk demanded.

Nils was jerked back to reality.

"What? Oh, nothing, Helge. I was only thinking."

"Yes," Helge said absently. "Well, we can rest the ship here tonight. Level ground, plenty of room for sleeping. Then, tomorrow . . ."

Helge's voice droned on, as he pointed to places on the trail that held potential hazard. Nils's attention strayed away again. It was like listening to a stranger talk about events that had no meaning. He devoutly wished that he was back in Norway among known places and events. Yet here he was, beyond the sea, on an expedition commanded by a man whose sanity must surely be questioned. Well, there was nothing but to play it out to the end.

"Are you all right, Thorsson?"

"Of course," Nils answered steadily. "Shall we move on with the ship?"

They turned back down the trail.

With pulleys, ropes, and levers ready, they continued the task of dragging the *Norsemaiden.* Nils tried not to look as Rafn's misshapen hand dropped free of the roller. He saw one of the men cross himself and pick up the crushed object, probably to bury it later. He hoped so. He had considered doing that himself.

It was about that time that a distant scream came from the direction of the *Snowbird.* Long, and filled with unmistakable evidence of pain and terror, it echoed along the ridge. Nils, like the others, pretended not to hear. Everyone knew that the stump of Rafn's right wrist was being treated.

The *Norsemaiden* crept on silently, the expression in the dragon's eye on her prow unchanging.

Odin, the Skraeling, seemed as silent and unchanging as the dragon's head, but Nils noted one difference. Odin's single eye constantly roved over the scene, taking it all in, missing nothing.

9

The accident had been quite disturbing to many of the crew. Despite this, there was a sense of optimism the next day as the *Norsemaiden* rolled the last few paces and dipped her breast into the lake. There was a cheer from the group on shore. It was a great accomplishment.

"See if she leaks!" Helge called to the two men on board.

Those still on shore held ropes to prevent the ship from drifting while the sailors scuttled from bow to stern in her belly, probing and checking.

"She looks good, Captain," one called.

There was another, smaller cheer. It would have been possible to repair the ship, to rebuild her, even, if necessary. This was good, however. She was still seaworthy, ready to explore the upper river.

Landsverk announced his plans for the upcoming journey that night. They would divide the force, the stronger portion to go with the *Norsemaiden* on her exploratory voyage up the lakelike river. The smaller force would remain behind with the *Snowbird*.

"Thorsson will come with me on the *Norsemaiden*," he stated.

Nils was astonished. This would leave the *Snowbird* with no one who knew navigation. Except, perhaps, for Svenson, whose long years on the sea furnished a great depth of practical experience. An uneasy thought crossed Nils's mind. Was Helge taking him because he distrusted him? Was Helge afraid he would take the *Snowbird* and leave?

"Svenson, you too," Helge continued. "The *Snowbird* will not be going anywhere."

It was uncomfortable. Landsverk appeared to be taking anyone who would be able to navigate the ship, to prevent its leaving. This seemed risky at best. There was always the possibility of danger upstream. What if the larger party never returned? The *Snowbird* would be stranded, with an understrength crew and no one really qualified to get them back even as far as Straumfjord.

Nils also wondered at the advisability of dividing the force at all. He had not foreseen that problem in the excitement of transporting the ship and the ensuing accident.

Rafn did seem to be recovering nicely. He would stay behind, of course.

Landsverk had been quite generous in providing wine to help alleviate the pain, and Rafn had remained drunk or asleep or both most of the time. He seemed morose during his lucid periods, depressed but accepting that which seemed unavoidable. Anyway, it could not be helped now.

They spent a day reloading the *Norsemaiden*, packing her cargo up the trail on their backs and stowing it again in the ship. There was an air of excitement, a sense of new beginnings.

Nils had regained some of his enthusiasm for exploration by the time they cast loose and moved into the channel next morning. He had talked more with Odin. There was, the Skraeling repeated, a chain of lakes, all a part of this river. Odin seemed confident that they could sail for "many sleeps" before their way would become difficult. The rapids they had passed, he assured Nils, was the only major barrier for a long way. In a newfound enthusiasm, Nils set aside the thought that they would have to bypass the rapids again on the way home.

He was beginning to trust Odin. Thus far, the Skraeling had predicted what was ahead quite accurately and truthfully. There were those who did not feel so kindly toward the stowaway, even now, when his information had proved correct. Some still growled that he should have been killed when he was discovered.

"The only good Skraeling is a dead Skraeling," was a quietly repeated saying.

Odin was quite aware of this undercurrent of distrust, but appeared not to notice. It seemed, however, that he had selected Nils as his protector, with Svenson a close second choice. In an unobtrusive way, he seemed to contrive to be near one or the other at all times. Nils wondered if Sven was aware of it, too. He must ask him, when occasion offered.

Nils had made a point of suggesting that Odin be utilized as a guide for the *Norsemaiden.* This would legitimatize his presence and furnish protection for the Skraeling. Still, he was not completely certain of the man's motives. Odin had said that he wished to go home. Was there more? The possibility existed that when they reached Odin's people . . . well, the Norsemen would be of no further use to him. They would be easy prey for the savages. That possibility now seemed less likely with each passing day. Odin was quietly cooperative, apparently trying to make himself inconspicuous. Gradually, Nils became less concerned about any deception on the part of the Skraeling. The man must be what he appeared, Nils concluded. An intelligent savage whose life had been hard, and who wished to return to his homeland.

With mixed feelings, he thought sometimes of Ingrid, her blue eyes, angelic features, and soft body. Usually it was at night, when he pulled his robe up around his ears against the night's chill. How that body could warm a man's bed, he would think. He wondered sometimes if she ever thought about him, and knew that he would come for her. He tried to forget her reputation, and the fact that when she left her husband to go with Nils, there would be unpleasant talk. Well, let them talk, damn them all. He would make his own decisions. He had promised to help the unfortunate girl and was determined to do so. He would then drift off to sleep to dream of the warm kisses that held so much promise.

It was early on the third morning above the Talking Waters that they first sighted evidence of human habitation. There had been a suggestion of smoke in the distance to the south on the first day. However, it thinned and disappeared so rapidly that Nils decided he had seen only the mists rising from the damp of the forest as the sun warmed the day.

They proceeded slowly, seldom using the sail. The country was much as they had seen before, beautiful, wild, and with no sign of human life. Nils mentioned this to Odin. The Skraeling looked directly at him for a moment, the one dark eye staring, questioning.

"But they are watching," he said quietly.

He pulled his cloak around him and turned away, to join Svenson at the rail.

"Wait," Nils started to call out. Then he checked the impulse. He would not go calling after the Skraeling in an undignified manner. Anyway, Odin would tell him what he wished to, and when. Nils rankled a bit at the situation, but decided there was nothing he could do.

It remained this way, an uneasy standoff between the two, with Nils still feeling that the Skraeling knew more than he was telling. It doubly bothered him that Odin, too, seemed concerned. Today, he decided, he would have it out, and find what the Skraeling knew. If they were being watched, by whom?

He was on the point of facing Odin with his demands when there was a cry from a lookout in the bow. Nils looked where the man was pointing. There, in a grassy meadow above the beach, stood three mounds, rounded and smooth, all alike and in a row. At first Nils thought this an unusual rock formation, but quickly realized that they were man-made. Huts of some sort? No, they seemed too small. He turned to Odin, who was staring hard.

"Odin, what—?" he began, but the Skraeling interrupted.

"Boats."

"Boats?"

"Yes. Made of skins."

He offered no further explanation.

Helge now ordered the ship to swing in to shore, and quickly selected a dozen men for a landing party.

Nils was scanning the terrain for other signs of life, but all seemed quiet. He studied the boats again as the ship drew nearer. They appeared quite similar in shape and size, rounded, and flat on the bottom, and a dull gray-brown in color.

It proved possible to bring the ship close enough to shore to use a plank. The heavily armed men trotted down the plank after Helge, and spread out to approach the boats. Even at the time, Nils felt a trifle uneasy at the warlike way Landsverk had deployed his party.

There was a flash of motion at the boats. A man scrambled out from under one of the upturned vessels and sprinted away.

"Shoot him!" shouted Helge.

A swarm of arrows buzzed after the fleeing savage, and he fell, face forward, and lay still. *Why*, Nils thought, *why would he have the man killed?*

There was more activity at the boats. Men came swarming out, perhaps two or three from under each boat, where they had been hiding, and a short but decisive skirmish ensued. The savages were cut down quickly, by arrows, then by swords and axes, before they had time to ready their own bows. It appeared to Nils that they had been completely unprepared for an instant attack at first contact, unready to do battle. Helge Landsverk was in the thick of the fight, savagely wielding a battle-ax.

One survivor, who had crept out under the far side of a boat, now jumped and fled. There was a shout, and men fitted arrows to bowstrings as the Skraeling ran, dodging and zigzaging across the meadow.

"Let him go!" laughed Landsverk. "He can tell the others what sort of men the Norsemen are."

The landing party picked up some of the stone weapons of the Skraelings, and a bow or two as curiosities. Helge ordered one of the boats carried aboard while he methodically destroyed the others with his battle-ax. He came back up the plank, his face shining with excitement and his eyes glittering.

"A fine engagement," he chortled. "Seven enemy dead, a boat that we can use, two more destroyed, and only a few scratches to us."

"Helge, is this wise?" Nils blurted.

"What? Of course. We have established our reputation as conquerors."

Nils's heart sank. A phrase from a generation ago, used as a prayer in the north of Britain, flashed through his memory.

"Lord, save us from the fury of the Northmen."

It was retold as a matter of historical interest now, a memory of a savage time. But, somehow, for Helge Landsverk, it had become a thing of the present. He saw himself as a leader of raiding and pillaging. This was no exploring expedition, setting up contacts for trade, Nils now realized. Landsverk was leading a raiding party.

But for what purpose? The old Norse raids along the coast and the isles netted plunder. Property, gold, foodstuffs. What could the plunder of these savage Skraelings yield? There was only one conclusion. It was the killing itself that appealed to Helge Landsverk.

Nils watched his friend as they drew in the plank and cast off. Helge paced up and down the *Norsemaiden* like a caged animal, his excitement not satisfied. What would he do next, Nils wondered. Was he really going mad?

He looked around for Odin. The Skraeling was standing at the rail, numbly staring at the carnage. Nils went to stand beside him. Contrary to his usual habit, Odin spoke first.

"This is very bad," he said quietly.

"Are these your people?"

The Skraeling looked up in surprise.

"No."

He seemed puzzled for a moment, and then a light seemed to dawn in the dark eye.

"Oh. No, not bad for them, Thorsson. Bad for *us.*"

The council was short and decisive at the village. The survivor related how his companions had been hacked to pieces, and the elders looked from one to the other around the circle.

"We still do not understand their purpose," one said.

"True, but they are vicious and cruel," another pointed out. "Blackbird saw one cut off the hand of his own warrior."

"The hand?" inquired the scout, who had been out of touch with the village.

"Yes, Blackbird saw them bury it."

There was much shaking of heads.

"It makes no difference what they want, now," Crow Wing observed. "They are too dangerous to ignore."

There were nods of agreement.

"Then we are all agreed?" asked the chief elder.

There was no dissenting vote, only more nods of approval.

"So be it," announced the elder, knocking the dottle from his pipe. "They must be killed."

10

They traveled some distance upstream after the skirmish, and then stopped for the night. Helge spotted a good landing site and wished to allow time to relax after the fray.

There was much amusement as the sailors attempted to learn the use of the captured boat. A thrust of the paddle had a tendency to result in a spinning motion of the craft, without any marked progress. Laughing, cavorting, intentionally falling into the water in mock helplessness, they were ready to abandon the boat and destroy it like the others.

"Odin!" someone shouted. "Here, Skraeling! Show us how to row the damned thing!"

Odin glanced at Nils as if for approval, then took a paddle and stepped into the boat. Without words, he dipped his paddle and took a curved, semicircular stroke, counteracting the spin of the vessel. He continued to stroke, demonstrating his skill, utilizing the momentum of the spin itself to change direction. His performance was so impressive that a half-mocking cheer rose from the onlookers. Nils was startled at the agility of the man.

Now those who had failed before must try again. Like children with a new toy, they cavorted and played until darkness prevented further activity. Some of the Norsemen were becoming quite proficient in handling the new craft.

Odin, as soon as attention turned from him, seemed to withdraw again, and became hardly noticeable outside the circle of firelight on the shore. Finally the camp quieted, with everyone exhausted from the excitement of the day. Nils rolled in his blankets, but lay awake for a long time. He was still quite disturbed over Helge's actions. This was not the purpose of the expedition, as he understood it, the killing of Skraelings. It made no sense at all. Even if plunder was the purpose, what did Skraelings have to plunder? Some dried meat, a few vegetables, some skin boats that were slow and hard to steer? He would talk to Helge in the morning. Maybe his friend could explain to him why this was *not* madness.

He turned to thoughts of the sensuous Ingrid. He lay there cold and frustrated until finally he fell asleep, to dream of wide blue eyes and a sad, alluring smile as she pleaded for his help.

He woke with a sudden start. Someone was touching his shoulder and urgently speaking in his ear.

"Wake up, Thorsson," Odin hissed. "They come!"

"What?" he mumbled. "Who? . . ."

He was confused, his mind fogged by sleep. He fought to clear his head.

The world was gray with the dim light of the false dawn. He looked first to the ship. She rocked gently on the water, her mast and proud dragon's head outlined against the gray of the sky. He turned to look at the sleeping forms of his companions, scattered around the now dead fire. Odin was still trying to get his attention.

"Thorsson," he pleaded, "wake up. They come!"

Nils sat up.

"Who comes?"

"The Skraelings!"

Odin had hardly spoken the word when there was a yell of alarm from a sentry, a cry that was choked off short. It was growing lighter, and as he scrambled to his feet Nils saw others doing the same, grasping for weapons, fumbling sleep out of their eyes. He heard the twanging of bowstrings and the soft buzz of arrows around him. Not until then did he begin to notice dark forms moving at the edge of the clearing, crouching close to the ground, encircling the camp of the Norsemen. Now the quiet of the dawn burst into sound. The shrieks of the wounded and dying mingled with the war cries of the attackers and the yells of the defenders.

Nils felt something pluck at his right ear, but ignored it as he grasped his sword and turned to face the rush of the Skraelings. Most of those closing in seemed to be wielding battle-axes, of the stone type carried by the men killed at the boats. One rushed at him with weapon upraised. He thrust upward into the man's soft underbelly, and jerked his sword free to swing at another who came at him from the right.

"Push them back!" Landsverk was shouting. "Attack!"

Nils was too busy defending to think of attacking. He stepped backward to avoid a swinging ax, and tripped over something to fall flat. The ax whistled through space occupied by his head a moment ago, and someone else struck the warrior down from behind. The dying Skraeling fell almost directly on top of him, and he struggled to free himself, pinioned by the weight of the man's body. The smell of the other's sweat was in his nostrils. He kicked free and scrambled to his feet, sword ready.

But now, suddenly, it was quiet. A few of the wounded Skraelings were dragging themselves away. Some lay dead, but the main force of the attackers had withdrawn, as suddenly as they came.

"They will be back," said Odin solemnly.

Nils wondered where Odin had been during the fight. It would have been quite risky for him. Either side might take him for an enemy, especially the Norsemen. Nils did not question Odin's bravery, but was a bit concerned as to where his allegiance lay. However, if the man had wished, the opportunity would never have been better to slip away during the battle. And he was still here.

"They will attack again?" Nils asked.

"Yes," Odin nodded.

Helge seemed inclined to pursue the retreating Skraelings, but soon gave it up. There were dead and wounded to care for.

"We will bury the dead," Landsverk announced.

Nils approached and drew him aside.

"Helge," he began cautiously, "Odin says they will attack again. Should we not bring the dead aboard ship and move on?"

Helge whirled on him, furious.

"Thorsson, I will not base my decisions on the advice of a one-eyed savage."

He turned and stalked away. In a short while, however, Nils was pleased to see that his friend's judgment had not entirely departed.

"Everyone on board," Helge shouted, changing orders. "Bring the dead and wounded."

They were in the midst of this task when a lookout pointed upstream.

"Look!" he called. "Boats!"

Around a shoulder of the shoreline, from out of sight, came two of the Skraelings' skin boats, each with three or four warriors. As they watched, there appeared a third, then another, and more and more.

"Hurry up," called Helge. "Prepare to cast off!"

Men stumbled up the plank, helping wounded, carrying dead.

"Bowmen!" Landsverk barked, "Be ready!"

Archers scrambled to the rail to be ready for the boats as they drifted past. Just as the first of the boats drew within range, there was a yell from shore. In a new attack, warriors pressed forward, pausing to loose arrows as they advanced. Then came a shower of arrows from the advancing boats. The last men were straggling up the plank now. Landsverk stood at the rail, watching the Skraelings run across the clearing, oblivious to the arrows buzzing past him.

"Come on, come on," he kept saying to the stragglers.

"For God's sake, Helge, get down," Nils yelled at him.

Just then Helge Landsverk straightened to his full height, spread his arms wide, and fell backward into the belly of the ship. Nils scrambled to look down. His friend stared back at him with a startled look of openmouthed wonder, through eyes that would never see again. An arrow's feathered end protruded from the base of his throat.

Nils's first impulse was to go to him, but he quickly realized that it would be useless. It took a moment longer to realize that he, Nils Thorsson, was now in command.

"Cast off!" he yelled. "To the oars!"

Slowly and clumsily, the ship began to swing into the open, as the few remaining oarsmen bent to the task. A handful of bowmen continued to return the hail of arrows that fell on the *Norsemaiden,* both from the boats and the shore. Nils saw one bowman drop his weapon and turn, grasping at his face, where the shaft of an arrow protruded between his clutching fingers. The man spun half around, and fell backward over the ship's side into the water.

He looked upstream again. More boats were still coming. Dozens, maybe hundreds, he thought. They *must* get the ship moving.

"Raise the sail!"

While sailors were trying to release the ties on the furled sail amid a swarm of arrows, a new danger threatened. An arrow thudded into the short foredeck, burning fiercely. Some sort of pitch or other inflammable material had been used to create a firebrand. It blazed and sputtered, melting and spreading on the planks of the deck, flames creeping outward. Nils yanked the shaft loose and threw it overboard, stamping out the blazing pitch. Another firebrand arched through the air and landed on the deck, and another in the hold. An oarsman jumped down to beat out the flames.

There were more thuds on the outside of the *Norsemaiden*'s hull. Curls of dark smoke indicated that the outside of the ship was in danger of burning, too.

"Get the sail up!" Nils yelled.

The oarsmen were beginning to fall into cadence now, but they needed the greater speed that the sail would afford to escape the swarm of boats that circled them. With agonizing slowness, the great sail rose and filled. The *Norsemaiden* creaked as she leaped forward in response. The steersman pulled her around toward the open water. Her prow sheared through the clutter of Skraeling boats that snapped at her flanks, and she broke free, still burning at a dozen places.

"Ropes and buckets!" called Nils as the Skraelings fell behind. "Stop the fires!"

They had headed downstream and across the lakelike body of water. This had allowed the most favorable wind for use of the sail. The steersmen kept their course down the middle of the channel, but there seemed to be no further pursuit. The oarsmen, now no longer needed, scrambled to help with the buckets. One by one the fires were drenched. The last one, below the curve of the stern, had burned nearly through the planking before it was discovered. The *Norsemaiden* would never be seaworthy again without major repair, even if they could get her back over the rapids.

At least, Nils thought, we have the *Snowbird.* He could bring the survivors home, perhaps less than half those who had sailed from Stadt so confidently, many months before. He must take stock of casualties now, and assume the duties of commander.

One thing was certain. The expedition was over, and they were going home. They had failed.

II

ils gathered the survivors on the shore beside the scorched and blistered *Norsemaiden.* There had been time, on the voyage back down the lake, to think about their predicament. He had begun to formulate a plan.

Now he paused to take a final count. Including the three men now left to guard the *Snowbird,* there were twenty-three, plus the crippled Rafn and the one-eyed Skraeling, who were of no practical use on the ship. There were not enough to man the oars in a thoroughly efficient manner, but they could get by. And of course, it might be possible, once they had managed to reach Straumfjord, to recruit a few crewmen.

He had mourned the loss of his friend Helge, silently, deeply, and personally. Even though in recent days Helge Landsverk had exhibited symptoms of irrational behavior, he was a friend. Nils kept thinking of him, not as he led the raid against the Skraeling boatmen, but as his childhood playmate. In his mind's eye, he could see the wide boyish grin, the mischief in the eager dark blue eyes. Eager, yes, that was it. Helge was a man who had always been eager for adventure, for new experience. He had been so until the last day of his life, when he had died directing the battle to save his crew and his ship.

What a responsibility, to fill the shoes of such a man. Nils was appalled by the enormity of the task. First, a decent burial for his friend. Then somehow, he must take the survivors home.

One thing was certain. They did not have the manpower left, at only a third of their original strength, to move the *Norsemaiden* around the rapids again. That thought had led him to the other part of his plan. They actually were ill prepared to bury their dead, even with many of the bodies missing. To dig decent graves for just the bodies on board the *Norsemaiden* would be a huge task for the two dozen men available.

There seemed a logical answer, then, for a useless ship and the burial problem that faced them. Why not combine these given factors to their advantage? They could stage a ceremonial honor for the dead, burning the ship as a funeral pyre. It had been a common thing a generation ago, to honor a dead chieftain in this way. As he thought about it, Nils came to the conclusion that Helge Landsverk would have relished this sort of departure. Yes, it was good.

"Tomorrow," he told his assembled crew, "we will burn the *Norsemaiden* as a funeral pyre to honor Viking dead. Then we will sail home on the *Snowbird*."

There were nods of approval.

"Then let us move all the cargo we can down to the other ship. And, on the return, carry brush and dead wood back to the *Norsemaiden*."

The crews turned to. Bodies of the dead were arranged properly on the foredeck. Everything useful that could be moved from the hold was brought out and taken ashore. There, the sacks, barrels, and bales were picked up by others and carried down the trail to stow in the belly of the other ship. As the *Norsemaiden* was emptied of cargo, her hold was filled with inflammable material, sticks, brush, and branches.

Odin joined the others at the task of carrying cargo. He seemed uncertain as to the purpose of all this, but willing to help. Once, as he passed Nils, he paused a moment.

"Why do we do this, Thorsson?"

"The supplies?"

"No, the dead."

"When we burn the ship with the dead on board, it is a way to honor them."

Odin's one eye widened. He still appeared puzzled.

"This is your way?"

"Yes, an old way of our people."

"It must take many ships, to carry your dead to the Other Side."

"It is not always done, Odin. Usually just for chiefs."

Odin nodded, understanding.

"So now, you honor your chief."

"Yes."

Odin nodded.

"He was a brave man," he observed. "A little crazy, but a brave man. I will honor him."

Now the Skraeling really began to work with a will. He brought logs and brush to help fill the hold, carried cargo, and more fuel on the return trip.

The work went well. The men moved up and down the trail between the boats, like a caravan of ants, marching busily in single file. Nils began to see that they would complete the work by early afternoon. It would be well to proceed with the funeral, and be done with it. If they could sail some distance downstream with the *Snowbird* by nightfall, so much the better.

The crews reassembled on the bank, and Nils and Svenson prepared to board the *Norsemaiden.* The captured skin boat would be towed behind to allow them to return to shore.

"Odin, you come," Nils commanded. "You can row the little boat back for us."

The Skraeling nodded and trotted up the plank ahead of them. The three pulled the plank aboard and cast loose the lines.

Rowing the *Norsemaiden* would be out of the question. They must unfurl the sail and catch the brisk breeze that was in evidence. Nils and Svenson estimated the angle and trimmed the boom, tying the sheets fast. Then they loosened the ties and began to unfurl the sail. As they tied off the lines and the *Norsemaiden* swung away from her last mooring, Svenson moved aft to his steering oar. He brought the ship about and headed her up the lake while Nils dropped below, taking a small pot of coals from the fire on shore.

As he poured the coals out and began to add tinder and small sticks, he heard chanting above. Flames began to lick at the fuel he was adding, and Nils tossed brush and more sticks from the waiting supply. His eyes watered as smoke began to fill the ship, and he quickly climbed out, beginning to cough even as he did so.

Svenson was tying his steering oar in place to keep the ship on her course. The singing or chanting continued, and Nils turned to see the Skraeling standing in the bow among the dead. Odin's arms were raised over his head as he sang, a sad, emotional dirge that could be nothing but a song of mourning in the tongue of his people. He was honoring the dead in his own way.

But now, flames were licking hungrily through the branches in the hold, leaping upward, fanning themselves as they grew.

Nils could feel the heat from below.

"Odin! Come on!" Nils beckoned.

The three men quickly assembled at the side and slid over into the skin boat. Odin took his paddle and Sven cut the craft loose from the ship. They sat for a moment, watching the ship draw away. Smoke poured from her hold, growing thicker as the larger timbers and then the ship itself began to burn. They watched, fascinated, as the dying *Norsemaiden* ran with the wind, carrying her cargo of dead toward their final reward, retreating into the distance.

There was an exclamation from Odin, and they turned to see him pointing downstream. Nils's first reaction was that of surprise at the distance they had come. He could barely see the crew on shore. More important, however, was the sight at which Odin was pointing. A gray plume of smoke rose from behind the trees, beyond the Talking Water. It greatly resembled the plume that retreated in the other direction.

"The ship!" Svenson exclaimed.

"Odin, get us back there!" Nils ordered.

"No, Thorsson, they would kill us."

"Damn your soul, I will kill you myself if you don't!" Nils snapped.

The Skraeling looked at him with calm resolve.

"There is another way around the Talking Water."

"Then take us there!"

Odin picked up his paddle and began to propel the craft downstream, working across the current, heading for the other side. It was too far to clearly see the crew waiting at the landing. Nils could not be certain whether they could see the smoke or not, from where they waited. If not, they soon would know. Just now, however, he felt that he needed to determine the fate of the *Snowbird.*

After what seemed an eternity, the little boat grounded on the other shore, and the three leaped out. Odin dragged the boat ashore and expertly flipped it over, pulling a leafy branch across it for partial concealment. He beckoned, and plunged into the forest along a little-used game trail.

They burst into the open below the rapids a little later, panting from exertion. Odin pointed. There in the distance against the other shore lay the *Snowbird.* She was dead in the water, burning fiercely along the entire length of her hull. Nils wondered for a moment what had become of the few men on board. For only a moment, of course. It was quickly apparent that they were either dead on board the burning ship, or had attempted to go ashore, where they would have met the attackers. Yes, beyond a doubt, they were dead.

Of the others, he was not so certain. It was possible that they had managed to mount a defense. Possible, even, that the survivors would scatter in the woods, some of them escaping. He felt an urgency to find out, to rejoin them, make plans, to find a way to survive.

"Listen!" Sven held up a hand and the three stood motionless.

Above the quiet murmur of the Talking Waters there came a more distant, more alarming noise. It took a moment to realize that the sounds, muffled and softened by distance and by the reassuring laughter of the water, were sounds of combat. There were shouts, screams, and cries that it seemed could not come from a human throat. Hair prickled at the back of Nils's neck.

"We must go and help them!" he exclaimed.

Odin looked at him with a stolid expression that was almost patronizing.

"You cannot help them, Thorsson," the Skraeling said sympathetically. "We must find a way to help ourselves."

They stood, watching the flames devour the *Snowbird* before their eyes. Nils had felt the crush of defeat as they brought the crippled *Norsemaiden* back down the lake. That was nothing like this, however. He had completely destroyed the expedition in his stupidity. He had lost his entire command, including two ships. One he had actually burned with his own hand. The other, he had left virtually undefended, and allowed it to be lost.

Even so, it was a little while before the enormity of the loss sank into his consciousness. He had been thinking in terms of his dereliction of duty, of the loss of prestige with the loss of a ship. Slowly, he realized that they were watching their only way home burn to the waterline. Without a ship, he, Svenson, and any others who had managed to survive until now had absolutely no way to return to civilization. They could not even get as far as Straumfjord. Worse yet, most of their supplies had already been loaded onto the *Snowbird*, and were going up in greasy smoke before their eyes.

How could he have been so stupid? he fumed to himself. He had actually burned a ship that might have gotten them home. Now they were stranded in the wilderness of an unexplored land, probably to be hunted down and killed like animals. For some reason, Nils recalled the old saying of his grandfather's, heard repeatedly throughout the years of his childhood.

"A man without a boat is a man in chains."

hey could see fires along the opposite shore as night fell after that darkest of days. They had watched the tragedy in progress as it unfolded before them. The *Snowbird*'s hull had burned to the waterline at her mooring, and scraps of her timbers were floating downstream with the current. The river that had looked so beautiful to Nils only days ago now appeared dark and ugly. Its pristine surface, clean and cold, was now dirtied with the greasy residue of burning supplies and human carnage. Black smoke still rose from the smoldering skeleton of the ship as darkness fell.

Skraelings moved along the shore, in and out of the woods, searching out survivors. Occasionally there would be a distant shout of triumph, a flurry of other shouts, and perhaps a scream, cut short in the middle. There was nothing they could do, even knowing well the meaning of the grim sequence of sounds.

Just before dark, there seemed to be a lessening of the search, pursuit, and killing. Skraelings began to sort through the supplies that had been stacked on the shore in preparation for loading on the ship. There began a methodical sacking and carrying along the trail. They would load the plunder into the boats above the rapids, Nils supposed.

He was extremely depressed. Had they been on the other shore, he would probably have attacked every Skraeling he encountered until he himself was killed. At least, he could have died fighting, as a Viking should: with dignity, with sword in hand, not cowering here in the underbrush, watching his world and his future disappear in black smoke.

A time or two, he was about to suggest it, but Odin, anticipating such an idea, firmly refused to permit it. In this, the Skraeling was supported by Svenson. Nils was outnumbered, and the use of the boat to cross the river depended on Odin's skill. So Nils sulked, suffering the dreadful guilt of responsibility that falls on a leader when things go wrong.

Sven sat quietly, muttering softly, occasionally crossing himself. Nils thought that he was praying, probably not only to the God of the cross, but to any of the deities in the tradition of the Norsemen who might have any influence. Sven seemed to hold no ill feeling toward the leader who had engineered the debacle. For this Nils was grateful, but it made his guilt even worse. Basically, both were numb with the enormity, the shock, and grief of the tragedy.

Just at dusk, Odin rose.

"I go to hide the boat," he said. "Stay here, no fire."

He flitted into the shadows, and it was a moment before Nils realized that the one-eyed Skraeling had virtually taken command of the situation. His temper flared.

By God, we'll see about that! he told himself.

It was perhaps fortunate that Odin had disappeared, because before he returned Nils's temper had cooled. When he took time to think, he realized that any slim chance of survival was totally dependent on the cleverness of this savage.

Time passed, and Odin did not return, Nils waited uneasily. Could it be that the Skraeling had abandoned them, to go off on his own? Or even worse . . . anger rose in him as the thought occurred. Would Odin betray them to the enemy to save his own worthless skin? It was possible. He fretted, pacing a few steps back and forth in the darkness.

When the drums started, it seemed to worsen their whole predicament even more. A dull throbbing, heard in the distance, like a barely perceived heartbeat. More accurately, *felt* rather than heard. It seemed to Nils that the throb was that of the earth itself, and it prepared to disintegrate under him. Then, with the beat of a humming sensation, rising and falling with the rhythm of the cadence. A chant or song, he realized. A celebration of victory. Or of defeat . . . he had never fully realized that before. When one side wins, another loses. Norsemen were not accustomed to defeat.

He glanced at the sky, at the position of the seven stars of the Great Dipper, wheeling their slow circle around the North Star. Come morning, he must have some decisions ready. He and Svenson might not even have a boat available to them, if the Skraeling did not return. Maybe they could make their way down the fjord on foot. It would be difficult, but he saw no other way, unless they could steal a boat from one of the villages downstream as they traveled. Even then, these native boats seemed so tricky to handle. . . . The entire situation seemed hopeless.

Suddenly, a shadowy figure materialized beside him. Nils jumped.

"Odin!" he whispered, startled. "What—"

"Ssh!" the quiet warning came in reply. "I have been to see . . . I will tell you."

The three sat close together while Odin told his story. He had crossed the river and observed the activities of the Skraelings.

"They sing, dance," he said. "For them, a great victory."

"Did you see any of our Norsemen?" asked Nils.

The Skraeling shook his head. "No. I am made to think they are dead."

Nils's heart sank, even though he already knew. He wished he could have helped.

"And the ship? The other one?"

He knew the answer to that, too, but had to ask.

"Burned and sunk," said Odin simply.

"What now?" asked Svenson.

"We try to get home," Nils answered, as confidently as he could. He realized that they could do nothing for the others now. "Odin, can you take us back to Straumfjord in the boat?"

"Maybe. Not now."

"What? What do you mean?"

"The Skraelings, there." He pointed. "We have to wait till they leave."

"But, can we not bring the boat around on this side? At night? We could slip past them and back toward the sea before they know."

"No. This path is not as good. We could not see well enough at night. In the day, they would see *us*. We wait."

Again, Nils experienced the flash of anger that his decisions were being made for him by this savage. But he had no choice. It was infuriating that the Skraeling was right, and that Nils could not argue with his logic.

"When will they leave?"

The Skraeling gave his characteristic little shrug, dimly seen in the starlight.

"Maybe today. Maybe two."

"We will need food and weapons," Nils observed.

They were poorly equipped, because when they left the main party their only purpose had been to fire the funeral ship and rejoin the others. Nils tried to remember . . . he had entrusted his sword to one of the other men, and had only his belt knife. Svenson, too, was unarmed, except for his knife, and Odin kept a blade at his waist. It took no stretch of imagination to realize that they were in desperate straits for such simple tasks as obtaining food.

"I have brought some," Odin said simply.

"Brought *what*?" Nils demanded.

"Sword. Ax . . . a little food."

"But how . . . where?"

The Skraeling shrugged again.

"It is much confusion over there. Dark . . . I picked up what I could."

"You went ashore? Among *them?*"

Nils's doubts began to return, in a strange mixture of pride in the man's accomplishment and a question of his motives.

"Of course. I look much like them. I stayed in the shadows. Everyone is picking up what he can."

It was logical, but such bravery! This man was truly remarkable, bold as well as clever.

"You have brought food, too?"

There was no urgency, no immediate threat of hunger. Nils could not have eaten now anyway, with the shock of destruction still upon him. But soon their bodies would need sustenance. Meanwhile, the fast would only sharpen their senses. Eventually, though, they must eat, and it would not be easy to procure food.

"A little," said Odin shortly. He pointed to a bundle, wrapped in skins and tied with a thong.

Nils wondered momentarily what it might be, but the thought was soon gone. When the time came, whatever was in the bundle might be edible or not. For now, there were more important things to consider. Survival, mostly. The boat, Odin had said, was well hidden. They must wait until the way was clear, and then row across the river above the rapids, carry the boat around the portage, and relaunch it below. As for when the way was clear, it seemed that they must rely on the one-eyed Skraeling. That, too, rankled in Nils's soul. He was not accustomed to asking for help in anything.

Yet he must admit that of their little party of three, Odin was the only one who was really equipped to make the decisions. Only Odin could effectively handle the boat. Only he could mingle with the other Skraelings undetected. He had proven himself already, procuring weapons and food.

"How long till they leave?" he asked again. "A day or two?"

"Maybe. I will watch to see."

Again, the frustration of becoming dependent on anyone, much less this savage whom he did not totally trust. What were the man's motives, anyway? He could merely have left them, or worse, brought back the enemies who even now were probably hacking to death any surviving Norsemen, between orgies of plundering the supplies. Yet he seemed to be trying to help them. Why was he doing so?

"Odin," Nils demanded with authority, "why are you doing this?"

"Doing what?"

"Helping us escape our enemies."

Again the shrug, with palms upward and spread wide. *That could become irritating,* thought Nils. It was not really an answer, but an evasion. It could mean anything.

"They are my enemies, too," the Skraeling reminded. "See?" He pointed to his shrunken eye socket.

"But you could have slipped past them and started back to your people."

"Yes. I thought of that. But you were good to me. You did not throw me to the fishes."

Nils thought that he saw a flash of humor in the one eye that looked straight into his. Straight through, perhaps. Every time the Skraeling looked at him, he felt that. What was it, this feeling that the man, even with only the one eye, could see directly into his soul?

"How are you called?" asked the Skraeling, unexpectedly.

"What? You mean, my name?"

"Yes, maybe so. How shall I call you?"

"Thorsson . . . Nils Thorsson."

The Skraeling nodded. "Thorsson . . . What means that?"

"I . . . well, Thor is one of our gods. The thunder-god. Thorsson means a son of Thor."

Odin chuckled, though very softly.

"So you are a son of thunder?"

"Maybe. I guess my name says it, no?"

"Maybe. Now, tell me, Son of Thunder, what my name means."

For a moment, Nils was puzzled.

"I am called Odin by your people," the Skraeling went on. "What means this Odin? No one ever told me."

"Ah! I see. Odin is another of our gods. The father of all the gods. The father of Thor, even."

The Skraeling was now thoroughly puzzled. "Why, then, am I called this? An honor?"

Disbelief shone in his one eye, and sarcasm in his voice.

"No," Nils answered. He was a bit embarrassed, though he was not certain why. "The god Odin has only one eye."

Nils was uncertain how this would be received, but he was surprised by the reaction. The Skraeling appeared delighted.

"Ah, I am Odin, father of the gods! It is good."

Nils started to tell the man that this was hardly an honor. The name had been given as a joke, a cruel joke that was designed to make fun of the man's infirmity. He had not completely realized that before. *That,* he thought, *was why I was uncomfortable when he asked.* He found himself searching for a way to apologize, but could not. Even more startling, maybe, was a new realization. Odin *understood* the joke, and even enjoyed sharing in it. Nils remembered again his thought that this was far from an ignorant savage. Odin was a clever man.

"Yes," Nils murmured in embarrassed agreement. "It is good."

13

ils chafed under the inactivity during the entire next day. If it had not been for his one-eyed companion, he might have acted unwisely. Repeatedly, Odin restrained him from exposing their position.

"No, Thorsson! Stay down!"

So they remained hidden behind the screening bushes along the river's edge. Three times boats skirted past the rapids and along the shore, circling, searching. Each time Nils was tempted to step out and scream a challenge. It would at least bring the conflict to an end. Once, even, when a boat with two heavily armed savages drifted within a bowshot of their place of concealment, he tensed his muscles to rise. But a hand gripped his wrist firmly. He tried to pull away, but the Skraeling was surprisingly strong. Angrily, Nils turned to meet the gaze of the single good eye. Odin's expression was stern, and his manner serious.

"No!" the man indicated by a shake of the head. He laid a finger to his lips to caution silence. Slowly, Nils's anger cooled, as the boat drifted past downstream.

The activity across the river continued. Dozens of warriors moved up and down the portage trail carrying plunder, loading bundles into the skin boats. Occasionally a heavily loaded boat would shove off from the opposite shore and move upstream, propelled by a skilled oarsman.

It was apparent that other warriors were still beating the brush where any surviving Norsemen might be hiding. It was difficult to gauge the extent of their success. Once a flurry of excited shouts seemed to indicate the discovery of a fugitive, but it stopped abruptly. Nils was not sure.

About that time, however, their plight really began to sink home to him.

The activity across the river, the boat that had come searching, even the massacre itself he had seen in a sort of detached dream. It was as if he had been watching a scene that had no real connection to him.

There is an illogical approach to life that makes the young among us consider themselves immortal. But there comes a day of reckoning when one realizes the truth of the fragile nature of our continued existence. It is a frightening transformation, too late for some—possibly only a heartbeat before the mortality is proven in the finality of death. Maybe there is not even the heartbeat's time for the realization before it descends.

For Nils Thorsson this was the day of realization. It did not come with lofty thoughts of Valhalla, but in a wave of perception that jarred him back to reality: *Those warriors on the other shore want to kill me!* Until now his training in weapons, the games and skills and contests, had all been in play. But this was the real thing. *Me!* No longer was his only problem how to get home, but whether he would be alive to try.

Nils shook himself. No, he must not think of failure. There *would* be a way, if he could find it. While he was alive, he would be trying. And, if it so happened, and this was the time when death overtook him, so be it. He would die like a Viking, with a weapon in his hand. Yes, outnumbered, hopelessly stranded, he could still show the Skraelings the pride with which a Viking dies, and could take a few along with him.

Nils glanced at Svenson. The sailor was sleeping, curled on a mossy hummock. For a moment, Nils resented such detachment, but then recovered his reason. Sven had survived many crises at sea and ashore, and his calm strength had carried him through. He was saving it now. *Yes,* thought Nils, *when the time comes, Sven will be ready.* The two of them could stand together and smite the Skraelings in a way they would never forget.

And what about Odin? Nils did not know what to expect of that one. A strange, complicated man, with many puzzling loyalties. There was actually no reason for him to be here. Odin, when he had crept away in the night, could have simply kept going, back to his own people. It was unclear to Nils why he had not done so. There must have been some glimmer of duty there. Gratitude, perhaps, for the shelter and protection that the Norsemen had given him at Straumfjord. Nils felt a twinge of embarrassment at that. All that had been accorded to the Skraeling was the right to sleep inside the palisade fence instead of outside. That was no great gift of kindness, to be repaid at the risk of one's own life.

Maybe there was more to this man. He had, Nils recalled, managed to learn the tongue of the Norsemen very quickly, and spoke it well, though he was sometimes frugal with words. Odin seemed also to take great interest in the sun-stone. The Skraeling seemed to realize its importance in some degree. And it was, of course, a great—

Nils rolled from his reclining position and sat up abruptly, his pulses pounding. *The stone! Where was it?* Then despair washed over him as he realized that the device had probably gone to the bottom of the fjord with the charred remains of the *Norsemaiden.* It must have been in Helge's pouch when they laid the bodies on the deck that had now become the funeral pyre. *Stupid, stupid!* he cursed himself.

"What is it, Thorsson?" asked the Skraeling, his voice little more than a whisper.

"What? Oh, it is nothing, Odin. Too late now. I was thinking of the stone. The sun-stone, you remember?"

"Oh, that. Here."

To Nils's shocked amazement, the Skraeling reached inside his furred tunic, drew out the leather pouch that held the stone, and handed it across.

"You were busy, so I took it," he explained, "from the other man's belt."

Now Nils's thoughts whirled in confusion. Had the man hoped to keep it for himself? That would be a likely thing. Yet his entire manner suggested otherwise. There had been no remorse, no guile in his face. It would have been possible, even, for Odin to deny all knowledge of the stone, so that he could keep it. Instead, at first mention of its loss, he had instantly produced it. There seemed to be not a hint of guilt, only the matter-of-fact statement, "I took it." It was as if the Skraeling felt a duty to care for such a valuable thing until it was asked for. *In the same way he is caring for our lives!* Nils thought. The whole thing was far more complex than he wanted to consider at this time, in his present state of exhaustion.

"Thank you. It is good," he mumbled, embarrassed by his suspicions.

Shadows were growing long now, and the Skraelings across the river seemed more quiet. The almost frantic activity of the day was slowing. There were not so many of them now, it seemed. Then he realized that they actually were fewer because many boats laden with plunder had departed. There would be celebrations in the villages upstream tonight. Supplies, weapons, souvenirs would probably be displayed and traded as the savages recounted their deeds of valor.

As darkness fell, they could see the fires on the other shore. *A fire would be pleasant,* thought Nils. His muscles were stiff, and still retained some of the chill from the previous night. He had not had opportunity to work that out, to warm himself with activity. Now came mosquitos to torture any exposed areas of skin.

The tiny creatures had been an annoyance the night before, but the enormity of what was happening had distracted him somewhat. Now they returned with a vengeance. If only he could stand in the smoke to the leeward of one of those fires for a little while, that would help.

Odd how such a thing becomes of such importance, he reflected. With his world crumbling around him, the most meaningful thing he could desire right now would be the warmth of a fire, and its smoke to drive away mosquitos. When big things are destroying one's life, one clings to small comforts.

The call of a hunting owl sounded from the timber behind them, hollow and ghostly in the gathering gloom. Odin looked up quickly, and then settled back.

"Kookooskoos," he said.

"What?"

"Kookooskoos, the owl. He cries out his name."

"Oh."

The call of the owl was slightly different from that at home, but he understood its similarity, too. And the Skraeling, whose world must also be collapsing, had recognized this cry as something that was *not* changing. Something stable and dependable, an ongoing scene of the nightly hunt that would continue for many lifetimes beyond their own. It seemed something stable, something to cling to, a dependable factor in a world gone suddenly mad.

As the darkness deepened, Odin rose and stretched.

"I go to see what is happening," he announced. "Do you want some food?"

Nils considered for a moment. He had progressed beyond the point where the hunger pangs gnawed at his stomach. He recognized the clarity of the senses that comes with fasting. He was not accustomed to thoughts of death or of the importance of a fire and its smoky protection. He had been told how fasting would improve and sharpen the senses, make a warrior quicker and more efficient. Well, this must be what he was experiencing now.

"No," Nils answered, "I will fast a little longer."

Odin looked over at Svenson, who shook his head in the negative. "I, too," he said.

The Skraeling seemed pleased, somehow, a reaction that puzzled Nils. Why should it matter? The conservation of their scant supplies, maybe?

"I go now," Odin stated. "I will come back."

He seemed to vanish silently into the night.

For Nils, there was less concern than there had been on the previous night. Where before he had fretted, suspicious that the man might not return, now he had few doubts. He did not fully understand why, but he was willing to accept that Odin had cast his lot with them. Since the Skraeling had returned once, there was no reason to think that he would not return again.

Nils settled down to wait. He had appropriated the sword that Odin had salvaged the night before, and now hefted it to test its balance. *Not bad*, he thought, *but not the best*. Maybe Odin would find a weapon of better quality. The Skraeling had been fascinated with the "big knife," apparently because he had not seen many of them. A heavy, double-edged sword of the Norse style was an excellent weapon for hand-to-hand combat, but this New World had called for little of that as yet. Bowmen would have been more important in the battle just past, if it had really been a battle. *Ah, how stupid*, Nils thought for perhaps the hundredth time, *to be caught off guard. And twice!*

He glanced over at Svenson, poorly seen in the dim light. The older man had taken the ax that Odin had brought back. It seemed appropriate, somehow. A versatile tool, it could be of multiple uses. Its great broad blade could fell trees, dress timbers, or split firewood. And when the time came, it was a weapon not to be discounted. *Like Sven himself*, thought Nils. The sailor's long years on the water had fitted him for the helmsman's tasks. In addition, he was quiet and dependable, and though Nils had never seen him in a fight, he had no doubt that the man would be a dangerous foe. He could imagine Sven's effectiveness with a battle-ax. . . .

A slight noise distracted him, and Nils dropped to a fighting crouch, gripping the haft of the sword.

"It is I, Odin!" came a soft call.

The Skraeling was breathing heavily, and seemed more excited than Nils had ever seen him.

"What—?" Nils began, but the Skraeling stopped him with a gesture.

"They have found the boat," he said quickly. "Chopped it."

Nils's heart sank. How could they travel now? That thought had hardly made itself known until a more urgent one sank in. Before he could voice it, Odin did so.

"If they did that," the Skraeling went on, "they know that we are here. Alive, and on this side of the river. Come, we must go."

14

din was assaulted with many mixed feelings. He led the way down the dim game trail, dodging low-hanging branches and brambles. Behind him, the two Norsemen followed closely. It had taken only moments to gather their pitifully few possessions and leave the hiding place that had sheltered them for a day. They must be far away by dawn.

Why am I doing this? the Skraeling wondered to himself. It would have been easier to leave the two whose lots had fallen with his. Their presence would probably make it more difficult to survive. He could not answer the reasons for his action, only that it seemed to be something he was compelled to do.

He had first sought the help of the Norsemen at their walled village because he was being pursued. Chased by these same enemies who had kept him prisoner and had blinded one of his eyes with a burning stick to teach him obedience after he tried to escape.

His second escape attempt had been successful, and that was good. He had no more eyes to spare if it had not been. His strategy had been to flee in the opposite direction from that which his captors would expect. Downstream, away from his own people. This had confused his pursuers, but not for long. Not long enough to lose them. He stole a boat and headed out into the sound, knowing that they could overtake him, with two paddlers to each craft instead of only one.

But then another idea had come to him. He was headed in the general direction of the settlement of the outsiders. He knew nothing of them, except by hearsay. Some were said to have white hair and light-colored eyes like those of old persons, though many could see quite well and appeared young. They might be dangerous, but so were the men who followed him, those who gouged out eyes as punishment. It would be no worse, to throw himself on the mercy of these light-haired strangers, rather than be caught.

And so he had made his way to the village of the Norsemen. Just in time, too. His pursuers were close behind when he reached the stockade. He had never been completely certain why the Norsemen let him in. Maybe it had been only idle curiosity. Whatever the reason, it was a fortunate thing. His erstwhile captors quickly decided that further efforts to recapture the escapee were useless. They disappeared, back the way they had come.

He had tried to make himself useful around the compound in any way he could. It was apparent that to many, even to those who availed themselves of his help with small chores, he was a lesser person. A nonperson, almost. He was called Odin, which he had not understood until recently. It was only a name, one to which he answered quickly to appear helpful and cooperative. It was in his best interest to do so. If these people shut him out, he was alone and virtually helpless again, separated from his people by distance and by the barrier posed by his enemies.

He longed to find a way to return home, but that could wait. The time must be right. Meanwhile, he had settled into a sort of temporary existence at Straumfjord, helping with menial tasks and keeping himself as unobtrusive as possible. He learned the strange tongue of the outsiders quickly. He had always been quick with languages, and this stood him in good stead. He pretended to understand less than he actually did. There was no special reason, except that it provided him a small bit of control over his life that he did not have otherwise. It also enabled him to learn more. People would carry on a conversation in his presence as if he were invisible. A nonperson . . .

When the young leader Thorsson had come to the settlement, Odin had seen an opportunity. A double chance, as it were. Here was a man who was sensitive and perceptive. In age, not much different than Odin. A bit younger, maybe, but his immaturity seemed tempered with tolerance and understanding.

Even better, the two ships of the newcomers were headed inland. It was a way past the dangers of his previous captors, back to his own people.

The decision to hide in one of the ships had been carefully considered. Odin compared his impressions of the two leaders. The one was dominant, bold, and had a charisma about him that would make his warriors follow him anywhere, no matter what the danger. But that one also seemed impulsive. Maybe a little dangerous, even. He considered the leader of the other ship by comparison.

This one, whom he now knew as Thorsson, had come to talk to him back at Straumfjord. He had talked to him as a man, not as something lesser. Thorsson would not be as showy a leader, not as dynamic, but he seemed more thoughtful. Steady. Yes, that was it. In an emergency the decisions of this one would be calm and sensible. Besides, he seemed less impulsive, less dangerous. Yes, Odin decided, he would hide in the ship of this one.

For a little while, when the stowaway was discovered, he had thought that it was over. He did not quite understand the anger and the threats that came pouring on his head. Was there something that he had missed?

But things had quieted. Odin was glad, of course, that he had chosen the ship of the more quiet and sensitive of the Norse leaders on which to hide. Had he been on the other, his flesh might already be feeding the fishes.

Which, of course, might yet happen. Things had gone from bad to worse, and then worse again. The burning of both ships . . . ah, that was too bad. Thorsson had not fully realized, maybe, the warlike nature of the enemy. Or their persistence. Odin could have told him. But no, Thorsson would probably not have understood. Some things must be learned by experience. Hopefully, that experience would allow for one's survival, so that it would be useful. Experience gained at the cost of one's life is certainly worthless, at least to that one.

Odin pushed on through the night, trying to put distance between the three fugitives and their pursuers. He was still not certain why he was risking his own life to try to save these two. Maybe just because he was stubborn, himself. But he had *liked* these men. The young leader would be great some day, if he survived, as he gained maturity. Odin felt a sort of responsibility for him, to bring him along with gentle help, seeing that he was properly guided.

It was a strange feeling, one he could not have described. Like the thing of the sun-stone, for instance. That was obviously a very special object, yet Thorsson, with much else on his mind, had forgotten it. Thorsson *needed* someone to think of and take care of such things, and Odin had done so.

The other man, Svenson, was one whom Odin had respected, too. Here was a quiet man who did what was needed, with strength and skill. A steady, dependable warrior, Odin thought.

There was one thing about this one that was quite striking, though. His hair. The Skraeling had become accustomed to the wide variety of colors found in the hair of these Norsemen. Many were almost white, as he had heard. But from there, the colors ranged through all shades of yellow and brown or black, sometimes. Some even showed highlights of red, but never had Odin seen such a head of hair as that on the Svenson man. Svenson's hair, by contrast to the bright yellow of Thorsson's, was fiery red, redder than the reddest fox or even the noisy red squirrels in the trees. In the sunlight, flames seemed to circle the man's head. At least, so it seemed to Odin. He had seen many things that were new and strange since he had been with the Norsemen, but this may have been the strangest of all. Except for the sun-stone, of course. That, thought Odin, was like a thing of the spirit. A stone that knew the direction of north!

He paused, about to take the next step, startled by a noise in the bushes. *I must be more careful,* he thought. He was annoyed at himself for having been lost in thought instead of paying attention to the possible dangers in the night. Such carelessness could get them all killed. Some small animal scurried away, a rabbit or a fox, maybe. Odin relaxed.

"What is it?" whispered Thorsson.

"Nothing. Some small creature. It is gone. Come, we must go on."

He was concerned that even at their best pace, the three were traveling ever so much more slowly than their pursuers could.

"Could we find a boat?" asked Thorsson.

Odin was startled for a moment. He had been thinking the same thing. This yellow-hair was quite perceptive, and that was good. Maybe these two were well worth helping. He would like to take them back to his people, to show the Norsemen where he had grown up. Also to show them off to his people, maybe brag a little, exchange some stories. It would greatly expand his prestige.

He paused, both in his thought and his stride. An idea . . . Yes, of course! Those who sought to kill them would expect the surviving Norsemen to try to return to the village on the sea. They would probably be unaware that a Skraeling was helping them. Yes, it had worked for him before! When he escaped, he had headed in the opposite direction from the one they expected. And he had succeeded. True, they had discovered the ruse, and had come after him again, but it had given him time. Time and distance.

Now here was a similar situation, though in reverse. The enemy expected the fugitives to flee downstream, and that was what they were doing. In the morning, the trackers would be hot on their trail. But why not double back? Confuse the trail, gain a little time to travel upstream, and try to rejoin his own people. True, it was not the direction that the Norsemen would wish. But, from the safety of Odin's own tribe, they could then plan their return to the Norse settlement.

"What is it?" Thorsson asked again, more impatiently this time.

"It is a plan, Thorsson. Until now we are just running, but I have a plan."

"What is it?"

"I will tell you later. For now, we go on as we are. But let us leave a plainer trail."

"Leave a *trail*?"

"Yes. To confuse them."

"It confuses *me!*" the Norseman protested.

"I know. We will double back later . . . try to lose them."

"But, I . . ."

"I will tell you, Thorsson, later, when we have time. But for now, we must keep moving. And leave a trail."

Odin reached out to break a twig that protruded in front of him. He almost chuckled at the consternation he hoped that this plan would bring to the enemy trackers.

15

Shortly after daylight they came to a small stream. It was little more than a rivulet that came trickling down the rocky hillside to tumble into the fjord below. But the Skraeling seemed pleased. He halted the others at the point where the path crossed the flow of water.

"Let us wait a little," he suggested, "for more light."

Nils did not understand, but was willing to stop. Even though he had considered himself in moderately good physical condition, he was nearing exhaustion. Svenson, too, was showing the effects of the past two days and nights. Nils looked at Odin with a new respect. When he had first seen the one-eyed Skraeling, his impression was of a ragged wastrel, a savage. He had assumed that the man had attached himself to the Norse settlement because he was unable to function on his own. That was a life of comparative ease for the Skraeling, doing menial tasks in return for the opportunity to beg from the settlers.

Only now had Nils begun to see how wrong he had been. This was no ignorant beggar, but a clever and inventive man. The Skraeling was much younger than Nils's original impression had told him, and far more intelligent. Odin was largely responsible for keeping them alive thus far.

The sun's rays were striking through the trees now, and scraps of scattered fog hung in the low places. It would have been a fine morning under other circumstances. Birds sang in the trees, and there was little in the beauty of the rocky fjord that told of the imminent danger that stalked the three fugitives.

"Now I will tell you," Odin began. "First, they will think we mean to return to your town."

"But we do!" Nils protested.

"Yes, it is so. And they can easily follow us, because they know that. But what if we go the other way, upstream, to confuse them?"

Nils frowned. "And be farther from where we want to be?"

"At first, yes. With *my* people. We will be safe, and when the time is right, we will bring you back to the village of your people. Down the river, in boats. But first, we must escape those who follow us."

"How do you know we are followed?" asked Nils.

The Skraeling chuckled. "I *know*. Besides, they found our boat. They chopped it."

"So, what is next?" demanded Nils, not quite convinced.

"I will show you. Watch what I do."

Odin walked to the stream, and carefully planted his foot so that it was mostly on a flat rock at the edge of the rivulet. But the toe of his moccasin protruded, and as he stepped forward, it touched the mud, leaving a partial track.

"You do not need to do that," Odin said. "One is enough for them to find. But now, see what I do."

The Skraeling stepped into the water and out onto the other bank, striding confidently down the trail a few paces. There the dim path seemed to disappear among a heavy growth of ferns, shrubs, and grasses. Nils knew that somewhere beyond, the trail would reappear, but what?

Now Odin stopped, feet firmly planted, balancing himself in midstride. Carefully he began to step backward, a deliberate step at a time. Each time his foot touched the ground, it was precisely in the damp track he had just made. Either that, or on an alternative spot, a rock or a clump of tough grass sod. When he reached the little stream, he stepped into the water with both feet, and beckoned to Nils.

"Now you, Thorsson. Make a set of tracks, but only that far. Then, come back in the same steps."

The scheme was plain now, and the Norsemen quickly followed his example, returning to stand in the icy water of the stream. Odin turned and waded upstream, motioning for them to follow.

"Now, leave no more trail," he said over his shoulder.

It would be good, thought Nils, *if that could be*. But he knew what meant. The less trail sign, the more time-consuming for those who sought them.

The water was cold, chilling the toes, then the ankles. In a short while Nils's feet were like wooden stumps. Doggedly, he followed the Skraeling, determined to show his resolve. Svenson brought up the rear, breathing just a little heavier at the steepness of the slope.

Odin remained in the cascading little stream for some time, stepping from one pool to another, letting the flowing water obscure their tracks. Finally they arrived at a spring that was apparently the source of the rivulet. Here, the clear stream gushed directly out of a hole in the rocks.

"We must leave no tracks here," cautioned Odin.

He led the way around the damp earth at the water's source, seeking rocks and grassy hummocks on which to step. Then he resumed the climb. Now, however, all three were careful *not* to leave the slightest sign of a trail. No more broken twigs or intentional footprints. Again, Nils noted the innate cleverness of the man who led them. If they survived, he now realized, it would be because of the skill of the Skraeling.

They neared the top of the slope, and Odin paused to caution them. "They will be watching the ridge," he noted. "We must not show ourselves against the sky."

They paused to rest after the climb, carefully screened by a thin growth of trees near the summit. The view below was immense. It was possible to see for a long distance both up and down the great waterway. Almost directly beneath them, the rapids of the Talking Water stretched across the narrows. Below and on the far side, a smudge of smoke marked the location of the burned and sacked ship. Nils felt yet another pang of loss and regret, mixed with guilt over his lack of judgment. His first and maybe his last command, and he had lost his ship.

Tiny moving specks on the water were identified as the small boats of the Skraelings. Not as many as before, but now Nils noticed a cluster of three or four just above the rapids on *this* side of the river.

"They look for us," said Odin simply, pointing in that direction.

"*Why?*" Nils wondered aloud. "Why is it so important to find a man or two?"

Odin looked at him with his baleful one-eyed stare, and gave his strange characteristic shrug.

"We killed them first. They want your people to know that cannot be forgotten."

"But if they kill us all, who is to know?" Nils persisted.

Odin nodded. "Your people would know when you do not return. But maybe they would leave one. Blind him, maybe. . . ." He pointed to his own shrunken eye socket. "Maybe cut off a thumb, so he cannot use a weapon. Maybe cut out his seed." He pointed to his groin in explanation.

Nils gritted his teeth at such a thought, yet he knew that his own people had inflicted the same sort of dread among the Britons. It had never occurred to him that he might some day be on the receiving end of such violence. It was not a good feeling. His thoughts of combat had been of charging into the fray, boldly killing or being killed, dying like a Viking. . . . This was not as he had expected.

Odin seemed mildly amused at his reaction. "Maybe we will get away, Thorsson," he said with a wry smile. "Now let us move on. We will stay on the high places, but try not to show ourselves. We go that way." He pointed upriver.

"How far?"

"To my people?" Odin shrugged again. "By boat, maybe three, four sleeps. This way, much longer."

Of course, thought Nils. *A man without a boat . . .*

"Maybe we can steal a boat," the Skraeling echoed his thoughts, "but not now. They will be watching the water. Now come!"

It was rough traveling along the crest of the headland, made even worse by the constant need not to expose themselves. It was already past midday when they had reached the ridge, and now the sun was lowering across the sound. Soon they must look for a place to spend the night. *Well, let Odin choose it*, thought Nils. *He knows this country.* Then again he felt mixed emotions. Gratitude for the Skraeling's help, but resentment that they should have to be dependent on the skills of this savage.

"Wait here," Odin said. "I will look ahead."

By this time the shadows were purpling distant coves and valleys, and the still of evening lay across the surface of the water below. In better circumstances, it would have been a setting of great beauty, to stand on this fine bold headland. But now, the darkening shadows lent a threatening tone to the whole panorama. Odin, who had gone ahead a little way, now returned.

"I have found a place to stop," he said simply. "Ahead, there."

He had chosen well, Nils saw. The place where they would spend the night was a broad shelf on the face of the promontory. Several paces in width at the widest point, its level area could not be seen from below. It was nearly a bow shot in length as it ran along the cliff's face. At the far end the ledge diminished to nothing, and at the point where they had stepped upon it, it was quite narrow. Persons could pass only in single file. Nils realized that there were many good things about this place. It was hidden from casual passersby. It was defensible, because the only route of approach was by the path they had taken. The cliff above protected from that direction, and the slope below was likewise too steep to climb. One man at the narrow spot could hold off any number of attackers.

One great disadvantage, however, was the lack of water. It took only a glance to see that the shelf was dry. No trace of a seep or spring was apparent. Any flow of water, of course, would have eroded the ledge through the many generations of its existence. *What an odd idea,* Nils thought. *We could not have both. Water or this shelf, but not both.*

"I go to bring water," said the Skraeling, who must have had similar thoughts. "There is a good spring below." He pulled an empty waterskin from his makeshift pack.

"Let us all go," Sven suggested. "Water is easier to carry in the belly than in a skin."

Odin smiled and nodded, turning to lead the way. In a short while all three had drunk their fill, and they returned to the ledge with a full skin of water.

"Now," said the Skraeling seriously, "I am made to think that we should all eat. We will need strength."

He produced some dark, greasy-looking sticks of a leathery substance and handed one to each of the others.

"What is it?" asked Nils.

"Meat."

Odin began to chew, and the others joined in the primitive meal as darkness fell and the night creatures began to fill the shadows with their distinctive cries.

"There are three of them," said the tracker, returning to the waiting war party. "One is very clever."

"What do you mean, Tracker of the Wind?"

"Two are the men from the big boats. I can tell by their tracks. Their shoes are different."

"But what of the other?"

Wind Tracker shrugged. These fugitives were forcing him to use every bit of the skill for which he was renowned.

It had been an interesting campaign. They had attacked the invaders in the raid at dawn and had caught them completely off guard. Even so, the white-hairs had fought well, and had managed to get their great boat under way. Then, for some strange reason, they had burned it. And after all the work of portage around the rapids! This had seemed a good time to attack the other boat, before the invaders had time to unite their divided force. That move had been highly successful, and had resulted in the capture of many supplies and many trophies of war. It was good, and there would be stories and songs for many generations in celebration of the great victory.

Some of the invading white-hairs had fled into the woods, and these were systematically hunted down and killed or captured for later amusement. Then came a discovery. One small boat, captured and used by the invaders, had apparently crossed the wide river above the rapids, and landed on the other side. There must be at least one or two fugitives over there. The leaders of the successful war party asked to utilize the skills of their best tracker to find these who had escaped the battle.

Wind Tracker was proud of his skill, and of the prestige that it had brought him. It had taken a lifetime to perfect, and he was not a young man. He rose to this challenge.

The scouts who had found and destroyed the small boat took him there. It did not take long to determine that the occupants of the boat had tried to hide it, and had then gone downstream around the rapids on foot. Obviously, they hoped to rejoin their own people at the settlement many days' travel downstream among the islands. He had to admire their determination, because that was a long way on foot, through very rough country.

It had not been long, however, before the tracker realized that there was something unusual here. At first there had been little attempt to conceal the trail. Then for a while, it appeared that there *was* such an effort. And abruptly, another change. The trail was quite plain.

At first he had thought that the fugitives believed themselves safe, and were becoming careless. But it seemed more complicated than that. It was a broken twig that had caused him to guess that he was dealing with an expert, and Wind Tracker rose to the challenge.

When a twig is broken by someone brushing past it, the break is in the direction of motion. He studied this twig for some time, broken and dangling by its strip of bark. There was something wrong about it. . . . Ah! He almost chuckled aloud as he realized. This twig had been bent *upward* until it snapped. So, it was not an accident, but a deliberate sign. Someone had taken this twig in his hand and broken it to *leave* a trail. But why? Wind Tracker squatted and held the broken and still-dangling stick in his palm, trying to read the thoughts of the one who had snapped it. It must be part of a planned deception, one for which he must be alert.

When the trail stopped abruptly, he was puzzled for a short while. He thought that he had lost it, but a quick circle revealed that the tracks led to a dense area of brushy growth and then simply stopped. If they did not go on, then, the tracks must go . . . *back!*

He dropped to all fours, examining the plain tracks in the game trail. *Yes, there!* Someone had stepped again in his own track. But not exactly. There were two overlapping impressions of the heel, not quite the same. Instantly he realized . . . the stream, the little rivulet that came tumbling down the rocks. Of course! Quickly, he trotted back. It was growing late, and if he could unravel this puzzle before dark . . . Well, a fresh trail is always easier.

He glanced up and down the rivulet. The fugitives would not go down toward the water, because of the boats of the searching parties. So, *up!* He began to climb upstream, wading from puddle to pool as if he were trying to hide his tracks. And there! Yes . . . a stone, no larger than his fist, lying in the shallow water. Growing on its surface was a single patch of lichen. But the lichen was under the water. It could not exist there for very long, so that stone must have been dislodged only a short while ago, and fallen into the pool.

He hurried on. Now that he knew more of the minds of the fugitives, he knew what he sought. Even so, it was probably only luck that caused him to spot the place where they left the little stream. They had reached the spring that was its source. Now, which way?

It was with some degree of surprise that he realized that they had doubled back. Then, when he thought again, maybe it was no surprise at all. Because, by this time he had become familiar with the tracks of the three men, and was beginning to know them well. Two were men of the invaders, one a trifle heavier than the other, with a wider foot that made a deeper track in soft dirt. The third, however, was probably the one who had laid such a skillful and deceptive trail. From the tracks of that one's moccasins, it was apparent that he was *not* one of the outsiders. This was one who knew the country, a native here. One of their traditional enemies, most likely. Special tortures should be reserved for *that* one!

Wind Tracker hurried back to where the dozen others waited. He would report his findings and then wait for the moon to rise. Now that he knew the fugitives so well, he could practically track them in the dark. He knew their direction, and game trails were few. He felt confident enough that he could gain nearly a day's time in the pursuit. And that would certainly present a surprise for the clever man, whoever he might be, who had caused all this trouble.

16

"Ah, their tracker is good! Much better than I thought," Odin said sadly. "They are here!"

He had returned hurriedly after an attempt to reconnoiter at daybreak.

"Did they see you?" asked Svenson.

"I did not think so, but . . ." he gave his characteristic little shrug. "Who knows? I did not think they should be here yet, either!"

"But how?" Nils wondered aloud.

"They had to find our tracks, where we doubled back, last night before dark. And then, travel all night. Their tracker is good. He saw what we were trying to do, and then followed us by moonlight!"

"Can we get away?" asked Nils.

"I think it is too late. I started on our back track, and heard them ahead of me. I hurried back here. Maybe they will pass us by."

The way that the Skraeling said it told plainly that he did not think so.

"What is there to do, then?"

"Hide here, be very quiet. Come, we will watch."

Odin led the way to the ledge, to an area where bushes screened the outer edge of the rocky shelf. He indicated that they should lie flat, unmoving, to watch.

"The trail goes on past us." He pointed. "Maybe they will follow it instead of looking for us. They know that we are trying to get back upriver, and following the ridge. Now let us be quiet. They will be here soon."

He had hardly finished speaking when a man stepped out of the woods where the trail opened onto the grassy slope below them. The man was moving rapidly, and he paused only to motion to those behind him as he trotted across the little meadow. Nils counted as more and more well-armed Skraelings crossed below them. *By Thor's hammer,* he thought, *a dozen . . . no, fourteen, counting the tracker!* Why so many to find three hapless fugitives? No sooner had the thought crossed his mind than he knew. These who had escaped must be made an example. The Skraelings could not do otherwise. Oddly, the thought occurred that this was not unlike Norse treatment of Britons and Welsh, and oddly this seemed to justify the action of the Skraelings.

Now the man in the lead, who had passed below them by this time, stopped to lean over and examine the ground. He held up a hand to the others to indicate that they should wait a moment, and then took a cautious step or two ahead. He peered at the shadowy forest, and seemed unsure. Then the man, obviously a tracker, turned to look up the slope.

For a moment it seemed that he looked straight into Nils's eyes, and Nils dared not even blink. There was a space of some fifty paces between them, but it seemed closer. The other men relaxed a little as they waited, and the tracker began to circle carefully, trying to pick up the lost trail of the fugitives. Nils knew that it could not be found, because it was not there. None of the three fugitives had walked in that area. He could follow the thought processes of the Skraeling tracker: *If there are no tracks this far, they have turned aside before this point.*

Yes, now the man was circling back toward the rest of the party. He called out something in his own tongue, and then, to Nils's consternation, pointed directly at the shelf on which they lay. Nils gripped his sword with sweating palms, trying to decide *when* he should leap up with a Viking yell in challenge to their attackers.

"Lie still, Thorsson!" whispered Odin, anticipating such a move. "Let us see. . . ."

There was a discussion below, some pointing in various directions, and everyone settled back, squatting on his heels while the tracker made one more circuit. Almost back to the point where they had left the trees he circled, and then suddenly straightened, calling out to the others. It was easy to see that he had found the trail that led to the shelf. Two men jumped up and sprinted across the meadow toward the other end of the formation. They would want to make certain that there was no escape route there.

Nils felt the trap closing around him. He glanced up at the rocky cliff above them. No, there was no escape there. Even if there had been handholds and places to step, any climber would quickly be riddled with arrows from below.

"This is not good, Thorsson," Odin observed. "They have said they will camp here. They know where we are."

"Yes, I saw that," Nils whispered irritably.

Now Odin stood up, in plain sight of their pursuers, and yelled something to the party below. There was a scramble of activity, and an arrow whistled past the Skraeling's head to shatter against the rock wall behind him. Odin picked it up and tossed it derisively over the rim. He shouted something to the bowman that could have been nothing other than an invitation to try again.

Now a man stepped forward who was obviously the leader of the party, by
his manner and by the deference the others showed him. He and Odin exchanged shouts for a little while. Nils decided to stand up, since there seemed
no point in doing otherwise. There was a flurry of noise from below, and now
Svenson, too, rose from hiding, to another volley of shouting. Odin and the
other leader continued to yell, and finally the man below simply turned angrily
and walked down the slope, motioning the others to do the same. They moved
to a flat area near the trees, and began to prepare their camp.

"What was all that?" Nils asked.

"He wanted us to surrender," Odin explained. "He said we would not be
harmed, but I have known them before." He pointed to his blind eye socket.

"What did you say to him?" asked Nils.

Odin shrugged, and a trace of a wry smile curled his lip.

"I told him that we do not yield to the sons of mangy dogs, and that their
mothers eat dung." He paused a moment. "We have to fight them anyway,
Thorsson."

"Yes, I know. It is good."

Actually, he was thinking that such a confrontation, such exchange of
insults, was not at all unlike it would have been in a similar situation nearer
home, somewhere in the Isles. He wished that he understood the tongue of the
enemy, so that he, too, could participate.

"When will they attack?" Nils asked.

Odin shrugged. "Not soon. They will let us worry about it for a while.
But they can wait until we weaken, when our water is gone."

It was a grim thought, one that Nils had not been able to face. The
fugitives were safe here, but had no way to replenish food and water. Time was
on the side of the enemy.

"We should keep watch, of course," Odin was saying. "They may try to
sneak up a man or two, just to bother us."

Nils nodded. Some things would be the same everywhere.

The first attempt came somewhat sooner than they expected. Svenson was
on watch at the narrow point where they had gained access to the ledge. It was
some time after dark, and the other two had retired for a needed rest after the
stresses of the past days. The camp below was quiet, too. Sven could plainly see
the recumbent forms around their fires. Yet the experienced old warrior knew
better than to accept appearances. This would be an excellent time for the
enemy to try a feint.

It was quite dark, as the moon had not yet risen. He had thought a little while ago that he had seen some movement around the enemy fires as the light of the flames died down, but he could not be sure. This would be the time, though, after the campfires' light dimmed but before the rising of the moon. And, since he could not see, he must *listen*.

Unconsciously, he leaned toward the steep part of the path that led up to the ledge, cocking his ear for any sound that did not belong. He thought . . . *Yes!* There it was again. The clicking of a dislodged pebble on the stony path. Svenson pressed himself against the cliff's face and gripped his ax. The sound was only a pace or two below him.

He felt, rather than saw, the dark form rise before him, only an arm's length away, and he started his swing. His adversary had obviously misjudged the position of the sentry. Well he might. Svenson had made himself quite visible before dark, but had shifted slightly after darkness concealed the move. The ax struck flesh and bone, and the first grunt of surprise changed to a mortal scream as the man fell, rolling down the steep slope. Judging from the sound, the Skraeling's dying form bounced and rolled for some distance before it came to rest. There was a soft moan, and then a flurry of whispers.

Someone below threw dry tinder on the fire, and light pushed the shadows into retreat as men came running.

The fugitives, too, hurried to join their sentry.

"Sven! Are you all right?" called Nils.

"Of course! We have one less to worry us!" Svenson chortled.

They could hear the voices below, as the other Skraelings tried to help the dead or dying man. There was an angry exchange of shouts between Odin and the attackers.

"It is good," Odin commented. "They know we are to be feared, now."

"But they can bring more and more," Nils observed.

"Of course, Thorsson. They know that, and we know that. But now, we have their respect."

By the time the moon rose to light the hillside, the Skraelings had carried their fallen warrior away. Nils was not certain whether the man was dead or not, but he knew of Svenson's strength and skill. They would not have to worry about that opponent.

One thing was becoming rapidly apparent to Nils Thorsson, however. It had taken only a little while to establish a relationship with the one-eyed Skraeling. There is a special bond between people who have fought together or suffered together. Or both. Add a common enemy, and an unorganized group becomes a team, a close-knit camaraderie. Already, the distrust that had surfaced in his suspicion of Odin was gone. The Skraeling had proven himself worthy of trust.

From an ill-suited trio of hapless fugitives they had undergone a great change. Nils had first become aware of it when Odin said things like "*we* should keep watch." Overnight the trio had become a unified force. There was now "we" and "they."

Nils knew that both he and Odin took pride in Svenson's victory over the attacker. He wondered a bit yet, with some degree of concern, about the leadership of their little party. It had bothered him at first that Odin seemed to be making the decisions for them. Even that seemed less important now.

For some reason or other, an old Norse legend popped into his thoughts as the moon rose and flooded the slope and the fjord below with its silvery light. A longship in new waters, it was told, had been hailed by strangers.

"Let us talk to your leader," the others had requested.

"We have no leader," the Norsemen had answered. "Among us, we are all equals."

17

When will they try again?" asked Nils.

Odin shrugged. "Who knows? Maybe they will not."

"But surely they will," Nils snapped irritably. "They cannot just leave us here!"

Even as he said it, he realized the truth. *They can.* There was no urgency at all, and the Skraelings could wait. Wait, until the beleaguered trio on the ledge was starved into submission. He wondered how many days' food there was in Odin's pack. Then he realized. It would not be food that would become the problem, but *water.* A man could go for a long time without food, but he must have water. Three days, it was said, was about the limit without it. Before death intervened, that is.

A stronger person might live a bit longer, a weak one a shorter variation.

Water was as necessary as air to breathe, to continue living. Its absence would bring death just as surely as the absence of air. A little slower, that was all.

It made him thirsty just to think about it, and he swallowed hard. It also called to his attention the fact that the dried meat and whatever else Odin might have salvaged for them to eat was likely to be just that—*dry.* That would result in more thirst. At least, so it seemed to Nils. Maybe it would be better to fast again. He could ask Odin about it. Surely the Skraeling . . . *Damn! I'm doing it again!* Nils fumed to himself. He was becoming far too dependent on this savage.

On the other hand, what choice did they have? He and Svenson could possibly survive, living off the country, though it would be hard. Add in a dozen enemy Skraelings, maybe a hundred, and it would be valuable to have someone who knew both the land and the customs of the Skraelings. Someone like Odin. Each time he tried to think about it, he came back to that inescapable conclusion. They *needed* this man. He might even be essential to their survival.

Nils had not yet reached a point where he was ready to consider seriously the thought that they might *not* survive. True, he had thought about it, but in a detached way. Were they not still alive? With the passing days, he had unconsciously settled into a pattern that would not admit failure. Just as success breeds success, survival feeds on itself, and where there is life, there is hope. It was not a matter of whether they would survive, but *how.*

By the third day, such resolve was becoming shaky. They could sit or lie on the ledge, watching the Skraelings in their comfortable camp below. It was necessary to be somewhat careful. If they exposed themselves too openly, or became careless, an arrow would come searching, buzzing like an angry hornet over the rocky rim. It was enough of a threat to keep their heads down.

Once Odin sent a shaft in answer, just as a gesture of defiance. It was not very effective, and one of his precious arrows was lost. Still, it was probably worthwhile. Their enemies had no way of knowing how many weapons the fugitives might have. Beyond one ax, of course. Sven's stroke must have made quite an impression, because no one had tried to ascend to the ledge by the path again.

Nils picked up an arrow that had been shot from below and examined its construction. The shaft had been broken when it struck the rocky wall behind them, but it might be repairable. The stone point, delicately chipped to shape, was bound into the split end of the shaft with a slender strip of rawhide. Feathers, spotted black and white, were similarly tied to the rear of the arrow. What sort of bird? At home it would have been the feathers of a goose. Possibly a heron. Then he recalled some birds that he had seen in a pen at Straumfjord.

Large birds, standing as tall as a man's waist. Their naked red heads had reminded him of the head and neck of a vulture, but the colonists had reassured him. These were no carrion eaters, but a valuable bird for food. Much like a large chicken, it was said. The meat was white, in contrast to that of ducks or geese. The colonists called the creature by its Skraeling name, which seemed to be an imitation of its own call, a sort of gobbling sound.

"Are these the feathers of the gobble bird?" Nils asked Odin.

The Skraeling nodded, but said nothing.

"Our people use those of a goose," Nils said.

"We, too, sometimes," agreed Odin. "You do not have this bird?"

"No. I saw them at Straumfjord."

Odin nodded. "They are good to eat." He looked at the broken shaft in Nils's hands. "Is the point broken?" he asked.

Nils handed the arrow to him.

"Did you want to shoot it back at them?" Nils inquired, half-amused.

"No. Maybe, but I am made to think not. That would tell them that we have few arrows. But the point . . . Yes, it is chipped, but it can be reshaped. I will save it."

Odin drew his knife and cut the rawhide lashing to free the stone point. Then he held it up for Nils to see. It was a light amber in color, well shaped and sharp edged. The Skraeling tucked it into the pouch at his waist.

It took a moment for the significance of this action to impress itself on Nils. Odin had gone to the trouble of saving the arrow point, to resharpen and use later. Therefore, he must think that there would be a "later." *Odin does not think this is hopeless!* Nils told himself. If he had known what the Skraeling really thought, he might not have had the strength to go on.

As it was, however, this ray of hope helped to distract him from the sticky dryness in his mouth. They were using only enough water to wet their tongues at dawn and dusk, and still the waterskin grew flat and slim. To add to that, the enemy below knew their plight, at least to some degree, and took advantage of it. At any time they could be sure that the fugitives were watching, they would go through an elaborate act, a big show of drinking from waterskins, splashing, throwing water on each other. Nils licked dry and cracking lips as he watched.

One of those below held his waterskin aloft and shouted something. He was dripping wet, hair, body, and leather garments.

Odin shouted back something, and the man appeared disgruntled for a moment. Only a moment. Then he gestured an obscene insult, and proceeded to slowly empty the waterskin on the ground. He yelled something, and then laughed uproariously, as if he had made a great joke.

"What did he say?" asked Nils.

"He said to come down and share the good fortune of their water," Odin said grimly. "I told him we do not need as much to wash our mouths, because we do not eat dung."

He was quiet for a moment, and then went on. "Now he said that if we do not want it, he will pour it out. And he did."

Nils licked dry lips again. He had suspected something of the sort. The taunting sight of clear cool water pouring out onto the ground was almost intolerable. He lifted his eyes to look beyond, and found that it was no better. Worse, maybe. The deep and wide river to the sea, its clear, cold water, appeared much like the fjords of his homeland. For an instant, he wished that he was a child again, sitting at his grandfather's knee, listening to the old man's stories. That had been a time of safety and security. There had been no Skraelings trying to kill him. The only terrors then had been in the exciting stories of his grandfather. Giants who lived in dark ice caves somewhere to the north. They had been scary, but even as a small child he had known that they were not real.

He wondered what his grandfather would have thought of the new discoveries. The colonies to the west, the newfound land and the continent beyond. Skraelings . . .

"Here," Odin was saying. "Put this in your mouth. Suck it."

Odin handed Nils a small round pebble, and another to Svenson. Nils turned it over in his hand. Nothing unusual about it. Just a stone, polished round and smooth by tumbling in the stream for many lifetimes. He put it on his tongue, and found that it fit well. He could visualize it between the ranks of teeth in his closed jaws. He pressed it against the arched roof of his mouth with his tongue. Yes, it felt good.

"It will make water," Odin told him.

Well, maybe . . . Nils had to agree that his mouth did not seem as dry, somehow. Maybe it was only a trick of his senses, but it did seem to help. A special kind of stone? Where did Odin get them? This sort of round stone was commonly seen in a small and rapid stream. Had Odin picked them up earlier?

"Odin," he asked, "tell me of these stones. Where did you get them?"

"The stream." Odin jerked his head in that direction. "They carry water."

"What? Water?"

The Skraeling nodded seriously.

"Theirs is the spirit of the water," he said. "They have lived there many lifetimes. How could it be otherwise?"

"But how?"

Odin shrugged his characteristic shrug.

"I do not know, Thorsson. I do not understand fire, either, but it warms me. Maybe this is spirit-water in the stone. It is not much, but it helps."

The subject was obviously finished.

The help given by the stones and their spirit-water was only temporary. In another day, it seemed no help at all. The waterskin was empty, and the parched throats of the beleaguered trio had begun to swell. It was difficult to swallow now. At dawn they licked dew from the grasses, but they knew it would not be enough. Nils recalled that he had not emptied his bladder for at least a day. There had been no need.

And he was growing weaker. This bothered him greatly. During the times when he despaired of survival, he imagined how he would go out, weapon in hand. Like a Viking . . . But if he became too weak to fight, it would be hard to die proudly. He was also finding that his thoughts were confused part of the time. This, too, worried him. To die was one thing. To die weak and confused was quite another. A drink of cool, clear water was becoming the most important thing in the world.

In his fantasy, he imagined that Odin could ask the Skraelings for water, in return for which the three would come out and fight. Then the dreamy confusion would pass and he would know that such a thing was ridiculous.

No, it would take something else, and as far as he could see, there *was* nothing else. If he was to go out proudly, he must do it before weakness and confusion overcame him. He hardly wondered what the others would do. They too were weak, and they talked little, now. Maybe they needed to talk about it. . . . Attack the enemy together in a last glorious fight.

Nils was curled up in the fetal position, half-asleep or half-stuporous, with such thoughts drifting through his head. It had just grown dark, and he was trying to make some sort of decision. What was it? Oh, yes . . . To attack the enemy. It should be at dawn. Dawn tomorrow, probably. He did not know if yet another dawn would find him capable of fighting, or even thinking. He wondered what his grandfather would have done. *Grandfather,* he thought, *help me, here!*

He began to think again about the stories of his grandfather. Stories of valor . . . fights against hopeless odds. Berserkers, fighting with superhuman strength in a trancelike state . . . *berserkers!*

Suddenly, he was wide awake, and his thoughts had cleared. *Yes! Thank you, Grandfather,* he said silently. Now, he must try to remember . . . how did they become that way? In his grandfather's story, they had stripped to the skin. . . . Yes, in midwinter, in the snow. That sounded good . . . you could eat snow. . . . *No, Thorsson!* he told himself. *Forget the thirst. Think!* The Viking warriors in his grandfather's story had stripped and become animals, almost. Animals with superhuman strength and courage, invincible, howling and screaming like madmen as they attacked. This had so unnerved the enemy that they had fled in panic and the day was saved. As Nils understood the berserker legend, though, that was not actually the purpose. It had only happened that way. The purpose was to die honorably, like a Viking, fighting for a cause against odds. By berserking, a warrior who for all practical purposes is already dead could enhance his passing. He could take more of the enemy with him.

What better situation than the one in which he now found himself? He had arrived at a point where he had to concede that it was over. There was no way in which the three fugitives could escape. They could stay on the ledge and die of thirst, or attack the enemy and die fighting. His Norse blood began to race at the mere thought that the one alternative meant curling up to die helplessly. It was not the way a Viking would choose. At least, he would retain that right, the choice of his manner of dying. He would concentrate on the frenzy of battle, and make himself known to these savages. He would give them a battle they would never forget. The tales of his valor and his death would be recounted for generations around the fires of the Skraelings.

Excitement rose in him. The urge to move, to shout, and dance was strong. Maybe it was partly the fasting. He had been avoiding the dried food from Odin's pack because it made his thirst more uncomfortable. Maybe that now accounted for the remarkable clarity of his senses. Now that he had reasoned out what he must do, the entire world seemed in harmony. He looked at the night sky above him, dotted with the myriad of stars. They seemed close enough to reach up and touch, now that he had the understanding of the way of things.

A night bird called, and he smiled at the very appropriateness of the sound. *Everything fits,* he chortled to himself. Now he must begin his final preparations. It was not long until dawn, and he had decided that dawn would be the time for his climactic triumph. Yes, as soon as it was light, he would begin.

Svenson rolled over and came sleepily awake. He glanced around at the empty place of Odin, who was on watch, and then at Nils, who was standing, staring into the sky.

"What is it?" Svenson asked.

Nils turned to look at him in the dim light of the waning moon.

"Sven," he whispered excitedly, "when dawn comes, I am going berserk!"

18

venson did not try to stop him, or to convince him otherwise. It was an honorable thing, a proud way to die. It was also a private thing, an individual decision. Svenson did not offer to join in the berserking, and Nils did not invite him to do so. When the fighting began, he assumed that the others would join in. Odin's arrows might work to good effect, fired from the ledge into a fight below. Sven would probably wade into the Skraeling attackers with his ax. If they did, it would be good. If not, so be it. The event that would be handed down in Skraeling legend would be that of the mighty warrior who had killed so many before he fell.

Nils waited until it was growing quite light before he began. The Skraelings were stirring in the camp below, rising sleepily and stumbling a few steps into the trees to relieve full bladders. *But I shall wake you!* thought Nils.

When the time seemed right, he stepped to the rim of the ledge.

"Gather here, you mangy sons of dogs," he yelled. "I will show you the event of your lives!"

He knew, of course, that none could understand him except Svenson. Yet the result was the same. The Skraelings began to gather and drift toward the slope, laughing and joking at this strange action of one of the fugitives.

Odin came running from his post.

"What is it?" he asked Svenson.

Svenson shrugged. "It is a way of our people. A warrior decides to die fighting."

"Now?"

"Yes."

"Oh."

The Skraeling seated himself to watch, but kept his bow ready. He was also near enough to the edge to see what was going on below. There were no arrows this morning. The enemy was concentrating on the figure at the rim of the ledge, curious as to what he would do next.

Now Nils began to dance and sing. It was a very crude thing, without much reason or sensibility. In fact, it had little except rhythm to characterize it. The words were partly threat, partly insult, and to a great degree, nonsensical.

As he moved in the rhythms of his improvised dance, he began to disrobe. He ripped loose the laces of his tunic and threw it aside. Then his shirt. Nils tossed the garment over the edge and it fluttered to the grass below. He loosened his belt and laid it aside more carefully, because it held his fighting knife. His leather pantaloons slipped to his ankles and he stepped out of them, now wearing only his wrapped footgear with the thongs that bound them to his ankles. They did not seem important now. Nothing did anymore, except the frenzy and excitement of the moment.

Nils would have had great difficulty in describing his feelings. He could not have said when it happened, or *what* had happened. He was standing on the very edge of the rocky shelf, screaming at those below. Screaming nonsense syllables that seemed meaningful though he did not know what they meant. As he had chanted, the words of challenge had become less and less coherent, replaced with nonsense. Some were completely foreign, gutturals and falsettos, growls and howls and screams.

Now his companions and enemies alike stared at him in wonder. The sounds issuing from his mouth seemed not to come from any human throat. They were animal sounds, and were now more like the howl of a wolf as the pursuit draws to a close and the kill is near.

The Skraelings below stood openmouthed in awe at the transformation. They could see the vacant look in the eyes of the white-haired stranger. His pale skin shone white in the morning sun.

Nils's reflexes were still functioning at their best, or perhaps better, even. By sheer instinct, his right hand gripped the sword and his left clutched the belt knife. Now, with hardly a glance below, he jumped from the ledge with a final roar of challenge.

The slope was perhaps the height of two men below the ledge. He struck the grass and rolled once, which brought him to a more level spot. He crouched for a moment on all fours to regain his balance, while yet another animal howl issued from his lungs. Then he stood erect, weapons ready, to meet the charge of the enemy.

And nothing happened. The Skraelings stood, watching, making no effort to attack. The white-haired figure rushed at them, and they fell away, hurrying out of his path. He tried again to attack, but the Skraelings dissolved again before his rush. He howled again, a frustrated challenge.

On the ledge above, Odin had watched with fascination. He had not expected the Norseman to be capable of such a ceremony. He did not know what he had expected. But surely, by all reason, the light-haired Thorsson should have been lying dead and dismembered almost before he struck the slope. He realized, of course, what held the enemy back. They had not expected, any more than Odin had, such a ceremony of the spirit.

Now Odin was thinking rapidly. The situation was critical, and could turn to disaster in the space of a heartbeat. They must do something. He glanced at Svenson, who was staring in openmouthed amazement. There was no time to communicate to him. Odin stepped to the very edge.

"Now hear me, below," he shouted in the tongue of the Skraelings' tribe. "It is well that you have not harmed this holy man."

He looked at their upturned faces. *Good,* he thought. *Now, if they will continue to listen.* The naked Norseman was standing there, swaying a little as he stood, exhausted from the spirit-visit that had just occurred. His howls were less pronounced, and he looked a bit confused.

"It is good that you have not harmed him," Odin continued. "Of course, you had no way of knowing his powers, so maybe he will forgive you this time."

There was a little nervous laughter, but many doubtful looks.

"This is a most powerful holy man," Odin went on. "You saw him turn himself into a wolf, almost, and begin his challenge on all fours?"

There were nods of amazement.

"What have you to do with this man?" asked their leader.

"I am his helper," Odin shouted dramatically. "So is this other, the Fire Hair, here." He pointed to Svenson. "He carries fire for our holy man."

There was a pause, and finally the Skraeling leader answered.

"I do not believe you. We only let him live on account of the spirit. Maybe we will kill him when it quiets down."

"Go ahead, if you want to take the risk," Odin shrugged. "But, to loose such a dangerous spirit . . . ah, you must be as crazy as he is!"

Again, nervous laughter.

"Look," Odin continued, "we all know how dangerous are the spirits that possess madmen. I am safe up here, but you would not expose yourself to this one by killing the body where it lives."

The looks below said that the Skraelings respected this line of reasoning, and Odin pushed on.

"You have no idea of this man's powers. We have seen him change the color of stones just by holding them in his hands. And Fire Hair, by the powers of his leader, can start a fire without even any rubbing-sticks."

There was a snort of derision, but most of those below seemed to take the whole thing quite seriously.

"What is happening?" asked the confused Svenson.

"I will tell you later. Do nothing until I ask it, and then do what I ask. You have your fire-maker?"

"Yes."

"Keep it ready."

He turned again to speak to those below.

"We will come down now," he said confidently, "but by the trail. We cannot fly like our holy man."

The Skraelings below nodded in acceptance, and the two gathered the cast-aside clothing of their comrade and made their way down the narrow path to the grassy slope below. The others kept their distance.

"It is good," said Odin, "that you did not try to harm him. I shudder to think what he might have done to you."

The leader of the Skraelings was staring, and now spoke.

"I . . . I *know* you!" he said. "You were our prisoner . . . the eye . . . you escaped!"

"Yes," Odin answered casually, "that is true. I have decided to forgive you for that."

An expression of rage came across the face of the other.

"*You* forgive *us*? Why should we not kill you right now?"

"If you think you want the risk. But I forget. . . . You have not yet seen the powers of my leader here. I am under his protection, and so is Fire Hair. He even changed my name! I am Odin, father of the gods!"

Odin felt that he was making an impression, but that he needed an example of some sort. This could still go either way.

"Let me dress White Wolf, the holy man," he suggested. "Sometimes he is dangerous for a little while after one of these spirit-visits. You have seen him act like a madman."

There were vigorous nods of agreement. Odin stepped very cautiously toward where the naked man stood. Nils stared numbly, exhausted from his strenuous effort.

"Here, Thorsson," Odin said gently. "Put on your clothes. You may have saved us. Now move very slowly . . . here, let me take your long knife."

He took the sword, though Nils held it tightly for a little while, not wanting to give it up.

"I will hold it for you, Thorsson, it is good," Odin continued. "Here, your shirt . . ." He turned to the leader of the Skraelings. "I need some water for the holy man," he said with authority. "He is always thirsty after one of these ceremonies."

The leader nodded and sent a man for a waterskin. Odin was pleased.

"It is good," he told Nils again.

"What? What happened, here?" asked Nils, bewildered.

"Yes, what?" Svenson added, still gripping his ax tightly.

"They think Thorsson is a holy man," Odin related quickly. "We are his helpers, so act so. I will tell you what we must do, and tell more later. Thorsson, are you all right?"

"I think so . . . a little dizzy . . . tired."

"You can rest soon. We need one ceremony. Can you show them the sun-stone?"

"Where is it?" asked Nils.

"I have it here. When I hand it to you, do the thing to make it blue."

The warrior returned with a waterskin, and Odin ceremoniously handed it to Nils. Nils sipped slowly, cautioned by Odin.

"It will hurt your stomach to drink too fast, Thorsson."

"It is good," Nils mumbled.

"The holy man says his helpers must have some, too," proclaimed Odin, taking the skin when Nils had finished. He sipped and handed it to Svenson.

"Now, after the White Wolf ceremony he likes to sleep a little, it takes much out of him. But he will give you a small demonstration of his power before he takes rest."

He took the leather pouch and made a ceremony of opening its drawstrings to slide the sun-stone into his palm. Then he handed it to Nils.

"Hold it high, Thorsson, so all can see," he suggested. Then he resumed the tongue of the Skraelings. "As you can see, this is a thin gray stone," he narrated. "Now watch it closely."

Nils rotated the object slowly, and as it neared the north-south alignment, there was a gasp from the warriors.

"It is *blue!*"

"Yes, it is as I told you," said Odin haughtily. "He changes stones with his hands. Now I must ask him to rest. It is enough for now."

The Skraeling leader nodded. "We will stand watch," he said. "Tell your holy man not to worry. We will protect him."

Odin stifled a smile. This had worked out much better than he could have foreseen. Already there was running through his head ideas of other ceremonies. Even the name, Thorsson, could be used. The son of Thor, god of thunder . . . Of course, White Wolf was good, too. But it was good to know the Norseman's name among his own people. That might be used later. And Fire

Hair . . . he would work on that, too. For the immediate future, it would be enough to have Svenson make a fire with his striker and flint.

But for now, some water, food, and rest. A great weight was lifting from them.

That thought was somewhat nullified through an offhanded remark by the Skraeling leader as they settled down to rest.

"You are still our captives, of course."

19

It was late afternoon now. Looking back on the events of the day, Nils Thorsson found that he could recall very little of how it happened. He remembered the decision to go berserk, and the excitement that began to generate as he prepared himself. Then it all became a half-forgotten blur, a dreamlike memory of howling and trying to fight. But his adversaries kept falling away, retreating out of reach as he attacked. . . . Like a dream.

Dimly, he remembered Odin, standing beside him and exhorting the Skraelings in their own tongue. He had not understood the strange power that his companion held over the enemy. It was even more confusing when he learned that this power belonged not to Odin, but to himself, Nils Thorsson.

"It is not mine, Thorsson," Odin explained. "Yours is the power. I am only your helper, as Svenson is."

Nils was uncertain. Was their one-eyed companion serious, or was this some bizarre trick to ridicule him? Odin seemed serious, and certainly the Skraelings seemed to treat Nils with a great deal of respect. A little fear, even. This sudden shift, from the surety of being killed by these people to being *honored* by them, was more than he could grasp.

They were captives. Odin made certain that he understood that, as soon as he was able. But prisoners who were allowed to keep their weapons?

"We are honored captives, Thorsson," Odin explained. "We will be treated well if we do not become dangerous to them. So be careful."

Nils had difficulty understanding their status. He himself seemed to be honored and feared, but to a degree, so were Svenson and Odin. The Skraeling tried to explain.

"You are regarded as a holy man, Thorsson."

"But *why?*"

Odin shrugged. "It happened that way. We were able to make it seem so."

"You mean, you told them this?"

"Well, maybe. Partly, anyway. But it is true, is it not, if they think it to be so?"

It was a puzzling question that had no answer.

"But what about you and Sven?"

"Oh, we are your helpers. I help you carry the things of your power . . . the sun-stone . . . your garments."

"Yes, I remember, now. You asked me to use the stone. But we knew north . . . and why did we *need* to know then?"

Odin chuckled. "We did not. I did not tell them of that power of the stone. Only that you could make it change color. We will save the north-finding power for later."

This man, Nils realized, had had a much greater part in their survival than he had realized.

"And what is Svenson's part in this?"

"He carries fire."

"Fire?"

"Yes. He had the little fire-striker, as your people use, with a flint stone."

"Yes, but—"

"These, whom you call Skraelings, start fire only with fire-sticks."

Odin gestured with his hands, showing the motion of a spindle in the socket of a fire-board.

"I do not understand, Odin."

"Well, I have told them that the Fire Hair can bring fire from a stone."

"Fire Hair?"

"Yes. I thought it would be good to have them think that this is why his hair is red . . . he is the fire carrier."

Nils smiled in amusement.

"Does Svenson know this?"

Odin glanced at Svenson, who was drowsing nearby. The entire experience of the past days had been a severe physical demand on them all.

"Yes, partly. I told him to take special care of the fire-maker."

"The Skraelings have not seen it yet?"

He hesitated a moment at the use of the term Skraeling to a Skraeling. Did that make sense? Could it be an offensive thing to Odin?

Odin seemed not to notice. "Not yet," he said. "I was saving that, too."

There was a mischievous twinkle in Odin's one eye. *He is enjoying this!* thought Nils.

Now the leader of the Skraelings approached, and spoke to Nils, a firm but respectful tone.

"He asks if you are feeling better," Odin translated.

Nils thought for a moment. He must be, but he could not even remember exactly how it had happened.

"Much better, I think."

Odin relayed the answer, and Nils began to think how he should handle this.

"Tell him," Nils requested, "that we thank him for his help, for the food and water, and we will be leaving in the morning to return to my people."

Odin's one eye widened. "I think this is not wise, Thorsson. We need boats—"

"Tell him."

Nils was feeling that he had lost control over his life, and felt a need to regain it. Maybe this sort of decision would make his authority felt.

Odin, obviously bothered by the request, still apparently relayed its main theme. The Skraeling leader retorted angrily.

"He says no," Odin reported. "He will not let us leave. He came to tell us that tomorrow, we go to *his* town."

Nils started to retort angrily, but then realized the futility of such an action. They had virtually no choice.

"We would seem to have no choice," he said. "Tell him we will come."

He never knew exactly how Odin relayed that speech, but might have been surprised. It was more like, *Tell my brother that we thank him for his hospitality, and are pleased to accept.*

The conversation continued for a little while, with Odin translating. Nils had the vague feeling that the interpreter was modifying the talk with his translation to meet his own desires. Probably, that of both parties. There was no way to be certain.

He did learn several things during the course of this conversation. The leader's name, which was a series of syllables without meaning to Nils, proved when translated to be Flying Squirrel.

"A squirrel who flies?" Nils asked Odin.

"Of course. You do not know them in your country?"

The whole idea seemed preposterous. Surely there was no such animal. A squirrel with wings? He dismissed it as a fantasy. Curious, though, that such a fantasy would be used as a name by the Skraelings. But he had yet another surprising bit of information to learn.

"Your name," said Odin, "is White Wolf."

"*White Wolf?* In the name of God, *why?*"

"Ah, you do not remember, Thorsson. You changed into a wolf, almost, howling and dancing. And without your garments you are very white, no? Your skin, your hair. So, you are White Wolf, in their tongue. Of course, I told them that among your own people you are Thorsson, son of the god of fire and thunder. This is part of the reason for your power as a holy man."

Nils was not certain that he understood that last statement. Did Odin believe that Nils had such power? Or had he only told the Skraelings that this was the reason? There seemed no point in pursuing it just now, and he let the matter drop. The whole thing was so confusing, so complicated, that Nils could not grasp it. He was still somewhat puzzled that they were alive. That had happened while he was dreaming or in whatever sort of trance he had entered.

That was another thing. Looking back, he realized that he had not really expected anything except that he would be killed when he attacked the Skraelings. He would take a few with him, die bravely, and make a lasting impression on the savages. But, he had been totally unprepared for the result, for whatever it was that *did* happen. He truly did not know, and it seemed unlikely that he would learn. The Skraelings, including Odin, seemed to accept the whole transformation as an important spiritual event, but not entirely unusual. Transformation? Had something like that really happened? Had he *really* almost changed into a white wolf? The whole thing was preposterous. Yet he remembered leaping from the ledge, rolling, and standing on all fours for a few moments while he howled a challenge. He could not remember it well, but . . . had he looked like a wolf? His memory was unsure, and Odin was vague about it. "Almost" a wolf . . .

Svenson was little help.

"What happened, Sven?" Nils asked the Norseman. "You saw it."

Svenson shook his head in bewilderment.

"I am not sure, Nils. We were all weak, dying of thirst."

"But did I look to you like a *wolf?*"

"Of course not. Well, not really. You were howling . . . on all fours. . . . Ah, Thorsson, I do not know *what* I saw. If they thought it was magic . . . or the work of the devil . . ." He paused and crossed himself. "I do not know. Whatever happened, it *saved* us. I will not argue with that."

"Nor I . . . but Sven, their attitude is so different. How can it be that what happened, whatever it was, is thought by them to be a miracle, but not unusual? How can *we* be honored, respected, feared a little, maybe, but still be *prisoners?*"

"I do not know, Nils. Their ways are strange. We know that." He was silent for a moment, then changed the subject. "Do you suppose there are any others still alive?"

Nils had wondered, too. Maybe Odin could find out, but he had hesitated to ask. Besides, so much had happened, so much that was hard to deal with anyway.

"I will see if Odin can ask them," he suggested.

The Skraeling was dubious at first, but quickly changed.

"Why not? I will ask."

He strolled over to talk to Flying Squirrel, they exchanged a little conversation, and Odin returned.

"He does not know, either," he reported. "There were some, at first. His people were hunting them down. Flying Squirrel and this party were following us, and the others were across the river."

He was quiet for a moment, and then continued. "I am made to think not, Thorsson. Not alive. There were few who could change into a white wolf, no?"

Thorsson was unsure whether this was a serious question or merely a bit of whimsy on the part of the Skraeling. Did *Odin* actually think he had seen it happen? Nils started to ask, but decided against it.

"We must consider," Nils said to Svenson as an aside, "that we are the only ones."

It was a hard thing to admit.

But what now? It was nearing sunset, and Flying Squirrel had told them that tomorrow they would start back upstream. Upstream, away from Straumfjord. Not that it mattered. They were still prisoners, even though honored prisoners.

"How far to the town of these people?" he asked Odin.

"A day . . . maybe two or three," Odin answered. "It does not matter."

Nils's anger flared for a moment. *It does matter,* he thought.

As if in answer to his unspoken protest, the Skraeling spoke again, more slowly, almost gently.

"It does not really matter, Thorsson. Farther from your people, closer to mine. We are *alive*. We will escape, some day. Then, we go . . . to your people or mine. It is no matter where, or when. For now, we are treated well, here."

20

It was three days' travel to the town of their captors. It was accomplished in the skin boats of the Skraelings, one Norseman sitting with two Skraelings who wielded the paddles. There were several other boats, loaded with plunder from the sacking of the supplies from the two longships.

It was quickly apparent that the three were to be closely watched. They were captives at best, even though with a certain degree of respect. During the first portion of the journey, that on foot back to the rapids, they were separated. On the trail, which permitted only single-file travel, there was always a Skraeling in front of each Norseman, and one behind. Nils noted that the same close observation was bestowed on their companion, Odin. Perhaps even more. Their captors seemed to distrust him somehow, though he spoke their language fluently. Maybe that was *why.*

Nils quickly realized that it would be of great advantage to learn their captors' tongue. He could communicate directly, then, without the troublesome translation through their fellow captive, Odin. Nils was feeling enough better now to begin to think of such things. Of the future . . . For a little while it had seemed that there *was* no future.

But now he had eaten and drunk, his strength was returning, and his kidneys were functioning once more. It was remarkable to him, how quickly his entire attitude improved with the simple act of emptying his bladder.

During a brief rest stop on the trail, the captives were allowed to mingle and communicate. This offered opportunity to speak to the others.

"Odin," he asked, "could you teach me some of the Skraelings' tongue?"

Odin looked at him in surprise.

"Why?"

"It would be easier if I could talk with them."

"Yes . . . but maybe we will not be with them long."

What does he have in mind? thought Nils.

"Escape?" he asked.

"Maybe. Maybe they let us go." He shrugged. "If you want to learn a Skraeling tongue, learn mine!"

"Your people speak a different tongue, then?"

"Yes. Did I not tell you that?"

"Maybe. Ah, Odin, much has happened!"

"That is true."

Now another thought came to Nils. If their captors were to let them leave, would it not be better to go downriver, toward Straumfjord, than away from it to Odin's people? Why would the one-eyed Skraeling think otherwise? Of course, Odin wished to go home, he supposed. But—

His thoughts were interrupted by their captors, who urged them up to travel again. Well, maybe he could speak with Odin later on this matter.

That opportunity came as they camped for the night. The three were permitted to communicate without interference. It was apparently only during travel. . . *They are afraid we will try to escape,* he realized.

They were given food and treated with respect. Even a fire of their own, against the chill of the night. There were three fires, each with its group of men. Nils had never thought about it before, but he began to wonder. At what point does a group need a second fire? A single fire is good for one or two people. Three, even. Maybe four, but beyond that point, there is a change in attitude. The campfire is no longer such a personal thing when so many share it. Its warmth and spiritual contact are spread too thinly for comfort. Emotional comfort.

He stared into the glowing coals as darkness deepened and closed around them. He was tired, from lack of sleep and from the physical strain of the day. Maybe that was the reason for the strange wandering of his thoughts. After several nights without a fire, the luxury of a campfire seemed beyond description. He stretched his tired muscles and extended his legs toward the fire to warm his feet. Even as he did so, he realized with some amusement that it was not merely for warmth. Not physical warmth, anyway. Partly, it was *light.* The cheery yellow flames pushed aside the shadows of the night, enlarging the circle where they now rested. It was a thing of comfort, and not merely physical comfort, but spiritual.

His thoughts along those lines had begun as the fires were lighted. Odin had suggested that Svenson *not* use his fire-striker.

"Let them do it. We will make a ceremony of the fire-striker later."

So the Skraelings had started a fire with their rubbing-sticks, and carried a blazing twig to the other fires. Nils noticed that Flying Squirrel, the Skraeling leader, took a pinch of something from a pouch to toss on the growing blaze of the first fire. A ritual of some sort?

"To honor the spirits of this place," Odin explained in answer to his question.

"What is the powder?"

"*Kinikinik.* Smoke."

"I do not understand."

"Made of dried plants, Thorsson. You do not know of this?"

"No." Nils was irritated at the condescending tone.

"You will see, later."

It was sometimes extremely frustrating to talk with this Skraeling. Yet they must trust him. Because of him, the two Norsemen were still alive.

And Odin was correct. They did see, later, the mystery of the *kinikinik* explained. At least, partly. It was just growing dark, and the party was settling in for the night. Most of the men had finished eating, and they gathered around the largest of the three fires. *Different fires have different purposes for these people,* Nils thought. This was a sort of social gathering at the end of the day. A larger fire was different in spirit, somehow, from the small private fire. It was almost a formal gathering, though men were laughing and joking as they assembled.

Flying Squirrel took out an object that seemed to have a small stone bowl at one end, attached to a stem about a hand span in length. From his pouch he took another pinch of the shredded plant material he had tossed into the fire earlier. He packed it into the bowl of the object. Nils glanced at Odin. The Skraeling met his eyes, said nothing, but motioned for him to watch. Now Flying Squirrel placed the stem in his mouth and took a burning twig from the fire to thrust into the bowl.

Fascinated, Nils watched while the man sucked smoke into his mouth and blew it back out in fragrant bluish clouds. The stem of the thing, he now realized, must be a hollow reed or pipe through which to draw the smoke. Others of the men around the fire had also taken out similar pipes and were beginning to light them.

Flying Squirrel now handed his pipe to Odin, who took a few puffs and handed it back. The other spoke a few words and declined to take it, gesturing toward the Norsemen.

"He says give it to White Wolf," Odin explained, passing the pipe to Nils.

Nils was unprepared for the sensation that resulted when he took a deep breath through the pipe. The smoke burned his mouth, his lungs, his nose, and he was seized with a paroxysm of coughing.

"Too hard," said Odin softly. "Be gentle with it. You do not know of these things, Thorsson?"

"No," choked Nils, wiping tears from his eyes. The Skraelings were looking on in amusement. "Why do we do this, Odin?"

The man shrugged, as Nils might have expected.

"It is a thing to share with others. It tastes good."

"Tastes?" There had seemed to be no taste at all, only irritation and heat.

"Yes," Odin insisted, "when you learn how to do it." He paused for a moment. "Of course, a pipe knows when a learner is smoking it."

He seemed quite serious. Nils experimented with a few puffs, and after the burning in his throat subsided, was actually able to taste the fragrance of the burning leaves. It was not completely unpleasant, though he could not identify the various aromas in the mixture. He started to hand the pipe back, but Flying Squirrel motioned to pass it on to Fire Hair. Svenson, having witnessed Nils's experience, did slightly better at learning the pleasures of *kinikinik*.

Odin spoke a few words to the Skraeling leader, who nodded in understanding. Nils turned to Odin in question.

"I told him," Odin explained, "that Fire Hair is more skilled in things of fire than you. Yours is a different gift."

Nils felt chastised, but said nothing. What could he say? He had not understood, and had drawn too deeply of the hot smoke. However, the Skraelings seemed to think nothing of it, beyond mild amusement. *Well*, he resolved, *I will do better next time.* And the smell around the fire as others smoked was not entirely unpleasant, he noticed.

"Tell me more of this, Odin," he requested.

"What is to tell?"

"Well . . . why did he throw some of this . . . *kinikinik?* Why did he put it on the fire?"

"A thing of the spirit, Thorsson. The smoke is pleasant to the spirits, and brings them close to us."

"It is a religious . . . a thing of the gods?"

Odin considered. "Maybe. Sometimes, like now, just to feel good. But that first pinch, when the fire was lighted . . . That says 'I am here. This is my camp tonight.' "

Nils pondered a moment, and then Odin spoke again.

"It honors the spirits of this place. We would not wish to anger them, no?"

"No, I suppose not. This asks their good feelings for us?"

"Yes, yes! That is it, Thorsson. It is good!"

Nils was a bit confused as to why he should be so pleased. Somehow, it was an honor to be praised for his insight. *Why*, he wondered, *is it so important to have the approval of this one-eyed savage?* He could not completely answer, but he was becoming more certain about one thing all the time. This man was far more intelligent, far more complex, than Nils had imagined. "Savage" was hardly correct. Was the entire world of the Skraelings as complex as this? Were there things that even Norsemen, with their highly developed knowledge and skills of navigation, did not understand as well as these Skraelings? Well, *kinikinik,* for one! He did not quite understand that yet. A substance partly for worship and partly for pleasure? And *what* plants were involved? Well, maybe later. He did not want to think about it, now. Or about anything. He was tired.

It was odd, then, that he now found himself sitting and staring at the dying fire. Colors shifted in the embers as slight changes in the breeze gently stirred them to life. His thoughts drifted back to his childhood, and to long evenings shared with his grandfather. He had loved to watch the glowing heart of the fire then, and memories came flowing back.

"A fire contains memories," his grandfather had once said. "Pictures of the past . . . Faces of friends and enemies, of good times and bad."

Nils had not understood until now, but now he did. He wrapped himself in a robe and lay on his side, staring at the fire, lost in thought and memory. Beyond the fire, a rhythmic snoring came from the huddled form of Svenson. Odin was quieter, but sleeping soundly. The others, if awake, were still. Nils was alone. It was a good feeling of aloneness, though. He reviewed the events of the past weeks in his mind. The shifting light and shadow of the dying embers seemed to parade them before his eyes.

The ocean crossing, the landing at Straumfjord . . . Its people . . . Karlsefni, the headman . . . Thorwald Ericson, the bold explorer . . . The warm body and warmer kisses of Ingrid, the blue-eyed goddess. Ah, to share *her* bed tonight! That in turn brought to mind her miserable husband, Olaf the cooper. He wondered if what the man had was worth the heartbreak of watching his beautiful wife flirt with anything that wore trousers. *Strange,* thought Nils. *I have less sympathy for her now.*

How had that happened? He would still try to take her home when he returned to their homeland, if she still wished it. Possibly this was the first time he had actually stopped to think about that. All his thoughts had been concentrated on getting back to Straumfjord. *But what then?* He had no ship. He had lost it. Lost his command. Guilt flooded over him, as he thought of the deaths of all the brave Norsemen in the crews of the two vessels.

And of the loss of his friend, Landsverk. Helge had been a little bit crazy, and had jeopardized the mission with his ambition. *No, I must not think ill of the dead,* Nils thought. *He was a brave man.* It was of some comfort now to think that Helge and the other brave Norsemen killed in the first battle had been given a heroes' funeral.

Some comfort, but not much.

21

The actual journey on the magnificent fjordlike river was almost pleasant. Nils's life and those of the people around him as he grew up had been focused on the sea. This was an opportunity to observe the boatmen of another people, to see their skills, their different methods of dealing with the same problems faced by those on the water anywhere.

He had already noted the skill with which they maneuvered the small round boats. Now he became even more impressed as they embarked above the rapids. A simple stroke or two at just the right time and place would right the spinning craft and steady her course. He recalled the clumsy efforts of the Norsemen in the first captured boats, trying to learn their handling. Now it occurred to him that those men, who had learned to paddle the Skraeling boats with such difficulty, were skilled sailors in their own right. But this was a *different* culture, a different way of doing the same things.

By noon of the first day of travel on the water, he had become quite impressed with the skill of these Skraeling boatmen. They had made good progress upriver, and stopped to disembark and stretch cramped legs. Odin was talking to one of their captors, and Nils saw them pointing across the wide river.

"What is it?" he asked.

"Your boat. The one that you burned for your dead."

"The *Norsemaiden*? What about it, Odin?"

"It went over there . . . stopped near the shore and burned."

"It is gone?"

"Mostly, yes. Part of it sank."

Nils had a strange sense of relief. For a dreadful moment he had thought that maybe that, too, had gone wrong. He imagined that the fire might have gone out, leaving partly consumed bodies aboard a still-floating hulk. But no, this was as it should be. Helge and the others, honored in death by the funeral pyre of their ship, bodies consumed by the cleansing fire as their spirits were carried aloft. Helge would have wished it so. Still, there was a sadness as they moved on after the pause. To Nils it was the final farewell to the brave yet troubled friend of his childhood. How different it might have been.

Nils saw familiar landmarks as they traveled, and in time recognized the spot where they had first encountered the Skraelings under the upturned boats. How long ago that seemed, like half a lifetime. Then, they had been an expedition of bold explorers, well provisioned, well equipped, and confident in the strength of their youth. He would have thought that nothing could threaten them. Now, only a few days later, it was all gone. Only he and Svenson had survived. The pall of guilt and sadness descended on him again, like a dark cloak thrown over him. He remained deeply depressed.

They did not stop at the site of that first skirmish, but proceeded on upstream. Nils assumed that their captors were from another village, and that proved true. By midafternoon there was an air of expectancy, much talk and joking. The Skraelings called across the water to each other, and there was a general feeling of happiness and satisfaction. *They must be nearing home*, thought Nils, whose spirits were falling even lower as those of their captors rose.

Now they were greeted by a couple of other boats from upstream, paddled by excited young men. The newcomers shouted and sang and turned their boats to travel with the returning victorious warriors. They stared at the captives, and there were busy conversations that obviously pertained to the Norsemen. Again, Nils was frustrated at his lack of understanding of their tongue. He would have liked to know what they were saying. *Damn that Odin*, he thought. *He could have begun to teach me!* His depression deepened.

They reached the shore where a crowd of people waited excitedly. It was a good landing, apparently much used. Nils could see a cluster of huts that must constitute the village, a little way up the gentle slope. Their captors were now scrambling out of the boats, pulling them up on shore. Flying Squirrel motioned to the captives to step out, and they did so, greeted by hostile faces. A woman spat at Nils, her spittle striking his cheek, to trickle down his jaw. He tried not to react, but wiped it away with his sleeve. Another held a stone knife menacingly in her hand, staring suggestively at Nils's crotch. He was more concerned about that one. It was a very uncomfortable feeling.

Then Flying Squirrel began to speak, and Nils watched the facial expressions change from hostility to wonder and awe. The woman who had spat at Nils looked positively repentant. The one with the knife, who had appeared more threatening to him, now lowered her weapon. Her expression was now one of curiosity. Curiosity and something else—respect.

"He told them about your great powers," said Odin at his elbow. "It is good. They will not harm us now."

That was reassuring, but it was still a tense situation, to be closed in on all sides by these Skraelings. A few days ago, any one of them would have gladly killed the intruders. Even with the protection of their strange mixed status as honored captives, Nils was uneasy.

The entire crowd moved up the slope toward the village in a confused procession. Children and dogs ran alongside, shouting and barking, respectively. It could have been a scene in his own country, Nils reflected. They could be Norsemen, Vikings of an earlier generation, welcomed by their families when they returned from raiding and sacking in Britannia and the islands. Now, of course, with the development of better navigation and the emphasis on trade rather than raiding, that day was passing. Still, it was a strange feeling, as if he were seeing his own past.

There was another thing that came as a surprise, somehow. Until now, he had seen no Skraelings at close range except fighting men. Here, there were old people, the children he had noticed before, and the women. He thought of the woman who had tried to spit on him, and the one with the knife. His skin still crawled, and the muscles of his groin tightened at the thought of her implied intentions. He wondered whether their captors would allow him to defend himself in an emergency. He would have to try it and see, he decided, if worse came to worst. And what that woman's hostile stare implied could have been a major tragedy.

He looked at her again, as the crowd moved along toward the town. A not unattractive woman, now that she was not quite such a threat to his manhood. Middle-aged, tall and proud, moving with grace and dignity. A woman who could take care of herself. Like one of the Norse women. There was a saying among the Britons, he recalled, a result of the traditional fighting along the coast and among the islands. "Never kill a Norseman, for then you will have to fight his wife." Maybe that was the case for this Skraeling woman. Had she lost a husband or son to the invaders?

Women were said to be experts at torture, and as bloodthirsty as any old-time Viking. Was there not a story . . . Yes! He had forgotten, in all the excitement of the expedition, and the hectic pace at Straumfjord. There had been a grisly murder a year or two ago, by a red-haired beauty who killed a rival woman with an ax. And was it not a sister of the Ericsons, Leif and Thorwald, who had done the killing? *By Thor's hammer,* he thought, *I think it was!* He could not remember the details, but there had been much gossip. He was glad that he had not thought of it while he was at Straumfjord with Thorwald. It would have been difficult to relate normally to the girl's brother.

He shrugged off the flight of memory, and returned to the present. *Yes,* he thought, *that woman, the one with the knife. She could and would use an ax on someone.*

While he was still thinking about the woman of the Skraelings, he noticed another fact. He had been thinking of these women as savages, either dirty and unkempt, or like the knife-woman, a dangerous warrior. He had not expected them to be attractive. But the little girls were pretty, as they ran along with the boys and dogs. And many of the older girls, blossoming into womanhood, were really quite attractive. The pleasing shape of a well-turned calf, the willowy swing of the hips drew his eyes. There were soft curves under soft buckskin dresses. Some were tall and slender, and the exotic dark eyes and long lashes in well-shaped faces were nicely framed by the gloss of hair as blue-black as the wing of a crow.

Nils was not certain why he was surprised. He did not know what he had expected. Maybe the long separation from women, on the voyage and then the expedition, after a frustrating stop at Straumfjord? . . . *No*, he decided, *that is not it.* It is true that chastity, like wine, makes a passing woman attractive. And the unfamiliar exotic appearance of these . . . *No, they really are attractive. Some of them downright beautiful!* He noted an inviting smile.

His reverie was interrupted as the crowd arrived among the houses. They were built of logs and chinked with mud, he saw, much like those that would be encountered in the more primitive parts of his own country. The thatched roofs, too, were similar. Some of the structures were of a size that would shelter a family, but some were larger. For an extended family, maybe. He thought of the communal structures at Straumfjord. There was also one long building that reminded him of a meeting hall, or longhouse.

"This is a meetinghouse?" he asked Odin.

The other merely nodded.

There was a brief discussion among their captors, some pointing, and more talk. Finally, Flying Squirrel, who appeared to be the village headman as well as the leader of the war party, spoke.

"He says that we will be his guests," Odin translated, pointing to one of the larger houses.

It appeared to be well kept, and there was a generally affluent character about it. A cooking fire smoldered outside, and women seemed to be tending it, even as they watched the proceedings.

"There will be a council tonight," Odin was saying. "We will be honored. I have thanked them for us." He paused for a moment. "I had thought to use Fire Hair's fire-striker now, but maybe at their council . . . Yes, that is better. Give them time to wonder!"

Flying Squirrel now beckoned, inviting them inside. They entered the house, and paused while their eyes adjusted to the dim light. Nils found the interior of the building much as he had expected. One major difference from those with which he was familiar was the absence of a chimney. But there was a place for fire, and an opening in the roof for the smoke to escape. The ashes were cold now. Apparently the Skraelings lived and cooked mostly outside in warm weather.

One of the women pointed to an area in a corner of the room.

"She says we may sleep there," Odin said.

There was a sort of ledge or bench that ran along the walls, completely around the room. This apparently served as furniture, in lieu of chairs, tables, and even beds. It was obvious that certain areas held sleeping robes, and that others were reserved for storage of food supplies.

Nils went over to the area indicated, dropped his few possessions on the ledge, and sat down. It was good to sit. Suddenly, he was exhausted, and wanted nothing but to sleep.

"Do not get too sleepy," Odin suggested. "We will eat, and then, the council."

"What will they do at the council?"

Odin gave his characteristic shrug.

"Who knows? They will talk. It is so with councils. They may ask us questions. We will show them the powers of Fire Hair."

There was a mischievous smile of satisfaction on his face. Nils did not ask further. There was no point in it. The one-eyed Skraeling would tell them what he wanted, when he wanted. That was mildly irritating, but Odin *had* kept them alive, and this was working as he had said.

There was one inescapable fact, though, Nils realized as he watched Odin settle their few possessions on the assigned portion of the ledge.

The bastard is actually enjoying this!

22

The council was held, not in the longhouse, as might have been expected, but outside under the sky. Odin had thought much about that, and finally inquired.

"Outside," Flying Squirrel answered. "Too hot and smoky inside."

At this season, that was true. Now, how to use their assets to create the best impression? Odin had planned to use every trick he could think of to amaze their captors, and as soon as possible. First impressions lasted, and there was no harm in trying.

"It is good," Odin smiled approvingly. "The Fire Hair wishes to make their first fire in this place tonight. He can light the council fire, no?"

Odin watched as the thoughts flitted through the chieftain's head. To his credit, it took Flying Squirrel only a moment to consider. There must be hazards, of course, in allowing the strangers full freedom. On the other hand, to challenge the power of the holy man, which was obviously so great, might bring even more risk.

"Your holy man, White Wolf, asks this?" inquired Flying Squirrel.

Odin nodded. "The lighting of the first fire is important to him."

"And to us," the chieftain agreed. "It is good. Let it be so."

Odin felt that the other had some doubts, but hesitated to challenge the unknown powers of the stranger's gifts. He had been prepared to call attention to the morning when the Norseman had almost become a wolf. There was a smug feeling of satisfaction that he had not even had to use that. But now, these people must be made to respect the powers of the other outsider, the fire-haired Svenson. Sven would not be completely safe from harm until he, too, had gained a certain amount of respect by some special deed. He approached the two Norsemen.

"I have told them," he explained, "that you have a custom of the lighting of a first fire in a new place."

"It is true," Thorsson answered. "We do have."

"Yes, yes," Odin hurried on, "we do, too. But we can use this, Thorsson. They will let Fire Hair—Svenson, here—perform it. And they have not seen your way of striking a spark with the metal striker."

"Ah, yes." Nils began to understand. "Sven, can you make it a real show for them?"

The old sailor smiled. "Of course."

"It is good," said Odin. "Just before dark. There must be enough light for them to see."

Svenson nodded, a mischievous grin on his face.

The crowd began to gather, and Odin accompanied Svenson and Nils to the spot where the council fire would be. A quantity of wood had been gathered to fuel the fire, and Odin busied himself with preparing the tinder and small sticks so that it would kindle quickly. A little opening under the stack of larger logs would provide a good place to plant the spark. He gathered more fine dry tinder than usual, to make the blaze flare up well. Dry grasses, cedar bark, tiny twigs. Normally, materials of this sort would be carefully saved and used in small quantities. Just enough, in fact, to allow the fire to start. This, however, was a special occasion, mostly to provide a spectacular show. Odin was careful, however, to arrange the fuel and tinder so that his lavish use of the finer materials was not readily apparent.

"There," he pointed, showing Svenson his handiwork. "You can put your spark in this little mouse nest of grass." Sven looked, and nodded eagerly in understanding.

More people were arriving now, reserving the best places to sit.

"Let us wait just a little longer," Odin suggested. "It would be good to have their chief here."

It was a matter of timing. To wait too long as darkness fell would destroy part of the impressiveness of the ceremony. But too soon, before the Skraelings' leader arrived, would be an affront to him. In addition, it seemed good to impress the leader with the fire-striker. It would seem to have great power to people who were familiar only with rubbing-sticks.

Odin began to prepare his scene.

"Here, Thorsson, you stand here. I will be there, on the other side, and Svenson, the Fire Maker, will be here. I will—"

His explanation was interrupted by the approach of Flying Squirrel, flanked by two of his warriors.

"It is good," muttered Odin to the Norsemen. "Now I will tell them—"

He broke off short and stood, raising his arms to get the attention of the crowd. Flying Squirrel and his party entered the circle and seated themselves. *Good. Not quite dark . . .*

"My chief," Odin addressed the leader, "and my brothers," to the crowd, "it is good to share your council fire."

He spoke in their own tongue, ignoring the sarcastic sneers on a few of the faces. It was to be expected that they knew the status of these three. Captives, though not without honor. But now, he must hurry on, before it became too dark.

"I speak for my leader, the holy man, White Wolf. Some of your men have seen his power. I, and this one, the Fire Maker, are very unimportant beside him. But enough. Tonight Fire Hair, the Fire Maker, will light the council flame. It is their way."

He made a grand sweeping gesture toward Svenson. The lighting of a first fire was completely familiar to the Skraelings, of course, and they sat waiting as Svenson knelt and readied his little scrap of charred cloth.

"He has no sticks," someone whispered. People began to stretch their necks, trying to see. There should have been a spindle, a fire-board, and a short bow. What? . . .

Svenson raised his hands and looked upward at the darkening sky, playing his part well. *Now*, thought Odin, *if his sparks will only fall right.* He held his breath. Svenson now took the nodule of flint in his left hand, and fitted the steel striker around the knuckles of his right. Very deliberately, he struck . . . once, twice, three times.

Odin saw the fat spark jump from the steel and land on Sven's charred cloth. Svenson, working with all deliberate haste, picked it up smoothly and placed it in a handful of cedar bark that he had prepared. Quickly, he folded the fluffy mass around the spark and lifted it high, blowing his breath through the shredded cedar, to fan it into life. White smoke poured from his hands, and just before the tinder burst into flame, Svenson bent to thrust it into the little grass pocket prepared by Odin.

Odin's one eye twinkled. *Just right!* There was a gasp from the front rows. It was apparent that this ceremony was something special.

"He did it with his bare hands!" someone whispered.

"No. He plucked it out of a stone."

". . . touched the stone three times . . ."

Everyone had seen it slightly differently. But their attention was now distracted by the fire itself. It seemed to leap into life, the orange tongues licking upward through the dry grasses and small sticks, leaping between the larger logs and thrusting out of the top of the well-built pile. Sparks flew upward toward the darkening sky, and the crowd stared in amazement at the speed with which it had happened.

During this distraction, Svenson quietly slipped the flint and steel back into his pouch and stood, hands raised toward heaven. The glow of the growing fire was pushing back the shadows now, enlarging the circle of light. The reflection of the flames on the red of Svenson's hair made it look alive, glowing in the twilight. People watched as the Fire Maker made a turn toward the crowd, a short bow, and sat down.

"What happened?" asked someone in the rear.

It had all been accomplished so quickly that those not watching closely had missed it.

"The Fire Hair just waved his hand and it blazed up!" insisted another.

Odin was pleased. It had gone well, and it was good to leave some observers dissatisfied. But he had accomplished his purpose.

Flying Squirrel was trying hard to appear unimpressed, but with little success. The blazing council fire spoke for itself.

"It is good," said the chieftain seriously. "Now, let White Wolf show the people *his* power."

Odin had not foreseen this, and he cursed himself for the oversight. It had not even occurred to him that the Skraelings might want to see more. Thinking rapidly, he tried to gain a few moments to plan something.

"What would my chief have him show?" he asked innocently.

Flying Squirrel thought for a moment, and then smiled.

"Let him change himself into a wolf!"

Odin thought for a moment. He must be very careful, now.

"My chief," he said as calmly as he could, "is this wise?"

Flying Squirrel appeared offended, but seemed to choke back a hasty retort.

"What do you mean?"

"You have seen him when the spirit takes him. He is like a madman. There must be some risk. . . ."

He paused, letting the thought sink in. Flying Squirrel looked uncomfortable, and finally nodded.

"That is true. Let him do something else."

"What would that be, my chief?"

Now Thorsson interrupted. "What are you talking about?" he demanded.

"He is asking that you show your power. He wants you to change into a wolf. I told him no, it is too dangerous."

"What? I cannot—"

"Yes, yes, Thorsson, I know. I am trying to think. Can you do the thing with the sun-stone?"

"Of course not!" Nils snapped. "It needs daylight. That is why it is called that, the 'sun-stone.' "

Now a new idea occurred to Odin. He turned back to Flying Squirrel.

"My chief, I have discussed this matter with the holy man. He says that to become a wolf is too dangerous to others. The children, here." He paused and gestured around the circle. There were nods of agreement, and a few looks of apprehension.

"So," Odin went on, "White Wolf thinks that you are right. It is best not to do that."

He hurried on, having planted the idea in the minds of the listeners that their leader had made such a choice in the interests of their safety. There was no way that Flying Squirrel could react except with thanks. The chieftain nodded. *He knows,* thought Odin. *He knows that I left him no choice but to agree. Very careful now.*

"We spoke of the changing of the colors of stones," Odin went on. "His power is of—" He had started to say "of the sunlight," but stopped himself in time. That might imply that White Wolf was powerless at night. That could be a dangerous idea.

Then the answer occurred to him, itself like a gift from above. He cleared his throat.

"His power is the greatest of gifts," he went on with confidence. "He will use it for the good of your people when he can. But, my chief, you know the dangers of *misuse* of such a gift. As your own holy men will tell you, to misuse such a gift is bad. He would not only lose it, but might sicken, or die."

He paused, hoping that the thought would occur to the chief that on White Wolf's dying, the evil spirit might be released to look for another body in which to dwell. That had worked once.

"Do you not think, my chief, that to change the color of stones for amusement of the crowd here might be questionable?"

He saw that he was reaching the chief. Flying Squirrel did not seem happy about it, but realized that Odin had left him with the decision-making power.

"That is true," the chief said crisply. "Let us not ask anything that is unsafe. Now, we go on with the council."

23

The Norsemen settled uneasily into the routine of their captors. It was exceedingly frustrating to go about the day-to-day living, not knowing what might come. Mainly, it was a boring existence. Their needs were cared for, they were respected, even honored to an extent, but their captors did not seem to have a plan beyond this.

Nils was picking up a few words of the Skraeling tongue, which helped some. Odin shrugged it off with a gesture that said it was a waste of time. Nils still did not completely understand why. He had the vague idea that Odin expected at any time to leave the hospitality of these Skraelings, if it could be called that. Yet nothing was happening, and that fact did not seem to bother Odin. Nils tried to question him about it. What did he expect, and when? He received no answers at all, which was even more frustrating than trying to learn the Skraelings' language without help.

"What happens will happen," Odin said, "when it is time."

There was a certain degree of hostility toward them, mostly from a few individuals. The woman with the stone knife still made him quite uneasy. She eyed his groin suggestively at every opportunity.

"She lost a son," Odin explained in answer to his questions.

Her attitude was understandable, then, Nils realized. He could even feel a certain compassion for her. This, however, was far overshadowed by his concern for the threat to his own private parts. He resolved to watch her closely, and to maintain his guard. He began to think of her as the Knife Woman, though he did not know her name.

Once, when the woman had been especially aggressive toward him, at least by suggestion, she was reprimanded by Flying Squirrel. She backed down, sullen and with a glance over her shoulder that was unrepentant. The point was clear. She waited only for an opportunity to act, to accomplish her vengeance.

Svenson was amused by all of this, much to the discomfiture of Nils.

"She wants you, White Wolf," Sven leered.

"It is not funny, Sven," Nils snapped at him. "You see how she looks at me."

"That is true," the sailor agreed. "I have seen women look at you there before, but they did not carry a knife!"

He slapped his knee and roared with laughter.

"You would not think it so amusing if your parts were the ones in danger," flared Nils.

"Do not talk so," cautioned Odin. "They must not think you are quarreling. Anyway, this woman will not be allowed to harm you, Thorsson. Just do not be alone with her."

Ah, so there is danger! thought Nils.

"Why me?" he asked Odin. "Why not you, or Svenson?"

Odin gave his shrug. "You are our leader, maybe. The one with power. She would cut off your power."

Nils's groin tightened defensively at the mere thought. Svenson chuckled to himself, but then quieted as both Odin and Nils turned a stern glance at him.

"Just be careful," Odin cautioned.

It was a warning that was not really needed. Nils's concern was already an active, constant thing.

Even so, their stay in the village of Flying Squirrel was not unpleasant. The wives of the chieftain were skilled in the preparation of food. Nils found some of the new tastes quite pleasant, and of variety that had not been available at Straumfjord. Or, he now realized, at home in Stadt. There were vegetables that he had never seen or tasted. One such item appeared to be a basic food for the Skraelings. It was a large gourdlike globe, yellowish in color, which was seen to grow on vines. The women were in the process of harvesting and drying fleshy slices of this vegetable for winter storage. Pumpkin, it was called. The seeds were also saved and dried. They, too, would provide food.

In and among the pumpkin vines were large numbers of another plant that seemed an important crop. Each stalk was as tall as a man's head, and along its sides were from two to four ears of grain, of a kind Nils had never seen. The large corns reminded him of teeth in shape and size. Maize, Odin called it. This grain was sometimes ground to a meal, but the women also cooked it as whole grains, mixed with yet another seed that was unfamiliar to the Norsemen. This was another vine, bearing pods much like those of peas or lentils. The seeds inside were larger, however, oval in shape and flattened. The mix of these beans with the maize provided a colorful and quite pleasant eating experience.

By contrast to these new vegetables and grains, the Skraelings seemed to have no source of meat except from hunting. It seemed strange that there were no cattle or sheep or poultry. The only domestic animals at all, in fact, were the few wolflike dogs that skulked around the huts.

Even so, there was abundant game. Deer were plentiful, as well as waterfowl. There was a large bird that was prized for its flesh and its feathers, larger than a goose but a creature of the forest. It was the same bird, he finally realized, whose feathers were used by the Skraelings to fletch their arrows.

The long days of late summer now began to grow shorter. Lines of high-flying geese trumpeted their way across the sky. Squirrels busied themselves with gathering and storing nuts. There was a restlessness in the air. The Skraelings accelerated their process of gathering, preparing, and storing food supplies for winter. Even the Knife Woman was too preoccupied to present a major threat to Nils.

There was at the same time an easing of the curiosity toward the Norsemen. Partly it was because everyone was busy with the harvest and its tasks. But it must have been also that familiarity, while breeding not necessarily contempt, certainly led to tolerance. The strangers were accepted for what they were. Outsiders, whose ways were strange and whose powers were great, were dwelling among them. Yet these men seemed harmless enough. White Wolf and the Fire Maker even took part in a hunt or two, which made their differences seem less.

As that change took place, there was another. Flying Squirrel recognized it, but was unsure what to do about it. He said nothing, for a leader does not admit that he is unsure. At least, not publicly. Most people still seemed unaware that a decision was needed. Thus it was easy to postpone such a step.

People will forgive many things in a leader. They will even forgive a mistake. One thing that is difficult to forgive, though, is the absence of decision. Even a wrong decision is better than none, because inaction gives the appearance of weakness. Flying Squirrel, being a wise leader, was aware of this, but was not certain what he wished to do. It was easier to let the days pass, and to see the calm acceptance of the strangers, than to face his dilemma. Sooner or later, he must decide what to do with them, but each day he told himself, *maybe tomorrow.*

All of this came abruptly to a halt one summer afternoon when he was approached by his head wife. Flying Squirrel was seated comfortably, smoking, when he saw her approaching. There was something about the way she walked that told him much. He wondered again at the many things a woman can express merely by the way she swings her hips. In the present case, Turtle Woman expressed stolid determination as she marched up to where he sat and planted her feet firmly before him. *What is it?* he wondered.

"Squirrel," she began, hands on her hips, "what are you going to do?"

"About what?"

"About these strangers. They are a bother to have in the lodge. They eat a lot, and we have none too much room."

Ah, he thought, *so that is it!*

"And winter is coming," she went on. "Are we to plan for them, too, this season?"

Well, it was out in the open. Now he must face it, though he realized that he had been avoiding the obvious. He took a long pull on his pipe and tried to look thoughtful.

"Yes, I have thought much on this," he said thoughtfully. That much was true, at least. He still had no real idea what he would do. Maybe he could distract her. "I thought you liked having the handsome White Wolf around," he teased.

"*Huh!* Much good it does me!" she retorted. "When I was younger, maybe." She tossed her head flirtatiously. Two could play at this game!

Flying Squirrel smiled. The outsiders had been with them nearly a moon, and had not been much trouble. From the first, he had seen this as a temporary situation, but he was not certain how he had expected it to resolve. Normally, they could have killed the intruders and it would have been over. He could have kept them as slaves, even, selling or trading them later. It was very fortunate that they had *not* tried either of those courses of action. He still shuddered sometimes as he thought of the narrow escape. How close they had come to attempting harm to the holy man, White Wolf, and his two assistants!

"What do you think I should do, Turtle?" he asked.

His wife shrugged. "I do not care," she answered. "But I must *know*. If they are to be with us for the winter, we must store more food."

She turned on her heel and strode away.

"I will talk to them of it!" he called after her.

Turtle Woman said nothing, and did not turn, but merely waved a hand. But the brief conversation had had its effect. There was still determination expressed in the retreating feminine behind. *It still looks pretty good, though,* he told himself with amusement. Well, he would do something.

He rose and sought out the one-eyed interpreter. That was a clever one! Squirrel realized now that they had badly underestimated him when they held him prisoner before. Too bad about the eye.

"I would speak with you," he greeted, halting before the tree where Odin sat.

"Yes, my chief?"

"It is about what you are going to do."

"I?" asked Odin innocently.

"Yes . . . you three."

"Oh. We are doing well, thank you."

"No, no. What will you do now?"

"Oh. I thought I might sleep in the sun a little while. Maybe smoke a little."

Anger rose in Flying Squirrel for a moment. Surely this man was not so stupid. *No, he is teasing me,* he thought. *He knows.*

"It is good," Squirrel said casually, holding himself in check. "And what, later?"

"Maybe a walk along the river."

"I mean . . . what of next moon?"

"Oh. I had not thought of that. Sleep some more, maybe."

It was more than Flying Squirrel could tolerate. He bit his lip for a moment, until he could retain his composure.

"Had you decided when you wish to leave?" Squirrel asked casually.

"You wish us to go?" Odin asked in surprise. "Ah, my chief, we would not wish to abuse your hospitality. My apologies, for myself and for my holy man. He did not know."

"It is all right," assured Flying Squirrel. He could hardly believe what he was saying. Almost an apology to one who had been a thorn in his flesh as they pursued the three fugitives.

"I am sad for this, my chief. Of course we will go. We did not realize that—"

"Enough!" said Flying Squirrel firmly. "Go, whenever you wish. We will give you supplies."

"You are very generous." Odin went on. "Truly a great leader. We are grateful for your hospitality. We will plan to leave soon. Two days, maybe?"

The chief nodded. "Where will you go?"

Odin shrugged, the odd little gesture that had become familiar now.

"I do not know. I will have to ask my holy man. To his people or mine, as he chooses."

"It is good," agreed Flying Squirrel. "You will need a boat, then?"

"My chief is too generous," purred Odin. "That is good, indeed. White Wolf thanks you, and will make a prayer for your long life and your health."

"It is good of him," Flying Squirrel found himself saying. *How did this happen?* He turned and walked back toward the lodge.

"What was that about?" asked Nils. "Something about a boat?"

Odin nodded, trying to stifle his triumphant grin.

"Oh, yes," he said calmly. "He offered us a boat and supplies if we will leave. And he said to thank you for your help and your prayers."

din was delighted with the turn of events. He had thought the situation through correctly, to its logical conclusion.

With winter coming on, their captors would not be eager to have three extra mouths to feed. Three extra men, who were in fact contributing nothing toward the well-being of the village, but would require substantial quantities of supplies by the time of the world's awakening in the spring.

Thorsson, to his credit, had suggested that they cooperate in the fall hunting that had been in progress. At first it had seemed like a good idea. But as he thought about it, Odin was convinced that it was not so. He wished to maintain a certain distance between their captors and White Wolf, the holy man. One obvious solution to the problem of winter supplies for the extra mouths would be to kill the honored prisoners. Odin saw that as a rather remote possibility. But, somewhere along the line, someone would think of it, and it would be suggested. Now, how to counteract such an idea?

He could see two possible plans. One would be to cooperate fully, join in the hunts, pour themselves wholeheartedly into the lives and the ways of their captors. That would be a reasonable course of action. Its disadvantages would be that the more firmly they became part of this village, the more difficult it would be to leave. In addition, Odin feared that familiarity would lessen the prestige that White Wolf now enjoyed. People would begin to regard him as a mere man, although one with great powers. It was to the advantage of the three honored prisoners to remain as aloof as possible. Maintain and encourage the air of mystery that they now enjoyed.

This line of thought had led him to the other extreme in his planning. They did not want to become part of this village, nor to become useful to have around. With this in mind, then, Odin was skillfully able to manipulate their status. They must not become helpful. Rather, it should appear to their captors that they were a mild nuisance. But not too much. . . .

To balance the nuisance factor, they must from time to time make their powers visible. That had been a matter of careful timing. When it seemed to Odin that the people around them were beginning to treat them with indifference, he would contrive something to draw attention. Their uniqueness was their protection. Thorsson had been saved by his appearance of madness. Now, anything that called attention to the differences of the Norsemen would act as protection. The greatest of fears for humankind is the fear of the unknown. So, he must prey on that.

Yes . . . just the right balance. Enough doubt to keep active a level of fear for protection. Along with this, the mild irritation, the nuisance of having the strangers present.

Odin worked hard at this two-pronged plan. He showed an unusual amount of deference to White Wolf, playing to the fullest the role of assistant to the holy man. Thorsson resisted some at first, but only had to be reminded that this was the impression that was keeping them alive. Well, maybe Odin *had* overstated that part to the Norsemen. At least, a little bit.

Svenson already treated Thorsson with respect. Odin did not completely understand the relationship between the two, but had a fairly clear idea in general. Thorsson had been the chief of one of the big boats, a leader of many men. Svenson had been one of his subchiefs, an older and skilled warrior and boatman. So their present relationship, the picture Odin was trying to convey, was not far off. The fire-haired one was a lesser chief, with special skills and powers of his own, while White Wolf was the primary leader.

From time to time Odin suggested things that would call attention to the differences of the Norsemen. He would ask Svenson, for instance, to play his role as Fire Maker sometimes. It was amusing to watch the looks on the faces of the observers. Odin himself was still impressed by the great power of the steel striker, though he tried not to show it.

Thorsson's best act, other than turning into a wolf, was the changing of the stone from gray to blue. It was such a special thing, so unreal, that it was good *not* to use it often. They had done it only once, the morning after they arrived at the village. The reaction had been great, beyond his expectations. Odin had a vague idea that the real importance of the sun-stone was not the color change. It was the fact that the stone could find north, even without sun or stars. He did not reveal that to their captors. No reason, especially, except that the more mystery, the better. *Do not tell all you know,* he thought. *Save part of it.*

As Odin planned carefully this part of his scheme, he also worked at becoming a minor nuisance. That part was thoroughly enjoyable to him. He attempted to remember all of the things that had irritated his mother the most when he was a youngster. As the memories recurred to him, he put them into action. He would allow a sleeping robe to slip to the floor, and then simply leave it there. He would contrive to waste just a little food, a last bite or two, left untouched. Sometimes he would have loved to finish his portion, but felt that the irritation caused by the waste was more valuable. Yet all the while he remained polite, cheerful, and grateful. A little demanding, perhaps. And the Norsemen would have been surprised at the demands that he made in their behalf.

"My holy man should have a softer sleeping robe. It befits his status."

Odin's slightly mischievous nature came to the fore as he enjoyed this opportunity. Not too much—that would be counterproductive—but just right. It was much like tuning a drum, he thought. Just the right tension on the skin of the drumhead. Too much, the laces would cut through the edges of the thin-scraped rawhide. Too little, the tone would be soft and flat. But just the right amount . . . Yes, if he could produce the correct amount of irritation, especially to the women of Flying Squirrel's lodge, it would be as satisfying for his purpose as the melodic ring of the well-tuned drum.

He had achieved results. The cross words and angry scolding of the women told him that. He was always apologetic, professing ignorance of their ways.

"Ah, I am indeed stupid! You must help me do better," he would exclaim, apparently in all innocence.

Odin had discovered, quite early in a mischievous childhood, that it is impossible to argue with one who agrees with you. He had put this to good use. When the time came for a reprimand from his parents, he would listen contritely for a few moments. (Timing was important.) Then, his large dark eyes wide with open honesty, he would look straight into the face of his mother and humbly phrase his reaction.

"You are completely right, Mother, and I am full of sorrow at my wrong."

It was a delicate thing—too open a confession would produce anger. But at just the right moment, and with just the right amount of self-deprecation, it always worked perfectly. There could be no further discussion, because there was complete agreement. He would watch the frustration in his mother's face, her helplessness when there was much more that she wished to say but could not. The skill with which he had come to do this had saved him much in the way of reprimand.

He had used the techniques before as a captive of these same people, and found that it worked well. In fact, if he had been content to continue as a slave, he could have survived in that way. But to him, life was somewhat more than survival. He had tried to escape, and had lost an eye as a result. He tried again, with greater success, fortunately. He had only one eye left.

When he had been forced to take refuge among the Norsemen, his old technique was again valuable. He appeared humble and cooperative to the people of Straumfjord, repentant when he made a mistake, and no great threat to anyone. He might still be there, he realized, spared much that had happened since, if he had been willing. But he had longed to return home to his people. He still hoped to do so.

Now, in the present situation, all his previous experience was proving valuable. An occasional mild scolding from one of the women was a sign of success with his carefully crafted plan of irritation. He could shut it off when he wished.

"I am truly sorry, Mother, it was stupid of me to drop such a beautiful sleeping robe to the floor. I must do better, to deserve your hospitality."

He would manage a look of complete repentance as the woman's temper cooled. But he knew that the nuisance factor was there. There was no way that these women would let the winter begin with these three strangers, even honored strangers, in their lodge.

And his plan had worked. They were about to leave, with the blessing, the protection, even, of the headman of the village. And with a boat and supplies! Ah, here was success beyond belief. He thanked the spirits who guided him for the success of his efforts.

There were, of course, a couple of things to be resolved. He must make certain that Thorsson was completely convinced of their course of action. Odin suspected that the Norseman might wish to go downstream, toward his own people. Well, that was a logical desire. The same as Odin's, actually, to return home. But there were advantages to the upstream journey. A return home would bring the protection of his own. Then they could plan the next step. At that point Odin would be glad to help the Norsemen do whatever they wished. Boats, supplies, assistance. He did owe them something. Besides, he rather liked them, both of them. Two very different men, but fascinating, each in his own way. Yes, he could help them return to their people, as they had unwittingly helped him return to his. It was good.

But he must be ready with his arguments for joining his people. He thought that he could do that. One thing he had so far avoided, though, in talking to the Norsemen. He was not certain that they understood that winter was almost upon them. He actually felt that they might not be able to reach Straumfjord before the first storms of winter. Well, if need be, maybe he could use that as an argument to join *his* people, who were much closer. Yes, that would be an argument to hold in reserve.

He turned to his other side in his sleeping robes, unable to sleep because of the excitement of the coming days. Two nights from now they would be camped upriver, on the way home!

He listened to the breathing of the others in the lodge, and to the soft snores of one or two. What more, now, should he be ready to do as they prepared to leave? Their supplies, the boat, weapons. Knives . . . For some reason, the thought of a knife brought to mind the one who was called Knife Woman by Thorsson.

He had a vague uneasiness about that. At first, it had been anything but vague. The woman, in her grief over the loss of her son, had been a real threat to Thorsson. She had apparently singled him out as the leader, one on whom she could wreak her vengeance. It was ironic that she had chosen Thorsson. He had had no connection whatever with the death of her son. From what he could learn, the skirmish in which the young man lost his life had been with the warriors of the other chief, the one called Landsverk. And that one was dead already. He had considered trying to explain it to her, but it seemed a futile effort. People are not rational over such things.

Well, she had calmed down now, to some extent. Maybe time was healing the wounds of her spirit. He hoped so.

There was one annoying thought that kept nagging at the dim recesses of his mind, though. What if the woman had only been biding her time? What if now, with the coming departure of the Norsemen, she saw this as her last chance for vengeance? It was a very disturbing possibility, one that he must consider carefully. It would be no surprise if the distraught mother decided to make one last try on the life of those whom she blamed for the death of her only son.

25

The parting was basically without regret. There were polite farewells, and the villagers gathered to watch the travelers embark. It was not from any sense of sadness, yet there was no animosity either. A certain sense of curiosity, perhaps. But basically, it was a fascination with the unusual and unfamiliar. The same attitude, in fact, that had hovered over their entire stay in the odd double role of guests and captives.

In the most basic of terms, it was a desire on the part of Flying Squirrel's people to avoid offending the outsiders. The unusual powers of the light-haired holy man and his assistants had been clearly demonstrated, had they not? Time had lessened the fascination, of course. The presence of the three had become a common sight. With familiarity, there was less of the awe and wonder that had marked the early days of their presence. No harm had come to anyone as a result of their stay, so they were not considered really dangerous.

Still, an aura of distrust had remained. In the presence of someone whose powers and gifts of the spirit seem almost limitless, it is only prudent to be cautious, is it not? What if, for instance, the strange holy man were to change himself into a wolf again? Little was known about that. White Wolf seemed calm and easygoing in everyday contact. Likable, even, though few dared to engage in much social interaction with him.

Yet there were many who wondered. Did the light-haired stranger have the power to *decide* when he would become a wolf? Or, did it just happen to him unexpectedly? Those who had been present spoke of how the holy man had seemed confused at the time. It had required the skill of his one-eyed assistant to explain what was happening. More importantly, even, once he became the white wolf, did he retain any control over his actions? Maybe, someone suggested, he became like the mindless animal who is stricken by the spirit that fears water, and whose bite causes certain death by the same spirit. There had been an incident only last year, when a crazed smell-cat had wandered into the village in broad daylight. It had bitten two people, a small child and her father, as he tried to intervene. Both had died in the anguish of the fears-water spirit. Could the affliction of White Wolf be similar? It was good that the war party had not killed him. Ah, what tragedy, if such a dreadful thing had been released.

So it was good, the people thought, that the strangers were leaving. They were not being driven out, so there was no resentment. But it would be more comfortable not to have them around, to be constantly in doubt as to what might happen next. At best, it had been a worrisome thing. At worst, an ongoing dread. So there was almost an aura of happiness over the departure. (Not too happy—one must not offend the spirits in question.) Such risks were avoided by the giving of small gifts to the departing strangers, such as food and ornaments of shell beads. One woman, who had noticed that the footwear of White Wolf had shown much wear, brought a new pair, sewn in the pattern of her people. The holy man seemed very grateful, and she was pleased to be the recipient of his smile. It should bring good luck, to be looked on with favor by so powerful a gifted one.

This same mixture of respect, curiosity, and a little fear and dread extended also to the Norsemen. They held the other side of the mutual distrust. It is always so when those of widely different customs meet for social interchange. We know what our own culture would produce, but are unsure of the other. In this short stay, it had not really been possible to progress beyond that point. And, it must be noted, without the presence of the one-eyed Odin, who knew something of both these cultures, it would not have been possible at all.

Even so, it was with an underlying sense of distrust on both sides that the parting took place. Flying Squirrel spoke in a dignified manner of the honor that had been his to host the stay of such an important holy man. And, of course, his important assistants, the one who makes fire and the one who understands the needs of the great White Wolf. (Let there be no misunderstanding, nothing to offend these outsiders as they left.)

By the same token, after translation by Odin, White Wolf gave an answering speech. It will never be known exactly how much of each side of this exchange was subject to editorial alteration by the interpreter. But is it not always so? Those who translate bear an awesome burden. Apparently, however, in this case the general tone was correctly exchanged, and understanding reached. The essence of the message was probably identical on both sides: *I do not really trust you, but I fear you a little, so I do not wish to offend you. I will thank you for the good we have exchanged and be pleased to part company with no further harm.*

Translated into more diplomatic phrasing, the speeches became, to all appearances, a congenial exchange of admiration and respect. And it was good.

There was one more thing. Flying Squirrel requested it with hesitation. In a way, he hated to give up all of the reflected glory.

"Would you ask your holy man," he requested, "if he would change the color of the stone for us again?"

Odin seemed to consider.

"It is not a thing to do lightly and without reason," he reprimanded gently. "But I will ask him. He may see fit to do so, in honor of this occasion. It might be good."

There were those who had not seen this striking ceremony before, and the gasps of amazement were quite gratifying as the sun-stone turned slowly from gray to blue, with the rotation in Thorsson's hand. That, too, was good.

The three men stepped into the boat and willing hands assisted in the shove away from the bank.

By the hammer of Thor, thought Nils Thorsson, *I am glad to be out of there!*

On shore, as the Skraelings watched the boat move up the broad river, there were many whose thoughts were remarkably similar. There was almost a unified sigh of relief. The people were pleased that no harm had come to them through the stay of the powerful holy man. Theirs was a good leader, they told each other. Flying Squirrel had managed the whole thing well, and without harm to any.

His wives, of course, were pleased. They hummed cheerfully as they turned back to their routine tasks.

"It is good," said the youngest of the wives to the others. "We have three fewer mouths to feed!"

She received a sharp glance from the first wife, but a smile and a nod from the middle one.

"It is best not to speak of it," that one said. "It would not do to offend. . . ."

"But they are only people."

"Are they? We only saw them around the lodge. You were not there, little sister, when he changed himself into a white wolf!"

Privately, Flying Squirrel was thinking thoughts that would have indicated great relief.

They are gone! Now we can return to our ways.

Things would never be the same, of course. They had met a powerful invader, with great boats and fearsome warriors using unknown weapons. And they had been able to destroy the invader! Apparently there had been only these survivors. Two, actually, because one was a member of a neighboring tribe. That one . . . *ah, a clever fellow!*

It was a great honor that he, Flying Squirrel, had been the leader of the war party that had captured White Wolf. It was an honor to have been the host of the three. It had also been an awesome responsibility, and he was glad it was now over. He had gained in prestige, and the honor would last for a generation.

It had turned out well, but a great load seemed lifted from his shoulders as the boat grew smaller in the distance. *It is good,* he thought.

And in the boat, Odin plied his paddle with true pleasure. He could hardly believe that it had come out so well.

His quick decision on the ledge at the time of their capture had been a desperate thing. When he had seen the war party hesitate and draw back, he had realized their dilemma, and had been able to take advantage of it. And it had worked! So well, in fact, that now he half believed that he himself had seen the transformation into a white wolf.

Since that time, everything had seemed to fall into place. Odin was beginning to think, in fact, that there are no coincidences.

Since he first met this Norseman, he now recalled, many strange things had happened to him, mostly to the good. There had been times when things *seemed* bad, but turned out well. Only a few moons ago he had considered that his situation was hopeless. Well, not quite. He had never *really* given up hope. But then came this Thorsson, who had talked to him as one would to another man. He was glad that he had hidden in Thorsson's ship, though there had been times when that had seemed a mistake that bordered on sheer madness. But since then, good things had happened, even when the situation appeared the worst. It would never do to *expect* such things, but now he began to wonder. *Maybe,* he thought, *just maybe this White Wolf is really a holy man. He is thoughtful, and modest, and does not misuse his gifts. Even when he was a leader, he did not misuse that power, as the other one did, the one who died. Did that one, the Landsverk, die because of his ways?* It was a thing to wonder.

Meanwhile, the paddles dipped rhythmically, and the boat moved on upstream. Odin watched the little streams of water flow quickly from the tip of Svenson's paddle in front of him. The Norsemen were quickly learning the use of the boat. He was glad that Flying Squirrel had offered a canoe, rather than the round skin craft. It was more difficult to build, and so represented a greater gift. Its long, narrow shape, however, was much better for a major trip than the other type. His companions had seemed pleased with the canoe, of course. It was much more like the shape of their longships, and familiarity gives a feeling of security.

He had been amused that at first the Norsemen had wanted to sit facing backward. That was still hard to understand. But they quickly learned the new technique, and were doing quite well with their share of the paddling. They would travel well today.

Odin was not certain how many days it might take to reach the village of his people. He could watch for landmarks later. But it had been a long time.

Three, no, four seasons ago. *Five*, next spring! He wondered about his parents, about his sister, just younger than he. She would be a woman now. And his older brother, who had just married before the attack that had cost Odin his freedom.

There was a girl, too, the friend of his childhood. They had talked of marriage. Hawk Woman . . . how beautiful she had been! He wondered how life had treated her. Ah, it was no use to wonder now. A woman as desirable as that one would be someone's wife by now. Probably have children . . . He dug his paddle into the water so vigorously that the canoe rocked and nosed out toward the center of the stream.

Careful, he told himself. *Give attention to what you are doing.* A deft stroke or two steadied the craft and straightened her course. *First things first*, he thought. *At least, I am going home!*

Odin's mood might have been more somber if he had been watching the shore. Behind a dark leafy screen in a little cove, a woman peered through the leaves to watch their canoe pass. Her face darkened with hate at the sight of the men who to her represented her son's death. There was no way, she vowed, that she would permit them to escape vengeance. She had been prevented from exacting physical retribution on them. That was as well, perhaps. It *was* danger-ous to release the spirit that dwelt in a madman. But now she had a plan.

Before dawn, she had crept quietly out of the village and launched her little skin boat, unseen. She might be carrying a few years, but she could still handle a boat. Had been quite good at it in her youth, actually. She traveled upstream for nearly a half day, and then drew ashore to hide the boat and wait. The canoe, with three paddlers, would travel faster than she, and she had no desire to be overtaken by them.

Her timing was good. She had barely settled herself to watch when the canoe came in sight. She touched her knife to reassure herself, and watched them pass. It was unfair, she thought for the hundredth time, that Flying Squirrel had prevented her vengeance. But now . . . her plan *would* succeed. It was based on avoiding close contact with the escaping spirit of White Wolf as he died. Avoid-ing *all* physical contact, in fact. It was not as good as it would have been to see the anguish in his face as she slashed away his manhood, of course. But less dangerous.

The canoe was out of sight now, and she carefully slid her boat back into the water. Hugging the shore, she followed their course, careful not to overlook the fact that they might stop to rest. She did not want to blunder onto them accidentally.

She tried to guess when they would stop for the night, halting to wait until they established camp. Then, as soon as it was dark, she moved on, slowly and carefully, searching for the smell of smoke or the glow of a campfire.

Ah! There . . . a flicker of light through the trees along the shore. She moved very slowly, urging the shell of her little boat against the bank. Only a little way up on the sand, for dragging a boat could be noisy. Now she hurried on to the upturned canoe, drawing her knife as she went. It had been a stroke of wisdom, she thought, this plan of hers. It would not require her to expose herself to the danger of the wandering spirit of madness. There would be no direct contact at all. She would only make tiny holes in the bark skin of the canoe. When they discovered the damage, it would be too late. She would be far away, and they would drown in the chill waters of the river. At least, she hoped so. Especially their light-haired leader. She hated everything about him, his light hair and skin, disgusting and pink. . . . This would be her revenge for the loss of her son. They might call her crazy, but no one else could devise a plan like this one, could they? She smiled in the darkness.

Suddenly she paused. *Was there a noise?* No, the sleepers were quiet, only the sound of their breathing broke the stillness of the clearing a few steps away. She almost returned to her task. She had made only two small slits in the canoe's shell, and another partway through. Such small holes would not be noticed. *Wait! The sound again . . . from the river!*

She stepped back toward her boat, which had been partly in the water, partly out. Ah, that was it. The craft was sliding farther into the water, making a soft noise on the sand as the little waves rocked it. She would drag it up a little way.

Just then a slightly higher ripple lifted the boat free and it curled out away from shore, turning slowly. The woman waded into the water to her waist, reaching for the boat. There must have been a hole in the river's bed, because she missed her footing and fell, her head going completely under water. She came up sputtering, still not particularly alarmed except for the noise she had made. The boat was drifting, an arm's length away, and she swam after it. She was a good swimmer.

But the boat was now moving into the current, elusive and just out of her grasp. A little more effort, another stroke or two . . . She was tiring now. Her arms and legs were stiff already from the unaccustomed exercise with the paddle all through the day. Now they failed to respond. She no longer had the resiliency of youth. The boat was farther from her now than when she had entered the water. She turned back toward the shore, to save herself. *Let the boat go!*

The shore was surprisingly far away. The deceptive current at this gentle bend of the shore had carried not only the boat, but the woman, too, well out into the stream. She struck out, swimming more weakly now. She could no longer raise her arms far enough for an efficient stroke. Then, it became too hard even to try. She relaxed, resigned to her fate. She had been guilty of poor judgment. The power of White Wolf's gifts as a holy man was greater than she had thought. He had won, after all. These were her last thoughts as the water closed over her head like a pall, and there was darkness.

26

It had been a new experience to learn the use of the canoe. As a boatman since childhood, Nils expected to adapt quickly to a new craft. He found, however, that this was far different. The thin shell of the bark canoe behaved unlike any boat he had ever seen. Its responsiveness, the way it moved under the stroke of the paddle, its sliding motion across the surface, were all a new experience. Along with the sensitive response of the craft came the inevitable disadvantage, however. It was also sensitive in balance. Any motion on the part of one of the passengers was magnified quickly. A casual shift in the weight of the canoe's contents instantly produced an alarming instability, a rocking of the boat that seemed out of all proportion. The natural tendency on the part of one experienced on the water was to shift his weight to correct the list. With the canoe, however, it was easy to overcorrect, producing an even more remarkable amount of sway. Once, Nils was certain that they would capsize the craft. There was actually a splash of water that poured over the side of the canoe to slosh around the bottom.

Nils was embarrassed by his ineptness in becoming familiar with the canoe. He felt somewhat better when it became apparent that Svenson, even with all his years of experience, was no better at it. There was simply an indescribable feel to the craft, one that must be experienced in its own right. It was quickly apparent that the very responsiveness of the canoe would make it fast and maneuverable. The two Norsemen had discussed this around the fire on the first evening.

"It is like a longship, Nils," Sven observed, "quick and fast. Their little round boats behave like a *knarr* while this is like a dragon ship."

Nils nodded. He could see the similarities that the steersman had quickly observed, now that Sven pointed them out. The shallow draft of the canoe, the way it rode on top of the water instead of *in* it, was like the longship. The squat, ugly *knarr*, with its cargo deck deep below the waterline, was slow and cumbersome by comparison. The two ships were for different purposes, the one for speed and mobility, the other for moving large quantities of freight, people, and livestock. And so it was with the small boats of the Skraelings.

"That is true," Odin said of the observations by Svenson, "and their spirit is different."

"Their spirit?" Nils asked. He was surprised that their companion understood the discussion of the types of ships. But now that he thought of it, he should have expected this. Odin was quite proficient in their Norse tongue. He had also been with the colony for some time. A boatman in his own right, the Skraeling had probably spent many afternoons watching ships maneuver in the harbor at Straumfjord. Of course he would have understood the variables involved. But this thing of different spirits?

"How do you mean, their spirits, Odin?"

Odin answered with his characteristic shrug.

"Each has its own," he explained. "The canoe has a quick spirit, the round boat a slow one."

Yes, that is true, thought Nils. *I never thought of it that way.*

"And each boat has its own spirit, too," Odin went on.

For a moment, Nils thought that Odin was referring to each type of boat. But no, the realization came quickly. Each *individual* boat . . . a different *spirit*? He thought of the *Norsemaiden* and the *Snowbird*, so similar and yet so different. Different *spirits*? Did this Skraeling understand that much about the handling properties of those two ships, both now gone to their watery graves? He shook his head to clear it. He knew that Odin was a highly intelligent man, but after all, things of that sort were beyond the understanding of most.

But Odin was injecting yet another idea, an extension of the concept of spirit as applied to boats.

"A canoe knows when a learner tries to use it," he observed.

"What?" asked Svenson.

"It knows. It tries him at first."

Ridiculous, thought Nils.

Then he thought again. The first time he had stepped into the canoe, his balance was not right. The craft had wiggled like a living thing, he could feel it vibrate from bow to stern, a tremulous wobble that was all he could do to stabilize. He had finally achieved stability, and . . . yes, he could see the simile . . . a living spirit.

"When you feel its spirit, it understands," Odin was explaining offhandedly, there at the campfire. "Then it becomes easier."

It was a reasonable, if simple way of looking at the situation.

"You have done well today," Odin went on, "and the canoe knows."

It was odd, sitting here at a campfire in the wilderness, Nils reflected. The odd part was that he was so pleased by this expression of approval. It made him proud, to be the recipient of a compliment from the Skraeling . . . from a *savage!* Somehow, it seemed quite logical, though in another way, it was not logical at all. Helge Landsverk would never have understood it at all, Nils reflected. Poor Helge . . . he had come so close, and had missed the mark so widely! What had it been? Nils wondered as he stared into the glowing coals. He and Helge had once been very close, much alike in their youth. At least, he had thought so. Yet, by the time of his friend's tragic death, there were many differences between them. How did he know now that Helge would never have understood the thing of the spirit that Odin had mentioned?

Maybe it was Helge's attitude toward people. That had changed, certainly. Once he had been a cheerful and friendly youth, liked and admired by all. A popular young man. More popular than Nils, actually, because he had been more outgoing. That had certainly changed. Not the outgoing part, but . . . well, the interest and concern for others, maybe. Yes, that was it. Helge had come to regard other people as something to be *used*, not respected. Used, to achieve his own goals. The incident of the severed hand drifted through his mind for a moment, a troubling commentary on the last days of the man who had been his friend.

"Let us sleep," said Odin shortly.

Nils wrapped himself in his robe and lay waiting for sleep to come. The soft night sounds and the crackle of the fire were a comforting lullaby. Through half-closed eyes he watched the ghostly flicker of firelight reflected from the trees. Somewhere a hunting owl called, and its mate answered. The quiet murmur of the water provided a droning background that lulled his senses.

He was almost asleep when he heard the splash . . . Ah, a fish, jumping to escape a larger one, probably. He listened, but it was not repeated. Still, he had the feeling that something was not right. Finally, unable to stand it any longer, he rolled out of his sleeping robe and stepped toward the river.

The fire was dying and the light was poor, but he could see the white of the canoe's birchbark shell. It seemed not to have been disturbed, and he moved on past its upturned hull and to the shore. There was something on the river's surface, maybe a stone's throw away, a mere blob of darker hue on the dark water. It seemed alive, seemed to move. There was a moment of splashing, and then quiet. The dark shape slid on downriver in the current, or disappeared under the water, he was not certain which. Anyway, his doubts were answered.

"Beaver," he grunted half aloud to himself.

Then he turned back toward the fire, and to the warmth of his sleeping robe.

The three travelers were on the river early the next morning. Odin was eager to put distance behind them. He had not given any definite answer as to how long a journey it might be to the village of his people. *Maybe*, thought Nils, *he does not know.*

Later, they wondered how they could have failed to notice the problem as they embarked. It should have been apparent. Looking back, they realized that there should have been footprints, but none of the three recalled having seen any.

They had embarked when the light was still poor, the rays of the rising sun filtering in crazy striped patterns between the trunks of the forest's trees. Odin, with all his experience in this woodland, was still distracted by the excitement of starting home. The other two were unfamiliar with the country, the weather, and the intricacies of the craft in which they traveled. So it was not unusual after all, maybe, that they noticed nothing.

To further complicate the morning, there were areas of patchy fog on the river and in low inlets, hanging like white smoke among the trees.

It was not long, however, before a problem became apparent. Odin had steered their course to a distance out from shore to avoid rocks, stubs, and snags that might rip the delicate underbelly out of their craft. They were not quite in the main current, which seemed to hug the far shore at this point. They were moving well.

"Ah! The fog is damp this morning," noted Svenson as they came through a wisp of the mist and emerged on the other side.

Svenson was seated in the middle, with Nils in front and Odin in the rear in the steersman's position.

"That is true," agreed Nils.

A little while later, Odin grunted to attract their attention, and pointed quietly with his paddle. Near the distant shore on their left, a large antlerless deer stood in the water with her calf by her side.

"Moose," whispered Odin.

The animal raised her large, ungainly head to stare at them as they moved past.

"Moose?" asked Svenson.

"Yes."

"It looks much like our red deer," Sven said to Nils, "but bigger, maybe. The stags have antlers, you think?"

There was a moment of confusion in language. There was difficulty in expression as the Norsemen's word for a male deer was tentatively clarified. Then Odin laughed.

"Yes, it is as you say. The father has big flat horns, so."

He placed his hands on his head to illustrate the appearance of the bull moose, and Svenson chuckled as he glanced over his shoulder. It was such diversions as this that prevented the immediate discovery of their problem.

Soon, however, there was an exclamation of surprise from Svenson.

"Water!"

"What?" asked Nils.

"Water! In the boat . . . that is why it seems so wet!"

Sven was shifting the bundles of supplies, which were packed around him. The change of balance rocked the canoe, and it took a moment to steady it. Water sloshed among the bundles, rolling back and forth on the flat bottom.

"We must go to shore!" said Odin quickly. He thrust his paddle into the water and swung the canoe's prow. "There!" he pointed at a level strip of shore. "No, too many rocks . . . to the left!"

The prow swung again. Water was deeper beneath them now, and the rolling weight was slowing their progress. The canoe rocked from the shifting mass of the water, and more water spilled into the left side as it dipped. Too much correction . . . now the right side . . . more water . . .

They were within a stone's throw of the shore when they capsized, spilling them into the water as the canoe rolled.

"Catch the paddles! Hold to the canoe!" called Odin.

They began to swim toward the shore, pulling the dead weight of the canoe and its sodden load. The three stumbled into shallow water and managed to drag the craft partially up on shore. Then they fell forward, trying to catch a breath, exhausted from the exertion.

"What happened?" asked Nils when he was able.

Odin shook his head, still breathing hard.

"We will see," he said. "But you see . . . why I . . . tied our supplies . . . to the canoe? They would be gone."

27

It took some time to dry their supplies and to inspect the damage to the canoe itself. The day was chilly, even with the fall sunlight, and they built a fire to assist in the drying process.

Odin crawled beneath the overturned canoe to look for leaks in the bark shell.

"Ah, here!" he said, from inside the hull, as a ray of sunlight shone through. "Can you see a hole from outside?"

"A crack," answered Nils. "A scrape or cut, maybe."

"Cut?"

"Yes. Like a knife!"

Odin scrambled out to examine the area of damage.

"You are right . . . a knife cut. Someone wanted this!"

It was a ragged slash, much like the cut from a sharp rock.

"Could we have struck a snag when we landed to camp?"

Even as he asked it, Nils knew the answer. The cut was *across* the long axis of the canoe. Any sharp obstacle that they might have struck would produce a lengthwise rupture, because of the forward motion of the craft. Besides, it appeared that there had been an attempt to hide the damage. The cut followed one of the dark rough stripes that patterned the chalk white of the bark. It had been a deliberate act, probably done with a stone knife. It was an alarming thought, that someone was still out there who had tried to harm them in this way.

But who?

Suddenly, the situation appeared more clearly to Nils. A knife . . . the Knife Woman! And the sounds that roused him as he drifted toward sleep . . .

"Wait!" he exclaimed. "Last night, I thought I heard something. I decided it was a beaver, but . . ."

Quickly, he revealed his suspicions. The others listened, nodding.

"This may be true," Odin admitted. "I did not see the woman when we left the village. She was ahead of us, maybe. Did you see her when we left?"

Neither of the others could remember that the Knife Woman had been present. And, with the intensity of her hate, it seemed unlikely that she would have let them go without a parting shot of some sort.

"Maybe she is still out there," said Svenson, glancing nervously at the dark forest. It was an uncomfortable feeling, and Sven was only voicing the thoughts of the others.

"Maybe," agreed Nils. "We must be careful."

"Yes," agreed Odin. "Some of their women can use a bow as well as their men."

"Can we fix the canoe?" asked Nils.

"Oh, yes. It will take us a day, maybe two." Odin was still examining the upturned canoe, and now uttered an exclamation. "Huh! Another cut!"

Soon they had found yet another, the third not quite all the way through the bark shell.

"Why would she stop?" wondered Nils. "It is as if she stopped before it was finished."

"I do not know, Thorsson. Something stopped her?"

They talked of it at some length, but came to no conclusion.

"Maybe we will never know," Odin observed. "She is a little bit crazy, and who knows what she might do? We must be watching."

"What do you need to patch the holes?" asked Nils.

"Not much . . . some sap from the trees."

"Pines? Pitch?"

"Yes, you call it that. The blood of the tree."

Nils had never thought of it in just that way. A tree . . . a plant, a living thing with life-blood, and a spirit of its own. It was a far different way of thinking, that of the Skraelings.

"What else?"

"Nothing much. The holes are small. A bigger hole would need to be covered."

"Covered? With what?"

"A piece of bark, over the hole. Hold it on with the pine sap. But we will not need that."

It was decided that Svenson would stay with the canoe, his back to the river. He would have to watch only half of the circle around him to escape any sneak attack. The other two would stay together as they went into the woods a little way, protecting each other. Nils could stand watch while Odin gathered the material that he needed for his repair.

None of the three saw anything unusual, but this did not lessen their concern. Knife Woman had already demonstrated that she could wait. None of them remotely questioned whether the danger was past. The risk was there, hanging over their heads, proven by the three gashes in the bark shell of their canoe.

Odin waited most of the day, after assembling his materials, allowing the damaged bark to dry completely. Toward evening, he took a brand from the fire and held it near each hole in the shell for a little while.

"To drive out any water-spirits," he explained in answer to Nils's question. "I want to do this tonight, because they will come in with the morning fog, and we would have to dry for another day."

And lose a day's travel, thought Nils. Of course . . . The Skraeling's approach to the world appeared to be a strange mixture of things of the spirit and things of the world. It appeared quite practical in application. *Why is it not so with us?* he wondered. *How did we come to separate these things?* He would have liked to talk to his grandfather about this. Odd, how each time a deep thought came to him, he was reminded of that wise old man. He had not fully realized at the time, the wisdom that was his for the asking. He had learned much without even trying. Even more, because his grandfather had demanded it. Ah, the long winter evenings when he had sat by the fire with the old man, drawing the runic alphabet on a smooth board with a charred stick. *Both* alphabets . . .

"You must learn both, Nils," Grandfather had told him repeatedly. "I am not certain this new set of runes will last. If it does, so be it. You will know it. But the old runes . . . They will be here a long time. You must know them, too."

Then they would play games, devise riddles and rhyming conundrums using the runes from both old and new. In an odd way, Odin reminded him of his grandfather. That was strange, that a person of his own age would affect him in this way. And a person of a completely foreign culture, too. Maybe it was a similarity in the way the two men had approached the world. He must think about this some more. Maybe he would talk to Odin about it. He wondered what his grandfather would have thought of that idea, and smiled at the thought. This recalled that both men had had the same wry sense of humor, which allowed them to *enjoy* the things of life. Things of the earth and things of the spirit . . . *or are these different after all?* he asked himself.

He was recalled from such abstract thoughts to watch Odin begin work on the canoe. The Skraeling warmed the pitch he had gathered on a bark slab next to the fire. Now he lifted it quickly and with a stick that he had shaped for the purpose, began to smear and poke the pitch into each of the defects. He set the remaining pitch near the fire again to keep it soft, and took a pinch of finely shredded cedar bark. With a clean stick, he began to force the bark into the crevice.

Nils's thoughts drifted back to the shipbuilders of his homeland. How many times he had watched the skilled craftsmen as they pounded shredded tow or oakum into the crevices of a ship under construction. *It is the same!* he realized. *Shredded fiber and pitch, used for the same purpose, to make a boat watertight.*

"What?" asked Odin, busily forcing his cedar bark into the crack before the softened pitch could harden.

"Oh . . . nothing," Nils answered. He had not realized that he had spoken aloud.

Odin reheated the second of his damaged spots and proceeded with the bark treatment. The third, not completely through the shell, he did not consider quite so important, but still used a pinch of the shredded cedar as a precaution. Then more pitch over all, and close attention while the patches cooled.

"It is good," Odin finally grunted. "In the morning, we move on."

They each took a watch, and none would have trouble remaining awake that night, at least while on guard. Svenson took the first part of the night, placing himself in a position of easy observation and defense, gripping his battle-ax tightly. Odin drew his robe around him, curled up near the fire, and within a few heartbeats, it seemed, his breathing was deep and regular.

Nils did not relax so easily. He wished that he had the ability to do so. This was part of the complicated man of contradiction that was Odin, the one-eyed Skraeling. Nils lay in his sleeping robe, staring at the night sky, thinking of how his own attitude had changed. When they first met, the Skraeling had seemed unimportant. A lesser person, an ignorant savage, not to be taken seriously. Except, of course, that he might be able to provide some information. Nils had thought of him as a nonperson, almost. There was a strange twinge of guilt. Had he not mentally criticized Helge for much the same approach?

With another guilty pang, he realized that he did not even know Odin's name. That appellation had been given the Skraeling by those at Straumfjord, as a joke. A cruel joke, one that called attention to a physical handicap. The loss of an eye is a serious thing, one not to be taken lightly. Here was a man who had been subjected to torture as a captive, and was then ridiculed because of it by yet another group. Nils wondered whether he could have survived to handle it as Odin had done.

Most compelling of all was that Odin, on learning the reason for his new name, had seemed *pleased.* "Father of the gods," he had proudly told their erstwhile captors. Nils wondered if the man realized that it was a thing of ridicule. Yes, surely. A man so quick and intelligent would quickly realize when he heard of the one-eyed Norse god, that it was a joke to call a half-dead refugee by his name.

Nils wished that he could ask Odin his true name, but was not certain that he should. It might be an embarrassment that he, Nils, was not prepared to face. Possibly Odin (or whatever his name) would handle it better than Nils. He had proven himself quick and resourceful. Nils was still not certain how it had all happened, that morning of the berserking. Sometimes he felt that there *had* been something of the supernatural. Another thing that he would have liked to discuss with his grandfather. Or maybe later, with Odin. Meanwhile, he would look for an opportunity to ask Svenson what *he* had seen, that morning on the ledge.

With these confusing thoughts drifting through his head, Nils finally slept. There were dreams, ones that he could not remember when he woke. Strange fragmentary dreams in which Odin appeared in a shipyard in Oslo, meticulously caulking the planks of a trim longship, readying her for a sea voyage. The Skraeling was talking to him, calling him by name as he worked, talking somehow of a voyage "home."

Then he woke, and it was in the present. The stars were still bright overhead. The seven stars of the Dipper had rotated around the North Star . . . yes, it must be past midnight. And the Odin of his dream, smelling of fragrant pine pitch, was touching him on the shoulder.

"Wake up, Thorsson! It is your turn to watch. We travel early tomorrow. I would hurry home!"

28

I remember this place!" said Odin, excitement in his tone. "The rock, there. Even that tree . . ." He pointed to a gnarled pine precariously clinging to the gray stone face of the cliff.

A stray seed, carried generations ago by the wind, or perhaps by a bird or a squirrel, had lodged in a crevice. It had found enough moisture and soil to sprout, and the probing roots, so tender yet so relentless, had found other small cracks in the stone that held water and debris. Through the seasons, the tree had forced the crevices wider, providing a better footing for its slowly enlarging root system. But it had been slow, limited to the nutrition that chanced to blow or fall into the crevices that furnished life.

"It is not much bigger," Odin continued.

He seemed to attach a great deal of importance to this place. He walked restlessly up and down the sandy shore, his eyes roving over the area, pausing on a thicket, a tree, a clump of late-blooming flowers. It was apparent that here was a place of memory for him.

Nils was gathering fuel for their evening fire, and Svenson was securing the canoe. Both were watching their companion as he experienced his memory trip.

"This place is special?" Nils finally asked.

"What? Oh . . . Yes . . . well, no, not particularly. I camped here once, as a child, with my parents. Its spirit is good, no?"

Yes, Nils realized, the *feel* of the place was good. Its spirit . . . There, again, was this custom of the Skraeling, thinking of all things in terms of their spirits. To Nils it seemed illogical, oversimplified, maybe even blasphemous to his family's newly accepted Christianity. Yet it was such an easy way to see things. It simplified communication, allowing for variance in philosophy and theology. He found himself falling into thought patterns that permitted spirits to inhabit not only people and animals, but trees, rocks, places. The river, even. It sometimes seemed like a living thing, and when its restless murmur lulled him to sleep at night, it seemed to be talking to him. Sometimes he felt that he could almost make out the whispering words. Odin had mentioned this, too.

"The river talks to us, and the wind, too. Hear? . . ."

Yes, when they were near a growth of pines, Nils had noticed the soft song, a hushed hissing whisper that was almost constant. He wondered if the song was that of the wind or of the trees.

"What does it say?" he asked Odin curiously.

The Skraeling's one eye stared at him for a moment, a slightly amused twinkle at the corner.

"It is not in words, Thorsson. It is in the heart . . . the spirit. It sings a feeling."

Nils understood the gentle reprimand. Yes, it was a wordless feeling, one that could not be expressed. *Grandfather would have understood,* he thought. Why he believed that, he was not certain. Possibly his grandfather had never been as certain about the new religion as the younger members of the family. The old man, like many of his generation, quietly accepted the new stories and prayers and rituals, but retained a large segment of his previous beliefs. Nils had seen nothing illogical in this. Different names for deities, maybe. His grandfather, though he would discuss many things in great depth, never seemed comfortable about this.

Nils roused from this nostalgic reverie of his grandfather as Odin spoke again.

"I do not know how the sun comes up each morning," the Skraeling mused, "but I am glad when it does. It feels good. The sun says nothing, in words. What feels good is its light and its warmth, no?"

Nils nodded. Were these not just words? What did it matter, he asked himself, if the feel of this camp on the river was called its *mood* or its *spirit*? It could be felt more easily than described, and the feeling was good. So was the sigh of the breeze in the pines. Now it occurred to him that he had been listening for words, when Odin mentioned its "song." But it was not a matter of words to express ideas. The ideas . . . the *feelings* were there, as the comfort of his mother's lullaby had been when he was a child. It was the feeling of the lullaby that he held in his heart. He now realized that he could not even recall the words to the bedtime song, only the warm and protective feeling. The spirit. It had been a long time since he thought of that part of his childhood.

Maybe it was like the chanting singsong of the priest when the family attended mass. That song was in Latin, he had been told. He had never quite understood why. What little he had been taught about the Savior led him to believe that the Latin had not been used by him and his followers. This he did not understand, but questions were not encouraged. It was true that the chanting ritual and the ornate pageantry of the Church brought forth great emotion in him. That feeling was a thing of the heart, a spirit that made him feel comfortable and fulfilled. So maybe that was it.

He had tried to speak of this to his grandfather, and that was the point at which the old man would seem to change the subject.

"There are many paths to the top of the mountain," Grandfather had once said, "but they all lead to the top of the mountain."

Young Nils had not understood what his grandfather meant by that. They had not been talking of paths and mountains, but it was a pleasant thought. He also did not quite understand why the conversation then turned to Grandfather's stories of the Olden Times, when there were gods and goddesses, whole families of them. Their trials and triumphs and adventures were amusing and interesting, and young Nils had loved to hear these stories.

Somewhere along the way, he realized that the telling of these stories by his grandfather was not totally approved by his parents. It became almost a matter of conspiracy, the old man and the boy sharing and enjoying together. It was an unspoken rule that when someone else approached, they would change the subject.

"It is much like the runes, Nils," the old man explained. "You need to learn both the new and the old."

The boy was confused. "Both alphabets?"

"Yes. And to know the old ways, too."

"Old ways of what?"

"Old ways of the gods . . . the earth. But . . . ach! Here comes your mother!"

And the subject would change. They seldom returned to the subject after such an interruption. Gradually, Nils realized that there were two different stories of how the world came to be. It did not seem to him that it made any difference, because both were pretty good tales. Grandfather's was the most exciting, but it seemed to be in disrepute, somehow, in favor of the other one about Adam and Eve and a garden somewhere.

Another mystery involved the reason the old runic alphabet was tolerated, but not the old creation story. Grandfather would only shrug and change the subject when asked. Nils always had the feeling that some day his grandfather would explain it to him, but that was not to be. The old man, who had become progressively more feeble and more forgetful, died during the winter of Nils's sixteenth year, and it was a great loss to the boy. There had been much that he wished to ask. Now there was no one to care, no one to whom he could turn. His own father was never quite approachable. Even that possible source of information was closed when Death again found his way to the house a few months later, and Nils's mother again went into mourning. Nils had never known his paternal grandparents, both having died before he was born, and now he felt lost.

Why am I thinking of these things? Nils asked himself. It had been a long time since he last did so. Well, the spirit-place that seemed to have meaning for Odin. Thoughts of things of the spirit . . . that may have started it.

Nils rose, tossed a couple of sticks on the fire, and turned back to his robe. He glanced at the rocky point where he knew Odin stood watch. The soft snores of Svenson came from across the fire, and all seemed good. They had seen no sign of the Knife Woman, but still kept close watch.

Two more sleeps, Odin said . . . one after tonight, and they would be among his people. That would be a great accomplishment, Nils thought. They would be safer than at any time since they lost the ships. Of course, he realized that he would immediately need to begin planning their return to Straumfjord. Not this fall, Odin had assured him. There was not time. But he wished to be ready by spring, so that he would lose no time. There was much to do, and he would have to arrange passage home for himself and for Svenson. He wondered how often ships from home would stop at Straumfjord next season. He did hope to find them berths on a longship. It would be a real comedown to leave home as master of a dragon ship and return in the wallowing sowbelly of one of the *knarrs.* Finally, he fell asleep, the clutter of thoughts racing through his mind. He awoke what seemed like only moments later, with Odin rousing him to take the morning watch.

The next morning dawned cold and overcast. The time since Nils rose from a warm bed to take the watch was among the most miserable times of his entire life. He had longed to go back to the fire, but had not dared to do so. It was too dangerous, in case they were attacked by the Knife Woman. Or by anyone else, of course, but there seemed little chance of that. Nils stood shivering, his robe tight around him, nose and toes tingling in the frosty night.

It was not fully light when he heard the cries of geese above him. Large numbers, by the sound. He could not see them, because they were above the low-hanging clouds, but he could visualize the long lines, their apex pointing southward. It was an exciting song, and had always stirred a restless feeling in him, a need to follow. Now, however, it struck him that the songs were new. These birds might not be like the great flocks of home, yet their habit, their migration, their song, all reminded him of home. How odd, he thought, that the sound that had always called to him to wander now called with a message that was almost the opposite. The slight twinge of homesickness gnawed at him, and he drew his robe closer.

How much longer, he wondered, *before the others wake up, and we can move on?*

29

As it happened, they did not move on that day. The cold drizzle changed to a wet slush that soaked everything and chilled the bones. Odin seemed disappointed, but shrugged philosophically.

"It is not fit to travel," he announced, and turned to gather more wood for the fire. He also began to construct a shelter.

"Hmm—yes . . . here and here," he mused to himself, examining the forks of a couple of small trees.

He began to cut a pair of poles, and propped the upper end of each in one of the tree forks.

"Now, let us put the canoe here," he indicated.

Nils was beginning to see the design of Odin's efforts now. They lifted the canoe, carried it, and placed it across the slanting poles. It would form a waterproof roof for Odin's shelter, big enough for them to sit under, and with plenty of space for their provisions. The Norsemen carried the supplies to the shelter while Odin completed its construction. He piled the brush he had trimmed from his poles along the back of the canoe, forming a rear wall for the makeshift lean-to. It required only a fire directly in front, now. That was quickly accomplished with brands from their night fire. Now they could spend the day in dry protection, comparatively warm and comfortable.

The day did seem to drag. They slept, ate a little, and from time to time, talked.

"Tell me of your people," Nils requested of Odin. Svenson was snoring peacefully near the other end of the shelter.

"Tell you of what?" Odin asked.

"What are they called? How do they live? What do they wear, what are their homes like?"

"Oh. Well, you will see, yourself, but . . . we call ourselves the People. That is true for everyone, no? We are the *People* and there are those *others* across the river, or in the next valley."

It was a strange way to express it, but it was quite true, thought Nils. He was thinking of his native Norsemen and their long-standing enmity with the inhabitants of the Isles and the coasts. English, Normans, Saxons, Scots, Welsh, Irish . . . *We* and *they*. It was no different here, it seemed.

"Your houses?"

"Much like the others, where we were. Like yours."

"Mine?"

"Your people. Straumfjord. But no wall around it."

"Yes. But we do not have such a wall in my own country."

The Skraeling nodded. "Nor do we."

"Your houses," Nils went on, "they are made of logs?"

"Yes. Sometimes bark." He paused and tapped on the shell of the canoe over their heads. "Like this. If we will use it only a short while . . . summer, maybe."

"A house for each family? Like the people we just left?"

"Pretty much so. One big house for meetings. Big enough for everybody."

Nils nodded. The longhouse . . . Another thought came to him.

"Do your people plant crops?"

"Crops?"

"Yes, like these. . . ." He pointed to the bundle of dried pumpkin among their supplies.

"Oh. Yes. Several different kinds. Potatoes, beans, maize . . . what you call corn. We hunt, too, for meat."

"Hunt what? Deer?"

"Yes. Deer. Moose, like we saw, sometimes bears. Ducks, geese, the gobble-bird."

"You said you would teach me your tongue."

"Oh, yes. That would be good. We can do that."

Even as the lesson began, Nils was thinking that the exercise would be useless. He did not intend to stay with Odin's people any longer than he must. A few weeks . . . through the worst of the winter. Just enough of the language to get them by.

Another flight of geese passed overhead, calling as they headed south, unseen in the low-hanging cloud cover. Nils felt the pull of their migratory instinct. Or of his own, he was not certain which. When they returned, though, he would be moving with them, he vowed. Not exactly with them . . . The return journey to Straumfjord lay north and east, while the migrating flocks would head almost due north. No matter. He would be starting home. He could identify with the feelings of Odin, who was going home now.

He, Nils, had until now been a bit discontented with that decision. Why should it be that they should now be hurrying to the Skraeling's home, rather than toward their own? He had felt that other options had not been considered, and the deep-seated resentment had smoldered in the dark recesses of his mind.

Now he began to see the point. Winter was coming, and its onset would be unpredictable. They dared not undertake the longer journey back to the sea and to Straumfjord at this season. Odin had tried to tell him that, but he had not been completely convinced, until now. But this day had made it easy to see. He watched a wet icicle grow, drop by freezing drop, dangling from a fragment of fiber on the edge of the upturned canoe. Finally he had to admit that this was the best course of action. He did not know the climate or the country, but Odin was one who did. Like it or not, they must take the Skraeling's advice to have their best chance at survival.

But now, the slush was turning to snow. By noon the ground was nearly white, except for protected areas where trees were thick. Svenson awoke, surprised and a bit alarmed.

"Snow?" he asked.

"It is nothing," Odin told him. "The ground is warm, and it will go away."

That prediction proved true. The snow had stopped by midafternoon, and before dark the ground that had been white was merely wet. They gathered armfuls of sodden wood and placed it near the fire to dry for the night fire. The sun actually peeked through the dissipating clouds for a brief while just before night, creating a gorgeous sunset. Nils watched it, wishing for a better view than one through the trees. A view over the sea, maybe, at the far western horizon. Still, it was a moving experience, and one that held promise.

The blazing display was short, giving way to the chill of a crisp autumn evening. They used their robes, not to sleep but to wrap themselves in for warmth as the meager warmth of the sun's dying rays began to diminish. Nils had given some thought before to the condition of his apparel. His footwear had worn out and had been replaced with the gift of soft native moccasins. He found that he rather enjoyed them. They were lightweight and comfortable. But his shirt was wearing thin, and would soon be in tatters. The leather tunic that he wore over it would be some protection, and his knee-length fur breeches still had some wear. Nils's questions to Odin about the customs of his people had been partly to learn of their manner of dress. The conversation had taken other directions, and he still did not know.

Odin himself wore a ragged assortment of garments, but these were largely castoffs from either their recent captors or from the Norse settlement. Nils wanted to ask about the possibilities of winter garments when they reached Odin's people, but did not know quite how to approach the subject. He drew his robe closer around his neck and shoulders, and resigned himself to some discomfort for the present.

"Do you think there is still danger from the Knife Woman?" asked Svenson as darkness fell.

Nils had not thought of that for some time. They had posted watch each night, but there had been no sign.

Odin seemed to consider for a moment, and finally spoke, slowly.

"I am made to think not," he said. "By now, she would make another try, or turn back. We have seen nothing, so maybe she gave up and went home."

"She did not seem the kind to give up," observed Svenson.

"That is true," Odin mused. "But would she not have tried again?"

"It seems so. We should keep watch, no?"

"Yes, one should stay awake," Odin admitted. "But travel would be hard today. That is why we are here. She could not travel either."

By contrast, the next day was ideal for travel—clear, crisp, and sunny. Odin seemed pleased with their progress, and his excitement was apparent when they camped for the night. It was understandable, thought Nils. What a thrill, to be coming home, after an absence of several years! How many, had the Skraeling said? Five? It occurred to him that he did not know whether Odin had a family. That thought was a trifle unsettling to him. Was he still thinking of this man as a nonperson?

"Tell us of your family, Odin," he suggested.

The Skraeling's one eye widened in surprise.

"Mother, father," he said simply. "A younger sister. When I left, anyway. Now, I do not know."

"You have no wife?"

Odin smiled, a little sadly.

"No, never. It is good, maybe. If I had one, she would have remarried by this time."

There was an aura of sadness that made Nils suspect that there was more to this story. There must have been a girl, a sweetheart, maybe. Odin had never said how he happened to have left his people. Only that he had been captured and was unable to return. Was this part of the story? Had he left *because* of a disappointing romance?

No, Nils told himself. *I am reading too much into this. Surely, the Skraelings do not have courtships like ours.*

This did not satisfy his curiosity, though. Odin's remark about a wife having remarried . . . Maybe that was it! A girl to whom the young man had been very close. Then, in his absence, no matter what its cause . . . Of course! Any woman in whom Odin had had a romantic interest would surely have married by this time. Five years, or more!

This gave Nils a whole new perspective on the impending homecoming. What a thing of dread this must be, mixed with the joy of reunion. His heart reached out, for the hurt in the heart of his companion. He could not totally relate, because he had never had a serious relationship with a woman. At least, not one of any duration. There had been girls, but none with whom he wished to share his future.

Abruptly, this brought him to thoughts of the blue-eyed Ingrid, wife of the cooper at Straumfjord. That seemed a lifetime ago, now. He had known her only a few days, had never been intimate with her, but she had had a profound effect on him. He had dreamed of her, sometimes, the lovely curves of her body, the shape of her long legs. The blue of her eyes, deep and full of sadness . . . He had promised to take her away. Maybe by this time *she* had found someone else. If there were someone who could do what she asked, he was certain that the girl would have gone with him. Nils held no delusions that Ingrid would wait. He wondered whether all women were like that. . . . Surely not. His parents had always had a steadfast loyalty to each other, so it must be possible.

Nils's thoughts returned to Odin, and he wondered again if there had been a woman. One like Ingrid, maybe, who had taunted and enticed and then stopped the sequence of events before it went too far. That sort of experience could make a man leave his own town in disgust, not caring whether he ever returned. He might reconsider later, and want to go home, but it would be apparent that such a woman must have *some* man.

These thoughts were becoming depressing, because he wondered now, who shared the bed of the blue-eyed Ingrid tonight?

din was becoming increasingly thoughtful as he neared more familiar territory. It had not been easy to sit still, or to sleep from time to time during the enforced day of waiting under the canoe. He had managed to conceal his true feelings from the others. It did not seem appropriate to him to appear as childishly excited as he felt.

Yes, childish. That was it. He had been little more than a child, he realized, when he last saw his home, friends, and family. He had not seen himself that way, of course. He had thought he was a man. But a man does that, Odin now understood. In the triumphant bloom of youth, he considers himself complete, not realizing his shortcomings. Because he has the strength of his elders, he assumes that he also has their wisdom. It requires some time and some bitter experience to learn that this is not true. Some, he had now learned, never know it. At least, he now understood his limitations. Anyway, he thought so. He no longer took himself so seriously. That, he had decided, is probably a young man's biggest mistake. Pride.

That is not quite it, either, he thought. There is a pride that brings self-confidence, and that is good. Pride in heritage, in strength, in accomplishment. Yet there is a pride in self that can become a hindrance, even a danger. *Maybe that is it. Self-importance,* his thoughts continued.

The paddles dipped rhythmically, and the canoe moved upstream. Certainly, his self-esteem was far different than the last time he had traveled this stretch of water, moving away from his people. It was almost embarrassing to think of the mistake that had brought on the tragedy of the past few years.

A quarrel, a simple lovers' quarrel, and a stubborn refusal on his part to admit that he might have been at least partly at fault. His heart was heavy when he thought of their angry parting. So heavy, in fact, that there had been a time when he thought he would never go home, even if he could. He could not face the shame of his youthful stupidity. That had been some years ago, however, when he still suffered under delusions of self-importance. It had been a gradual thing, the realization that in the fullness of all things, it did not really matter very much. It had taken some severe, ugly, and very painful lessons to arrive at his present way of thinking, and it had not been easy.

It was possible, now, for him to take a certain wry amusement from his earlier mistakes. That had sustained him, sometimes. The one mistake at which he could not smile, however, was the one which had turned his life upside down. He had abandoned the most important things in his young life over a simple thing like hurt pride. *Of course,* he told himself, *I would have realized it.* But of that, he was not certain. How long would it have taken him, he wondered, if he had not been captured? Would his temper, his hurt, have cooled and allowed him to go home, to apologize to Hawk Woman? Even now, there was a spark of anger when he thought of it. She should not have teased him and threatened to marry Old Dog. Even though he had realized long since that it had been a taunt, a thing to make him angry and jealous, it still hurt. She should not have hurt him that way.

As a logical extension of that angry thought came the next, each time he relived the scene. *I should not have told her what she must do.*

"You have no right to tell *me!*" Hawk had hissed at him, eyes flashing fire. "You do not own me. I will do as I wish, and marry who I choose."

If he had not been so angry at the time, he might have realized that she would not be serious about Old Dog. Dog would eventually find a wife, but certainly one with the desirability of Hawk Woman would not have been interested. Yet this, too, bothered him. Was this idea yet more evidence of his youthful pride, his thinking that he, the man now called Odin, was more important than one with lesser skills, less athletic ability, and less handsome features? He had considered himself superior to Old Dog . . . even the young man's name had been a cruel joke by the other boys, he now realized. Dog was not handsome or skilled, and was actually clumsy in his motions. Like . . . well, like an old dog.

This one question still haunted him, after all the years. *Had* Hawk Woman actually been serious? She had always been a girl with a great instinct for mothering. An injured puppy, a baby bird . . . any creature in need, it seemed, could count on her help. But *Old Dog?* It had tortured him for years, this question.

He had, in his rage, taken a boat and started downstream. It had been an irrational, possibly stupid thing to do, he now realized, but he wanted only to get away. It had not taken him long to realize, however, that it was not solitude that he sought. It was a desire to disappear, to punish Hawk Woman for her cruelty to him. *She will be sorry,* he vowed.

Soon, he was not even certain of that. Sitting by his lonely campfire he had come to the conclusion that it was *he* who was now sorry. Hawk Woman was at home with her family, while he shivered in the night's chill and slapped mosquitoes. And the longer that he stayed away, the more stupid it would make him appear.

He had already decided to turn back, that night so long ago. He had been ready to apologize, to admit that he had been angry and jealous, and that he surely had no right to tell her what she must or must not do. He had decided at his fire that night that with the coming of dawn he would be on the river, going back upstream, to repair the damage to his life that had been caused by pride and jealousy. It was almost at that moment that the chance had been taken from him. The warriors had burst out of the bushes, subdued him quickly, and tied him. He had fought. That, too, was probably a mistake, he now realized. He had managed to inflict enough injury to his attackers to anger them, and the torment and subsequent torture had begun. He was probably fortunate to be alive, even.

These events had destroyed the possibility of reconciliation with Hawk Woman. Probably forever, he knew. There were many times through the years when he was certain that an opportunity would never present itself. He had been carried by ongoing events progressively farther from home.

Until now. The coming of the light-haired Thorsson had somehow begun a time of change. True, there had been some times when it had not seemed good. Each time it was so, however, something good seemed to emerge. Even now, they traveled back toward his people, something that he had almost believed could never happen.

There were many things that he had seen in the past few moons that he had thought could never happen. The changing color of the sun-stone . . . The white wolf episode . . . There had been no chance that the three fugitives could have survived that. Yet it had happened. Truly, the man now called White Wolf must have a powerful gift of the spirit, Odin had decided. It was thrilling and exciting to be associated with such a man, and he was proud to have been chosen to be a part of it.

All in all, he was returning with a certain amount of triumph. He was the helper to White Wolf. He had survived captivity, enslavement, and torture. He had lived with and observed the customs of the Norsemen, as had no other of his people.

A major concern for him was the manner in which he would be accepted by Hawk Woman. His parents, his friends, all would welcome him home. He was not so handsome as when he left. The empty eye socket with its shriveled and scarred lids was not pretty. He had seen it, reflected in a still pool. That would evoke only sympathy from his parents. Friends, too, probably. But, as for Hawk Woman, how would she see it?

Then he would become irritated with himself. What did it matter? She would be someone else's wife now. Whose, he could not even imagine. Surely not Old Dog . . . The thought made his stomach tighten. He had spent many nights of sorrow through the years, lying quietly awake in the darkness, thinking of Hawk Woman in the arms of another man. *Any* other man. His heart had always been heavy at such thoughts, but until now there had always been a possibility, a slight chance that she had not married, that she had waited for him. As long as he did not know for sure, that chance existed.

Now, however, the closer he came to home, the more he was forced to realize that it could not be so. One of the most eligible, beautiful, and desirable young women of the village would not be still unmarried. He must resign himself to that. It was hard to do so and still smile, though. This was one area where he could not quite avoid taking himself seriously. The best that he could do would be to conceal it. At that, he was an expert. To conceal emotions was to survive, and he was a survivor. It would be hard, but he had done it before, and though his heart was heavy—

Odin paused, his thought interrupted by a flash of motion in the trees along the shore. Or had he only imagined it? He wished for the keenness of vision that he had once possessed, as he studied the forest. The leafy colors were turning, showing startling hues of red and yellow and brown. It was hard to distinguish shapes among such patterns. A deer? Bear? He blinked his one eye to clear it, but still could distinguish nothing. Maybe he had been mistaken.

The observer drew back into the red-orange of the thicket, stepped to the shadowy shelter of a giant spruce, and watched the canoe slide past and out of sight. Only when he was certain it was gone did he make a further move. Then he trotted a few steps to a well-worn trail, set his feet upon it, and began a systematic routine. He loped for some time, an easy distance-eating pace through the trees and along the slope. Then, breathing heavily, he slowed to a walk for a while, resting even as he continued to move in long strides. When his breath began to come easily again, he shifted the bow to his other hand and resumed the loping gait that covered so much ground. When opportunity offered, he cast a glance at the river, but he did not pause to study it. It did not matter.

The young man did stop at a clear spring beside the trail, cupping water in his hand to rinse his mouth and spit. Then a little more water, swallowed this time. Not too much . . . His entire stop could have been measured in heartbeats, before he turned back to his mission.

It was a little past midday when he jogged wearily into the village, between the lodges and toward the center of the community. He did slow to a walk as he neared the council house. He must let his breathing slow, because he must be able to talk.

Several older men were sitting in the sun outside the longhouse as he approached, relaxing and sociably smoking. They looked up, nodded a greeting, and waited for him to speak. The young warrior pointed downstream.

"Someone comes . . . Strangers," he said, still breathing deeply.

"How many? Where?"

"One canoe, three men. They dress strangely."

There was more interest now, and a readiness to move into action if necessary.

"Where?"

"Downstream . . . half a day. I have run. They will be here tonight."

"Are they heavily armed?"

"I could not see. Not for war, I think. But they are very strange. The hair of one is white."

"Ah! They are old men?"

"I do not know. The white-hair does not move like an old man. And the other . . . maybe he wore a fox cap, but it seemed to me that the red fur *grew* on his head."

The little group of elders chuckled, and the scout turned away, insulted by their disbelief.

"It is as I say," he said over his shoulder. "You will see."

31

Word spread quickly through the village, and observers were posted to give information about the progress of the strangers. It was possible, of course, that the canoe containing the travelers would not even stop. The village was not readily visible from the river, being a couple of bowshots upstream on a small tributary.

It was a matter of some import, then, when the canoe veered directly into the stream's mouth and toward the landing. There seemed to be no major threat in the coming of a canoe with only three men, whose actions were not particularly suspicious. It was prudent to be cautious, of course. The watcher at the river tensed when the canoe altered its course and came straight toward him. It was not long before the newcomers were close enough for him to see their faces. He gasped and drew farther into the bushes that concealed him. It was as young Black Hornet had said. The man in the front of the canoe *did* have hair that was almost white, yet he did move like a young man. They had laughed at Hornet, and he had gone home in anger. Now someone would have to apologize. The watcher turned his attention to the man in the middle. This one did seem a bit older, but the fox fur cap . . . Ah, it *did* seem to grow directly from this man's head! Again, Hornet had been right, or so it seemed.

The scout turned attention to the steersman in the back of the canoe. This one seemed familiar, somehow. His face, his manner . . . He wore ragged and disheveled garments, but not quite like the others. The canoe was sliding past at close range now, and the scout studied the profile. *Do I know this man?* He thought . . . *A man with one eye?* He could recall no one. Then he wondered . . . *Did he lose the eye since I knew him?* He studied the profile again and almost gasped aloud. *Walking Bird!* Close on the heels of that thought hurried another: *But he is dead!*

Something that was almost terror gripped the young man as he turned to run. *If Bird is dead and this is his ghost, then the others must be also from the spirit-world*, he thought. *They are coming for someone!* This was such a dreadful idea that he sprinted all the way to the village and arrived breathless and unable to speak.

"I . . . They . . ." he gasped. "They are coming!"

"Who? The canoe Hornet told of?"

"Yes, yes!" His breath was beginning to come more easily now as he became calmer in the presence of other people. "Walking Bird . . . one of them is Walking Bird."

"No, no. Walking Bird is dead."

Now doubt gripped the young scout. He hesitated a moment, then spoke. "His ghost, maybe. Or somebody who looks like Bird."

There was a chuckle around the circle, and he felt an uncomfortable mixture of anger and embarrassment.

Even as this occurred, several men were reaching for their weapons and moving toward the landing place. No matter who or what, someone was approaching, and they must be prepared. A few children started to follow the warriors, and a mother called after them.

"Be careful! We do not know who these men are! Best you stay here."

There seemed to be no real danger, however. Anyone intending harm to the village would surely not approach openly this way. And, with only three, at a disadvantage in the canoe as it neared shore . . . The appearance of the newcomers suggested more interest and curiosity than any threat of danger. Their confidence, too, was reassuring. The strangers seemed open and friendly.

It was only prudent, however, to meet the unknown with a show of strength. A dozen men with weapons ready formed a casual half circle around the spot where the canoe would ground. It was one of these who first voiced recognition.

"*Aiee!*" he cried. "It is . . . Walking Bird, is it really you? We thought you dead!"

The canoe touched the bank, and the white-haired man in the prow leaped nimbly ashore to pull the craft farther up the gentle slope. The other men moved forward and stepped out, too. The one who had been the steersman was smiling and laughing now.

"It is long since I was called Walking Bird," he answered, "but I am the same one."

There was a volley of questions. A couple of boys who had followed the greeting party despite their mothers' cautions now ran to spread the word of Walking Bird's return. They could scarcely remember such a person, or his disappearance. The story of the unfortunate young man, however, had been used as an example to frighten children into obedience ever since.

"Walking Bird has come home!" the boys called.

People began to stream from the houses and hurry toward the landing place.

"Is it true?" a woman asked one of the youths.

"Of course! I heard him say so!" the boy called over his shoulder as he ran on.

The crowd gathered quickly, and the scout who had been ridiculed now hurried to bask in the pleasure of vindication.

"Is it not as I said?" he demanded. "It is Walking Bird, a white-hair who is not old, and one who grows fur like that of the fox upon his head!"

"On his face, too!" said an astonished bystander.

Now Walking Bird was holding up a hand for silence.

"He has lost an eye!" a woman whispered to her companion.

"Yes. Too bad! He was a very handsome boy."

"He still is . . . as a man, I mean. Some woman . . ." She rolled her eyes suggestively.

"True. Was he not friendly with Hawk Woman, before she married Dog?"

"Yes, I think so. Something like that. They quarreled and he left, was it not?

"That is true! I had nearly forgotten. Odd that he would return just now, no?"

"Ssh! He is going to speak!"

The repatriated Walking Bird now began to talk, his voice choked with emotion.

"It is good to be home, my friends," he said. "Many things have happened, and I will tell them later. First, I would see my parents."

"Ah, Bird, your father is dead," an old man spoke. "My heart is heavy for you. He was my friend."

Walking Bird swallowed hard. "And my mother?"

"She is well. Your sister, also. But it is good that you have returned. They need you."

"Who are these others?" someone asked.

"The white-hair is called White Wolf," he said quickly. "He is a great holy man. The other is Fire Maker. I will tell you all of this tonight, but now let me find my mother."

He brushed through the circling crowd and hurried toward his mother's lodge. The crowd began to scatter. They would go their separate ways, spread the news and gossip, and then reassemble at dusk to hear the story of their lost son who had now returned.

The people gathered early to find a good seat. There had not been such excitement in a very long time. Rumors flew, especially about the strange-looking companions who had accompanied Walking Bird. No one had seen men of such an appearance. White hair, though young . . . Blue eyes that are not blind. There had been rumors of outsiders from far away, who had established a town on an island in the salty ocean to the east. That part was probably true, but no one had taken seriously the story that their hair came in many different colors. Now they must accept that maybe that was true, also. The strangers had followed Walking Bird to his mother's lodge, taking their packs with them. Well, soon the people would hear the story.

It was nearly dark now. The fire had been lighted, and flames reached hungrily up through the pile of sticks and logs. A stick burned in half, allowing the pile to settle into a new position as it dropped. A shower of sparks hurried aloft like living things, to be lost in the darkness above. Or, maybe, to join the myriad of stars that spread like strewn sparks across the deep blue-black of the sky.

The crowd's murmur rose a little in anticipation as the returned Walking Bird approached, flanked by his mother and sister, and his two companions. There was joy in the eyes of the women, who clung closely to the repatriated Bird.

He walked through the crowd, pausing to speak to friends and acquaintances as he passed. The pause was longer as he greeted the leader of the town. He had already paid his respects, in accordance to custom, but now spent a little more time and effort to honor the man's position and prestige. Then he took his place before the assembled circle, carefully selecting to best advantage the light, the dark background of trees, and the position of the rising moon. Walking Bird was a natural showman, and would take advantage of every factor possible.

The crowd quieted, waiting in anticipation.

"My brothers and sisters," he began, his voice choked with emotion, "much water has flowed down the Big River since I left this, the place of my childhood. Many things both good and bad have happened to me. But now I have come home, and it is good.

"Now, it is usual for our storytellers to begin with the story of our Creation, of how our People climbed into this world of sunlight from the world below. The roots of a giant grapevine formed our ladder. We have heard that story many times, so I mention it in passing, though briefly. It is enough, for there is much more that I would tell."

He paused and took a deep breath.

"You have noticed that I have lost an eye. I will tell of that, but first, know that the loss is partly gain. I am no longer Walking Bird. My name, given me by the people of my companions here, is Odin, father of the gods."

There was a murmur, and he waited for it to quiet.

"These others are special men," he went on. "The white-hair, who is called White Wolf, is a very powerful holy man. I have seen him change into a wolf when I thought . . . But forgive me, I am getting ahead of my story. You will see his powers later. The fire-haired one is his assistant, as I am. You need not fear either of them. They are our friends and allies.

"But now, I begin my story. When I left this village and the home of my parents, I started downstream in a little boat. I was very young and very foolish, though I thought otherwise at the time. My heart was heavy and I wished to be away from here. Ah, I have learned much. Enough, my friends, to realize my stupidity."

There was laughter, and he waited for quiet.

"I traveled for three days," he continued, "before I began to see what I was doing to my life. I had determined to return. . . ."

The story droned on, the listeners enthralled with the tale and with the manner of its presentation. The fire crackled and sang its soft songs to accompany the narration. Behind the speaker, a blood red full moon showed its glowing arc, turning to silver as it rose above the fringe of trees.

Far back in the crowd, beyond the circle of light created by the story fire, a woman listened. Her attention was fastened on every word of the speaker. Hawk Woman had been told that he was back, but she had not seen him until now. It had been a long time since they quarreled, and she had shed many tears. She had not intended that it should end that way. Now, though she was glad that Walking Bird was alive, her heart was heavy with a new hurt.

She shifted her baby on her lap, rocking it gently to prevent it from fussing. She wanted to miss nothing that the storyteller said.

32

Nils Thorsson sat, alternately staring into the fire and watching the crowd. The people of Odin's village seemed completely absorbed in the storytelling. That was to be expected. One of their young men who had been lost and who was believed dead had now returned, with strange companions and a new name.

It was apparent that Odin was a good storyteller. The man did it with a flourish, an enjoyment that verged on excitement. Such enthusiasm was easily transmitted to the crowd, and people hung on his every word.

It was more difficult for the Norsemen to remain attentive. They knew only a few words of this language. There were times when Nils thought that he knew which part of the account was in progress, but he was not certain. His attention wandered. He was seated between Svenson and the mother of Odin. They had been told that Odin's father was dead. Somehow that information had struck deeply into his emotions. From time to time Nils had thought of his own parents and his home. Usually it had been in times of peril, or when he was sure that he was about to die. At these times he would picture them in their grief, wondering about the circumstances of his death, knowing that they could never know the details yet hungering to do so. This made him long for home, to be a child again so that he could run to the welcoming arms of his mother for comfort and protection.

Watching the reunion of Odin with his family had stirred such feelings to a remarkable degree. One meets a person, knows him for some time, yet many times does not think of his family, his home, or wonder about his childhood. There is a tendency to assume that this person arrived as he now is, fully grown, skipping over the formative years. Nils had been somewhat embarrassed before, in regarding the one-eyed Skraeling as a lesser human being. He had slowly realized the quickness of Odin's wit, the keenness of his mind. Both Nils and Svenson owed their lives to this man several times over.

Now it seemed strange to see Odin, once called Walking Bird, in the bosom of his family. In an odd way, Odin's mother reminded him of his own mother. She would have related to the unexpected arrival of foreign guests in just the same manner. The woman, still handsome in her middle years, bustled around the lodge preparing food for the guests and for her long-lost son. In this, she had been assisted by her daughter, the sister that Odin had mentioned before.

Nils leaned back to steal a glance at the girl, her face flushed with the flickering glow of the firelight. She was completely absorbed in her brother's story, her expression changing from interest to anxiety to amusement as the tale unfolded. He watched her for a little while, trying not to stare. Her attention was so completely focused on the storyteller that she seemed completely unaware of all else. *How beautiful*, Nils thought, *how very beautiful*. He had certainly not expected this. From Odin's infrequent mention of his younger sister, Nils had expected a gangling child. Actually, he had thought almost nothing at all about what sort of a person this sister of Odin's might be. A child . . .

"She grew up," Odin had said as they were introduced.

That was obviously a monumental understatement. This was no knobby-legged teenager, clumsy in her attempts to adapt to her new growth. Here, instead, was a beauty, in the first fullness of the flowering of young womanhood. Long-legged, yes. He had seldom seen such well-turned calves and ankles, or such length of thigh. Her buckskin dress could hardly conceal the exquisite artistry of the soft curves beneath. That was only the beginning. The rest of her body, equally well formed, seemed to flow with a willowy grace as she moved.

There was a catlike dignity in the way that she walked, stood, or sat. It was sensuous without appearing seductive, pure and unconscious in its quality.

Now, while her attention was diverted, he took advantage of the opportunity to study her face. In profile, her perfectly chiseled features were striking. Many times Nils, in observing a woman, had told himself, *Surely this is one of the most beautiful women in the world.* Yet now all others paled to insignificance beside this, the sister of his friend. Even the image in his mind of the golden-haired Ingrid, wife of the cooper at Straumfjord, suffered by comparison. The face at which he covertly stared now was veritable perfection. Large, deep-set eyes with long dark lashes, a well-formed nose between high cheekbones, full and sensuous lips . . . He could imagine the ecstasy of nibbling at the ripe fullness of that lower lip.

He was absorbed in that pleasant fantasy, then, when the girl suddenly turned and looked straight into his eyes. Nils had a brief moment in which he experienced a wave of guilt. It was much like the feeling when he was a child, and had been forbidden to play near the fjord. He had done so anyway, encouraged by some older boys. Fortunately, no harm had resulted, but they had been caught. He had been deeply hurt by the look of disappointment in his mother's face. It was like that now. He had been trapped in an activity that might not be forbidden, but he was not sure. At worst, he might have violated custom in some way by ogling the girl. At best, he feared that she would be offended by his blatant stare. He reddened under her gaze. He might be able to protest his innocence to her brother, but he would never forget the startled and surprised expression on that lovely face.

Then, to his amazement, she smiled. The smile still held traces of surprise, but it was a friendly, open smile without anger or resentment. It was contagious, and he smiled back. A bond of friendship passed between them in the odd way that it sometimes does, a sort of recognition without any implication of anything else. Nothing seductive or suggestive, just the acknowledgment of another human being's presence, one that might be interesting. In that moment both knew it for what it was, and it was good.

I do not even know her name! Nils thought. He now had a tremendous longing to learn the language of his friend. The girl's name had been spoken, but it was a group of meaningless syllables to him. No one had made an effort to translate. Well, he would ask later, but he looked forward to being able to talk with this fascinating creature.

The two people of different worlds turned their attention back to the storyteller, still smiling. Nils wondered if Odin had said something about "White Wolf" in the course of his narrative, to cause the attention of the girl to turn his way. He thought not. No one else had turned at that moment. He felt that more likely, the force of his thoughts had attracted her. He had reached out, and she had answered, though not in exactly the same context.

A thought struck him: *Do these people have something that we do not? Some understanding, maybe, of the nature of the spirit?* Odin sometimes talked about "things of the spirit," which Nils found rather confusing. Did this spirit-thing extend to communication? Did they have a way to speak without words?

He shook his head to clear it, and turned his attention back to the storyteller. They had spoken little since arriving here. Odin had been completely occupied with the enormous task of relating again to his people, and had had no time for anything else. *Will it be like that for me, when I return home?* Nils wondered. Of course, Odin had been absent for several years. *But I might be, too,* he thought.

He glanced at Svenson, who was nodding sleepily at his elbow. The old sailor's head sank lower and lower, then suddenly rose with a jerk as he opened his eyes wide again. Sven glanced from side to side to see if anyone had noticed, but then slumped again and quickly resumed his nodding.

Now, Nils noticed, people were beginning to turn and look at the two outsiders. Odin was pointing. There were gasps of amazement. Yes, now it must be their part of the story. He nudged Svenson with his elbow.

"Wake up, Sven."

Svenson came awake. "What?"

"Wake up. Odin is talking about us."

"How do you know?"

"People are looking this way. I think he is telling about how we three fell together."

"Yes . . . it may be. What should we do?"

"Nothing, I suppose. Look dignified?"

Svenson, feeling all eyes on the two of them, waved a nervous greeting. Nils followed his own original suggestion and tried to appear stern and dignified, with moderately good results.

Odin asked them to stand and join him as he told of the climactic events leading up to and following their capture. Now there were many expressions of amazement. Some of the few words of this language known to the Norsemen were their own names, White Wolf and Fire Maker. This part of the story could be followed to some extent. They saw the storyteller recount the changing of the color of stones and Sven's creation of fire by bringing it directly from a flint nodule. Now the onlookers were staring at the newcomers with something akin to awe. Nils caught the phrase "holy man," and tried to behave as if he knew what that role entailed. He had had some practice in this, during the time they had spent in the village of their captors. Yes, he thought that he could continue in this role, with the help of Odin. Such honor was certainly a pleasure.

Just then his glance caught the eye of Odin's beautiful sister. She was looking at him almost worshipfully, as if he were some kind of a god. *No,* he wanted to say, *I am nothing like that! I am a man, an ordinary man, but one who wants very much to know you better.*

He must talk to Odin as soon as possible, he knew. He must learn the girl's name, and more importantly, ask about the customs observed by young men and women among these people. In this, he did not want any mistakes.

There was one other conversation that evening, a very short one, but of great significance to the returned Walking Bird, now Odin. In turn, it would become of importance to the Norsemen.

The gathering was over, and the crowd was breaking up, people going to their various lodges. Several people hung around the dying fire to welcome their friend home. There had been little time until now. He had barely had time to visit with his own family and introduce the newcomers before the story fire was lighted. There had been no time for news of friends or for village gossip. This came to an abrupt end as a boyhood friend greeted him warmly.

"Snake!" Odin cried. "It is good to see you. You had just married—"

"Yes, and now I have two daughters."

"It is good! Ah, I cannot believe! You, a father!"

The other shrugged. "It is as it should be. Have you seen Hawk Woman yet?"

Odin's heart jumped. "No . . . I . . . I had supposed that she must be married."

"Yes, yes, of course. She married Old Dog, the year after you left."

Grief descended over Odin like a thrown robe. Why had he come back at all? He had known that it must be. His thoughts raced, wondering how he could leave. No, he could not, he must care for his mother! The idea of seeing Hawk Woman day after day, and seeing her go each night into the lodge of another . . . *Old Dog?*

Snake was talking, but Odin's thoughts prevented his hearing. His heart was very heavy. Now Snake was shaking him by the shoulder to get his attention.

"What? I am sorry, Snake. I was not listening."

"No one has told you, then? Yes, she married Old Dog after you left."

"You just told me that," Odin snapped angrily.

"But you did not listen to the rest. Old Dog died last winter, in the Moon of Snows. Hawk Woman's time of mourning is past and she needs a husband. You have come home at a good time."

Odin's heart, as heavy as stone a moment ago, was suddenly as light as the breath-feathers of Kookooskoos, the owl.

Part II

33

ils Thorsson sat on the curving slope of the lodge's domed roof, watching a line of geese high in the blue. The birds were so far above him that he could barely hear their barking cries as they hurried southward.

You had best hurry, he thought. *Winter comes!*

After the first light snow of autumn, experienced as they traveled, the weather had moderated again. Days were warm and nights cool. The stillness of the air and the sights, sounds, and smells of autumn made it a joy to be alive. At home in Norway, this would be called the Second Summer. It did not happen every year, but when it did . . . ah! was the sky ever so blue, the changing colors of the trees so rich? There was an all-pervasive feeling of well-being now, a sense that all things are in order. A confidence. Yes, that was it. He had not felt so confident since their disastrous expedition had left Straumfjord.

There was a pang of sadness and pain at the thought. The pain of guilt and failure swept over him for a moment, as it always did at the memory. Two lost ships, the dozens of good men . . . Helge Landsverk, his friend.

But what could I have done? he asked himself. By the time he, Nils, had assumed command at Helge's death, the final events were already in motion. It had taken some time to accept this, but he found that now he was more willing. His periods of guilt and regret were shorter. And, as Svenson said, they were lucky to be alive at all. While it is good to die bravely, as Sven had once noted, one is still dead. And they, at least, were alive. Alive, to relish this uncommonly good weather, this Second Summer, here in a strange land, among strange people.

Odin's people. The Norsemen had been welcomed, honored, treated with awe and respect. *It would be interesting to know,* Nils pondered, *what Odin had told his people.* Maybe he would know, some day. They were attempting to learn the language. Svenson, who could speak several of the dialects of the Norse coasts, was learning quickly, Nils a bit more slowly. *Some people,* Nils reflected, *have a gift with languages.* He had already decided that Sven had such a skill. Sven could communicate quite well almost anywhere, even in the islands. One of the sailors had once told him that Svenson could even talk to the Welsh.

Odin, too, seemed to have this gift of tongues. The Skraeling could communicate quite well in the language of the Norsemen, with hardly an accent.

Skraeling. Nils thought for a moment about their use of the term. *The skraelingar, the "lesser people."* True, some of the natives were shorter in stature than the Norsemen. But some were not. In the first usage, the newcomers had undoubtedly seen some of the shorter natives, and remarked on it. The name had stuck, modified, perhaps, by the tendency of the old Norse raiders to regard anyone else as lesser people. *Yes, that must be it,* Nils thought. The modified meaning, unconsciously classifying all others as lesser humanity . . . Skraelings, the Lesser People . . .

Once more, Nils felt the odd embarrassment that had occurred before. It was in essence the admission to himself that he had terribly underestimated the wisdom and cleverness of Odin. A cleverness, he knew, that had saved their lives.

Nils still rankled a bit at their enforced stay here. If he had been able to choose, they would not have made plans to winter here. He was beginning to tolerate the idea more easily now, however. Odin's explanation made much sense, when one actually looked at the situation. It was practical. Of course he had realized that from the first. It had helped considerably, though, that Odin's beautiful sister was present during most of every day since they had arrived. Add to that the beautiful Second Summer . . . well, being there was, after all, not bad.

It was different. That had become apparent very quickly when they arrived two weeks ago. The very form of the houses seemed strange. Rather than dwellings for individual families, these were large structures that served for several couples, their children, and assorted relatives. In that respect, the lodges were used much as the communal structures at Straumfjord. That, it appeared, was a temporary arrangement by the Norse colonists. This, among Odin's people, seemed to be a long-established way of life. Nils wondered, with a certain degree of embarrassment, how it would be possible to make love in a big single room with no privacy. That question had occurred to him at Straumfjord, but he had cast it aside in the presence of more urgent activities.

The gentle breeze shifted a little, and smoke from the square hole in the lodge's dome drifted toward him. Nils blinked, coughed, and moved his position to a better place, upwind from the smoke hole. Below, he could hear the murmur of voices as the women prepared food. He tried to identify the voice of Calling Dove . . . that was her name, he had learned. He loved the sound of her laughter, and of the melodious syllables. He did not even understand their meaning, but their sound was pleasant to him. As pleasant as her smile, and the way she moved. He must learn more about the customs of courtship here among Odin's clan. It would not do to push too rapidly. *Go slowly, Thorsson,* he told himself, *until you understand their ways.* In simplest terms, it could be dangerous to do otherwise.

He had asked Odin to tell him of these people, and of their ways. Odin merely gave his characteristic shrug, looking a bit puzzled.

"What did you wish to know?"

"Well . . ." Nils stammered, "what do you call yourselves?"

Odin responded with a nod and a series of syllables that had absolutely no meaning for Nils.

"What does it mean?" he asked.

"I do not understand, White Wolf. What is it that you want to know?"

"Well, what is its meaning?" Nils paused in thought, then continued. "Ah! Our name, that of the Norse, is from the *direction*. You know, north, the North Star . . . *Norsemen.*"

Odin nodded. "I see! I did not notice that! *North.*"

"Good. Now, what is the meaning of your name for your people?"

Odin's puzzled expression was the same as before. "The People," he said.

"No . . . I mean . . . look, Odin. Those who held us captive, before? What are *they* called?"

"Oh. They are called the same."

"The *same?*"

"Yes." Odin spoke a few more syllables that had no meaning for Nils. "They call themselves that. To them, it means the People . . . same as ours."

"But you . . . what do *you* call *them?*"

Odin smiled, and his one eye twinkled. "Many things, sometimes. Mangy dogs . . . dung eaters. Worse. But I know what you mean, Thorsson. They are the Downriver People, to us. But for each, his own are the People, no? Do you not call yourselves that, sometimes?"

Well, yes, thought Nils, recalling the pride with which his grandfather often referred to "Our People" and their exploits.

"Yes, that is true," he admitted. "I understand. A little better, anyway. 'The People.' "

This may have been a turning point for Nils Thorsson. He began to realize the pride with which these people regarded themselves. *The People.* It was a thing that a Norseman could understand. This pride had enabled Odin to survive, to refuse to surrender, to overcome all the misfortune that had befallen him. That was the reason for the man's joy in his new name . . . Odin, father of the gods! It was as if he wore the name, originally a cruel joke, as a badge of honor. Yes, that was it. Odin wore the name as he wore his empty eye socket, a symbol of his pride and his survival. From that day on, the realization of a kinship of spirit drew him closer to this remarkable man of the People, and to the People as a whole.

There were eight of the big lodges in this village, and he estimated about twenty people living in each. Maybe a hundred fighting men. Or hunters, as the case might be. A few men seemed to have more than one wife.

"How is this?" he asked Odin.

"The women are sisters. The man of that one—the fat one, there—was killed by a bear. So her sister's husband takes her in."

This seemed logical. Another thought occurred to Nils.

"Odin, are there others of the People? Other towns?"

"Oh, yes. Another, a day upriver, and one across the river."

"The same size as this town?"

"One a little bigger . . . maybe ten lodges, when I left the People. The other, six or seven."

"Their lodges are like these? Yours are much different from the Downriver People."

Odin's eye twinkled at the usage.

"Of course," he said simply.

Nils had never seen houses like these domed structures before. Except for lack of privacy, it seemed an effective way to build. Four stout posts stood near the middle, forming the four corners of the smoke hole. Poles slanted like rafters from a circle that formed the outside wall. Then smaller poles were laid, covered with matting woven of rushes and piled with dried grass for insulation. Dirt dug from the inside was heaped over the roof like a dome, placing the floor a little below ground level. Sod was laid over this dirt to complete the structure. It was actually quite comfortable, Nils found.

Privacy was achieved by separate compartments around the walls. These were made of skins over a framework of sticks, and were just large enough for the beds of three or four people, a family group. Odin, Svenson, and Nils had been provided with such a cubicle for their sleeping robes in the same lodge as Odin's mother and sister.

That part was not easy for Nils. Through each day he was in constant contact with Calling Dove. At least, with observation of her graceful form and friendly smile, and the sound of her voice. Then at night he would lie in the darkness, waiting for sleep to come, listening to her breathing, knowing that she was almost within arm's reach on the other side of that leather curtain. So near, yet so far . . .

To add to his frustration, there was a young couple whose cubicle was directly across the lodge, who seemed exceptionally inclined to romance. Nils gathered that they had been married only a short while. Every night, it seemed, they retreated to the privacy of their cubicle before anyone else. There were remarks and jokes by the others. Nils could not understand the words, but the meaning was plain. The young couple, only slightly embarrassed, would retort with remarks of their own and then disappear for the night. Sounds of giggling, scuffling, and heavy breathing came from the little skin tent at intervals. All of this was very disconcerting to Nils, who could imagine the rapturous events taking place across the big room.

One night the scuffling and giggling were more active than usual, and more prolonged. *This is more than a man should be forced to endure,* he thought as he lay awake in the darkness. *I must talk to Odin soon.*

Svenson's soft snores and the deep breathing of Odin sounded in the cubicle of the three. Nils thought that no one else was awake in the entire lodge except for the athletic couple across the fire. Then, just as the sounds in the darkness seemed to reach a peak, there was a momentary silence. In this short space of quiet, he heard a sound that was perhaps the most frustrating of all. From the other side of the thin leather curtain at his elbow came a soft feminine chuckle that he recognized as quite familiar. He was greatly tempted to reach under the curtain's edge and feel around in the darkness. His hand actually moved in that direction, but he hesitated.

No, he told himself sternly, *but I will talk to Odin tomorrow!*

34

Walking Bird, now known as Odin, father of the gods, was almost ecstatic over his good fortune. His return to the People had been beyond his wildest fantasies. He was somewhat embarrassed that his long separation from family and friends was because of his own stubbornness and stupidity. Family and friends, however, seemed unaware of that factor. Unaware, or perhaps forgiving. There was a willingness to forget and forgive in the happiness of his homecoming.

That homecoming, he realized, was a major event in the lives of the People, as well as in his own life. He had returned with an astounding story, a prolonged story with several individual parts to it. Any one of the separate phases of that story would have been good. His capture and repeated attempts to escape . . . His eventual success, flight and his sanctuary among the Norsemen at Straumfjord . . . The voyage of exploration, the great canoes with winglike sails that caught the wind . . . The destruction of that entire expedition, and the escape of the three survivors . . .

Ah, he had not even had to exaggerate any of it in the telling! Best of all, he had brought with him the living proof of his story in the form of the two Norsemen. He had found it unnecessary even to demonstrate the powerful gifts of White Wolf. The appearance and demeanor of the light-haired holy man were enough to convince the People, once they had heard the story.

Was he really a holy man? Odin had spent much time in thought about that. At the time of the White Wolf episode, Odin had initially thought that he, Odin, was performing a deception on their enemies. He had deliberately led them to believe that certain things of the spirit were happening. But somewhere along the line, reality had become blurred. Odin had lost track of what was real and what was part of his subterfuge. In his sincere efforts to convince their captors, he had been drawn into the story so completely . . . Ah, one *must* believe, to tell a story well. There were times when he himself believed that he had seen Thorsson turn into a wolf. In the final analysis, did it really matter? Events had occurred that brought about astonishing results. If he, in attempting to interpret those results, had brought about a belief on the part of others, so be it.

There are many things in the world that cannot be explained, but that cannot be denied, either. Maybe some of these that defy explanation should merely be enjoyed. The colors of a sunset, the whisper of the breeze in the pines on a warm autumn afternoon, the uniform lines of migrating geese high above . . . how were they able to space themselves in such exact formation? Odin had wondered about such things all of his life, and had eventually decided not to worry about it, but just to accept it. Some things are not meant to be understood. The sunset will occur, the breeze will still whisper to the trees, whether anyone understands that conversation or not.

And, Odin had decided, it is the same with things of the spirit. It did not matter whether Thorsson had *really* become a wolf, or had only *appeared* to. The result was the same, and it was good. Whatever the powers of the Norse holy man, they seemed beneficial to Odin. Had it not continued to be so? The most recent discovery, on his return to the People . . . Ah, had there really been any chance that Odin's childhood sweetheart, with whom he had quarreled, would prove to be just emerging from her time of mourning for a lost husband? Hawk Woman had just become eligible for resumption of their once thwarted romance.

The two had talked, embarrassed at first. Very quickly, however, it seemed that they had resumed a conversation they had stopped only a little while ago. Soon they were chattering and giggling like children again. The resumption of their interrupted romance was a subject of great interest and of joy to the People. Even the infant, who looked much like her mother, gazed at Odin with mischief in her large dark eyes, and smiled. And he found that that, too, was good.

Who was to say? Was all of this, these good things happening to him, just by chance? Or were they somehow resulting from his association with White Wolf and the unknown strength of the holy man's powerful gifts? In the joy of the homecoming, he did not know and did not care. But he was thankful. Next season when the People carried out their annual celebration of thanks for the return of the sun and the awakening of growing things, he would offer prayers and sacrifices. Yes, to the spirits that guided the lives of the People, and to those of the Norsemen as well. He must find out more about their gods.

Perhaps he had been neglecting the newcomers, Odin thought. Once he had arrived home, he had been almost totally absorbed with reunion. Everyone wanted to talk to him and to listen to his tales of adventure. That was exciting and flattering, but it had begun to be a nuisance. He needed time to spend with his mother, his friends, and most of all, with Hawk Woman. It had become apparent at their first conversation after his return that they would be together. It was, however, for her to say when, and in the hope of a speedy resolution to that question, he was spending much time with her.

Therefore, White Wolf and Fire Carrier had been left to fend for themselves much of the time. Certainly, they had seemed to have no problem in adjusting to their new surroundings. Odin had expected none, because he had seen these two adjust quickly to the ways of fugitives, and again to those of their captors. One thing he had not anticipated was the reaction of children toward the Norsemen. To the children of the People, the most remarkable thing about the newcomers was their appearance. Their light-colored hair and eyes, and the bushy beard that grew directly from Svenson's face seemed to fascinate the young ones. It had not been so with the children of their captors, but of course that had been a different situation altogether. That stay had been based on mutual distrust. Yes, that must be the difference.

Still, it had been startling to see the rapidity with which the children related to the strangers. To Svenson, especially. Within three days, Sven's every move was followed by a handful of children. When he sat, his lap was quickly occupied by at least one or two small ones. He reacted warmly, which in turn pleased the children. They laughed and teased and playfully tugged at the beard of the "Fire Man." He in turn teased them, and it was not unusual to see a child riding on his back as he made his way around the village.

"Does Svenson have children at home?" Odin asked Nils.

"Yes, three or four. They are grown, I think."

"It is good to see him with the little ones," Odin observed.

The mothers, cautious at first, soon relaxed, seeing the obvious quality of the relationship. One extra advantage in all of this was that Svenson's use of the People's language was greatly helped. Naturally quick with language anyway, he rapidly began to communicate with his young followers in their own tongue. This in turn helped Nils, who was not quite so gregarious.

In half a moon, both were beginning to communicate, gradually improving their understanding as their usage increased. Nils had discarded his linen shirt, which had become threadbare, and was wearing a buckskin shirt that had been offered by Odin's mother. Little by little, the two were becoming more comfortable with the customs and dress of the People. Odin felt pleased at that, and it helped to soften the slight pangs of guilt that he felt at having neglected them.

One of his concerns dealt with how well the outsiders would winter. There was a closeness, a forced association that was always somewhat of a problem in winter. During the Moon of Long Nights and the Moon of Snows there was frequently a period when no one could move farther than the adjacent lodges.

Sometimes not even there, for a day or two. The People spent the time in visiting, telling stories, smoking, or gambling. Even so, tempers often became short before spring allowed more freedom of movement. By that time the lodges would have become stagnant and foul smelling, like the den of an animal. It was a joke among the People that some tolerated all of this better than others. Even so, it was an annual problem that was understood by the People. Odin's concern was that it might not be understood by the newcomers.

Yet, surely, he thought, they had crossed the salty Big Water in their great canoes. That had taken many days, he understood. And they had had no women to comfort them, to warm their beds on the long, cramped sea voyage. That was another thing. The way things were now progressing, Odin felt that before Cold Maker swept down in full attack, Hawk Woman would have announced her intention to remarry. That was a matter of great anticipation for him. But what of White Wolf and Fire Carrier? How great was their need? He did not know their customs. He had seen the way Wolf looked at Calling Dove, and was not certain that he approved of such intentions toward his younger sister. After all, he did not even *know* the Norseman's intentions. He could see the admiration and desire in the blue eyes, but what did it imply? A temporary dalliance, or something based on a sense of responsibility toward one's bed companion? Odin was concerned, but did not know how to approach the subject with the Norseman. Even more disconcerting was the look in the eyes of his sister when she looked at White Wolf.

If these two did consummate the desire that shone plainly in the eyes of both, what then? What would happen when spring returned with the accompanying opportunity for travel? Would the two Norsemen immediately insist on starting back to their own people? Probably. If so, what of Calling Dove? Would the Norseman consider her his wife, and take her back with him, away from her people? Or would he feel no lasting ties, and leave her behind like a cast-off garment, possibly with child? Odin was wise in the ways of the world, and was not unaware of that strong possibility. It is the way of things, he knew. But he had never looked at the ways of men and women in just this way before. *This is my sister,* he wanted to shout. He found himself feeling a resentment toward White Wolf that was quite uncomfortable. And the man had done nothing to deserve it. Well, not yet.

Maybe, thought Odin, *maybe I could talk of this with Hawk Woman.* Yes, that seemed to be a good thought. Maybe, even, Hawk Woman could inquire discreetly about Dove's feelings in the matter. *Yes, women do discuss such things,* he thought, *more readily than men.* He would ask her to approach the subject with Calling Dove.

Feeling somewhat more confident, he went to look for Hawk Woman. He found her gathering sticks for fuel in the edge of the woods, her baby asleep in the cradleboard on her back.

"Let me help you," he offered, starting to pick up branches to begin his own armful of wood. "I would talk with you."

"And I, with you!" she said, smiling. She paused, studying his face. "You are very serious!"

"Yes," he said. "It is a serious matter."

"What?" she asked, sobering. "When we should marry?"

Odin was caught completely off guard.

"No . . . I mean, yes . . . I . . . well, no . . . I . . ."

"Stop!" she chuckled, placing a finger on his lips. "I think we should marry now. Soon, before snow flies." She studied his face for a moment. "Was there something else?"

Now he recovered his composure, and smiled at her.

"If there was," he told her, "I have forgotten."

35

din and Hawk Woman consummated their marriage late in the Moon of Falling Leaves. There were jokes about the timing of the event. The next cycle in the unwritten calendar of the People would be the Moon of Madness. There were those who said that it would be more appropriate for this long-troubled romance, to wait until that time. Others were of the opinion that the couple wished to avoid such a connotation.

The Mad Moon is a recognized phenomenon. It is at this time that the creatures of field and forest are stricken with irrational behavior. Squirrels scamper frantically, storing large quantities of nuts, only to forget many of their hiding places. Grouse fly senselessly, often colliding with trees, rocks, or brush and falling crippled or dead.

Deer, elk, and moose travel widely, searching for something. Possibly they are troubled by the remnants of a migratory urge that still moves some species of their kind. The same urge, maybe, causes man to watch the long lines of geese high above him and feel the longing to follow them. Males of the deer family are also stricken at this time with the mating urge. Bull elk have been bugling their searching challenge across mountain and meadow, causing the hair on human necks to bristle in a primitive emotion felt by our ancestors a thousand lifetimes ago. Usually shy and retreating from potential danger, at this time the male deer become aggressive and dangerous. They will fight all comers for the females, for territory, or merely for supremacy. For a while, they become almost as irrational as man himself.

For man, the Moon of Madness is aptly named. There is something, maybe, about the obvious shortening of the length of the days that fills us with dread at this season. It is apparent that the Moon of Long Nights is near at hand. The sun itself is dimming, and there is an unspoken fear in us all as the longest night of the year approaches. *What if this time, the sun is really going out, like an untended lodge fire? What if it does not come back?* It is no coincidence that even modern man, with his brightly lit environment, feels this dread. Madness in men still reaches its peak in the waning yellow sunlight of late autumn and early winter.

So, the good-natured jokes of the People, tossed at the reunited couple, revolved around this seasonal phenomenon. Were they reacting to the mating urge of the deer, it was asked? Someone pretended to examine the head of Odin for sprouting antlers. This joke became even more hilarious when Svenson mentioned that in the country of the Norsemen, men sometimes wore headdresses with horns or antlers.

"As part of the marriage?" a woman asked in amazement.

"No, usually to fight," Sven answered.

"Ah, Fire Man, your ways are strange!" laughed a little girl.

Svenson had been called by several names since their arrival. Fire Keeper, Fire Carrier, Fire Hair . . . It was a matter of finding one of the variants that fit well. All were equally appropriate. To some extent they would be used interchangeably, as formal names and nicknames or pet names are used in all cultures. In the end, it was the name chosen by the children that seemed to stick to the fire-haired Svenson. "Fire Man."

Nils Thorsson, by contrast, was White Wolf from the first day. There was a certain quality about his demeanor, a dignity that implied special qualities. From the time of their arrival among the People, Odin had continually capitalized on this situation. It had been quite effective among their enemies, and now lent an air of mysticism and magic. The People were impressed. It was an honor that a holy man of such great prestige would spend a season with them. White

Wolf was feared a little at first, because of his great and unknown powers. He was said to be a bit crazy, but are not many holy men slightly mad? They dwell on a different level of the spirit than everyone else. Odin, of course, did nothing to discourage such attitudes. In a short time, the People had begun to see that the holy man, while he possessed qualities of the spirit, was predictable, quite human, and not particularly threatening, a man to be respected and treated with honor rather than fear.

White Wolf himself was slightly unnerved at the distraction caused by the marriage of Odin. He was pleased for his friend, of course, but it was apparent that Odin had better things to do than to act as a social advisor for the romantically inclined Norseman. He decided to postpone his questions for the present, to learn as much of the language as he could, and to observe the ceremonial aspects of the marriage as best he could. He was still receiving a covert glance and occasionally a warm smile from Calling Dove. *She is interested,* he thought. But what to do next? In his own Norse culture he would have found occasion to draw her aside and make a romantic advance or two, to see what might develop. Here, he was unsure. Well, he would return the smiles, watch, and wait. Meanwhile, he would observe the customs of his friend's marriage.

The actual ceremony was quite simple. The couple, assisted by family and friends, constructed one of the skin cubicles that furnished sleeping quarters around the outside wall of the lodge. There were brief prayers and ritual chants that White Wolf did not understand. The parents of the two spread a sleeping robe over the backs of Odin and Hawk Woman as they knelt in front of the sleeping cubicle. Hawk Woman had moved her few belongings into the lodge shared by Odin's family.

The imagination of White Wolf became a great nuisance to him as he saw the couple enter into their newlywed marital bliss. It seemed unfair to him somehow, that Odin and Hawk Woman, yes, and the noisy young couple across the big lodge, were sharing their respective sleeping cubicles in ecstatic romance. He, Nils Thorsson, shared his with Svenson. Sven seemed mildly amused by his frustration, but aside from an occasional ribald remark, showed only good-natured recognition of the activity in the curtained cubicle. Nils wondered if, at Svenson's age, such things were forgotten. Surely, Sven could not be much past forty. Was that too old for such activity? Of course, there had been that old lecher who had lived down the street from Nils's parents when he was a boy in Stadt. What was his name? No matter. The old scoundrel had seemed ancient to the neighborhood boys, who joked and laughed about his exploits. There seemed to be a constant assortment of young women coming and going around the house of that old goat. He seemed to have no family but plenty of companionship. What did he have, Nils had often wondered, to attract such a parade of femininity? Money? Maybe, but there had to be more to it than that.

He chuckled to himself at the memory, still somewhat confused. *Why,* he wondered, *are some men so attractive to women?* It seems to have little to do with mere physical appearance. That is part of it, of course. But beyond that, some men . . . In school, he had noticed, some of his fellow students as they matured . . . Jenson, and yes, Knudson, too, had nearly had to fight the women off. He had never understood that. Women were polite to him, but never aggressive in the way they were to the occasional man who had that special something. *But what is it?* he wondered. *Women sometimes have it, too.* Some women attract men like flies, and that, too, is not entirely beauty. A way of moving? Maybe . . . the way she walks, the inviting way she stands . . .

Ingrid, the blue-eyed goddess, popped into his mind. Yes, she would be attractive to any man alive. He could become aroused merely by thinking of her. And he had kissed her only once. . . . She had kissed him, actually. Yes, she certainly had that special something, whatever it may be. He wondered what she was doing now. Had she found someone to take her back to Norway? Who now shared her bed? Again, his heart reached out in pity to her husband, Olaf the cooper. What was the problem in that marriage? Was it only that Ingrid was so attractive to men that someone was always trying for her? It was with a small feeling of guilt that Nils recalled that he would have happily bedded with her himself. In fact, he had virtually pledged to do so. But now . . .

He wondered when, if ever, he would be in a position to do so. He had nothing. No ship, no possessions, no way to get himself home, really, much less the ability to help anyone else. Maybe he could rely on the kindness of a shipmaster. . . . One of the Ericsons, possibly, on promise of payment when they got back to Stadt. But would such a promise obtain passage for Ingrid, too? She already had a reputation for trouble. Quite possibly she had already offered someone else the opportunity to share her bed in return for passage. What if he managed to return to the colony next spring, only to find that the lovely Ingrid had forgotten him and departed for home with someone else? It was possible, though something deep within him still wanted to deny it.

What am I thinking of? he asked himself in irritation. It bothered him that he was worrying so much about who was sleeping with whom. But he understood why. He had seen, first, the happy young couple across the lodge, who were so blatantly noisy in their lovemaking. Then, the brief courtship and subsequently happy communion of Odin and his bride. And he, Nils, had nothing.

Calling Dove walked past, and glanced his way. She could certainly remove all thoughts of Ingrid, or any other woman, for that matter, with a glance or a smile. Still, he realized, he was not any closer to a real relationship than he had ever been.

From all indications this had the makings of an extremely frustrating winter.

Well, for now he would concentrate on learning the language. At least, he would try.

36

The Moon of Falling Leaves brought about, among other things, a late fall hunt in which the Norsemen participated. Both were familiar with the use of the bow, and two extra hunters were a welcome addition to the productivity of the village.

The newcomers had requested to be allowed to help in this manner. They had realized the effect that two extra mouths to feed would have during the lean moons of winter. This led to a discussion of weapons, and considerably broadened the knowledge of the Norsemen about their hosts.

"What use is the long knife?" asked a curious warrior, looking at the heavy sword, salvaged after the massacre and now in the possession of White Wolf.

With appropriate translation by Odin, Nils attempted to answer.

"It is used in fighting," he explained.

"Ah! Nothing else?"

"Not much. Cutting meat, sometimes."

The other nodded. The shiny blade of the sword seemed to be a matter of great curiosity to these people.

"It shines like a small fish in a clear stream," one of the men said in awe, translated in turn by Odin. "He also asks what you use in hunting."

"The bow, sometimes a spear. You have seen."

"Yes," Odin agreed. "But your bows are different, no?"

"Some. Longer, maybe."

"So it seems to me. But I have watched your people use the bow, Thorsson. Do they not hold the string in a different way?"

There followed a morning of demonstration and experimentation. The Norsemen were accustomed to a grip that held the arrow between the index and the middle fingers. The third finger assisted in drawing the string. The Skraelings seemed to draw the string with four fingers, but pinched the arrow between the thumb and the index finger. Each tried the other's method, shooting at grass-filled target skins, laughing at the ineptness of the others, and at their own clumsiness. The Norsemen found that it was easier to draw the short, heavy bow of the Skraelings if they used the grip on the string favored by the bow's owner. They had more difficulty with the release, however. It was hard to let go with all fingers at exactly the same time. This affected accuracy considerably. Ah, well, it would take time.

Nils reflected for a long time on this. He had been quite proficient with a bow at one time, but had neglected it in recent years. Svenson, by contrast, was so completely oriented to the sea that he had little interest in the bow. It was simply not a practical weapon. If a conflict came to a battle, Sven much preferred an ax for hand-to-hand combat. He eventually decided that of the weapons available for hunting, a spear was more to his liking.

One of the factors involved in Nils's ultimate choice of weapons was availability. There was no European longbow to be used. He was familiar with the differences in style and construction, but not to the extent that he would consider making a bow. No, it would be better, he decided, to adapt his skills to the use of the weapons available to him.

He began to practice. In the hunt they were planning, he must be considerably more proficient than he had shown himself at the target bags. Arrow after arrow he shot, gradually improving his accuracy.

As he was better able to control his aim, however, another problem arose. The tips of the fingers on his right hand were becoming sore and swollen. The unaccustomed friction on the bowstring was becoming a source of pain. At first he attributed the discomfort to the fact that he had not used a bow for some time. After all, it is necessary to develop calluses at appropriate friction points in the use of any tool. Until then, skin protests against the insult of repeated irritation by blistering.

Gradually, Nils realized that the new grip itself was partially responsible. Areas of his fingertips that normally would not contact the taut rawhide thong were forced into friction on the release. Stubbornly, he kept on, gritting his teeth against the pain as he drew the arrow to his ear.

"It is enough, Thorsson," Odin said finally. "If you tear the skin off your fingers you cannot shoot at all. Try only a little every day until the skin hardens some on your fingers."

Reluctantly, Nils put the bow aside.

The Norsemen had been somewhat surprised to find that the Skraelings seemed to have no metal tools or implements at all. They had noticed this lack among their captors earlier, but had not fully realized its significance. Now, as they examined and tried to use stone-pointed arrows, they began to understand. This also helped to explain the preoccupation of the men over the shiny blade of the sword, and with Sven's ax. As this situation sank into Nils's understanding, he approached Odin to verify his impressions.

"Your people have no metal at all?" he inquired.

The Skraeling looked puzzled for a moment, then amused.

"Why would we want that, Thorsson? Our knives cut well, our arrows kill, no?"

Nils had no answer, but Odin continued.

"You see that some of our things are of metal. I am made to think that it is softer, though, than your long knife."

Nils now recalled that he had indeed seen bracelets and necklaces that seemed to be made of copper or brass. Yes, *softer* metal. He was dimly aware that a much hotter fire is necessary to process iron ores than to melt the softer bronzes, but it was a subject of which he knew little.

But yes, this all seemed to make sense when he thought about it. Odin's people had some access, probably through trade, to small quantities of copper. It would be considered of great value because of its scarcity, and would be used for ornaments and jewelry. Not for weapons. He had once seen a bronze ax head, said to have been used by his Norse ancestors, but that was long ago. Modern skills had produced fine steel for weapons such as the sword he now possessed.

Nils thought, too, about Odin's odd remark, *Why would we want that?* in reference to metal weapons. He would have scorned, at one time, any suggestion that in a modern world knives, arrow points, even axes of stone, would be practical enough to use. But if one had nothing else . . . No, that was not it . . . He had seen the flint knives in use, and watched their efficiency. The glass-hard, serrated edges were remarkably suited to skinning a deer or moose. A flint arrow point sliced through the hard skin of a target bag with deadly efficiency.

He recalled that not too long ago, he had thought of the one-eyed Odin as an ignorant savage. It was embarrassing now to realize how wrong that had been. Odin was probably as clever as any man he had ever known. Was it possible, then, that he had misjudged the entire situation? Was this simply a *different* civilization than his own?

No, he was not ready for that. Nils shrugged the notion aside. These were pitifully primitive people, without even a written language. His own modern culture, by contrast, boasted the skills of navigation, development of the swift and maneuverable longships, scientific discoveries like the *solarstein*. Not to mention the cultural advances, poetry, literature. Not only one runic system, but two, the old and new alphabets. This made him think of his grandfather and of the evenings by the fire. He had loved the riddles, puzzles, and conundrums made possible by the two sets of runes.

No, that was far above the level that could be achieved by these simple people. Nils shoved the subject aside in his mind's furthest reaches, burying it with other forgotten or outgrown ideas. Still, he reflected, it would have been interesting . . . He would have liked for his grandfather to be allowed the opportunity to meet Odin.

There was one other thing that Nils observed just prior to the day of the hunt. It seemed inconsequential at the time.

He had been practicing with the bow, and had stopped when his fingertips began to protest. As he walked back toward the lodge, he encountered Svenson, who was seated in the afternoon sun, carving on a wooden stick. Sven was constantly whittling or carving. It was a way to pass long days at sea, the old sailor had explained. His artistry was much admired by Odin's people, and especially by the children to whom he gave simple carved toys.

The creation in his hands, however, was something different. It was not ornate, merely a smooth stick of hardwood with rows of notches. Nils now recalled that he had seen it before. It had not had nearly so many notches. But that had been some time ago. Why hadn't Svenson finished it, whatever it was?

"What are you making, Sven?" he asked.

"What? Oh, nothing. A calendar."

"I don't understand."

"A habit, Nils. At sea, it is hard to keep count of days. There is the ship's log, of course, but for myself . . . I used to . . . Well, look. Each of these little notches is a day, then the deeper ones are Sundays. Today is late October, about the twenty-third."

"You have kept count?"

"Well, yes. Not really, at first. I may be a day or two off. I just thought it would be a good idea to keep count. I tried to guess as near as I could when I started."

"But that was back in the other village?"

"Yes. I thought—"

"A good idea, Sven. I should have thought of it myself."

It was somewhat embarrassing. Nils, as leader of the expedition, should have been thinking of such a thing. He would want an accurate estimate of the time elapsed in each phase of their travels and adventures.

"It is good, Sven. Please continue this. It will help when we tell our story back home."

Svenson nodded. Nils felt that the sailor did not completely understand how important such a record might be, later.

Or, maybe he did. Nils himself had not even thought of it. What a leader . . .

By comparison to all that the Norsemen had learned about the People and their weapons, the hunt itself was almost an anticlimax. There was not much organization about it. The scouts had been observing a band of about a dozen deer. The animals were, in their customary way, preparing for winter by gathering in a loose herd. They established territorial claim to a strip of dense brush and timber in a sheltered gully. It was, Nils noted, much like the behavior of the deer in the forests of his faraway homeland.

The plan, such as it was, would space hunters around the edges of the little valley, advancing toward the middle.

"Be careful not to shoot anyone," cautioned Odin.

It was a moment or two before Nils realized that this was a joke. A half-serious joke, to be sure, a way of reminding themselves and each other that there was danger in the hunt. The responsibility was not to be taken lightly.

Nils found himself, shortly after daylight, stepping quietly with the other hunters, moving into position. The air was crisp, and a warm mist hung over the river and layered like fog among the trees. His hands trembled a little, not entirely from the chill of the autumn dawn. The excitement of the hunt made his heart beat faster.

A long whistle, like the scream of a hawk, drifted across the valley as a signal, and the hunters moved forward. Odin was on Nils's left, and Svenson beyond. Sven had decided not to attempt the use of the bow. His progress with that weapon still left something to be desired. The old sailor gripped a spear. Nils smiled to himself at the incongruity of the red-haired Svenson, dressed in rough native skins and carrying a primitive stone-tipped weapon. Sven would have been more comfortable with an ax, probably, but a broadax is hardly suitable for hunting deer.

Nils glanced to his right, making certain that he was keeping in line with the others. His eye caught that of the nearest hunter. The other man acknowledged the glance with a nod and a nervous smile.

Ahead of them, some large creature moved noisily through the underbrush. Nils caught a glimpse of a tawny form, but it was gone before he could raise his bow. There was a distant shout, and then suddenly a frightened doe burst out of the brush, leaped between Sven and Odin, and was gone. No one had been able to release a shot.

The hunters paused, and the noise of creatures running through fallen leaves came rapidly closer. Nils half raised his bow. *There* . . . a shadowy form flitted among the trees . . . a yearling buck, with spike antlers no larger than a man's finger. The animal was fat from the summer's lush feeding. It was looking back the way it had come, toward the noise of distant shouts. Nils lifted the bow, released his arrow, and missed.

The buck seemed not to notice. Maybe . . . he reached for another arrow, and the animal, attracted by the motion, turned its head to look. At that instant, an arrow from the bow of Odin struck it just behind the foreleg. The deer took three long leaping jumps directly toward Nils, and then fell kicking in its death struggle.

Other deer were crashing past between the hunters. Now the shouts were closer as the hunters from the upper end of the valley approached. Nils took a shot at a fat doe. He thought that he struck his target, but the animal turned and ran toward the hunter on Nils's right. The man drew his bow.

Nils's attention was diverted by a yell of genuine alarm from somewhere in the thicket. He turned to see a dark shape crashing toward where Svenson stood seeking an opportunity to use his spear. But these cries of warning . . . there was something wrong here! He could not tell what. His meager understanding of the language was a great hindrance. Annoyed, he focused on the hurrying dark shape, and at last he realized the danger. A *bear*.

Apparently, by sheer accident, the net as it tightened had enclosed not only the band of deer, but a wandering bear. Nils was not certain that Svenson could see what sort of danger faced him.

"Look out, Sven!" he yelled at the top of his lungs. "A bear!"

Svenson did not even look around. Nils expected him to run, but this was not the way of the old sailor. He held his ground, and then to Nils it seemed that Svenson actually stepped to meet the creature. Surprised, the bear stopped and rose to its hind legs, as tall as a man, roaring its challenge. With a mighty shove, Sven drove his spear deep into the soft underbelly of the animal. The bear roared again and struck out at its tormentor, striking a glancing blow to Svenson's shoulder as he tried to dodge away. Even so, he was flung like a rag doll. He rolled and rose to run, but it was unnecessary. The bear had collapsed, rolled over, and now lay kicking feebly as its eyes became vacant and began to glaze.

37

I t was all over very quickly. Excited hunters were crowding around Svenson, who stood swaying like a tree in a high wind. His right shoulder was bleeding, and his leather shirt was in tatters. Several long parallel cuts from the bear's claws knifed across the smooth white skin of his shoulder and back. Sven seemed weak and confused, and a couple of hunters helped him lie down.

Yet at the same time there was rejoicing and celebration. The hunt was good, and it was apparent that Fire Man's injuries would not be serious. The leather shirt had given some protection, and this was only a skin wound. To people whose everyday lives are filled with violence and danger, such a wound is nothing. More important is the courage and bravery of the hunter who sustains the wound. Already there were shouts and chants of honor to be heard as word spread of the bravery of the fire-haired outsider. In time, the song of Fire Man and the Bear would become part of the legendry of the People.

The success of White Wolf, too, was a cause for celebration. His arrow *had* flown true, and his quarry, after running wildly for some fifty paces, had collapsed. It was identified by the individually marked arrow. It was good that an outsider, unskilled in the use of weapons of the People, could prove himself in this way. The People rejoiced for him, and his prestige increased.

Women were coming now to the area of the hunt, beginning to skin and butcher the harvested game. The men were assisting with the heavier work, rolling the larger animals to allow easier access to skinning and removal of the entrails. The mother and sister of Odin quickly stanched the bleeding of Svenson's shoulder and bound it tightly, using strips from his tattered shirt. After making him more comfortable, they were joined by Hawk Woman, and turned attention to the carcass of the bear. Its fur was growing long and thick in preparation for winter. It would make a warm robe, to be worn with honor by Fire Man.

Nils was not certain how many deer kills there were, scattered through the woods in the little valley. At least four, he thought. He could see people gathering around a fallen buck in a clearing a bow shot away. There were the two near at hand, and Odin had mentioned another kill farther up the valley. Maybe there were more.

Since the women were occupied with skinning the bear, Nils turned his attention to the deer that had fallen to his arrow. The throat should be cut to bleed out the carcass. Odin joined him, after assisting in positioning the bear for skinning.

"It is good, White Wolf," he laughed. "A good hunt!"

They began the process of butchering, and Calling Dove, sister of Odin, joined them.

"Let me help," she said quietly, with a shy smile.

Though she spoke in her own tongue, her meaning was clear. Nils smiled at her, excited by her nearness. His blood was still racing from the thrill of the chase, and he found it translating in a strange way. It was an urge to celebrate the successful hunt by enfolding this desirable woman in his arms and . . . He stopped short. *What an odd thought!* The young woman turned her glance away from him, and seemed embarrassed. He wondered if his thoughts had been so obvious that she had seen . . . that she *knew* what he wanted to do. That in turn embarrassed him, and they avoided each other's eyes.

Odin, meanwhile, had severed the head of the deer, and propped it on the ground before him in a lifelike position. He began a half-chanting singsong in his own tongue. Nils realized that this was a ritual of some sort.

"What are you doing?" he asked when Odin paused.

The Skraeling looked surprised.

"The thanks and sorrow," he said.

"I do not understand. This is a ceremony?" Nils asked.

"Of course. You do not do so?"

"I . . . I am not sure. What did you say? What are the words?"

Odin thought for a moment.

"Well, something like, *'We are sorry to kill you, my brothers, but we must eat your meat to live.'*"

Nils had been thinking of something like a prayer of thanksgiving. This was foreign to his experience.

"An *apology?*" he blurted.

"I do not understand," Odin answered. "What is 'apology?' "

"It says 'I am sorry.' "

"Yes, maybe so. It tells the deer-people why we kill them."

Nils was speechless at an idea so foreign to him. He remembered just now that as a child he had watched Holger, the butcher, cut the throat of a sheep. The animal's soft gentle eyes had looked startled, then frightened for a moment as the lifeblood began to drain. It had struggled a little, then quieted, and the spark of life-spirit inside had flickered briefly. Then the eyes had become flat and dead, even as he watched. There was nothing left inside, no spirit. And he had felt sadness. Even though he knew that this represented mutton for the table, he felt sorrow. For a long time, an occasional bite of meat would seem to become larger in his mouth as he chewed, when he thought of the eyes of the dying sheep. He had told no one. It would not have been seemly. . . .

He was pulled back to the present by Odin, who had asked him a question.

"What?"

"I said, do you not have such a custom?"

"No . . . no . . . I am sorry, I was thinking of . . . of something else."

"Are you all right, Thorsson?"

"Yes, of course. But you asked . . . no, we have nothing like that. We might say prayers in thanks when we eat."

"It is good," said Odin simply.

Nils was not certain what was "good." The prayer of thanksgiving, or the apology to the spirit of the slain animal? He did not want to ask. But he wondered. Would he have felt better over the dying sheep if he had known of this? If he could have said, "I am sorry, but you provide food for us." Maybe someday he could talk of this again with Odin. Maybe when he knew the tongue of the People better . . .

The skinning and butchering progressed. The work was hard, but the occasion was joyful, a celebration. There were jokes and laughter and teasing of each other among the young people. Nils could not help but notice the similarity to the festivities of the marketplace at a harvest day celebration. There was everything but the dancing in the streets. *But probably that, too,* he thought. These natives seemed to celebrate everything with ceremonial dance.

A young man carrying a haunch of venison paused in flirtatious conversation with Calling Dove, and Nils felt his hackles rise. The excitement of the hunt had stimulated him in a romantic way, and must do so to others too. His resentment of the young man rose as Dove smiled and answered his good-natured banter. The youth moved on toward the village, and Calling Dove glanced at Nils.

"What is it, White Wolf? You look angry!" There was concern in her face.

Even his meager knowledge of the tongue of the People let him understand this. Yet how should he answer? He wished that he could tell her how he felt, wished to shout, *No! You must not flirt with the young men. You are mine!* He realized how ridiculous such a thing would be. He did not even have the ability to put together such a tirade in the People's language, much less the right to do so. He felt very foolish.

"I . . ." he mumbled. "Nothing. It is nothing."

She looked at him, puzzled and a little sad, he thought, before she turned back to her work. There was something left dangling unsaid between them, an uncomfortable feeling that there was more. Dove glanced up and their eyes met again. Both started to speak at once, then they laughed together.

"You first," he indicated clumsily.

The girl looked him full in the face, searching for words. When she did speak, it was slowly and deliberately, so that he would be sure to grasp her meaning.

"White Wolf, the man is a friend. Nothing more . . . do you understand?"

There was a sympathetic smile on her lips, an entreating look in her eyes. His heart soared like an eagle.

"It is good!" he said.

And it *was* good. Unfortunately, he had very little idea how to push his advantage now. He looked over to where Odin was skinning his own kill, and saw that the other had been aware of the entire episode. Odin was chuckling in amusement. This irritated Nils. Why would a friend treat him so?

Damn! He *must* learn more of the courtship customs of the People. Nils was pleased for Odin's good fortune in his reunion with a childhood sweetheart, but there is a limit to the happiness that one may have for someone else. He must approach Odin directly as soon as possible, and demand an answer to some of his pressing questions. *How does one go about a courtship?*

Maybe today he could make an opportunity. Yes, he would do just that. As soon as the bulk of the immediate work, the heavy part of the butchering, was in hand, he would approach Odin and demand a conversation.

With the reassurance of this decision, Nils was able to make himself useful. He helped to position the animal for cutting up into more manageable chunks. He carried a haunch back to hang it in a shady spot near the lodge, and returned for another. He paused to talk with Svenson, who appeared to be feeling somewhat better. At least, his color was returning.

It was past midday before the last of the meat and the hides were transported to the village. Now the task of slicing, drying, and curing by smoke was beginning. He could finally seek out Odin for answers to his pressing questions.

He encountered his friend as Odin returned from the scene of the hunt with the skin of the great black bear on his shoulders. He was breathing hard from the heavy load.

"Ah!" grunted Odin, swinging his burden to the ground. "There is nothing as hard to handle as a fresh bearskin, no?"

Nils had little experience with fresh bearskins, but it was easy to see the difficulty. The hide was thick with its layer of prewinter fat. In addition, it was shapeless and slippery, sliding out of one's grasp, as hard to manage as a large fish. There are no handles. It would be the same with the fresh skin of any large animal.

The women began to spread and stretch the bearskin on a grassy spot, preparing to peg it out for scraping and dressing.

"Odin," said Nils, "I would talk with you of something."

"It *is* good," agreed Odin. "Let us walk."

They strolled out from among the lodges and toward the river.

Nils spoke, nervously.

"Odin, I want to ask—"

"Wait, Thorsson. First I want to tell you something."

"Yes?" Nils inquired, too impatient even to wonder what.

"It is about my sister, Calling Dove. She is much pleased with your ways, and would be proud to have you look upon her with good feelings."

"But . . . I . . ."

"No, no, say nothing now. Think on this. If you wish to do so, I will tell you of our customs."

Nils Thorsson tried hard to maintain his composure. *Yes, yes!* he wanted to shout. *I do wish it!* As he hesitated, Odin went on.

"Now, what was it you wished to talk about?"

"Oh . . . that . . . It is nothing, now. I must think on this!"

Outwardly, he hoped to appear calm and in control, but again, his heart soared like the eagles.

Three of the leaders of the People drew aside that evening to talk of the events of the day.

"They are brave and strong," said Big Tree.

"Yes," agreed Clay, "but would you want your daughter to marry one?"

"I have no daughter old enough, Uncle," chuckled the younger chief. "But I see your point. There are things about them that we do not know."

"That is true," agreed Singing Moose, keeper of the traditions of the People. "Their ways are very different."

"I am made to think," pondered Clay, "that there are two questions here. First, is there danger to the People in the power and strength of their gifts? Especially those of the one called White Wolf? The other, that of our women. I have seen that the daughter of Red Fawn looks with desire on the White Wolf. He is the most powerful, I think. Should this be allowed?"

Big Tree nodded. "I have seen this, too. Maybe we should talk with the girl's family."

"Her brother?"

"No . . . he seems under the spell of the white-haired one. Her mother, maybe. Yes, let us talk to Red Fawn."

"It is good. But what of the other thing?" asked Clay. "Are they not dangerous in their power?"

"I am made to think not," said Big Tree quickly. In his position as headman of the village, he welcomed the presence of two such fighting men.

"Well, so be it," agreed Singing Moose. "If they become dangerous, we can always kill them later."

"That is true," agreed Clay, the holy man. "Now, let us talk to Red Fawn about her daughter."

"We have seen," said Big Tree carefully, "that your daughter, Calling Dove, looks with desire on the outsider, White Wolf."

The woman drew herself up proudly.

"And what is that to you?" she demanded.

Big Tree was caught completely off guard, though he should not have been. Red Fawn was about his own age, and he remembered well from their childhood that she spoke her thoughts plainly. There had been a time when . . . but Fawn had matured earlier, and had married another. She was widowed now, and still quite attractive, but . . . He brushed such thoughts aside, stammering to answer the question that was really not a question.

"Well, I . . . we—"

"Why should it concern you," she went on, "with whom she beds? Or with whom I bed, either, Big Tree?"

She whirled on her heel and strode away, anger showing plainly in the

swing of her hips. Big Tree watched her go, trying to ignore the chuckles of the
two older men.

"Well," Big Tree said finally, "it is as Moose says. We can kill them later if
we need to."

38

Events moved so swiftly after the hunt that Nils's thoughts were a blur of
confusion. A blur of ecstasy, actually.

The People were quite matter-of-fact about the marital union. It was simply announced that White Wolf and Calling Dove would wed. The ceremony
would be before the chill of winter actually descended, so that the young couple
might share the warmth of each others' bodies. Above all else, the People were
practical.

It was frightening, to see the rapid planning and preparation for this major
life-change. There were times when he wondered if this step was an act of
complete idiocy. When they had first joined the People and he had seen the
sheer beauty of Calling Dove, he had been thinking in terms of a temporary
liaison. The fact that she was Odin's sister bothered him a little. One simply
does not seduce the sister of a friend, with the full intention of leaving her later.
And of course, part of the long-range plan of the two Norsemen was to return
home as soon as possible next spring. Still it seemed to Nils that the availability
of women in this setting was relatively easy. He did not fully understand the
customs, but it was apparent that the women had a great deal to say about their
choice of sexual partners.

Following this line of logic, as well as his own instincts, it was only a short
step to another conclusion: It should not really matter whether he intended to
leave her in a few months or not. Likewise, it did not matter that the girl was
the sister of his friend. It was *her* choice.

Reassured by this idea, he was able to wrestle with his conscience more
easily. If the girl did not object to the possibility . . . no, the *probability* of his

leaving, why should he worry about it? He thrust the last of his nagging guilt feelings out of sight and resolved to forget them. He was relatively successful, at least for the moment.

Nils still had questions. The most urgent was *when?* Now that the matter was decided, his excitement grew with his passion. He did not want to be too blunt, and it was quite frustrating that every cautious inquiry was met with a casual nonchalance on the part of Odin.

"Later."

The People seemed to have little concept of time. The sun was in the east for morning, overhead at midday, and sank in the west in the evening. The moon marked the months for them, but one day was much like another. He could get no answers about how many days until anything would transpire. He recalled that it had been so when the expedition started upriver. He had asked Odin how far to the Talking Water, and Odin had answered in "sleeps." This had been frustrating, and was even more so now. "Sleeps" had taken on a whole new meaning now that they would soon be shared with the lovely Calling Dove. But *when?*

"When it is the right time," Odin answered with his noncommittal shrug.

"But should I be doing anything?" Nils asked in frustration. "Any ceremony? Among my people, a man tries to show his strength, to win a woman's heart."

Odin nodded. "That is good. You have done that, Thorsson. The hunt . . . Before that, our escape. But Dove sees you each day, too. That tells her that you are a good man."

"But I am not good with your tongue, Odin. I am made to think that I learn very slowly."

Odin appeared mildly surprised.

"So?" he asked. "Do you not hear much of what is said?"

"Yes, maybe. I hear more than I can speak. It is easier to hear words than to find them."

"That is true. It is always so with a new tongue."

This conversation utilized the Norse tongue, in which Odin was fairly proficient from his years at Straumfjord. That had been easy at first, and they had casually continued such usage.

"Odin," suggested Nils, "maybe I should try harder to learn your tongue."

Odin shrugged. "It is good, maybe. I will speak to you only in the tongue of the People, no?"

Nils had not intended to go quite that far, but the idea was good.

"Maybe. But you would help me if I need it?"

"Of course. But your wife . . . my sister . . . she will teach you much!"

Odin chuckled at his own double meaning, and Nils reddened.

"No, Odin, I—"

"Of course, Thorsson. I mean, *now.* You asked what you can do to know her better? Talk to her. That will let you learn quickly, too. It is good. And I will speak only in my own tongue."

Somehow, Nils felt that he had just crossed a bridge and had burned it behind him. Of course he would still have Svenson. . . . But no, to make this work, Sven should use the People's tongue, too. The sailor was already better than he at its usage. Yes, he would mention it to Svenson.

Sven, whose wounds were healing rapidly, agreed with the general idea of the proposal.

"I may forget sometimes," he chuckled, "but so be it. A good idea. When is your marriage to happen?"

Nils sighed in frustration.

"I do not know, Sven. Do you notice how time means nothing here?"

Svenson nodded. "One day is much like another, no? Like being at sea, maybe. I like it, though."

"But you should still keep your calendar."

"Oh, yes. But you know, Nils, with no hourglass, even a sundial or an hour candle, each day is all one."

"Yes, I had thought that, too," Nils agreed. "But I wish sometimes—"

Svenson interrupted. "Does it matter, though? When the sun goes down, it will get dark."

Nils laughed. "Sven, you are fitting into this much better than I."

"Of course. I have had more time at sea. That breeds patience."

"That must be true. Well, shall we try talking in their tongue?"

"It is good," agreed Svenson in the People's tongue, with a shrug and a guttural grunt like that of Odin. "And you know not the day of your marriage?"

Nils chuckled sheepishly, and answered in the same language. "I do not know that in either tongue. When the time is ready, Odin says."

"And you are ready now, no?" Svenson teased.

"Yes, maybe so," Nils replied, embarrassed and uncomfortable.

It was actually not long before some of the answers to these questions were apparent. A day was set, three sleeps from the present. There were preparations, of course. Calling Dove and her mother were busily sewing, preparing new garments for the ceremony. Garments for both, in fact. They were much like any other garments of the People, but perhaps finer, softer, and sewn with more care. There were decorations, too.

A strange creature furnished these decorations. It was the size of a small dog, but its way of walking was slow and clumsy. The animal reminded him of a similar creature that was familiar to the Isles, a spiny dweller of hedgerows, called by the natives there a hedgehog. This similar beast was even more spiny, bearing sharp, barbed quills as long as a man's finger. He had seen a young wolf dying because it could not eat, with these barbs sticking out of its lips, nose, and tongue.

"Wolf tried to bite the spine-dog," Odin explained. "One does not do that!"

Fortunately, the spine-dog was not an aggressive beast. It seemed to eat mostly the bark of young pine trees, and was active primarily at night. It was largely ignored or avoided by the People.

Even after he had learned of the spine-dog, Nils did not make the association between its quills and the decorative designs on garments, bow cases, and arrow quivers. He was astonished, then, when one day he encountered two young women tormenting one of the creatures. The spine-dog, a big specimen, was crouched against the base of a large rock, its quills erect and threatening. Each of the women held a pole with padding of dry grass wrapped tightly around the end. Each time the spine-dog tried to flee, the women would thrust their poles at it to prevent its escape. It would then whirl, lashing out with its thorny tail at the padded sticks.

"What are they doing?" Nils asked in amazement.

Odin laughed. "They are gathering quills."

Nils saw now that the padded end of each pole was bristling with the white spines.

"Why?"

Odin pointed to the colorful decorations on his moccasins. "For this."

It had not occurred to Nils to wonder about the source of the decorative material. It had no real similarity to the quills of the spine-dog.

"They will soak the quills in water, cook them, maybe, color with plant juices, pound them flat—"

"Wait!" Nils interrupted. "Why do they not just kill it? Then they would have all its quills."

Odin shrugged. "Sometimes they do. In a bad winter, we eat the spine-dog sometimes. But he does not taste very good. His best quills are in his tail, and those are the ones they want."

The women now backed away and began carefully plucking quills from their padded sticks. The spine-dog made his escape and disappeared into a dense pine thicket.

"See?" laughed Odin. "He can grow more quills for them now."

Nils shook his head in wonder. Practical, that was it, maybe. This strange game had done exactly what was desired, no more, no less. These people and their ways were so different, yet in some respects, so similar to those of his own. The annual shearing of the sheep at home for their wool, the subsequent preparation of that wool into yarn, to be dyed, woven. There were many similarities here.

He had thought these natives to be simple people. Simple in many ways, maybe, but he was constantly learning things that surprised him. Their customs, while more primitive than those of his own people, were certainly as intricate. But *different*. He wondered if there was anyone in Stadt, or in all of Norway, for that matter, who could take a shard of flint and fashion a knife that could dismember a deer as efficiently as those he had seen. And the quality of the leather produced by these people was softer, better, maybe, than that at home! Well, he would watch and learn for the next few months. There would be interesting tales to tell when he returned home.

One thing Nils found disturbing as the days passed and the time for his union with Calling Dove came closer. He saw no preparation, no effort to construct another cubicle in the lodge for the new couple. That had been done with no hesitation for the three men, when Odin rejoined his people. A new partition had been erected for Odin and his bride. But there was no one who seemed to think of the fact that he and Dove would need a place to sleep. There must be something that he did not understand about the customs of the People. For Odin and Hawk Woman it was a remarriage of sorts. Did that make a difference? In the back of his mind a nagging doubt bothered him. Was the first union of this couple as they wed to be a *public* affair?

This began to concern him greatly. At best, romance in the lodge with other families was only semiprivate, even with separate compartments. Yet this was such a sensitive subject that he hesitated to inquire.

But, even so, if there was no other cubicle, the possibilities for living arrangements for Nils and Dove were quite limited. Surely they were not to be expected to share the cubicle where Nils now lived with Svenson. Not impossible, of course, but quite unsatisfactory. Another alternative would be for Nils to move into the living quarters of Calling Dove. The disadvantage here was apparent. Dove shared her cubicle with her mother, Red Fawn.

It was not that Nils particularly disliked his prospective mother-in-law. Actually, he felt that he could be quite fond of her. Red Fawn, in her middle years, was still quite attractive. She was well respected, and highly intelligent, it appeared to Nils. She had raised two children, both of whom were well above average in wisdom and in appearance, even with Odin's missing eye. But no matter how pleasant, how likable, how capable such a woman might be, a man would hesitate to share a bedroom with his beautiful new wife *and* her mother.

Nils felt that he was at a decided disadvantage in this odd situation. He was communicating better each day with Calling Dove, but to inquire of her might be construed as disapproval of her mother. The same with Odin, who would have been his first choice as a confidant. He felt close to no one else here. Snake, the boyhood friend of Odin, was a possibility, but Nils did not know him well enough for such intimate discussions.

Svenson! Sven would not know the customs, but at least would understand this dilemma. Nils reverted to their own tongue for this conversation.

"Sven," Nils asked when they were alone, "something worries me. No one seems to think of building a sleeping place for Dove and me. Should I be doing that?"

"Ah! You grow impatient, no?" laughed Svenson. "Of course they have thought of it. She will move into our compartment. Has no one told you?"

"No . . . I . . ."

What could he say now? He was angry, angry at the situation, and at Sven for taking it so lightly. The sailor was actually leering with an evil grin as he chuckled. Nils would never have suspected that a perverted streak of voyeurism would reveal itself here. He felt his face redden with rage.

"By God, Sven . . ." he began, glaring at the other.

Svenson now backed off, his face serious.

"Wait! Ah, you really do *not* know! You have been too occupied with your bride to notice, but I thought someone would have told you. I am to marry with Red Fawn! I will share her bedchamber, and Calling Dove will join you in this one, no?"

39

With such questions as sleeping arrangements now based on better understanding, the late autumn became a time of romance. The warm weather held, though nights were cool and crisp. Mornings were beautiful and invigorating. Steamy fog rose from every body of water to hang in misty layers over ponds, streams, and over the river. This effect and its ghostly landscape lasted only a short time each day, until the sun's rays began to warm. When the air was as warm as the water, it stopped abruptly. The last scraps of fog faded among the trees like the last grains of white sand slipping through an hourglass. Another day had begun.

Most of the common chores of preparation for winter had been completed, and even preparations for the double marriage. The day had been set. Nils Thorsson's occasional bouts of apprehension were somewhat offset by Calling Dove's attitude. She seemed not only to see his feelings, but to understand. She was spending a little more time talking to him as he tried to learn her language. They laughed together at his halting efforts. Dove found things to show him, things in which they could both take pleasure.

"See?" she pointed proudly.

She had seen a pair of fawns, half-grown now, their white spots nearly obscured by longer winter hair. They were grazing quietly in a clearing near the lodges, dimly seen in the morning mists.

Nils's first reaction was that she wanted to show him game to shoot. But that was not her attitude, he quickly realized. This was simply a thing of beauty, a scene to share. It was startling that the animals would be so near. It was as if they knew that the People had no need for more meat now. They were still cautious, of course. Any slight sound brought both graceful heads to attention, ears flared. A jay called its raucous alarm, and both deer looked and listened attentively until it was apparent that any danger would be to a jay, not to deer. Jays, Nils knew, are notorious for false alarms anyway, usually to distract from their own depredation.

The fawns resumed grazing, tails still flipping nervously, ready to signal the need for flight if it became necessary. They were only a stone's throw away, and Nils was certain that the animals were aware of the presence of the couple.

Dove had led him by the hand, moving quietly to their present position, half concealed by leafless bushes.

"Two," she said, indicating the number with her fingers. "Twins."

"Twins," he repeated. "It is good."

She smiled, pleased, and the light in her eyes, soft yet exciting, made him feel weak-kneed. It was an expression of absolute devotion.

"Yes, it *is* good," she said softly. "A good sign, no?"

He understood the words, but it required a moment to understand her meaning.

"Oh. For us?"

She was pleased that he had grasped her meaning. "Yes. A good sign!"

It would be a long time before he fully understood. For the People, twinning among the deer was a predictor of good things to come.

"The deer-people know," Odin told him much later. "When there are good times ahead, with plenty of food, they will have twins."

For now, Nils saw this scene only as a sign of a rewarding union for him and Calling Dove. This would be appropriate to the thinking and the ways of the People. Not too different, after all, from the folkways of his own people. Either way, it *was* good. The morning of shared beauty, the growing closeness of companionship, the touching of their spirits in a way beyond and above the daily need for communication. He saw, understood, and realized that her thoughts were the same. He leaned over and kissed her.

Calling Dove looked startled, and pulled away for a moment. Her tongue delicately touched her lips, and she seemed lost in thought.

"That is not our way," she said thoughtfully, "but it is good!" She moved toward him, and her kiss was more responsive this time. "I must think more on this," she said, pulling away gently. "Oh, look!"

The two big fawns had suddenly focused their attention on a thicket a few paces from where they grazed. It was not a matter of alarm, because they now moved *toward* that thicket. A large, well-formed doe slipped quietly into the clearing. Her color was more reddish than most, and her underparts almost white. She was sleek and fat, a beautiful specimen.

"Their mother," whispered Calling Dove.

One of the fawns attempted to nurse, and the red doe kicked at him irritably. The girl chuckled. "She is tired of feeding three!" she observed.

"But a good mother," Nils answered. "She is fat, and so are her children."

"Yes," Calling Dove agreed. "That is a good sign, too."

They smiled at each other and kissed briefly. Activity was increasing around the lodges, and a dog barked in the distance. Instantly the deer were alert, and their tails stood erect in the signal for danger. Even so, there was no undue alarm in her gait as the doe led her fawns in retreat. In a moment, they were gone.

"May you winter well, Mother," Nils said softly, half to himself.

"What?" Dove inquired.

He realized that he had spoken in his own tongue.

"Oh. I only wished them a good winter."

The girl smiled approvingly, and clapped her hands like a child.

"It is good! We have a song to the deer: '. . . may your children be fat and your women happy . . .' It is much the same."

Yes, it was, thought Nils. He had surprised himself a little. His remark to the doe was like something Odin would have done. He was trying to understand the People, but in so doing, he was slipping into their ways of thought, maybe. He wondered what his grandfather would have thought. Nils had often been frustrated at his grandfather's endless riddles, conundrums, and stories that forced one to think. Only in retrospect had he become aware of the value of such teaching. He had not even realized that it was teaching until after his grandfather's death. Then, it was too late to tell him, to thank him again for the pleasure and benefit that had been learned by what had seemed only play. *Play is the work of children,* grandfather had said. It had taken a long time for Nils to begin to understand the implications of that. Maybe he never would, completely.

By the day of the ceremonies, Nils was thinking of nothing beyond that day. Nights were cool, and the thought of a warm female body next to and intertwined with his was certainly desirable at the very least. That it would be someone whose presence was pleasant and whose company he enjoyed as a friend was an added benefit. And, to have that warm body belong to one of the most beautiful women he had ever seen . . . Ah, what more could a man ask of life?

The ceremony he had witnessed before in the marriage of Odin and Hawk Woman. This time, he understood more of the words. Not all, but it was a meaningful prayer, he realized, about the lives of a loving couple warming their lodge against the chill of winter and hardships of life. He was touched by the beauty of the words.

In the absence of families for the Norsemen, they were asked to stand in for each other. The ceremony of union for Svenson and Red Fawn was presided over by Nils and Fawn's children, Odin and Calling Dove. Then the roles changed. Red Fawn and Svenson spread the robe around the shoulders of the younger couple.

The People withdrew from the lodge out of deference to the privacy of the newlyweds. In summer, it had been explained, each couple would have gone out alone for a day or two. At least, for a night. At this time of year, it was not practical, so the other inhabitants of the communal lodge simply went elsewhere for the night. The other lodges could accommodate them for a short time. There were many ribald jokes, of course, about moving out to avoid a sleepless night, but it was all in good spirit.

Nils found it embarrassing to think of making love in the cubicle next to that of his wife's mother. What if he were not able? . . . No one else seemed concerned. It was a mildly amusing distraction, no more. Simply another basis for jokes at the expense of the newlyweds. It was the source of much vulgarity from Svenson, and more ribald jokes. Sven suggested, tongue-in-cheek, that a contest was in order.

"Svenson, that is enough," Nils roared, reverting to the Norse tongue. "You are a dirty old sailor! Now stop it!"

The People stared, wide-eyed, not understanding the apparent anger. Svenson became more serious.

"Of course, Nils. You have to see that this is not easy for Fawn and me, either."

Nils had not thought of that.

"I am sorry, Sven."

"And I . . . I suppose this is easier for the women . . . they grew up this way."

"Maybe so."

It was reassuring to Nils that Svenson seemed to have some dedication to his marital union, too. That had been of some concern to Nils. Sven had a wife at home. Of course a sailor, gone for many months or even years at a time, was expected to seek comfort. It was usually the comfort of a temporary liaison. Nils liked to feel that his relationship with Calling Dove was something better, on a higher plane. It was reassuring, then, to hear Svenson refer to "Fawn and me." Somehow, it made things seem more right.

It did not, however, remove his anxiety about the merely semiprivate nature of their sleeping cubicles. After all, it was only a thin wall of hanging leather that separated the beds. He was sure that it would inhibit his ability to become aroused.

He need not have been concerned. Soon after they crawled into the darkness of their cubicle, he felt the arms of Calling Dove encircle him.

"Now," she whispered, "show me more of the mouth-on-face thing."

He complied, and found that she learned the art of kissing quite rapidly.

The noises from the other side of the curtain, which he had feared might inhibit his ability, seemed to have the opposite effect. The sounds of pleasurable union stimulated his own imagination. Through the night, each time there was activity next door, he would wake, or Dove would wake him, and in their newfound excitement with each other . . . Toward morning he began to wonder if they could keep up with Svenson.

He was drifting back to sleep after such an episode near daylight, sleepily thinking of the memory of Sven's ribald comment about a contest. It had angered him at the time, in the tenseness of the situation. Now, in his present state of complete relaxation, it was mildly amusing.

Calling Dove, also near sleep, threw her knee across his thighs, laid her head on his shoulder, and nuzzled her face into his neck. There was an erotic sensation to the silky feel of her hair across his bare chest, but at the moment, there was absolutely nothing that he could have done about it. He stroked the knee gently, and was asleep in an instant.

40

When Cold Maker finally descended on the People after the prolonged Second Summer it was with a vengeance. There had already been a few heavy frosts, and on many mornings there was a rime of furry white on trees, bushes, and dead grasses. For Nils Thorsson, now White Wolf, it was reminiscent of late autumn among the deep fjords of his coastal homeland.

But, when winter came on in earnest, everything changed. The welcome sunlight that had warmed each day to a comfortable level became shorter in duration each day now. Its quality changed too, from the golden light of autumn to a watery yellow, barely warming the bones by evening. There came a day when they did not see the sun at all. The sky was a leaden blue-gray, and the chill breath of Cold Maker came whistling from the northwest, gaining in intensity through the day. By evening the whistle became a howl, like that of some enormous wild thing. It roared across the rocky headlands, screamed through the pines and the leafless trees, even stripping some of the dead leaves that still cling to the oaks through the winter. The broad surface of the river was whipped to a frothy pattern of whitecaps running before the wind. Nils thought with sympathy of ships trapped at sea, trying frantically to tack into a safe harbor in the face of the mighty gale.

Then suddenly it was still. The People ventured to look outside for a little while. There was a frantic last effort to bring firewood into or near the lodges, and while people still scurried about at these chores, the snow started to fall. At first it was slow and gentle, an occasional puffy flake drifting downward through the trees like the breath-feathers of the great white owl who accompanies Cold Maker from the north. The flakes became thicker, and in a short while it was possible to see only a short distance. The People called warnings to each other, and drew inside the lodges, fastening the hanging double doorskins tightly to hinder the entrance of cold. The temperature was already plummeting.

Now, for the first time, the Norsemen began to appreciate the effectiveness of the half-buried earth-lodge. The houses of their homeland, built of stone or logs, had seemed comfortable enough most of the time. In a storm like this, however, cold always crept in around doors and windows. Nils could remember his mother stuffing rags of cloth around window casings and then drawing a heavy drape for extra warmth. Here, there were no windows to allow the assault of Cold Maker. There was the square smoke hole above the cooking area, which also provided a fire for warmth. There was little chance of Cold Maker's gaining entry there. The only other means of ingress was by the doorway. There was a heavy leather curtain at the outer end of the short tunnel of descent into the lodge, and another at the inside wall. The dead space between formed an effective barrier to the cold wind. The People settled in to wait out the storm. It would be the first of many.

Days and weeks passed, the progress of time marked by Svenson on his carved stick. The Norsemen fell easily into the lax, easygoing lifestyle of the People. Both had, of course, the advantage of a recent marriage to distract them. Jokes and teasing about that continued. The other inhabitants openly compared the prowess of the newlyweds to that of the noisy couple across the lodge.

But it was impossible to sleep or to make love all of the time. Long gray days, with thin gray light filtering through the smoke hole, needed some distraction. No sooner had Nils realized that, than he also saw that the People did, also. *Of course,* he thought. *They have lived this way for generations. They will know.*

Some of the People had pastimes that were obvious. Many of the women spent time in sewing or in perfecting the designs for their intricate quillwork. Stone Breaker, an older man who lived in the southwest portion of the lodge, worked occasionally at his trade. He made knives and arrow points, and complained occasionally that his light was poor. Nils suspected that Stone Breaker's more intricate pieces were deferred until they could be worked in open daylight.

Between storms, there was always a flurry of activity. The People moved out into the snow, gathering wood, trampling down paths from one lodge to the other, and improving the paths to areas just outside each lodge where they could tend to bodily functions.

It was important to keep the paths open between lodges for social reasons. On most days, except for the very worst, there would be a social gathering of some sort in one of the lodges. Attendance was loose and optional. Usually the men gathered to smoke and gamble with sticks or plum stones, and the women would draw aside to gossip. Children, of course, have few problems in passing time together. They play, spontaneously and joyfully.

Occasionally, though, there would be a story fire. That was more structured. Nearly the entire village would assemble in one of the larger lodges, and the storytellers would hold forth, each in turn. There were three main tellers of stories, the most important of whom seemed to be Singing Moose. The others, both younger men, deferred to his expertise. Sometimes some other person related a tale. Occasionally it was Odin, who of course had many tales to tell of his adventures. Nils recalled the outdoor story fire at the time of their first arrival. Nils had understood very little of that evening's talk, but now felt that he was able to grasp much of the speakers' narration. He noticed that it was customary, at any given story fire, for the first speaker, usually Singing Moose, to open the occasion with a recounting of the story of Creation. Then there would be a brief history of the Peoples' adventures since, before progressing to specific tales.

"Why is this?" he asked Odin.

The Skraeling looked at him with surprise.

"How else would the children learn of their people?" he asked.

Yes, Nils could see a pattern here, and felt that it was good.

"In the beginning," Singing Moose droned one evening, "the People lived under the ground. All was darkness and cold. There was water, because there was a great lake under the ground there. But few plants grew, because there was no sunlight. A few mushrooms, some fish from the lake. Then one day, one of the young men saw something like a rope hanging from the roof of the great cavern in which they lived. He pulled on it, and found that it was solidly attached, and that there were other branches to it. He tied some of these together, and started to climb up, up toward where the ropes disappeared into the darkness. No one knew, you see, how high the roof might be."

Nils smiled to himself as he saw small children tip their heads back to study the shadowy rafters above.

"Finally," Moose continued, "the young man saw light above. He was afraid. . . . What kept the fire from falling down on him as he climbed?" The children were wide-eyed. "But he kept on, pulling himself toward the light, and at last he saw that it was a hole, leading out into the world above. He peeked out, and saw that he had been climbing the roots of a giant grapevine. In fact, grapes grew everywhere, and there was sunlight, and much game to eat."

Vinland! thought Nils. *This sounds much like the description brought home by the first Norsemen. A land of grapevines!*

"Well," Moose went on, "the young man took some grapes back down, and everyone tasted some, and it was good. They began to climb the grapevine. One after another, they crawled out into the world, and they began to dance and sing and to hunt and pick grapes and to build lodges. That, too, was good. Then, a tragedy . . . A fat women was climbing the vine, and was nearly at the top, when her great weight broke the vine! She fell back into the darkness, and no one else could come through. But those who had already come through became the People."

"What happened to those below?" a little girl asked anxiously.

Singing Moose shook his head sadly. "No one knows. No one even re-members now the exact location of the hole. Maybe it crumbled away when the vine fell. But coming outside brought problems, too. Winter, enemies, wild animals like bears and wolves . . ."

"But my heart is heavy for those below," the little girl protested.

Moose patted her head. "And so you should be, child. But that is another world. This one is ours."

Nils was pondering this story, heard for the first time in its entirety and with understanding. *It is a sort of reverse Garden of Eden,* he thought. *How strange!*

But Moose continued.

"About half of those first People were left behind. They built a village like this on the shore of the lake below. After death, we rejoin them there. Except, of course, for those who have been very wicked in this life. They find that they cannot cross the lake to get to the village."

Someone requested that Odin recount the story of the time White Wolf changed himself to an animal to confound the enemy. This was the first time Nils had heard his story retold when he was able to understand the storyteller. It was somewhat startling to him, the mystical, supernatural aura that Odin was able to create. By the time the story reached the point where he had jumped off the ledge and attempted to attack the enemy, he almost believed it himself. *Had* he changed into a wolf? His memory for the event was faulty, from weakness, fasting, and whatever else it was that had occurred in the berserk episode. After all, no one really knows what happens to give the berserker his superhuman strength. At least, Nils had never heard an explanation. It was a creepy feeling, to hear this description from the viewpoint of Odin, with the strong influence of the mysticism and spiritism of the People. Maybe it *had* happened that way.

Now Singing Moose was speaking again, and Nils was brought quickly out of his wandering thoughts. *He is speaking to me,* he realized.

". . . so, White Wolf, will you honor us by telling of your people? Their Creation story?"

With something like panic, Nils pulled himself back from his daydreams. He started to protest that he could not, but then realized that only a short while ago he had actually been comparing Moose's story of Creation with his own. Yes, he could tell them of Adam and Eve, and the Garden.

It was just then that he happened to think of his grandfather. He was never certain why, but he remembered that the old man had loved to tell the tales of the Norse gods. Grandfather had honored and respected the God of Christianity, because his family did, but he had loved the old legends, too. Nils had always suspected that his grandfather was never completely convinced that one story was right and one wrong.

"Men call God by different names," he had once told the boy, "and He speaks to them in different ways."

It was like the many paths up the sides of the mountain, maybe. All lead to the top. No sooner had this idea struck him than he knew what he must do. He would tell the story that he felt would be most reasonable to the minds of the People. And, of course, the most interesting.

"In the beginning . . ." he began, and paused for a moment. "My brothers and sisters, I may need our friend Odin to help me with this story. My lips have not learned your language. But I will try. Now, in the beginning, there was only darkness. No earth or water or air. In the darkness was a being, the Allfather."

He paused, unsure of himself and his translation. Odin spoke a few words to clarify. It occurred to Nils that up to this point there were many similarities in the various stories.

"Whatever the Allfather willed, it happened," he went on. "So, there came to be, in the middle of the darkness, a deep gully . . . a canyon. . . . To the north of it, a spring of water and fog. The water froze to ice, and great pieces fell off into the canyon all the time. It made a roaring sound, but the canyon was too deep to see the bottom. To the south of it was a bright world of light and fire. It was a warm place, guarded by a giant whose weapon was made of fire. Sparks fell from him onto the ice with hissing sounds and the ice melted, but only part of it. The steam froze again and began to snow, to fill the deep canyon. In the middle of all this there came to life a great creature called Ymir, from the frozen clay. He was an ice-giant."

The listeners were spellbound by the enormity of the Norse story. Nils was glad he had chosen this one over that of the Garden of Eden, whose warm and idyllic setting would be hard for the People to understand. Sometimes, in the chill of winter, the Garden was hard for the Norse to understand.

"This ice-giant," he went on, "looked around for something to eat, but there was nothing. Then he noticed a great animal, just created like himself. From her came four streams of milk, and he saw that this was good. He called her Audhumla, the nourisher."

There was a short pause at this point while Odin and Nils conversed in the Norse tongue. The concept of a cow did not translate well. Finally Odin spoke to the assembled People.

"My friends, it is this among the people of White Wolf and Fire Man: When I was living there, I saw these animals. The people there keep them as we keep dogs, and they squeeze milk from their udders."

There were gasps of amazement.

"No, no, it is true," Odin assured them. "I have seen it. This animal is much like the hump-backed buffalo that we see sometimes from farther west. Now, let us listen to more of White Wolf's story."

The crowd quieted expectantly, and Nils continued.

"This cow, the nourisher, was also looking around for something to eat," he went on. "She began to lick at a block of ice, melting it a little, and soon there was seen a head like that of a man, but it was a god-being. He stepped free of the ice. Meanwhile the ice-giant had fallen sleep, and there began to form other frost-giants from his body. From the sweat under his arms, a boy and a girl. From between his toes, a six-headed giant, who was the start of a race of evil giants."

There were more gasps.

"Now," Nils went on, "there was the god from the ice block, who soon had a son, Borr, and he was good. The ice-giants were evil. This started a war between the gods and the giants. Three sons of Borr finally killed the great Ymir and rolled his body into the canyon. This ended the war, and they began to make the earth out of the giant's parts. His blood and sweat formed the ocean, his flesh the land. His bones are the mountains and hills, his hair and beard the trees and grass. They painted the inside of the giant's skull blue, and it is the dome of the sky. The clouds are Ymir's brains. Four very strong little men were put at the four corners to hold the dome in place. Their names were North, South, East, and West."

He paused, and a murmur ran through the crowd.

"What about people?" someone asked.

"Yes, White Wolf," said Odin, to whom much of this was new. "What about people?"

"That was not yet," Nils explained. "First, there was—"

"Enough!" stated Singing Moose. "My head is tired from such a story."

He rose and left the lodge. Others began to drift out, too. Now Nils was concerned. The listeners had certainly responded well, but had he somehow offended the honored storyteller of the People? Should he have *not* tried to tell the Norse story of Creation?

· 41

inging Moose needed some time to think. He had not been offended, actually. It was more as if he had been overwhelmed by the enormously powerful stories of the outsider, White Wolf.

It was a good thing, to have an honored guest such as this light-haired holy man. An honor for the People. It was also good that White Wolf and yes, the other, too, the one called Fire Man, were fine providers. They had proved themselves in the hunt, in both skill and bravery. These two had vast powers. White Wolf was regarded with awe because of Odin's eyewitness tales, and the People had *seen* him change the color of a stone. Fire Man's powers were different, but equally impressive.

The People had been afraid at first, of men with such gifts. Even with the reassurance of Odin that they could be trusted, it was an uneasy time. It was soon apparent, though, that Odin was right. These holy men were, after all, men. They were kind to children, and both had now taken wives among the

People. From what Moose had heard, they treated the women with respect. That, too, was good. It was known that some tribes did not.

So, it had become an interesting, stimulating thing to have these outsiders among the People. They had learned the language quickly, though they were still not skilled in its use.

One thing, however, that had never even crossed the mind of Singing Moose, was that he would be challenged as a storyteller. Moose had inherited this vocation from his father, and he in turn from *his* father, for many generations back into the Old Times. It was the responsibility, the duty of the story-teller, to teach and pass on the story of the People. Their Creation story was a good one. He had always enjoyed telling it to visitors, and listening to theirs. In addition to the underground lake account and that of the grapevine ladder, there were many other stories of the People. Some of these were for amusement, some for instruction, some for both. Children loved the stories of foolish Rabbit, back in the time when the animals talked and could converse with man. How Bobcat lost his tail . . . How Coyote stole fire . . . Good stories.

It was good to hear the stories of others, too. That was always a pleasure. He had inquired of the stories of White Wolf's people out of curiosity. The outsiders now seemed to have enough use of language to share their stories. Now Moose was wondering if he should have done so. Even with the language difficulty, White Wolf had told them a story so powerful . . . *Ah!* Gods and giants and ice caves and dwarfs . . . For the first time, Singing Moose was afraid. Always in the past when other storytellers were present, it had been an easy, friendly give-and-take. *Ah, your story is a good one. Now here is ours.* . . . And others had good stories, too. Some were closely alike, others had interesting variations. In one Creation tale he had heard, people came from the sky, sliding down its dome to reach earth. None, however, had threatened him as a story-teller of the People. Until now. He had been unable to absorb any more, and had caused the story-fire session to end. He needed to think. There was always an interest in new stories from outside, but never an absorbing acceptance like this. And if the outsiders were to stay, what would happen? Would they *prefer* the stories of White Wolf? In a generation or two, would the origins of the People be forgotten? It was a heavy responsibility for the old storyteller to bear. He wished that the light-haired outsider would just go away. Let everything be as it was, as it had always been. Maybe it would be best for the People if some tragedy were to fall on the two outsiders. Maybe he could . . . He thrust that thought aside.

One thing he could do, however. He would share his concerns. Moose was

one of the three most influential men in the village. The others were Big Tree
and Clay. Tree was the headman of the village. He was young, strong, a good
headman. Not much of a thinker, Moose sometimes believed, but that was not
his real strength. He was a leader, and could inspire people to do better than
they really should be able.

Moose sought out Big Tree to seek his counsel. The day was sunny though
cold, and they stood outside to breathe the fresh, crisp air and to indulge in the
luxury of private conversation. Somewhat to the consternation of Moose, Tree
seemed to recognize no problem at all. He had apparently overcome any jealou-
sies over the marriages of Calling Dove and Red Fawn. The headman was as
entranced by the stories of White Wolf as anyone else.

"Is that not a good one, about cutting up the giant to make the world?" he
chuckled. He pointed to the sky. "Look, there are a few of his brains in the sky
now."

Singing Moose glanced up at the few puffs of convoluted clouds against
the blue of winter sky. Yes, they *did* resemble brains. That was the problem.
. . . He saw no use in talking further to Big Tree. Maybe Clay would understand the danger here.

Clay was older, a contemporary of Singing Moose, and he was a holy man.
They had long been friends.

"Let us walk and smoke," Moose suggested. They could stroll for some
time along the tramped-down paths around and between the lodges. It would
provide privacy, too. They walked and smoked, not talking for a little while.

"I am made to think," Clay said finally, "that your heart is heavy. What is
it, my friend?"

Moose smoked a little longer, and then spoke. "You were at the story fire?"

"Yes. It was good." His tone was noncommittal.

"Yes . . . too good, maybe."

"How can this be?" Clay asked.

"Maybe the People will follow the stories of White Wolf instead of their
own."

"Well, they are good stories," admitted Clay. "The buffalo licking the ice
away . . ." he chuckled at the thought.

This did not help the heavy feeling in the heart of Singing Moose.

"You think their stories are better!" he accused angrily.

Clay took a few more steps and then paused, puffing his pipe. A woman
carrying wood came toward them, and they nodded a greeting, stepping aside to
allow her to pass. Then the holy man answered, slowly and thoughtfully.

"Not better, my friend, or worse. They are *different*. Strange creatures, strange ways. But do not all storytellers tell the *same* story?"

"What do you mean?" Moose was unconvinced, and a bit ruffled.

"Well, look at it. White Wolf's story has ice-giants and gods who are of the fire . . . the sun, no? They battle, good and bad. Is it different than ours? We have Cold Maker, in his lodge in the north. He comes out and tries to drive Sun to the south. Then Sun wins, and drives Cold Maker back to his lodge. It happens each year."

Moose was not quite convinced. "But White Wolf has not told of Sun."

"True. I am made to think that he will, though. Do you not think so?"

"Maybe. There is more to his story."

"Yes. But do not all people tell the same story as it seems to *them*?"

Moose nodded, grudgingly, and then Clay resumed his conversation.

"Now, friend Moose, consider *my* problem for a little while."

"Your problem?"

"Of course. You think you are the only one? Look, here comes a man who is strange in appearance, who changes stones to different colors with his hands, who can even turn himself into an animal and back again. You think this is not a danger to my importance among the People? Is his gift stronger than mine? Is he more powerful?"

Clay paused, but Singing Moose, staring at the snow, said nothing.

"I had thought," Clay went on, "that I might kill him, or have someone do it. Maybe both of them, the Fire Man too. That would remove the threat, no?"

Moose stared at him in astonishment, and Clay continued.

"I thought then about it, and that they are younger and stronger than I. Maybe they would kill me, and my family would mourn. And I thought too that maybe the powers, the spirit gifts of White Wolf are stronger than mine, anyway. Maybe I could not kill him at all. And if I used my gifts to do him harm, that is bad. To use my gifts for evil might kill *me*."

Moose was still speechless. He had had no idea that his friend had suffered much the same problem as he himself.

"So," Clay went on, "I came to think that it would be unwise to test his power. He has his gifts, I have mine. They are different. Maybe one is stronger, maybe not, but they are *different*. White Wolf can change the color of stones. I can listen to Kookooskoos in the night, and talk to him. Maybe both are good, but different. The same with Fire Man. We make fire with sticks, Fire Man with his striker, but it is all fire."

"What are you saying, Clay?" Singing Moose asked, still confused.

"Only that they are different. They have shown no wish to harm us. They have helped us in the hunt. I am made to think they are not a danger to us. White Wolf's power is no threat to me, as long as mine is not, to him. It is the same with the stories."

"But . . . how?"

"Wolf's people tell the story one way, you tell it another. Same story, same purpose. I am made to think so."

Singing Moose walked along in silence. Maybe so. He was surprised that his friend had already seen the threat, and had reasoned out this answer. The holy man's danger had been greater than his own, maybe, because of the possible clash of power in the strength of their respective gifts. He happened to glance at his friend and was surprised to see a gleam of mischief in the holy man's eye.

"Besides," said Clay, "Kookooskoos tells me I am right."

Moose was not certain that Clay was serious, but said nothing.

"Tell me," Clay went on, "when will we have another story fire? I want to hear about Sun, and Moon. And you know, Wolf has no people yet! And is it not interesting, the Allfather looking over both good and bad?"

Moose nodded, still perplexed that his friend had already been through all of this soul-searching.

"We will speak of all this again," said Clay confidentially, "but let us listen carefully to their story. Maybe we will still need to kill them."

But this time, Moose was sure that there was a gleam of laughter in the eyes of the holy man.

"White Wolf, tell us more of the stories of your people," a woman asked.

It was several days since the last story fire, and even more of the villagers had gathered. Some of those who had not been present when White Wolf told his story, the Creation story of his people, were quite eager to hear. The rest wanted to hear more. For generations, the People had heard their own stories recounted by the storytellers, with only slight variations. They had exchanged stories with neighboring clans. Once in a long time a traveling trader from a faraway tribe would stop for a day or two, with stories that were new. That was always an exciting time.

White Wolf had initially been regarded with a certain amount of fear because of his powers. Gradually the fear had been replaced by respect, as the People realized that he was not particularly dangerous. A turning point in his relationship with the People, however, occurred when he spoke at the story fire. Even with his halting use of the tongue of the People, even with the frequent necessity for him to consult with Odin about words, the stories were powerful. White Wolf had told of the very beginnings, as seen by his people. It was gigantic and exciting. And it was apparent that there was more, much more.

"His story has not even told of Sun yet," someone had noted.

"Nor humans!" another offered.

"Yes. Maybe we can ask him."

Singing Moose did not seem to mind that an outsider had such compelling stories. The People had wondered about that at first. Old Moose had abruptly called a halt to the stories, and there were some who thought that he might be angry. Apparently he was not, however. When the woman requested more stories from the outsider, many people looked toward Moose to see his reaction. If they expected resistance they were disappointed. There was only a bland expression on the face of the old storyteller.

"Yes," he said, "let us hear more. How did your people discover Sun?"

Nils hesitated for a moment. He had not foreseen the interest that might be generated by his recounting of the Norse legendry. He wondered whether he could remember enough to keep the story afloat.

"Ah . . . yes!" he said thoughtfully, "I had told how the gods decided to make a world from the parts of the dead giant, Ymir?"

There were nods of agreement, and he continued.

"It was good, but it was still dark, so they gathered sparks from the south-giant's flaming weapon, and flung them into the sky. The two biggest were the sun and the moon. But they just floated around, with no direction. Someone must guide the lights across the sky. Two young giant-people were chosen, Mani for the moon, and his sister, Sol, for the sun. Each day they—"

He paused in consternation. He had talked himself into an impossible corner. He had been about to search for words to say "they drove chariots." Golden chariots, the story said, drawn by powerful steeds. Until now, when he needed a word he did not know, he had merely asked Odin to supply one. But now, how could he tell a story of golden chariots to people who had never seen a chariot, or even a wheel? For that matter, even a *horse!*

Odin was looking puzzled, and Nils turned to Svenson. No help there! Svenson was almost overcome by amusement, trying hard not to burst forth in his boisterous laugh.

"Sven," Nils said curtly in their own tongue, "help me, here!"

Svenson spread his hands in a helpless gesture, his big shoulders shaking with restrained amusement.

"It is your story, my friend!"

"Well . . . I . . . well, the young giants carried the sparks. . . ." (*Torches! yes, torches,* he thought.) "They made torches, and each day they run across the sky and around the other side."

Svenson could not restrain a guffaw of laughter. "Good!" he called. "That will do!"

The People were puzzled. Some laughed nervously, following the lead of Svenson, but not quite understanding the joke. Was it something about Fire Man's connection with the heavenly fires?

Nils plunged doggedly ahead, past his predicament now, and able to return to the original version.

"They had to . . . to run very fast, because they are always chased. The Wolves of Darkness follow them, to try to swallow the lights. Sometimes the wolves catch up, and . . . Well, you have seen. The wolves take a bite or two. Then the people had to make a great noise. The wolves spit out the sun or moon, and it is whole again."

There was a murmur of quiet conversation, excitement in the tone, and some puzzlement. Svenson spoke aside and in Nordic.

"Nils, you don't have any people yet. Who makes the noise?"

Nils was annoyed. Sven was having far too much fun over this.

"Do you want to tell this?"

"No, no," the sailor insisted. "My job is to make a fire, remember?"

Nils regained his composure and continued.

"Fire Man says that I have left out some of the story," he admitted. "That is true. At first, there were no people to make noise. It was a very dangerous time. But as soon as they had daylight, the gods saw that something was going on in the rotting flesh of Ymir. There were maggots. These grew and became small creatures that looked like men and women, but were not. Some were ugly and loved the darkness, some were beautiful and loved birds and flowers and sunlight. So the gods gathered them all and sorted them. The dark ones are the . . ." (What could he call gnomes and trolls?) "*Kobolds,*" he decided, using the Norse word. "The others are . . . faeries."

The People were wide-eyed.

"The Little People!" someone said softly.

"You know of this?" asked Nils, surprised.

"Of course, Thorsson," Odin said aside. "The Little People. I did not know you have them too. Ours can cause mischief and harm, but can help you if they want to."

"It is much the same, then."

Odin nodded. "Go on about humans."

"After a while," Nils continued, "the gods saw that the earth was a good place. They would come down sometimes, using a bridge. . . ." At this point he paused, not knowing the words, or even sure that the People knew the concept of a bridge. He consulted with Odin.

"Yes," Odin assured him. "To cross a stream . . . a log . . ."

The next idea was harder. How to describe the rainbow that formed a bridge from heaven? With hand motions and words like "colors in the sky," he managed to convey the meaning.

"The gods would come down to walk along the shore," he went on, "and one day Odin and two others—more of Odin later—but on that day they came upon two trees, called Ask and Embla. They seemed to have human form, so Odin gave them spirits, and the wood came alive and became First Man and First Woman. These, then, bore all the humans of the earth."

42

As long, dark, and frustrating as the winter was, it eventually began to show signs of lessening. There had been many days in the month that the People called the Moon of Snows when the sun did not show itself at all. Svenson said it was January. After long periods of no sunlight, when a clear day did occur it was almost a futile effort. The pale and watery rays of a yellow sun that rose only halfway above the horizon toward the zenith did little to warm the drifted world.

Next came the Moon of Hunger. In most years, Odin explained, food supplies ran short. There would be starvation among the People. But this had been a mild winter, and in addition there was plenty of meat. By the odd coincidence of their arrival here, much of the credit for a good year had gone to White Wolf, the powerful holy man who had joined them. Probably Nils Thorsson was only partly aware of the respect and prestige with which he was regarded. For one thing, he was almost totally absorbed in a delightfully sensuous and romantic marriage, and had little else to distract him. He had enjoyed the story fires, and the People seemed entranced by his tales of Norse legendry. He wished sometimes that he could recall more detail, but his listeners did not seem to mind. It was all new to them.

There finally came a day when Nils stepped out of the lodge into a morning that was different. There was a slight breeze, but it came from the southwest. And it was *warm.* Not really so, he noticed, but there was a different feel about it, somehow. He was standing, puzzling about this, and squinting his eyes against the glare of sunlight on snow, when Odin came out of the lodge, allowed the doorskin to fall into place behind him, and straightened. He took a deep breath.

"Ah! It is the time of awakening!"

"What? What do you mean, Odin?"

"Do you not feel it? A different spirit . . . Sun renews his torch and pushes Cold Maker back to the north. It is the Moon of Awakening."

Yes, thought Nils. *March.* He had begun to notice, or thought he had, the almost imperceptible lengthening of the time of daylight each day. The sun rose just a trifle higher. With the navigator's eye, he noted the position of a tree's shadow on the snow-covered dome of the lodge. Yes . . . it was nearing the equinox, probably. Had he thought of it, he could have constructed a pole marker whose shadow would have told him the exact day. Well, no matter.

"Cold Maker will make another attack or two, maybe," Odin was saying, "but no matter. Sun has won again."

The concept was little different from that of the tales of Nils's childhood. Hrae-svelger, the corpse-swallower, had been placed in charge of the north wind by the disagreeable god Winter, enemy of the gentle goddess Summer, mild and lovely. Disguised as a giant eagle, Hrae-svelger would raise his great wings to fan sweeping blasts of icy wind. Nils had not thought to tell that tale at the story fires. Cold Maker . . . The People would be able to relate to Hrae-svelger. Maybe later, he would try to remember more of that one.

For now, though, the idea of the coming spring was suddenly thrust upon him. It was almost a surprise, in a way. In his mind had been the vague idea that when spring arrived, he and Svenson, and perhaps Odin, would travel downstream to the colony at Straumfjord and seek passage home. Odin, assuming he had chosen to guide them at all, would then return to his People. That had seemed a simple enough plan. Now that the time was drawing near to put it into motion, it began to seem far more complicated. He had a wife, and so did Svenson. Actually, the thought of *not* returning to Straumfjord had never occurred to him, and did not now. Home was his eventual destination. What tales he would be able to tell to his drinking friends back in Stadt! The sadness, of course, would be that Helge Landsverk was no longer among them.

But his friends would find his tales fascinating. The escape and pursuit after the loss of both ships, their capture, and the travel on upriver to live for a season with the Skraelings, and even to have married one of their women . . . It did not feel right, this line of thinking. He could not quite understand what it was that bothered him, and could certainly not have put it into words.

Sometimes he felt as though he were two different people. One was Nils Thorsson, from a respected old Nordic family. Well educated, a ship's master and navigator, a man from a race of conquerors, respected and feared everywhere. Feared because of the past, of course. The courage of the Viking marauders in the recent past was changing quickly in these modern times. The courage had translated itself into bold ventures in exploration and trade. When he thought of all that was being accomplished, he gloried in the privilege that he possessed. To be a part of this magnificent age was an honor beyond belief.

That was sometimes. At other times he found himself thinking of a completely different identity. He was no longer Nils Thorsson at those times, but White Wolf, a respected man of the People, and husband of Calling Dove. He loved that identity, that of husband to the most beautiful woman he had ever seen. Why, then, did he feel sadness when he thought of himself in that role?

It came to him finally, on this day when the world began to come awake. That event made him think of travel back to Straumfjord. Now it would be possible to make such plans, but he found himself torn by this other part of him, the part that identified him as White Wolf. It had been far too easy to set the planning aside, to defer it because nothing could be done through the winter months anyway. That, he now began to see, had been only a convenient excuse for lack of decision. Or maybe he was falling under the influence of the People. They lived from day to day. With the exception of storing food for winter, there was little planning at all. That had frustrated him at first, but the enforced inactivity of winter and the exotic distraction of his marriage had made it much more comfortable.

Now, however, they must make plans. He must thrust aside the temptation to let things slide along as they had all winter. He was having a great deal of difficulty in understanding *why* he dreaded facing these decisions. It finally occurred to him that it was because of Calling Dove. He had fallen into an easy companionship with her, and had become so comfortable in it that he did not really want it to change. Yet it must, in some way. He must consider the reality of parting with the woman who had become one of the most important persons in his entire lifetime. He did not want to think about it, but a tiny voice deep in his mind kept whispering, *You have to.*

Maybe Svenson could be of help. He had the same problem. Well, nearly the same. Except, of course, that Sven had a wife in Stadt and a wife here. It was not really the same problem at all. Sven must have realized from the start that his was a temporary union, a convenience that provided a pleasant interlude while they waited out the winter. Probably Red Fawn knew this, too. She was a practical woman. It was with something of a shock that Nils realized that there was a sort of unspoken understanding between those two. They would be together while circumstances dictated it. When the time came, they would part. Nils would have to admit, it seemed, that among Skraelings there were really no ethics like those of civilized people, and among sailors, very few.

One possibility continued to suggest itself to him. Maybe Calling Dove could return to Stadt with him. He had never suggested it to her, but then they had never discussed the reality of his departure either. And, while Svenson might not be able to take his Skraeling wife home, was there any reason that Nils Thorsson could not? He wondered what his mother would say. She had always wanted him to be interested in that buck-toothed Hingerson girl with the funny eyes. How would she react to a daughter-in-law such as Calling Dove? He must think more about this.

He must also, of course, talk to Odin and to Svenson, make some solid plans, and consider a boat and some supplies.

First, though, he must talk to Dove, explain to her the necessity of rejoining his people. He would be able to convince her of the advantages of civilization, he had no doubt. She would probably be pleased that he wanted to take her with him, wanted for them to stay together. She did not even know what she was missing. The thought began to please him, and he began to dream of the things that he could show her, share with her. The great ships, the cities, the exotic foods and clothing.

Maybe it would be better, he now thought, to plan their departure, at least in general terms, and then surprise her. The idea pleased him. He approached Svenson first.

"Sven, we should be making plans to travel."

Svenson nodded noncommittally.

"Yes."

Nils was puzzled at the reaction.

"Have you talked to Odin?" Sven asked.

"Not yet."

"Let me know when," the sailor said. "It is probably too early yet."

"Of course. But we should plan. Odin will know what to expect of spring storms."

Svenson nodded again. Somehow Nils had expected him to be eager to get back to the sea. Was he afraid of the dangerous river passage, down past the rapids and the area of their disastrous defeat? Surely not. Maybe Sven was feeling his age. He was no longer a young man.

"I will talk to him, then," said Nils, feeling uncomfortably that the conversation was not finished.

As it happened, there was no opportunity to talk to Odin for a few days. Every time he attempted it they were interrupted, or were unable to draw aside alone. He almost had the impression that Odin wished to avoid this conversation. That seemed unlikely, though, since Nils had not even had a chance to tell Odin what he wanted to talk about.

During the few days, he had time to do some thinking. There was much to be said, after all, for discussing the impending departure with Calling Dove first. With this in mind, he asked her to walk with him. It was sunny, as the days had been, though nights were still quite cold. This was the warmest day yet, and there was actually enough melting of ice and snow to initiate a steady drip from the tree branches. A few birds, stimulated by the awakening of the season, began to sound their territorial songs, and Dove laughed happily.

"It is good," she said.

"Yes. But I have something to tell you."

"Good. I, too!" She stopped and turned to face him. "I will speak first, for this, too, is good, my husband. Listen: I am with child!"

She pointed to her belly, still flat and trim.

"Are you sure?" he mumbled, completely stunned.

"Of course! What is it, Wolf? You are not happy?"

"Yes . . . yes, very happy. Only surprised."

"Why?" She giggled, her glance coy but teasing. "How could it *not* be so?"

His head whirled. He was unable to grasp all the differences in his plans that this would entail. Could he attempt the dangerous journey with a pregnant woman? He felt confusion, resentment, and a little anger.

"You are not happy!" Dove accused. A tear glistened in her eye as she whirled on her heel and strode away.

43

ife was difficult for Nils Thorsson for the next few days. He had spent a
delightful winter snuggling in the warmth of the sleeping robes and then
in the warmth of a vital relationship. There had been, of course, the cyclic
inhibition of complete romantic fulfillment. Even then, there was an intimacy,
an understanding of a promise of better things soon.

Now, however, even that was gone. The delicious comfort of warm and
softly rounded curves, cuddled against and around him in a myriad of ways,
might as well be forgotten. He could not understand how a body that had
seemed all softness and warmth now presented only the jab of knees and elbows
when they entered their cubicle at night.

To make matters worse, the entire lodge seemed aware of it. He received
dark, critical glances from the other women. One old woman had an extremely
annoying habit of staring at him with a frown, then shaking her head and
clucking her tongue as she turned away. He was not certain what the sequence
of mannerisms meant, but of one thing he was certain. It was not good. It was a
clear sign of disapproval.

One of the worst things about it was that Nils had virtually no idea why
he was subject to such ostracism. He had done nothing to deserve it as far as he
could see. He had not even begun to tell Dove about the impending choice, to
leave the People or not. There were many possible variations on that decision,
but he had not even approached the subject. He went over the scene in his mind
again and again. Things had been fine, they were talking and laughing, happy
together. Then, before he could mention the subject that must be discussed,
Dove had proudly told of her pregnancy. His reaction, then, must be at the root
of the problem. But what had he done? What had been expected that he failed
to fulfill? It was not as if he was opposed to this turn of events. Surprised, yes.
Speechless for a moment. And in that moment, something had happened. The
moment was gone, the warmth had been destroyed, and he was somehow the
culprit. He had tried to plead his innocence, but Dove only pulled away, angrier
than before. Even to look at her, to catch her eye brought tears sometimes.

Could there have been something he should have done, a ceremony or
ritual of the People, unknown to him? A response to be carried out when the

husband was informed of the pregnancy? Surely Odin would have told him. He would inquire of Odin. Meanwhile, he would inform Svenson that they could not make any plans quite yet.

It did not help that Svenson seemed to think the entire situation humorous.

"Yes, I heard," Sven chuckled. "Your bed is not as warm as before, maybe?"

"Sven, this is not funny. I do not understand it. What did I do wrong? I had not even mentioned leaving for Straumfjord."

Svenson was laughing openly now, his blue eyes, squinting almost shut with mirth, tears of laughter streaming down his cheeks.

"Ah, Nils, it is not that you did *wrong*. It is that there are times when a man can do no *right*. Dove is newly with child, no?"

"Yes. But, I—"

Svenson waved him to silence. "Nils, at this time a woman is like this. You say 'Good morning,' she cries. You ask what is wrong, she says 'Nothing.' Well, not always. Sometimes she says 'If you do not know, I will not tell you!' Then you tell her you love her. That has always worked before. But now, she says 'Don't touch me!' That is the way women are."

"*That* is it, Sven? It lasts for nine months?"

"Oh, no. Three or four, maybe. Then things are better. I am not sure when."

"Not sure? What do you mean?"

"Usually I was not there. Why do you think a sailor goes to sea at that time, Nils?"

Svenson slapped his knee and roared aloud, as if at an old joke. Then he paused in thought.

"You know, I *was* there once, Nils, when my wife was carrying Tomlin . . . no, maybe it was Johann. About the fourth month, I think, she decided I had been wronged and tried to make it up to me. Ah, she was hungry. I could hardly keep up with her. But it was very nice, trying."

Sven had stopped laughing and seemed lost in thought. Here was a side to the old sailor that Nils had not seen.

"They are in Stadt?" Nils asked.

"Yes. The boys are grown, almost. They will take care of their mother."

An odd statement, Nils thought. *Does he not expect to get home?*

Suddenly, the sailor's mood changed.

"Well, do not worry, Nils. It will be better. Do not argue, do not try to understand. It is a woman-thing."

Nevertheless, it was a puzzling thing. *Why are men not warned of this?* Nils thought. Immediately he realized the answer. There is no way to tell of some things in life. They must be experienced. He had not expected to experience this particular phenomenon in a far country in a strange and primitive culture. Another thought occurred.

"Why are all the other women angry at me, Sven?"

Svenson smiled wryly. "That is part of it . . . the woman-thing. They follow her moods. Soon, when she treats you kindly again, they will, too."

Nils was not certain about this. Just to be sure, he decided to talk to Odin.

"Odin, I had thought to talk with you about leaving. Traveling back to Straumfjord."

Odin said nothing, but there was a look of concern on his face.

"Now, that seems not to be a good thing to do," Nils went on. "You know that Dove—"

"I know, Wolf." Odin seemed to brighten.

"I had thought to take her back with me. I have never had a chance to speak of it to her."

"You have troubles too?" Odin asked.

"What do you mean?"

"My wife . . . Hawk Woman is with child, too. I did not think the journey a good thing. I feared you would want to go."

"But you spoke of troubles?"

"Yes. She is not the same, Wolf. I am told by the old men . . ."

"Yes, I have talked to Sven. Fire Man. He says it is so. . . . That is why sailors go to sea."

Both men chuckled. It was a comfort to have their fears accounted for.

"Fire Man says it is soon past. It is the same with the People?"

"Yes. We just wait, are very quiet, and things get better."

"It is good. I am ready!"

"I, too."

Both men felt considerably relieved, from reassurance, and because the clumsy topic of a possible journey back down the dangerous river to the sound had been postponed. Not indefinitely, of course. When the time was right they would consider again. Maybe it would still be possible to reach Straumfjord this season. After all, it was completely downstream. *Then on home the next season,* Nils thought.

All such thoughts became of very little consequence when the enemy attacked.

· · ·

The enemy had never come this early. The river was still frozen, though there were signs of melting. Great cracks were beginning to form a pattern across the windswept surface. Deer, bear, and moose, which had frequently been seen crossing the river on the ice, now avoided it. There were ominous crackling sounds from time to time, starting at one particular point and running an irregular jagged course across or up and down the stream.

Still, the ice was solid and thick except for the holes that the People kept open for water. There would come a day soon when the ice bridge across the river would go out, breaking into blocks and pieces to be swept downstream in a grinding roar toward the sea. Nils knew what to expect, having seen it each season in his homeland. He estimated that it would be a few days yet.

It was after the breakup of the ice that the enemy might be expected to attack. That was almost an annual ritual. When boats could be used, their old enemy downstream would almost eagerly take to the water to raid their neighbors in a celebration of the season. For now, it was considered that only a token watch be posted on the river. The ice was a barrier that adequately protected the People from the threat of attack by warriors in boats.

And it was, but the attack this time was not by water. Later, it was discovered that the raiding party had traveled from downstream on foot along the ice pack, probably coming ashore in areas of questionable stability. When they neared the village they then split up, moving through the woods to surround the lodges. Some had used snowshoes.

It had always seemed to Nils that the heavily domed earth-lodges were quite defensible in case of attack. Only one enemy could enter a lodge at a time. On the other hand, no one could see out, either. Or come out to fight, except one at a time. Nils had taken little note of that.

It was just at dawn. Thin gray light was beginning to filter through the smoke hole above, and the People were stirring. Someone threw a couple of sticks on the embers of last night's fire, and firelight began to pervade the lodge. A man rose to go outside and empty his bladder. Nils, after a restless night with less than satisfactory snuggling, was rolling out of the cubicle. In his mouth was a bitter taste that is the result of such a night, and his eyes were dry and scratchy.

Then came the scream. It started as a warning cry, and ended in a death-scream. Almost at the same time, someone threw a robe or skin of some sort over the smoke hole. The newly kindled fire was producing quite a bit of smoke, which began to layer out at the top of the lodge. Still, it took a moment for Nils, in his sleep-fuddled condition, to realize fully what was happening. Almost as he grasped the truth, Odin was shouting the warning.

"Attack! We are attacked. The enemy is here!"

Odin was grasping a spear, and an emotion something like terror gripped Nils. He felt that the thick earthen walls and roof that warmed and protected were now closing in. The lodge was becoming a death trap. They must fight their way outside, even knowing that an armed enemy would be waiting.

"Sven!" he yelled, but Svenson had already grasped his battle-ax and headed for the doorway. Odin was at his side.

"Wait!" called Nils. "All at once!"

Hawk Woman joined them, to draw the skins aside. The four huddled for a moment in the short tunnel inside the outer door. Nils shivered, not only from the outside cold, but from the surge of excitement that swept over him. He gripped the sword.

"Now!" yelled Odin.

Hawk Woman yanked the skin curtain aside and the three burst into the open. An arrow whispered past Nils's ear and thunked into the doorskin. Sven roared a challenge and waded into a tightly crowding cluster of enemy warriors with his ax, taking great sweeping swings that wrought havoc. Nils was only dimly aware of this, and of Odin's use of the spear, because he was hard-pressed. The first man to come at him was too close to swing the sword. Nils thrust instead, and the momentum of the man's rush made the withdrawal slow. Almost too slow. A man rushed at him from the right, swinging an ax or war club. The enemy was almost upon him before he managed to free the heavy broadsword for a backhand swing. The man fell, and Nils advanced a step, hacking right and left in the dim light. Another arrow whizzed past. Some of the enemy were shooting from a little distance away, but must be hampered by fear of hitting their own warriors.

Apparently the counterattack had been completely unexpected in its ferocity. The cluster of warriors who had waited outside the door had expected something less dangerous. Men and women coughing and choking, blinded by smoke, perhaps. This was not to their liking. Those still able began to fall back.

Another man, with a bow in hand, joined them through the tunnel and began to shoot at the retreating enemy. There were shouts by the invaders that could mean nothing except a warning to each other to retreat.

Now for the first time Nils could look around to see how the other lodges were faring. One of them had the smoke hole covered, and a woman was climbing the dome to remove it. He turned to look at their own, to see Red Fawn jerking the skin aside. A column of smoke rose heavily in the still morning air.

"Look!" said Fawn, pointing to one of the lodges. Flames were shooting out of the smoke hole in a roaring inferno. People were running to help, but were waved off by Big Tree.

"It is too late! Let it burn!"

The inhabitants were stumbling out, clutching what possessions they had managed to grab. The enemy had been able to enter that lodge and subdue most of the inhabitants who were still inside. They had thrown a quantity of wood on the fire, and as it blazed up, tossed on everything at hand. It was apparent that the four support posts of dry cedar were burning fiercely. The lodge was gone.

Even so, it was nearly midday before the domed roof collapsed, sending a shower of sparks skyward in the fat column of greasy smoke. The People were still trying to determine the extent of their losses; but the plaintive wail of the Song of Mourning was heard everywhere.

44

ut *why*, Odin?" Nils was unable to understand the attack and the carnage.

Odin shrugged in his familiar gesture.

"Who knows? They attack us sometimes. Not this early. Sometimes they steal girls. Ours are prettier than theirs. Sometimes in autumn, for crops."

"Do you attack them?"

"Not much. We are more peaceful."

It was still a confusing situation. Norsemen, in these modern times, were rapidly replacing attack and pillaging with more peaceful trading. Even so, the tradition was there. Nils had grown up hearing stories of surprise raids along the British coasts, of unexpectedly fabulous looting. And occasionally, the empty sack at the end of a bloody fight. That was always told as a huge joke on the attackers. In his mind, though, was the tradition of raiding for booty. Even though he personally did not condone it, he could understand it. But to raid someone as these enemies had done, knowing that there was little to steal . . . The whole thing was repulsive to him. What could be the gain?

"Are these the ones who held us captive?" he asked.

"Yes. Our name for them means the Downstream Enemy," Odin explained.

"Could it be that they are angry that we escaped them in the way we did?"

"Maybe. Yet they are warlike anyway, Thorsson. You saw how they attacked your people."

"Yes. But they had reason for that."

"That is true." Odin nodded thoughtfully. "Yet I am made to think there is more."

He remained in thought for a moment, and then his eyes widened.

"Maybe . . . maybe, Thorsson, they are worried about your power. The power of White Wolf. Maybe they wanted to keep it from growing."

"You mean . . . to kill *me?*"

"Maybe. You and Fire Man. That would give them great honor."

Nils thought about that for a moment. It was a chilling thought, one that was decidedly uncomfortable. It would help to explain, though, why one main portion of the attack was centered on the lodge where the Norsemen lived. There could have been spies, watching. Yes, it would be a matter of saving face, perhaps, for the enemy to track down and try to kill the "holy men" who had bested them.

Odin was laughing now. "That is funny. You and Fire Man helped lead the defense. The Enemy lost again. That tells them your power is greater than they thought, even."

Svenson had joined them, and now shook his head ruefully.

"If that is true, they will want to kill us even more now."

Odin sobered. "That is true. We must be on guard."

"Odin, it is not good to bring this danger on your people," Nils said. "Maybe we should leave."

It was an impulsive statement, and Odin's responding glance was almost indignant.

"Why? They would still seek to hurt us, and we would have two fewer warriors. Besides, your families . . ."

"Forgive me, Odin. It was a stupid idea."

Odin diplomatically refrained from agreeing, at least not aloud.

The rising and falling wail of the Song of Mourning was still sounding through the village as the evening shadows lengthened. Every lodge, and nearly every family, had been affected. It was fortunate, most agreed, that the killing was not worse, considering the timing and the nature of the attack.

The bodies of the fallen had been wrapped for burial and tied securely.

Then they were hoisted into the trees outside the village, and tied to crude scaffolds in the branches.

"The earth is frozen," Odin explained.

"They will be buried later?" Nils asked.

"Yes. Much later, maybe."

The one lodge that had been destroyed completely was still burning inside. Even now, a day later, smoke and flame belched up through openings in the dirt of the collapsed dome. The homeless ones had been taken in by friends and relatives. They had lost everything.

A young man approached the Norsemen and Odin as they talked.

"There will be a council tonight at the lodge of Big Tree," he stated. "I was asked to tell you." He turned and hurried on to finish spreading the word.

The lodge was crowded. It was the largest in the village, but everyone would want to be present for this most important council.

"They will decide nothing," one old woman complained. "They never do."

Still, she moved along with the others, packing closely into the dim lodge. The air was heavy with the smell of winter's smoky fires and unwashed bodies. One cannot bathe often when the river is frozen.

"Leave the doorskin open!" someone called. It was done, and the fire began to blaze up for better light, as well as a better movement of air up through the square smoke hole.

Nils and Svenson joined Odin just inside the door, but the headman motioned the three forward. They found places near the fire, between Clay and Singing Moose.

Odin saw immediately from the seating and the expressions on the faces of those leaders that serious discussion would happen tonight. He was apprehensive, at least a little bit. The more he had thought about it during the day, the more seriously he was taking the idea that this had been a vengeance raid.

The Enemy had been engaged in a war of extermination with the Norse outsiders. There had been few survivors, possibly only these two. He, Odin, had helped them escape, partly by trickery. He *did* think that there were powerful spirit-forces at work here, but that was a different matter. The three *had* survived, but now, in thinking back, would not the Enemy be wanting to complete the unfinished war? They must have spent the winter convincing each other that they had been tricked. To finish the war of extermination against the invaders, the Enemy must track down and kill these two. And of course, Odin himself. They would blame him for any trickery that was involved. Yes, his position was almost as perilous as that of the two Norsemen.

Odin was not certain that he saw any reasonable solution. Well, he would wait and see how the discussion would go in the council. Maybe he would gain some ideas.

Finally Big Tree rose and held a hand up for quiet. His pipe bearer filled and handed him the council pipe, and Tree lighted it with a stick from the fire. Then he blew a puff to the four winds, to the sky and the earth, and handed it to Clay, who repeated the ritual.

"You know the reason for this council," Tree stated after the pipe had made its circuit around the front row.

There was a brief murmur, which subsided spontaneously.

"We have been attacked, and hurt," he went on. "Now, what is to be done?"

"Were the other towns attacked?" someone asked.

"Other towns?" whispered Nils to Odin as a buzz of conversation circled the lodge.

"Yes," Odin answered, also in a whisper. "You know, the People have two other towns. . . ."

"We think maybe not," Big Tree answered to the assembly. "We have sent runners . . . one has returned, from the western town. They have seen nothing."

"But what of the other town?" a woman asked. "The Enemy would have to pass there to come here!"

"She has relatives there," Odin whispered.

Big Tree shrugged. "We will have to wait," he said. "Let us go on with the talk."

"But it makes a difference," a man protested. "Is this a war, or only a raid?"

"*Only* a raid?" snapped Big Tree, obviously irritated. "They can come again!"

There was silence for a moment and then an old woman spoke.

"All my life I have seen these raids. They steal our crops . . . our children . . . my own sister was stolen by these Downstream Enemies when we were children. Is there nothing we can do?"

"Attack *them*!" shouted a young man. "Give them a taste!"

"Let us go slowly," said Clay, speaking for the first time. "The other towns must be willing to join us if we choose that."

It was a gentle reminder that the Enemy was far more numerous and more powerful than the People. All of the People must be in agreement, even the other towns, because they would quickly be involved.

Now a young man rose to speak, and received the nod of recognition from the headman.

"My heart is heavy to speak of this," he said, "but maybe they were after White Wolf and Fire Man."

Bedlam broke loose after a brief moment of shocked silence. There were shouts of agreement and of protest. Odin was startled that there appeared to be others who had considered this possibility.

Big Tree, to his credit, handled it well. *Maybe*, thought Odin, *I have underestimated him.* Tree spread his palms and spoke quietly as the noise died.

"And what is that to any of us?" he asked. "These men are of the People. They have joined us, married with women of the People. They helped in the defense. We are honored to have such holy men among us."

There were nods of agreement.

"Maybe they envy us," Tree went on.

"But if these outsiders were not here, maybe we would not have been attacked," shouted an angry man.

He was hooted down immediately, but Nils rose to speak.

"My brothers," he said, "if we are a danger to the People, Fire Man and White Wolf will leave!"

Shouts of protest rose. It was obvious that most of the People believed that the advantages of the Norsemen's presence outweighed any dangers. After all, here were two experienced fighting men, who had been a valuable addition to the defense only yesterday. There were still, however, a few who seemed unconvinced.

"But would we have been attacked without them here?" the angry man persisted.

"Maybe not," Big Tree said calmly. "We will know more when our runner returns. If the other town was bypassed, then White Wolf and Fire Man must have been the Enemy's target."

There was a shout from outside. "The runner comes!" said a man in the doorway.

"It is good!" said Big Tree. "I hoped for this."

The exhausted runner slipped inside, breathing heavily. There was not a sound while the crowd waited.

"The town . . ." He panted. "Was *not* attacked!"

There was an uneasy exchange of glances around the lodge. If the Enemy had bypassed a closer village to attack this one, it must be that the suggested theory was correct. The attack must have been aimed at saving face by searching out the last of the Norsemen. This was the murmur that traveled like lightning through the crowd. Big Tree held up a hand, and the murmuring grew quiet.

"Then what shall be done?" he asked.

Undoubtedly there were those who would have comfortably solved the dilemma by casting out the Norsemen. They were silent, however. The tide of opinion seemed to flow against the use of that solution. Besides, few would dare to challenge the power of White Wolf's gift. An uncomfortable silence hung in the air for a few moments. Then Clay, the aging holy man, cleared his throat to speak. In a way, it was a relief of tension that anyone would break the uneasy stillness. That it would be this respected elder of the People was doubly good.

"No one has noticed," Clay said solemnly, "that it may have been our brother Walking Bird, now called Odin, that they sought."

There was a startled exclamation or two, followed by a muttering that quieted as he continued.

"Think about it, my friends. This man of the People has defied them for many seasons. They captured and tortured him, took his eye. He escaped, and made them look foolish. Then, with the help of the powers of White Wolf and Fire Man, he did it again!"

There were chuckles now, and a sense of pride and accomplishment. Odin marveled at the old man's skill in dealing with people. He was overcoming some of the insecurity, fear, and dread of the Downstream Enemy by poking fun at them. And in a serious, even a solemn way.

"It probably does not matter," Clay continued. "They do seek a vengeance against us, this town of the People. Whether against our brother Odin or our new brothers, does not matter much. They will come again, and will be angrier because they have been shamed."

Clay settled back as if he had finished talking.

"So, what do you suggest, Uncle?" someone asked.

Clay shrugged. "That is for us to decide in council. I do not know. But we must choose what we want to do. . . . Prepare to fight to defend ourselves, or prepare to go somewhere else."

Odin smiled to himself. He wondered if Clay and Big Tree had discussed all of this previously and had already reached a decision. It was possible that Clay was acting a role, forcing the People to think. Odin had already come to a conclusion, one that would shake the world of the People to its very core. It was a decision, though, that must not be suggested by anyone directly connected with the source of the problem. That eliminated himself, the newcomers, and their families and friends. Maybe even the storytellers, though Singing Moose was not likely to suggest ideas anyway. The storyteller's function was to retell and inform, not to suggest innovation.

Odin waited for someone to speak, and a man rose, hesitantly.

"Did not the People once have a wall of logs or posts around the village to defend it?"

There were murmurs and nods.

"We could do that again," he suggested. "Cut trees, build a wall."

Now there was a mixture of nods and hoots of derision as the man sat down.

"Yes," said Big Tree. "It would be hard work."

"But we must defend ourselves," someone called.

"Of course. But there is much work this season already," said another. "Two of the lodges are old, and need rebuilding. Another burned yesterday. Could we cut enough trees before the Enemy comes back?"

Odin happened to be watching the face of Big Tree at the moment, and saw a fleeting expression of pleasure. Now he was certain. This man, too, had been speaking a part, playing a role in the decision that seemed the logical one to Odin. If it had been planned in advance, as he suspected, it was going well.

"That is true," Big Tree was saying now, "but what else can we do? Move somewhere else?"

"It is easier to build new lodges than to repair old ones," someone noted.

"But where?"

Now the air was filled with comments, questions, and discussion.

"Here!"

"No, a safer place."

"Huh! Where would that be?"

Yes, thought Odin, *I was right. It has been planned. And very skillfully, too.* By the time the voting came, everyone would think that the move was his own idea. Big Tree was certainly a more capable leader than Odin remembered. Or maybe he, Odin, had merely grown in understanding.

Whatever . . . tonight or tomorrow the People would vote to move their village, and that was probably good. He was uneasy, though, about the reaction of the Norsemen, the adopted brothers of the People. As he saw it, any logical move would take them farther from what they wished, a return to their own people.

But that, too, was good. At least, if he could prevent their becoming too upset about it.

45

It was with something of a shock that Nils realized what was happening. The matter under discussion was whether the People should move or not. A move was probably a good idea, it seemed as he listened to the discussion.

Sometimes the more complicated arguments were difficult for him to follow. Eventually he began to realize fully the significance of the direction in which public opinion was moving. They were not talking about a move to another site for rebuilding the town. This would be a move to another *area*. It did not take him long to realize that the People would not choose to move *closer* to the enemy. Any move would be away from this threat. And farther, of course, from the colony at Straumfjord, and passage home.

He had struggled with the necessity to stay with the People for a time because of Dove's pregnancy. He had come to peace with that, convincing himself that it was temporary. But a move such as that which was being discussed was something else. This presented a threat. It was not merely a postponement of any return home, but a long-term impediment. His main concern revolved around one question: *Where* would such a proposed new location be?

Everyone seemed a bit vague about it. It was not a matter of a reluctance to discuss the plan. Rather, it seemed to be that even in a decision of this importance the People saw no urgency. It was a part of their approach to the world, their lack of dependence on time.

"It is not time to think of that yet," Odin had told him.

Nevertheless it was frustrating to Nils. More so than to Svenson. Sven had adjusted more easily because of long days and weeks at sea, Nils decided. The old sailor seemed to feel no more urgency than Red Fawn did, or Odin, or any of the others.

Nils sighed deeply, and toyed with the knife in his hand. It was a good weapon, a Norseman's belt knife that had been carried by one of the attacking Enemy. The first man, the one who had met the point of Nils's sword . . . It was heavy, well balanced, of good steel, and still held an edge. He was pleased to have acquired such a knife, because he had none since their disastrous defeat last season. Its blade was as long as a hand's span, and its hilt felt good in his grip.

He wondered about the Norseman who had worn it. All the way from

Stadt he had carried the knife, only to lose it and his life on an uncharted river in a violent land. Had there been any meaning in the life of that nameless sailor? Or in his own? Nevertheless, the knife was somehow reassuring, a tie with home, so far away.

The council had adjourned without a decision the night before. Delegates were coming from the other towns to take part in the discussion. There was still a possibility, it seemed, that the People would go to war. It appeared unlikely, though, Nils thought. The idea had been all but rejected last night in favor of a move of some sort. Surely delegates from towns not involved in the violence would not choose a warlike position.

That in turn lent credibility to the idea that a move was imminent. Such a decision was unsettling, to say the least. It was even more so, however, when Nils realized the significance of participation by delegates from other towns. These people were not thinking in terms of a short distance, but a major relocation. He sought out Odin, only to find his friend rather uncommunicative.

"Who knows?" Odin shrugged.

"But, Odin, the people from the other towns . . . will they move, too?"

"Maybe."

"Maybe they will leave their towns?"

"That is for them to decide."

"Odin, you think the People will decide to move, no?"

"Maybe so." The answer was cautious.

"So . . ." Nils decided to try another tack. "How far?"

"How far what?"

"The *move*," Nils snapped irritably. "How far will we move?"

Odin suppressed a look of surprise.

"Oh. I do not know."

"And the other towns? Could we join one of them?"

"Maybe," Odin said carefully. "Thorsson, that is why they come to the council. I do not know."

Somehow, Nils felt very strongly that Odin knew much more than he was willing to say. Maybe it would help to talk to Svenson, but he could not find Svenson. Fire Man was somewhere with Red Fawn, it seemed, talking with some of the people who were arriving from the other towns.

It was evening before those for whom they waited were fully assembled. The newcomers were openly curious about the Norsemen, leading Nils to wonder what they had been told. A few of the visitors had been here before, and would have described the adopted warriors who had joined Big Tree's band.

"Yet they see, even though their eyes are blue?" he heard a woman ask her companion.

"Yes, it seems so."

"And they have the hair of the old?"

"This one, yes. You have not seen the hair of the other. It is like a flame. He is called Fire Man."

"Because of the hair?"

"Partly, maybe. But he can also shoot flames from his fingers, I am told."

"*Aiee!* They must be very powerful!"

"It seems so."

The two moved on, and Nils relaxed. It had been a strange experience. The two from one of the other towns had carried on a conversation about him as if he were not there. It had been very uncomfortable, to hear and understand, yet pretend that he did not. He was not certain why he had done that. Out of embarrassment for the strangers, maybe. It was happening before he realized it, and then what could he say? *I understand what you are saying about me?* It had been easier to appear ignorant of the content of their conversation.

He was amused by some of the remarks that day about the hairy faces of the Norsemen. The People seemed to have very little facial hair. The Norsemen had thought at first that Skraelings had none at all. Later, it became apparent that the People did indeed have sparse growth on their faces, but that it was plucked periodically, as one plucks a goose. He and Svenson had discussed that. Nils had actually considered the procedure, and denuded a patch on one cheek. Sven, laughing, refused even to try it. His beard was much heavier than that of Nils, and the task looked too imposing.

"Besides, am I not Fire Man?" Sven joked, fluffing his luxuriant bush proudly.

In the end, both had decided that it was far easier to let nature take her course. The People were now quite accustomed to their full beards, except for newcomers who now came from the other towns to the council.

Tension and excitement increased as the time neared. If it had seemed crowded in the lodge before, it was doubly so now. It became necessary to exclude some of the children, not because they should be denied the council, but because there was no room. Seats were needed for the delegates.

It was a strange council all around, Odin noted. In his lifetime, there had never been such a council, one at which the air was so thick with the enormity of the decisions that were to be made. *Maybe,* he thought, *maybe it is only that I now see the importance.* But no, that was not it. There had never *been* a decision so important.

The crowd quieted, the pipe circulated, and the discussion began. Visiting headmen made brief speeches pledging unity. No one seemed to want to approach the major issue that all now realized as the decisive question. Finally it was broached by one of the visitors.

"We have heard," said Black Squirrel, "that you are thinking of a move."

It would have been possible to hear the falling of a breath-feather, so still was the big lodge. Big Tree waited a little while to answer.

"That is true," he said finally. "We are made to think that the Downstream Enemy will come again. We need to build three lodges anyway, so it is this: *Where* shall they be built?"

"You would be welcome to join us," said Spotted Hawk, headman of the other town, "but I am made to think that is too many. We would all have to go too far in the hunt."

There were nods of agreement. Too large a band required more food than could be hunted or grown in a reasonably sized area. Hunters would have to range too far for their own safety.

"That is as we have thought," agreed Big Tree. "But the three clans of the People must not lose each other."

"That, too, is true," agreed Black Squirrel. "But, let us say what we are all thinking. If you move, Big Tree, then we should all follow you."

"No, no!" insisted Big Tree. "I do not ask that your clan follow *me*. It is only that the People stay together. We must, because alone, we are weak. Whatever we decide, we must stay together. Close, but not *too* close."

"How is this, Uncle?" asked a young man, using the traditional term of respect for an older male.

"It is this way," explained Big Tree. "We cannot just start. When the time comes to plant corn, we must be *where* we can plant. Then we must stay there until after harvest, and then decide where we winter. We must have time to *build* lodges for winter."

Odin watched the headman closely. *He has thought of this for a long time,* he realized. *Before the attack, maybe.*

That led Odin into an entirely new area of thought. Already, he had decided that a major move would be good for the People. The People were largely peaceable and nonviolent. They were dependent in large part on their crops, but were often raided by the Downstream Enemy.

He had seen and realized much during his years of absence. The People, he realized, were surrounded by more aggressive tribes. The recent raid was confirmation of his theory. The coming of the Norsemen was yet another factor. He had been fortunate, he now realized, that he had not been killed at Straumfjord. Or thrown out, to be killed by those who had pursued him.

But they had taken him in. Out of pity, maybe. More likely, simple curiosity. He had furnished the colonists an opportunity to observe one of the Skraelings, as they called him. They had considered him a savage, a lesser human, and he had survived by trying to be what they *wished* him to be. He had always thought that eventually he would be able to make his way home. The Norse expedition up the great river had been his opportunity.

Odin often wondered what would be the situation if he had not fallen in with these two, White Wolf and Fire Man. He had come to a conclusion long ago, that it would be good for the People to relocate to the west, away from access by water. They were being pushed more aggressively year by year as the Downstream Enemy became stronger. Add to that the coming of the light-haired foreigners in their great canoes. That expedition had been destroyed, but there would be more. There might be a great war between them and the Downstream Enemy. And when the bull elk fight, anything underfoot is trampled.

He liked these two strangers, White Wolf and Fire Man. Their association had been beneficial to all of them. Lifesaving, in fact. They were now family, relatives by marriage, and that was good.

Yet he was not certain that he trusted any others of the Norsemen. Some were good, some bad, of course, like any other tribe. His doubt was stirred in uneasy remembrance of the Norse headman who had led them into disaster. Landsverk . . . was that his name? That one was a little bit crazy. What if others like that one came?

No, it would be better for the People to avoid an area where it appeared that two violent peoples were headed for war. To do that, they must relocate. But where? He had long considered that. They were restricted by the terrain in some directions, by the water in others, and the Enemy in still another. There was basically only one way to go—west.

He had talked to a traveling trader once while a prisoner of the Downstream people. The man had carried red stone for medicine pipes, and knives and arrow points of flint from far away. Strange colors of stone, unknown here. Pink, black, white . . . The trader talked of a trail that led to the west, an ancient trail, used for many lifetimes. There was plenty of game to the west, the trader said, open country and fewer people.

That was inland, of course, away from home, for the Norsemen. Maybe he could convince them that it was a temporary move.

His thoughts were jarred back to the present by the words of the headman.

"I have been told," Big Tree was saying carefully, "that there are fewer people and more game to the west. There is an ancient trail that leads there. I am made to think that the People should go west."

Aiee! thought Odin. *Did he talk to the same trader?*

"What about the crops?" someone called.

"We move until planting time," Tree answered instantly. "Then stop until harvest."

"And stay there to live?" another voice challenged.

"Maybe . . . Maybe, if it is good. Move on, maybe. We decide when the time comes."

I have surely overlooked this man's leadership, Odin was thinking. *I can help him.*

But for now, he had a more pressing problem. He must convince White Wolf and Fire Man that this was a wise decision. Already he could see that it would be a difficult task.

46

There was very little argument. It appeared that the headmen of the other towns of the People had also realized the threat that hung like a cloud over this, their traditional home. The other towns, too, had their number of old lodges that must be replaced. They faced the same problems, the same threats, as the town of Big Tree.

There was discussion, but it centered around preparation for the move, and *how* it would be carried out, not *whether*. Preparations began immediately. It was noted that a few days would be required to ready their belongings for travel. Much would be discarded. There were wails of protest from some of the old women, whose lives had been stable but were now beset with change. Yet even as they raised their voices in dire predictions of disaster, they started to pack. A sense of excitement and adventure began to make itself felt. New scenes, new sights, sounds, and smells. It would be like a visit from a traveling trader, but better. Everyone, from the oldest grandmother to the smallest child, would be a participant in the great adventure. They would *live* it, not just hear of it from a trader who had experienced it.

Odin waited, and it was as he expected. White Wolf approached him, his brow furrowed with concern.

"Odin, tell me of this," the Norseman began. "We did not understand all of the talk in the council. A move is planned. Is this a custom of the People?"

"Sometimes," Odin replied casually. "Not every season. But some of the lodges must be rebuilt, and the enemy—"

"We move because of the attack?" Nils interrupted.

"No . . . well, partly, maybe. The Enemy has become stronger. It seems good to avoid trouble, no?"

"But where will we go?"

"That way," said Odin, waving a hand in a generally southwestern direction. "There is more space there." He watched carefully and waited for the expected reaction. It was not long in coming.

"But that is farther from *our* people, from Straumfjord!"

Odin pretended surprise. "Oh! Why, yes, so it is, Thorsson. But what other direction is there? The water, the Enemy . . . that is the only open trail. But look, my brother, the People cannot go very far. We have to plant the corn, no?"

Nils Thorsson thought about that for a moment, and Odin was pleased to see the understanding in his eyes. It was a recognition that here is one inflexible event in the world. The corn, a necessity to the People, must be planted every season. It must be done by human hands, for there is no wild corn, as there are other wild plants from which to gather food. So it was with great satisfaction that Odin watched the understanding in the blue eyes of the Norseman. From understanding to acceptance is not a long step.

"When must the corn be planted?" asked Nils.

Odin tried hard to appear nonchalant, to hide the pleasure that he felt. This question indicated acceptance. He shrugged.

"When the time is ready."

He was prepared for the look of annoyance. These light-haired outsiders did not take well to the fact that many times it is not possible to plan very far ahead. He had noticed that about them when the three had been fugitives after the battle. Well, they were learning much, though they were still impatient. This one, more impatient than Fire Man.

"How do you know when it is time?" Nils asked irritably.

Odin shrugged again.

"Many ways. How warm, how wet, how warm the earth . . . They will decide."

"They? Who are they?"

"The women. The grandmothers."

Odin saw the resignation in the Norseman's face, and relaxed. He knew that look, from association with these outsiders. It was a look that indicated *I do not understand, but it is something I must accept.* Odin was pleased when he saw that, because it indicated a move toward accepting the *attitude* of the People.

Nils nodded, and Odin felt that it was time for a little more information.

"There is a trail," he explained, "used by travelers and traders. We will follow that. We will have scouts out in front, a day or two. They will be looking for a place to plant."

The Norseman nodded again, but there remained doubt in his face.

"Then after the harvest, what? We build there, winter there?"

Odin tried to conceal his delight at the use of the expression *we.* It indicated a great deal of acceptance.

"Maybe . . . We decide."

"Whether to stay there or come back?"

"Mmm . . . Yes, maybe." He would not at this time mention that the real decision was whether to winter there, or to go farther west before making winter preparations. The adopted warriors were beginning to fit well into the routine of the People, and Odin wished that to continue. There was no harm in mild deception, he thought. At least, until family ties were more firmly established.

Later, he could decide how to introduce gently the idea that the People did not really intend to return to this area at all.

"Where is this trail, Odin?" asked Nils.

It was a week later now, and the People were ready to leave. It had been said that they would meet the travelers from the other towns "on the trail."

"It is right there," answered Odin, puzzled. He was pointing to the path that led out of the village to the west. There was another that led southeast, and still another that meandered northward.

"But those are just the paths that we use for hunting, paths along the river."

"Of course. What did you think?"

Nils had been thinking in terms of a highway. The People spoke of the route as if it were a well known and important thoroughfare, the Southwest Trail.

"In our homeland," Nils began, "there are trails that are traveled by many people."

"Yes, it is as this."

"No, Odin. By horses and carts and wagons." *Chariots,* he had started to say. But he had no words for these things. It had not, until just now, fully occurred to him that these people had never seen a horse or a cart. Well, Odin himself had seen carts at Straumfjord, maybe. There were cows and oxen there. Had there been horses? Nils could not remember. The short stay at the colony now seemed a lifetime ago.

"Odin," he said, "do you remember, at Straumfjord, the animals that pulled the carts?" He now reverted to the Norse tongue, realizing that Odin would know those words, though they might not exist in the language of the People.

"Yes, the same kind they squeezed milk from!"

"Well, yes." There was no need to go into the distinction between a milk cow and an ox. "Did you see another kind that was used to sit on and travel?"

Odin was silent for a moment. "Maybe so. I think there was one. It died, soon after I went there."

"I see." It was possible that the colony had possessed a horse or two, but found them impractical. Need for transportation was limited when compared to the need for food and shelter.

He began to understand. With no large domestic animals and no wheeled vehicles, all travel must be on foot or by boat. A broad highway was not only unnecessary but virtually useless. But another thought occurred to him.

"The trail follows the river?"

"Yes. That is how we find it, no? Do not all trails follow rivers?"

Nils thought for a moment. Yes, the roads of his homeland were dependent on the terrain. Now that he considered it, the rivers were usually the prominent feature of the landscape.

"Yes," he admitted, "that is true."

He was still confused, however, about the other towns and how the different parties would link up to travel. He voiced his question to Odin, who squatted, brushed a smooth place with his hand, and began to scratch lines in the dirt with a stick. Nils realized that it was a crude map.

"We are here," Odin indicated, pointing to the tip of one of the lines. "This is our part of the trail. It meets those from the other towns here, and here. They are like streams that start in different places and come together as they flow. The Southwest Trail has others coming in along the way, like a river."

Nils nodded. He had always thought of a road as reaching from one point to another. Most journeys are for such a purpose. Here was an entirely new way of thinking. A road need not start at any one point, but at several places. As the separate paths joined together, the trail would be plainer because of the wear of use.

It now occurred to him that it was probably the same at the other end, too, with many branches. It was like a tree, maybe, with roots joining to form the trunk, and then separating into individual branches again above. No, there was a difference. Traffic on a road flows both ways. There is no up or down, except for variations in the terrain. He turned his attention back to Odin.

"The scouts are already out," the Skraeling was saying. "Some, two days ahead. They will find places to camp, tell us where the others are . . . the other towns."

It began to make a little sense, as he thought about it. Within the loose, easygoing framework of the People's lifestyle, this was a considerable amount of planning.

Another thought came to him. If they were to follow the river, why not use boats? He asked the question of Odin.

"We are too many," Odin explained simply. "There are not enough boats to carry all. The Downstream Enemy uses boats more than we do, Thorsson. They live near the sea."

Yes, he could understand that. He had seen the efficiency of the Skraeling boatmen as they attacked the longships. The People were not quite the sailors that their enemy had proved to be. This thought sent a pang of nostalgia through him. His background had fitted him better for an alliance with boatmen. But he had no regrets.

"Odin, what about other people that we meet?"

"What about them?"

"Are there enemies?"

"We do not know yet. Maybe. Maybe friends."

"But—"

"Look, Thorsson, we have many men. These, and those of the other towns. Who would attack such a big party?"

There was something to be said for such logic, but still . . .

"Do you speak the tongues of these people?"

"Some," Odin said. "Those nearby. We will use some signs."

"Signs?" Nils was puzzled.

Odin shrugged.

"One cannot know all tongues. So, everyone uses signs. Is it not so where you come from? With the hands?"

Realization began to dawn. Nils had noticed that the People, especially some individuals, accompanied conversation with many hand gestures. And yes, now that he thought of it, when they had been among the Downstream Enemy, it was so there, too. "Tell me of this, Odin."

"There is nothing to tell. To eat, drink, talk . . ." He made hand gestures as he said the words. "That is all!"

"But there are many things not so simple, Odin. That bird, there! How do you say 'bird'?"

Without speaking, Odin raised both hands, thumbs together and fingers spread like . . . like *wings. Bird!*

The conversation was interrupted by a distant shout, and the People began to shoulder their packs and prepare to move out.

Well, thought Nils, *we must finish this later.* Such a useful thing! How had he failed to learn of it? He consoled himself with the fact that there had been no reason to use it. Through the winter months there had been no outside contact.

But I will learn of this, Nils promised himself.

47

A major concern as the People began their trek to the southwest was the danger of attack. Hopefully the scouts, well in advance of the column, would be aware of questionable areas and could pass word of warning. Even in an apparently safe region, it was important to keep the column closed up.

Such a procession necessarily moves at the pace of the slowest individual. The warriors moved up and down the column, assisting the elderly, encouraging children.

"Stay together, now."

Older children ran playfully up and down the trail, accompanied by the dogs. It was part of the great adventure.

"That will soon slow," remarked Svenson to Nils. "They will sleep well tonight!"

"We will, also," Odin noted.

They chuckled and moved on.

Smaller children were carried part of the way when they became tired. There were frequent rest stops, usually at a spring or other source of drinking water. Nils wondered how many generations had used this trail through the wilderness. There were indications of old fires and campsites at favorable watering places.

It was a pleasant day, warming as the sun rose higher. Overhead, geese honked their way north. The willows were showing the fresh yellow-green of new buds, and the scent of fresh loam underfoot promised warmer weather ahead. To the right of the trail, the broad expanse of the river was frequently visible through the trees. Nils watched a fish hawk as it hovered, then descended in a long smooth glide that terminated at the glassy surface of a smooth stretch of water. A taloned claw struck down and backward, barely breaking the surface, and the hawk rose, carrying a fish.

Nils smiled. He had seen fish hawks before, in his homeland, but had never seen the actual strike and the catch. He had grown up largely in the city, among the wharves and docks of Stadt. There was excitement in the bustle of the city, the trade and commerce and the coming and going of the ships. But this had been an excitement of a different kind, and it was good. He hoped to see more.

It was shortly after midday that they arrived at a fork in the trail, and the leaders called a halt.

"What is it?" asked Nils.

"We wait for the others," Odin explained. "The other towns."

It was not long before they heard the soft murmur of a large group of people moving along the trail that joined here from the south. Dogs barked, and were answered by other dogs. Soon the two groups were mixing, greeting friends and relatives, and sharing tales of experiences on the first morning of travel.

High overhead, an eagle soared on fixed wings, uttering a long-drawn cry. The direction of flight was southwestward.

"It is a good sign," observed old Clay, the holy man.

After a short rest for the newcomers, the procession moved on, following the trail that was now broader and plainer.

"The scouts say the others are ahead of us," Odin remarked to Nils. "We will join them by tonight and camp together."

"That will be many people," Nils said. He could estimate that if the other towns were the size of their own, several hundred people would be involved.

Odin glanced at him. "Yes," he answered. "This is a big move, Thorsson! But we are large enough to protect ourselves, no?"

Yes, thought Nils, *there is security in numbers.* He still had some questions in his own mind about what sort of danger the People might expect, where, and from whom. It seemed, however, that he was unlikely to obtain any answers from Odin at this time.

He tried questioning Calling Dove, but she casually shrugged off his inquiries as if she had no idea. *Maybe she does not,* he finally decided. At any rate, he elected not to pursue it with Dove. She had enough to concern her, probably, with her pregnancy. Her belly was not beginning to enlarge much yet, but she tired easily. He was concerned for that. There were others in the procession who were with child, though. Surely the People knew the limits to which they could be pushed.

There was one bright spot in all of this. Her mood was better. She appeared to have passed the point of irritability that had characterized her early pregnancy. Now, though she was tired at the end of a day's travel, so was everyone. The irrational anger and tears were becoming less frequent. Nils appreciated that greatly, though he did not understand it. No mere man ever does. He wished to tell her how he felt, but it was difficult. He did not want to risk a mistake that would send her into one of the tirades that had marked her early weeks with child.

He resolved to walk softly and to watch for ways to help her as best he could without making it a major issue. This seemed to work satisfactorily, at least most of the time. Day by day, her moods improved. They began to enjoy each other again, and the sharing of a sunset on a smooth stretch of the great river. They chuckled at the long-legged clumsiness of a newborn fawn, following its mother to the water's edge. They watched the geese overhead.

Nils showed her the sun-stone, and the secret of its blue color when it was aligned to the north.

"It points the way, like the geese!" she exclaimed excitedly, clapping her hands like a child.

"Yes, that is its use."

"Not just to show your power?"

"Well, that, too," he admitted modestly, with a chuckle.

She laughed and tickled his ribs, and he decided that possibly their relationship was to survive the throes of early pregnancy after all.

In a few days a routine had been established, and travel seemed easier. It had been the uncertainty, the change in day-to-day activity from the town to the trail, that had been disconcerting. But, for a people whose existence is based on meeting the problems at hand day by day, change is easily faced.

Now they settled into each day without discussion. Rise at dawn, move out on the trail as quickly as possible . . . more quickly now than at first. Even with the combined bands from three separate towns, and the large number of people involved, it was becoming easier. Travel, rest, move on . . . Sometimes wait for the scouts to verify the trail or some questionable situation, move on . . . Camp before dark to allow time to gather firewood, move on at dawn.

Sometimes they passed towns of other tribes. Most of these had been known to the People for many generations. In addition, the scouts had made advance contact, paying their respects to the headman of each village and explaining the purpose of the People's trek.

Twice in the early days they camped near towns that seemed to be much like the People. The language was similar but not quite the same.

"It is like Norwegians and Danes, maybe," observed Svenson. "Almost but not alike."

Other villages seemed to be close allies, but spoke an entirely different tongue. Most of the People understood them well and talked easily to them.

"We have lived near them for many lifetimes," Odin explained.

The weather was a great help, and they were putting much distance behind them. It was to be expected that they would encounter some rain. Maybe cold and sleet, even, but for the first nine or ten days' travel it did not happen.

Then came a day when the dawn was dark and gray-blue instead of golden. Wind howled through the budding trees, and the People drew robes around them and huddled against the chill.

"Cold Maker comes once more," said an old woman. "He sees a chance to catch us in the open."

Nils recalled that this one had been one of the more vocal against the move from the very first.

"No good will come of this!" she predicted.

They waited, and soon the word was passed: No travel today. There was a stir of activity to seek out the best places to camp before the expected cold rain would begin.

It started as a fine mist, deceptive in its softness. Invisible droplets hanging in the air so saturated everything that the whole world seemed sodden. Objects that were still and unmoving began to appear frosted with moisture. The tiny droplets merged, becoming visibly wet. Soon these coalesced into larger, fatter drops, which formed rivulets that trickled down tree trunks, down the spread robes that formed makeshift shelters, and began to puddle on the ground. There was still no real indication of falling moisture. It was simply hanging free, soaking the air, the trees and rocks and bushes, and the garments of the People.

They crouched under the scant shelter of their spread robes, and prepared to wait out the weather. Fires blossomed here and there, providing warmth and light and helping the mood.

By noon it was growing colder. The air was still now, and it was apparent that the moisture in the air was no longer hanging, but drifting gently downward. The twigs on the bushes near the place where Nils and Calling Dove huddled together appeared wet and shiny. Still, it was some time before he realized that the shiny coat was not merely water, but ice. He reached out to touch a twig and found that the coating was thickening rapidly. By a unique combination of weather patterns, moisture was falling as fine droplets of water and then freezing as ice instead of snow. The Norse tales of ice-giants, gnomes, and dwarfs flitted through his mind. Maybe it was only because he had recently recalled those myths and legends for the story fires that he felt a sense of dread. Yet there seemed something evil about the silence, and the thickening of the icy coating on the world.

He glanced at Dove, and she snuggled closer and smiled.

"Cold Maker is not to be trusted," she said.

Yes, he thought. *That is a good way of saying it. Treacherous . . .*

He drew the robe more closely around them and tossed another stick on their little fire. The hiss of the icy fuel on the coals was like the sound of something evil. Nils found himself wishing for the comfortable warmth of the crowded earth lodge.

There was a sudden rumble to their left, and a scream split the silence. Nils tossed aside the robe and sprang stiffly to his feet, reaching for his sword. But it was nothing that a mere human could fight. A huge cedar tree, weighted slowly by a thicker and heavier coating of ice, had split apart. A great limb in the top, as thick as a man's thigh, had broken away from the trunk. Ponderously propelled downward in a rolling motion by the tons of ice that coated every branch and twig, it struck the limbs below it. These in turn gave way, in a grinding, churning avalanche of greenish ice and timbers, to strike the ground with an earthshaking force.

It was fortunate that those who had taken shelter beneath that tree were not crushed. But it was understandable, Nils saw. The heaviest buildup of ice was, logically, on the north side of the trees. The best shelter was on the south, facing away from the stirring of any north breeze. This had spared those who crouched under the south branches of the stricken tree.

Nils saw that one of those was Clay, the holy man. The old man scrambled free of the debris and retreated a few steps to look back.

"No one is injured?" he called.

"No, Uncle," someone answered.

"Good. The signs are good, then!"

Nils thought that perhaps that interpretation might be a bit too optimistic. From somewhere farther down the trail came another grinding roar, and another.

48

Ultimately, the interpretation that was placed on the ice storm by the People was mixed. The Norsemen noticed how much their thinking was influenced by their holy man. Is it not always so?

"It is good," Clay had explained. "We have only to look at all the destruction. Many trees have been crushed, yet we have no loss of life!"

"So the signs are good, for our journey?" a woman asked.

"I am made to think," said Clay, "that this is the meaning: There are dangers on the trail we travel, but we will escape them. Not all of us, maybe, but yes, *the signs are good!*"

It was another day before travel was possible. The trail was too slippery underfoot, and even then, there were places where the way was blocked by fallen limbs and trees. Some could be moved aside, but in places it was necessary to move out and around, or over. It was very frustrating to Nils. By the end of that day's travel, they had covered less than half the distance that they normally achieved. This did not seem to bother the People, beyond the mild inconvenience.

"Some days travel is good, some not so good," Odin said philosophically.

They traveled on, and the weather continued to warm. They encountered rains, but the season had taken the chilling bite out of the wind. The flow of air was from the south or southwest, a refreshing breeze that held promise of better things to come. Nils felt it, smelled and savored its qualities. He was regarding this breeze from the viewpoint of a sailor. How best would he set the sails, how would he navigate the broad river that was still a prominent feature on their right as they traveled? It was apparent that the river *was* navigable. In his mind's eye, he could see the longships, their bright sails bellied before the wind, slicing through the clear waters of the great river, pushing upstream to trade. He wondered about the depth. In most places, it appeared, there would be plenty of water for even the draft of the heavy *knarrs* with their freight. They had been following the river almost continuously, and he had seen no rapids since the Talking Waters, the site of the expedition's destruction.

But now, in the optimism of springtime, his imagination soared in flights of fancy. Suppose, after he and Svenson returned to Straumfjord, they could interest someone in financing an expedition. Even a ship or two, to ply this inland waterway. It *could* be done. They *had* done it, in fact, the transport of a ship around the rapids. Why not leave a vessel or two in the upper waterway, and transport only the goods around the rapids? This would open lines of trade into the interior. This country seemed rich in furs. There might be ores. Yes, he recalled the copper ornaments worn by some of the People. There must be metal ores. Iron, probably, somewhere. The People only lacked the tools and the sophistication to mine it.

Yes! If he could get the backing . . . Start small, trade metal tools for furs. It would be necessary to have a treaty with the Downstream Enemy, of course. Then expand, open mines. A smelter upstream, maybe. Plenty of trees for fuel . . . Maybe they could *build* a ship or two on the upper river!

"What is it, my husband?" Dove asked at his elbow.

"Uh . . . what?"

"You seem far away." She cuddled provocatively against him.

"Oh . . . I was only thinking. It is a good country, no?"

"Yes," she said simply. "It is good."

They were on one of their frequent rest stops. He looked at her, and saw that she looked tired.

"You are all right?" he asked.

Dove smiled. "Oh, yes. Tired. But it is late in the day. We will stop soon to camp."

He could understand that she might tire more easily now. Her pregnancy was just beginning to show a little. Not in an enlarging belly. Not yet. The change was in her balance, her way of moving, her walk. He recalled now that the old women at home in Stadt always said that a woman walks differently when she becomes pregnant.

"There is a pride in pregnancy," he had once heard a woman say. She had been a friend of his mother's, and the women had not known that young Nils was eavesdropping on their conversation. There were four of them.

"Pride?" asked one of the others.

"Yes! A woman throws her shoulders back, head up, shows the pride in her pregnancy."

One of the other women snorted indignantly.

"Huh! That is not pride, Helga. It is *balance.* She throws her shoulders back to keep from falling on her face with the new weight in front!"

The women had laughed, and Nils crept away, afraid that his presence would be discovered and disapproved. Odd that he would remember that now, so far from home. Yet it was true that he understood it better.

He wondered what Calling Dove would think of his previous flight of fancy. Would she be able to envision ships in the broad river below? Then it struck him: *Of course not.* Dove had never seen a ship. Neither had any of the People, except for Odin. Possibly one or two others. It gave him an odd feeling. Maybe he should try to tell her, to explain the great longships and his ideas for establishing trade up the inland waterway.

"Dove," he said, "You have heard your brother tell of the big canoes of my people?"

She nodded. "Yes, what of them?" Her face was interested, curious.

"Nothing . . . I was thinking. We could bring them upriver, here."

Dove looked confused. "Why?"

"To trade!"

"Oh."

It was clear that she did not understand the significance of trade. Trade for the People was limited to an individual trader with his goods in his backpack.

"You see, my people—Fire Man's and mine—we came in the big canoes."

Dove still looked puzzled.

"Yes, so it is said."

There was a long call from the trail ahead, and people began to rise and prepare to resume travel. The rest stop was over.

"I will tell you more of this later," he promised, as they picked up their packs.

Maybe he should talk with Sven about his ideas. Yes, he would do that at first opportunity. They moved on.

That evening he found an opportunity to talk with Svenson. The old sailor was only moderately interested.

"Yes, it could be done. We did it. But by Thor's hammer, Nils, that was hard work!"

"But Sven, the trees around the rapids are already cut now. We would not have to do that again. And once we have a ship in the upper river . . . Or we could build one above the rapids."

Svenson nodded. "Yes . . ." That idea seemed to intrigue him. "That is true, Nils. I am no shipbuilder, but maybe, after we get home, we could find a crew of shipbuilders. You know, I have thought . . . The ship we burned, the *Norsemaiden.* She is above the rapids."

"But she burned, Sven."

"Yes, but I have seen ships burn before. They can burn only to the water line, no? Besides, many will sink before burning that far. At least, her planks would be usable. Maybe some ribs. It is worth a look. We can look on the way back to Straumfjord."

He paused, and his eyes widened, then began to sparkle with excitement.

"The *Snowbird!*" he muttered. "Parts of her frame might be usable, too. Sister ships, built from the same plan . . . Nils, we might be closer to this than we think! It would be easy to carry planks and timbers around the rapids to use above. Easier than new timbers, and much easier than a whole ship."

It was pleasing to see this excitement in Svenson. But the dream was a long way off.

"Sven, we would need shipbuilders, sawyers, carpenters, ropes and lines, sails. . . ."

They looked at each other, and both laughed.

"It *could* be done, though," Svenson said.

"Yes, it could! First, though, we have to get back to Straumfjord."

"And we cannot do that right now," the sailor finished.

"True. But on the way back to the colony, we can look at the ships, what is left of them."

On this sobering thought, the discussion ended for the present. This had introduced a new idea, however. With such grandiose plans ahead, it would be doubly hard to travel in the opposite direction day after day. Svenson apparently felt this, too.

"First," he said, a twinkle of humor in his eyes, "we have to plant the corn."

Both laughed.

"What is it?" asked Calling Dove. "What were you and Fire Man saying?"

They had reverted to the Norse tongue for the conversation, and no one but Odin could have understood. He was not present.

"Oh, nothing," Nils told her. Then he relented. "No, we were talking of ships. The big canoes. And of returning to our people."

Dove's face fell, and tears glistened in her eyes.

"No, no," Nils assured her quickly. "Not now. Later, maybe. Fire Man just now said that soon we must plant the corn."

"That is all?"

"Yes."

"Then what is the joke?"

He thought for a moment.

"The joke," he explained, "is that Fire Man knows nothing of planting corn."

Now her face relaxed, and her eyes twinkled with mischief.

"That is true," she laughed. "But neither do you!"

It was the next morning as they prepared to travel that Nils noticed Svenson chipping at the trunk of a giant spruce with his ax.

"What are you doing?" he asked curiously.

"Marking it," Sven said simply.

"But why?"

"Look at it . . . tall, straight. . . . It will make a good mast."

"A *mast?*"

"Of course. When we begin our shipbuilding."

It took a moment for Nils to realize that Sven was completely serious. In another moment he realized that this *was* an exceptional tree, well suited to the purpose Sven envisioned for it.

"But this far inland?" he asked. "Why here?"

"Why not? A deep channel, here. As good a place as any to build ships."

The old sailor straightened from his task and Nils saw the mischief in his eyes.

"No, seriously, Nils," Svenson went on, "if we do build, we can cut and float timber down the river to wherever we wish. This is an especially fine mast. I thought to mark it, in case we need it."

"I see."

Nils did not see, entirely, but could partly follow the logic of the sailor. One thing he did not fail to notice. The mark or blaze that Sven had carefully chipped on the tree was on the side toward the river.

They might be traveling by land just now, but to Svenson, the only proper way would be by water. *A man without a boat is a man in chains,* echoed the old saying in the recesses of his mind. Odd . . . He had thought that Svenson was tolerating their predicament better than he. He wondered if the sailor even realized the depth of the powerful urge that called them back toward the sea.

But the People were beginning to move out for the day's travel. Svenson finished with a last careful chip or two, and thrust the ax in his belt to pick up his pack and join the others.

49

They had seen and visited with several different tribes or nations as they traveled. Their reception varied considerably, from warm welcome to outright hostility. On the whole, however, their manner of approach seemed effective.

Initial contact was by a pair or a trio of scouts, a day or two ahead of the main party. In principle, they approached the leaders of the village ahead, and asked permission to pass through their territory. "We mean no harm, we are only passing through," was their message. Odin was often called upon to participate in this diplomatic gesture, because of his experience with other cultures and his language skills. He was also regarded as one of the most skilled in the use of hand signs.

Nils was rapidly learning the hand signs. It was a pleasant way to learn, as Calling Dove took a great interest in teaching him. Very quickly he progressed from the obvious signs for "eat" and "drink," for "sleep," "talk," "man," "woman." Woman . . . the hand sign was a motion with the right hand, as if combing long hair. He found this a charming thing, especially when demonstrated by Calling Dove. She did it as a demure gesture, her eyes averted flirtatiously, with a provocative smile. She *was* "woman."

Other signs were not quite so obvious. There was one that he saw used whenever another people was being discussed. The index and middle fingers of the right hand were used to touch lightly the back of the left hand, in a stroking motion. He inquired about it, and after a bit of confusion in language, he began to understand that it meant a group of people.

"Our people? The People?" he asked.

"Yes, *any* people," Dove assured him.

He was still unsure, and Dove seemed to have trouble explaining, so she called to her brother.

"Oh!" said Odin, reverting to Norse to explain. "It is 'tribe' or 'nation.' That sign, then the sign for *which* people."

Quickly, he demonstrated several signs. People of the Forest; Bird People; People Who Are Downstream Enemies.

"This is 'enemy'?" Nils interrupted.

"Yes. This is 'friend or brother. . . .' " He raised his right hand with index and middle finger extended. "Then 'no.' Together they say 'not friend . . . enemy.' "

"What is the sign for *the People*?" Nils asked.

"We call ourselves the People," Odin said, "but everyone calls himself that. Others use this sign for *us*."

He made the sign for "nation," then a cupped hand for "drink," and finally a motion with his right hand, palm down, fingers fluttering.

"Running water?" Nils asked.

"Yes. River. 'People Who Live by the River.' "

"But others live by the river, too."

"Yes. Sometimes it is slow to understand. But others are called by other names. Like our not-friends."

"And what do you call my people, the Norse?" Nils asked, curious.

Odin laughed. "That is not sure yet. 'People of Big Canoes.' Sometimes 'People with Hairy Faces, People with Light Eyes.' Any of those signs. Maybe put in the sign for 'stranger.' Would it not be plain who is meant?"

"So, the signs change?"

"Of course. New things happen. The coming of your people . . . After a while everyone will use the same signs. But not always."

"Not always?" Nils was puzzled.

"Look, your name . . . You are Thorsson, and sometimes Fire Man calls you Nils. But now you are White Wolf. I was Walking Bird, but now am Odin."

Nils was thinking of all the variant names by which Svenson had been called by the People, finally settling on Fire Man.

"But these are names," he pointed out. "Other things do not change, do they?"

"Oh, yes. To Dove you are husband, to Fire Man, you are friend. And to me . . . brother, almost."

Nils was deeply touched. He did not know what to say. Was this usage because of the marriage relationship, that which would be "brother-in-law" at home? He did not want to read too much into such wordage. "It is good," he finally mumbled. But he still had questions.

"But still, almost-brother," he began again, "these things are about names and people. Some things do not change. A dog is a dog, no?"

He pointed as one of the dogs wandered over to lie down in the sun, taking advantage of the rest stop. Another, nearby, wriggled a little to ease the discomfort of the pack that it carried. Most of the larger dogs had been called upon to help transport the belongings of the People when they started their trek.

"Ah, but is it?" asked Odin, mischief in his one eye. "There are two, there." He pointed to the animals lying in the sun. "One carries a pack, one not. One is yellow, one black. Big, small . . . I think, Wolf, that a dog can be many things —tall, old, angry, hungry. . . ."

"Yes, yes, I see." At least, Nils was beginning to understand.

"Even the People. Hand signs for ourselves. We might use this— 'mother. . . .' " Odin placed his right hand on his left chest, then the sign for "tribe" and then "mother" again. "The Mother Nation . . . *Us.* But to others, we are 'People of the River.' To some, even, maybe we are 'not-friend . . . *enemy.*' "

It was many more days' travel before there began to be discussion about stopping for the season, to plant the corn. The leaders of the People consulted often, and old Clay, the holy man, performed ceremonies designed to assist in the decision.

There were several factors involved. They must choose a place where the ground could be tilled, yet one not used already by local inhabitants. It would be an advantage to be *near* growers of corn, however, to see how *they* managed the planting and the harvest. All of this must be done without presenting a threat to the occupants of the area.

Nils did not quite understand all of this. He listened to the discussions around the fire, still limited to a degree by the newness of the language. He was taken completely off guard, therefore, when the problem suddenly began to involve him.

Nils had been lost in thought as the drone of conversation mingled with the crackling of the fire. It was warm, and he was a little drowsy, his mind far away. Suddenly he realized that everyone was looking at him.

"Wh—what?" he mumbled. He turned to Odin.

"The holy man asks you, White Wolf," Odin said seriously, "when should we plant the corn, and where?"

There was a moment of panic. Nils sat with open mouth, trying to think what to say. He had never even *seen* corn planted, had no idea.

"But——" he stammered, helpless.

Odin came to his rescue.

"Say nothing for a moment, Thorsson," Odin said in the Nordic. "Act thoughtful. I will help you."

"But what can I say? I know nothing. . . ."

"Never mind. I am not sure what is happening here. Right now we must play for time while we think on this."

"Where is Svenson?" asked Nils. Maybe Sven would have an idea.

"Not here. He and Fawn . . . you know, they spend much time alone." It was one of the common jokes.

"I will just tell them I know nothing of this!" Nils said.

"No, no. Do not do that. This may be a test of your powers."

"My *powers*?" Nils's heart sank. "I have no powers, Odin. What? . . ."

"Wait. This is not a thing to deny. Let me answer for you. I am your assistant, no? We can set it aside to give time to talk of it. You have the sun-stone?"

"Yes."

"Get it out, hold it up."

"But there is no——"

"*Do* it!" said Odin firmly.

Nils fumbled in his pouch and drew out the stone. Solemnly, he held it aloft, knowing full well that he could learn nothing in this way. But the gasps of wonder and the attentiveness of the crowd told that Odin was on the right course. To further add to the impressiveness of the ceremony, many of the observers were of the other bands, and had never seen the wondrous stone before.

Of course, nothing happened. But now, Odin began to speak, in his own tongue. His voice was deep and solemn and carried a tone of authority, seeming to explain the ceremony.

"White Wolf is asking," he announced. "He uses the sun-stone." He waited, using the pause to best advantage.

"Tell . . . them," said Nils in Nordic, beginning to catch the idea, "that this . . . is the first part. . . . The second . . . requires . . . the sun. . . ."

Nils spoke in a singsong chant, as if the words were a ritual.

"It . . . is good," crooned Odin, his response also a part of the same ceremony. Then he bowed to the stone, to the fire, and spoke to Nils again, still in the Nordic chant. "Now . . . I will explain . . . that . . . the ceremony takes . . . a whole day. That . . . will give us . . . time to think on . . . this."

There was rapt attention on the part of everyone in the crowd as Odin relayed the message from the holy man.

"White Wolf will continue the prayers and ceremonies. Some will require the skills of Fire Man, too. Tomorrow night at the fire, he will tell of his vision."

Nils lowered the stone very slowly and with much ceremony, and returned it to its pouch. The crowd began to stir and to break up. He saw Svenson who appeared to have just rejoined the crowd around the fire, making his way toward them.

"What are you doing?" Svenson demanded. "What in the name of Asgard is going on?"

"I do not know," admitted Odin. "Maybe I can try to find out. Do not speak of it with anyone except each other."

He turned and disappeared into the crowd.

It was next morning when the three drew aside, apart from the camp. There would be no travel, it had been announced, until a decision was reached.

Odin had quietly talked with Snake and others of his friends, but no one seemed to have any information. The scouts had seen an area some two days away that looked promising. There were not many people there, and they seemed peaceable enough. But it would be a major decision, the commitment to a season's crop in this place—in *any* place. Everyone, thought Odin, was feeling the insecurity of new surroundings. It is one thing to go out into the unknown with the secure knowledge that it is possible to return. It is quite another when the entire future depends on a decision like this. A mistake, a failure of the year's crop, and the People would starve. Some of them, at least. True, there had always been good years and bad years for growing. Yet it had been within the framework of a known area. This was a different sort of risk, and they must not fail.

These were the thoughts that had kept Odin awake. The decision must be made, and it would be by the council, greatly influenced by Clay in his position as holy man, and by Big Tree as headman of the band. The other headmen would also have a voice, as well as holy men or women from the other bands. Still, the impetus to move had been initiated by Big Tree and Clay. They must take a leading role in this decision. It was a tremendous responsibility.

Odin wondered whether there was political pressure from the other bands. Maybe that was it. The other leaders might be, by implication, at least, letting Big Tree know that this decision must be the correct one. There might even be warnings. *Yes*, he thought, *that must be it!* Whether there were warnings or not, there was a great deal of pressure here, the pressure of responsibility. Odin tried to place himself in the position of Big Tree, or of Clay. They would want to spread the responsibility, in case things did not work out well.

And what better way than to shift part of the blame to the outsider, the strange and powerful holy man, White Wolf? He did not want to believe this, but he must be realistic.

Clay had shown a great tolerance toward the outsider, but was he now changing his attitude? Did the holy man fear the power of White Wolf, and wish to destroy him? Possibly, but that did not seem right. It was more likely that Clay was seeking support. *Yes* . . . If Clay could enlist support for his decision, the support of White Wolf and his popular assistant, Fire Man, it would feel good to the People. If the season became a success, it would enhance the power and prestige of them all. Of Big Tree, too. He wondered why Clay had not simply approached White Wolf and discussed this. It did not take long to realize that Clay would seem to be talking from a position of weakness. The holy man could not risk his prestige in this way.

The rest of the story that now thrust itself on Odin's thoughts was darker. Downright ugly, as he considered it at greater length: If the season became a total disaster, Clay and Big Tree would have someone to blame.

He wished that he could take the Norsemen to talk with Clay and Big Tree, but he quickly rejected the idea. He could not risk the prestige of White Wolf in such an approach. That would imply weakness in White Wolf.

No, he, Odin, must find a way to handle this. He must do it without letting the Norsemen know the darkest of his thoughts. And without jeopardizing the prestige of anyone involved. It would be a very interesting summer, an exciting challenge.

He looked at the waiting faces of the two Norsemen.

"I am made to think," he began, "that Clay would like to have your support."

"Then he should ask for it!" Svenson blurted.

"No, he cannot," Odin explained. "That would look like weakness."

"But how could we be of help?" Nils asked. "We have never even seen corn growing!"

"That is true. And you must say so." *That will remove much of the responsibility,* he was thinking. "But you must make it appear that your prayers, your sunstone, your powers all say that Clay has the gifts to tell *him* what to advise."

"And what if the choice is a bad one, then?" Svenson demanded. "What if the crop fails?"

"Then," said Odin, "we are all in trouble."

50

venson, it was decided, would begin the ceremony with the lighting of the fire. Odin explained to the gathering crowd that it was prudent, in a case of this magnitude and importance, that all the powers available should be called upon.

He had also taken Nils aside and solemnly consulted with him about how to approach the ceremony.

"But there is no ceremony, Odin!" Nils protested.

"Then you must make one. It is important that they know it is very serious before you say what your gifts tell you."

"My gifts can tell me nothing about corn!"

"That is true. So let us talk of what is good to say about it. Corn has much to do with the gifts of Clay and Big Tree, no?"

"Yes," agreed Nils, "I suppose so."

"Then you can tell them that. . . . That you have consulted your gifts, which tell you to follow *theirs.* Yes, that is good! If anything goes wrong, it is *their* advice that caused it."

Odin was growing excited. *He is actually enjoying this,* thought Nils. *This is his way in emergencies!*

"Now," Odin continued, "let us talk of your ceremony."

"But I have told you," Nils protested again, "there is none."

"I know, Thorsson, but there must appear to be. Is there a song, a chant, something you could sing?"

Nils began to understand. It would be in Nordic, not understood by anyone except Svenson and Odin. *Much like the Latin liturgy at Mass in church,* he thought. There was a brief pang of guilt at such an analogy, but it passed quickly. The purpose, though, was surely the same. This must be a solemn, prayerful chant. It need not make sense to the listener. It would be better *not* to. Any rhythmic chant, a collection of nonsense syllables, even, that would establish a mystical aura, lending credibility to what he would say. That itself seemed simpler now, with the general theme in mind. Yes, maybe he could do it.

But what chant? A poem or song? It need not make sense, because the listeners did not know the Nordic tongue anyway . . . some childish nonsense rhyme?

Strym-strahm pamadiddle lolly-body rhigdhym . . . fragments of a childhood nonsense rhyme flitted through his head. It was meant to be sung, but he could remember no more of it. The tune, but no more of the words.

He thought of the twinkle in the blue eyes of his grandfather as the two of them had sung this rhyme together. Nils could have been no more than four years old. . . .

"You have thought of a chant?" asked Odin.

"What? Oh. No, but I will find one."

He was thinking now of long winter evenings around the great fireplace. One of the favorite pastimes in winter in the Northland was that of riddles. Often these were phrased in runic rhymes. They made no sense until they were solved. The cryptic message was then plain, but not until the trick was exposed. His grandfather had loved these games. Nils had realized in later years that it was because it had forced young minds to learn to *think.*

"How much dirt," one riddle had asked, "in a hole a hand's span wide, a span long, and a span deep?"

That one did not rhyme, but was always amusing. There was always some-one present who failed to realize that if it is a *hole,* it is empty, and contains no dirt at all. But this was not quite what he sought. True, it did deal with digging in the dirt. Presumably, planting corn does, too. Yet Nils was not certain that he could make this sort of riddle sound serious enough to pass as a ceremonial liturgy.

Something more mystical . . . It need have nothing to do with the plant-ing of corn. Well, it *could* not, since he knew nothing. But it need have no connection with the sun-stone or with anything else. It must only suggest a mystic, spiritual *something*. He thought of how impressed the People had been with his stories of the Norse gods and goddesses. Surely there must be some way that he could utilize that interest.

Then it came to him. There were riddles and cryptic puzzles that dealt with the Creation story and with the gods. These were always presented in a confidential mystic tone, a singsong rhythm that was much like a chant. *Yes, that would be the way.* It struck him as amusing that for him the question had become the answer.

"What is it, Thorsson?"

"Nothing. I have thought of the ceremony I will use."

"It is good. Be sure to use the stone!"

"But it will show nothing in the dark."

"I know. But pretend it does. They cannot see it anyway, and do not know your words. It makes it better if they think you see things that they do not."

Nils had to admit that this made good sense. He spent the rest of the day rehearsing in his mind, remembering the words of the little childhood riddle. Not that that mattered. The listeners would not know them anyway, but he felt that he could carry it off better if it made at least some sense to *him*.

Svenson played his part well. After the first time or two that he had kindled a fire with flint and steel, he really began to enjoy his status. Nils had been amused at the sailor's ceremony. For Sven did have his own ceremony now. He had ceased to use his steel at all except to create the impression of a mystic skill, the gift of fire that gave Fire Man his name.

This special council fire was duly kindled, and soon the flames were licking hungrily upward through the carefully stacked fuel.

Big Tree requested the answer he sought from White Wolf. With a great deal of ceremony, Nils stood and positioned himself to best advantage. Light, dark, the fire with its sparks ascending to the black dome above.

He raised his arms high, and began to chant the old riddle in the singsong cadence that his grandfather had always used. It dealt with the tales of the Wild Huntsman of the Northland who rides through the sky on the wings of the winter storm. The howl of the winds mingles with the baying of his hounds. The Huntsman is no less than the god Odin himself, astride his great eight-legged steed, Sleipnir. He carries the magic spear Gungnir, and a white shield held on high.

As a child, Nils had always felt a chill at the mention of the Wild Huntsman, and would creep close to his grandfather. Even now the hair stood on the back of his neck as he chanted. The chant, however, was not of the story, but was the riddle itself:

> *"Who are the two who ride the Thing?*
> *Three eyes they have together, ten legs, one tail,*
> *And thus they travel through the land."*

It was easy for Nils to become caught up in the dread that he had felt as a child, and for the emotion to show. His listeners were spellbound. Though they did not understand the words, the emotion in the voice of White Wolf was apparent. Even Svenson stared, openmouthed, and he must have heard the story before.

Nils repeated the chant a time or two, and then turned to Odin, who handed him the sun-stone with great ceremony. Nils held it aloft and stared at it for a long time, utilizing the pause for effect. There was complete silence, broken only by the crackle of the fire and the distant call of Kookooskoos, the hunting owl. Its hollow sound lent an even greater sense of mystery.

Finally, Nils lowered the stone. He began to speak, this time in the tongue of the People.

"I am made to think, through the power of my gifts, that it is this way with the planting of corn: Corn is of the People. Your nation, not mine. So, the knowledge of corn comes not to me, but to our brother, the holy man, Clay. His powers are great, and it will be given to him where and when to plant. I am made to think that his gifts will let him advise us well."

He cast a quick glance at Clay, but could tell little. The leathery old face was serious, but from the quick glance in the flickering firelight, Clay did not seem displeased.

Odin seemed quite satisfied, and Svenson wore an amused expression.

Big Tree rose.

"It is good," he announced. "The signs are good. Tomorrow we will move on, into the place that has been found by the scouts and approved by our holy men. I thank you, White Wolf, for your help."

The council was over, and people began to rise and go to prepare for tomorrow's trek. Nils glanced over at the old holy man, and their eyes met for a moment. Clay nodded ever so slightly, possibly a greeting, possibly a nod of approval. Maybe both. Nils could not tell, but surely there was no disapproval here. He nodded back, and they went their separate ways.

Svenson and Odin fell into step beside Nils. These were the only two, he realized, who had understood a word of his chanting.

"You did well," Sven chuckled. "Your riddle made a good ceremony!"

"That is true," said Odin thoughtfully. "It is good." He seemed preoccupied.

"I looked at Clay," Nils said. "I think he was pleased."

"That, too, is good," said Odin enthusiastically. "Yes, White Wolf, I am made to think you have done well tonight. But I have a question."

"A question?" Nils asked, concerned.

"Yes." Odin paused for a moment, as if hesitating to speak, but then plunged ahead. "What is it," he inquired, "that has three eyes, ten legs, and a tail?"

Nils started to answer, but paused. How could he explain the legend of the Wild Huntsman? An eight-legged horse with a one-eyed rider, to be explained to a man who had never seen a *four*-legged horse?

"Odin, it will take time to tell of it," he said. "It is a man with one eye, and a beast with eight legs."

Odin thought for a moment, and then nodded, as if in complete understanding.

"The man sits on the beast," Nils pushed on, feeling a need to explain.

"Of course," Odin agreed. "It is a story, no?"

How easily the acceptance came, Nils noted. For the Skraeling, it was not necessary to understand it all, only to hear it, to enjoy it. *It is a story.*

Well, yes, Nils thought. *A good story.* Maybe he would tell that one, sometime around the story fire.

51

The planting of the corn was hard work, undertaken with much ceremony. Everyone was involved. It was a ritual, a repetitive thing that caused the back to ache and muscles to tighten from bending and digging and planting.

First each "hill" must be prepared. Every sprig of grass or other growing plant was plucked from the soil, and the dirt mounded up into a little hillock a hand's span across. Then a hole, poked with a stick. In the hole, a bite of meat or fish. Three seeds, in a triangle around it. The rich humus drawn over them and patted smooth. On to the next . . . In every third hill were placed three pumpkin seeds.

"Why do we put the piece of meat in the hole?" Nils asked his wife, who worked at his side, on all fours.

Dove was growing larger with child, and he could tell that she tired more easily. She straightened and stood for a moment on her knees, stretching her back. He could imagine how she must feel. His own back muscles were complaining of the unaccustomed strain. She smiled, a tired smile.

"We are asking Earth to give us food," she said simply. "We show our willingness to share by feeding her first."

Nils nodded. He did not really understand all of this logic, but it was a part of the People. He was beginning to accept, and realize that there were things about his wife's people and their customs that he would never understand. Many of their rituals . . . Not formal ceremonies, but merely simple things, like the pinch of tobacco tossed into a new fire when it is kindled, to honor the spirits of the place. The apology to a newly slain animal whose meat is needed for food. This, the sacrifice of a bit of food to the earth, to thank in advance for the crop.

He noticed, too, that the People talked to the world around them. A thanks to the river for a cool drink, a thank-you to an unseen spirit for the beauty of a sunset.

"Listen, the wind is talking to us," Calling Dove had once said to him.

It had been during their courtship on a warm afternoon. They were seated on a quiet hillside a little way outside the village. Behind them was a dense thicket of pines, and the singing of the gentle breeze through the fragrant pine needles made a constant murmur.

"What does it say?" he asked, amused.

She had shrugged, and had given him an evasive answer.

"It says many things, no? A promise of happiness together, maybe. . . ." She paused, and seemed embarrassed. "Who knows what the wind says?"

She averted her eyes, and changed the subject slightly.

"Did you know that once we could understand and speak all tongues?"

"How is this? Those of all other people?"

"Of course. And of all the animals—they talked to us, too—and the trees, the river's whisper. Those still talk to us, you know, but we no longer understand."

He thought of that now, as the two of them stood on their knees in the loamy soil that would bring forth the year's crop. At least, that was what the People were *asking* it to do. It was neither a solemn churchly ritual or a superficial, flippant act. It was quite matter-of-fact, like asking a small favor of a friend. Yet with it was the expression of appreciation, too. *Thank you . . .* It was a prayer of thanksgiving, given in advance, symbolized by the bit of food beneath the corn seeds. There would be more giving of thanks later, after the expected richness of the resulting crop.

Just now, he was tired. The muscles of his back ached, and his thighs cramped from the unaccustomed position. He could see the others moving slowly across the field, digging, mounding, dropping a bit of food, planting the three seeds, covering, moving on. The sun was low, shadows growing long. They would not finish today.

They did finish, finally. It had taken several days, and it was good to complete the task. There was a certain satisfaction, to look over the gently rolling terrain, to see and smell the freshly turned earth and the slightly curving rows of hillocks.

Now the People began to look to the sky for signs of rain. It was not long in coming. The entire sequence was as if the People expected it to happen exactly that way. They awoke with scattered clouds, high and thin, to the north and west, increasing quickly in density and coverage. By midday the sky was gray and overcast, and the air was heavy. Birds that had been singing their territorial calls were quiet. The People hurried to put finishing touches on their brush-and-pole shelters, tying loose edges, testing lashings.

Then came the rain, with wind, lightning, and thunder. It was slow at first, but became heavier and heavier, a hard, pounding, driving rain.

"What if it washes out the corn in the little hills?" Nils asked.

Dove laughed at him. "We want it to rain now. Everything is ready."

"But . . . *this* hard?"

She laughed again. "Maybe not. But it is good. The Rain Maker's drum will waken sleeping corn. You will see!"

Even so, he was startled when, a few days later, spears of bright green thrust upward through the mounds of soil. The rain had lasted three days, and it appeared that this was a good sign. It was also quite a shock to the Norsemen to see the rapidity of the growth.

"I can almost *see* it grow," Nils said to Svenson. "Sven, there is nothing like this at home, is there?"

Sven shook his head. "I know nothing of such things, Nils. Mine has been a life on the sea, not in the dirt."

The disdain of a sailor for those who till the soil was evident, even though Sven had helped with the planting. Nils was certain that, as sore as his own muscles had been, the aging limbs of Svenson had felt it more keenly. The sailor made only one grumbling remark, though.

"By the hammer of Thor! It's a sight easier to furl the sail!"

In a few more days, it seemed, the corn plants were knee high, reaching toward the sky. Pumpkin vines reached along the earth, their tendrils searching. *For what?* Nils wondered. Yet he knew. It was for space. He could understand that spirit. It was his own, the urge to reach out. . . .

He paused, surprised at himself. He had actually been thinking in terms of the *spirits* of the pumpkin vines. The priest at the church back in Stadt would not approve of such thoughts. That devout cleric might even have called it blasphemy. But the priest would not understand the People, either. They were of different worlds. Yet it seemed easy, standing here at the edge of the growing crop field, to see it as the People did. He felt glad, and even a little proud, maybe, that he was a part of this. That the sweat of *his* labor had contributed. That *his* gifts of food, given to Earth, were being acknowledged. And it was good. . . .

"*Thank you!*" he murmured, half aloud, unsure to what deity or spirit he was speaking.

Svenson said it was the month of June. Nils was willing to take his word for it, because Sven was the one keeping count with his calendar stick. It did seem likely, because the flowers in the area were blooming in profusion. Some were similar to those at home, others completely different.

"Yes," said Odin. "It is the Moon of Flowering."

As it would be at home, Nils thought. The People always seemed to have a way of coming straight to the heart of anything.

In a few weeks the corn was taller than their heads. Twice the People had weeded the field. It was a chore, a boring and mindless task. Worse, even, than the planting. Here, every sprig of green that did not belong must be removed.

"It is much easier now than later," Calling Dove had assured him.

But now, it seemed, there was no more work to be done until the time of harvest. That was good, he thought, because Dove was moving with increasing difficulty as her pregnancy continued to grow. The rains had come at irregular but satisfactory intervals during July, which Odin called the Moon of Thunder. The People seemed pleased with the progress of the crops. The pumpkin vines were covered with bright yellow blossoms, which were soon followed by swelling green globes. Bean vines, planted on tripods of sticks around the edges of the fields, were bearing heavily.

Corn, however, seemed to be the main crop of the People. At the top of each stalk a sort of bloom appeared, jutting upward like a handful of sticks.

"That will become the grain?" asked Nils.

"No, no," Dove laughed. "The corn grows down here, on the side of the stalk."

She pointed to enlarging cylinders that had the appearance of leaves at first glance. No, a *bundle* of leaves, with a tuft of brown hairlike material protruding from the tapering tip.

"Then what is this other?"

"The corn has two spirits," Dove told him. "There must be both, this at the top and the part below. Like you and me—" She pointed at her swollen belly. "Man and woman. But I am made to think that corn does not have as much pleasure."

It took a moment for him to realize that she was teasing him. Then he smiled sheepishly, and Dove laughed aloud at the success of her joke.

"But the corn," he protested, after they had laughed and shared her teasing. "Its bloom is in one place, its fruit in another?"

"Of course," she insisted. "Is it not always so with corn?"

Nils did not know. He had never seen corn growing before. But he could think of no other plant with this characteristic. Maybe he could talk to Odin about it, or to Sven. Yes, Svenson had seen much of the world, and might know of this. He would ask.

All of that was forgotten, though. He had not had an opportunity to talk to Odin that evening, and Dove woke him out of a sound sleep in the night.

"My husband . . ." she whispered.

"Yes . . . what? . . ." He fought to awaken. "What is it?"

"It is my time, maybe. Will you tell my mother?"

Now he was wide awake.

52

It was a woman-thing, the birthing of the child. Quickly, Red Fawn arrived to assist her daughter. The husband was banished from the lean-to shelter that was the summer dwelling for the couple.

Nervous and at loose ends, Nils wandered a little way and stood looking up at the night sky. What was he supposed to do now? Someone approached, and he was glad to recognize Svenson.

"The time has come, eh?" Sven spoke. It was not really a question, only a greeting.

"It seems so. I was wondering what I am expected to do. You are a father, Sven."

The old sailor chuckled. "Yes, but I was always at sea when the time came."

"But surely there is something I could do."

Now Svenson laughed aloud. "I am made to think," he said thoughtfully, using the idiom of the People, "that you have already done what was expected of you, several moons ago."

He slapped his thigh in amusement.

"It is not funny, Sven," Nils snapped. Somehow the usual ribald jokes did not seem appropriate now.

"I meant nothing, Nils. Calm down. They can handle this. And we could do nothing. Look, let us go and sit on the rocks, there. I will stay with you."

Sven pointed to a jumble of boulders against the shoulder of a little hillock a bow shot away. The area was only dimly seen in the pale light of a new moon, but it was a familiar place. Nils nodded and moved in that direction. He glanced at the sky and noted the position of the Great Bear. The Seven Hunters, the

People called the same constellation. Odin had told them how the Hunters go out each night, to circle their lodge at the Home Star. Once in each day and its night, the Hunters make their circuit, circling the sky forever. It was of interest to Nils that the People recognized the importance of the Polestar, though they did not use it for navigation.

But he was not thinking of that now. His quick glance told him that dawn would be coming soon. Not that it mattered much, in the present situation. He had only looked from habit. Yes, even now the velvety blackness was fading in the east to a leaden gray. He looked back toward the shelter and saw that Red Fawn had built up the fire. A few other people were stirring.

Someone else approached, and Nils felt a bit of resentment. No one had a right to bother him at a time like this. The irritation passed as he recognized Odin, who silently fell in beside them.

"Odin, is there something that I should do?" Nils asked.

"No, you have done your part," Odin said.

Sven chuckled, and Nils's irritation flared again. *Mother of God,* he thought, *it is no different anywhere!*

Odin seemed to sense his anger, and spoke again.

"It will go well, almost-brother. Our family's women birth easily. It is in their body to do so."

Nils wondered at such a curious remark, but Odin continued.

"She is long, from arms to hips, like our mother. This gives easier birthing."

"I have heard that, Nils," Svenson said. "A long-waisted woman . . . easier labor. I do not know, but it looks good. Long waist, long legs . . ."

"Can we speak of something else?" Nils snapped irritably.

"Of course," Odin answered. "Of what, Thorsson?"

Nils shrugged uncomfortably. "I do not know. I am sorry."

"It is all right," Odin soothed. "We do not need to speak at all. But we will stay with you. A man needs someone."

"Thank you," Nils mumbled.

"Let us smoke," suggested Odin. He brought forth a pipe and his pouch of tobacco mixture.

"Shall I start a fire?" asked Svenson.

"No, I have one," said Odin.

He was carrying a gourd full of ashes, and now drew out a stick which had been buried in the gourd. He blew on the stick to brighten the fiery coal at its tip, and then held it carefully to his freshly filled pipe. A few long draws produced an answering glow in the pipe's bowl. He took another puff or two and then handed it to Nils, who in turn puffed and passed the pipe to Svenson.

By the time the pipe had made two or three rounds, the yellowing of the sky in the east was becoming more prominent, and the prospective father more calm. Conversation came easier.

"When is the time to come for your wife?" Svenson asked Odin.

"Who knows?" shrugged Odin. "I had thought by now, but Hawk Woman says no. She says soon, though. She has birthed before, you know."

"Yes, I know. Her daughter grows quickly this season."

"That is true! Like the corn, no?" Odin chuckled. "The old ones say that one has babies for only a little while. Then they are grown. You know that we call her Yellow Corn, because of this?"

They all chuckled, Svenson with the most understanding.

Nils appreciated the company and the attempt to distract him, but still he could not keep his mind from the intense scene being played out in the shelter below. He thought of the wife of Vili Heinesson, a neighbor back in Stadt, when he was a child. *Inge, that was her name.* A beautiful young woman, an object of admiration and one to stir the pulse of a young boy whose maleness was just beginning to make itself felt.

The death of Inge Heinesson had had a profound effect on him. It had troubled him greatly to think of that lithe and handsome female form stilled in death. He missed her, though he barely knew her, and she had probably been completely unaware of the boy who worshiped her from afar. Of course she *had* smiled at him that once, when they nearly collided in the street. He still remembered that smile, open, fresh, and confident, that of a happy, secure person.

But she had died in childbirth. He did not know the details. His parents and the other adults had spoken in hushed tones, and seemed not to think of the feelings of young Nils. They did not know that he had secretly loved this fine woman, or that he had gone to the barn to cry out his grief alone.

He had felt a tremendous sympathy for the bereaved husband. He had wanted to tell Vili Heinesson that he knew, and understood. It would have been completely inappropriate, of course. Still, he had wondered then and afterward if Vili actually knew how special had been the beautiful young woman who shared his bed.

Nils had held a great deal of resentment a year later, when Vili Heinesson remarried. He was certain that Vili was disloyal to the memory of Inge.

It had been a long time now, since he had thought about that tragedy in his young life. No one else had known his feelings and would ever know. It only came back now because of his concern. Was he being punished for his coveting of Vili Heinesson's wife so long ago? How severe would the punishment be?

His concern and his dread became greater as time passed. It seemed an eon ago that the three had walked out here in the dark of the predawn morning. It was growing lighter, but the sun was still not showing above the distant hills. The pipe came around again. He took a quick puff and passed it on to Sven. He rose and paced.

What if—he dared not form the thought—*what if Calling Dove met the fate of young Inge Heinesson? What would he do, if he lost her?*

He had never stopped to realize how Dove had become a most important . . . no, *the* most important part of his life. If anything should happen to her . . . *I must not think such thoughts!* Tears came to his eyes. *If only I could do this for her!* he thought.

"Nils! Nils! Are you all right, boy?"

Svenson was shaking him by the elbow.

"What? I was thinking of something else, Sven. What is it?"

It was Odin who spoke.

"They are calling to us." He pointed to the distant camp.

In the growing light, Nils saw a figure outside the lean-to shelter. He thought he recognized the stance as that of his wife's mother. She was waving her arms at them.

"Deer says to come on down," Svenson observed.

Could there be trouble? Were his worst fears to be realized?

Nils leaped to his feet and ran, his heart pounding in near panic. *Something is wrong!* He nearly fell from his downslope momentum, but recovered his balance. How frustrating . . . Like a dream, in which one tries to run but can only move slowly. He was only dimly aware of the others behind him. There was no way for them to understand his dread.

He loped across the level meadow and drew closer. It was with great relief that he saw a smile on the face of Red Fawn.

"Is it . . . is she? . . ." he panted.

Red Fawn merely pointed to the shelter.

Calling Dove lay there on the robes. She looked tired, but had never seemed so beautiful to him as she did now. He saw that her abdomen, covered by a sleeping robe, was flatter now. For some reason that thought was the first to make itself felt, even before he saw the smile on Dove's tired face. More slowly than that, even, he realized that she held a bundle in her arms. Gently, she turned back a corner of the soft robe.

A pair of wide, dark eyes peered out of a face like that of a little old man. Some babies arrive in the world under protest, squinting and yelling at the light of day. Others are born with a knowing look, curious about all that lies before them. This child was of the latter.

"Your son," said Dove. "He is beautiful, no?"

The child's dark eyes seemed to look straight through to Nils's soul, as if it knew and understood all his feelings.

"Are you all right?" he asked her.

"Of course! Tired . . ."

The other two men came up behind him, and stopped.

"They have a son," Red Fawn explained.

Nils turned to look at them, not knowing what to say. At that moment, the rim of the sun peeked over a notch in the distant hills, touching the trees and the brush shelter with a golden glow. It may have been responsible for the tears in the eyes of the new father. Or, maybe not . . .

"It is good," he said in the language of the People.

"Yes," agreed Red Fawn, "it is a good sign."

53

The harvest came soon. Too soon, it seemed, for there was much happening. White Wolf and Calling Dove were preoccupied with the small manchild who had joined them.

"He is a good baby!" decreed Red Fawn, after the manner of grandmothers everywhere.

But it was true. The infant boy was called Bright Sky after the manner of his birth at sunrise. He might have another name later, Dove explained to her husband. This was merely a baby name. It did seem appropriate, however. Never had Nils seen an infant whose eyes were so intense and inquisitive. He smiled very early, and had a look of perpetual understanding that made him seem an adult who merely lived in a small body. Such infants, though somewhat rare, are a joy, not only to their parents, but to everyone with whom they come in contact.

In addition to this preoccupation with their own child, there was the birth of another, a girl to Odin and Hawk Woman. It was not her first child, but it was a completely new experience for Odin. Nils was able to return the support he had received from Odin on the occasion of Bright Sky's birth. That was a good feeling.

Seldom if ever was there a new father who was so overcome by the significance of the birth of his child. Odin had reveled in the experience of being a parent to Hawk Woman's older daughter by her previous marriage, but this was different. This was his own flesh and blood.

To the People, there was little difference, and to give Odin the credit deserved, in a short while there was none to him either. In a few seasons, few would remember that the two daughters of Odin and Hawk Woman had had different fathers. But today, it was important to Odin. This was his first such experience. He suffered all the anxiety and the joy that he had shared with his almost-brother a short time earlier.

But then came the harvest. Both women were gaining strength and their babies doing well, and both would take part in this, the most triumphant of annual festivals.

It was at this time that Nils first realized that there were several types of corn. He had wondered, when the planting was taking place, why there had been such care to lay out different fields. They were separated by specific distances, paced off carefully by Clay, the holy man. He had not paid much attention, but had assumed that this was to designate the ownership of the different plots. The space between, however, had been planted to beans and squash of several varieties. Even so, he paid little attention.

Now, however, he noticed that the corn from different plots was quite different in size, shape, and color. He asked Dove about it.

"For different uses," she told him.

"But it is all to eat!"

She laughed at him, but then relented. "You have never seen the harvesting before, have you?"

"No. It was past that time when we joined the People."

"And that was good," she laughed. She seemed apologetic that she had not realized, and hurried on to explain. "This kind is best for ground meal . . . this to cook whole. This one for *hominy*."

"*Hominy?*"

"Yes, you have eaten it. The hard skin is taken off with ashes from the fire!"

He did not remember. He was realizing how little attention he had ever paid to what he was eating. If there was food, he ate, and asked no questions. When he had become involved in the growing of the crop, his attitude had changed.

Another thought came to him as he helped to gather the ears, pull the husks back, and tie them together to hang in bundles. How was ownership established?

Calling Dove looked at him in amazement at such a question. "It belongs to the People!"

"You mean, everyone?"

"Of course. Everyone eats, no?"

And everyone plants, he thought. This was a strange idea, that of community property. He turned it over in his head for a little while.

"Who decides its use?" he asked finally.

Again, Dove studied his face as if such a question were unheard of.

"The women, of course."

The *women?* He had been with the People for nearly a year, and was only now learning some things about their ways. The absence of the idea of property was completely foreign to him. But surely . . . Yes, there *was* a recognition of personal property. Weapons, clothing, such things. But the food supply belonged to all. So did the lodges, he realized, though each person or family owned a certain area. Maybe "owned" was not the right word. The rules of ownership were quite specific, he now decided, and actually quite strict. When applied to the few items of personal ownership, the rules of ownership were totally inviolable.

"Then why," he asked Dove, "is it so important to separate the different plots?"

Again, she looked at him as if the question made no sense.

"To keep them apart."

"But both belong to all!"

"Yes," Dove said cautiously, "but that has nothing to do with it!"

"Wait . . . then why keep the fields separate?" he demanded.

"Because they are *different!*"

"Different?"

"Yes. I have told you, Wolf, this for meal, this for hominy. . . ."

They stared at each other for a moment, in complete lack of understanding.

"Their *spirits* are different. They must not be allowed to be together," she went on.

Slowly, he began to grasp the idea. He was no farmer, but he knew that among livestock it was good to keep bloodlines pure. Could it be the same with plants? He could think of no comparable instance at home. Of course, here was the strange situation with the corn, when the flower and the fruit are at different places on the plant. Was that a part of it?

"How long has it been so?" he asked.

Dove shrugged. "Always, maybe. The People planted corn after they came out of the ground."

He decided that he must ask Odin about this. It was a thing so completely foreign to him that he was lost in trying to understand it. For reasons still unclear to him, it was necessary to keep the various types of corn from mixing. He could recall nothing similar in the grains familiar to Europe and the Isles. Had he simply overlooked it? Wheat, oats, and barley were quite similar in appearance, though there was nothing like this crop with its huge ears and large hard kernels.

In fact, now that he thought of it, almost none of the crop plants grown here were remotely similar to those at home. Beans, squash, the great golden pumpkins . . . *There* was an oddity! The largest vegetable he had ever seen. Some were so big that it would be hard to encircle one in a man's arms. And they grew not in the ground like a turnip, or in a leafy head like cabbages, but on a *vine.* Even to a man not familiar with farming, it was apparent that there was much more here than he had imagined. Primitive though the Skraelings might be in some respects, there was a vast amount of special knowledge and skill involved. Yes, he would speak with Odin about it, when an opportunity offered. Maybe, when it was time to return home, he could take seeds of some of these crops. As a curiosity, at least, corn, beans, and pumpkins.

In the process of the harvest, Nils also noticed that the colors of the corn became important. There was a ceremonial significance, apparently, a religious meaning in the fact that some types were white, some red, some yellow. This was not exactly the same as the *use* of the different types. Ah, well, no matter . . .

All of the crops were gathered now, except for a few pumpkins still in the fields. There began to be discussion about what the People should do now, and where they should winter. Almost immediately, the People split into two factions. Those who had spent more time on the improvement of their shelters wished to winter here, where they were. The others, who had assumed that they would travel on before cold weather, argued to move immediately, so that suitable winter lodges could be constructed elsewhere. Arguments became heated.

"The People have seldom moved very far," Odin explained to the Norsemen. "The towns have been where they were, longer than anyone's lifetime."

Only now did the magnitude of this move begin to make itself felt to Nils. For the People, it was bigger than a lifetime. It was no wonder that it was causing argument and divisiveness. Especially since the People were unused to long-range planning anyway. Their easy, day-to-day style, governed only by the seasons or the availability of game, did not lend itself well to planning decisions.

Finally a council was called. There were many who spoke, telling and retelling their arguments. It was long and boring to the Norsemen. It seemed that the discussion would never end.

At last, however, a tentative agreement was reached. The headmen and holy men from the three towns would meet in discussion and prayerful consideration. After the appropriate ceremonies and spells, a course of action would be recommended. It was much like the decision earlier about when and where to plant. There was one important difference, from the standpoint of the Norsemen. White Wolf was formally invited to be a part of the meeting of this inner council.

"It is good," Odin told him. "You were being tested, last spring. Now the crop is good. Your power has been shown."

"But what do I do?" Nils asked.

Odin shrugged. "Nothing much, maybe. Look wise, nod sometimes. I will help you. First tell Big Tree that you need your assistants. At least, me . . . That is good, to help you understand what is being said. I can speak for you, if it is needed. Yes, this is good."

The inner council was quite informal, slow-paced, and deliberate. The pipe was passed, discussion ensued, and opinions were exchanged. Nils was startled when finally Big Tree turned to him suddenly.

"How are your thoughts on this, White Wolf?"

Nils gulped, then paused a moment to collect his thoughts.

"My brothers," he said slowly, "I am still an outsider. I do not know your weather, as I did not know your crops."

"Do you wish to do your ceremonies?" asked Big Tree.

"If the People wish it," Nils answered. "But I am made to think the answer would be the same. My gifts are powerful, but not as great as those of these other holy men in decisions of the People."

"It is good!" whispered Odin in Nordic. "Offer again to ask your guides."

"Still," Nils continued, "I would ask the advice of my guides if this council wishes."

"White Wolf," one of the holy men from the other bands spoke, "I am told that your ceremony changes the color of a stone."

It was a question, of a sort. Probably, it was based on curiosity.

"That is true," said Nils.

"Yet we have not seen it happen," the other said thoughtfully. "In the spring, your ceremony? . . ."

The question was left hanging, an open challenge now. This man was questioning the validity of the powers of White Wolf. He must be faced.

"My brother," Nils began, but Odin interrupted angrily.

"Wait! You have no right—"

"Stop!" The booming voice of Big Tree broke in. "Cat Skin, *I* have seen the powers of this holy man. *I* have seen the stone change. White Wolf will show you his gifts at the right time. This is not the time. You should know better than to ask another holy man to prove his powers!"

There was a heavy silence, finally broken by Odin, who spoke directly to Cat Skin.

"White Wolf will show you when the time is right, Uncle."

The disgruntled holy man merely nodded. Nils hoped that he had not made an enemy here, though he did not see what he could have done to avoid this confrontation.

Eventually, the decision was made to winter where the People were now camped. There was a scurry of activity, to build protection against the onslaught of winter.

It was only as they waited expectantly for Cold Maker to attack that Nils realized something. In all of the discussion, the choice had been considered that of staying here or moving on. There had not even been a mention of going back toward Straumfjord. Even staying here seemed to take them farther from the return journey home.

54

There seemed to be little organization among the People, once the decision had been made to winter where they now camped. It was understandable. The major responsibility for the year, the growing and harvesting of the grain, was behind them. There would be some hunting, maybe a fall hunt, but with the grain safe and the pumpkins and beans ready for storage, there seemed no urgency. Always before, for several generations, the People had merely readied the big communal lodges for the winter. They were already built, ready to move into when Cold Maker came roaring down. Now few people seemed to notice that there was no such refuge.

There was, of course, a scurry of activity to improve the flimsy family dwellings of brush and skins. It was apparent to some, however, that this would not be sufficient protection. Odin, who had seen more of the world than others of the People, was quite concerned over this lack of foresight. He attempted to initiate the construction of more substantial shelter.

"But we are not to stay here," a man protested. "It is useless to build a town."

This was, admittedly, a valid point. The construction of the massive earthlodges, sheltering as many as fifty people of an extended family group, was a major undertaking. It required heavy digging and moving of earth, not to mention the felling of sizable trees for the central posts and roof beams. This was not to be the answer, Odin realized. The problem, as he finally identified it, was that the People had no ready alternative. In his methodical way of thinking, a problem must have a solution. Hence, an alternative shelter of some sort, to be used for a season.

He considered the dwellings of the Downstream Enemy, which were adequate. Not as good as the lodges of the People. They had a tendency to be cold and drafty. Not as warm, even, as the structures built by the Norsemen at Straumfjord.

The thought had come to him unexpectedly as he pondered the situation. Now it had all his attention. There were things about that construction that he could not quite remember. . . . Four posts, at the corners rather than the center. More along the long walls. . . . Most importantly, these were structures that the colonists had built for exactly the same purpose that the People needed now: shelter for the winter. The Norse were building more permanent dwellings now, but the big longhouses had housed the entire colony at first. He must speak with Thorsson.

"I am not sure," Nils mused in answer to the question. "I am not a builder of lodges, you know."

"But you have lived in them."

"Yes. I see the need for this, Odin. Let us ask Fire Man."

Between the three of them, they began to piece together the general idea for a longhouse. It would be above the ground, to avoid the heavy digging. A row of posts to form each side wall, poles for the peaked roof. There would be an almost solid wall of poles, tied in place to form the sides and the flat slope of the roof. The cracks would be chinked together with dry grass and plastered outside with mud.

"The walls would be of stone in a place where we would stay longer," Nils commented.

Odin nodded. "I am made to think we can do this, Thorsson."

Svenson's battle-ax now came into a more peaceful use, that of felling and trimming trees for poles. Others of the extended family lodge watched for a little while, and then began to join in the construction. The longhouse rose quickly. Big Tree came to observe, and in another day or two another structure was rising a few paces away. The people working on this one were the relatives of the headman and his family.

People from the other towns came, saw, and started their own shelters for the winter. There need not be so many lodges, or so large as the permanent earth-lodges. These were for one winter, it was already understood.

Odin had some concern about the project. Not about the longhouse shelters. That was working well. His concern was twofold. First, that this construction might prove too successful, leading some to avoid the building of proper lodges later.

His other concern was about the two Norsemen who were now part of the People. He had seen the doubt in the face of Thorsson, now White Wolf, his sister's husband. Not doubt about the winter shelters, but about the original move. He, Odin, had deliberately been quite vague about the long-range goals of the People. He had implied in talking to the Norsemen that it was likely that the People would move back to a place near the coast in a year or two. That, he knew, was unlikely. He must, without seeming to do so, try to bring the outsiders into the ways of the People so completely that they would not *want* to go back.

He was not certain that he could do this. It was a great help, of course, that both had now married into the People. He was pleased at that for a number of reasons, and doubly so that White Wolf and Dove had been blessed with the child. That would make the ties stronger. So far, so good. Odin dreaded, however, the coming of spring after this winter in the new semipermanent houses. What would be the reaction of White Wolf and Fire Man when they learned that they had been misled? He did not relish the thought of their anger, which would surely be directed at him. He thought many times about how he would meet their accusations. Injured innocence? A protest that he had not known the general plan? Maybe he could convince the two that the entire move was for *their* protection. No, they would hardly believe that.

Well, there was nothing to be done, really, until after winter, and the People were ready for winter.

The longhouses were finished none too soon. Cold Maker's first probing thrust was not severe, but was a reminder of what lay ahead. It lasted only two days, a hard freeze and a light dusting of snow, followed by crisp nights and sunny days. The reminder served to bring about the final preparations for winter, and a last hunt or two.

One of the interesting developments before Cold Maker settled in for good was that of contact with those who lived in the area. Their initial contact had been cautious, but when the locals found that the People did exactly as they said, some degree of trust had developed. There were frequent visitations back and forth, and much trading. Interest in the others' crops was strong on both sides. They exchanged the seeds of corn and beans, and compared their various types of squash. They compared tools and weapons, and traded for arrow points, furs, and ornaments. They smoked together, and exchanged pipefuls of smoking mixture, and sometimes pipes or pipestone for carving.

They engaged in games and contests, shooting arrows at a target, throwing spears, running, wrestling. One of the games that was demonstrated by the hosts was played with a ball made of rawhide, thrown with sticks that were looped on the end and laced with thongs to form a sort of net. Some of the men of the People tried it, but the rules seemed quite intricate and the skills were totally unfamiliar.

More popular were the gambling games. Some were familiar to both groups. The stick game was popular, in which one player conceals several sticks in his fists, with only the tips showing. The other players attempt to choose the longest stick.

The plum-stone game, too, was seen often. Seven of the seeds were chosen, and each marked on one side with a dot of red, to contrast to the yellow of the natural color. The seeds were tossed on a flat surface by each player in turn, and the yellow or red surfaces showing were counted accordingly.

Virtually all communication was by hand signs and obvious motions. The two groups seemed to have no words at all in common. Even the tongue of the Downstream Enemy was closer to that of the People. But it seemed to make little difference. Odin wondered whether, if they had summered here in a season of poor harvest or scarce game, their hosts would have proved as friendly.

One thing was certain. The children had no problems between them. Like children everywhere, they became friends instantly, with the universal communication without words that is known to the very young and is usually lost with the coming of age. They skipped in circles, learning the playtime songs of the others, whose words had no meaning to them, but whose pleasure was apparent.

"This is my friend," one small boy proudly introduced another to his parents.

"It is good," smiled his mother. "What is his name?"

"I do not know," the child answered, "but he is my friend."

The decision to winter here and move on at the first opportunity in the Moon of Awakening was explained as soon as possible to the other group. This was undoubtedly a great help in avoiding friction. There were, of course, some misunderstandings, but it was in the best interests of both groups to avoid conflict. So cooler heads would prevail and the angered parties were separated and placated.

As the weather worsened, it was more unpleasant to undertake the trek across the ridge to the homes of the other group, so contact had a natural tendency to lessen. In fact, when Cold Maker howled, it was far easier to stay inside except for necessities. On better days a supply of wood was gathered, so that on worse ones, with wind-driven snow, sleet, and ice, it was possible to stay inside.

Days were growing shorter. It was the Moon of Madness, when everyone is uneasy. Grouse flew wildly into obstacles that they would avoid at other times. Deer were rutting, the bucks fighting for the favors of the females, oblivious to any outside danger. The bugling call of the great bull elk and the even larger moose were heard often.

Humans, too, became irritable. The migrating geese had virtually all passed overhead. The realization that it was really time to brace for the on-slaught of winter hung heavily over the People. Svenson said it was late November.

"What do the people call our December?" asked Nils.

"I do not know," Sven answered. "Let us ask."

Odin chuckled. "Ah, yes, the Moon of Long Nights. It is not a good thing to think of. The sun is dying. . . . Maybe this time it will really go out, no?"

How like the feeling at home, Nils thought. *Maybe this is the time that the frost-giants win after all.*

55

ell us more of your stories, White Wolf!" Odin requested.

It was a cold and snowy evening, but some of the families from one of the other longhouses had come over to smoke, gamble, and socialize. There were even a few men of the local tribe who had come over to visit. The snow had begun, and they had elected to stay over, rather than risk the trek back over the ridge in the increasing storm.

Somewhere in the distance, a wolf howled, and another answered. The wind, too, seemed to answer the wild cry as it moaned around the square smoke hole in the roof. Nils thought of the Wild Huntsman of his homeland, with his pack of wolflike hounds, flying on the winds of the storm, hunting for lost souls. It would be on just such a night that his grandfather would have retold that story, while the children huddled closer to the big fireplace with the boar's head mounted over the mantel. The baying of a hound before the storm was still considered a bad omen. He had promised to tell Odin more fully of the Wild Hunt, but the right occasion had not yet happened. Maybe this would be the time.

He used both the language of the People and the hand signs, to try to allow the visitors to participate, too.

"In my homeland," he began, "a night such as this would bring back this story. You hear the howling of the wolves, no?"

There were nods of agreement, and the listeners stared in rapt attention. Now, how to explain about the horse. . . .

"There are ways in our homeland, mine and Fire Man's, that are not found here. This you know already."

More nods.

"One of these is a creature, much like an elk without antlers."

"Like the female elk?" a listener asked.

"Yes, much like that. But the males have none, either."

"*Aiee!* How do they fight?"

"They do not fight much. They bite, and strike with their feet. But let me tell you . . . our people ride on the backs of these animals."

There was a murmur of disbelief, and some low chuckles.

"For what purpose?" a listener challenged.

"To go from one place to another. Or to hunt . . . this creature can run very fast. A hunter can *chase* the game, instead of driving it."

He saw that this was a difficult concept for the People, that of a hunt on horseback. Even the idea of a beast that can be *ridden* was apparently difficult for them to imagine. He glanced at Svenson, who was greatly amused by his predicament. He would be no help, here.

It was Odin who came to his rescue.

"Wait!" Odin called out. "My brothers, I have seen some things myself. White Wolf's people *do* have several kinds of animals, which they keep as we keep dogs. Now let him tell the story. It is not good to doubt before he begins!"

The listeners quieted a little.

"Thank you, my almost-brother," Nils began again. "Where was I? Ah, yes . . . our people sometimes hunt while riding on these creatures. This is one of our old stories, of a great holy man, a god-spirit, almost. He rides a beast that instead of four legs, has *eight,* so it can run twice as fast. He and his wife, with their pack of wolf-dogs, ride the wind in their hunt on a night like this. That is why we hear the howls of the wind and of the wolves. . . . Hear them?"

As if to punctuate the story, a distant howl drifted through the smoke hole. There was complete silence now from the listeners. Once they had gotten past the initial premise of a beast that can be ridden, there was no problem. It was a story, and even a creature with eight legs presented no reason for disbelief.

"Now you wonder, what would they hunt on this stormy night, and *why?* This is the answer. . . . They hunt not for game, but for the lost spirits of the dead. . . ."

There was a gasp from the listeners.

"Spirits?"

"Yes . . . they gather the lost, and take them away."

"To where?"

Nils was at a loss for a moment. For one thing, he was not certain how the original story ran at this point. The Huntsman was Odin, but he did not want to confuse the listeners by using the name of his wife's brother. But where did Odin take the souls as he gathered them? He could not remember that he had ever heard. To Asgard, home of the gods? To Valhalla? No, that was only for heroes fallen in battle, not for lost souls. How could he resolve this? The listeners waited.

Again, it was Odin who came to his aid.

"To the Other Side?" he asked.

Nils thought for a moment. He was aware of some of the customs of the People, and had seen how they cared for their dead. "Crossing over" was the expression they used. Yes, to the Other Side, the spirit world. This would help with the understanding of his story.

"Yes," he agreed. "He gathers spirits who have trouble finding their way, maybe, and helps them cross over."

Somehow, there was a big difference here, in the two cultures. Here, death was mourned, but as a loss for the living. The spirit would cross over to the Other Side. The dark chill of the Huntsman was a thing to be dreaded, which was somewhat different in tone. Nils had not realized this difference until now. The god Odin, though the patron of disembodied souls, was seen as dark and foreboding in his role as the Wild Huntsman.

Whatever the differences, his story had had a profound effect on the listeners. They huddled around the fire, and drew closer as the wind howled.

Then Odin spoke. "My almost-brother," he began, "tell us how this holy man of yours received such powers. Surely that is in your story."

Nils paused to think. It had been a long time since he had sat at his grandfather's feet to listen to the old Norse tales. Surely there must be one that would fit . . . the early stories around the events of Creation . . . Odin . . . Well, it would be necessary to explain the connection with his wife's brother to use it, but . . .

"You know," he began, "that my almost-brother here is called Odin because of his one eye. That is because the god-man in this story, who had the same name, Odin, had but one eye. This story is of how he lost the eye, but gained some of his gifts.

"One day he was walking, and came to a famous spring called Mimir, whose waters held the secrets of all wisdom. No one had ever taken a drink of this water, because it was guarded by a *kobold*." He paused, searching . . . had he told them about the idea of gnomes? "A small man with great powers. Had I told of them?"

"Of course, Wolf. One of the Little People," Odin prompted.

"Ah, yes, that is true. You have them, too."

There were nods of interested agreement. A distracting thought flitted through his head. *Does everyone, all cultures, have Little People?* The Irish have their leprechauns. Maybe the Little People are real. He drew himself back to his story. He must think more on that theory later.

"This little man guarded the spring, letting no one drink. Odin asked for a taste, and the *kobold* offered a drink in exchange for one of his eyes!"

There were gasps of surprise.

"Now, Odin, knowing that the waters would give him all the wisdom in the world, thought this was a good trade. He popped out one of his eyeballs and handed it to the *kobold,* who dropped it into the spring. It is still there.

"Now, with all the wisdom, this Odin was able to see that he still did not *understand.*"

There was a pause while the latter-day Odin helped to translate for the listeners the fine points of knowing, seeing, and understanding. Then the story continued.

"To give him more understanding, then, the holy man decided to fast and pray. He went to a great ash tree that shaded all of the world, and hung himself by ropes over the great canyon called Nifl-heim. He had wounded himself with his spear, to show that his heart was right for this. For nine days he swung there in the wind, without food or drink, praying, thinking, fasting, asking for help.

"When he finally cut himself down, he had been given great gifts. He now knew that he did not *need* to understand, only to trust."

"It was a vision-quest, then!" exclaimed Odin. "A young person goes out alone, fasting, to do this!"

Nils had never thought of it in that way. He was aware of the quest, as practiced by the People, but had never realized the similarity.

"Maybe so!" he agreed. "But this other Odin was also given other gifts, too. He came down from the tree with a set of magic signs, to be painted or carved. They were called runes. They could be used to cast spells, to tell the future, and they had great power."

It was apparent that the People were quite impressed.

"These are the source of *your* powers, White Wolf?" asked someone.

Nils thought for a moment before answering. It would be wise to maintain the aura of mystery that had come to surround his "powers."

"Partly," he said casually. "Those old runes and their meanings were partly forgotten. Some have been handed down through many lifetimes. I was taught their use by my father's father."

Nils had not expected for this casual storytelling to become so impressive to his listeners. They seemed fascinated by the idea of signs and symbols with magical powers. He was unprepared for a reaction of this sort, and rather puzzled by it.

Slowly, he began to reason it out. The People had no written language, though a few of their traditional symbols apparently had meaning. He thought of explaining that the runes had changed, over a long period of time, from magic and mystery to a means of expressing messages. The "new" runes, primarily for communication . . . *No*, he decided. It would be far too complicated to explain. He felt that he was already in over his head. But there was really no need, anyway. Why should he answer questions that were unasked?

Besides, there was the advantage of maintaining his own status as a holy man by implying magical gifts or powers. He had not begun the evening's stories with this idea in mind, but it had happened that way, and he was not quite certain just how. There was hint of mystery in that, even. How had it happened? He had certainly not caused it. Not intentionally, at least. He felt a recurrence of a feeling that he had experienced before for short periods of time. Mostly, since he had met the People. It was a feeling that he was caught up in a series of events over which he had no control at all. There was a strong temptation to fight it, to deny it. Yet equally strong was the feeling that denial would be useless, and understanding impossible. It was much more pleasant, it seemed, to relax and be carried along on the current of whatever it was that was happening.

It had been an evening of great power and mystery and magic. He felt very close to some of the truths of eternity that all men seek. Yet there was the strong feeling that many things are not meant to be learned or understood. The thought came to him that he felt much like the mythical Odin, dangling over the bottomless abyss, realizing the limitations of understanding. That, of course, was the point of the story.

Just then, the present-day Odin caught his eye, across the fire. Odin was looking at him and smiling knowingly. Singing Moose, the storyteller of the People, was beginning his tale of how they had acquired fire.

But Odin held his gaze on his friend for a moment, and silently communicated by a simple hand sign.

"It is good!"

Nils felt it too. Something had happened tonight, something that was important. Odin knew, as did Nils, but Nils was not sure what it was that they knew.

56

With the first signs of the Moon of Awakening, there began to be talk of travel. Odin was quite uneasy as to how the Norsemen would react. He found himself trying to avoid the inevitable confrontation. He knew, possibly more than most of the People, that it would be important to travel as fast and as far as they could before they stopped for the season to plant.

There was also a faction that was prepared to argue, favoring another year in their present location. That, of course, would be a mistake. The entire success of their friendly relations with those who lived across the ridge depended on the temporary nature of their stay. The People had initially stated their intention to move on. To do otherwise now would discredit their honesty. Their leaders knew it, and would not allow consideration of anything else. At least, Odin hoped not. It could lead to a dangerous confrontation, if not managed skillfully. A visiting nation of strangers might be treated with friendly curiosity if they were only passing through. Even if they stayed for a season, with appropriate diplomacy. Any longer, and they would appear to be a threat. No, they must move on, and as soon as it became practical.

Some of the more foresighted of the People were already packing. Each day brought a little thawing in the middle of the day, a steady patter of dripping snow-melt from trees and bushes. Falling drops punched small round holes in the smooth surface of the snow beneath. That, too, began to melt, first in tiny rivulets, joining into larger ones, which hurried downhill toward the great river.

Most of this runoff refroze each night, with resulting slippery footing. Certainly, it was not yet time to travel. It was time to think of it, though. Before long there would be patches of bare earth showing, and sprigs of green awakening from beneath the white robes of winter's snows.

As Odin had feared, Nils sought him out with questions. The confrontation could be postponed no longer.

"Has it been decided when we move?" the Norseman asked.

"No, White Wolf. It is not yet time."

"I know, but some have begun to prepare."

"That is true. But as you can see, it is not yet good to think of travel."

He motioned casually toward the sodden slope behind them, still largely covered with drifts.

Nils nodded.

"When the footing is better," Odin went on. "We can tell when the time is approaching."

Nils sighed impatiently. "Which way will we take?"

Now, thought Odin, *comes the difficult part. What if they demand to return?* Well, he might as well meet the question head-on. He feigned surprise.

"Why, on the trail," he pointed. "It goes two ways. We have seen one of them. Now, we try the other. Is it not so with your people, Thorsson?"

Nils had increasingly been called by the name that Odin had given him, White Wolf. Many of the People knew no other. Odin himself usually used Wolf, or White Wolf. Now, however, maybe due to the subject, he found himself slipping back into the usage that had begun at Straumfjord. It was partly unconscious, but he continued it for a reason. To be called by his Norse name might recall Nils's reason for his being here, exploration and discovery. At least, Odin hoped so.

The Norseman frowned. "I had thought of returning," he said flatly. "The trail here leads farther southwest."

"Have you talked of this with Calling Dove?" Odin asked.

"No . . . I thought to speak with you first. But the baby is old enough to travel."

Ah, thought Odin, *that answers one question. He does not intend to leave his wife.*

"Yes," Odin agreed, "but I had wondered. When you do go back, who do you plan to take? You spoke of the child. . . . His mother, of course. Fire Man?"

The Norseman appeared indecisive. "I suppose. We have not talked of it."

"Ah . . . and Red Fawn? Would she wish to go?"

"I do not know. She would go if she and Sven wished it, I suppose."

Odin nodded thoughtfully. "That is four, not counting the baby. Two small boats, or one of the bigger ones . . ."

"Well . . . yes . . . I had hoped that maybe you would go to guide us."

Odin appeared to consider a little while. Actually he was using the time to create a doubt. He knew quite well that it would be possible to guide them to Straumfjord and then return to his family, but he wished to make it appear as complicated as possible.

"Let me see," he said thoughtfully. "Myself, Hawk Woman, the children . . . Four more . . . Six grown people and three small children altogether. A big party, White Wolf. It becomes more dangerous with the children. The Downstream Enemy, you know." Maybe he could take a risk here. "Of course," he continued, "you and I and Svenson could go, and then I could return."

That remark fell into the conversation like a heavy stone into a still pool. The look on the face of the Norseman was quite gratifying, a look of distaste, almost of horror.

"No! I would not leave my wife and child."

Odin smiled inwardly. He now knew that he had won. He had correctly judged the relationship between White Wolf and Calling Dove. Well, he might leave a chance open for now. . . .

"Maybe," he suggested, "after the People find a place and settle there, we could make a trip back."

"Yes!" The Norseman jumped at the bait. "I can make some maps to take back. It is good, Odin!"

Yes, it is good, thought Odin. *That is resolved for the season.* Svenson would probably go along with whatever Thorsson decided. It was quite apparent, however, that as Fire Man, Sven was quite content in his present situation. He and Red Fawn seemed pleased with each other. Fire Man was increasingly popular with all children. Yes, he should be no trouble.

Nils approached Svenson with some misgiving. He was not certain how the old sailor would react.

"Sven," he began, using the Nordic tongue, "we must talk."

Sven appeared concerned at the serious tone.

"Yes?" He was whittling on a stick, and paused to brush away the chips in his lap.

"You know," Nils began, "that the People are preparing to move on."

"Yes. So?"

"Well, we had talked earlier of going back to Straumfjord."

"You mean, *now*?" Sven asked.

Now Nils was pleased. This might be somewhat easier than he feared.

"Not necessarily. After all, we *are* exploring new country, are we not?"

"Of course," Sven agreed.

"We can map the river, no?"

"Yes," agreed Svenson. "Did you know they talk of a sea of fresh water farther upriver?"

"Ah, I had forgotten that! Maybe we should learn more before we go back?"

"I am made to think so. See the People established . . . that will give us a base . . . a port. . . ." Svenson began to whittle again.

It had been easier than Nils thought.

"But you do want to go back? Later, I mean?" he asked.

"Of course. But we came to explore, no? We are learning much here, Nils. Are you making maps?"

"Ah . . . I had not. It would be good to do so."

"Yes. I do not know the runes as you do, Nils, but I can help you with maps, maybe. Will you draw on skins?"

Nils had not really considered this, but now began to wonder. He could hardly approach the quality of a parchment for his map, but a skin could be painted. All that would be really necessary was a directional arrow to indicate north, and lines to show the seacoast, the river, and the direction of flow. It should not be difficult to make such a map.

He had found himself staring at a small tree, one of the birch used to make boxes and containers of various kinds. Larger trees of the same species were used for canoes. The white bark was scarred here and there by the teeth of deer and elk that had chewed at it in winters past. Curiously, those scars were black, as if they had been painted on the smooth white surface. *Painted! Why not?* The idea grew quickly. A pair of square pieces of the bark, laced loosely together along one side . . . the inside surfaces could be painted with the map, and then tied shut to protect the diagram.

"Sven!" he said. "Look, the birch tree, there! Could I not paint the maps on birchbark?"

"Why not? The People paint on it, to decorate their boxes and packs, or anything else."

"It is good! I will try it."

He was thinking of something else, just noticed. Twice in this short conversation, Svenson had used the term "the People." That in itself was not unusual, but it was the way Sven said it. It was a hard thing to explain, but Nils had a strong impression about it. Sven said it as one would say *"our* People." A slight inflection of the voice, a subtle thing, a mere suggestion of a distinction between "we" and "they" . . . "ours" and "theirs." Sven had not really said "our," but "the." It was only an innuendo. Maybe, even, Nils was picking up on something that was not really there. Yes, that must be it.

He walked away, satisfied that he had been imagining the reaction by Svenson. He must have been mistaken.

Then he stopped short. He had forgotten for a moment that he had come to explain to Sven why it was best not to go back downriver just now. Before it was finished, Sven had been telling *him* the advantages of remaining with the People another season.

Now how had *that* happened?

57

I t was easier this time, to prepare and to begin travel. Last season the first few days had been a total disorganization. Now the People were seasoned travelers. Within a day or two the march had fallen into an efficient pattern. The distance covered daily was much greater than it would have been a year ago, and the confusion much less. The scouts were now more experienced, and consequently more skillful at their tasks.

The roadway spread before them, running parallel to the river. It was not a road built by anyone's intent, simply one that existed, shaped through eons of time by generations of moccasined feet. Maybe by bare feet, before that. Bare feet and the hoofed or clawed feet of the creatures that sought the easiest path from one place to another.

Basically, it is so with all roads. No one knows who was the first to use them. It happened many lifetimes ago, maybe at Creation itself. All creatures, seeking an easy path, follow that taken by someone or some*thing* that went before. The trail may change sometimes. An individual, dissatisfied with the path he follows, sees a better way. At least, he thinks he does. A short-cut, when weather permits . . . A longer but more comfortable way around a muddy area. The trail divides and comes back together again, to unite for a while.

An old trail, like that followed by the People on this journey southwestward, has changed many times through the ages. Climate changes, political changes take place, new groups come into the area, old enemies become allies, or vice versa, and trading patterns change. Still, over all, there are people who wish to go from one place to another despite disadvantages or risk, and the trail remains, becoming a roadway that will be used for centuries into the future.

Sometimes the People encountered lone travelers or small parties on the trail. A trader, alone or with a partner or perhaps his family. All of these used the hand signs fluently. They exchanged news and information about the trail, the weather, and the availability of game. Most of these travelers had passed along the trail many times. There are always restless spirits who must do this, who would be hopelessly lost if they ever settled down.

There are others, of course, who would be equally uncomfortable if they were unable to settle down. These must sink roots into the soil of a *place* that becomes their heritage. Mother Earth nurtures them and enables them to become identified with place. They become part of it, and it, part of them.

Mankind probably needs both of these spirits to grow. One extreme represents stability, the other exploration, a reach for that elusive something that is just over the next hill, or maybe just beyond the stars.

Travelers whom they met on the trail now more frequently mentioned the great freshwater sea. How far? The question often met with a shrug and a question in return: "How fast are you traveling?" The rate of travel of a large group is limited to the speed of its slowest member.

There came a time when people they met on the trail began to refer to "where the trail turns south." This seemed to be an important landmark.

"Why does the trail turn south?" someone finally asked.

"It cannot go on west," the trader signed. "There is the Big Water, the Ontario. One must travel south many days. Then the trail turns west again. How far will you go?"

"It has not been decided. We have to stop and plant soon."

"Of course . . . But there is a longer season as you go south. You should do well."

That was the attitude of every trader they had met, an eternal optimism. It *must* be so, for a trader, Nils thought. He must not hesitate to go into strange country. But precisely because the trader is occupied with what he does, he is considered immune to many of the local feuds and conflicts. He serves a useful purpose, which is respected by all, because he is needed.

"Is there danger where we are going?" Nils asked.

The trader laughed. "No, I trade with all."

"I mean, danger for *us*."

"Oh . . . I am made to think not. Your scouts, a day or two ahead, talk well with the signs."

"What nations will we see?" asked Odin.

The trader paused in thought. "Many different ones. Some are related." He thought a little longer. "Each is known by several names. One they call themselves, then maybe two or three others they are called by different neighbors." He spoke several names aloud, sometimes accompanied by a hand sign. "Abnaki . . . you have seen them—People of the Rising Sun. I am told you wintered near some of them. Mohauck, People of the Flint Place. Not the same as Mahican, Wolf People. Their tongues are different. Some say they are treacherous, but I trade with them. Delaware, related to them, also called Wolves. Oh, yes . . . after you turn south you will meet Chalagee, People of the Caves."

"*Aiee!* They live in caves?" asked Odin.

"Some do. It is a place of caves. Mostly in towns, sometimes a wall of poles around it. And they build mounds." He made the hand sign for a little hill.

"Hills?" asked Odin. "Really? They build them? Why?"

"It is part of their worship. A house on the mound for their holy men."

"We do not know of these Chalagee. Are they dangerous?"

"Not really. They are strong fighters, but not warlike, I think. They use a hollow stick to shoot darts at rabbits."

There was a pause while the problems of translation were attempted. The People were unfamiliar with the blowgun.

"Of course, they use a bow and arrow for deer," the trader went on. "And they are growers. Then, if you go on west, you would find Erie, Long-tail Cat People. Even farther, the Illinois nation, several different nations in one. But not this year. Your people cannot travel that far this year."

"It is good to know these things, my brother," signed Odin in thanks. "Come, will you eat with us?"

"It is good," signed the other.

It was only a few days later that the scouts sent back word that they had reached the place where the trail turned south.

"I have seen the Big Water," the messenger said. "The other side cannot be seen! It is *big!*"

"Have you met some of the people along the trail?" asked Big Tree.

"Yes, some. We told them of our plans. Some are called Mohauck. They have flint to trade. We might think of that as we go through their country."

"It is good," said Big Tree. "Any others?"

"We were told there are Delaware, the Wolf People. They are related to the Abnaki."

"The ones with whom we wintered?"

"Yes . . . they are the same, but different, maybe."

"But you see no danger from any of these?"

"It seems not. All appear to be friendly."

"It is good."

When the People first saw the huge body of water stretching before them, it was a time of great excitement. Some of them had seen the ocean, where the Big River empties into the sea and the water is salty. Even those were impressed by this magnificent expanse of open water.

"You really cannot see the other side!"

"And this is where the Big River begins?"

"We are told," said one of the scouts, "that there are other lakes beyond this, bigger still."

"*Aiee!* How can it be bigger than something that is too big to be seen already?"

Mostly, there was only stunned silence at the magnificence of the view.

To the Norsemen, such a body of water suggested only one thing: the possibility of putting a ship on it.

"It would have to be built here, on this lake," observed Svenson. "We have passed too many rapids."

"Yes," agreed Nils. "If there had been only that first one . . ." He let the sentence go unfinished. As they had traveled, it had become apparent that the river, which seemed so fine for navigation, had a number of difficult areas. For some distance it would be wide and deep, but then a stretch of rapids would interrupt the smooth waters. It would be possible to take a boat, even a sizable ship, around the rapids. They had done it. Once, surely. A second place, possibly. But here, on this magnificent river that in long stretches appeared perfect for the use of their longships, were not merely one or two impassable areas, but at least three. Probably more.

They had not spoken of it, but both Norsemen now realized that their dream was beyond reach. Ships might sail certain stretches of the river, might sail this inland sea, but not in continuity. Without speaking of it, Nils had several times thought of the old saying, *A man without a boat is a man in chains.* Somehow, it did not seem to carry the importance that it once had. He was experiencing a different kind of freedom.

Now, however, the sight of this great body of water stirred his Norse blood. How could one look on such a sight without one overpowering desire, to put a ship on it? In his mind's eye, Nils could see the billowing red and white sails of the longships cleaving their way through the blue waters of this unknown sea.

"Is it really fresh water?" he asked one of the scouts. "Not salty?" That was the thing that seemed most incredible.

The scout shrugged. "So they all say. We have not been clear down to the edge. But it must be. Our Big River runs out of it, does it not?"

"Where can all this water come from?" Nils wondered.

The scout looked at him strangely, and pointed to the sky. "Up!" he said. There was general laughter.

It was tempting to try to go down to the lake's edge to verify the puzzling

freshwater description, but it did not seem practical. The trail ran along the
ridges far above it, turning south rather abruptly at this point. They would
follow along the very irregular east shore at some distance away. Then, it was
said, the road would turn westward, and continue along the south shore, between the lake and the mountains. Maybe, thought Nils, they would have an
opportunity for a closer look. Surely there were inlets on this lake that would
make wonderful harbors.

Meanwhile, days were growing warmer, the grass greener. Soon, they would
have to choose a place to plant their crops.

58

T he scout trotted into the walled stockade around the town and made his
way to the lodge where the leaders waited.

"They continue to come this way," he reported. "It is as we heard. They
are many."

"These are the same who lived near the Delawares last season?"

"Not the Delawares," said another. "Somebody else . . . an ally of the
Delawares, was it not? No matter. These are the same."

"But what do they want? Why do they travel? And with families?"

"It seems so," the tired scout answered. "I saw women and children."

"Then they do not intend war."

"Does anyone know whether they planted last season?"

There was silence for a moment.

"They must have," said an old woman. "The Delawares grow only enough
for themselves."

There was general laughter.

"Not really Delawares, Mother," said a younger woman, "but you are right.
They must have planted to sustain themselves. How many are there?"

The scout shrugged. "Many . . . hundreds, maybe."

A murmur ran through the group, followed by a silence.

"If they are only passing through," said an old woman, "they would not be dangerous."

"That is true," said another. "But if they are growers, they must stop soon to plant. Then they would be here for the season. Is there room enough or game enough?"

"Do we know what tongue they speak?" someone asked the scout.

"Only that it is strange to us," he reported. "They use some hand signs, and some of the trade language. At least, so the Mohauks say."

"You have talked with them?"

"No, no. I spoke with a trader who had. The trader thinks that these whom he calls River People come from farther east, beyond the Abnaki, even. He thinks they are peaceable. He had traded with them."

"Ah! Does he know *why* they are moving?"

"He thought maybe they were driven out by an enemy."

"Defeated?"

"Maybe. Or to *avoid* a war. He did not know."

"There are more people all the time," observed an old man. "It is more crowded than in my youth."

There were nods of general agreement.

"The trader said he knows of others who are moving," the scout interjected. "People to the south of us are crossing the mountains, moving west."

"There is more room there?" another asked.

"Maybe so. At least, fewer people."

There was a brief silence, and then a question.

"Well, what shall be done?"

"I am made to think," said an old man, "that we should know more of these people before we decide."

"Yes . . . where are they now?"

"They have passed the place where the trail turns west, and are several days along it," the scout explained.

"Ah, they draw close! Could we capture and question one of their scouts?"

"Maybe. They travel two or three days ahead. I have seen them."

"*Talked* to them?"

"No, I avoided them."

"How do they act? Warlike?"

"Who knows? They are well armed, but I have talked to no one who knows of trouble with these people. They are just cautious, maybe."

"Yes, they have to be. Especially, if they seek a place to plant. How soon must they do that?"

Several people glanced around at one of the *kutani,* a priest or holy man who had said nothing yet. His garments marked his difference in calling. He wore a capelike robe woven with feathers and strips of fur. His was the responsibility for ceremonies for the crops, for needed rain, and for time of planting.

"I do not know their crops," he observed, "but I am made to think that corn must be in the ground soon. Half a moon . . . maybe a little longer."

"So, they must find a place very soon, no?"

"That is true. Our planting is nearly finished."

"Look!" a woman said. "We could not kill them *all* and it would be dangerous to try. Maybe we could get rid of them faster if we help them find a place to plant."

"But then they might want to stay!" protested another.

The argument rambled on. Finally it was decided. They must learn more of the intruders, and the most practical approach would be to question the advance scouts.

"What if they resist?" someone asked.

"Then we capture one. . . . Or kill him, if he seems too dangerous."

There was a chuckle, at the thought of one or two scouts presenting a danger to the warriors of the Real People.

"Well," said one of the elders, "let us catch one and see!"

The trail had broadened into a well-used thoroughfare in this area. After the People reached the westward bend of the road, it was apparent that it was heavily traveled. They met more travelers, in ones and twos like the traders they had seen previously. There were also other parties of varying sizes. Some may have been hunters, moving into an area favorable for a day's hunt. Others included women and children. People looked at the procession of outsiders curiously as they passed, sometimes smiling and signing a greeting. It was obvious that the presence of the People was of no surprise to anyone they met. The approach of such a large body would be news that had traveled quickly up and down the trail. Probably, word had spread in other directions, too. There were spurs and branches along the way, leading to other areas.

At the point where the route turned westward, a well-traveled branch split away to wind into the mountains to the south. The main trail seemed to continue to the west, however. There had been only one brief discussion before the People chose their route. Their most urgent need for the coming summer was a place to plant. Certainly, the likeliest spots would be in the rolling plain between the great lake to their right and the mountains to the south. It was really no decision at all. One seeks flat lowlands to plant corn, not mountains. They moved on westward.

Now, however, there was beginning to be a certain urgency. It was time to plant. They must find a site. The complicating factor was the presence of unexpectedly large numbers of people. The entire area seemed heavily populated. On some days they had passed not only several dwellings, but several clusters of lodges as well as a village or two. Still, information that they gleaned from traders suggested that there was more room and fewer people to the west. They moved on.

There was growing concern, however. In strange country, the seasons might be quite different. Not everyone was aware of this, but there was quiet discussion, always skirting around the question: How long is it until we *must* plant, or lose the crop?

Odin, more widely traveled than most of the People, was quite concerned over this. He sought out Nils one evening as they camped.

"White Wolf," he began seriously, "you have traveled much."

It was an odd statement, coming from Odin.

"Of course," Nils answered, puzzled. "We are here, no?"

"No, I mean . . . I am not sure what I mean, Thorsson."

Odin usually called him White Wolf, or simply Wolf. The use of the Nordic name sometimes indicated that Odin was in a very serious or philosophic mood. They sat in silence for a little while, watching the stars appear over the lake to the north. It was a warm evening, the air soft and quiet. The busy sounds of a large encampment were settling to a muted hum as darkness deepened. Halfway up the deepening vault of northern sky hung the North Star. Now Odin pointed to it.

"There," he said, "the Real-star."

"Yes," Nils answered after a long silence. "What about it?"

"It is always there, no? All others turn around it."

Nils was puzzled. "Of course." He had become aware in the past year that the Skraelings were far more knowledgeable than he had supposed. At least, more aware of the movements of the heavenly bodies. Even so, the observation that the North Star does not move like the others is a primitive thing. His puzzlement and surprise was that Odin would remark on a thing so simple. There must be something else. He waited, and in due time Odin spoke again.

"Thorsson, is the Real-star not lower in the sky here?"

Nils was caught completely off guard. He had come to realize that this was a highly intelligent man, but this question indicated a great depth of thought.

Odin was showing an understanding, or at least a glimmer of knowledge that involved the basic principles of modern celestial navigation.

"Yes," he said. "We are farther south."

Nils would soon be almost embarrassed by his lack of understanding of Odin's knowledge. He was still thinking to himself that it was clever of a primitive Skraeling to notice such things. But now Odin continued.

"And as we go farther south, the Real-star is lower, no?"

"Yes, that is true. When we sail on the sea, we use that to—"

Odin waved that aside, as if it were unimportant. "And this," he continued, "because we are farther from the lodge of Cold Maker in the north."

It was a statement, not a question. A statement that reflected the childlike simplicity of the Skraelings. Nils smiled and nodded patronizingly. Therefore, the next comment from Odin was a surprise, a complete shock.

"So," said the Skraeling, "that is why we can expect a longer growing season here."

Nils's mind whirled in confusion. He knew nothing of growing seasons, but it was apparent that once more he had badly misjudged Odin, and probably the People as well. The simple remark about Cold Maker was not childish whimsy at all. It was merely a way to express an understanding of the principles of climate in relation to latitude.

"So," Odin went on thoughtfully, "maybe we have more time to find a place to grow, more time than we thought."

Nils thought for a moment. The logic seemed to escape him.

"I do not know," he admitted. "Does the corn always ripen in the same number of days?"

"Yes, mostly. Some kinds shorter, some longer. And some difference with what sort of season, how much rain."

Nils had no comment. This was far more complicated than he had imagined. Odin was nodding to himself, lost in thought.

"Thorsson," he said finally, as if he had solved his dilemma, "here is my thought. If the corn takes the same number of days, but the season *has* more days, we could plant earlier, *or later*. It does not matter so much, here."

The Skraeling glanced over to see if an answer was forthcoming, but it was not. Nils's knowledge of agriculture was limited. He was aware that different crops are grown in different places, but the complexity of it all! He had not really wondered about it, but now he felt a little foolish. He had just learned something. He had been taught some very important principles by an illiterate Skraeling, a man he had once regarded as an ignorant savage. Nils hoped that his embarrassment would not show in the gathering darkness of early evening.

Odin seemed not to notice.

"I think I will go with the scouts tomorrow," he said thoughtfully. "I would like to see how the crops of those who live here are planted."

59

din was glad that White Wolf did not express interest in the idea. It was one thing for an extra scout to travel out ahead of the column. It would be quite another if the extra scout had blue eyes, yellow hair, and facial fur. It would be much better not to confuse further the initial contact with these Chalagee by the presence of the Norsemen. Man fears that which he does not know, and fear leads to unpredictable behavior.

He sought out Big Tree and told the headman of his idea. It was received with approval, although not with wild enthusiasm.

"Yes, it is good. See what you can learn."

The scouts were more interested. It would be pleasant to have a companion with whom to visit on the trail, and Odin was generally popular among the People. He would depart next morning with the runner who had returned to bring the latest news. There was a constant rotation to relay information daily, a shuttling of messengers back and forth from the advance scouts to the column. Usually there were two warriors together at the front at all times. If some misfortune befell them, one would try to return word to the main party.

So it was that Odin had decided to accompany the runner as he returned to the front to relieve one of the others.

"You will be careful, my husband?" Hawk Woman asked seriously. "I do not want to lose you again."

"Of course, Hawk. This is nothing. I will maybe not even talk to anyone among these Cave People. We just want to see their crops."

This was not quite true. He did intend to make contact, and possibly negotiate if he could. This had intentionally been left somewhat vague when he talked to the headman. Actually, Odin was looking forward to the challenge of meeting and communicating with these people.

"I will be careful," he assured his wife as he lifted the small traveling pack to his shoulders. "I will be back in two, maybe three days."

"It is good to have company," said the scout as they jogged along the well-beaten trail. "To travel alone is not my favorite thing."

Odin nodded. He was having a little trouble matching the stride of the runner. He was in fairly good condition, but this steady jog-trot for half a day at a time was using different muscles. There was little possibility of communication as they moved, because it required most of the breath in his lungs just to keep the pace. He resented, just a little, the youth and vigor of his companion.

They stopped to rest, and the tired muscles of his calves and thighs reminded him again that it had been some time since he had used the message-runner's jog. That was a task for younger men, like this youth by his side. That one now glanced at the sun, rose, and started on.

It was midmorning of the next day when it happened. The three men of the People had suspected since the sun rose that they were watched. There was much evidence of human habitation, but they had seen few people, except for the occasional travelers on the road.

On either side of that road were plots where fresh dirt gave indications of planting. Corn, probably, Odin thought. He had examined the little hillocks, taking care not to disturb anything.

A time or two, they had seen a hint of motion that suggested that they were watched. They discussed this, and decided to continue at their deliberate pace, an easy walk.

"It is often so," one of the scouts told Odin, making much of his experience on the trail. "They will contact us later, maybe. See, on the rocky hill to the left . . . do not be too obvious. There is a man in the rocks, watching us."

"He is not well hidden," observed Odin.

"Yes. He wants to be seen, to see what we do, how we act."

"There are probably more who watch from hiding," said the other scout. "They will meet with us when they are ready."

The whole experience was unsettling to Odin. He could not forget his capture and servitude by the Downstream Enemy, and all of his troubles since. To walk calmly, knowing that they were watched by the eyes of unseen warriors, was quite difficult for him. These strangers, of a powerful and unknown nation, could be very dangerous. Now *his* fear of the unknown made his palms sweat and his stride unsteady. Irritated at himself, he squared his shoulders and trudged on. He had chosen this, and would see it through.

They approached a place where the trail passed along the base of a rocky slope that rose sharply on their left. The way narrowed to pass between this hill and a rough, brushy gully on the right.

"Look!" said one of the scouts. "On the left."

At the crest of the hill, where a flat ledge formed the rim of the slope, stood a man. He was completely exposed, pointedly watching them. He carried a bow, and a knife or short ax at his waist. He was naked except for a breech-clout. The warrior made no move to raise his bow, or to make any other threatening gesture. There seemed nothing about him that would arouse suspicion. He continued to watch.

"He seems friendly," said one of the scouts.

"Yes, but he is farther away than a bow shot," the other answered sarcastically. "That makes him look friendlier. But he wants us to watch him."

"Should we stop and wait?" asked Odin.

"Maybe. But let us keep moving as we have been a little longer."

"I am made to think," said Odin, palms still damp, "that the rocks on the slope below him are a size to hide men."

"That is true. Let us be careful."

They were approaching the point where the trail squeezed narrow at the base of the slope. It would actually be necessary to step to the right around one of the great stones to continue. This block was a little less than the height of a man. It appeared to have broken away from the ledge near where the warrior stood, to roll all the way down to where it now rested. It had been there for a long time, possibly for generations, as indicated by the beaten path that curved around it. Other stones were scattered all the way up the slope, furnishing hiding places, a perfect place for ambush.

Nervously, Odin tried to estimate how many warriors might be hidden on the hillside. Could it be that these Chalagee made a routine practice of waylaying travelers at this point? It was natural to watch the man who stood in plain view at the top, distracting suspicion from the hiding places where warriors might be concealed.

Odin was about to speak a warning when the attack came. The warrior above suddenly raised his hand in a signal, and there was a rush of activity. Not from the obvious hiding places on the slope, but from behind the travelers. Men rose from the brushy draw to the right of the trail, weapons at ready. At least ten, Odin saw quickly, some armed with bows and others with spears. It was hard not to stare at the sharp flint points that now approached them in a half circle, penning them against the steep slope. A clever ambush, leaving no place to retreat. He tried to keep his composure, lifting his right palm in the hand-signed greeting.

The scout on his left suddenly seemed to panic. There had been no confrontation of this serious a nature before, and the young man apparently found the tension intolerable. He tried to run, only to find his way blocked by a large Chalagee with a spear. He turned, frantic now, with the warriors closing quickly, and tried to slip between two of them. His retreat was blocked again, and the scout rushed desperately at one of the attackers.

"No!" yelled Odin. "Stand still!"

But it was too late. The young man was beyond reason, irrational with fear. As he raised his hand to wield his knife, the more experienced Chalagee calmly stepped aside and swung a war club. The heavy hardwood ball at the end struck the scout full in the face with a sickening sound, and he fell, to lie twitching in the dust of the trail.

The full attention of the attackers was now turned to the other two. Odin still stood, his palm raised. The other scout quickly followed his example. There was a tense moment while no one moved, and then Odin began to sign, very slowly and carefully.

"We come as friends."

There were a couple of grunts of amusement, and one of the Chalagee pointed to the still form in the dust.

"That one was not a friend. He tried to kill me."

"He was afraid," signed Odin.

"And you are not?"

There was general laughter.

"I would be foolish not to be," Odin signed carefully.

More laughter.

"But reasonable men will talk," Odin went on. "May we talk?"

"Drop your weapons," ordered an older warrior who appeared to be a leader.

Odin did so, and his companion laid down his bow, also. The weapons were quickly retrieved by the warriors, and one stepped forward with a thong, motioning as if to tie their hands.

"Wait," signed Odin. "I cannot talk with my hands tied."

There was a chuckle, and the leader nodded. "That is true," he signed. "But you can talk later. For now, quickly: How are you called, and who are your people?"

"I am called Father of the Gods," signed Odin proudly. "Our nation is sometimes called River People, in the country where we lived."

There was a nervous giggle from one of the young warriors, which brought a stern glance from the leader.

"Why Father of the Gods?" he signed.

"It was given me by our holy man," Odin signed. "I am his assistant."

"You are a priest?"

"Yes," Odin signed simply.

"We would hear more of this," said the Chalagee leader, "but later. Now we tie you."

"Wait," signed Odin. "Let this young man go. He will tell our people not to enter the land of the Chalagee until we have permission. Our people mean no harm, my chief. We came ahead only to ask. You still hold me, no?"

The leader thought for a moment, and then shook his head. "No!" he signed. "We tie you both. After we have talked, we will see."

"But—" Odin had no desire to be tied. That was not a good part of his past experience.

"Silence!" the Chalagee signed firmly. "The question is not whether you are to be tied, but whether you will be allowed to live!"

Odin fought down the temptation to run or to attack their captors. He glanced down at the still form in the dust, whose face was crushed to a bloody pulp.

"It is as you say, my chief. But we have nothing to hide. Our hearts—"

The other interrupted with an impatient motion, and Odin quickly held his wrists forward to be tied.

"No," signed the Chalagee. "Behind your back."

60

There was some concern among the People when the expected scout did not return to report what lay ahead. Big Tree consulted quietly with other leaders. Even though there was a concerted effort to avoid alarm, rumors spread like a forest fire through the camp, growing as they spread.

What was known as fact was simply that the usual messenger had not arrived last evening. Sometimes the runner was late, but this time he had not arrived at all. A late-night council had been held, it was said, among a handful of the leaders. This led to the announcement that there would be no travel today.

It was then that the wildfire rumors roared into a flame of speculation and fantasy. It was discovered that Odin had accompanied the scouts, and that none had been heard from since. There was a general feeling that something was known by the leaders that was being withheld.

"Why did this Odin go with them?" demanded a man from one of the other towns. "What concern is it of his?"

No one seemed to know. With no activity to occupy them, the People grew more restless. By noon there was still no word, and a move was under way to demand a council.

Hawk Woman approached the little campfire where Nils and Calling Dove sat.

"You have heard nothing either?"

Dove shook her head. It was really a useless question. If either family had heard, the whole camp would have known. Hawk Woman sat down, and placed her baby to play with Dove's child nearby.

"Did my brother say when he might return?" asked Dove.

"Two or three days, maybe." Hawk Woman tried to sound confident.

It was not so much that Odin had not returned. He was not really expected. But the messenger . . .

"I am sure he is all right," Hawk Woman went on. "I do not expect him yet."

There was an uneasy silence, finally broken by Dove.

"Do you think something has happened to the runner?"

They glanced uneasily from one to the other.

"Maybe," said Hawk Woman. "Maybe he decided to stay over at one of the towns along the trail."

They all knew that this was wishful thinking. Something was wrong.

"There are bears here, no?" asked Hawk Woman.

"Not many," said Dove. "Too many people live here."

"That is true," Nils joined in the conversation. "We have to think that people are the cause of this."

"But the danger to my brother," Dove said carefully. "Is there not more danger to the runner than to those who go to talk?"

They exchanged glances, all of them hesitant to answer.

"There is no way to know," Nils said finally.

Hawk Woman drew herself up in an expression of confidence.

"My heart is good for this," she insisted. "My husband is strong and clever. He has been in worse places and his guide was strong."

"Will the leaders send someone to see?" asked Nils.

"Maybe," Dove told him. "They will decide at the council tonight."

As it happened, there was no council. Events happened too quickly. The weary runner, battered and scratched and reeling from exhaustion, stumbled into the camp a while before sunset, the appointed time for the council. He was taken directly to the campfire of Big Tree, and a crowd began to gather.

"Catbird is dead," the runner rasped hoarsely. "Odin and I were captives." He displayed raw friction burns where the thongs had tied his wrists. There were excited murmurs.

"You escaped?" asked Big Tree.

"No, they let me go."

"What about my husband?" demanded Hawk Woman fearfully.

"He is alive. He talked to them." There was a look of wonder on his face. "Odin made them to think that it was good to let me go and keep him."

"But *why*?"

"I do not know. He said to me— Wait! Where is White Wolf?"

All eyes turned to the Norseman.

"He said to tell you that this is as before."

Nils was puzzled. "As before?" What could that mean?

Big Tree interrupted. "Did he tell you what we should do? Send a war party?"

There was a ripple of approval.

"Yes, a war party!"

"They cannot treat the People so!"

Big Tree held up a hand for silence.

"Wait!" he demanded. "Let him talk."

"Odin did not say that," the scout went on. "I am made to think it would be a mistake. These Chalagee are very powerful. Their town is enclosed by a wall of logs."

"Logs burn!" shouted someone.

"Yes, and they will kill our brother Odin if we attack them," said Big Tree indignantly. "Now, let Black Hornet tell us. What did Odin send us, what message?"

The scout shrugged. "Very little, my chief. They did not want us to talk to each other. We were separated."

"But you said he spoke of White Wolf?"

"Yes. I did not understand that. Odin told them much of White Wolf, our holy man. I could tell that from watching his hand signs. Then as he passed me, he said in our own tongue to tell Wolf. They hit him then, and me, too, for trying to talk."

"Tell Wolf *what?*" demanded Big Tree.

"As I said. 'This is as before.' I did not understand. They were captured before, maybe."

Big Tree turned to Nils. "Does this have meaning for you?"

Nils racked his brain. Odin must be trying to get a message to him.

"I am not sure, my chief. We were captured before, but—"

"But you escaped."

"Yes. They let us go, really."

"You used your powers?" asked the scout. "I was made to think he meant something like that."

"Like what?" asked Big Tree.

"Well, he was telling them . . . I could see the signs, though I was tied a few paces away. He told them of Wolf's powerful medicine, and that he was the holy man's helper."

"And he said to tell Wolf that this is as before?"

Understanding was beginning to dawn to Nils. It was not the most comfortable of realizations, but he could see no other interpretation. Odin had convinced their captors, after the fight where the ships were lost, that it was dangerous to threaten the white-haired stranger. It must be now that Odin was attempting to create a similar setting, one to impress the Chalagee.

The more he considered this, the more the puzzle seemed to come together. Odin, finding himself a captive in a threatening situation, would do his best to think his way out. It had happened by accident before, the berserk incident. Odin had seized on that and turned it to their advantage. There were things about that which Nils still did not understand, but no matter.

What did Odin expect him to do now? Surely not the berserk thing. Yet he must do something. Odin had indicated that to the scout, or had tried to do so, even at the price of a beating. But *what*? *This is as before.* He reached back in his mind, trying to remember the events following their capture. He had been confused and numb after fasting and working himself into the berserker rage. Odin had established the mood before Nils was actually rational again. And how had he accomplished it? There was the suggestion that to kill a madman would loose a dangerous spirit, searching for a new abode. No, that did not seem to fit. Later, a little at a time, Odin had suggested demonstrations of the power carried by the "holy man," White Wolf. They had made a solemn ceremony of the sunstone, and later of Sven's fire making.

Suddenly it came to him. Odin was laying a foundation for a similar demonstration. Captured, questioned, and mistreated, Odin had played for time. As he did so, he had begun to drop hints that would excite the curiosity of his captors. Nils turned to young Black Hornet.

"Tell us," he said, "what Odin was saying to the Chalagee. You saw his hand signs?"

"Yes, some. He was tied, much of the time. But what I saw, he was telling of you, White Wolf."

"But *what*, of me?"

"Of your powers . . . the blue stone."

"Did he also tell of Fire Man?"

"Yes! Yes, I am made to think he did. How Fire Man uses no rubbing sticks, but brings fire from his hands!"

Big Tree interrupted. "Does this have meaning for you, Wolf?"

Nils nodded. "I am made to think so. Our brother wants us to . . . to use our gifts, as we did once before."

"How is this done?"

There was a pause as Big Tree realized that he had come close to asking about another's spirit-gifts. That would be quite rude, even in the urgency of the present situation.

"I mean," the headman went on, "what is needed now?"

"I am made to think," said Nils with great dignity, "that I must go to him."

"It is good!" announced Big Tree. "We will send a party of warriors with you."

Now a plan was forming, one that would create the greatest impression on Odin's captors.

"No, my chief. This is a thing of spirit, not of weapons. I will take Fire Man. Hornet can show us where to go. Maybe one warrior."

There was an instant reaction from one of the men in the circle.

"I will go," said Snake, boyhood companion of Odin and Hawk Woman. "Odin is my friend."

"When will you go?" asked Big Tree.

"Tonight," Nils answered. "There will be a moon later. Let Hornet rest while we make ready."

Svenson approached and spoke to Nils in their own tongue.

"What are we going to do?" he asked.

Nils looked at him, and noticed a gleam in the eyes of the old sailor. Sven, too, had realized what Odin intended, and was actually enjoying the excitement.

"We can plan the details as we travel," Nils said. "This has to be a good show, Fire Man."

Svenson nodded.

A day's travel to the west, Odin shifted his position, trying to ease the strain on his muscles. The abnormal angle that was imposed by his fetters was uncomfortable at best. After long periods of time it became almost unbearable.

All in all, he had not been treated badly, he reflected. He had been subjected to much worse in his previous captivity. These people had beaten him only a little, and then not with weapons, but only their hands. They had given him food, and had even untied him to allow him to eat and to make hand signs for a little while. There had been two episodes of questioning.

He had a strong impression that these people were primarily curious about the nature of the newcomers into their territory. That was as it should be. They would need to determine the purpose of this nation of people on the move. Would the People represent a threat to the Chalagee? And if so, what sort of threat? One of war, or merely an occupation of territory that was needed for crops? Yes, it was easy to see their concern.

The frustrating thing was that he could have answered their concerns if they had allowed him. Their meeting had started in a very unfortunate way, with the death of young Catbird. Odin regretted that, but he saw no way that it could have been avoided. He had the idea that their captors regretted the killing, too.

But after all, Catbird *had* attacked the man, driven by panic. That was no way to begin diplomatic negotiations.

Odin had felt from the beginning that his questioners were so impressed by that event that they were not listening to him. It was some time before an idea began to form in his mind. If he could arouse the curiosity of their captors, impress them, somehow. From that point, his plan fell rapidly into place.

He had already tried to convince them to release Black Hornet. That, he insisted, would let the People know of the power of the Chalagee, as well as their generosity.

"Why are you willing to be a captive in his place?" he was asked.

"Because my heart is good. The Chalagee will see that I speak truth."

He began to gain confidence after the thought came to him to use the expertise of the Norsemen. It had worked before. The problem was to get word to them. His captors seemed unwilling to let the two prisoners converse at all. He now hoped that the brief message that he had given to Hornet had been understood. If so, he believed that by tomorrow evening he would see White Wolf and Fire Man. If the message was not understood, then the People would probably send a war party. That, in view of the strength of the Chalagees, would be a great mistake.

Well, he could do nothing for now but try to rest. Finally, he drifted off into fitful slumber.

61

Odin lay, or rather propped himself against the wall of one of the lodges, hands still tied. After a fitful night of interrupted slumber, the day had dawned at last. At least, the bright rays of the sun gave him a sense of optimism that he had almost lost in the chill hours before dawn.

This should be the day that someone from the camp of the People would come. He hoped that the scout had understood his message, but could not be sure. After being cuffed for trying to communicate, there had been no further opportunity to attempt it. If he had realized that their conversation could be only a few words, he might have handled it differently. "Tell White Wolf to bring the sun-stone," maybe. Or perhaps, "White Wolf and Fire Man must bring their medicine." As it had happened, his only chance to say anything had been the partial idea, "Tell White Wolf it is as before." He would have continued with more detail, but the conversation had been interrupted. It was difficult now even to remember at what exact point he had been cut off. He *had*, he was certain, been able to say that this situation was like their previous captivity. The nagging doubt was whether the scout had understood enough of that interrupted statement to inform White Wolf properly. Today would tell. By sunset . . . well, if the People decided to attack the Chalagee he might be dead by sunset.

He would think of other things. A few paces away, three youngsters sat and watched him, chattering among themselves. There were two boys and a girl, probably of eight or ten summers, he thought. One of the boys carried a stick of about his own height. By the way the youngster handled the object, it seemed to be something of importance. It was regarded with respect, somehow.

Puzzled by this, Odin focused his gaze on the youth and his stick. Could it be a weapon of some sort? Then he saw . . . yes! A hole in the end. The stick was hollow. He recalled now that a trader had spoken of this weapon of the Chalagees. It was primarily used for hunting squirrels or birds, the man had said, had he not? A puff of breath through the hollow tube would blow a small arrow as fast as the eye could follow.

Now that Odin realized what sort of implement the young man held, his attention was totally absorbed by it. He did not know just how dangerous the blowgun might be. To add to his discomfiture, the boy kept swinging the tube slowly back and forth, pointing it at the captive. It was very disconcerting to watch the round mouth of the weapon move toward a position where it pointed directly at him. Then it would sweep on past, Odin would relax, and the children would giggle. He must have shown his concern more than he realized, because the game was repeated. The boy pointed his blowgun, as if threatening, and then lowered it, and the others laughed.

If his hands had been free, Odin could have talked to them in signs. That was impossible under the circumstances. He also realized that his reaction was important. If he showed his concern, the game would continue. He tried to appear calm, even bored, lifting his gaze to watch a fluffy white cloud high overhead. He was dimly aware that the boy with the blowgun was moving it around, but he determined not to look.

There was a light *thunk* beside him, and he glanced down involuntarily. Only a hand's span from his left shoulder, a dart protruded from the bark-covered log of the lodge wall. It was slender, as long as his fingers, and a fluffy little plume of feathers or thistledown was tied to the shaft. The children were laughing in delight at his reaction, and a chill came over him. This could be a dangerous situation. He was virtually defenseless, and at the mercy of children who might not be possessed of good judgment. If the darts could kill a squirrel or a bird, they could do much damage to unprotected flesh. A deep wound to the chest might collapse a lung. Or a wound to the face . . . he cringed at the thought, and then the full import of his danger descended on him. *His eye . . .*

Odin had adapted fairly well to the loss of his eye some years before. He could still see, and he was still alive. With the inborn stubbornness that was his, combined with a basic optimism, he had made a success of survival. Now, however, he faced a situation even worse than his mutilation at the hands of the Downstream Enemy. He glanced again at the slender dart beside him. If he were struck in the eye with such a missile . . . It was too horrible to contemplate.

He watched, fascinated, as the boy chose another dart from a pouch at his waist, and inserted it into the rear end of the tube. Then the game began again. The wavering mouth of the weapon swept slowly across him. The girl was giggling. Odin could hardly stand to watch as it pointed directly at his face. There was no way that he could defend himself, even to raise a hand to stop the dart, to protect his vision. He could turn his head to give partial protection to the eye, exposing the already blind side. That was little comfort. In so doing, he could not see his tormentor. Such a position would also expose his ear. In the mind of a youthful tormentor, that opening might be an inviting target. Odin shuddered again. That polished hardwood dart . . . Ah, he must not even *think* such thoughts!

He tried to estimate a position for his head that would at least partially protect his eye, yet not expose his ear to direct danger. It was not easy, and even more difficult to remain calm. He was sweating profusely, waiting, knowing that soon, or maybe later, another dart—*thunk!* He looked quickly. This one was at his other shoulder, again about a hand's span away.

Somehow, it was reassuring. The boy was apparently skilled with the weapon, and was merely teasing him. Odin was able to regain some of his composure while the youngster reloaded. Again, the tube of the blowgun scanned back and forth across Odin's bound figure. With a little more confidence, he managed to maintain an expression of pride and dignity. There was actually a look of disappointment on the face of the Chalagee boy.

Then, an idea seemed to dawn. The boy lowered the aim of the tube. Odin was sitting propped against the wall, knees bent slightly, and spread apart by a couple of hand spans. It took only an instant for Odin to realize that the blowgun was pointed directly at his groin. Instinctively, he clapped his knees together, protecting his private parts. The children howled with laughter.

Now a new dimension of danger was added. He had reacted so definitely that they were amused, and this was not good. They now knew that they could affect his mood and his reactions in another way, by a threat to his manhood. He stretched his legs out flat in front of him, knees together. The blowgun hovered with its aim at his lower abdomen. Even that, he knew, could be a dangerous wound.

The boy apparently tired of waiting for Odin to spread his knees again, and loosed another dart.

This one struck the ground just beside his right hip. It was close, too close. He flinched involuntarily, and there was more laughter. This had missed his thigh by less than two fingers' width. Odin tried to tell himself that it was good, that this proved the boy's skill, but he was not convinced.

Now the other boy, who had been quiet, seemed to initiate a conversation. It seemed to involve the blowgun. In a little while the first boy handed the weapon to the other, a bit reluctantly, Odin thought. It was disconcerting to see that this one handled it clumsily, as if it were unfamiliar to him. It was certainly not reassuring, then, when this boy reloaded the tube and began the taunting game again.

The first dart missed Odin by an arm's length. It quickly became apparent that it was a mixed blessing, however. The studied preparation by this boy as he readied his next shot said plainly, "This one will be closer."

Even as he realized this, Odin was unprepared for the sharp jab of pain that struck his left shoulder. The shaft of the dart was protruding completely through the meaty part, with the ball of fluff sticking like a bur to the front of his buckskin sleeve. He realized that he had cried out involuntarily, and regretted the loss of dignity.

Odin need not have worried. It was apparent by the look on the shooter's face that the boy realized he had made a great mistake. He almost threw the blowgun back to its owner as he jumped and ran. The other two followed in the twinkling of an eye, and Odin was left alone. That was a relief, but the wooden skewer in his shoulder would not let him enjoy the fact that the children were gone.

A woman looked out of a doorway to glance around the area. Almost as an afterthought she turned for a look at the captive, and stopped short in amazement. She hurried across the open area, talking loudly to no one in particular.

She paused to study the plumed darts in the wall and the one in Odin's shoulder. For a moment, she seemed to consider pulling it out, but decided against that course of action. Instead, she raised her voice in a call for help, and people came running.

There were exclamations of surprise and even of irritation, much gesturing and pointing to the darts. Odin had the impression that his tormentors were known, and that they were probably in trouble. Meanwhile, the jab in his shoulder that had struck like a swarm of hornets had now steadied to a dull ache, except when he tried to move it. Then it was a massive thing, spreading up his neck and down his arm. He did not see how such a tiny wound could cause such misery.

An older man joined the crowd, and the others parted to let him approach. The man examined the skewer, shook his head, and muttered something. Odin had a strong impression that this was a sort of holy man, but different than the *kutani,* the Chalagee holy men who lived in a special lodge on a hillock at the edge of the town. This one seemed more like the men of the People who had the gift of healing.

Now the old man gently touched the dart, then grasped it firmly and gave a quick jerk. There was an instant when Odin felt that the bone itself was being pulled out through the skin, but there was quick relief. The old man brought out a gourd with a greasy salve and rubbed some of it on the wounds, both front and back. Odin nodded his thanks, and the medicine man returned the nod.

People began to drift away, sometimes laughing. To Odin there was very little humor in the situation, but he understood. He wondered what sort of punishment might be directed at the youngsters.

Even more, he wondered what the People were doing. He glanced at the sun. Shortly past noon, it seemed. Sometime between now and dark, he should know something. He hoped it would be good. He did not know, even, if White Wolf had received his partial message.

He shifted his position to wait again, and his shoulder throbbed dully.

62

The hill up ahead," said Black Hornet, pointing. "That is where he stood. They were hiding to the right, there, when we came along the trail."

It was a well-planned ambush, Nils saw.

"And they killed Catbird?"

"Yes, with a club . . . in the face."

"Yet they did not try to kill you, or even harm you?" asked Nils.

"No. I was made to think that they only wanted to capture us. Catbird tried to escape. He attacked one of the Chalagee."

Nils nodded. It seemed likely that the plan had been capture, but something had gone wrong. The favorable part of the situation was that the Chalagee had released the scout, with a message that they wished to talk. That was a start. The darker side was that the Chalagee still held Odin, and there was no way of knowing his status or condition. That was a worrisome thing.

There was also the concern that the situation they were walking into could become very dangerous. They had seen signs that they were being observed all through the morning's travel. Now they were nearing the place where the scout party had been ambushed, and Hornet was becoming quite uneasy.

"Hornet, if they wished to kill you, they would have done it," Snake told him.

The scout smiled ruefully. "I know. But you were not here, Snake. To see Catbird struck down . . ." His sentence died uncompleted.

"They will probably contact us at the same place, no?" Svenson suggested.

"Yes, I am made to think so," Hornet said nervously.

"It is good," Nils spoke. "Let us move up near where the trail bends around the rock there, and stop to wait."

Before they reached that point, however, the sentry at the top of the hill stood to allow himself to be seen. It was apparent that it was a deliberate move.

"There! It is as before!" said Hornet excitedly. "We were watching him and the slope above the trail, and they came from the other side, behind us."

"From those bushes?" asked Snake, being careful not to point.

"Yes, to the right of the trail."

"It was well-planned, no?" Snake observed.

"Yes," Nils agreed. "Let us keep walking, but stop before we reach that point."

The four men did so. When they were about a long bowshot from the spot where the ambush had taken place, they paused by common consent. At first nothing happened. They stood and waited, trying not to let their nervousness show. The observer on the hill waited, too.

After what seemed an eternity, a warrior emerged from his concealment in the bushes and stalked over to stand in the middle of the trail, facing the newcomers. Soon he was joined by others, six in all, who drew up in a casual line across the trail, blocking passage. They waited.

"Let us move toward them," suggested Nils.

He raised his palm in the hand sign for peace, and stepped forward. The Chalagee party waited for them to approach. Svenson was carrying his battle-ax, and it was apparent that the warriors were curious about such a weapon. No more so than they were about the appearance of the Norsemen. There was a murmur of talk among the Chalagee warriors, which was cut short by the older man who appeared to be their leader.

Now, thought Nils, *it begins*. He must think and act as Odin would do, playing the part that fate had assigned him. He tried to consider himself the powerful holy man that Odin had envisioned.

"We fight only if we must, to defend ourselves," he said quietly. His companions nodded.

Nils walked to within a few paces of the warriors and then stopped, assuming a firm stance in the middle of the trail. His right hand was still raised in the peace sign, but there was no response yet from the Chalagee. Well, he must do *something*.

"Our brother here says that you hold my helper. How is this?"

He tried to look confident, and to appear in command of the situation, which of course he was not. The party of the People was outnumbered, and facing well-armed, capable-looking warriors. If it came to a fight, however, Nils thought that they could handle themselves well. Svenson alone was probably worth two men. But of course, he reminded himself, if it came to a fight, they had already failed Odin.

In his opening gestures, Nils had tried to seek the initiative. His question as to Odin's capture was expressed in the hand sign for an inquiry. The same gesture asks *how, where, who,* or *why*. A stronger, more demanding question, perhaps, than one could ask in words. In effect, it was a demand: *Explain your actions!*

This seemed lost on the Chalagee, who completely ignored the question.

"How are you called?" he demanded. "You have come onto Chalagee land."

Nils took a deep breath. He did not like the part he was forced to play. He was not even certain how to play it. He wished that Odin were here, to tell him what to do.

"I am White Wolf, of the River People," he signed. "This is Fire Man, my helper. You have my other helper, Father of the Gods. *Why?*"

Again, he used the demand.

If the truth were known, the Chalagee leader was probably more shaken over the meeting than the Norsemen. They had not half believed the tales of their captive. A holy man with white hair and facial fur . . . Another, whose hair and face-fur gleamed red like the fire. That one carried a strange weapon, too. At least, it looked sharp, like a weapon. One would certainly not want to learn of it in a wrong way.

"It is all as the captive said," one of the younger warriors whispered in wonder.

Blue Tree motioned him to silence, but he had been thinking along the same lines, himself. It was expected that any captive would make exaggerated claims to try to improve his status. No one had really believed the one-eyed father of gods, as he called himself. It was quite disconcerting, then, to find that so far, every absurdity that the man had voiced was precisely true. Maybe they should have treated him with more honor. . . . No, probably not. The captive had not really been hurt. Too bad, though, about the blowgun dart. Children sometimes show poor judgment. Luckily, there had been no major injury.

But just now, it was time to think of other things.

"The one-eyed one is our guest," Blue Tree signed. "Come, we will take you to him."

Two warriors stepped forward as if to take the weapons of the travelers, but Svenson hefted his ax in an unmistakable gesture, and the young men stepped back. They glanced at their leader, who shook his head.

"It is not needed," he told them.

"Tie their hands?" asked one.

It was a stupid question. How could they tie the hands if the would-be captives were still armed? But here was an opportunity to curry favor with a potentially powerful holy man. Blue Tree spoke both in his own tongue and in signs.

"Of course you need not take their weapons," he said, as if that had been the question. "These are our guests."

He turned back to Nils.

"Come, White Wolf. We will take you to your brother, Father of the Gods."

He led the way along the trail and they followed, the two parties still eyeing each other suspiciously.

It was really not far to the stockade that surrounded the village. It was strategically placed beyond the ridge, not openly visible from the road. The village, however, overlooked the trail, allowing easy observation of the traffic at any time, merely by stepping to the crest of the ridge. At the nearest point, the trail was only a bowshot away.

Children came running to see what was happening, and the Chalagees warned them back. By the time they entered the stockade and made their way toward the center of the town, a sizable crowd had gathered, trailing along with the principles. There was an excited buzz, many of the remarks obviously directed to the striking appearance of light-colored Nordic hair and beards.

Their escort stopped, and a man who seemed to have more authority now emerged from one of the houses to approach them. In a few moments, there seemed to be a loosely organized party of leaders, including a couple of women.

Nils repeated the peace sign, which was now returned courteously. He decided to try to take the initiative.

"How is it," he asked, "that you hold our brother? And you have killed another. We come in peace!"

The others exchanged glances.

"What do you want?" one of the leaders asked suspiciously.

"We would talk. But first, our brother, Father of the Gods?"

The man who had just spoken turned and made a gesture, and a couple of warriors led Odin, his hands tied behind him, from behind one of the lodges. His glance met Nils's, and the old glint of mischief showed that Odin was basically unharmed.

"It is good," Nils signed. "May he now be released?"

"We would talk," said the other.

"That, too, is good," Nils agreed, "but let us free my brother's hands."

The man seemed to consider for a moment.

"The fire!" Odin called.

Nils nodded to indicate that he understood.

"My chief," he signed, "let us have a council fire. Fire Man, here, will make one while we prepare to talk. Is there a little wood?"

"Yes, of course."

He motioned, and a couple of older children scurried to bring an armful of sticks.

"Here?" signed Svenson, asking permission. The leader nodded.

Nils watched as Sven began his preparation. He had been amused before at the natural showmanship of Fire Man. Svenson, in the few times that he had used the flint and steel as a demonstration, had managed to make an impressive ceremony of it. Even so, it was quick.

Sven lifted the tinder of shredded cedar bark toward the sky, tucked his scrap of charred cloth into it, and knelt to strike the spark. Never had a spark flown so well. One or two strokes, and Sven palmed the steel to lift his tinder, blowing his breath gently from beneath as he offered it to the sky again. A dense white smoke, a burst of flame . . . He thrust the little blaze into the cone of small twigs that he had prepared, and stood, arms spread to indicate that his ceremony was finished. There was a murmur in the crowd. The rapidity with which the flame-haired stranger had kindled a fire, and even without the use of rubbing-sticks, must have seemed miraculous.

"It is good, Fire Man." Nils turned to the Chalagee leaders. "Now you have freed my brother there. Let us talk."

Odin was allowed to join them, rubbing stiff wrists as he did so.

"You are all right?" Nils asked.

"Yes. We talk later. Show them the stone."

"Do we need it?"

"Maybe. We can start the council first."

The Chalagee were showing signs of irritation, and Nils turned back to them.

"It is good. Now, let us talk."

They seated themselves around the fire, the People on one side and the Chalagee on the other.

"Now tell us," the man who had done most of the talking signed, "how it is that your people have entered our country."

Nils shrugged, as if it really made no difference. "We are only passing through." He started to go on, but was interrupted.

"To *where?*"

"We do not know, my chief. When we find the place, we will know it."

"It is a quest, then?"

"Yes," whispered Odin. "That is good."

"Yes, my chief," Nils signed. "We have heard there is more room, not so many people, to the west."

"That is true, maybe."

"Our people, called the River People by some, do not want the land of others. Only a place to plant."

"What do you plant? It grows late for planting."

Nils glanced at Odin.

"Corn, pumpkins, beans," signed Odin. "We had hoped to ask the advice of the Chalagee, for this one season only. Is there a place to plant and maybe winter, then move on?"

The Chalagee exchanged glances.

"We must consider this. You would hunt?"

"Some. Mostly, a place to plant," Odin signed.

"Wait," signed the Chalagee. "Who is the leader here?"

Nils and Odin exchanged glances.

"Neither, my chief," Odin signed. "As I have tried to tell you, this is White Wolf, a holy man. Fire Man and I are his helpers. These others are warriors of the People. Our leaders are camped a day's travel away."

"Yes, we know. Well, let us talk of this, and we will meet again in the morning."

He rose, indicating that the council was over.

"Someone will show you where to camp tonight," he said as he turned away.

63

The corn was well sprouted now, pointed sprigs of green pushing up through the black loam to reach toward the sun. And it was good.

It was good, too, after the initial period of suspicion and distrust passed. The Chalagees had, after meetings that seemed to go nowhere, suddenly announced their willingness to help the People find a place for summer camp, as well as an area for planting.

"Their ways are very strange," observed Calling Dove.

"That is true," said her husband. "We talk, the leaders talk, we seem almost ready to agree. Then they say, 'We will think on this, and talk again tomorrow.' They never decide anything."

Dove laughed. "That is your way, my husband, to decide *now*, before thinking. My people go more slowly."

A year ago she would not have thought of teasing him so. The heat of
their romance had, while not cooling at all, ripened into one of solid friendship
and understanding. She could tease him and know that he would understand
and appreciate the humor in it. Then they would laugh together, and tickle and
giggle like children. It was all a matter, she had learned, of *when* to tease him.
Sometimes it was not the right time, if she found him too serious. But she was
learning. She had an increasingly better feel for her mischievous antics. It was
merely that she must be cautious. To initiate such an episode when he was lost
in serious thought could provoke an angry retort, and White Wolf would pout
until evening. Usually, after darkness fell and they sought the sleeping robes she
could find ways to influence him, and correct her error.

The occasions when she was guilty of errors in judgment were fewer now,
however, and the resulting periods of sullen noncommunication were shorter.
Their relationship was ripening, and Dove knew that her marriage was the envy
of many young women. Older ones, too, probably. She often smiled quietly to
herself at such thoughts.

Today, she was not quite certain. She had ventured to poke fun at the
tendency of the Norsemen to make sudden decisions. That was their way. The
way of the People was easygoing, more accepting. Why make a decision until it
is really necessary? They had discussed this, though not at length.

This time, he was very quiet after her gibe at his impatient tendency to act
on impulse. She studied him covertly. No, he was not angry. Just lost in
thought. That was good. Still, it was a relief when he spoke, quietly and
thoughtfully.

"But the Chalagee are different from either. Maybe . . . Dove, do you
think they have some ritual by which to make decisions?"

"What do you mean?" she asked, puzzled.

"Well, it is as I said. We meet, then they stop the council, and nothing is
decided until the next day. Or even longer, sometimes. Then, when they come
back, they have decided. What did they *do*, between? Is there a ritual, or a casting
of . . . of a spell, or something, that tells them?"

There was a slight problem with finding words for such complicated ideas.
White Wolf had learned the basic tongue of the People, but things like ideas
require more words. Still, he was doing well, she thought. Dove watched an eagle
soar across the valley and land ponderously on her nest in a tall spruce.

"Or," continued Nils, thinking aloud, "do they get their answers from
dreams?"

Dove was startled. That was a possibility, of course. "Do *you*?" she asked.

She was still in awe of his powers as a holy man. That was a subject that she had never dared to bring into their conversations. It was too great for her to comprehend, and she was far more comfortable if she kept that part of White Wolf completely outside their relationship.

"No," he said quickly. "Well, maybe sometimes."

He was distant, lost in thought. Dove waited, unsure.

"There is a saying among my people," he went on, slowly, "about 'I will sleep on it.' An answer to a problem is easier after sleep, sometimes."

Dove nodded. "That is true. But . . . dreams?"

"Dreams, visions, maybe it is all the same. Do you think so?" he asked.

"Maybe. But you think the Chalagee might do something to help them dream?"

He considered a little while. "I wondered," he said finally. "They always seem to wait overnight. A prayer, maybe? It is not long enough for fasting."

"I do not know, Wolf. But they will tell us when they are ready."

"*If* they decide to," he corrected. "If not, we will never know."

They chuckled together, and turned back toward the camp.

"The corn grows nicely," Dove observed.

"Yes! Their *kutani* told us well on that."

Diplomatic relations had gone well, except for the tragic death of young Catbird in the first encounter. That had been accepted as a misunderstanding by both sides, and regrets exchanged. There had been no further incidents. Actually there had been little social contact at first. Both groups were cautious. A major factor, however, was the fact that the planting must be done immediately. The People worked hard and long, while curious Chalagees watched their methods. As growers themselves, they could relate to the planting of the crops.

Now, with the fields of the various types of corn sprouting well, there was a little more time to relax and become acquainted with these strange people on whose hospitality their season's success depended. Later, it would be necessary to weed the fields, but not yet.

"There is to be a story fire tonight," Dove said conversationally. "Hawk Woman told me. Shall we go?"

"Are Hawk and Odin going?"

"Yes. You know how Odin likes the stories."

They chuckled together again.

"Yes. He will probably want me to tell those of my people, no?"

Dove laughed. "Probably. But Wolf, yours *are* good stories. Oh, yes . . .

Hawk says the Chalagees' Creation story has them coming from the sky, not the earth!"

"Really? How does she know?"

"My brother heard it. You know, he talks to them."

"Odin talks to everyone, no?"

She laughed. "Yes, but Odin is cautious. And very skilled."

"That is true. Well, let us go. I would know more about this coming from the sky. My people tell of a path from sky to earth, you know."

"A road?"

He paused, having no words. He tried to describe the Asabru, the rainbow, a "bridge" formed of light, air, and water.

"Oh, yes!" she exclaimed. "Maybe that is how the Chalagee came down, no?"

Nils smiled at the eager interest in her eyes. "We will see," he said.

The story fire was well attended. It was the first major social event between the People and their Chalagee hosts. It was held on neutral ground, near the Chalagee village, largely because of the great number of people involved. There was no gathering place large enough inside the stockaded village.

Several storytellers would be involved. Singing Moose of the People and First Cloud, one of the older Chalagees, would apparently be the featured speakers. Another man from the other village of the People would also contribute.

The fire was lighted, the pipe passed, and First Cloud began his story. He used both words and hand signs. Some of the People were learning the Chalagee tongue, but mostly their communication was by the simplified trade language. They had picked up this tongue as they traveled, the past two seasons. So there was little difficulty in following the tale of the storyteller. It was helped, of course, by hand signs. Occasionally, when a word or an idea was obscure, Singing Moose would try to assist with a word or phrase in the tongue of the People.

"In the beginning," First Cloud intoned solemnly, "the earth was only water."

The People glanced toward each other in amazement. They had heard several widely different stories of the Creation, but never anything like this. Even White Wolf's stories of fire and ice . . . But it would be impolite to interrupt, and to their credit, the People maintained their composure.

"Our people, the Real People whom you call Chalagee, lived in the sky above the Sky Dome."

There was a pause for clarification. The listeners were unfamiliar with the concept of the Sky Dome, and there was a short discussion with signs and attempts at various tongues.

"It is like a blue bowl or basket," explained First Cloud, "upside down over the earth. It is made of solid stone. Sun crawls across the Dome each day, and under the western edge. She stops for a little while at midday, straight overhead. Her daughter's lodge is there, and she stops to eat."

The listeners were puzzled. This was a very unusual story, unlike any they had heard. True, the sun *does* seem to pause at midday, but . . .

"Now," First Cloud continued, "let us go on. Our people, the Chalagee, were on top of the Dome. Down below, there was only water, with the Sky Dome floating on it. No place to stand. So, what to do? They sent down a diving bird, the Loon, to see if there was a bottom. It did not even come back up. The Beaver tried, but could not reach the bottom. Finally, the Water Beetle, grandson of Beaver, stayed down a long time, and came back with a little glob of mud. Another dive, a little more mud, spread out on the surface. Another dive, and yet more.

"Then the Great Buzzard decided to help, by fanning the mud with his huge wings to dry it. Back and forth he flew, again and again. His wingtips brushed the drying mud on each downstroke, making valleys and canyons, and pushing up ridges and mountains between. So, it is as you see it now."

"This was here?" someone asked.

"No, this was an island, far to the south, where Water Beetle brought the mud. We came here later. But land was formed more than one place, no?"

The listeners nodded, and First Cloud continued.

"Now there was land, and our people began to slide down the outside of the Sky Dome, to stand on solid ground. For protection, they crawled under the edge, inside the dome, and we are still here."

The People were staring up at the dark sky, studded with stars. The idea of a huge stone Dome was strange to them. More strange, maybe, than White Wolf's stories of giants.

Singing Moose interrupted, politely and gently.

"My brother," he inquired, "where does Sun go at night?"

"She crawls under the edge of the Dome, and up over the top, back to the east side. She pushes it up, just far enough to slide through."

There was laughter. Not impolite laughter, but laughter that indicated amused interest in a good story.

"For us," observed Singing Moose, "Sun is a young man with a torch. He goes on *around* the earth, sleeping on the other side. Or, doing something else. No one is sure what. Some have tried to find out."

"Yes," answered First Cloud. "Some of our people have tried to follow Sun, too. A party of brave warriors once followed her to the west, and saw the edge of the Sky Dome lift for her to slide under. One tried to follow Sun, but the Dome dropped down and crushed him. The others heard him scream, but of course it was dark, when the Dome closed. All night they had to wait, until Sun crawled through in the east to light the day. They could see his feet and legs sticking out from under the rim where he was crushed. No one has tried it since, to see what is outside the Dome."

"How far is it to the wall of the Dome?" asked Singing Moose. "We are traveling westward."

"Yes, I know," said the storyteller. "We do not know how far. But in the story of the warriors who went west, they left as young men, and those who survived came back as old men. It must be very far."

There was silence for a moment, and Singing Moose spoke again.

"Could it be," he asked, "that the things they had seen made old men of them?"

The Chalagee storyteller smiled, half to himself, and a bond of understanding seemed to flow between the two.

"I have wondered that, myself," First Cloud admitted. "Maybe both are true. The rim of the Dome is half a lifetime away, and there are things to the far west that turn men old and gray."

Calling Dove leaned closer to her husband. She wondered if he felt, as she did, the occasional chill, making the hair prickle at the back of her neck when she thought of the unknown future to the west.

ils sat alone, staring at the expanse of scenery before him. The harvest was in, and the People were again preparing for winter. The decision had been no major surprise. It was only that he had been somewhat startled when he realized, *after* the fact, that he had expected such a decision, and had not even questioned it.

What had happened to him? To his determination to return to Straumfjord and eventually to Stadt and home?

They had spent two growing seasons on a sort of aimless migration westward. There was not, had never been, any clear purpose in this move, as far as he could see. It was hard to determine any ultimate goal that the People might have had. He suspected that there was none, except to move from an area that was becoming dangerous to their way of life.

It was not that the People were simplistic, as he had once thought. They were quite complicated, actually. He was not able, even now, to understand all the subtleties of their culture. He had been drawn into it unwittingly, not really understanding that he was being used. He recalled with some degree of amusement how Big Tree had involved the Norsemen in the decisions regarding last season's planting. There was a certain degree of doubt involved, and the clever leader had managed to spread the responsibility for possible failure.

As it happened, the resulting success had strengthened the prestige and importance of all those involved, Tree, and the Norsemen, Odin, and Clay, the holy man. Only now he realized that there had been a quiet power struggle in the tribe, a striving for political prestige between the two bands. He wondered what might have happened if the crops had failed. But they had not. It had been a good season, and the prestige of Big Tree had grown. With it, the prestige of White Wolf, the holy man, and of his assistants. Big Tree now called on them for support without hesitation. This was no problem, at least so far, because Big Tree *was* a good leader. All the support that was needed was to say, in effect, "Yes, it is as Big Tree says." Or, "Clay has given wise counsel."

It had been amusing to watch the change in Svenson. The sailor had adapted quite rapidly to his new role as Fire Maker. The ritual with which he used the flint and steel was a masterpiece of showmanship. Sven had also seemed to fit easily into his marital relationship with Red Fawn. It was as if the two were a couple of middle age who had been together for many years.

A bigger change in Svenson, however, was one that had occurred slowly, almost unnoticed. During the first season of the migration, the sailor had pointed out all the features of the river and of the great freshwater seas. Sven had suggested ambitious plans for shipbuilding and trading, and had made maps on birch bark. True, Nils admitted himself, he, Nils, had been enthusiastic, also. It was easy for seagoing men to become excited by the great vistas of clear cold water and untouched forests.

Nils was not certain when it had happened. He had been preoccupied with other things, the planting and harvest. He was still surprised that he could have been caught up in that. And the relationship that had been established with the Chalagees this past season, uneasy at first, then quite sociable. He found himself looking forward to a winter of socializing and trading of stories with these Chalagees, so different than any other Skraelings they had encountered.

Whatever had happened, it had changed his own attitude and that of Svenson. They seldom talked anymore of plans for shipbuilding or trading. He wondered, even, if Sven was still drawing his maps. It did not seem as important as it once had. They had not talked of such things for a long time. This seemed odd, now that he thought about it. When this prolonged journey with the People started, one of his foremost thoughts was that of when he and Svenson could return to Straumfjord. Now their visit to the colony seemed so long ago, so far away. There was a dreamlike quality in his memory of the place. The beautiful blue-eyed woman . . . It took a moment to recall her name . . . *Ingrid!* Yes, that was it. Her memory, once the most important thing in his life, had paled to insignificance. What had he seen in her? Possibly only a warm body in his bed.

This in turn brought his thoughts back to Dove. Despite the initial language problem, theirs was an extremely close relationship. At least, he thought so. He had nothing for comparison, but he could not recall ever noticing a marriage like theirs, either among his own people or among Dove's. The marriages of Odin and yes, that of Svenson and Fawn were good, but surely not as exciting as this. And it was still growing. They now had longer discussions, made easier by more language familiarity, hence better understanding. Nils was pleased to find that Dove was a highly intelligent woman, whose depth of thought often put him to shame. She had, for instance, finally reasoned out why the Chalagee seemed indecisive. She told him about it, eyes sparkling with mischief.

"Do you know why they always stop the council without a decision? They have to ask their women!"

Nils snorted indignantly. "You are joking!"

"No, I think not. Watch, next time. I am sure that their women have great influence. You know they follow family through the mother's side?"

"Yes, so it is said. But the People hold women in high regard, too." He had been pleased to note that. The Norsemen had been in contact with some nations who regarded women as without much value. As property, almost. By contrast, strength and confidence were considered highly desirable among the Norse. "Are you sure of this, Dove?"

She laughed. "No, of course not. It would not be polite to ask. But watch, and see if you think so."

He had watched, and though it was never proven, Nils was inclined to think that his wife had hit upon a valid theory. They said nothing to anyone else, for there was no purpose in doing so. This remained one of their private secrets, shared only with each other.

They had many things that were shared only between them. The child, Bright Sky, now in his second year . . . ah, what a feeling to watch him explore the world. Sky was quick to learn, and had an easy, humorous approach to all things. His hair was a few shades lighter than that of any of the People. This seemed quite important to Calling Dove. It was also noted that the eye color of this special child, a strange dark gray-brown at first, had continued to change for a while. After several moons it could be seen that the color was to be one unfamiliar to the People. Brown, yes, but with an odd cast in certain lights that was suggestive of green.

Life was good. He shifted his position in the warm autumn sunshine, enjoying the view of the hills and the lake. Autumn color was painting the hillsides with splashes of bright orange, yellow, and red, in stark contrast to the dark green of spruce, cedar, and pine. Three crows beat their way lazily across a distant clearing to land in a dead tree at the other side. *What does a crow think?* he wondered, and was immediately startled at such a thought. *I am thinking like the People,* he told himself, unsure whether this was good or a cause for alarm. Or whether it mattered. His entire outlook had changed materially, he now realized. It had been some time since he had found a chance to get away by himself, just to think.

He was not certain of when or *how* his thinking had changed, but he knew that it had. There was that time when, listening to the strange tales of the Chalagees' Sky Dome, he found himself looking forward to exploring toward the unknown west. There had been a slight twinge of guilt. He should have been trying to plan their return to Straumfjord. Of course, Svenson had not mentioned it, so it was easy to postpone any such plans. There were better things to think of and to plan.

He was aware of someone approaching up the slope, and he turned to look. It was Dove.

"Ah!" she greeted. "Here you are."

She seated herself beside him, pausing a moment to catch her breath. "May I watch the sun with you?" she asked. "Ah, it is beautiful here, no?"

Shadows were lengthening, and the western sky was blossoming into brilliant color, its hues rivaling even those of the oaks and maples on the hillsides.

"It is good," he said softly, slipping an arm around her trim waist.

To himself, he was thinking along another line. Why bother to think of trying to return to Straumfjord right now? Winter was coming, precluding travel. Anyway, Svenson had not mentioned it for a long time. Maybe he would not bring up the subject until Sven did.

He snuggled Dove's firm body against his, stroking the soft buckskin over her thigh, feeling the firmness of her muscles.

Another thought struck him, which might have caused him concern if it had been more than a fleeting idea. It was there for a heartbeat or two and then lost in the urgency of the moment. *Why*, he thought, *would I want to go back to Straumfjord?*

Part III

65

he sight of the river stirred powerfully within the very depths of his being. Nils glanced at those around him, wondering if his reaction would be noticed. He saw no indication that anyone even cared. Each was preoccupied with his or her own reaction to the sight.

The arrival of the People at the river was not unexpected, of course. They had known of the location of the Big River, the Missi-sepee, for a year now. The scouts had even traveled there to evaluate the route. They returned, greatly impressed. The river, they reported, was not as wide as that where they had lived before, or as swift. Surely, not as clear and cold. In fact, this river seemed sluggish by comparison. And muddy. Maybe that gave the impression of dark secrets and shadowy depths. No, that was not quite it. . . . Majesty, maybe. But a certain threat, too, a doubt about what things might lurk in the dim hiding places at the bottom of this great stream.

Nils, though a veteran sailor, now found himself shuddering a little. What was the story of the Chalagees that had so impressed the children a few years ago when the People had spent a season there? A giant leech, big enough to kill a man, lying on the bottom of the lake, waiting for unsuspecting prey . . . Some of the children would not go near the water for weeks. He understood that dread now.

It was not that the river appeared threatening. Actually, it looked quite calm. Yet there was a hint of power, the merest suggestion that here was a sleeping giant that when roused has a ponderous feel to its spirit, like that of a sleeping winter bear. Or like that of unknown things lurking in the depths . . .

He shook his head to try to rid himself of such thoughts. After all, he had crossed the entire ocean, had he not? A mere river . . . He tried to shrug off the dark thoughts. Maybe he had been ashore too long. How many seasons had they traveled now, since leaving the sea? Five . . . no, six! It seemed a way of life, now. Travel, find a place to plant, raise a crop, spend the winter, move on. One place, they had spent two seasons. It had looked as if the People might stay there. There had even been a start on building permanent lodges. That had drawn the attention of their neighbors, and the situation had become tense. The People certainly would have been strong enough to stay by force, but it hardly seemed worthwhile. They had held a council and decided to move on.

It had been a hard thing when they left the last of the big lakes behind. The feeling of loss at the separation was left unspoken, but it was there. Mishi-ghan, that place had been called. Nils recalled still the last look over his shoulder at the great expanse of water behind them, growing smaller in the distance as they traveled. It had been hard to leave the water behind. *A man without a boat* . . . He said nothing to Svenson but wondered whether Sven, too, had felt the loss.

There were many things to take the place of his love for the sea. His family, for instance. He could hardly believe how rapidly Bright Sky had grown. Nils felt a warm glow of pride when he watched the children at play, saw the confidence with which the boy carried himself, his growing skill with the bow . . . ah, it was good. Best of all, maybe, was the shared joy with Calling Dove, as together they watched the development of this child that was a part of themselves and a product of their love.

Yes, there were many things to offset the loss that he had felt at leaving the sea. The actual ocean was far behind, of course. Still, until they left the place called Mishi-ghan, they had never been out of sight of the water. At least, not for long. There was the continuum of the gulf, the river, the chain of freshwater seas . . . but when they left the last of those behind, there had been a land-locked feeling that was new. He had quickly overcome it, or at least, he had thought so. He had felt no special affinity for the rivers and streams that they had encountered. *Maybe they were not large enough,* he thought to himself. This one was. If not in size, certainly in *spirit.*

Nils had, a little at a time and without realizing it, accepted one of the basic premises of the People: Everything has a spirit. Every person, animal, every tree and rock, every *place.* If he had been asked, he might have denied it, because this was not a part of his childhood learning. Yet he had no hesitation in thinking of a glowering sky, an angry sea, or a place whose mood or feeling was joyful and comforting. Or sometimes, maybe, foreboding. He had not actually reasoned out all of his feelings on this, but he was dimly aware that his tendency was to go along with the thinking of his wife and her people. It was easier than questioning.

Thus, when they talked of the annual war between Sun and Cold Maker, he understood. They watched the shifting weight of advantage in each individual battle, and he could relate this to his grandfather's stories of the Norse gods and their battles with the ice-giants. Was it not much the same story? Each season the forces of cold and evil attempted to push down into the area where the People were. Sun would retreat to the south, the rays of his torch becoming weaker with each confrontation. Sometimes it seemed that the pale and watery yellow rays of Sun's fire would go out entirely.

But by the Moon of Hunger, when supplies were growing painfully short, it usually could be seen that there was hope. With the coming of the Moon of Awakening each season, it could be seen that Sun was growing stronger. Cold Maker began to retreat toward his ice caves in the frozen north. He did not go willingly, of course, but snarling and snapping vindictively as he went, like a wolf driven from his kill. There would be intense confrontations as Cold Maker retreated, but they were usually short, for the Moon of Awakening was the beginning of the new growing season, the new year.

That was when they had begun to travel this year, as usual. They had reached this, the Big River, in the Moon of Greening, and it was apparent that there were some decisions to make. Nils was waiting, like everyone else, watching the children at play. It was midday, and it would be late afternoon by the time the last of the stragglers rejoined the main column. Probably there would be a council.

As if in answer to that thought, Odin joined him.

"There is to be a council tonight," the newcomer stated. "How is it with you, Wolf?"

"Good. I was looking at the river. I thought it might be bigger."

"I, too. Its spirit is powerful, though."

Nils nodded. "I wondered if others felt that, too. It speaks to me in a strange way. You feel it, too, no?"

"Yes," Odin said thoughtfully. "It speaks, but I cannot hear what it says. That is why we have the council tonight."

"What will be decided, Odin?"

"Who knows?" Odin shrugged, with a wry smile. "Maybe nothing. But they will talk of whether to stay and plant on this side of the river, or to cross first. Big Tree will ask what your medicine says, maybe."

Nils nodded again. That had become an expected thing. Usually it was no problem, merely to agree with what seemed the most logical course of action. That would have been discussed in advance between Big Tree and Clay, the holy man. Sometimes, it was not so apparent.

"What is your thought on this, Odin? Do you know what Big Tree wants?"

"No. I am made to think that he wants to hear how the People are thinking."

Nils nodded agreement. Big Tree, a good leader, was certainly capable of using that approach.

"We have half a moon," Odin went on, "maybe a moon, before we *must* plant. To cross, we would need to build boats. And we do not know how welcome we would be on the other side."

That was a big question. Would the first few of the People on the other shore be in danger from the local natives? There would be a little time before they could land in force to protect those who followed.

"Could the People build boats in half a moon?" asked Nils.

"Maybe. Yes, I think so. But we still have to find a place to plant."

"Have the scouts crossed?"

"Yes. Two of them, I think, in a skin boat. They did not talk to any one."

"You have heard that?"

Odin smiled. "No, but if they had talked to anyone, we *would* have heard, no?"

The council was one of dissent and argument. Very quickly, three factions emerged. One group wished to stay on the east side of the Big River for the season. Plant crops, harvest, and then move across the stream to winter on the west side.

An equally vocal group argued for an immediate crossing, to plant for the season on the other side.

A third faction, represented largely by the other clan, was highly critical of the leadership of Big Tree.

"There has been no planning," one of their leaders observed.

It was a calmly stated accusation, but guaranteed to strike fire among the loyal followers of Big Tree. It was apparent that a political power struggle was under way. Big Tree, trying hard to maintain his composure, reacted calmly, asking for comment, nodding in answer to statements made with emotional fervor. He seemed to remain calm, but if one looked closely, his seething anger could be seen. His teeth were clenched, indicated by a bunching of muscle along the jaw and in front of the ear.

Nils was quite aware of this, and watched Odin closely for a reaction. He was certain that Odin's loyalties lay with his own, in support of Big Tree. However, he was unsure as to the headman's preference. Although Big Tree was a strong and clever leader, he sometimes had a tendency to give too much leeway in decision making to the crowd. At least, that was Nils's opinion.

There comes a time when a leader must *lead.* A decision made by a good leader is usually respected, even if it is wrong. The thing that will not be tolerated is a lack of decisiveness. The leader must act. Nils had, several times over the years, thought that Big Tree had come perilously close to that point. Yet, each time, there had been subtle maneuvering in the council, and by various means, Big Tree usually achieved his preferred goal.

This time, it was not so sure. For one thing, Nils thought, Big Tree had not made his preference apparent. This in turn made the leader appear weak. Even so, Nils had to admire the man's composure as he presided over the council and faced the challenge to his authority.

Odin now asked for and received the right to be heard. That was a bit unusual, Nils thought. Usually Odin merely listened in council, and must be somewhat concerned about the direction the discussion was leading, to take this step.

"My chiefs," he said calmly, in an almost puzzled tone, "I am ready to cross, if it is so decided." He turned to face those who were urging such action. "But I have no boat. May I use yours for my family?"

There was a momentary pause and then general laughter, growing from a chuckle. It was known that there were no boats, except for one or two that the scouts had used to look at the west side of the river.

"If we are to cross," Odin went on, "we should not be sitting here talking. We should be building boats." More laughter, and Odin continued. "We have come a long way, these past seasons. Big Tree has brought us safely here. Now let us help him take us on."

Nils could see the satisfaction in the face of Big Tree, the little crow's-feet of amusement at the corners of his eyes.

"It is as our brother says," he noted. "We are arguing whether to use boats that we do not even have." He turned to Clay. "Holy man, can we build boats before the seeds must be planted?"

How clever, thought Nils. In his own country, a clash among leaders might have led to violence, and overthrow of one or the other. Here, the diversion of

the discussion to a common problem, that of the boats, had avoided it. Once
more, he was impressed with Odin's skill, as well as that of Big Tree. The need
for boats would be there, regardless of other decisions. Let *that* become the
primary concern.

Clay, in his answer, was quite vague. "How quickly," he asked, "can we
build boats? How many do we need?"

There was a murmur of excited discussion, and it was apparent that the
confrontation had been avoided.

"It is good," stated Big Tree, without any reference to *what* might be good.
"Let us think on this, these boats, and speak of this again tomorrow."

There was some grumbling as the council adjourned, but mostly excitement over the coming adventure, no matter when.

66

T he day for cooling tempers proved quite successful. When the council
reconvened, there was really very little to decide. People were already
starting to build boats. This also had another effect, possibly one anticipated by
Big Tree. It was apparent that boats could not be built quickly enough. They
must cross the river, find an area in which to plant, settle there, and have the
seeds in the ground within half a moon. There was simply not enough time.

This may have been the reason that the discussion was now at a much
lower intensity. There was little argument. Even that was limited to *how* to
accomplish the tasks before them, rather than what those tasks should be.

All of this was satisfying to the Norsemen. There was a sense of accomplishment, to be on the water again, and to be building boats. Nils realized that
he had left the lakes behind with regret. Svenson, too, had cast backward glances
that held a look of longing when they left the freshwater sea called Erie behind
them. They had followed its shoreline for two seasons. It had been then, with
the shining water fading behind them in the blue haze of distance, that the
Norsemen had stopped discussing their plans for shipbuilding. Nils had not
realized it at the time. It was not a conscious thing. There simply was nothing to

discuss, with no large body of water at hand. Their conversations turned to other things. The children, the crops, the day-to-day problems of the People.

It was a land of a different sort that they had crossed after that. Flatter than any they had seen, yet rolling, gently rounded hills, often covered with grass rather than trees. This seemed to be an ideal setting for grazing animals. They now saw herds of humpbacked oxlike creatures, much larger than deer or elk. The local tribes hunted them aggressively, and the People followed their example. The flesh of these creatures, the Norsemen found, was much like beef. It was not long before the People discovered that the skins of these shaggy oxen provided warm robes when tanned with the fur still on. The meat dried well and had good keeping qualities. The Moon of Hunger had not been quite so threatening for the past few seasons. The herds were filling a need.

There had been less notice, therefore, of the absence of the bodies of water that were so important to the Norsemen. They were preoccupied with the excitement of the hunt. True, the brief contact, the sight of the inland sea at the place called Mishi-ghan, had stirred their seafaring blood. But it, too, had been left behind.

Now the primary task for a little while was the building of boats. Sven was in his element again. Though not a boatbuilder, he was certainly a boat user. As such, he had a great interest in the proceedings. With this came more discussion between the two Norsemen.

"Nils," said Svenson, "have you thought of the danger to the first boats to cross?"

Nils had, actually, but had said nothing. Still, it made him quite uneasy to think of the first boat as it pulled up to shore. The small round boats would carry no more than three people. Two would be left on the other shore while one boatman returned for more passengers. If any potential enemies were there on the west bank to meet them . . . Well, the two who were left there alone would be at great risk.

"But surely we will have contacted whatever people live over there," Nils suggested.

"Maybe."

There was silence for a little while. It was apparent that even with several boats, there would be danger. Even if several crossed at once, they could not all land at the same place. The warriors who landed first would be scattered up and down the shore, two by two. Nils paused to think of how such a landing would be carried out by a Norse exploring party. The situation would be different, of course. A landing party from one of their ships would consist of perhaps a dozen men. Well armed, they would approach the shore in a longboat, running the prow up on the beach. Warriors in the front of the boat would jump out to face any threat and to protect the others as they moved forward.

But there were no longboats here, and they lacked the tools as well as the skills, to construct them.

"I was thinking," Svenson said. "What if there is treachery? We do not know these people on the other side."

The sailor must have been thinking along the same lines as he had, Nils mused. Probably there would be no conflict, but the uncertainty was a matter for concern. And the time to be concerned, obviously, was now, well ahead of time. It would certainly not do to discover treachery with their fighting force divided and part of it marooned on the enemy's side of the river. If there were to be enemies, of course. Yet safety would lie in preparation.

"It would be good to have a longboat or two," Svenson observed.

"Sven, we cannot build longboats," Nils retorted irritably.

"Of planks, no," the sailor mused. "But Nils, remember the bigger boats that the Downstream Enemy sometimes used? They were shaped like a little ship. A longship."

Nils nodded. "And made of bark, were they not?"

"Yes, I think so. Canoes, they were called. Could we not build one or two of those?"

"Maybe. Let us ask Odin."

Odin was agreeable, and understood the premise immediately.

"Yes. War canoes . . . the Downstream Enemy uses them."

"Yes," said Nils. "They were used against us. Did they not carry eight or ten warriors?"

"Yes," Svenson agreed. "Two abreast, no?"

"We will probably not need to fight," observed Odin, "but it does no harm to appear ready."

"Besides," Nils added, "we can land a party on the other shore, and then carry larger numbers faster, back and forth."

"And supplies and baggage, too," Sven agreed. "Odin, can we build a canoe? Maybe two?"

Odin nodded. "I have seen it done. It should not be difficult. Two is good, I think. And it seems we are to be here for a season. The bark must be stripped at the right time."

So the plan began to take shape. The People would plant, hunt, and construct boats. Attempts would be made to contact the inhabitants on the west side of the river, to reassure them of the peaceful intentions of the newcomers.

They decided quite early that there would be no crossing of the stream without the consent of the council. They could not risk another accident like that which had nearly destroyed their initial contact with the Chalagees.

The initial flurry of boatbuilding subsided, due partly to the necessity to concentrate on planting. The other factor was the scarcity of fresh skins for building the small round boats. But now that there was no hurry, the People settled into their traditional pattern of letting tomorrow take care of itself.

There were contacts across the river from time to time. A traveling trader, headed west, stopped for a day with the People, exchanged stories and traded. He had come from the north, and was carrying several pieces of a soft red stone. Pipestone, he called it, showing a pipe that had been carved and polished. It was smooth and warm to the touch.

"Its spirit is good," Odin noted.

The trader nodded. "And very powerful!"

"White Wolf, you should have a pipe of this stone," Odin insisted. "It would make your gifts even more powerful!"

They haggled a long while, Nils somewhat reluctant. The main stumbling block was that the trader held his wares in such high regard.

"Such stone comes from only the one place," he explained. "The farther from that quarry that we go, the more value it has. No, I do not even want to trade it now. It has greater worth to the west."

So the trade was never consummated at that visit. More valuable anyway, perhaps, was that this man had been across the river before.

"You are preparing to cross?" he asked, noticing boats in various stages of construction.

"Yes, but not now," Odin explained. "We will grow crops, winter here, then cross next season. Can you tell us of the people over there?"

The trader looked surprised. "You have not met them yet?"

"No. Our scouts crossed, saw that there are people, but we were not ready. . . ."

"I see. Well, they are called Hidatsa."

"What is the meaning?" Odin inquired. "We have been calling them Minitari, They Who Have Crossed the River."

"I do not know," said the trader. "But they are much like you, who are here on the east bank. How do you call yourselves?"

Odin shrugged. "The People, like everyone else. Right now, we are the People on the Bank."

"Hidatsa," an old man in the circle recalled. "When I was a child, there was such a town. They moved. . . . I had forgotten."

"It is good!" a woman said. "Those on the other side of the river will be friends!"

"Maybe not," said Odin. "We must be careful. They might be much like us, but more warlike."

"Look," offered the trader, "I will take you to them. I have been there. Take us over in one of your boats, and I will help you meet them."

There was enthusiastic agreement. It was admittedly a thing for the council, but there was already discussion of who should be included in the party to make the first contact. It was quickly apparent that it would require more than one of the small boats.

"Two, maybe," Odin suggested. That would allow a greeting party of four of the People, along with the traveler, his wife, and their goods.

All subject, of course, to the action of the council. But the council agreed readily.

It was a tense moment when the two boats grounded on the west bank. They drew the vessels up on the shore to wait.

It was not long. Suddenly armed warriors rose up out of the grass and from behind bushes. Odin's heart pounded in alarm. Had the trader betrayed them? Surely not. A trader who would do such a thing would never be trusted again by anyone. He glanced nervously at Big Tree and the two other warriors, Snake and Red Hand. They, too, looked quite anxious, but were trying to maintain their dignity.

"How are you called?" demanded one of the Hidatsa in hand signs.

The trader stepped forward, his right hand raised in greeting.

"I am Trader. Remember? Last season?"

The other nodded, but very cautiously.

"And these others?"

"They are people of the other bank. They mean no harm."

"Let them speak for themselves."

"It is good," signed Odin, stepping forward. He used both hand signs and spoken words. "Our people are traveling to the west. We have stopped to plant, and would cross next season. If our brothers across the water do not object, of course."

"Your tongue is much like ours," the Hidatsa responded, ignoring the inquiry. "Where do you come from?"

"Far to the east. A salty shore."

"Ah! We, too. But look! We, too, must grow corn. Will there be enough? Or enough room to plant?"

Odin was thinking quickly. If that was to be the problem, a fear of how much food, and whether there would be enough.

"I am made to think," he began, "of one of our holy men. You may have heard of him—White Wolf?"

There was no sign of recognition, so he continued.

"This man has white hair and fur upon his face. Blue eyes, too, though he is young and very powerful."

"It is not true."

"Yes, yes. He comes from beyond the salty water."

"What is this to us?"

"Nothing . . . But I am made to think of one of his stories. He tells of a great leader of his tribe, long ago, who fed a great number of people, many hundreds, maybe, with only a few fish and some corn cakes."

"That is nothing," sneered the other. "We once had a sack of meal that was bottomless. It never became empty."

"Ah! Where is it?"

The Hidatsa looked irritated. "We no longer have it," he admitted. "It is a story, from long-ago times."

"It is good," Odin observed. "But no matter. The stories are much the same, no? It is possible to feed many in one way or another."

"That is nothing. I would hear more of your holy man who has blue eyes yet sees."

"We can bring him," Odin offered. "See for yourself. We will have a council, and story fires. And we will bring food."

The other man now smiled for the first time. "It is good!"

A day was set for the meeting, and the four men of the People returned to the boats.

"If they are to be friendly," Nils said thoughtfully, "will we need the canoes?"

The season was not yet right for the stripping of bark, and they had done nothing except begin to look for appropriate trees.

"I am made to think," Svenson offered, "that it might be good to have a canoe anyway. Have you wondered, Nils, where this river flows?"

Nils was startled. The obvious answer lay before them. Rivers flow to the sea. The sea had been the very life of Svenson until the past few years. Now his longing to return to it must be very powerful. Many times Nils himself had felt it, though the urge had become lesser now. But it was there, lying just below the surface. It was an instinct, an inherited urge, like that of the wild geese. No, more like that of the salmon, swimming upstream to return to the place of their birth. Except that, for the Norseman, the return was downstream. Back to the sea.

"Yes," agreed Nils. "We need a boat."

67

wo boats would be needed, it was decided. Two of the long canoes, that is. Many families had already started to build the small round skin-covered boats, but they could hold no more than two or three people. Still, they were useful, because they could be constructed and used that summer. This would allow an occasional exploration and more contact with the people on the other side of the river.

They had made that contact with the Hidatsa, with the help of the traveling trader. Not quite the same, their way of speaking, but nearly so. There would be a slightly different inflection, a variant pronunciation, a few words used by one of the groups but not the other. It was apparent to all, however, that they were kinsmen, and it was good. When the planting was finished and the fields had been weeded for the second time, there were no pressing tasks to occupy their days.

Or their evenings. Often a flotilla of round boats would make its way across the river in the afternoon, to remain for an evening of storytelling. Usually the People would stay the night, rather than cross the river in darkness.

Nils was glad for this. He still had a dread, perhaps a premonition. It lurked in the half-formed fears among the cobwebbed recesses of his mind, a gnawing suspicion of the dark waters. He could convince himself that the Chalagee story of the giant leech was just that, a story. Still, he could not entirely escape the dread of some evil thing lying in wait. *How odd,* he thought. *Is this part of growing up, of realizing one's mortality?* It was not a thing that weighed heavily on his thoughts, however, or that was with him constantly.

He participated in the storytelling, at the request of Odin. The two related groups had stories that were quite similar, of course, but the Norse legendry was completely new to the Hidatsa. They listened in rapt wonder at the tales of Sol and Mani racing across the sky, pursued by giant wolves who would devour their light.

"It is true!" exclaimed an old man of the Hidatsa. "I have seen it myself, as a boy. Sun nearly went out, swallowed by a great darkness. This was the creature, the giant wolf told of by our guest! Is that not right, holy man?"

"So say the legends of my people," Nils agreed. "But the wolf spit it back out, no?"

"That is true! We all sang and beat the drums and prayed. It has been so always, maybe. It always succeeds."

There was a glint of mischief in the eyes of the old man, and Nils felt a kinship. This one might not be a storyteller, but he certainly had a sense of the dramatic.

"Tell them of Nidhug, the dragon," whispered Svenson. "The People have not heard that story, either."

Nils nodded. "My people tell of an end to the world," he went on. "Fire Man has asked me to tell of this."

His listeners were wide-eyed.

"When is this to happen? Soon?" someone asked.

"No, no. It has already happened, long ago," Nils explained.

"Then how are we here, White Wolf?"

"Well . . . I . . . it was restored," he mumbled. "But you are ahead of the story! Listen . . ."

He recounted briefly the tales of the ice-giants, and their wars with the gods and the forces of warmth and light.

"It is like Cold Maker," he explained, "forcing Sun south in winter. My people have told of that. But there was a tree, a giant ash tree called Yggdrasil, whose leaves shaded all the earth and the heavens. And it was good. But at the base of the tree lived a great beast, who gnawed at the roots."

"Yes. A beaver?"

"No, no. Not a beaver," Nils insisted.

"But a beaver does this, Wolf."

"Yes, but this is a monster creature, who breathes fire and smoke."

"Ah! We have none like that!"

"That is true . . . but this is a story, Uncle."

"This animal is a spirit-beast?"

"Well, yes . . . a spirit."

The other man nodded, and Nils continued. He had not thought of this tale for a long time, and was feeling his way, trying to remember.

"The humans on the earth had become so evil," he related, "that all the spirit-beings and Sun and Moon were sad. Some of their brightness was lost, and this let the forces of cold become stronger. This terrible winter lasted for three years, and it caused much hardship."

There was a sympathetic murmur in the crowd. This sort of hardship was a thing they could readily understand.

"It was called the Fimbul," he continued. "Snow fell from all four directions at once, and there were bitter winds. A thick layer of ice covered all the earth. Yet, after three years of this terrible Fimbul-winter, it started all over again. All hope was lost. The people of the earth turned to even more evil, and there was much killing."

Old women clucked their tongues and shook their heads at the thought of such a situation.

"Under the darkness of these long winter nights, many evil things were done. Now, you remember the wolves who try to eat Sun and Moon? They were fed by a giant woman, and their food was the bones and marrow of evil men, murderers. With so much to eat, they grew and grew and became huge monsters. Finally they did swallow Sun and Moon, and there was darkness. Earth shook, stars fell. Just then the monster Nidhug gnawed through the great ash tree and it fell."

The crowd before him was tense, waiting. Suddenly, Nils realized that he had talked himself into a hopeless corner. The next part of the story was to tell how the red clarion-cock above Valhalla crowed the alarm. This caused Heimdall, the sentry of the gods, to blow a blast on his horn to announce the Rangarok, the Last Battle. Heimdall's horn had never sounded before, because its only function was to announce the end.

With a momentary panic, Nils realized that he was about to tell this story to people who had never seen or heard a horn of any kind. Or a rooster, for that matter. He paused, confused as to how to proceed. He glanced at Svenson, who seemed to be enjoying his plight immensely. Well, maybe he could move on quickly.

"The sentry of the gods gave the alarm," he went on, "and they rushed out to fight the evil ones: giants, wolves, and the great snake who lived in the ocean's depths. But wait . . ." He turned to Odin. "I have never told the People of the great snake?"

Odin shook his head, puzzled.

"He lives in the bottom of the sea," Nils explained. "His writhing causes the waves, no?"

He realized now that many of the details of Rangarok, the last day, were nearly impossible to recount. The battle involved horses and chariots, and many things for which the People had no words. No concept, even. It was much like the time when he tried to tell of Allfather's eight-legged horse to people who had never seen a four-legged one. This struck him as amusing, now, and he began to see a great truth. All of the detailed description was mostly for effect. The main part of the story, the important part, was that of the battle, a struggle between good and evil. He had never fully realized before, the purposes behind the tales of his childhood, the lessons learned from his grandfather. The old tales of the Norse gods were to *teach.*

He took a deep breath and continued.

"There was a great battle then, between Good and Evil. The earth caught fire, and all the forests burned. The warriors of evil had won. But everything began again. After a while, green sprouts began to show, and flowers and trees, and good spirits recovered. Finally they were able to force the giants to live in faraway mountains, and the gnomes—the Little People—to live underground."

"Ah!" said the old Hidatsu who had shown such interest. "We know of them. I am made to think, White Wolf, that many of our stories tell of the same things, yet with different stories."

"Yes, it must be so," Nils agreed.

"And it is good," said the other. "We would hear more."

But it was now growing late, and further stories would be told at another time.

It was autumn before Odin told them that soon it would be time to obtain the bark for canoes.

"The tree must be asleep," he explained. "If not, it will be sad and weep, and then its spirit will get angry and cut slits in the canoe."

Nils did not understand all of this, but he knew better than to question it. Through the years of experience with Odin, he had learned not to doubt. If the man said there would be holes in the canoe, it could be accepted as truth. The holes would be there. Why and how were really unimportant. It was easy merely to accept the idea of the tree's resentment over the violation of its outer garment.

It was no great surprise to him, then, that when the time came, Odin performed an apology. It was quite similar to that over a kill for meat. Odin addressed the tree in just the same manner.

"We are sorry to take your robe, my brother. We require it for the things we must do. May your people have sunlight and rain forever, and be many."

They had previously selected the trees that would be used, tall, straight and round, and with as few side branches as possible.

"The fewer patches, the fewer leaks," Odin said.

The building process was somewhat longer and more complicated than Nils had imagined. It was necessary to shape the bark shell of the craft as it dried. Odin pried and propped and tied, tightening a thong here, loosening one there, adding a stick to establish width or depth. Svenson was active in the process.

"A bit wider in the midships," he suggested. "That will lose a little speed, but make her more steady."

The old sailor confided to Nils in the Norse tongue an old saying of seafarers. The basic principle that he had just stated, that of speed, width, and stability, Sven said, applies to ships and women alike. Odin, being fairly fluent in their tongue, chuckled with them.

"Maybe," he agreed, "but not always. And this is not a thing to tell a woman."

"Especially one who is wide amidships," Svenson added. "You might learn her speed very quickly."

"What is the joke?" asked Red Fawn, who approached just then.

Svenson was more embarrassed than Nils had ever seen him. He reddened, mumbled, and seemed completely at a loss. Odin came to his rescue.

"Fire Man was telling me," he explained, "how his people think of a ship as a woman. See?" He pointed to the trim, graceful lines of the canoe. "It is shaped much like their longships. You have not seen them, Mother, but the ships are beautiful and graceful. Like a woman."

Fawn smiled, reached over and patted her husband lightly.

"It is good," she said. "That is a nice thought, Fire Man. I will remember it." She cast a flirtatious sidelong glance at him. "How is the boat coming?"

"It goes well," answered her son. "Soon we will patch with pine tar and try her."

"Her? Yes, I see. . . ."

When they finished the canoes a few days later, Odin painted a large eye on each side of the prow. Nils asked about this.

"To let it see where it is going," Odin explained. "Your ships have an animal's head on the front, no?"

Nils thought of the gargoylelike carvings on the prow of the Norse long-ships. Dragonships, they were sometimes called, for this reason. He had never thought much about it. It was simply a custom. How had it started? And was it not, after all, much like the custom just carried out by Odin?

"Come," said Odin, "let us try them!"

68

The first launching of one of the canoes was a momentous event.

They had had some experience with a canoe when they left the Downstream Enemy long ago, but that was a smaller craft. It could be handled much more easily, and during the journey upstream to reach the People, there had been no occasion to lift or carry it. Odin, who was the only one present with any real experience, instructed the others.

"Stand beside the canoe, like this."

"Facing the *stern?*" asked Svenson in Norse. "The river is behind us!"

"Yes. You will see. Now, bend over and put your hands on the sides, so. . . ."

He reached across to the opposite gunwale of the craft with his right hand, and placed his left on the closer side, next to his knee.

"Now," he went on, "I will count. On three, we all lift the canoe, turn it, and hold it over our heads."

"Wait," protested Svenson. "How can this be? We will be twisted!"

"No, no," Odin laughed. "As we lift, we turn, too. We will be facing forward."

Sven still appeared to have his doubts, but the canoe was not heavy. A boat of this size built of planks could not be lifted by three men.

They bent and gripped the sides, and Odin counted. "One . . . two . . . *three!*"

Together they lifted and pivoted, turning the canoe bottom up as they did so. It was much easier and less complicated than Nils expected. In the space of a heartbeat, the three were now facing forward, holding the canoe aloft over their heads. Svenson laughed with delight.

"It is good!" he shouted.

Cautiously, they moved toward the water, careful not to fall into step. Odin had explained that earlier. If their steps were exactly matched, the rhythm would cause the weight of the canoe to begin to swing. That would make it much harder to control, because they would be fighting not only the weight but the motion.

"It is like carrying a long beam or plank," Svenson noted to Nils. "It is the same thing. The men on the front and back ends are careful not to be in step."

Nils had never had much experience in carrying long planks, but he could see that the principle would hold true.

They reached the river, and Odin gave his instructions. "Now we turn and put it down just as we lifted."

"Turn to face backward?"

"Yes. I will count."

In another moment, the canoe stood on the bank, her prow pointing into the river. It was apparent that the maneuver was quick and efficient, and would be even more so with practice. They slid the craft into the water, careful to keep a grasp on the upturned stern.

"Now we must take care getting in," Odin advised.

"Of course," Sven agreed.

The principle was much as they had learned before. Place a foot directly in the middle to achieve balance. Step forward, one foot exactly in front of the other, sit or squat to stabilize the tremor and sway of the canoe in the water.

Again, Nils was impressed by the feel of a canoe under him. It was a living thing, with a spirit of its own, and he could sense the life as he adjusted his position. There was a melding of the gentle lapping motion of the river with the tremor of the canoe, and the reaction of his own muscles to the rhythms of these motions.

There was a good feel to it, one that had been absent for a long time. He had not realized how much he had missed it. And this feel, that of the big canoe, was completely different from the feel of the somewhat smaller one they had used before. He mentioned this to the other two as they pushed off to try a run up and down the shore.

"Of course," Odin agreed. "The spirit is different."

"Yes, the size and width."

Svenson chuckled. The old sailor had an instantaneous feel for this.

"No, no, Nils. That is only a small part of it. It is as Odin says, her *spirit* is different. Remember, the *Snowbird* and the *Norsemaiden*? Built to the same plan, alike yet different in spirit. Ah, they are like women in *many* ways!"

It had been some time since Nils had thought of the two ships. That seemed another world, so far away in time and place. And yes, in spirit, too. How odd, that here in the interior of this world so different, that Sven's words would set him off on flights of fancy. Maybe it was the gentle motion of the great river, maybe the union of the spirits of river and canoe.

Maybe it was merely the heritage of the Norsemen, out of reach but not forgotten. Under appropriate circumstances, it had awakened in a powerful surge. The pulse of Nils Thorsson began to quicken with the feel of a boat under him. He did not realize how much he had missed this feeling.

It is good, he told himself softly, as the strange mixture of two cultures spread warmly over him.

"What did you say, Wolf?" asked Odin, plying his paddle as steersman in the stern.

"What? Oh, nothing, I only said 'it is good.' "

"Yes," agreed Odin. "It is!"

Nils realized that they were talking of different things.

They spent a little while learning the ways of the new canoe, up and down the river for a few bowshots' distance each way. Quickly, the three learned the feel of the craft, her responses and their own.

"I do not know about the other one," observed Svenson, "but this one is good. Maybe we did not need the other."

"Maybe," Odin answered. "But it is nearly finished. We can use two."

There were a few places in the canoe's hull that leaked a drop or two of water as they maneuvered up and down the river.

"Mark them!" Odin advised. "Here!" He tossed a piece of charcoal to Svenson. "A little pitch from the pine tree will stop that. But we must take it out to dry."

They marked the tiny leaks and headed back to the landing area. Their families waited there, excited over the achievement.

"It is good!" cried Calling Dove, clapping her hands like an excited child. "A beautiful thing!"

"May we ride in it, Father?" asked Bright Sky, as he stood with the daughters of Odin.

"Not now," Nils told them. "We have a few small leaks. We will fix those, and next time we launch her, yes! We will all go."

They drew the canoe up on the bank and turned it over to dry in the sun. Svenson stepped over and gave his wife a quick hug.

"Ah, Fawn, she is a fine craft," he told her. "You will see!"

Nils sat that evening, staring at the coals of the dying fire for a long time. Dove came to sit beside him and leaned her head against his shoulder. She was silent for a long time. The fire made little crackling noises, and from downriver a night bird called.

"What is it, my husband?" she asked.

"What is what?" he asked. "The bird?"

"No, no. I spoke of you. You are troubled?"

Nils was startled. He had been so deep in thought that it had not occurred to him that anyone else might notice.

"No, not troubled. I was only thinking."

"Of what, Wolf?"

"Of, many things . . . the canoes . . ."

She had realized that this must have something to do with the canoe. He had not been quite the same since they returned from the river after the trial run. But she knew him well. When he was ready, he would talk to her, so she merely snuggled closer against the chill of the night. He reached to toss another stick on the fire. Most of the People had retired to the longhouses, and the village was quiet.

"Are the children asleep?" he asked.

"Yes."

She wanted to ask him to come in and join her in the sleeping robes, but felt that he had something that he must think on, so she waited, staring with him into the bright glow of the fire. *What is it?* she wondered. *What does he see in the fire?* And the answer came to her: *He is thinking of his people, his home. . . . The canoe has done this!*

For a moment, she felt a wave of resentment. Of anger, almost. Was this to come between them? Maybe she could destroy the canoes. Then the situation struck her has ludicrous. Could she have actually felt a pang of jealousy against a *boat?* The thought flitted through her mind that the Norsemen *do* think of their boats as female. *No! This is stupid,* she told herself. There were things that she could do for him that a boat certainly could not. It would help if he would come to bed.

But this was not unpleasant, to share his warmth and that of the fire, with his buffalo robe drawn around the shoulders of the two of them.

"I am sorry," he said suddenly. "I was thinking of my people."

Ah, I was right, she thought. A touch of fear crept into her consciousness. *In what way? Is it now that he will leave?*

She hesitated to phrase it, even in her thoughts, but her fear was becoming quite real. Now that he had the boats, would he some day soon decide that it was time to go home?

Hot tears filled her eyes, and she hoped that he would not notice as they overflowed and slid down across her cheeks. She was glad for the darkness as the flames died.

He stirred and stretched his legs in front of him, preparing to rise.

"Come, let us go bed," he said.

At least, Dove thought, *I have him for now.*

This was an advantage that she must not overlook. If she could make his life pleasant enough, he might not *want* to leave.

69

Calling Dove might have been even more concerned if she had known her husband's actual thoughts. He was not thinking so much of his people and his home as he was of the geography of this place. The river, it appeared, was flowing in a southerly direction. The smaller streams that they had seen in their travels for the past year had done the same.

Gradually, an idea was forming in his mind, a general idea of the configuration of this great land, that which they called Vinland. The Norsemen had crow-hopped across the Atlantic, colonizing as they went. Eric the Red, fleeing from the law, had done so. His sons, Leif and Thorwald, had continued the push westward. Iceland, Greenland, Newfoundland, Vinland . . . It was only now, however, that Nils had begun to see the immensity of this Vinland. It must be much larger than Greenland, even. He had doubted the stories of the People at first, that the land stretched westward a lifetime's travel. After all, stories are meant to be exaggerated. But here, it seemed, all things were bigger than the story. The immensity of the inland seas of fresh water had not been fully realized. The land, too . . . Vast stretches of mountains and prairie, reaching on westward forever, it seemed.

Nils had begun to ponder the stories of nations and clans that they encountered. They *still* talked of the wider lands to the west. No one they had seen knew where it might end.

And now, this river. He had noted as they traveled a slight rise, or divide, between the lakes and the rolling plain to the south. There were small streams flowing northward, but mostly, the watershed seemed to be to the south. These streams, then, must flow into a large body of water somewhere in that direction. He had considered what it might be. More of these strange freshwater seas? It was possible, of course. Anything was possible, it seemed, in this land so different from anything known in Europe. However, it seemed unlikely to him. He was certain that they had crossed a divide, and that the watershed where they now camped was sloping south. South, *away* from the freshwater seas, and probably back to the ocean.

What was needed, he knew, was a map or chart of some sort. The impression that the river had made on him was greater than he realized, and he found himself thinking in terms of navigation. He knew that they had traveled quite a distance to the south. The position of the Polestar said so. He had paid less attention to it for the past year or two. He had been preoccupied with the problems of the People, and with the delights of watching his son grow and learn.

Now, however, the river had quickened his seafaring blood. He had almost forgotten the uneasiness that he had felt when he first saw it. No longer did he wonder what lay in its dark channels. He was amused, almost, that he had felt that dread. It was certainly inappropriate for a seafarer. A river, especially one of this size, is a highway to the sea, and its pull was becoming stronger. Maybe the canoes, too, were a factor. Give a boatman a boat, and it opens the world to him. And, though these canoes were intended primarily to help the People in crossing this watery barrier, he began to see other possibilities.

"Sven," he asked, "do you still have your charts?"

The sailor looked a bit startled, and somewhat apologetic. "Yes," he answered tentatively. "I have not kept them up. You want to see them?"

"Yes. I would talk with you of this, Sven. This river flows south, no?"

"Of course."

"And where does it go?"

Svenson shrugged. "Back to the sea."

Nils was startled by that answer. The sailor had not said "to the sea," but "*back* to the sea." This would suggest that Sven, too, felt something of the pull to explore the waterway.

"Do you remember," Nils went on, "how some of those at Straumfjord were talking of how big this Vinland might be?"

Sven nodded, puzzled, but said nothing.

"Karlsefni thought it might even be a new continent," Nils went on. "Maybe it is."

"It seems so," Svenson agreed. "But what—"

"Let us look at your charts," Nils suggested.

Svenson fumbled among his belongings and came out with the birchbark maps. The two men withdrew to a quiet place and Sven opened the bundle.

"I have not made an entry since before we saw the lake at Mishi-ghan," Svenson admitted.

"No matter. I wanted only the bigger picture. Let us align it with north."

Quickly, with the use of the sun-stone, the map was oriented and they began to study its features.

"The river would be about here, no?" asked Nils.

"Yes, off the map, there."

"Let us put it on the sand, here, to draw a little more." He picked up a stick. "Now, here would be Mishi-ghan, at about the edge of your map, no?"

"Yes," Svenson answered, "about there."

"And let us draw in where we think the coast might be."

"To the south?"

"No, the east. Straumfjord is here, no?"

"Yes, of course."

"And we know something of that coastline. The Ericksons have sailed southward along the coast, have they not?"

"Yes, Thorwald said—" Sven began.

Nils motioned him to silence, now warming to the excitement of his theory.

"So, they will be exploring in this direction. The coastline runs southwestward as far as they had sailed."

"Yes . . ." Svenson agreed, beginning to understand.

"Now, if we follow this river, it will lead to the sea. The Ericksons will be exploring around the coast, trading—"

"Nils, it has been six years!" Sven sputtered.

"All the better! They will have colonies. Maybe at the mouth of this very river. They could sail a longship this far upstream, even. We might meet them!"

Svenson was staring in openmouthed astonishment.

"You want to go *down* this river?"

"Why not? We have the canoes. It would be an easy thing. Float along . . . Sven, I am made to think that this river is our way home!"

"But . . . but Nils, what if they are *not* there?"

Nils shrugged. "No matter. We follow the coast northeast. Somewhere, we will meet our people. Sven, they must have more colonies by now. Leif is as anxious to colonize as Thorwald is to explore."

"That is true," Sven agreed, beginning to catch the excitement of the grandiose idea. "But we do not know how far."

"Of course. But we can reach the sea without much effort. And think . . . We can hand Thorwald Erickson a chart of the interior!"

Both chuckled. That in itself would be a crowning achievement. Yet Svenson still had reservations.

"But Nils, your family . . ."

"We *take* them. Look, Sven, we have two canoes. Each can carry five or six people and their baggage. Some goods to trade, maybe. You and I, Odin and his family . . . we need him to help with languages."

"You have spoken to Odin of this?"

"No, the idea is new to me, too. I have said nothing to Calling Dove, even."

"You had best do that, my friend," Sven chuckled. "But yes, I think this thing could be done. Had you thought of when?"

"No. But the People plan to cross the river as soon as the weather opens up. The Moon of Greening, maybe?"

"Probably. As soon as the ice clears the river."

"Good. We could help get everyone across, and then start downriver in the canoes. We would be heading into warmer climate, and would have all season to reach the ocean. Sven, we can do this!"

Svenson was becoming more enthusiastic, but had a few reservations.

"Nils, before we launch this trip, we must talk to the women and to Odin. What if they do not want to go?"

Nils thought for a moment. "Let us talk to Odin first. We can see if he thinks this could be done."

It was not yet evening when Nils drew the Skraeling aside and briefly explained their theory. Odin's one eye widened with wonder.

"You have talked with Dove about this?"

"No . . . I . . ."

"You would leave your *family?*"

"No, no, Odin. We would all take our families."

"Oh. That is different, then. Maybe . . . yes, it could be done."

"To the sea?"

"Yes. The Hidatsa have talked to people who say there is a salty sea to the south."

"I knew it!" Nils exclaimed triumphantly. "It *can* be done! Will you help us, Odin?"

Odin appeared lost in thought for a little while. "Yes," he said finally. "But this is a very big thing, Wolf. We must go slowly, talk with our wives. There is a little time before we must decide. But yes, I will go. Your people were good to me. And I am made to think this can be done."

Nils's enthusiasm was tempered somewhat by Odin's remark, "Your people were good to me." He was a bit embarrassed at his own feelings when they first met. He had considered the Skraeling as a lower-class being than himself, a sort of half-human barbarian. The others at Straumfjord had had even less regard for the Skraelings. Now this man was one who had not only saved his life repeatedly, but who was a friend. Possibly, Nils thought, the best friend that he had ever had.

"So," Odin went on, "let us talk with the women. We will speak of it later."

They rose to go back toward the longhouse, and Odin spoke again.

"Does Fire Man know of this?"

"Yes. We decided to talk to you and then to the women."

"It is good. This could be a great quest, Wolf."

Nils smiled. He could see that this was beginning to stir Odin's imagination, too. His own excitement was mounting, and he was becoming more confident of ultimate success.

He did not know, of course, that Thorwald Erickson had been killed in a battle with Skraelings some years before, that the colony at Straumfjord had been abandoned, and that Leif Erickson had seriously curtailed his explorations.

More important than any of these facts, however, was one that he did not even suspect. The great river that appeared to be their highway home led not into the ocean traversed by the Norsemen, but into the southern gulf.

70

Once the decision was made, the period of waiting began. It was easy for Nils to become impatient. The People with their easygoing ways settled in for the winter quite comfortably, but it was harder for him to do so. Up to a point, he could adopt the day-to-day attitude of his wife's people, but this was different.

He began to wonder how he had managed to refrain from such impatience for the past few years. The possibility of returning to the sea and maybe even on to his native land was a stimulating thing. Though he did not realize it at the time, it may have been the journey itself, not the goal, that inspired his excitement. It was a wonderful vision that now challenged his imagination. He could imagine a gathering of ships' masters back in Stadt. He had listened sometimes as a boy, while the older men told tales of the sea. But there had been none that could even approach the tale he and Svenson could tell now. They would have maps and charts of the great inland waterways, and of the river by which they had returned to the sea. They would proudly introduce their families. It would also be good to watch Calling Dove and her mother as they discovered all the miraculous things of the modern world.

Odin had not yet decided whether he and Hawk Woman would go on to the home of the Norsemen or not. There were the two girls to consider, ages six and nine. Their presence might complicate such a journey beyond acceptable limits. Hawk Woman was reluctant.

"We will see," Odin said cautiously. "If we find that this can be done, then will be time to decide."

This, of course, was logical. Odin had the ability to see beyond the immediate, acquired from bitter experience. Nils found it interesting that Odin had no hesitation at all about the journey itself. He had only a reservation about what course to take at the other end.

"We are traveling anyway," Odin explained. "This is only a change in direction. If there are problems, we can return to the People."

Yes, Nils reflected, *I had not thought of that.* But if, for any reason, the voyage downriver seemed not to be practical, they, too, could turn back. Even if it had been a season or two, they could return to wherever the People had decided to settle.

That, too, was a matter that was much discussed that winter. There was a general feeling that once across the great river, the People should begin to look for a permanent site on which to build. Maybe this was far enough to go, and it was time to put down roots again. That, of course, would make it easier to rejoin the People if it became necessary. Nils wasted little time on such a thought, but it was there, to be noted in passing.

One thing that was noted this winter was that there seemed to be less snow in this area. There were discussions around the fires. Younger people felt that this might be only normal variation from one season to the next.

"No, I am made to think not," said old Clay, the holy man. "The snow is not nearly so deep here, or for the last two winters."

"Do you think this is because we are farther south, Uncle?" asked Nils.

The old man looked at him in mild surprise, and took a puff or two on his pipe before answering.

"Maybe," he finally said, "but maybe not. There is not so much water here. Cold Maker likes ice."

Nils thought of the ice-giants of his own mythology, and it seemed logical enough. It takes water to make ice, so in terms of a mythical being who depends on ice, it was much the same. The remarkable thing was the similarity of the two stories.

"You think, Uncle, that this is why the snow is not so deep here?"

Clay's eyes twinkled as he shrugged his shoulders. "Who knows? But it is not. That is enough for me."

Nils smiled. He was thinking of a saying that he had heard somewhere, about looking a gift horse in the mouth.

"Yes, it is good, no?" he asked.

Still, the questions lingered in his mind. Was the climate changing as they moved westward? How much effect did latitude have as they moved southward? And the lakes . . . was Clay's suspicion valid, that water *brings* snow? He realized that he might never know for sure. Some day, someone might.

There were snows, of course, some driven by icy winds and drifting enough to become a nuisance. Still, this was not as bad as many winters that they had experienced in their own country. And the ice on the river was never quite frozen solidly enough to attempt a crossing on foot. The People ventured to walk on the ice near the shore, but farther out it became less trustworthy, and to be avoided. It was only two seasons ago that a tragedy had occurred.

Three small boys had been playing on the ice. As the lone survivor related the story, the other two had been challenging each other, to see who could go farthest out onto the frozen water. They became more daring, even as the ice began to speak in musical creaking tones. He had not seen a crack appear, but suddenly one of his friends plunged through into the icy water and disappeared. The second ran to help him and another fracture claimed him, too. The sobbing boy who told the story related how he had screamed and run for help. Men came running with ropes and poles, but there was no sign of the victims. The river's current and Cold Maker's chill had claimed their victims.

The People had become more cautious about the treacherous ice of the frozen rivers. There seemed no doubt that something was different about the climate here.

Nils and Calling Dove talked often of the coming journey. She had misunderstood at first. He had started to explain to her what he had in mind when he noticed that her eyes were filled with tears. She was trying to choke them back, with little success.

"What is it?" he asked, concerned.

"You are telling me that you are leaving me?"

"*What?* No, no, Dove. I . . . oh, no!"

"But the canoes . . . the river . . . you said—"

"Dove, I would not do that. I want to be with you!"

She brightened for a moment, but then showed concern again. "Then you are *not* going?"

"Yes . . . that is, I want to go, if you will come with me."

He had not decided what to do if she refused, and her manner concerned him greatly. But only for a moment.

"Oh!" Dove said, wiping her eyes. "Of course. Who else is going?"

"The others are talking of it, too. Your brother and Hawk; Fire Man and Fawn. The children, of course."

She gave him the smile that could always cure any ill for him, solve any problem. He had not seen that smile recently, he recalled. He was confused for a moment before the truth dawned on him, and then a great sadness swept over him. Had she actually believed? . . .

"You thought I would *leave* you?" he blurted.

She did not answer immediately, but her tears told the story, coming now with a rush, in a mixture of laughter and crying. He gathered her in his arms.

"I . . . I thought maybe—" she stammered.

"Ssh . . . No, no, Dove," he crooned, holding her close. "I would not—" he broke off, unable to speak further.

Now they were both laughing and crying all at once, and holding each other tightly. Finally she pulled away and brushed the tears from her face.

"It is good," she giggled. "Tell me now, Wolf, how it is to be, this great adventure."

Nils warmed to his subject, telling her of his theories about the river and its course, of the trading voyages of the Ericksons, and how he expected to meet his people on the coast.

"I do not understand the big canoes," she said. "My brother says they have wings?"

He tried to explain the use of sails, and found that Dove grasped the idea quickly.

"Yes," she said, "it is easier in a canoe, to go with the wind than against it."

"Right! And if you held up a robe, it would go faster!"

"But what if there is no wind, Wolf?"

"Then they wait. But there are long paddles. Men can use those."

Dove nodded. "I will know more when I see it. But tell me, you want to go away in this big canoe? *All* of us?" She smiled as she spoke the last, now much more confident.

"Well, yes. I would want to show you my home, where I was a child. I want my people to see my beautiful wife, and our good son."

She laughed again. "It would be good for him to see these things, Wolf. And for me. But what if your people are *not* there, at the salty water?"

"Then we come back, up the river. Find the People again."

"You make it sound very easy," she chuckled.

"A little harder to paddle upstream," he admitted. "But we have done harder things."

"Yes, that is true. So what is needed now?"

"To wait until the Awakening, mostly. Then we use the canoes to help the People cross the river. Then, start."

"We will need food, extra garments. . . ." she mused.

"Yes, some. We can hunt as we travel."

"It is good!" she exclaimed, jumping to her feet with finality. "I will talk to Hawk and to my mother. We will begin to prepare for the journey."

She walked away, happy now. He could tell by the strength of her stride. He marveled once again at the way a woman speaks with her body. The swing of her hips can express her mood. Anger, frustration, happiness, sorrow, or the joy and seductiveness of life itself. He admired the graceful curves of her body, and was reminded once more how very fortunate he had been to find such a woman. There was a slight pang of guilt that he had caused her to have doubt and sorrow. Even though it had been unintentional, he regretted having brought her pain. But she now understood, and was happy again, and that was good.

Preparations began immediately. At least, discussion did. There was plenty of time, the whole winter, almost. But the three women began to talk of the great adventure.

The children, too, were excited. Their enthusiasm lessened somewhat when they realized that the proposed departure was several moons away. Bright Sky and the two daughters of Odin and Hawk Woman became celebrities in their circle of friends. There were many children who envied them this opportunity for great adventure. Some, of course, were jealous, and tried to raise doubts.

"What if you are all swallowed by a great fish?" asked Blue Feather, one of their playmates.

"My father would not allow it," Bright Sky retorted. "Anyway, there are not fish like that in the river!"

"But what about downstream, or at the salty water? You do not know, Sky. And maybe not fish, but other creatures. Remember the stories of some of the people we visited last season? Giant lizards? Arrgh!"

He made a horrible grimace and spread his fingers, clawlike.

"Stop!" demanded Sky. "If there is much danger, we would not be going. Anyway, my father and Odin are great warriors, and holy men besides. Fire Man, too! Their gifts are strong."

"Do not listen to him, Sky," said Oak Leaf, Hawk's daughter by her first marriage. Oak Leaf was two years older, and was already mothering the younger two who would be going in the canoes. She turned to young Blue Feather.

"Let them alone," she warned. "You will have me to answer to!"

Blue Feather might be jealous, but he was not stupid. He wanted no part of such an argument. He turned away, disgruntled.

"Well," he shot back over his shoulder, "there might be monsters!"

Oak Leaf took a step toward him, and he quickened his pace.

"I am going," he protested. "I only said there *might* be!"

Nils had watched and listened to this entire exchange, unseen. It was amusing to see the children as they worked out their differences. These were certainly three capable youngsters. Good to have on such a journey. Oak Leaf had certainly put down the boy who was teasing. That one was like her mother, Hawk, and was not to be trifled with. He admired the women of the People for this quality, much like that of the Norse women.

He turned away, still unseen, a half-forgotten thought still in his head.

What had the boy Blue Feather said? *You do not know,* suggesting unknown monsters in the lower river. Nils shrugged it off, or tried to do so. But that old nagging doubt, born when he first saw this river, came creeping back.

Nonsense! he told himself. Had he not braved the perils of the North Sea with its great whales and other unknowns? Yes, and bested it, too.

71

At long last the days began to lengthen. It was by only a few moments at first, hardly distinguishable unless one really paid attention. Before many days had passed, however, the change was becoming apparent. The Moon of Long Nights was over. Sun had turned the course of the battle once more, and would now drive Cold Maker back to his retreat in the icy mountains somewhere in the north.

It was such a welcome thing that it was easy to forget what lay ahead—The Moon of Hunger.

During the few years in which the Norsemen had been with the People, there had not been a really severe winter. This had been discussed around the fires during the social "smokes," but only casually. There were some, mostly the elders, who advised caution, but beyond that, little concern. What is not an immediate problem can be dealt with later, no?

Each bright and sunny day lent optimism, and a careless attitude. It was easy, then, when trouble came, to think that there was no hint of warning. It should have been apparent, in retrospect, that the Moon of Hunger had been given such a name for good reason.

The morning dawned warm and sunny on that unforgettable day. Children played and adults greeted each other happily in the promising warmth. The color of the sunlight was changing, it was noted, recovering from the watery yellow of winter, to return to the rich golden tones of Sun's renewed torch.

The breeze was gentle, and came from the southwest. By noon, however, there came a stillness in the air. A vague anxiety crept through the encampment.

It was noted that the birds, singing their mating and territorial songs a short while earlier, were now silent. People who were observant also saw a change in their behavior.

Nils had been talking and smoking with Clay when the change occurred. The old man gestured casually toward a brilliant male cardinal. The bird had been singing from the top of a nearby cedar a little earlier. Now it was on the ground beneath the tree, searching for any of its blue fruit that might have fallen there unnoticed.

"Look," the old holy man pointed. "Does Red Bird know something?"

Nils watched for a moment. Even after he had been with the People for these several years, sometimes he remained puzzled over such an enigmatic remark.

"What is it, Uncle?" Nils asked. He had now come to the point where he was no longer embarrassed to reveal that he did not know. His respect for the wisdom of the People had grown. It was different from that of the Norse, but wisdom is wisdom anywhere, he had decided.

The old man watched the bird a little longer before he answered. A gray bird of about the same size, with a white breast and rusty sides jumped from the cedar's lower branches to join the scarlet forager. The cardinal struck out at the newcomer threateningly, and the towhee retreated, but only a little way. There were more important things to do than fight.

"They are searching for food . . . eating," Clay explained. "There must be a time coming soon when they cannot."

Clay moved from his comfortable position against the wall of the longhouse, out into the open to observe the horizon. He looked first to the southwest, then to the west. These were the likeliest directions from which a storm might come at this season. Turning on, he surveyed the northern sky, his gaze sweeping on toward the east. Rarely would weather breed in the east, though, at any season. He stopped suddenly, and his eyes returned toward the northwest.

"There!" he said simply, pointing.

Nils studied the horizon. There were a few high clouds, a thin veil that seemed no threat. Sunshine could filter through those to help warm the earth. Then he saw what had attracted the holy man's attention. A dirty gray-blue line stretched across the far horizon. It appeared to offer no immediate threat, but as a sailor, Nils knew that this was the sort of sign to take seriously.

"There . . ." the old man repeated.

Even as he spoke, there was a stirring in the still air, a mere breath, as if now discovered, Cold Maker must move quickly.

"Cold Maker comes," said Clay.

"How long, Uncle?"

"By evening, maybe."

The stirring of the warm air now began to chill. Nils turned back to glance at the dirty gray cloud bank again. Was it possible that it had grown in the few moments since Clay had noted it? It seemed so.

"He moves quickly," Clay noted, verifying Nils's impression. "We will need firewood tonight."

It was not long before the People noted the chill in the air, and the growing darkness to the north and west. There was a scurrying to bring fuel into the lodges. It was made more difficult by the fact that the winter had depleted the available supply. With warm weather, it had appeared that the necessity was past for the season. There had been no urgency. Now, there was.

People cast anxious glances over their shoulders as they hurried back from hasty foraging up and down the river. The dark blue-gray mass of cloud was now growing rapidly. Nils was reminded of some of the stories they had heard around the campfires of other tribes and nations in the past few seasons. A great monster, who could swallow the sun, the earth, the sky itself . . . It was easy today to understand the origins of such tales. To watch the rapidly approaching storm front was frightening. It seemed a living thing, evil beyond compare, writhing in hideous shapelessness with the threat of unspeakable danger.

The camp was still bathed in thin sunlight when the first flakes of snow began to fall. These were not the fat moist flakes that foretell a quiet snowstorm. They were small and dry, buffeted on a nervous wind that curled and buffeted and changed direction every few heartbeats. Nils thought of the Norse tales of earth's destruction, the terrible Fimbul-winter when snows came "from all four directions at once."

The People cast last anxious glances outside, and drew the skin curtains behind them to settle in while the storm ran its course.

They could tell when the main force of the invasion struck. The winds rose to a howling, shrieking terror, buffeting the longhouse. Hungry demons blew frosty breath through cracks and crevices that had gone unnoticed until now. Little piles of dusty-dry snow began to form along the inside of the north wall, making miniature drifts on the floor. Anxiously, people hung skins over the worst of the cracks to defend against the icy winds of Cold Maker's assault.

When darkness fell, the storm was still raging. Actually, it was difficult to tell when night did come, so dark had it become outside. For a while the smoke hole in the roof revealed a dark blue-gray sky with hard-driven snow whipping horizontally across it. Then that background changed gradually to black, laced with the continuing sweep of dry white powder.

The People slept, wakened, replenished the fire, and slept again. Morning came, they rose, ate a little, and watched the square of the sky become gradually lighter. The blowing snow was diminishing, and the howl of the wind was less frightening. Shortly after noon they ventured out, into a heavily drifted world bathed in sparkling sunlight.

Hawk Woman stepped into the open and raised a hand to the north in an obscene gesture.

"We have beaten you, Cold Maker!" she shouted.

There was general laughter, but Nils noticed that there was no happiness in the face of Clay.

"What is it, Uncle?" he asked, aside.

"I do not know, Wolf. It is good to see the sun, no? But the cold is still here. I am made to think that maybe this is only a trick of Cold Maker's. Was that only the first feint of the battle?"

The chill that struck through the heart of the Norseman was not entirely from the weather. Clay, he had noted, had an instinctive feel for such things. If the old man was voicing this sort of caution, he must feel something that was not readily apparent to others. And now that it had been called to his attention, Nils realized that it was actually no warmer. It only seemed so, now that the wind had died.

Clay proved right. Within a day, another wave of cold swept down, worse than before. If the first sortie had seemed like the dreadful Fimbul-winter, this was doubly terrifying. There was much complaining about the drafty quarters of the longhouse. It would not be so uncomfortable in an earth-lodge, many noted.

Some went even further. "Why are we traveling anyway?" demanded an old woman. "We have left good places, where we could have built real lodges, and for *this*?"

A certain amount of grumbling was to be expected. Nothing could be done immediately, so they bundled up more tightly and listened to the howl of the demons outside. The storm lasted longer this time, and the snow grew deeper and more drifted.

Firewood had been seriously depleted, and there was a concerted effort to stockpile more as soon as the storm lessened. It was even more difficult now, because of the deep and drifted snow. Much of the wood being brought into the longhouses now was that which had already been rejected as too rotten or too green.

The respite was shorter this time, too. The storm seemed to turn, even as it passed. There was a brief time of calm, but it was soon shattered by another blast. Even those who had not become very apprehensive until now showed faces lined with anxiety. When would it stop?

It was after the third onslaught that Calling Dove approached her husband to tell him of a threat he had not even considered.

"Food is running low."

"But . . . Dove, there are packs of corn, beans . . ."

She nodded. "But those are for planting. If we eat those, we starve *next* winter, because we have no crops."

He began to see the problem that they faced. It might approach the point where some would starve, with the food that could have saved them right before their eyes.

"This is the Moon of Hunger, in most winters," Dove told him. "This time, it is the Moon of Starvation."

The women began to ration the remaining supplies more carefully. Many of the adults almost ceased eating altogether, to save more food for the children.

"They are the future of the People," explained Red Fawn.

Still the vicious weather continued. Day after day, the cold remained, and wave after wave of storm and snow swept down from the north. Nils wondered how long this could go on, and looked for old Clay, without success.

"He is gone," said a little girl.

"Gone where? When?"

"Before Cold Maker's last visit."

"Where did he go?"

The child shrugged and waved a hand vaguely to the north.

"To fight Cold Maker," she said. "He was singing."

"Singing?"

"Yes, Uncle. The Death Song."

> *The earth and the sky go on forever,*
> *But today is a good day to die.*

The song with which a warrior of the People enters into a battle to the death . . . Nils realized that what the child said was true. Clay would battle to the death with Cold Maker. Whether the old holy man could make a difference in the course of the storm was in question, though Nils had seen some amazing evidence of the power of Clay's gift.

What could not be denied was that Clay had given life to a child. One who could survive on the food that it would have taken to feed the aging holy man.

72

As quickly as Cold Maker's last dying thrust of winter came, it was gone. From one day to the next, the sun shone, mild southern breezes warmed the earth, and the People moved out into the sunshine.

There was mourning for those who had succumbed. Two in one of the big longhouses, one old woman in another, a sickly child who had never been quite right. There were others. . . . In most of these cases old people had simply stopped using the food that would feed the coming generation. Cold Maker, with his devious ways, had attacked some quietly, smothering their last breaths from inside their very bodies as their lungs filled with fluids that could not be coughed out. Even some children fell to this sneak attack. In those cases the loss was most pitiful, that a child should be taken before it had a chance to grow and live.

Nils remembered something that Singing Moose had once said about the death-dealing congestion of the lungs.

"It is the enemy of the young, but the friend of the old," Moose had pointed out.

Nils now thought about that, even as the high-pitched wails of public mourning hovered over the camp. The enemy cold had struck down some young children. He was only thankful that none had been of the immediate families of those he loved.

The other thing that he was beginning to understand, though, was the attitude of the old. Most of those who had recently died *had* seemed to welcome it quietly, as a friend. The fact that they had stopped eating surely hastened the process, but there was something else at work. Somehow the will to die seemed to *cause* it. It usually happened quietly, with no fear or anxiety apparent at all. In this respect, the attitude toward death was much like that of his own people, and he admired it. Of course, a Norseman would prefer to go out bravely, with a weapon in his hand, fighting with his last breath. Quiet submission was a less acceptable mode.

Old Clay . . . *There* was a man! Nils could visualize how it must have been, the old holy man striding into the teeth of the gale to challenge Cold Maker's power on his own terms. Surely there was a place in Asgard's great hall of fallen heroes for such a man!

Nils smiled inwardly at such thoughts. The man was a *Skraeling!* There had been a time when he would have thought that it was ludicrous to think of a Skraeling, an ignorant savage, approaching the throne in Odin's hall to be welcomed as a hero.

Now, thanks to his almost-brother who had been named Odin as a cruel joke, Nils had accepted many things. Things that he did not understand, maybe, but that he had to accept because he had seen them happen. *Maybe,* he thought, *it is like the* solarstein, *the sun-stone.* He did not understand how the crystal knew north, either, but he was willing to use it.

The People had other gifts, he was sure. Gifts that could not be described, even. Like those who could die when they chose. Was this simply *because* they chose to will it at that time? And he was sure that Clay had been able to foretell the future. *How?*

One other thing was a puzzle to him. As he thought of Clay, and his courageous challenge to Cold Maker, Nils wondered at his own reaction. He had thought of Clay approaching the Hall of Heroes. *Why not the throne of God?* He, Nils, had been raised a Christian. Why, now, did he find himself thinking in terms of the Norse religion of his grandfather? More and more, he was becoming convinced that Grandfather had been reluctant to give up certain of the old beliefs. The old man must have had a hard time not to inflict more of his own philosophy on his young grandson. Only now was Nils realizing it.

What would his mother think, for instance, of Nils's theory that the People could welcome death by willing it so? Or what would the priest have said? Nils had the uncomfortable feeling that such an idea would have been branded as heresy. He would have been accused of blasphemy and would have said many Hail Marys before it was over.

And the visions and dreams that seemed to play such a part in the lives of the People . . . These seemed quite useful sometimes. His feeling about this was colored with a tinge of guilt, because he knew what the priest would say about that. It was demonism, pagan worship, and the work of Satan, at the very least. The immortal souls of the People (if indeed Skraelings *have* souls) were doomed to hellfire and damnation. They must undergo the transformation that would bring salvation.

Again, that pang of guilt. He did not feel that he was qualified to bring Christianity to the Skraelings, and would not want to try. That was the job of the priests. His feeling of guilt, however, was not over that. It was that he wondered whether anyone *should* try to bring them salvation. From what he could see, the People were doing quite well. He and Svenson had adopted their ways in large measure, rather than vice versa. It had been easier.

He thought of the Creation stories around the fires of the past few seasons. Why had he chosen the Norse mythology to relate to them, instead of the Christian legends? He was not sure. Maybe because the Norse tales had seemed more appropriate at the time, for a primitive people in a harsh northern clime. No matter. His tales of ice-giants and gnomes had been accepted eagerly. He had considered, a time or two, telling the one about the Garden of Eden, Adam's rib, the apple and the snake. Maybe sometime.

The sudden thought came to him that the sometime must be *now*. As soon as the ice on the river was open, they would be gone. Possibly to return later, though that was a bit vague as he thought of the future. Well, there might not even be an opportunity to tell that story. Some day he would share it with Dove.

As he thought about the immediate future, though, another doubt struck him. It had been some time since he had the dream, but it had occurred several times since the People had reached the great river. He shuddered a little as he thought of it. Especially since he had been thinking of the importance of dreams to the People. Were they more attuned to such things, and to the possible meanings?

It was always the same, or quite similar. There was water, and he was in a boat or canoe. Sometimes, even, he seemed to be *in* the water itself. There was a dread, a fear of an undefined Something, an evil presence in the dark depths. The first time he had experienced the dream, he had thought that it was connected to the Chalagee story he had just heard. The giant leech that lies in wait in the dark waters was a gripping tale, guaranteed to make the listener shudder with dread of the unknown. It had been puzzling to him, and humorous in a wry manner, that such fear was worse than the dread of sea monsters in the ocean's depths. The risk of an encounter with a whale as long as the *Norsemaiden* was nothing compared to thoughts of a slimy Something of unknown size and shape. . . .

The dream itself had been vague and poorly defined, too. Some visions are starkly real, as clear as any seen in reality. Even more so, maybe. Others are shrouded in a misty nothingness that shifts and shimmers, ebbing and flowing, while the mind of a mere mortal tries to cope with its mysteries.

Nils's dream was of that ethereal quality. The action in it was slow, painfully slow, each and every time. He sat on or in the water, watching wisps of fog or mist curl lazily along the surface. It was warm, damp, and sticky. He held something in his hands, it was never clear to him exactly what. A weapon? A pole or a canoe paddle, maybe. There was always the feeling that whatever its purpose, the object was useless in the present situation.

He was never certain in the dream where the creature came from. . . . Out of the mist and fog, or rising from the depths of the dark water. It did grow larger as it grew nearer. A giant armlike projection tipped with jagged claws thrust up from the water's surface, towering over his head and descending on him to drag him under. There was a vague feeling that in the water around him were other similar appendages, all grasping at him, hungry for his life.

He had awakened with a little cry of fright, to find himself in familiar surroundings, with Dove sleeping quietly at his side. She stirred sleepily and rolled over to open her arms to him.

He had lain there in the darkness for a long time, puzzling over the dream. It had been so real, so terrifying. Dove's warm body next to him was a great comfort. Dove . . . *She* had been at risk in his dream, too!

Nils had told no one of that dream. The People had some taboos about the sharing of such things and he was not quite certain how they might apply here.

The dream had recurred several times since that first frightening experience. It was always a fearful thing, but he recovered more quickly now. Sometimes there would be many moons without it followed by recurrences almost every night for a while.

There were a number of unique things about it. Perhaps the most puzzling was his perception of the appendages that reached for him out of the water and the mist. He had begun with the assumption that his dream dealt with the giant leech. Such a creature, slimy and dreadful, could suck blood from an unsuspecting victim painlessly, without his knowledge. It could be as round as a ball, or long and slender, changing shape at will from one moment to the next. And how big would such a creature be? The largest leech that he had ever encountered was smaller than his fingertip. It was firmly fastened between his toes after a swim in a muddy pond, back in his childhood. He had felt nothing at all. He had seen larger ones, years later, in a jar in Stadt. Even these were smaller than a man's little finger. Maybe the fear of the unknown extended to size. . . . Would the giant leech be larger than a man?

There was another puzzle about it, though, that seemed even more troublesome to him. It dealt with the quality of the terror that reached at him in the dream. A leech could, he conceded, assume almost any shape that might suit its purpose. Any of the shapes, though, would be limited by the texture of the creature. With no bones or shell, its shape would always be soft and slithery . . . slime. Though the thought of being dragged beneath the water by such a creature made him shudder, he could not quite reconcile it to the dream. An arm or tentacle of the leech, no matter how big, would be soft, slimy, and elastic, even though it might be powerful and sinewy.

That did not fit the impression he had of the creature in the dream. The arms that thrust at him, seeking to drag him under, were not of such a texture. They were hard and horny, with jagged claws and irregular projections. It was an inconsistency that bothered him almost as much as the dream itself.

Now, as the time neared to begin the trip downriver, the dream was recurring frequently. Nils decided that there was something about it that he was missing. He must look for advice. But where? Clay would have given good council, but Clay was gone, having given his life in the battle with Cold Maker. There was a holy man in the other clan, but Nils was reluctant to speak of such things to someone he hardly knew.

He often discussed things that related to the customs of the People with Calling Dove. Somehow, that did not seem appropriate in this case. Even less so, the thought of discussing the dream with Svenson. But he must. . . . Then it came to him. *Odin!*

Of course! Nils wished now that he had considered this before. Odin would take him seriously, could tell him of the Peoples' customs, and might have a very good feel for the meaning of the visions.

Nils went immediately in search of his friend, and found him sitting on a rock, watching the river. Great chunks of ice were floating down the middle of the channel. It would be necessary to wait until the current cleared somewhat.

"Ah! How is it, almost-brother?" Odin greeted.

"It is good," Nils responded easily. "How is the river?"

"Still rising a little. See, the ice is in the middle."

The flotsam of ice, fragmenting and grinding itself smaller as it melted, would seek the banks of the river when its level started to drop, Nils knew. There must still be much melting upstream.

"We will see," Odin said philosophically. "When it is time . . ."

He trailed off in word and thought.

"Odin, I would speak with you of something else," Nils began.

The Skraeling glanced up, but said nothing. Nils began to blurt out the story of his dreams of the giant leech, pouring it out, cleansing his soul of the torment. At last he paused, exhausted from the emotion of the effort.

Odin stared at him for a long time, and finally spoke.

"My brother, why did you not . . . No, I understand. . . . Ah, I wish Clay could help us."

"What could this mean?" Nils demanded. "And I did not know whether I should tell anyone such a dream."

"Dove?" asked Odin.

"No, I have not told her."

"My friend," Odin began thoughtfully, "I do not know. This seems to be . . . But you say the creature does not *look* like the leech of the Chalagees?"

"No, it does not," Nils stated positively. "This is . . ." He paused as the importance of his words sank into his mind. "Odin, this must be *something else!*"

Odin nodded. "I am made to think so. Could it be just the dangers of a journey?"

Nils thought about it for a moment. "Maybe." That must be it. Any journey might be fraught with danger of some sort. Unknown dangers. Yes, that must be it. He had misunderstood the dream, confusing it in his mind with the story of the giant leech. Yes, it was much clearer, now. He wished that he had spoken to Odin before.

"It is good!" he said with a smile. He felt better than he had for many moons. Maybe, now that he had acknowledged the warning vision for what it was, it would cease tormenting him. Maybe . . .

lanning now became easier, with the concern behind him that had been brought about by the weather. He looked forward with an eagerness that he had thought he possessed, but which had obviously fallen short until now.

Specific needs for the journey came to the attention of the party, and with this, Nils was in his own element. Supplies were prepared and stowed in the rawhide carrying packs that were characteristic of the People. A herd of buffalo, migrating slowly northward with the greening of the season, provided a good spring hunt. Packs of dried meat and pemmican were prepared and set aside for the journey.

Nils began to think about specific decisions. Who of the party would travel in which canoe? He mentally evaluated the group, and began to divide and assign positions in the two canoes. All, of course, would be subject to Odin's approval. He was far more skilled in this sort of travel than any of the others.

The canoes could carry as many as six people, one in the prow and one astern. Four could sit in the middle, by twos, side by side. That, of course, with no baggage, but they would have a considerable amount. He paused to count the people involved. Dove, Bright Sky, himself, three. Odin and Hawk Woman and their two daughters would make seven. Sven and Red Fawn, nine. *Yes, it is good,* he thought, and smiled to himself. He was thinking like his wife's people. But it was true. There should be adequate carrying space for the nine people who would go, and the baggage they required.

Then he began to think of specific seating arrangements. He would speak with Odin later, but this was a way to vent his enthusiasm, planning in his mind. Odin would serve as steersman in the stern of the first canoe. The other steersman could be either himself or Svenson. Maybe they could trade off. Or, Red Fawn was quite able to serve in that capacity. Any of the other adults could handle the prow of each canoe, and that would leave five people to sit amidships with the baggage. Three of these would be children. Yes, it was a very satisfactory plan. He would speak of it to Odin soon.

First, of course, they would assist the People in crossing the river. They were still waiting for the ice to clear and the river to subside from its swollen condition. But it does no harm to plan, and Nils's mind was racing eagerly ahead. They would set the last boatload of the People on the west bank, go back to load the canoes, and start downstream, riding the current of the river on the great adventure. He was aware of his childish exuberance. In fact, he reveled in it. Combined with the skills of his Norse heritage, it would stand the party in good stead. He felt invincible, sometimes, glorying in the strength of his young manhood. What a thrill, to have conquered the dangers of this new world!

He had not the slightest doubt as to the success of the mission. The maps and charts that he and Svenson had created during the long winter appeared more convincing each time he looked at them. He thought of the calendar, and the likeliest time for exploration along the coast. Yes, summer should find much activity. It was entirely possible by now that there was a regular trade route up and down Vinland's east coast, with Straumfjord the axis of the operation, and the bulky *knarrs* stopping along the coast as a routine operation.

But he must not count on it, he realized. It would be good, but more likely the first Norsemen they would encounter would be an exploring party in a dragon ship. One of the Ericksons, probably. Thorwald's enthusiasm for exploration of the continent was well known, in contrast to Leif's more conservative tendency to establish settlements as he went. *Yes*, Nils fantasized, *probably Thorwald.* Would it not be a great triumph if they happened to meet Thorwald Erickson as he sailed up the great river? What a delightful scene he could imagine.

Good day, Thorwald, he would say. *How goes it with you?*

And Erickson would be speechless with astonishment, and Nils would continue.

I thank you for the sun-stone. It has been of great help in mapping the continent. Here are our charts. . . .

But that line of thought brought the memory of Helge Landsverk, and he felt again the sadness and failure of that doomed expedition. *No matter,* he told himself defensively. *This one will be a success.*

He returned to reality from his daydreams as Svenson approached. The old sailor appeared concerned.

"What is it, Sven?"

"I would talk with you, Nils."

He had seldom seen Svenson so serious. Was there something wrong?

"Yes?"

"It is of this voyage downriver," Sven began hesitantly. "Is it really . . . does it? . . . Nils, do we really want to do this?"

Nils was caught completely off guard. This was unlike Svenson, who had never before hesitated to accept *any* challenge. What had changed? He studied the older man as if he had never seen him before. Sven's image in Nils's mind had always been one of gentle power. It was a childish image, perhaps, dating far back. Yes, he had built an idea based on the old sailor's appearance and good humor. As a teenager, Nils had imagined that Thor probably looked much like this. The red hair and beard, the burly good nature of the man, his strength and determination. Nils had outgrown that mental picture as a childish diversion. At least he thought he had, until now. He had never told anyone of this daydream of Sven as Thor, but now he found it was still there. He still thought of Sven as invincible, unafraid.

"What do you mean, Sven?"

"I am not sure, Nils. At one time, I would have been as eager as you."

Nils did not know what to say. Could it be that Svenson was afraid of such an adventure? He would certainly not accuse him.

"We might get home," Svenson continued, "or, maybe not. But would it really matter?"

"I do not understand, Sven. What are you saying?"

"Well . . . I suppose . . . is it worth the effort and risk?"

"Sven . . . your family . . ."

Ah, maybe that was it! Sven had a wife and children at home. Unlike Nils, who could return home with an exotic foreign wife, Svenson could not show up at home with Red Fawn. She must be left behind. That problem had not occurred to Nils. He now saw that he had touched on the heart of the matter.

Sven took a deep breath. "Nils," he said, "we have been gone seven years. You know that they think us dead, because those at Straumfjord will have heard of the battle. Now, Gudred—my wife, you know—we have always had an understanding. If I was lost at sea, she would remarry without hesitation, no?"

"Yes, but—"

"Nils, she is remarried now. Our youngest child is grown."

There was silence for a little while, and Sven continued. "It is better if she thinks me dead. Less problem for her."

"And for you and Fawn?" Nils asked. He was uncertain as to what he thought of this.

"Maybe," Svenson admitted. "We are very happy together. Nils, I have slept more nights with Fawn than with Gudred. Besides, I am feeling my age a little. My bones are stiff on cold mornings. To give up a warm bed and a good life to brave an unknown river . . . it sounds like a big journey."

Nils had not thought of Svenson's ever aging, but now he took another look, in a new light. Yes, the bright red of Sven's hair was yellowing along the temples. There was a streak or two in his beard. The whole picture, Nils realized, was a bit incongruous. Here was an aging sailor, in the buckskins of a Skraeling, with his hair plaited in the style of the People, as was his own. The whole thing was striking Nils as funny, and he smiled.

"Nils," Sven went on, "you are young and strong. You should go home. Ah, what tales you can tell! But tell them I died bravely, they will mourn, but they will be happy. Gudred will probably be pleased that she does not have two husbands!"

Sven chuckled now, and Nils could see how this course of action would simplify the old sailor's last years. Probably quite a few of them. Though, as he thought of it, Sven had been to sea before Nils could remember. He must be how old? Possibly fifty?

As if in answer to these thoughts, Sven spoke again, very seriously. "I told your father, before your first voyage to the Isles, that I would look after you," Svenson admitted. "He was my friend, as well as my employer. But now I am made to think that you can take care of yourself. I will help you get started, if you are set on going, but I see no need for either of us to go."

"Sven, I have to. I can let our people know much about this new world, no?"

Svenson nodded. "Of course. I thought you would feel so. Besides, it is an adventure. Ah, you are as bad as the Ericksons," he teased. "But I will help you when you start."

Nils nodded, lost in thought. This put an entirely different light on the makeup of the party. Four adults, three children. It would be a more dangerous combination. Not insurmountable, but something to think on. He would talk to Odin about it, and soon.

"It is good, Sven," he said.

"Remember, though," Svenson said, "when you tell them of my death, make it good!"

"How would you like it?" asked Nils, laughing. "Overrun by hordes of enemy warriors?"

"Maybe," agreed Svenson good-naturedly. "Weapon in hand, like a Viking, fighting till his last breath." His face lighted. "I know! Tell them I died, ax in hand, against the giant bloodsucker of the Chalagees!"

Sven doubled over, chuckling in amusement at his own cleverness.

Nils sat unnoticed, in shocked silence. Of all the stories that they had heard over the years, how had Svenson happened to think of that one? A chill crept up the back of his neck, and his skin fairly crawled in dread.

"What is the matter?" asked Sven.

"It is nothing," Nils lied. "That is good. How did you choose that story?"

Svenson shrugged. "Who knows? It is a good story. I dream about it sometimes."

Sven said it casually, but Nils wondered. Was there more concern in the old sailor's eyes than in his voice? Was this the reason, or one of the reasons, for Svenson *not* to start the long journey downriver?

Was Svenson's dream as terrifying as his own?

74

ow Nils faced a dilemma. The decision of Svenson not to try to return to civilization was a complete surprise and shock. As he began to think about it, however, Nils could see Sven's position.

It was not a matter of abandoning his family at home in Stadt. Not entirely anyway. That family had been without its husband and father for a long time. Legally, he was dead, lost on a voyage to the unknown. A sailor's wife, it was assumed, would remarry after a decent time of mourning. That time could vary, but in this case there was the additional weight of the news that must have reached home. The expedition on which Svenson had sailed had been destroyed by Skraelings during the exploration of Vinland. There were no known survivors.

This news would have reached Stadt by way of Straumfjord within a year, probably. Gudred Svenson would have been free to marry six years ago, now, and undoubtedly would have done so. For Sven to return now would create more problems than it solved. What would Gudred do with two husbands? There were many pitfalls, both emotional and legal, here. The woman would probably have to choose between them. . . . Maybe Svenson's way was best, to spare her that torture, and himself the pain of possible rejection.

There was another factor, too. Sven's marriage to Red Fawn appeared to be a happy one. To go back to Stadt, Sven would have to leave Fawn. He could not take a wife home to where another wife waited. But, by leaving Fawn behind, he would make *her* eligible to remarry. And what if Gudred elected to stay with her present husband? Sven would have nothing at all. If he could avoid all this potential hurt to so many people, why not? It seemed the wisest choice.

All of this reasoning, however, made Nils's choices no easier. He did not relish the idea of an expedition with only two men, and five women and children. Not that the women would be any burden. They were both as capable as any man. Still, their primary concern would be protection of the children. This was as it should be. But that would leave only himself and Odin for defense if necessary. It was not an insurmountable situation, but it made him uneasy. This was a far different scenario than when Sven and Fawn would have provided two more unfettered warriors for defense of the party. He must think carefully on this, and discuss it with Odin.

As it happened, Odin approached him first.

"My almost-brother," the Skraeling began, concern showing in his face, "I would speak with you."

Nils nodded. "You have talked to Fire Man."

"Yes . . . But that is not it."

Nils experienced a moment of panic. There was *worse* news?

"What?" Nils demanded. "How bad?"

"Not really bad," Odin said. "But bad just now. Hawk Woman is with child."

Nils felt his plans crumbling, his world falling apart under him. There was a rush of anger for an instant. The actions and desires of others were taking from him all the power of decision that he thought he had. It had been hard enough to justify a journey into the unknown with the children, but with a pregnant woman?

"How far?" he asked numbly.

Odin gave his characteristic shrug. "Two, three moons, maybe."

Nils calculated quickly. That would put the time of birthing in the autumn. In the Moon of Falling Leaves, maybe. Or in the Moon of Madness.

The whole thing was madness. A twinge of resentment made him wonder if Hawk Woman had intentionally accomplished this to defeat the expedition. She would be at her largest and most unwieldly shape just at the critical part of the voyage on the lower river. It would be possible for her to go. The women of the People often did hard work and even travel during a pregnancy. But it would limit her effectiveness in defense, in handling the canoe.

"Hawk's heart is glad," Odin said. "But she knows that is not what you would wish. For that part, she has sorrow."

Nils was embarrassed that he had suspected her of duplicity in the timing of this pregnancy.

"Tell her it is nothing," he mumbled.

Odin nodded, and both were fully aware that such a statement was ludicrous under the circumstances.

"I am made to think," Nils said slowly, "that this ends the journey down the river. Shall we use the canoes to help the People across and then leave them behind?"

"Maybe not," Odin said thoughtfully. "You and I . . ."

"You would leave your family?" Nils asked, shocked at the idea.

"No, no, only a little while," Odin said. "You and Dove go on, I come back."

"But we could not handle two canoes."

Odin nodded. "That is true. And we would need two. One to go on, one to go back."

"This cannot be, my brother."

"Yes, I know. Unless . . . maybe another man or two . . . maybe Fire Man would go, and come back with me."

"Maybe. Let us ask him."

Svenson was thoughtful about it, but it was apparent that his heart was not really in it.

"Nils," he explained, "I can still do what is needed, but my joints tell me that they have seen many winters."

Nils was amused at the manner in which the old sailor used the way of the People to explain his position.

"There are many snows in my hair," Sven went on. "See? If I am needed, I will try, but on cold mornings, I am moving very slowly. Could you find another man?"

"Sven, there is none like you," Nils assured him. "But I understand. Do not worry over it. We will find someone."

Sven seemed greatly relieved.

The search progressed without much success. They did not want to attract too much attention, but word spread quickly. There were several young men who approached them, eager for adventure but lacking the responsibility and maturity that was needed.

Conversely, anyone reliable enough to be considered was also responsible enough not to be interested. Nils was dejected, ready to give up on the entire plan, abandoning all hope of returning home.

Then he was approached by a man who might prove to be just what was needed.

"You remember me? I am Snake, friend of your friend, Odin."

"Of course. How is it with you, friend of my friend?"

Nils did not know the man well. Snake was quiet and thoughtful, one easily overlooked in the everyday activities of the People. He belonged to a different lodge than that of Odin and his family, and consequently their contact had been irregular. Still, he knew that Snake was well respected, especially by Odin, and that the two had been boyhood friends.

"I have been told," Snake began carefully, "that you look for someone to go downriver with you."

"You know someone?"

"Myself."

Nils had been curious as to this man's interest, but this was a surprise. He tried to think . . . did Snake have a family? Yes, surely. A wife, anyway.

"You have talked to Odin?"

Even as he asked, Nils knew somehow that Snake had not. He would not presume on friendship to accomplish a purpose such as this.

"No."

"What of your family?" Nils asked bluntly. This would tell him more without revealing his own lack of memory. There was something . . .

"My wife was taken by Cold Maker this past winter, you know," Snake said, his face drawn with emotion.

That was it! Nils told himself. *I knew there was something!* At the same time he was embarrassed that he had been so thoughtless.

"Yes," he said sympathetically, trying to salvage a bad mistake as best he could. "My heart is heavy for you. But your children?"

He devoutly hoped that he remembered correctly, that there were children.

"They are with their mother's family," said Snake. "They are well cared for."

"It is good," said Nils, happy to have survived the treacherous moments of this conversation. "Now, about our journey. I must talk with Odin, but . . . do you know the canoe?"

"Some. I have used the round boats."

"Good. I will talk to Odin."

Odin was delighted at the prospect of having his boyhood friend as a companion on the downriver journey.

"Yes! Thorsson, I could choose no better man!" Odin said excitedly.

They began again to plan the details of loading the two canoes. There would be plenty of room now, with only four adults and young Bright Sky. One canoe would have been enough, except that Odin must have a means to return upriver.

"You would not need to go," Nils suggested. "Dove and I can handle our canoe."

Odin was quite definite on this, however. "No!" He smiled the mischievous little smile that had become familiar to the Norsemen. "Someone must look after you. Dove cannot do it alone."

"How far will you go?"

Odin shrugged. "Who knows? When the time comes, we will all know. Then Snake and I will go back."

It seemed a good plan. Preparations went forward, both for the river crossing by the People, and for the downriver trip. Svenson helped with the planning of the latter. He hovered and helped and gave advice, fussing around like a mother hen. Nils knew that Sven must have mixed feelings about this parting. He had such feelings himself. Nils could not remember a time when he had not known Sven. To part with him now would not be easy. He could imagine, too, the old sailor's emotions. Sven must refuse the call of the sea that had been his life, and that must be difficult for him. But with the help of such a woman as Red Fawn . . . Probably, Nils reflected, a good woman would be the only thing that could tear Svenson from the arms of his mistress, the sea.

Finally came the day when Odin approached with a gleam in his one eye.

"I am made to think," he said simply, "that our time to leave is near. There is only a little ice in the river this morning."

They had noticed that the river's level was falling. Ice and debris no longer rode the main current in the center of the stream, but floated lazily out toward the banks.

"When?" asked Nils.

Odin shrugged. "The holy men will decide. Big Tree may ask you, too, since Clay is gone."

Nils nodded. "What should I say?"

"Whatever seems good. Three days, maybe. That will let you change it if you need to."

"Good. I will talk to Fire Man, too. But Tree may not ask me."

Odin nodded. "That is true. Listen to your guide."

Nils recalled that from time to time Odin had made such a remark. He was aware that the People had a high respect for things of the spirit, for dreams, and for the protection of one's personal guide. Many signs were interpreted as warnings, others as omens of good luck. He had not taken these seriously at first, but they were so much a way of life for the People.

He must talk at greater length with Odin about this. Maybe during their time together on the river there would be an opportunity. Just now, however, such ethereal musings were overshadowed by the one at hand. In a few days they would start the greatest journey of his life. He was going home.

75

That night the dream returned to haunt him. This time it was even more frightening than before. He did not waken as quickly, and it seemed that he could not waken at all. It was the sort of dream where the dreamer *knows* that he is dreaming, but can do nothing about it. This makes the fear even worse, because of the helpless feeling that he has lost all control.

The dream was much the same as it began. Dark water, glowering sky, a foggy mist over the water. He could not tell whether this was ocean or river. *Odd,* he thought, *I have never wondered before.* A light drizzle was falling, it seemed. More properly, hanging in the air. Fat droplets of mist seemed suspended permanently, soaking everything, making a sodden world even wetter.

He was being carried along, and seemed to have no control. His paddle . . . *yes, it must be a canoe paddle in the hand* . . . was useless against the mighty pull of the current. *A current* . . . *It must be the river, then.* Just as he realized this, still in his odd dual role as observer and participant, it happened. Dark tentacles thrust up out of dark water, reaching, writhing. . . .

This was the part where he had always wakened. The conscious part of his mind, the part that knew it was a dream, waited, but it did not happen. In a panic, he felt that he was trapped in the dream. The reaching, grasping thing from the river's depths thrust up, searching. This tentacle had risen from the left side and behind him. Now it reached *over* him, grasping at the figure in front of him.

This was the first time that he had been aware of another person in his dream, but he could see her dimly through the mist . . . a woman. The reaching Thing grasped at her, and he tried to scream a warning, but it was too late. The woman turned her head and the terror in her eyes was horrible to see.

"Dove!" he screamed.

Just then something reaching from behind struck him, grasped, and pulled him under. The dark chill of the waters closed over him, and he was drowning. He struggled, kicking and fighting his way, trying to reach the surface. But he was being pulled deeper, tangled by the clutching fingers of the creature below. He fought, even as consciousness was slipping away. . . .

"Wolf! Wake up!"

Dove was shaking him, holding him in her arms now, and the darkness around him was the dark of the lodge, not that of the water. Gratefully, he drew a deep breath.

"Dove . . . I . . ."

She held him tightly. "What is it, my husband?"

Someone tossed fuel on the embers of the fire in the center of the longhouse, and a flicker of yellow began to light the area. It was a great relief to see the familiar surroundings.

"What is it?" called Red Fawn from their curtained cubicle nearby.

"A night-vision, maybe," Dove answered. "I do not know."

"Yes . . . yes, it is good now," Nils mumbled, embarrassed at the commotion. "It was only a night-vision."

People were settling back into the arms of slumber. There was some grumbling, but not much. The seriousness of a night-vision was well recognized. Above all, it was a very private thing. If the dreamer chose to tell it, so be it, but if not, it would be a serious breach of custom to inquire.

"A dream? A night-vision?" Dove whispered.

"Yes . . . I will tell you. . . ."

"Ssh . . . you do not need to."

"Yes, I want to. You are in it."

"Later, then. Now, rest."

She lay beside him and snuggled him in her arms, and it was good.

He lay in the darkness a long time, staring at the dim flicker of firelight on the ceiling around the blackened smoke hole. Dove's muscles relaxed, her breathing became regular, and he knew that she had fallen asleep again. He would tell her of his recurring dream in the morning. Meanwhile, it seemed unlikely that he would be able to sleep. The dream . . . *What could it mean?*

• • • •

"You had a bad night?" Odin asked casually as they rose for the day and began to move around.

Both men had gone outside to empty their bladders. No one else was within hearing. Nils realized that Odin's comment was not really a question, but a statement, to open a conversation about the incident that had roused the whole lodge.

"Yes," Nils answered. "Odin, I would speak with you of this . . . the night-vision again. The People see them as very important."

Odin looked startled. "Your people do not?"

"Not the same, maybe. This is a thing that Clay would have known about."

"That is true. But we do not have Clay."

"Let me tell you of this dream, Odin." He quickly sketched the basic points of the dream, as Odin's one eye widened in wonder.

"The same, but now drowning . . . Maybe this *is* a warning, Thorsson!"

To Nils it was almost a relief to have that suspicion actually voiced. Now he realized that he had been unwilling, or perhaps unable to face that possibility as a meaning in the dream. Odin was standing there, lost in thought, pondering the situation. Another man approached the area sleepily, and nodded a greeting as he prepared to answer his call of nature.

Odin rearranged his own private parts in his breechclout, and motioned to Nils to follow him. This, the area where men came to empty their bladders, would become busy, and they needed privacy for this discussion. They moved a little farther from the lodges.

"I am made to think," Odin began, "that we need the advice of a holy man. *Another* holy man. Clay is gone. There is one in the other band, Broken Tail, who could help, but you cannot go to him."

"Why not?"

Odin looked at him with displeasure. "It would lessen *your* powers. Not really, but the People would see you differently. No, we must not risk it."

"But Odin, I—"

Odin waved him aside. "No, Wolf, you have convinced the People of your gifts as a holy man. To ask help from old Broken Tail would make it seem that your powers are less than his."

"But they are!" Nils started to protest. "I have no special gifts."

"Ah, but you do," Odin insisted. "We are alive because of it. It is good, of course, that you are not too proud. Still, you must accept that your gifts are real. To yourself, anyway. Now, let us think on this. You need Broken Tail's help, but cannot ask for it."

He seemed lost in thought, and then suddenly brightened.

"Ah!" he exclaimed. "I know . . . you cannot ask without showing weakness, but *I* can!"

"What do you mean, Odin?"

Odin was becoming enthusiastic now, as he usually did over a new and exciting idea.

"I will tell him it was *my* dream!"

"You think—"

"*Yes!* That is it, Wolf. You must tell me more, all about your night-visions. Then I tell it to him, as mine!"

Nils began to understand. This would not be as good as a firsthand discussion with the holy man, but would have to do. He could understand Odin's reluctance to lose the prestige. The two walked a little farther and he began to relate to Odin all the details that he could remember, from the first time that he had experienced the dream. Odin was impressed.

"Ah, this is a big thing," he observed. "A warning, I am made to think. And you see it from outside yourself?"

"Well, maybe. It is like both, Odin. I can watch what is happening to myself, but I *feel* it, too."

He shuddered at the thought of the trapped feeling, of being dragged under and drowned.

Odin nodded. "Now," he said, "let me tell it to you, as I will tell it to Broken Tail. See if this is right: After we left the Chalagees, I began to have this dream. . . ."

Odin sat across the little fire from the holy man, uncomfortable under his stare. There was obvious suspicion in the eyes of Broken Tail.

"Why do you come to me?" the old man demanded.

"Our holy man, Clay, has given himself for the children during the Hunger Moon. He went out to fight Cold Maker."

"So it is said. But you have the great holy man, White Wolf, no? Are you not the one called Odin, his helper?"

"That is true, Uncle."

"But when you came to me you called yourself Walking Bird. *Why?*"

"That, too, is true. But I meant no harm. That *is* my name, or was until I was called Odin by White Wolf's people. I used my old name to approach you, Uncle, because this is a personal thing."

Odin could see that the old man was quite suspicious. He had decided that his approach should be as near the truth as possible, but already he was becoming enmeshed in falsehood. This would not be easy.

"Why would you come to me," Broken Tail inquired, "instead of asking the great White Wolf?"

There was a trace of a sneer in his voice. Odin saw that the suspicion was against White Wolf. Did the old man think that the Norseman was trying to steal his powers?

"Uncle," he began, "White Wolf has no wish to harm you, or steal your powers. He will start downriver soon. I go with him a little way. But my dream is of the river. I need to talk to a holy man who is *not* to be with us."

Broken Tail thought for a moment, then nodded, very tentatively.

"Maybe so. And you have not told White Wolf of your dream?"

"No, Uncle." He hated to voice an outright lie, but . . . well, it was true. He had not told *his* dreams. Actually, he had none to tell.

"Well, let me hear it. It is of the river, you said?"

"That is true, Uncle. It began after we wintered near the Chalagees. Each time, I am sitting in the water. In a boat, maybe . . ."

He went on, including all the detail he could remember. The eyes of the holy man widened in wonder as he continued.

"And you have seen this many times?" Broken Tail asked.

"Yes, Uncle. The last time, last night. That was the first time that I felt that I was drowning."

Broken Tail nodded. "And then you wake up?"

"Yes, Uncle."

"Mmm . . . This is a warning. Let me ask my bones."

Broken Tail began to putter around among his belongings, and finally drew out a small container that rattled when he shook it. Odin was familiar with such a ceremony, and it appeared that this one was little different from those he had seen before. The holy man made his sweeping cast and the tiny fetishes skittered and jumped across the painted skin. Then came the studied interpretation.

"Well," he said at last, "it *is* a warning. There is something that I cannot understand. It is as if someone else is warned. . . . I do not know. And I see death, but not for you."

"For *whom?*" blurted Odin.

"I cannot tell. That is what I do not understand."

"You think White Wolf should not go on the river?"

"He must decide that. The death picture is distant, both in time and in persons. I have never had this kind of a reading from the bones."

Odin thanked the holy man, rose, and started to leave, but Broken Tail stopped him.

"I am made to think," he said seriously, "that you should tell White Wolf of your dream. He may have more to tell you."

76

ils had not had the dream since they began the journey. He thought that a good sign, and so did Odin. It seemed that, even with the misleading information given to old Broken Tail, they had learned one thing. The dream was a warning of dangers to be met on the downriver voyage.

"Do you want not to go?" Odin had asked after relating his conversation with the holy man. "Broken Tail says there is danger, maybe death, but not to me."

"But he thought it was your dream," Nils observed. "The danger is not to the one who had the dream, and that one is me. *You* may be in danger. Do *you* want not to go?"

They discussed and argued, but finally agreed on one thing: They did not and *could* not know for sure. It was quite frustrating.

Nils had felt it necessary to inform Calling Dove of their concerns. She was well aware that the night-visions had been disturbing him. It was only fair to tell her the whole story, and he had done so. She did not seem concerned, even after they told her of the subterfuge they had foisted on Broken Tail. She had laughed at that.

"But it was good," she admitted, "not to show weakness. Of course, there *is* none," she hurried to say. "But I mean—"

"Yes, Dove, it is good." Nils laughed. "But really, what do you think?"

"I am made to think," she said soberly, "that the dream, no matter who had it, says only 'be careful.' Is that not what Broken Tail told you, Odin?"

"Yes, that is true, maybe," said her brother. "He mentioned death, but not to me. Not to Wolf, that is."

"Could it be to others in the party?"

"It could. There is always danger on a journey, no? A holy man is almost sure to say so. But not to us, I am made to think."

Dove rose, clapped her hands, and laughed.

"So," she said simply, "let us go!"

The day was pleasant. Warm spring sunlight flooded over his left shoulder and chest as the sun rose higher, swinging from east to south as it climbed.

Three days they had been on the river now, and Nils felt that the voyage was going well. The work was easy, almost nonexistent, because they needed only to ride the current. Occasionally he would dip his paddle to ease the craft back into the mainstream of the river's flow. But there was plenty of time to enjoy the day. When spring finally arrived it had come with a sudden enthusiasm that was almost bewildering. Trees, grass, and early flowers seemed to come to life all at once.

As the Moon of Awakening gave way to the Moon of Greening, long lines of geese high overhead swept northward, trumpeting their presence. To Nils, their cries, particularly those of the snowy birds with black-tipped wings, sounded like the barking of distant dogs. Since they had been on the river, he had noticed a great variety of waterfowl in small groups and in pairs. There were at least a dozen kinds of ducks, as well as herons, cranes, geese, and a myriad of smaller shorebirds along the banks and sandbars.

Animals, too, came to the river to drink, and to stare at the passing canoes. Deer were abundant, and a larger deer that the People called *wapati*. Buffalo, in bands and larger herds, were seen frequently.

"It is good," Odin observed. "We will have no trouble hunting when we need to."

There were also, in addition to the deer and buffalo, the hunters. Bears were common. Mostly they were the familiar black bears, with the expected variation in color from honey colored to dead black. They were much like bears at home, amusing to watch at a distance. Once, though, they saw a bear that was new even to Odin. The canoes rounded a slight curve and saw the creature in shallow water, apparently searching for shellfish or some small creatures that might inhabit the shallows behind a sandbar. This bear appeared much larger than any they had seen. Its color was dark with a grizzled or frosted appearance over the entire coat. Most impressive, however, was the reaction of the animal to their presence. It rose to stand, not on all fours, but on its hind legs. Even allowing for the water in which it stood, it was apparent that this animal would be much taller than a man, perhaps half again as tall. It showed no fear at all, only curiosity as the canoes drifted past.

"Ah! That is a *real* bear!" Odin called softly.

Later they would see another, a mother with cubs. The Skraelings were much impressed with this animal, the "bear-that-walks-like-a-man," and Nils no less so. He had never seen so magnificent a creature.

There was also a great variety of fur bearers, which Nils noted for further reference. It would be good to be able to list those valuable for possible trade. Otters, beavers, a variety of foxes, a large spotted cat with a short tail and tufted ears, and once, a lion with a long tail, crouching to drink at the water's edge. Yes, this could be a very interesting country for fur trade. If they could find a port at the mouth of this great river . . . Or, as an alternative, it appeared that the river could be navigated by Norse ships. Not *knarrs*, maybe, this far upstream, but surely by longships, with their shallower draft and maneuverability. He was becoming excited again at all the information that he would be able to furnish when he returned to civilization.

He wished that he had someone with whom to share it. He missed Sven, the only one in his recent life who would have understood his eagerness. He wondered how Sven and the People were faring. Big Tree had given the impression that they would not move far after crossing the river. They had established a good relationship with the Hidatsa, and might stay near them, at least for a season or two. In the back of Nils's mind was the idea that he should know the general location of the People for the time when he and Calling Dove would return. It seemed logical to think of that. Dove would not want to leave her family forever. And it would be good to visit. He was a little more reluctant to admit that there was a possibility that he could not find his own people. If not, he and Dove could return, back upriver, and rejoin the People.

But that was far ahead. He dipped his paddle and gently turned the prow of the canoe back into the current to keep it from slipping broadside. It was a comfortable way to travel, and the pace made it easy to observe their surroundings. They had passed a sizable town the day before, with many lodges. He had been anxious for a little while, but needlessly, it seemed. Odin, in the leading canoe, had made a big show of the hand sign for greeting and peace. The people who gathered on the shore waved and returned the sign. They drifted on past, and it was over.

Twice, they had seen smaller encampments or villages with only a few lodges or huts. There was no reason to stop, Odin said. Later, when they wanted information about the lower river, they could stop for a council.

Nils shifted his eyes from an eagle with a white head and tail, perched in a dead tree at the river, and glanced at the people in his canoe. Dove, in the prow, her dark hair shining like the wing of a raven as she held her paddle, ready to assist if necessary. Now she turned partly around to call Sky's attention to the bird.

"You see the eagle?"

"Yes. I would like to see another bear-that-walks-like-a-man."

"Maybe we will see more. I am made to think, though, that we do not want to see that one up close, no?"

"He would make a good sleeping robe," Bright Sky retorted. "When I am grown, I will kill one for you."

Dove laughed, her deep-throated rippling chuckle. "Save that for your wife, my son. I am only your mother!"

Nils smiled to himself. *Life is good,* he thought. These two, with whom he shared the canoe, had become the most important individuals in his life. He could not imagine a world without them. What a great adventure for Bright Sky, to experience a voyage down the great river at this age. Some of it the boy would not remember, but much of it would be retained and treasured for the rest of his life. *My son,* Nils thought, still amazed when he realized that he would return home a family man. He wondered what his parents would say about Calling Dove. They had rather favored the girl at Stadt . . . what was her name? No matter, she could not have held a candle to Dove. He looked at her back, the graceful curves of her body. He had never seen a woman so desirable. More so now than when they met, even.

He must think of something else. It would only be frustrating to become aroused right now. He lifted his eyes to the trees along the shore, looking for new and different creatures to distract his attention. Small and colorful birds sang, a squirrel scampered along the branch of a mighty sycamore, but these things were really too far away.

For a little while, it was amusing to watch three crows chasing and harassing a great silent-winged owl, the hunter of the night. Nils wondered how the owl had been caught without cover in the daylight. The annoyed hunter finally escaped his tormentors in a clever way. He flew *across* the river, just above the water. The crows could not dive at the owl, because of the risk of overshooting their quarry and falling into the water themselves. Once on the other side, the owl sailed gracefully into a thick clump of cedar. The crows gave up the chase and recrossed the river, still complaining loudly.

Bright Sky laughed. "Kookooskoos is clever!" he noted.

"Yes," answered Dove, "but not too clever. He was caught outside in daylight, when he should have been in his lodge!"

Nils smiled, pleased that their son was observant and that he was learning. What a wonderful teacher he had in Dove. Nils's heart reached out to her, and he longed to hold her. In many ways, this canoe travel was frustrating. To be this close to the woman he loved, almost close enough to touch, for long periods of time, but unable to do so . . . He wondered if he could be so attracted to any other woman, ever. *Had* he ever been? He thought not. There was Ingrid, the blue-eyed goddess at Straumfjord. She had certainly impressed him at the time, but how fortunate that nothing had worked out with her! In the wisdom of hindsight, he realized that a woman like Ingrid meant only trouble. She was seeking merely a way home, and would probably have slept with anyone who was able to accomplish that. Once more, he felt sorrow for Olaf the cooper, her miserable hardworking husband. But once home, what would she want next, and who could gain it for her, with the implied reward? Ah, he had been lucky to avoid her trap. He wondered whether she had snared someone. Probably, for she had been ready, willing, and certainly well equipped for the task. Ah, what a face and body!

I must stop such thoughts, he told himself. Maybe the inactivity was a part of the problem. A person becomes bored and his mind wanders.

Such thoughts were interrupted by Odin in the other canoe. He drew out into slower water and let Nils drift alongside.

"My legs are stiff," he called. "Shall we stop on that sandbar ahead?"

"It is good!" Nils called back, guiding his own canoe out of the main current. It would be a relief to stretch his legs. Sky, too, would benefit from a chance to run a little.

The two canoes nosed into the bar side by side. Snake and Dove jumped out and steadied them while the others stepped forward and onto the sandy strip.

"Ah, it feels good to stand up!" said Dove. "It is good, my brother."

Odin was glancing at the sun. "It is a little past midday," he noted. "Let us build a fire, eat a little."

The fire, while not needed for warmth or cooking, was a way to establish their presence. *Here I camp.* It would help to appease whatever spirits might inhabit the place. Bits of food would be offered through the fire, and maybe a pinch of tobacco. One could not be too careful. . . .

77

Nils lay awake, snuggled in the sleeping robes on a sandbar on the east bank of the Big River. Beside him, Calling Dove's soft regular breathing told of restful sleep. He could clearly see the still forms of the others, around the coals of the dying fire.

He was unable to sleep. The moon was full, and was silvering the whole world with its soft light. *What is it about such a night?* he wondered. He had experienced such a feeling before, on calm moonlit nights at sea, or on the fjords at home. Something about the full of the moon, maybe. It was a time of excitement, of restlessness that he could not explain. It was as if he did not want to sleep, because something might happen in the magic of the moonlight. Something that would be so wonderful that it would open to him all the mysteries of the universe.

He wanted to shout, to howl at the moon, like his brother the wolf, heard in the far distance across the river. A band of coyotes answered from nearer their camp, the chuckling chortle that made two or three sound like a dozen. Odin would have been amused had he been awake, Nils knew. It was Odin who never let him forget the bizarre event, the berserk when Nils had earned his name, White Wolf. The one-eyed Skraeling, now his closest friend in the world, had teased him gently ever since about his affinity for the wolves.

"Your brother, the wolf," Odin always said, when the spine-chilling song floated across the mountains and valleys. And Nils always felt that although Odin said this in mild amusement, he was quite serious. There had been a bond of spirit, somehow, since that day. It was an ethereal thing. There were times when Nils had observed Odin telling other tribes they met about the incident. He knew that Odin's main purpose was to impress the strangers with the power of the People's holy men. But there were times when he thought that Odin actually believed his own story, that the light-haired Norseman *had* changed into a white wolf.

Sometimes he even wondered himself. Something *had* happened, that fateful day when death had come so near. It was mildly disturbing that he still had no memory of it. Odin always told him not to worry about it, or to try to understand it.

"Some things are not meant to be understood," Odin had told him. "Just enjoy the results!"

Maybe it was like the night of a full moon, he now pondered as he watched the still yet exciting night around him. He remembered the old women back in Stadt talking of someone who was moonstruck, a little bit crazy. He felt that way tonight, but it was a wonderful, thrilling sort of craziness that made him feel he could do anything. He felt that way now. He rolled over and sat up, careful not to disturb the sleeping Dove. He wanted to see better, to experience this night. The moon was setting in the west, turning from silver to flame as it neared the dark treetops across the river. Its reflection fell across the water in a sort of pathway that seemed sprinkled with magic. The ripples in the water's surface distorted the image so that it shimmered and danced, yet remained there, stretching all the way across the river to end at the sandbar under his feet. He had the strange feeling that he could set his steps on that silvery trail and walk across, clear over the river and up, over the dark trees on the other side, up and into the moon itself.

He almost decided to try it, but it was only a passing thought. He shook his head to clear it. Was he going crazy? Moonstruck, whatever that might mean? Or, in this strange land, so different from the land of his youth, did the moon affect people differently? He looked at the still forms around him, all resting peacefully. But he was the only Norseman here. *Does the moon here affect only Norsemen?* he wondered in his flight of fancy. But there lay young Bright Sky, sleeping peacefully beyond his mother. Sky was half Norseman, yet seemed unaffected.

Odin's words came back to him. *Do not try to understand . . . just enjoy. . . .*

Maybe that was the answer. Nils had been raised to learn and understand the latest in Norse achievements as their ships probed the seas around Europe and the North Sea. He felt a need to understand everything he saw or did. The People, on the other hand, seemed to have a feel for things of the spirit. Not to understand, but only to enjoy. He envied Odin sometimes his ability to listen and enjoy stories of other tribes they visited, without wondering which story was right. Nils's Christian teachers would probably have been scandalized by his own tolerance of others' legendry. But his grandfather would have understood. Maybe that was what his grandfather had tried to give him, with all the tales of the Norse gods and goddesses. He had not fully understood at the time Grandfather's reluctance to take the new Christianity too seriously. Now . . . yes, that must be it. . . . Grandfather was afraid that it would thwart the imagination. If only one story can be true, all other versions are lost. He was aware that his parents' generation quietly disapproved of Grandfather's stories, but was only now beginning to understand why. His grandfather had given him a rich legacy, which had stood him well in learning to live with the People.

"Thank you, Grandfather," he whispered to the setting moon. He did not understand exactly why, only that he did not need to understand.

The moon was lower now, partly hidden by the trees. The silvery pathway had turned reddish and was now breaking up in dull rusty fragments as the moon disappeared. The gray-yellow of dawn was paling the eastern sky, and the day was coming, and it was good.

He looked again at the river, and it murmured gently to him. A fish jumped beyond a log that lay partly on shore downstream, and he heard the splash of a beaver from another area. The coyotes were silent now, ready to turn the world over to the creatures of the day. An owl passed soundlessly overhead, a ghostly form on soft-spread wings.

The river . . . his dream . . . He had not even thought about it for some time. Travel was going well, the weather had been good, and he had not dreamed at all. Could it be that, having been warned, he was now to receive no more warnings? What a strange thought! He must be thinking more like the People, *expecting* spiritual help, or mystical information. He was sure that the priest would have disapproved, and muttered about demons. The priests seemed to worry a lot about demons.

But the river, and the dream. No one had mentioned the danger that old Broken Tail had warned about, since this voyage began. Nils had not thought of it, because he had not dreamed. *Should* they be worried? Or, at least, concerned?

As he was thinking these thoughts, Dove stirred behind him and sat up sleepily.

"You are awake," she said.

"Yes," he told her, "I was watching the moon."

"But it is gone," she said, puzzled.

"Yes. Just now." He wished that he had wakened her to share the beauty of the night. He was afraid, though, that she might not have appreciated what he felt if she had been wakened from a sound sleep to experience it.

He wondered something else, now. At the time that Odin had talked to Broken Tail about the dream, Dove's reaction had been strange. She had acknowledged that the dream meant danger. Yet she had been eager for the trip, and had not mentioned it again. Was he missing something here?

"Dove," he began, "you remember my dream of the river?"

"Yes! You had it again?" She seemed concerned.

"No. I have *not*, and that is strange, too. But you said something. . . . Broken Tail warned of danger, but not to me, or to the dreamer. You remember Odin told him."

"Yes," she smiled. "That was clever of you and my brother."

"It was his idea. It *did* lead to questions. Danger . . . to *whom?* Not to the one with the dream, we thought."

"I remember."

"But Dove, we have not spoken of this since, you and I. Are you not worried about the danger?"

"I had not thought about it," she pondered.

Why not? He wanted to shout. *You have been warned, but are not worried?* He decided to try another approach.

"Dove," he said, "I wonder who is in danger. I dreamed the dream that Broken Tail heard, and he said the danger was not to me. Odin does not believe he is the one. Maybe it is you, maybe our son . . ."

Dove was quiet for a little while, and then answered, slowly and thoughtfully.

"My husband," she began, "I know that you are a great holy man."

"No," he protested, "that—"

She waved aside his protest. "I understand that a holy man must be humble about it, even deny it, as you do. That is part of your gift, Wolf. And holy men among your people are probably different, too."

Yes, he thought, *you have no idea.*

"Now," she went on, "think about this dream, and of any holy man trying to tell you of it, and of our journey."

"What do you mean?"

"Remember when you told me of this, and we agreed that any journey has danger?"

"Yes, but—"

"It would be foolish for a holy man *not* to mention it. If someone is hurt or killed, the holy man should have warned him. He would lose the respect of others if he did not warn. So a holy man always says that, no? If nobody is killed or dies, it is forgotten. Maybe he is even praised for stopping it!"

Nils began to understand. It was a clever approach, and even more clever of Dove to have reasoned it out. But a question or two remained.

"Dove," he persisted, "there is something else. Broken Tail warned of danger, not to the dreamer, not to me or maybe to Odin, but to someone else. How is this known?"

She smiled quizzically. "Let us think about that, Wolf. First, I do not know the ways of holy men, as you do. Maybe Broken Tail has a way to tell. But think about it. If you were explaining a dream, would you tell anyone, especially the party's leaders, that they will die?"

He was silent, thinking hard, and Dove continued.

"Of course not. It would hurt the party's success. But you *would* warn of death, in case someone is killed. If they are not, the party is a success because it was avoided. If they *are* killed, the holy man has said so."

"But what if the leader is killed?"

"Ah, then the holy man has warned of it, but did not clearly see *who*. Or, something else interfered. The holy man is still right."

"You mean, Dove, that your holy men *have* no real powers?"

Her eyes widened in astonishment and alarm. "Oh, of course not, Wolf. Where did you get such an idea? Of course they have gifts of sight, and powers to make things happen and to tell what will happen. But they must also know how to explain, how to tell others. Is it not so with your holy men?"

Now Nils felt he was more confused than ever.

"Maybe so," he agreed.

The holy men of the People *did* have powers of some sort. There were things he had seen that could *not* have happened, except that he had seen it. Things he could not explain, but that were real.

"It is like your sun-stone," she was saying. "I do not know how it knows north, but *you* do. That is why you are a holy man."

He saw no reason to tell her again that he was not really a holy man, and that he had no idea how the sun-stone could find the North Star.

78

With the conversation behind him about the warning and the dream, Nils began to enjoy the journey more. On the long overland trek he had forgotten, almost, the pleasure of travel by boat, especially for a Norseman. His preoccupation had been with adjusting to the culture of the People, to his marriage, and family life. Ah, that *was* a distraction.

Now the tasks of travel were slight. The river was doing most of the work, and he had time to look around him, to think, to watch the creatures who made their lodges along the great watercourse. The days were thoroughly enjoyable, with warm sun and fresh breezes and the scent of blossoms in the gentle air. He had never before realized that there was a sweet fragrance, like that of honey, in the flowering of grapevines. The flowers themselves were quite unremarkable, small and greenish in color, but their fragrance seemed to affect him beyond all belief. It carried a sense of romance that kept him constantly alert and acutely aware of the presence of the woman who sat in the front of the canoe. Maybe it was partly her natural perfume, the powerful yet almost unnoticeable woman-scent, that drew him.

More likely, however, it was simply that she was Calling Dove, his wife, his friend, mother of their child. It was very difficult for him to watch her lithe movements, hardly more than an arm's length in front of him, without becoming aroused. He knew the feel of those well-shaped arms that plied the paddle, as they had often embraced him. The feel of the sensuous body . . . He must not think such thoughts now. Maybe tonight they could slip away from the camp for a little while.

Dove glanced at him over her shoulder and smiled. He smiled back, wondering if her thoughts might be along the same lines. He hoped so. It was early in the day, though, and they would travel far before he had a chance to test that theory.

They were on a smooth section of water that stretched on southward without any perceptible current. He knew it was there, however, because he could feel its pull on the canoe.

One of the big white-headed eagles hung high over the water, held in precisely the same position by a fluttering motion of its wings against the wind. It was much like the action of wind on a sail, he realized. He studied the angle of the wings, thinking how one might adjust a sail, angling it to port or star-board to catch just the right forces. . . .

The eagle suddenly folded its wings and dropped in a long sloping glide toward the water, faster and faster, like an arrow in flight. Nils began to wonder if the bird could pull out of the dive before it struck the surface. Then a slight change in the fixed angle of the wings, and the path of flight leveled in a powerful curve just above the water. A wingbeat or two and the bird swept across the smooth surface, little more than a hand's span above it. A taloned claw struck downward, there was a quiet splash, and the bird rose, a flopping fish clutched tightly in its fist. The fish was large, and the eagle struggled to gain altitude. For a moment Nils thought it would drop its prize, but it deftly turned the fish to face forward, into the wind of its passage.

Yes, he thought. *The fish is shaped like a boat. It cuts the wind like the prow of a ship!* How clever of the eagle to know how to use such principles to help her carry a load. She flew quite easily now, gaining altitude as she headed toward a nest in a towering cottonwood at the river's edge ahead. Nils could see two or three small heads poking up over the pile of sticks to greet the returning parent, clamoring for the food she brought.

He smiled. He had noticed that his powers of observation were improving. There would have been a time when he would not even have noticed the eagle. Now he not only saw and watched it, but felt a strong sense of *enjoyment* over the success of the eagle's hunt. He felt like congratulating her, a fellow hunter, for a job well done.

What was it, he wondered, that was allowing him more insight, more enjoyment of the world around him? He thought of Odin, and how the man seemed to see and understand everything, even with his one eye. It must be that the People looked at the world a little differently. . . . He could not define just *how.* It was much like the way a good sailor relates to the sea, it now occurred to him. Yes . . . An amateur tries to *fight* it, the wind and waves and currents. The one with skill and experience learns to use all of these forces, to become one with them.

On a smaller scale, he realized, it is much like learning to use the canoe. The first time he had stepped into a canoe, the thing had seemed alive, over-responsive to his every motion. It had been necessary to attune his entire body to its motions. As he did so, it became easier.

"You must talk to its spirit," Odin had told him, and so it had been. When that communication had been established, the canoe became like part of him, and he of it.

Could it be, he now wondered, that it was so with the *world,* too? In a way, he had always considered himself, as well as everyone else, as outside the world, or at least separate from it, even though living in it. What was it that he saw or felt in the approach of the People?

Finally it began to dawn on him. This was something that could not be put into words. Something, maybe, that could not even be understood. But the People seemed to feel no need to understand it. It must be like trying to understand the spirit of the canoe as its tremulous wobble tests the senses of the inexperienced. Then he becomes one with the canoe and . . .

Nils realized that he was close to the attitude of the People now. Not of understanding it. He might never do that. But he was, it seemed, *experiencing* it. Without realizing exactly when or how it had happened, he had slipped into their ways. He was not acting *in* the world, but was a *part* of it, and it a part of him. Their spirits were one, though still identifiable, and it brought a joy and comfort, at the same time an excitement. He was seeing more, feeling the spirits of the creatures he saw as they traveled, understanding the mood of the beaver whose tail slapped the water of a still pool as it dived.

For the first time he realized the importance of the apology over a kill.

We are sorry to kill you, my brother,
but our lives depend on your flesh. . . .

We are not in the world, but part of it! he thought. He must have been learning this lesson without realizing it, over the past few seasons, he now saw. This had led to the increased acuteness of his observation, the greater enjoyment of things he saw. Like the eagle . . . Yes, he had, without thinking of it, wished her good hunting! It was a strange and exciting discovery, to know that such a thing had happened to him.

His thoughts were interrupted by a call from Odin in the other canoe. "Wolf!"

There was no real urgency, merely an effort to get his attention. Nils looked that way, a stone's throw to his left. Snake, in the prow of Odin's canoe, did not speak but lifted his paddle to point to the northwest. Nils turned to look over his shoulder. In the far distance a low cloudbank lay along the horizon, gray and ugly. He realized now that the air was still, and that the warm and gentle breeze they had enjoyed for most of the day was now quiet. Stray puffs of wind from odd directions were stirring the tops of the willows.

"Let us camp," called Odin, indicating a long stretch of grassy meadow along the bank by pointing with his paddle. "Rain Maker comes."

The wind changed, even as they swung the canoes toward shore. Indecisive gusts steadied and merged and became a chill wind, now from the northwest. The distant cloudbank was growing alarmingly by the time they landed. Orange fire flickered in the blue-gray mass, and there was a low growl, a rumble that was felt rather than heard.

"Rain Maker's drum," grunted Snake as he dragged the canoes well up on shore.

"Gather some wood," Odin called. "We can start a fire before the rain comes."

As it happened, they could not. The wind whipped violently, blowing sparks away and extinguishing them before they could light the tinder.

"No matter," Odin shouted into the rising wind. "But here . . . Keep the wood dry!"

Quickly, they established a makeshift camp. The two canoes were overturned and placed against the dubious shelter of a thin fringe of willows. At least this would break part of the force of the northwest wind that was sweeping down on them.

Their baggage and the hastily gathered firewood were shoved under one of the canoes, while the humans took shelter under the other. They wrapped themselves in their robes and sat facing away from the storm's advance. Young Sky crept between his parents, and Dove gathered him inside the folds of her own robe.

The crash of Rain Maker's drum was closer now, and the individual flashes of lightning were followed more closely by the thunder. Fat raindrops were beginning to beat a tattoo on the upturned canoes. They could see the advance of the front of the storm on the river's surface. Wind, stirring the smooth water into ripples, and then the sharp line that formed the border of the raindrops . . . Ahead of its advance, only wind-driven ripples, behind it, the river beaten to a froth by the driving rain.

It came from behind them, but there was a strange twist to the passing storm front. The rain swept along the river to the east of them before it struck full force on their shelter. This enabled them to watch its progress for a little while. The rain crept like a living thing down the river. The water where it was being beaten was writhing like a being in torture. Nils gazed in fascination as it swept on.

On a narrow point of land across the wide river stood a lone tree, a giant cottonwood. He was watching the storm approach that point when there was a blinding flash, and a crooked finger of fire jabbed downward from the glowering sky. It touched the top of the tree in the distance, and half of the majestic old giant seemed to fall away, to fall ponderously to the earth. A heartbeat later, the deafening boom reached their ears. In another instant, the entire scene was obliterated by the gray curtain of driving rain that swept over their camp from behind.

"It is good not to camp under such trees," observed Snake. "Rain Maker's spears of fire are drawn to them."

Nils was busy drawing his robe around himself, Dove, and young Sky, and paid little attention to such wisdom. It was much later that Odin assured him that yes, the cottonwood *did* attract the fiery spears of Rain Maker.

They huddled together under the canoes, trying to stay as dry as possible. The driving wind shifted and tore at them, and at times the rain seemed to fly horizontally. Then suddenly, the air was still. The rain slackened, and Odin poked his head outside.

"What is it?" Calling Dove asked.

"I do not know. Something is not right," Odin answered thoughtfully. "The spirit . . ."

They could all feel it, the sense of expectancy in the still air. There was a strange greenish glow in the sky, and objects at a distance appeared distorted and otherworldly.

"We should build a fire now," Odin said. "Let us announce our presence here before something else happens."

He drew dry tinder and kindling sticks from beneath the other canoe, and his fire-making sticks from his pack. Before the flames were fairly started however, there was a sound, a rumble like distant thunder. It grew, seeming to shake the very earth, and came closer. They exchanged anxious glances, and Bright Sky crept close to his mother.

The noise now was like the bellowing of a hundred buffalo bulls all at once. The frightening thing was that its source seemed to move nearer, coming toward them from the southwest. Odin hastened to feed his fire, and Snake stood with upstretched arms, eyes closed, chanting a prayer for their safety.

Nils, like the others, was completely puzzled, as well as frightened. This was unlike any sound he had ever heard, a combination of a rumbling of the earth under them and the primal scream of a giant creature, mixed with the mutter of thunder that rolled on without pausing.

In a few moments it became apparent that the source of the sound was to pass south of their position. They could follow its course, from the southwest, approaching the river, then seeming to *cross* the stream without pausing.

The wind had quickened again, and though they searched the distant scene for the cause of the horrible shrieking sound, they could see nothing. Their view was partly obstructed by the heavy timber just downstream, and further by the low-hanging clouds that layered out above the water.

Then, as mysteriously as it began, the sound was gone, decreasing rapidly in volume as it continued to move on to the east. They looked at each other in wonder.

"What was it?" asked Nils. In the back of his mind the episode seemed like the passing of a huge living thing, howling in rage as it went. It had conjured up for him the tales of Norse mythology and the supernatural monsters that threatened the earth and humankind. Nidhug, the great dragon of Nifl-heim. Was this to be the end of the world?

There was no reassurance in Snake's remark at just that moment.

"Strange things must live here!"

79

The party had begun to regain some confidence by the next morning. The storm had passed on, and the day dawned bright and sunny. To Nils, his fears began to look a little foolish. He wondered about the rumbling, roaring sound that they had heard. Maybe, though, it had not really been so bad as it seemed at the time. That must be it. It was hard to take such things seriously in the bright sunlight of a new day. Birds were singing and the breeze murmured gently in the willows, answered by the whisper of the river in its own language. It was good.

No one spoke of the frightening experience of the evening before. They loaded the canoe and shoved out into the river again. It was not long, however, before the incident was recalled forcibly. They had gone only a few bowshots' distance downstream, around a bend of the river, when Snake suddenly gasped and pointed.

"Look!"

On the west side of the river there was an opening in the timber that came down to the water's edge. Not a natural gap in the trees, but a newly torn pathway, perhaps a hundred paces wide. They could see where it came over a hill some distance from the river. From that point all trees were gone, twisted off at the ground to leave only jagged stumps. Some were as thick as a man's outstretched arms could reach.

Nils shuddered. It was easy to imagine some gigantic creature crawling from the river, destroying everything in its path. But wait, had the sound not moved *toward* the river? Maybe it had come out and then returned by the same path. Was it now hiding directly *beneath* them? His skin crawled at such a thought. The dream . . . no, this did not seem . . .

"Look! Across the river," Dove said, her voice tight with emotion. "Where it crawled out again!"

All eyes turned toward the distant east bank, where the path torn by the giant Thing resumed, in exact alignment with the one on this side.

"It *crossed* the river!" said Snake. "Did it swim?" There was a moment of silence before he added another question to the one that still hung unanswered in the air. "Or did it *fly*?"

No one was paddling or even guiding the canoes. They drifted, staring in awe at the evidence before them on either side of the river.

"Should we land?" Nils asked Odin. The thought of what might lurk in the dark waters was not a comforting thing. A creature so big, larger than the greatest whale ever seen! And the trees . . . What had happened to them? Did the monster *eat* huge trees? He could remember no specific tales about the dietary preferences of Nidhug the dragon. It had, however, gnawed off the roots of the giant ash tree Yggdrasil, the Tree of Life. But surely, that was only a story . . . was it not?

"Let us go on," Odin suggested. "There is no reason to stay here on its trail. It may come back!"

They drifted on, and the newly torn pathway through the forest was quickly lost to view. It was some time, however, before they all breathed easily again.

That night, far downriver, they slept the sleep of exhaustion. Nils doubted that he would rest well, and dreaded the possibility that his dream might return. But it did not happen.

It was the following afternoon that they saw a cluster of lodges on the shore. No more than four or five, it appeared at first, but then, as they drifted on around a long point of land, more appeared. Then still others.

"A city!" Nils murmured, half to himself.

There were rumors, gleaned from people they had encountered farther north, of a "big camp" at the junction of two rivers. Another big river was to join this one, it was said, and between the two, "many people, big lodges." Their communication, limited to hand signs, had exchanged basic ideas. In no way, however, had there been any inkling of a population center like this. It was still distant, lying in the haze over the river, but he could see earthen terraces, large mounds that appeared to be manmade structures, and a variety of large buildings. *A city!*

Most of the earthworks lay in the delta between the two rivers. He could plainly see the large river that joined the one on which they traveled. It was nearly as large, and seemed to flow in from the west.

The other canoe drew alongside.

"Wolf," Odin called, a note of concern in his voice, "I am made to think that we should not go there!"

Nils was startled. Odin had seldom hesitated to approach anyone openly. Such an introduction had usually been respected in their travels. What was different here?

"Why?" he asked, surprised.

"Let us talk later," Odin said quickly. "Cross over, now."

He did not even wait for an answer, but thrust his paddle into the stream and with a powerful stroke or two guided the craft into the current. Nils followed. Odin was quite correct on one point. If they intended to avoid the city below, they must cross now, before the current carried them into the waters around the city itself.

By the time they crossed the main current and neared the east bank, they were almost exactly opposite the city's levees and earthworks. A few boats moved along the river, their occupants apparently engaged in fishing. They would not pass closely to any of them.

"Now," Nils spoke to Odin. "What is it? Why are we over here?"

"No reason, maybe," Odin said. "But I am made to think so. People who build such things are very powerful. We are too few to defend ourselves. My sister . . . your son . . . I thought it would be safer."

It seemed logical, now that he thought about it. They had no way of knowing the temperament of whatever king or lord might rule over such a place. To satisfy their curiosity might become quite a dangerous thing. Norsemen were accustomed to meeting other nations from a position of armed strength. Odin, by contrast, knew the dangers of being too vulnerable in such a meeting.

"It is good," agreed Nils. "Let us go on."

He had a certain degree of disappointment. It would have been an exciting thing to walk the streets of that city, to look more closely at their structures, talk to their leaders. Well, maybe that could come later. It was apparent that a longship, possibly even a *knarr*, could sail up this river to dock at some of these earthworks. He would speak of this with the Ericksons. If they made contact soon, maybe they could return, even this summer.

The city was receding behind them now. Beyond a wave or two from other boatmen as they drifted past, they had had no contact at all. The clusters of dwellings were fewer here, and by midday they saw hardly any. It was late in the afternoon that they came to a small group of thatched lodges, and Odin suggested that they pause here for a little while.

"They can tell us of the people upstream, maybe," he noted.

The canoes nosed in, and they were met by a group of people on shore, who approached cautiously.

"They seem friendly," noted Odin, as he raised his palm in the hand sign for a peaceful greeting.

It was obvious that no danger would be likely from a party traveling with a woman and child, so these people showed little suspicion.

"You are traders?" signed one of the men.

"No, only travelers," Odin signed in reply.

The people from the huts seemed mildly disappointed, but beckoned them ashore.

"Where are you going?"

Odin shrugged, indicating some doubt.

"How far to the big salty water?" he signed.

The others laughed. "Many sleeps," one signed. "Many moons, maybe."

"Many *moons?*" Nils asked aloud. "Is that what he said?"

"Yes. I will ask him again."

"Maybe not moons," signed the man in answer to the repeated question. "But many *sleeps.*"

"It may be farther than we think," Nils observed aloud.

"True. But they may like to tell it bigger than it is, too," Odin answered.

"Ask about the city," Nils suggested, and Odin did so.

"Yes, very big," the man answered.

There followed a rather unsatisfactory hand-signed conversation, in which very little information was gained. They gathered that the people of the city were of a different nation, who were sometimes dangerous. Beyond that, the skills to explain were lacking.

"Can they tell us of the Thing that broke off the trees?" asked Nils.

Odin relayed the question, and the man nodded excitedly.

"Yes, yes . . . in the storm!" he signed.

"They know about it," said Nils. He turned to the man and used hand signs. "What creature is this, who eats big trees?"

There was laughter from the others.

"The wind," their spokesman signed.

"No, wind would not do that," Nils protested.

"Yes, yes! Wind-spirit," the others insisted. "Very powerful!"

The man moved a forefinger in a rapid circular motion, pointing to the ground.

"Does he mean a whirlwind?" Nils wondered aloud.

"A special wind?" Odin signed the question.

"Yes, eats everything!"

"But not an *animal*?" Nils signed.

The man looked doubtful for a moment, then shook his head.

"Not animal," he signed. "Wind-spirit."

At least it was somewhat reassuring. The dreadful fear of unknown creatures from the bottom of the river was abated somewhat. A wind, even a devastating whirlwind, was one thing. A giant serpent or dragon or some unknown dweller in the slime was quite another.

"Let us ask him more about downstream," Nils suggested. "Not how far, but what is there?"

Odin nodded and signed the question.

"More river . . . towns . . . peoples." The man used the sign for tribe or nation.

"Danger?" asked Odin.

"Some," the other shrugged. "Always, some."

"What people?" Odin signed.

The other man repeated the people or nation sign, and then made several signs that were unknown to the travelers.

"We are called River People where we came from," Odin told him.

It was apparent that this meant little to the others.

"All people here are river people, maybe," Nils said. Odin agreed.

"Which of those you told us of would be dangerous?" he asked the man.

The answer was a quizzical look, followed by one of the signs already used, but unfamiliar. It consisted of placing both palms on the forehead and pushing the hands up and over the top of the head, as if combing the hair backward.

"I do not know this," Odin signed. "Hair?"

"Yes," the other nodded, "cut . . . hair."

"The People Who Cut Their Hair?"

"Yes. Cut very short."

"Where are these people?" Odin asked.

"Downstream, many sleeps."

"At the salty water?"

"No, not that far."

They resumed travel, somewhat reassured about the whirlwind. Nils had a strong suspicion, however, that nothing else they had learned was very reassuring.

80

They saw no more of the wind-creature that had wreaked such a trail of destruction through the trees along the river. Nils could not help but wonder what might happen to people whose lodges or towns chanced to be in that path. A force that could devour great oaks and sycamores would hardly pause for mere humans and their lodges. The deeply banked earth lodges of the People, so strange to him at first, now seemed a thoroughly practical answer to such dangers.

The others spoke of this recent event very little. It was a danger that had been avoided, and there was no point in discussion. The escape itself was a thing for which they were grateful. However, had they known of the deadly wind, what could they have done?

"There was nothing we could do, Wolf," Dove told him, "so why worry about it? It would happen or not anyway, no?"

This approach seemed quite reasonable. It was neither a denial nor a helpless resignation. In an emergency, if something *could* be done, any one of the People would be good to have beside him. In many ways, this philosophy reminded him of his grandfather again. *Do what you can, then face the rest without regrets.* Grandfather would have liked the People.

What an odd idea, he told himself.

But there were many other things to think about. The travel, the occasional times when they paused for a day to hunt for fresh meat. The warm sunlight on the river, cool evenings around the fire, nights when the moon was nearly full, and bathed the world with silver . . . And, of course, the questions that set his thoughts in motion. Where were his own people and where would they encounter them? It would probably be the Ericksons, he thought. Sometimes he tried to guess which of the brothers would be the one to explore the coast southward as far as the Great River. Leif, sometimes called Leif the Lucky, was certainly bold and courageous in his voyages. And lucky. Nils had never met Leif, but had been greatly impressed by the enthusiasm of Thorwald, the younger brother. Thorwald was more interested in the importance of exploring the land they were calling Vinland.

Yes, probably Thorwald would be the one. It seemed likely that he would choose to map the coast, to find what sort of place this Vinland might be. Leif would be more inclined to concentrate on colonizing the islands. Nils daydreamed again about what amusing sort of greeting he would use when they met. *Good day to you, Thorwald. How is it with you?* He smiled at the thought of the surprise he would see on the face of Erickson.

There was a chance, of course, that the meeting would be of a different sort. Maybe they would simply come to a settlement, like Straumfjord. He had no idea who might be the headman of such a colony. Well, he would see. . . .

Another idea troubled him slightly from time to time. As they paused to contact natives along the river, no one yet seemed to have any idea of how far it might be to the ocean. They were still traveling on the river that would lead them back to the sea. Now he began to wonder whether the Great River might flow into the sea on the *opposite* side of this unknown land. Several facts made him doubt it. The big river that had joined the one where they traveled had come from the *west*. Its size spoke of a great expanse of land in that direction. Also, their direction of travel was still almost directly *south*. If it had chanced to turn westward in its flow, Nils would have assumed that his theory was wrong. He would have turned back.

As he pondered that possibility, another thought struck him. Odin had said nothing about when he and Snake would turn back. Nils finally asked him.

"I do not know, Wolf. I had thought maybe by this time. Did you want to go back?"

"No, no. I only meant . . . you have been away from your family so long. . . ." In truth, he had not thought of turning back, but now was forced to consider it. Maybe this was too big a chance to take. It was already apparent that Vinland was much bigger than any of them had imagined. "Do you think we should?" Nils asked.

Odin gave his quizzical shrug.

"Maybe a little farther. For Snake and me, I mean. You could go on, or back with us. What does Dove say?"

"We have not spoken of it. I will talk with her."

But he kept postponing that discussion. He was not sure why, except that he was not sure what Dove would want to do. Actually, he was no longer certain what he wanted to do, himself. The voyage was pleasant and easy. To go back upstream would be harder work. There had been a few summer storms, but none as bad as the first one, when the wind creature had howled its way past their camp. So day by day, the decision was postponed. Odin, too, seemed reluctant to turn back.

"A little farther," he would say. "Then Snake and I will turn back."

But they had not done so. It was much later, midsummer now, and they had traveled a long way. Nils was becoming discouraged. They had passed another of the cities like that first one at the junction of the two rivers, only yesterday. Again, they had been reluctant to stop, because of their vulnerability. It had been so each time they passed such a settlement, and they had gone on, passing four or five cities in the past moon.

Each time, Nils had studied the waterfront, wondering whether the facilities might be used for ships. At several places, he thought it possible. How glorious it would be, if they rounded some bend of the river and encountered one of the Norse longships, moored safely at the wharf of some unknown city here on the Great River! That was too much to hope.

They stopped once more, to question the dwellers of thatched dwellings on the west bank. It was like all the other conversations, carried out in hand signs, with few answers that they had not heard before. Yes, there was a salty sea, Big Water, far downstream. How far? Many sleeps. What else? A big river, from the west, joining this one . . . two, maybe three sleeps.

Nils was confused. For a moment, he felt as if they were reliving this voyage over and over. It had not been unpleasant, except for a storm or two, which had passed quickly. But more recently, he was becoming impatient. *Nothing happens,* he thought irritably. *It is the same day after day.*

In his musings, he felt that it was as if the river were flowing in a circle, that they were doomed to travel forever, pausing every few days for hand-signed consultations that were exactly like the last. Their goal seemed no nearer. Maybe he should have *insisted* that they stop at one of the cities. Such people would have more experience with traders, and would know of what is going on in other places, maybe. They might even know of Norse contact downriver. Their reasons for not stopping at one of those cities had centered primarily on Odin's reluctance. That, too, was uncharacteristic of the man. Did Odin know something that he had not communicated? Nils asked him, finally.

"No," Odin answered blandly. "But I am made to think that the danger is more than any help we would get."

He said it with such finality that Nils did not push it further. Odin had changed much as a family man. He was cautious, far less likely to take risks than he had once been. In a way, Nils wondered how Odin had ever agreed to accompany the voyage. A sense of responsibility to his sister Dove, maybe, or to his almost-brother, White Wolf. Odin had saved his life long ago, but it must have been a hard decision this time, to leave his own family to fulfill what Odin must see as a responsibility.

Even so, Nils made up his mind that before they saw another of these cities, he would try to convince Odin of the importance of questioning *those* people. Otherwise, this could go on endlessly.

One difference about this most recent stop, however, was the news of another big river ahead. He had tried to sketch in an ongoing map the mouths of the streams they had encountered. Somehow, these local natives seemed more impressed by the *size* of the river two or three sleeps below. Maybe this one *would* be really large. Maybe he would have to revise his ideas of Vinland's size yet *again.* Everything they had encountered seemed to indicate an immense land to the west. Well, they would soon see. About the river, at least.

They had also inquired about dangers downstream. Yes, they had been told, be careful of storms. *Of course,* Nils thought irritably. *We know that!*

"Oh, yes," the other man added as an afterthought, still in hand signs. "You know of the people there?"

"What people?" Odin signed the question.

The answer was the sign for tribe or nation, followed by one they had seen before. It was the two-hand motion of cutting hair, back over the head.

"The Hair-cutters are below?" Nils asked.

The other nodded.

"Beyond the big river's mouth," the man signed. "Where the two come together."

"And they are dangerous?" Nils asked.

"Sometimes. Maybe not."

So, the Shaved-heads were in the area two sleeps downstream, and could be dangerous. At least, they were unpredictable, according to this informant.

For some reason, Nils felt good about this. At least, it presented a change. Even something that could be risky seemed better than the sameness that had become so intolerable.

There was an extra possibility here, too. A large and well-known nation, recognized even many sleeps upstream, would be powerful, it seemed. So, they would be well informed. They might know of the distant sea, and possibly of any dragon ships that might have been in the area.

Nils hoped that he could convince Odin of the importance of this contact. He must talk to him before they reached this new "big river."

81

The storm came in quietly, as many had done on the long river trip. This was initially a gentle rain, completely unlike the crashing assault that had struck them far upstream, with the destructive whirlwind.

A major difference was the character of the storm. That well-remembered strike by the forces of Rain Maker had come in noisily, with the roll of thunder and the spears of fire. This storm crept in by night, almost without notice. They woke to find the world covered by a gray blanket of low clouds, silent and sullen. It hung broodingly over them, dark and menacing, nothing more. It seemed to be waiting.

When the rain began, it was hard to notice, even. There was no change in the wind, because there was no wind. It was such a fine mist that it appeared more like a heavy dew, settling on the leaves of bushes around them, on the upturned canoes, on everything. Droplets of water grew fatter, until their weight became great enough to force them to drip from dangling leaves to splash to the ground.

The campfire was one source of comfort in this sodden world. The little party retreated to the partial shelter of the canoes and faced the warmth of the flames. It was not really a cold morning, but the shadow of the fog was a depressing thing, a chill that gripped the mind as well as the body. It seemed to penetrate all the way through, clear to the bone, though it was as much mental as physical.

Their fuel supply was low, because it had been intended to move on with the coming of day. Now travel seemed inadvisable. They ventured out long enough to find more firewood. It was sodden and wet, of course, but Snake arranged part of it around the fire to dry, so that it would be ready when needed. The flames hissed and crackled, steam mixing with rising smoke to layer out over the dark brooding river.

By midday the rain was falling steadily. Not a hard and pelting rain, like some they had experienced, but a steady, unchanging patter that seemed to have no end. This continued through the day and into the night. Daylight of the next day revealed little change. They began to wonder about the danger of flooding.

"Should we move to higher ground?" Snake asked, of no one in particular.

It was Odin who finally answered. "I am made to think not," he said thoughtfully. "The valley is wide. If the water rises, it would be slowly, no? We would have time."

This seemed a logical assumption, and they settled back to wait. By evening of the second day, however, Nils was becoming impatient. He knew quite well that it would be imprudent to start into unknown waters during a storm of any kind, but . . . Well, tomorrow might be better. For some reason, he thought of an old sailors' saying that his grandfather had used. *Three days' rain will empty any sky.* Would such a truism still hold in the strange lands of this new world?

He did not know, but there were certain things that he had begun to notice during this summer of travel. He was helped considerably in this by his experience at sea. Such things became second nature to seamen. Here, all storms seemed to come from the west. Sometimes more northwest, sometimes southwest, but it was a general weather pattern. With this in mind, he had begun to watch westward during a storm, to see the broken patches of lighter blue that would herald its passing.

This time, he searched in vain for such a sign. The heavy gray blanket simply seemed to hang there, unmoving. He had the odd feeling that its very weight prevented any change in the storm's position. It was soft and bulky in character, and wide. *How far westward does it extend?* he wondered.

It was like a person whose bulk is so great that he must move slowly. He, or *she* . . . Mrs. Johannson, a friend of his mother's, had been so fat that he had marveled at her size when he was a small child. "Large," his mother had always said, but Nils knew. . . . *Fat.* The woman's legs were like hams, her arms above the elbow larger than his young waist. It was fascinating to watch the woman get out of a chair, all of her flesh quivering and jiggling at once, yet not going much of anywhere. His mother had cautioned him not to stare, but it was very difficult.

Somehow this storm was like that, sitting heavily over them, unable to get up. He smiled grimly to himself. It was amusing how his childhood experiences came back at odd times to apply themselves to the present situation.

But how long could this storm sit here? It was a little bit discomfiting to think of the biblical story of the Flood, when it was said to have rained for forty days and forty nights.

On the morning of the fourth day there were signs of thinning in the clouds to the west. Maybe if they could move on, they could slip out from under this cursed blanket of gray. They decided to try it, and were quickly on the river.

They had found that they could make better time by utilizing the river's current to carry them. With this in mind, they usually sought the best flow near the center of the stream. It was pleasing to note that there seemed to be little debris there. Flotsam near the center of a stream would indicate rising water. A subsiding flood deposits its refuse on the banks. So they were apparently not embarking on water that was flooding, and that was reassuring.

It was not until afternoon that Nils began to suspect that all was not quite right. He had expected clearing by this time, but it had not happened. There were lighter and darker times, as clouds seemed about to open, but then crept back to cover the patches of blue. It was growing darker again, and the overcast seemed lower and more threatening. He was about to suggest that they look for a place to camp before the rain resumed, when Odin pointed ahead with his paddle. Ahead, and to the right.

It was difficult to see, from their position low on the water, but Nils quickly grasped the situation. Even with the poor light, he could see the widening of the great stream. Could this be the ocean that they sought? No, of course not. The expected river from the west? Yes, they must be looking across its mouth. Now he could dimly see the line of trees on the other shore. There seemed to be a fog bank, or maybe a light shower in progress.

"Let us pull to shore," Odin called.

They turned toward the west bank, to land before they reached the questionable currents where the rivers would mix. But it was too late. In a few moments, Nils saw that they would be carried past the junction before they could land. It was of no major concern. They would simply stay out in the main current until they passed the junction. He started to call to the other canoe, but

Odin waved to indicate that he, too, understood. They would land farther downstream.

Nils could see, now, the point where the waters began to join. There was a subtle difference in the color of the water, the suspended mud a different shade of red-brown. Other factors quickly became apparent to him, flitting through his consciousness like the flicker of lightning. The river from the west carried a large quantity of debris. There were rafts of dead sticks, leaves, and dead grasses, the trash picked up by rising flood waters. Occasionally, larger logs, dead trees, and a bloated carcass of some small animal. The bulk of this flotsam was near the center of the river's mouth. *The flood is still rising,* he thought.

Alarm had not struck him yet. That came quickly now, however, as he saw the river's surface straight ahead, broken by a series of treacherous whirlpools and back eddies where the two powerful currents joined. Floating logs and other debris were being pulled into the whirling vortex, sucked under to be carried downstream. The more buoyant pieces would come thrusting upward below, the heavier somewhat later.

"Pull to the left," he yelled at the other canoe, slightly behind and to his right. If they could move far enough out into the main current, they could avoid the dangerous spot.

Dove, in front of him, was already struggling to turn their course, and he joined in the effort. In their eagerness to change direction, they made the needed correction too quickly. The powerful current caught the stern of the canoe and swung it to the right, bringing the craft almost broadside to the river's flow. Nils struggled to regain control of the now unstable canoe. He had time for one quick glance behind him, to see what was happening to the others. Odin and Snake were being carried directly toward a whirling mass of logs and limbs and trash. But then there was no time to think of anything but the threat to their own canoe.

He managed to swing the stern at least partially, aligning the canoe with the current. The alarming rocking motion subsided a little, and he was able to look ahead. They were nearly far enough left now to escape the unpredictable whirl of the joining current. A little more . . .

It was then that he saw it. Just ahead, a large eddy of some sort. Maybe there was a sandbar deep under the surface that was affecting the flow where the new current joined. He caught a glimpse of the giant swirl, with large logs and trees bobbing like living things, to be sucked under again. He tried to maneuver, but felt that he had completely lost control.

Then, to his horror, he saw a great clawlike arm reach up out of the swirling flood, to grasp at the canoe. It was plainly the limb of a giant old tree, carried by the powerful current. But its broken branches held a close resemblance to grasping fingers. He tried to pull aside as Dove dodged the tip of the branch, but had little control. Beside him another broken stub thrust up out of the depths, close enough to touch. Its rotting bark glistened with moss and slime from the river's bed. It grated along the side of the canoe, grinding with a snarl like that of a living thing. The canoe shuddered from a new impact, and another branch of the old giant jabbed upward through the floor of the craft. In a panic, Nils realized that this tree must be rolling along the bottom, propelled by the current. Their canoe was trapped in its branches, impaled and dragged.

Even as their predicament became clear to him, the canoe was twisted and pulled slowly under. He heard Bright Sky's scream, cut off sharply as the water closed over him, and saw Dove lunge to grab the boy. Then Nils himself was dragged down, fighting, striving to free himself from the grasping arms of the creature in his dream. This was the meaning of the dream, then. *Not* the giant leech . . . of course . . . *this!* He was fighting, disoriented, unable to determine which way the surface might be . . . panic. . . .

So this is how it feels to drown. . . .

82

alling Dove was a strong swimmer. She was of the People of the River, and she had been around water all her life. Children of the People could swim almost before they could walk. When the accident began to unfold, she did not immediately fear for her own safety. Hers was the self-confidence required in an emergency. She knew, or thought she knew, that she could save herself. Her concern was first for her son, and next for her husband.

She lunged to grab the boy as he was pulled under, kicking herself free of the doomed canoe as she did so. Her shoulder struck one of the limbs of the rolling tree and she pushed away from it, glancing behind as she did so. She saw

White Wolf pulled under, tangled in the clawing branches. She could have screamed in her anguish, but made no sound. It would not be appropriate to waste effort in anything so useless. Dove did not stop to think this, but it was an instinct of survival. Above all, the People were survivors.

She began to swim toward shore, still holding Bright Sky with one hand. He was helping, swimming strongly, and she felt a momentary thrill of pride at his skill and stamina. Her heart and spirit reached out, searching for her husband, but she was unable to concentrate on that for the moment. She reassured herself that he was strong and brave, and that his power as a holy man would help him. At least, she devoutly hoped so.

They were being carried rapidly downstream by the current, and Dove struggled to escape its pull. If she could only reach the calmer water nearer the shore, it would not require so much effort. She could tell that Sky was tiring. She could not see the other canoe. To make matters worse, a sudden squall sent a patter of rain that obscured almost everything in sight, pelting the river's surface into a frothy mist. They struggled on.

Out of the mist and rain loomed a log, floating downstream like every other bit of flotsam. Dove pushed toward it. This was unlike the mighty tree with the clawing branches. It was a trunk, no more than four paces long, partly rotting away. It could almost be encircled by the arms. She grasped a short stub that protruded from its bole, and placed Sky's hands on it. He grabbed at it eagerly, and held fast.

"Do not climb on it," Dove cautioned. "Just hold on."

"Look!" said Sky, indicating with a shake of his head.

There, at the other end of the log crouched a large spotted cat. It was easily bigger than the boy, and potentially quite dangerous. Bobcats, known for ferocity when at bay, are equally recognized for quickness. And, for unpredictability. Dove stared hard into the yellow eyes, noting also the flattened ears held close to the head. The creature was ready and willing to fight.

"Move slowly," she cautioned Sky quietly, "or stay still."

The cat curled its lips in a defiant snarl, still unmoving.

"My brother," Dove spoke softly, "we have the same problem as you. We would share your log for a time, and then we go our separate ways, no?"

The only answer was a low hiss and the continued unblinking stare.

"It is good," she said, as if she had received the desired answer.

Very slowly and deliberately she began to swim, thrusting with her legs and pushing the log ahead of her, toward the unseen west shore. She paused to glance around for any sign of the others, but could see nothing. Once she thought she heard a shout. She would have answered, but dared not startle the cat at the other end of their log. It could easily decide to attack if it felt threatened.

It seemed like a long while before the curtain of rain lifted a little way to show a fringe of willows ahead. It was even longer until they drew near the shore and Dove began to look for a place to land. Not that she had much control, but she would try to reach the shore where they would not have to fight their way through a thicket.

A sandbar loomed ahead. Almost at the same moment, the log struck bottom, sending an impact that was felt rather than heard. At the first hint of grounding, the great spotted cat leaped to the sandbar. It was gone, disappearing into the thicket along the bank.

Now she could call out without fear of causing something worse. She raised a long shout, then waited for an answer and tried again. There was only the quiet murmur of the river and the cries of birds as they began to come out after the shower.

Well, she would try again later. Now there were things to do. They must try to build a fire, which would not be easy with the sodden timber.

"Come, Sky, we will find some dry tinder."

"Will my father find us?" asked the boy, teeth chattering.

"Of course. Wolf can do anything. We must make a fire to guide him."

Dove wished that she could be as confident as she tried to sound. It was certainly not time to mourn. *We have been separated,* she told herself, *that is all.* It was impossible for her to think otherwise about so bold and strong a man as her husband. Had he not been a leader among his own people, before? Odin had great confidence in him, did he not?

She could not push from her mind her last glimpse of White Wolf as he sat in the back of the canoe, trying to dodge the clawing arms of the water-logged old tree. It had reached for him like a living thing, intent on his destruction. She was certain that the canoe was destroyed. She had heard its frail shell crack. A tear came to her eye as she thought of her husband dragged under, fighting for breath. . . .

I will not think so, she thought savagely. It would not only be disloyal, but she owed it to young Sky not to reveal any doubts she might have.

And what of the others? She had no idea what might have happened to the other canoe. It had encountered water that was not quite so treacherous. Or was it? The tricky currents were so deceptive. There had been so little time, so little to see! Her heart was very heavy.

"Come," she said to Sky. "Here is a log that may have a mouse nest."

That would do for tinder, she was thinking, *if we can find one.* But then she would need dry twigs and some softwood for rubbing sticks. She had a small knife that she always wore in a pouch at her waist. It was fortunate that she had not lost it. But the day was drawing to a close. It must be, because they had been on the river for some time before the accident.

Also, where would they camp? The sandbar would be the best place for a signal fire, to be seen by anyone on the river. But the flood was still rising. The sandbar might be under water by morning. Well, she had no fire yet, anyway. Build a fire on higher ground first, then another on the sandbar. . . .

"We will camp here," she indicated, pointing to a partly sheltered grassy knoll. She took a moment to establish the route of retreat to even higher ground in case . . . well, maybe it would not come to that.

She kept looking toward the river at every opportunity, hoping for some sign, but there was none. Finally she resigned herself to the task at hand, and turned to the attempt to build a fire. It would be a long cold night without one. Even in this warm autumn, a night's chill could be quite uncomfortable. And they had no robes. Their comforts of that sort were probably at the bottom of the river, or lodged in some pile of driftwood far downstream.

Dove was able to kindle a fire before dark, for which she was grateful. The hollow end of a large dead log furnished not only the dry, finely shredded tinder of a mouse's lodge, but an older structure. A pack rat had crammed the log with its characteristic armful of small dry twigs. She constructed makeshift fire-rubbing sticks, and in a short while had a blaze going. She removed the thong from her fire bow and tucked it back into her pouch. She might need it again.

Carefully, they nurtured the fire with the dry sticks until some of the wetter fuel was dried enough to ignite. By the time darkness fell, their night's supply of firewood was toasting and steaming, drying by the heat of the fire. Its warmth lifted her spirits some.

"When will the others come?" asked Sky.

"I do not know. Maybe we can build a signal fire!" Dove jumped to her feet to put the plan into action. At least, it would occupy their minds.

They carried dry wood to the sandbar, and some twigs, building a pyramid of small sticks with tinder inside. Then, a square of larger sticks around it, leaning inward. Finally, she carried a burning stick from the campfire and thrust it into the tinder. The fire leaped quickly this time, catching the partly dried fuel. Sky spread his hands to the warmth as Dove looked up and down the river. She saw no signs of activity.

"Mother, I—" Sky began, but she interrupted.

"Ssh . . . I thought . . . Did you hear someone call?"

Both listened a little longer, but they heard nothing.

"Maybe it was only a night bird," she said finally. "Well, let us build up this fire and then stay at the other one. The wind is cold here."

She was practically certain that she had heard a shout, but hesitated to say so. It was as if too much confidence might make it untrue. She could see for some distance up and down the river, though not well in the fading light. But the signal fire was well located. They could build it up before complete darkness, and it would burn for some time. Just before they left it for the night, she shouted a few times, waiting for an answer that did not come.

They made their way back to the campfire, away from the chill breeze on the river. Dove squatted by the fire, and drew her son close to her, giving him the warmth of her body as well as that of the fire. Her buckskin dress had partly dried from the activity and from the heat of both fires, and she was a little more comfortable now.

She devoutly hoped that the others had seen their signal fire. There was no way of knowing, of course. She and Sky would stay here, keep the fires going. Tomorrow she must think of food of some sort, in case they were not found. She tried to ignore the gnawing doubt that maybe the others had not survived. Or not *all* of them.

Sky was asleep now, snuggled against her. Her muscles were cramped, but she did not want to disturb him, and the ground was too wet for either of them to lie on. She finally compromised by sinking to a sitting position and extended her legs to ease the muscles. She managed to feed the fire a stick or two, and noticed that the stars were out, the clouds moving on to the east. A beaver splashed on the river, and from somewhere in the distance came the booming call of a night heron. A coyote gave its chuckling cry.

She was dozing off when she was rudely awakened by a screaming cry near at hand. It took her a moment to realize its source. A hunting cat . . . Possibly the one with which they had shared the log. She smiled, and rocked her sleeping son gently.

"Good hunting, brother," she murmured softly.

A short while later there was another sound, the dying scream of a rabbit. Their friend the bobcat had found good hunting.

Now, if their own peril could come out so well . . .

din had seen the other canoe trapped and crushed by the rolling tree. The grasping arms . . . later he would realize the significance of the accident in connection with Wolf's dream.

Just then, however, he had been preoccupied with saving his own life and that of his companion. Trapped in an odd whirl of the new river's cross current, the canoe had shot helplessly past the dangerous tangle and on into the center of the combined stream. He could feel the powerful current catch the craft and speed it on, overtaking and passing the doomed canoe of Wolf and Dove. He caught only glimpses of someone struggling in the water. He could not tell who.

Their paddles were useless, puny against the might of the current. The canoe seemed to take on a life of its own, surging on downstream, out of earshot of the others. He called out, but felt the futility of the effort. He was not even certain whether he might have been heard.

It was some time later before the two men, exhausted and shaken, managed to bring the canoe out of the powerful current and into a quiet backwater near the west bank. Snake looked over his shoulder, eyes wide.

"Let us go ashore."

"It is good!" answered Odin, though there was very little in their situation that fit such a term.

"Did you see?" asked Snake.

"Yes. We must look for them."

"The tree . . . it was alive!" Snake muttered, badly shaken by the tragedy he had just witnessed.

They drew the canoe up on shore a little way, and then stretched themselves on the ground, still breathing heavily. Odin found himself shaking as his tired muscles quivered in the ecstasy of relief from straining.

"I saw your sister grab the boy," Snake panted. "Did she reach land?"

"I did not see," Odin answered, "but she is a strong swimmer. Maybe so."

"What about White Wolf?"

"Ah, I do not know, Snake. He was caught . . . pulled under. I fear for him."

"But the holy man said—"

"I know. But we know, too, what we *saw*. Still, his gifts are powerful. I have seen him—"

"Yes, yes! You saw him change into a wolf, no? Maybe he could change to a beaver or an otter, even a fish!"

Odin saw that Snake too was greatly impressed with the mystic powers of their companion.

"Yes, maybe," he agreed. "But Snake, even though Wolf has great power, he needs help. And we must find my sister."

They were recovering now, breathing more normally. The discomfort of protesting muscles was subsiding.

"We must go," Odin stated, rising stiffly and beginning to shove the canoe back into the water. It would soon begin to grow dark.

"Let us stay near the bank," Odin said as they stepped into the canoe. "We cannot fight the current."

"Do you think they were swept out into the middle, as we were?" Snake asked.

"I cannot tell," Odin shrugged, "but maybe not. We were pulled past them . . . no, I am made to think they are all behind us, alive or not."

He hated to think in such terms, even, but they must be realistic. The chances of survival for any of the people in the other canoe were pretty grim.

They made their way along the shore, searching for any sign of the lost ones. It was more reasonable to do so than to watch the flotsam out in the main current. Any object there after the accident would be far downstream now. If it were a person, that person would be dead. Even so, they cast a glance toward midstream occasionally, but saw no bodies. That, at least, was gratifying.

Evening was drawing near when Snake suddenly exclaimed and pointed ahead. Something light in color, trapped against the roots of a large tree that stood partly in the water.

"The canoe," said Snake softly. "Part of it."

They circled past it, looking, searching. The stark white of the birchbark gleamed like bleached bones in the deepening dusk. It was an ominous sign.

"Let us get a little closer," Odin suggested. "Is that the front or the back part? It is twisted."

They moved in, searching for any bit of information they might find. This section of bark had once composed perhaps a third of the canoe's length.

"The back," said Snake. "It has no eyes."

So it could not see, Odin thought. The symbolic eyes had been painted on the prow, to look forward. This, then, would have been the rear portion of the canoe. *The part where White Wolf sat.*

Snake, sitting in the prow of their own canoe, was practically close enough to touch the torn shell when he jumped suddenly. His movement was so violent that the canoe rocked alarmingly.

"What is it?" asked Odin, who could not yet see closely.

"Someone . . . there is somebody under it!" Snake exclaimed.

Now Odin could see what had startled his companion. A hand jutted from beneath the bark shell, grasping the roots of the tree in a last dying effort.

"Who? Can you tell?"

Snake gingerly grasped the edge of the shattered canoe and pulled it aside. It floated, drifting clear, to reveal a human form.

"White Wolf!" Snake gasped. "His powers . . ."

Odin's heart sank. They had come so far, survived so much. And a man of the water, one who had crossed the sea . . . Maybe this was a fitting end. But they had been brothers, almost. He knew the intensity with which White Wolf must have clung to life. It was apparent in the way the grasping hand still held tightly to the tangled cottonwood roots. He could imagine that grasp tightening rather than loosening as consciousness faded. The flowing yellow hair and beard were muddy and matted now. Tears filled Odin's eyes, and he lifted his head to begin the Song of Mourning for his almost-brother.

"He lives!" Snake gasped.

Hastily, Odin wiped tears aside and looked more closely. Yes, clearly Wolf was trying to raise his head. There was a low moan.

A stroke or two of the paddles beached the canoe. Snake pulled it ashore while Odin splashed back into the water.

"Wolf! It is Odin! Wake up!" Odin pried loose stiff fingers and half carried, half floated his friend to shore.

"We need a fire," he said to Snake.

Snake trotted off to look for fuel and tinder, while Odin continued to rub and massage Wolf's chilled limbs. Wolf opened his eyes, confused, poorly focused, only half-conscious.

"Dove?" he whispered. "Where is Dove?"

"We will find her, Wolf," Odin said shakily, wishing that he could sound more confident than he really was.

Snake returned with a handful of dry grass and some bark and twigs, and began to prepare the tinder. Odin reached into his pouch for fire-making tools. When they had parted far upriver, Fire Man had insisted that he take the steel striker and nodule of flint. It would be much quicker now than trying to construct the rubbing-stick bow and fire-sticks.

Just as the welcoming warmth of the fire began to grow, Odin thought he heard a distant shout. He answered, but heard nothing further. The fine drizzling rain, which had been starting and stopping, seemed a little heavier just now, and he crouched nearer the fire. They had spread a robe and placed it around White Wolf, who was slowly regaining his senses.

"What about Dove and Sky?" he asked again.

"We do not know, Wolf," Odin told him. "It is too dark to search now, but she is strong. We will find them as soon as it is light."

When Dove opened her eyes, the sun was shining, and it was warm. She had not expected to rest at all, but exhaustion had done its part. It must have been nearly morning when she closed her eyes for a moment, and now . . . She turned to look at Bright Sky, curled up beside her and sound asleep.

What about the others? she wondered in a mixture of urgency and sorrow. The other canoe? White Wolf? She rose and fed a few half-burned sticks into the embers of last night's fire. What should she do first? Try to search, or look for some food?

Dove looked again at her son, still sleeping peacefully, and then stepped the few paces back to the sandbar. The fire had burned low, and she thought of building it back up. But no, a signal fire was not so effective in daylight. A *smoke* . . . Yes, she could do that with the other fire. She took a long look up and down the river, and returned to their sparse camp. A few more sticks, intentionally wet now, and an armful of green leaves and grass. Thick yellow smoke rose straight upward in a fat column, to fan out in a layer high above on a gentle breeze not felt here at the ground.

It is good, she thought. For now she would stay here, maybe look for a rabbit or some frogs. If no one came, then they could look elsewhere later.

She found some berries, which were being enjoyed by the birds. The fruit was unfamiliar to her, but by custom, if other creatures ate it without harm, it was safe to try. Sky was awake now, and they picked and ate for a little while. The berries were seedy, but good. *Anything would taste good,* she thought.

It was well toward midday when she heard the sound of someone approaching. Her heart beat faster. Who . . . Her brother? Her husband? She jumped up from where she had been feeding the fire, and faced the opening of a faint game trail near them. The soft rustle continued, coming closer. *What if it is a bear?* She had not considered that possibility.

The bushes parted, and a tall, nearly naked warrior stepped out, followed by three more. They were armed with bows, and she saw that their hair was cut very short except for the strip up and over the center of the head. *The Hair-cutters,* she thought. She gave the palm-forward gesture for peace and then started to sign boldly.

"I am Calling Dove, of the River People," she began. "How are you called?"

The four stared at her for a moment, and then one began to sign. He did not answer her inquiry, but asked questions of his own.

"Where is your man? What are you doing here?"

"We were on the river. Our canoe broke up in the flood. Will you help me find him?"

There was no answer for a few moments, and then the tall warrior who had signed before did so again.

"There is no need. He is probably dead. We will find you a man."

A couple of the others smiled at their leader's unkind joke. Calling Dove did not like the quality of their humorless grins, or the way their eyes kept roving over her body and legs. Even worse, she had no weapon except her small knife.

84

hey came ashore here," said Odin, pointing to the tracks in the sand and gravel of the bar. "They had a signal fire last night."

"Both of them?" asked Nils anxiously. He was still feeling a little weak and shaky, but was recovering quickly. The warm sunlight seemed to have restorative qualities.

Odin nodded. "Both are active, Wolf. It is good. I am made to think they came on that log, there."

"Then where are they?"

"I do not know. Let us look around. Something is wrong."

"Why did we not see their fire?" asked Snake.

Odin glanced up and down the river. "We were downstream. There is a little bend in the river here. See, the trees . . . Their fire was hidden from us."

"But they did not spend the night here, in the open," Snake replied. "Where did they go?"

"They must have had another fire," Odin decided. "Stay here, let me look for tracks."

"Should we call to them?" asked Nils.

"No," Odin advised. "Let us learn more, first."

He picked up his bow and slipped into the timbered strip. It was only a short while until he returned, though to Nils it seemed much longer.

"I have found their night fire," Odin said quickly, concern showing in his face.

"What is it?" asked Nils.

"They are gone. Tracks of others, maybe three or four men. Come."

Quickly, they drew the canoe ashore and concealed it in the thicket.

"What if the flood rises and takes it?" asked Snake.

There was only a brief hesitation.

"Tie it," said Odin. "That tree, there. But more important is to find my sister."

They made their way along the dim trail to a clearing, where the acrid scent of dead ashes hung faintly.

"Here was their fire," Odin pointed. "The ash is still warm. They sat here for the night." He pointed to an area of flattened grass near the fire.

"They had no robes," Nils noted.

"True. But a good fire. Dove is clever, Wolf. But look, here. Tracks not theirs . . . see . . . three, at least. I think four men."

"There is no sign of a struggle," Nils observed. "Is there?" he added, unsure of his tracking skills.

"No," Odin agreed. "They left with no struggle. There would be no reason to struggle. She was outnumbered, and had no weapon."

"Her knife," said Nils. "She would have her little knife."

"Yes, unless she lost it in the accident. But come, we need to follow them. They left on this trail."

He indicated a game trail that seemed to lead vaguely westward, away from the river.

"Let me go ahead to look for tracks," Odin suggested. He studied the trail before entering the dark tunnel-like course through the woods.

"Ah!" he exclaimed. "She leaves sign! They went not by choice, but are not mistreated. Not yet, anyway."

That was not very reassuring to Nils.

"How can you tell this?" he demanded.

"No struggle. No choice but to go. But she leaves signs for us to find, that these others will not see."

"What?" Nils asked.

"We must hurry, Wolf, but look . . . this twig. It is broken, but not just by brushing past it. Someone took it in a hand and bent it *upward* to break it. But come, let us go."

Odin disappeared into the dim shade of the forest. Nils took a long look at the broken twig, dangling loosely on its thin strip of bark. It told so much, yet so little. He followed Odin, and Snake brought up the rear.

"They stopped here," Odin pointed out much later.

It was nearly noon, and the captors of Dove and Bright Sky were moving swiftly. There was a spring here, and more signs of travel. The game trail had become a path.

The three dropped their packs and drank at the spring, then sat to rest while Odin explained some further observations.

"I am made to think this is a hunting party," he explained. "Four men. I am sure of that now." He paused to point to moccasin tracks beside the spring. "They are probably one sleep from home, and this trail is known to them. The spring . . ." The others nodded and he continued. "Dove still leaves sign, so they are captives. These men will not let her wait for us."

"You think they will reach their lodges before night?" asked Nils.

"I am made to think so, Wolf, but not long before. They hurry a little."

"They may think they are followed," Snake noted.

"That is true," agreed Odin. "We must be careful not to come into an ambush. But I am made to think this: They think their safety is in reaching home. That makes them hurry."

At the next stop, Odin was not so confident.

"Ah, this is not good. They have learned that she leaves a trail for us to follow."

He pointed to a bush beside the trail with many broken twigs. The appearance was as if some large animal had forcefully damaged it. Odin reached behind the bush and brought out a clublike stick. Obviously, it could have been used to create the damage to the bush that had caught his attention. He tossed the stick aside and seemed to study the bush itself.

"Ah! Here," he muttered. He pointed to a single broken twig, its tip completely missing. But on the remaining part, the curl of bark told plainly that it had been broken upward and quite deliberately.

Nils began to understand. One of Dove's captors had seen her break the twig, and they had torn it away and vandalized the bush to conceal her sign.

"Let me look ahead again," Odin suggested, disappearing on down the trail.

He was soon back. "They still hurry. Maybe more now," he panted. "They are close to home. If it was a long way, they would stop to wait and fight. This is not good. They travel faster now. We must stop and plan."

"Stop?" Nils's patience was wearing thin. "Should we not hurry *faster?*"

"Look, Wolf, now they suspect they are followed. We do not know what Dove might have told them, so let us think on it. She might try to put them off guard by saying she was alone with her husband, and fears him lost."

"But she knows they might have seen two canoes," reminded Snake. "Then she might tell them there are more, *many* warriors."

"That is true." Odin glanced at the sun, lowering in the west. "They have not harmed her. I am made to think we should let them reach their village, and then see how it is."

Nils was not pleased with this decision, but realized there was little alternative.

"What weapons do we have?" Odin asked. "Two bows, mine and Snake's . . . Wolf, it is good that your long knife was around your neck. Shall we make a spear out of it?"

Nils still carried the short swordlike weapon that they had salvaged after the massacre. It had been an object of wonder to all tribes they had encountered. None had been familiar with metal objects except of copper, used mostly for ornaments.

During this river trip, he had once dropped the weapon into shallow water. It was easy to retrieve, but it brought concern. What if the water had been deep? From that day on, the big knife had been carried on a thong around his neck, wrapped in a skin sheath. It had been a mixed blessing. He had felt for a moment while he was drowning that he should drop it to free himself of the weight. No matter. Now he was glad to have it.

"I will use it this way, if we fight," he told Odin. In a battle such as they might encounter, a sword, even a short one, would be quicker than a spear.

They moved on, well aware that those they followed might be watching. It was still well before dark, though, when they saw a smoky haze ahead.

"That must be their town," Odin said. "I will go ahead and see what I can find."

"No, I go," Snake protested. "You are a tracker, but I have two eyes. Better for looking at far things. I will go."

He turned and started away.

"But—" Odin began.

Snake turned with a smile. "It is not time to argue, my brother."

That, certainly, was true. And Snake's scouting skills were well respected.

"Let us meet on that rise to the west of their town, after dark," Snake pointed. "Be careful."

And he was gone.

"Almost-brother," Odin said seriously, "let us plan. After we get them out, where to go."

"How can we plan?" Nils asked.

"Much, we cannot. But a place to meet. That hill where we will meet Snake might be good."

"But that is farther from the river!"

"Of course. They will expect us to go back. We head west, it delays pursuit, because they do not think we would go that way. But it is only a meeting place."

Nils nodded.

"Odin, who are these people?"

Odin gave his quizzical gesture.

"Who knows? I am made to think they might be the Hair-cutters we heard of. They were said to be undependable." He rose. "Well, let us go to meet Snake."

This was little comfort. They circled carefully, and arrived at the little hill just at dusk.

"Be careful," cautioned Odin. "They might use this for a lookout, too."

They saw no signs of scouts, however, and the view of the town was good. The light of the setting sun behind them was a great advantage.

"Their lodges," observed Odin, "smaller than ours. They are covered with . . . what? Skins?"

"Not a thatch," Nils answered. "Grass, maybe. Yes, woven grass. Like square robes made of grass, tied over poles, maybe."

"That would not be very warm in winter."

"True. But, my brother, we are far south now. Winters are warmer here, maybe."

Snake suddenly appeared, seemingly out of nowhere, in the deepening dusk.

"They are here," he said. "I saw them. They are unhurt."

"Where?" asked Nils quickly.

"The lodge on the far north," Snake pointed. "They are guarded, but not closely. There are many warriors here."

"Can we get them out?"

"I do not know, Wolf. The Shaved-heads may know we are coming. They will have many warriors ready."

"They are Shaved-heads, then?" asked Odin.

"Yes, I saw them." Snake made the hair-cutting sign they had seen before.

"We cannot attack them," Odin mused. "I am made to think that maybe we should just walk in, in the morning, and ask for our woman and child."

Nils was astonished. "They might kill us! What good—"

Odin held up a hand to stop him. "Almost-brother," he said with a smile, "do you not remember how your power impressed the Downstream Enemy long ago? You still have the sun-stone, no? And I can do Fire Man's ceremony. Yes, we can do this thing. Besides, that will let my sister know we are here."

"We have nothing to trade for them," Snake noted.

"A canoe, one day away," Odin said.

"But then we are on foot."

"We are on foot now, Snake," Odin smiled. "Let us see what happens in the morning."

Nils spent a sleepless, uncomfortable night, wishing for a fire, wishing for many things. He silently breathed a prayer to whatever gods might be appropriate, and wondered if Odin might have more of a plan than it appeared. He devoutly hoped so.

85

The three entered the village of the Shaved-heads pompously and with great dignity. They had circled back to the east side before daylight, to appear from that direction.

Nils's palms were moist and clammy. The emotion and uncertainty of the situation were weighing heavily on him. One quick glance around the town . . .

There, that lodge . . . The one where his wife and son lay captive. He must not look at it again, because the Shaved-heads must not learn what the newcomers knew.

They walked boldly past an astonished sentry, who seemed thoroughly confused. Should he stay on watch or challenge the trio, or merely accompany them into the village? He compromised with a halfhearted challenge, and then trotted along with them, signing questions. *Good,* thought Nils. It was good to have an adversary uncertain, off-balance.

Odin stopped and casually, almost haughtily, signed a question at the young man.

"Your leader?" he asked, pointing to one of the larger dwellings at random.

The warrior nodded, and Odin walked with confidence toward the lodge. A crowd was beginning to gather, and a woman looked out the door and quickly withdrew. There was a conversation inside, quick questions and answers, and a tall Shaved-head stepped outside. He straightened to face the newcomers.

"Greetings, my chief," Odin signed, trying to take advantage by opening the dialogue. "We come in peace. Our leader, here, is White Wolf, a famous holy man. We seek—"

He was interrupted by an impatient gesture from the Shaved-head leader.

"Stop! Who are you? What are you doing here?"

"This is what I am trying to tell you, Uncle. We are called People of the River."

"There is no river here."

"True. We were on the Big River, and an accident . . . our boat was broken."

The expression on the face of the Shaved-head was grim. "What is that to us?"

"Nothing, Uncle. But we seek a woman and child. The wife of our holy man, here. We were separated in the flood, and the woman and child came this way."

"There is no such woman here," the other signed. "You are mistaken."

"He lies," Snake said quietly. "I saw—"

Odin held up a hand to his companion. "I know," he agreed, "but let me—" He turned and began to sign again. "It is good to know, my brother. But the powerful gifts of our holy man have pointed us this way. We would ask that you let us camp near you, and continue our journey tomorrow."

The Shaved-head leader looked a bit uneasy. "What gifts?" he asked. "Who is this old man with the white hair on his face?"

"Ah, you have never heard of the great White Wolf, Uncle? The most powerful of all holy men!"

"Talk is easy," scoffed the other. "I have seen nothing!"

"We will tell you all," Odin signed, "but let us have a council fire. Here! I will start one."

He selected an open spot, sank to a squatting position, and drew out a handful of tinder and sticks and the striker. "Could someone bring more wood?" he asked.

In the space of a few heartbeats his kindling was blazing. Snake, who had carried a few sticks the diameter of a finger, handed them to Odin, who added them to the fire.

It had all happened so quickly that the observers were silent, lost in wonder for a few moments. Now a murmur of excitement began to ripple through the crowd.

"What is this?" demanded the leader. "This is your power? Anyone can build a fire!"

Odin looked up in innocent surprise. It was apparent that the Shaved-head leader was impressed but was determined not to admit it. Odin decided to use this for all it was worth.

"This?" he signed. "No, no, of course not. This fire . . . White Wolf has given me just enough power to start fire with my hands. So much easier than rubbing sticks."

The Shaved-head nodded, as if he saw such things every day. "Tell me of your holy man," he signed. "His hair is old, his eyes are blind, yet his skin is young."

"His eyes?" Odin pretended to be puzzled. "No, no, Uncle. These blue eyes are not blind! They have a special vision. White Wolf can see into the souls of men!"

There was a gasp of surprise around the circle, but the leader remained unconvinced.

"Can he not talk for himself? And I have still seen none of his powers."

"Ah, I had hoped this would not be needed," Odin signed sadly. "He is a little dangerous sometimes. I am his assistant, and talk for him so that he can think on holier things, but—"

"Enough talk!" interrupted the Shaved-head. "Show me!"

"Uncle, it will be as you say. I have, with my own eyes, seen this holy man change himself into a white wolf. That is how he got his name. But he is dangerous, then. These people, the children here . . . Also, a leader of your wisdom must know the dangers of misuse of such powers?"

Odin could see that the Shaved-head was growing more impatient. It was time to go on with the plan they had devised. He spoke quietly to Nils. "It is time for the stone." He turned back to the Shaved-head.

"Here, Uncle!" he signed, as if a great thought had just come to him. "There is a simple thing that White Wolf can show you. He can change the color of stones by holding them in his hands."

Nils stepped forward, drawing the sun-stone from the pouch at his waist. They had done this before, and he now understood much more of the ceremonial effect that was needed. The stone could be aligned to the north very quickly, but more slowly was much more impressive. He held it up for all to see, then high over his head, and began to rotate it.

"A chant would be good," Odin said quietly. "I will do it!"

He raised his voice in a long, quavering singsong melody. He half expected to be stopped, but the Shaved-heads could not know what he was singing.

"We have come to help you, my sister. Be ready to go when we come. Watch well. We do not know yet how it will go."

He continued to chant, mixing nonsense with a repetition of the message.

Now the stone was nearing the alignment that would give the color change. Nils knew the general direction of north, and was ready. The dull gray of the translucent stone flickered to blue, back again as he manipulated it, and finally steadied to a radiant blue tone. The crowd gasped. Even their leader seemed impressed.

Nils had followed the lead of Odin so far, but now an idea struck him. He had noticed that when the stone was aligned, it was pointing almost directly toward a tall tree on a distant ridge. Now he raised his voice in a soft ritual chant.

"Odin, the tree on the ridge to the north . . . The star will be straight over it. I will tell them that."

"It is good. . . ." chanted the holy man's assistant.

Nils lowered the stone, and for the first time turned directly to the Shaved-head leader.

"The color of a stone means nothing," he signed. "Its purpose is to let me see the stars in daytime." He swept an arm in a dramatic gesture. "There!" he went on. "There is the Unmoving Star, the North Star. There above the tree!"

It was a moment before the onlookers began to realize the importance of this. They were staring northward, straining to see what was obviously *not* visible. Gradually they began to realize that this strange holy man was right. He had never been here before. He had no other way of knowing that the North Star did indeed hang above that tree on the ridge.

Their leader could not help but be impressed, but was reluctant to admit it. "It is only a guess," he signed. "Why should I not kill you and take the pretty stone?"

Even his own people were shocked. To challenge a holy man of such powers . . . ah, could this not be dangerous for them all?

The visiting holy man shrugged and smiled. "My brother knows the danger of trying to use another's gifts," he signed. "Would you risk it?"

"I only asked," the Shaved-head answered quickly. "It is good . . . for you to stay here tonight, that is. But we have no woman. That is another thing. Now our young men will show you where to camp. But the day grows later. Let us sit and talk, and our women will bring food."

The hand-signed conversation was mostly about the weather and the season, very light talk. They exchanged Creation stories, including Nils's tales of the Norse frost-giants, and Odin's of the grapevine. The Shaved-heads were greatly impressed.

Their own story told of a race of subhuman beings who climbed from underground, up a giant red oak tree, up three more layers of existence, and reached a place in the sky where they were given souls. Then they descended back to earth and divided into two bands, the Peace People and the War People. All Shaved-heads are descended from these two groups, the storyteller said.

"That is a very good story," Odin signed. "Tell us . . . from which of those does your band come?"

The Shaved-head leader gave a contemptuous grunt. "The War People, of course!"

It was long after dark now. The people of the village had looked and marveled at the North Star, precisely where the holy man had said. They had discussed and argued, and had now gone to bed.

The strangers had made their camp outside the perimeter of the lodges, in the place assigned. They were quiet and presumed to be sleeping. A sentry watched them from a little distance.

White Heron had called a quiet council of a handful of the most respected men in the band. There was a brief ceremonial smoke, and Heron began the discussion.

"You have seen our problem," he said simply. "What is to be done with these strangers?"

No one spoke for a little while.

"Otter," said an old man, "you should give them the woman and boy."

Black Otter bristled. "No! She belongs to us! These men will travel on in the morning."

"But Otter . . . the holy man sees the stars in the daytime. He knows you have the woman," said another.

"He cannot see through the walls of my lodge," Otter retorted. "We have kept her quiet. My brothers and I found her. She is ours."

"I am made to think," said the elder statesman, "that she is bad luck. You should give them up."

"And if I refuse?"

Heron spread his hands in a gesture of helplessness. "Then it is your problem. You and your family. We will not let you bring trouble on the whole band."

"You would tell the strangers where the woman is?" demanded the enraged Otter.

"Maybe we should kill the three men," suggested another.

"But this holy man appears dangerous," yet another voice joined in.

Finally White Heron silenced the discussion. "Let us sleep. See if they move on in the morning. But Otter, you and your family have brought this on us. If there is trouble, it is on your shoulders!"

86

ove sat in the dim corner of the lodge, her eyes fixed on her son and the threat that hovered over him. She was completely helpless to assist him, her hands tied behind her.

The threat was real. An old woman knelt behind Bright Sky, her left hand grasping his hair as he sat between her knees, pulling his head backward to expose the throat. A flint knife in her right hand rested under Sky's left ear, ready for the fatal slash.

One of the men had confronted Dove a few moments before, and had bluntly explained the situation in hand signs. "Any sound from either of you, the woman cuts his throat. Tell the boy."

Dove spoke softly but urgently. "Be very quiet, my son. Do not make any sound."

There had been a growing sense of expectation in the village since shortly after they arrived. She and Sky had not been harmed, although they were pushed around somewhat roughly. But then had come this change in attitude, the strong impression that they were waiting for something or someone. It did not take her long to realize that whatever it might be, it had a direct connection with her and her son. It must be, then, that their captors had discovered something that presented a threat.

It could be only one thing: There were other survivors of the ill-fated party after the accident on the river. The men had followed her trail of broken twigs.

Her heart had been heavy all during the day, as they traveled farther away from the area where she would have searched. Her main concern was for her husband, but she knew Wolf's medicine to be strong. Her last glimpse of Odin had shown his canoe being swept on downstream. He and Snake had probably survived.

She had no idea whether the survivors were being brought in as captives, or just what their status might be. As she thought about it now, however, she began to realize: *If they were captives, there would be no reason to keep us quiet!* Her heart beat faster with hope, then with dread. The men—whoever might have survived the dreadful river—might be walking into a trap. She must . . . but she could *not* warn them, without watching her son die in the hands of a cruel stranger. Tears of anger, frustration, and fear welled up and flowed down her cheeks.

Excitement outside began to grow, and she realized that the newcomers, or newcomer, must have entered the village. Sky rolled his eyes to look at her, and she shook her head in a warning. He *must* make no sound.

She could see nothing. The position in which she had been placed had been selected so that she could not look outside. For the same reason, no one outside could see the captives. She listened to the mutter of talk among the Shaved-heads, and realized that their leaders must be talking in signs with the newcomers.

Another quick glance at her son . . . Dove did not want to appear too concerned, both for his sake and for the old woman. The flat, unemotional expression of that one told that she would slit the boy's throat without hesitation if the situation called for it. Sky's face, though showing fright and concern, certainly revealed no panic. Dove tried to appear more confident than she felt, nodding to him reassuringly. It was a terrible moment, one which could result in the deaths of her entire family in the space of a few heartbeats if things went wrong.

Again, the urgency of the situation thrust itself upon her. *Who* was out there, trying to negotiate with her captors? She fought down panic, and forced herself to think more calmly. Since they were here, at least one of her companions, it must be that they were aware of her capture. Of course, they had followed the trail. Knowing this, they would negotiate cautiously, while they tried to learn where she and Sky were being held. Probably they knew already, because all three of the men were clever and observant.

She still did not know how many of the three had survived, or whom it might be. Her greatest concern in that respect was for her husband. She had *seen* him pulled under. But of the three, his was the most powerful medicine. She must hold fast to the faith that he *had* survived. Whether by his great physical strength or by his spirit-powers, it made no difference. He could change himself into a white wolf. Why not into a fish if he chose, to swim out of the danger?

Outside, there seemed to be some kind of a decision. Movement, a milling around of the crowd, and then she heard an excited ripple in the crowd. Then a long pause. She heard the crackle of a newly kindled fire. Yes, of course. They would need a fire for council. Probably Odin would start it with the striker, making a great ceremony out of it.

As if in answer to her thoughts of a ritual, there began a singsong chant outside. Quickly, she recognized the voice of her brother.

"We have come to help you, my sister. Be ready. . . ." Odin chanted.

His song went on, mixing his message with sounds that were pure nonsense, to keep the rhythm of the chant. Now there was a pause in the song, and a gasp from the crowd. The fire? No, that had been already crackling. Something else . . . She did not know the fate of her husband, but now that question was answered in a wonderfully reassuring way.

"Odin, the tree on the ridge to the north . . ."

Tears of relief flowed freely, and she tried to stifle her joy at the sound of his voice. All three must be alive, then.

There was more conversation outside, but it was in hand signs, so she could not tell what they said. But her confidence was rising. The others were all alive, and she had faith that they would devise a plan. She must be ready.

The council outside dragged on. They were probably exchanging stories, and that was good. It gave the men of the People a chance to learn all they could about these Shaved-heads. Her own situation had relaxed now, too. The old woman put her knife away and released young Sky, who crept over to sit beside his mother. There were more signed threats, and Dove nodded agreement. She spoke softly and briefly to Sky, urging on him the need to continue his silence. The old woman stared harshly at them, and finally signed once more a demand for silence. Dove nodded agreement. Now they must wait. For what, she was not quite sure, but when it happened she would know, and she and Sky must be ready.

The three men of the People readied for the night with a great show of preparation. They spread sleeping robes around their small campfire, gathered a pile of sticks, and appeared to settle in. They even carried a brand from the council fire to light their small one. To use the striker again would be to draw more attention, and they wished to be as inconspicuous as possible.

They were busily planning, though.

"You see the lodge where they are held?" Snake asked.

"Do not look at it," Odin warned.

"Of course. But see, it is on the edge of the town. We could come around behind it."

"They will be looking for that," Nils protested. "They are probably watching us now."

"That is true. But something to take their attention away. A fire, maybe?" Snake pointed with a toss of his head toward the nearest of the grass-thatched lodges.

"Yes!" Odin agreed. "But that will make them very angry."

"They will want to kill us anyway, when we free Dove," Nils said.

"Yes. We must be ready to move all at once," Odin agreed. "And they may be tied."

"Let me see what I can learn," Snake suggested. "When the fire darkens some, I will go. I am made to think that one man watches us from the trees to the north, there."

"Yes, I saw him, too," Odin said.

The autumn night was uncomfortably cool, but they made an extra show of preparing beds and bringing firewood. They moved around, changed places, anything to confuse an observer, while pretending that they did not know they were watched. They rolled themselves in their robes and allowed the fire's light to die. Then one of them rose to replenish it.

By the new light the observer saw two other sleeping forms on the ground, but was unaware that one of those beds had no occupant. That robe was arranged with sticks and a rawhide pack to appear that someone slept there.

Snake returned during the next period of darkness, sliding back to his bed and rearranging the robes. Then he sat up, threw a couple of sticks on the embers, and began to tell of his findings.

"One man watches us, as we thought," he said. "Another, near the lodge where Dove and the boy are. That one is lazy, half-asleep. This one, more dangerous. I am made to think we must take down both."

The planning continued, quiet talk as they openly warmed themselves by the newly rekindled fire. The position of the Seven Hunters told that the night was more than half over.

"Afterward, we should start back east, the way we came," Odin suggested. "They will expect that. Then circle, meet at the hill, and go northwest."

"But that is not where we want to go!" protested Nils.

"True. And they know that," Odin explained. "That is why we go that way. The first thing is to escape these Shaved-heads. Then we decide what is next."

Nils had to agree that it made good sense, though it was frustrating to head in a direction away from where he wished to go. But first, they must escape.

They stretched, yawned, and lay down in their robes again. As soon as it was dark enough, Snake wriggled out. The other two waited, quiet but sleepless, waiting for Snake's signal, the cry of a night bird. That would signal . . .

"There!" Odin exclaimed. "Snake's signal. We go!"

They parted, Odin with the fire-starter and Nils to circle to the rear of the lodge where his wife and son lay. There he would meet Snake, who had disposed of the sentry who watched them, the dangerous one. The night bird's cry signaled the completion of that grisly task.

Nils skirted the village and approached the lodge carefully. He did not know where the watcher might be. That clump of trees? There was the sound of a scuffle, and then silence. He knelt, close to the ground, to see in silhouette an approaching figure against the starry sky. He made a slight squeaking noise, like that of a deermouse, and saw the dark figure turn toward him.

"Snake?" he whispered. "Here!"

The warrior knelt beside him, breathing a little hard.

"It is done," said Snake. "Now we wait for Odin's fire."

Dove lay in the dark, listening, waiting. She could hear the breathing of other people in the lodge, and the soft snores of the old woman with the knife. Bright Sky snuggled against her, twitching nervously in his sleep. Gently, she touched him with her elbow. She did not know whether he would live to see morning, or whether she would see morning herself. She only knew that sometime before the dawn came, there would be an attempt to free them.

She wished that her hands were free, so that she could defend herself and her son when the time came. Well, Wolf would surely realize that they were helpless. She would stay alert and try to be ready. Meanwhile, she worked quietly at her bonds.

Now she noticed the square of the doorway, where the doorskin hung. It was fitted loosely, and there seemed to be a crack of light that was growing lighter. Surely it was not yet dawn. No, a fire! Of course! Her heart leaped, and she sat up. Bright Sky came sleepily awake.

"Ssh, my son," she whispered. "Hold tightly to my dress, and stay with me. Your father will come soon."

Nils watched, waiting for the spark that would begin the events that would lead to their escape or to their deaths. Snake crouched beside him, breathing more calmly now.

"There!" Snake whispered.

A flicker of light blossomed at the far side of the village. It took only the space of a few heartbeats until there was a shout, then another. People were running, screaming, the whole town coming awake. They must hurry. As Nils tore aside the thatch at the back of the lodge, hacking at it with his short sword, he prayed that no one had been designated to kill the prisoners in case of an escape attempt.

He half crawled, half rolled through the opening and collided with some-one in the darkness.

"Dove!" he called softly. "Where are you?"

"Here . . . right here. My hands are tied, Wolf!" Quickly, he slashed the thong and she gave him a quick hug.

"Where is Sky?" he asked.

"Right beside me. He understands."

A dark form rushed at them, a weapon upraised, and Nils hacked at it with the sword. His attacker screamed and fell.

The fire some distance away was shedding a growing, flickering light now. Figures in the lodge were silhouetted against the lighter square of the doorway, as someone tore aside the hanging skin.

"Out," urged Nils, pushing Dove and Sky toward the hole in the thatch. "Snake is outside."

A woman rushed toward them, swinging a short knife of some sort. Dove turned back.

"Wait!" She spoke a one-word exclamation. With the fury of a wolverine, she was on the woman. Dove seized the outstretched arm, pulled the woman forward, tripped her, and wrested the knife from her hand, all in one motion. She paused for a moment, apparently considering further mayhem, as the other woman lay gasping, the breath knocked from her lungs.

"Dove! Come on!" Nils cried urgently, pushing Sky on out through the hole.

Reluctantly, Dove turned away.

Outside, they drew in deep breaths of crisp night air and Snake led the way out of the village.

"Where is my brother?" Dove asked in alarm.

"He started the fire," Nils explained. "He will join us later. Now let us hurry!"

87

They were almost clear of the area around the village when it happened. Snake, in the lead, was suddenly confronted by a large dog. The creature did not appear ready to attack, only to bark. Snake raised his bow and launched an arrow to silence it.

Somehow in the poor light and flickering shadows, his aim was not true. It was not a complete miss, which might have been better, as it turned out. The dog gave a yelp of pain, and then began a thin, high-pitched squeal, running in a small circle and biting at the arrow in its flank. This would surely alert any pursuers to the direction of the fugitives' retreat.

Nils ran forward, swung his sword, and the dog stopped in midcry. But even that, he now realized, would help the Shaved-heads locate their position.

"Hurry!" he called.

They heard the sounds of people running toward them now. Three or four warriors, maybe. Nils could hear them calling to each other. He turned to Dove.

"We are to meet Odin on that hill," he pointed. "Go on. We will follow."

"No!" she insisted. "We must stay together."

Now he saw in the dim starlight that she carried a war club. Apparently she had picked it up as they left the lodge.

"It is good," he said, thinking to himself that it was not.

They could see the warriors rushing toward them now. Snake loosed an arrow and the first man stumbled and fell.

"Behind that tree, Sky!" Nils cried, giving the boy a gentle shove. Then he turned to face an assailant who rushed at him, swinging a club or ax. Nils ducked beneath its arc, coming too close for such a weapon to be effective. They grappled, wrestling for advantage. Nils thrust at the man's legs with the sword, and knew from the other's flinch that he had inflicted damage. He kneed the man's groin, and as the Shaved-head doubled in pain, clubbed the sword's hilt on the back of his enemy's neck and the blade swung again. He turned to help the others.

Snake was just finishing off another attacker, but yet another rushed him from behind. Nils started to his aid, but before he could reach the struggle, Dove stepped from behind a tree with a long looping swing of her war club.

Quite possibly the Shaved-head never saw it. There was a sound like the bursting of a ripe pumpkin as the club struck him full in the face. He tumbled backward from his interrupted momentum, and struck the ground with a loud thump.

"Come," said Snake, trotting on.

They would be tracked, but it would take a while, and their pursuers could not begin until daylight. By that time, they could be far away.

It was not yet dawn when the hurriedly assembled council met. White Heron was seething with rage.

"Three men, a woman, and a small child!" he ranted. "We have six, no, seven warriors dead! Four in the woods, two sentries, and one in his own lodge!"

"But Otter—" someone began.

"This is no longer Otter's trouble," Heron sputtered. "They have shamed us. We must catch them, teach them that no one does this to our people."

"Kill them all? The woman and child, too?" asked another man.

"She is mine!" protested Otter.

"Otter, you no longer have a say in this!" snarled White Heron. He paused, thinking. "Maybe we let one go, to tell that no one dares challenge us."

"Maybe the woman, after the warriors finish with her?" suggested someone. There was a chuckle or two, but no one dared to say much, with White Heron in his present mood.

"Maybe," Heron agreed. "But first we catch them. I will lead, and we will take . . . not too many. . . . Ten, twelve . . . A tracker . . . is Ferret here?"

"Yes, Uncle," answered the tracker.

"Good! You will go?"

The tracker nodded.

"It is good. We start when there is enough light."

The fugitives paused on the hilltop as the yellow first light began to dawn. They had spent most of the remaining darkness laying out the false trail back toward the river.

"Not too plain, but show the tracks of us all," Odin had advised. He had joined the others soon after the skirmish in the woods.

Now they stopped to rest and wait for light before starting on into unknown country. The pause would not be long, but they would need every bit of strength in the next days.

Snake was a little apart from the others, head bowed. Odin glanced at him, then took a longer look, rose, and walked over to where he sat.

"Snake . . . what . . . *aiee!* You are hurt!"

There was a wide stain of blood around a hole in Snake's buckskin shirt.

Snake nodded. "An arrow . . . it is still inside."

"But you said nothing!"

"What was there to say? There is nothing to do."

"You broke the arrow off?"

"No. Pulled it out. The point stayed in. I can feel it when I take a deep breath. That is harder now, too."

"What can we do to help you?"

Snake smiled. "Nothing. You know that, my friend. Today I will cross over and be with my wife."

He coughed, and wiped blood from his lips. Odin knew that his lungs were filling with blood, slowly drowning him.

"I will wait here," Snake went on. "If they find the trail soon enough, maybe I can take one or two to the other side with me."

Nils came over to join them. "What is it?"

"An arrow," explained Odin. "He is dying."

"But . . . when? When did it happen?"

"It does not matter, Wolf."

Snake appeared to be weaker now. "Go on," he told them. "You can be far away by dark." He paused to catch his breath, and smiled grimly. "I can be, too, I am made to think."

There was little more to be done or said. They made the injured man as comfortable as possible, and left him a waterskin and a few bites of dried meat.

"I will not need that," Snake protested.

"That is for your journey to the Other Side," Odin said.

"But that is a short journey, my friend." Snake smiled weakly.

Dove paused a moment, trying to hold back tears. "Thank you," she choked.

"It is nothing," Snake told her.

They crossed over the ridge and found a trail heading northwest.

"Let us try not to leave too many tracks," Odin cautioned. He would bring up the rear, destroying such sign as he could as he went.

Their hearts were heavy as they moved on.

Snake was drowsy. He had lost track of time, but knew that he slept and wakened, and slept again. Now something roused him, the alarm call of a crow in a tree a little distance away. He looked up at the bird.

"Thank you, Grandfather," he muttered.

He moistened his lips and waited, looking down the hillside along the trail toward the village. He was pleased to see that the sun was low in the west. Pleased for a number of reasons. It meant that his friends were far away now. Also, that the approaching Shaved-heads had spent an entire day trying to untwist the false trail. They would approach now into the sun, and would not see him until too late.

He fitted an arrow to the string and raised the bow, hoping for the strength to draw it. The first of the war party emerged from the trees and came toward him. The crow flew away, cawing loudly.

"Yes, I see them," Snake said.

The man in the lead seemed completely unaware as Snake held his breath and drew the arrow to its head, wincing against the pain in his chest. The string twanged and Snake knew that his arrow flew true. Otter fell backward, the feathered shaft jutting from just below the vee of his ribs. The other warriors scattered and flattened to the ground, as Snake lifted his voice in the Song of Death.

> "The earth and the sky go on forever,
> But today is a good day to die."

He tried to fit another arrow, but his sight was dimming and his fingers would not follow his instructions. He stared at his hands as if they belonged to someone else and he now saw them for the first time.

The warriors spread out across the hillside, but it was a little while before they realized that a lone man stood in their path. Or rather, lay there. When they made their final rush they found him staring at the sun, with a contented smile on his face.

White Heron stared at the dead man, and for a moment it seemed that he would attack the corpse.

"Son of a dung-eating dog," Heron hissed between clenched teeth, "you have beaten us. But your friends will regret it when we catch them."

88

I am made to think that we should mourn for our friend Snake," said Calling Dove, as the fugitives stopped at dark.

Unfamiliar country was questionable for travel at best. In the dark of night, it was impossible. There would be no moon, and they had decided at one of their brief rest stops to camp for the night when darkness fell. They should still be well ahead of their pursuers.

There had been a slight hope before the escape that there might be no pursuit. The intensity of the fighting, the loss of life, had eliminated that hope. The erstwhile captors of Dove and Bright Sky would not likely forgive such a defeat.

The fugitives had several advantages, if only at first. The surprise of the escape had apparently been successful, and it would have taken a little while to organize the pursuit. Then, Odin's clever tricks with the misleading trail could be quite important. And if Snake still lived when the Shaved-heads solved the mystery of the trail they followed, he would have found a way to delay them further.

All of these things were short-lived advantages when their entire plight was considered, however. They had not discussed it very much, but it was plain that their situation was desperate. It might be not whether they could escape, but how long they could survive at all. They would talk of it tonight, Nils knew, and make such plans as they could.

"Is it wise," he asked, in answer to his wife's statement, "to raise the sound of the Song of Mourning?"

Odin shrugged. "Why not? We are well ahead of them. Maybe a day, even. We see no signs of other people here. Yes, I think we should mourn our brother."

"We cannot do it right, for the three days," Dove admitted, "but we can show that our hearts are good."

So they carried out a semblance of the ceremony of mourning, there in the darkness of a cold and uncomfortable camp, and then sat to talk.

"Can we not have a fire?" asked Sky. "It is cold."

"Not tonight," Odin told his nephew. "We do not know the spirit of this land yet."

"But is that not the purpose of the fire, Uncle, to learn of its spirits?"

"Yes, Sky, but there are the men who hunt us, and we do not know where they are. So . . . maybe tomorrow. Here, wrap in your robe."

The boy was soon asleep, tired from the long day and hard travel. The three adults drew a little aside to talk of their predicament. All of them realized that the future, if any, was quite bleak.

"First," Odin suggested, "let us decide where we would go, and then how to do it, no?"

"We have the canoe," Nils observed. His heritage still spoke strongly to him. *A man without a boat . . .*

"But it is not here," Dove spoke. "It is two sleeps away, on the other side of the Shaved-heads."

"That is true," admitted Nils. "But would it not be good to double back? Confuse them?"

"I am made to think," Odin mused, "that they would expect that. Let us think, now. . . . Our first thing is to escape those who follow us. Maybe they will lose our trail, but I think not. And they know the country, while we do not."

"So what are you saying?" Nils demanded.

"That to use the canoe, we must be alive. Also, they may have destroyed it, or taken it away. We cannot depend on it. So let us set the canoe aside for now." He paused to chuckle grimly. "The thoughts of the canoe, anyway."

Nils nodded agreement. "So?"

"So," Odin said simply, "the Shaved-heads are that way, we go the other way."

"Farther away from our canoe!" snapped Nils irritably.

"Until we are sure we are no longer followed," Odin answered. "Then, if we want, we could go back and look for it."

It was plain that the canoe, which seemed to Nils the answer to their problems, was seen quite differently by Odin. To him, to return to the area where they had left the craft actually presented more of a problem than it solved.

"But we do not know the country ahead," Nils argued.

"And we never will, if we are dead," Odin retorted. Then he took a more persuasive tone. "Look, almost-brother. We do know some things about this country. There is a river to the north of us, the one that runs into the Big River, the one that ate your canoe! We can go northwest toward it, while we escape the Shaved-heads. Then we can decide whether to follow it down, past them again, or follow it *up*, back toward the People."

"But the People are far upstream on the Big River."

"Yes, but on this side of it. We will have to winter somewhere else anyway, Wolf. I do not want it to be near the Shaved-heads."

"I had hoped to winter with *my* people, Odin."

"I know. But Wolf, we seem no closer to them than when we left the People. We are not to find them this season."

It was the first time that this idea had been voiced, and it dropped like the chill of ice sliding into the North Sea. There was, too, the unspoken implication that did not escape Nils: if it is *ever* to be.

"We can try again, my brother," said Odin gently, "but another season. For now, let us escape these Shaved-heads, no?"

Nils was quiet for a moment. Always, Odin had a way of cutting straight to the heart of a matter. He was right, of course, and now Nils was wondering how he had overlooked the obvious for so long.

"It is good," he said in resignation.

"At least, what we must do," Odin agreed. "Now let us rest. We must travel as soon as light allows."

"Their tracker is skillful," said White Heron. "It must be the one-eyed one. I am still not made to think that the white-hair sees well with his blue eyes."

"He sees some things," said one of the other men. "The woman is his."

"*Was* his," snapped Heron.

Another spoke. "Maybe the man who killed Otter was their tracker. That would make it easier."

White Heron looked at him with indignant scorn. "That one was already dying when they laid the false trail," he pointed out. "Besides, it is never easy, when the enemy is this skillful."

"If the white-hair is truly a holy man," said still another, "is this not dangerous?"

At this, White Heron became furious again. "*I* am dangerous!" he shouted. "If we cannot catch or kill these few, who have killed our warriors and set fire to our lodges, we are not *men!*"

There was little more talk of that subject as they prepared to camp for the night. They were tired, having pushed since dawn. It had been late in the day when they found the dying Snake. Even in dying, he had taken another strong warrior with him. It had consumed even more daylight, for caution was required to assure that no one else lay in ambush. Finally, they realized that their quarry was gone.

And then, there was still the need to assure themselves that the fugitives had really headed northwest.

"Why would they go that way? They would want to return to the river!"

Painstakingly, they had untangled the trail, and by dark, those whom they followed still traveled northwest. The war party had not followed far, because of the tricks and deceptions in the trail. A deliberate moccasin track here, a broken twig there, a suggestion that the fugitives had turned off on a branch of the trail that led somewhere else. With each of these distractions, White Heron had become more furious and more determined.

Now they camped for the night. It had become too dark to untangle false trails.

"We will do better tomorrow," promised Heron. "We know them better now, and they are less than a day ahead."

It now appeared that those they followed were really headed north and west. An old trail meandered in that direction, used by deer and elk. It was roughly parallel to a more well-traveled trail along the river in that direction. The river trail, although plainer and usually easier, lay low and muddy at some seasons. This year, the heavy autumn rains had caused flooding, and the lower trail was virtually impassable in spots. In a time such as this, it was customary to revert to the higher trail, which followed along the uplands that paralleled the river. This upland trail was harder going, rocky and steep in places. But there were advantages to the fugitives. Higher points of observation allowed them to observe any possible pursuit. The rocky terrain allowed more opportunities to tangle and confuse their trail. There were, of course, more opportunities for ambush, so those who followed must be more cautious.

But how do they know this? White Heron asked himself angrily. *Are they not outsiders here?*

There was a glimmer of doubt in the back of his mind. Was this strange light-haired holy man *really* as powerful as his one-eyed assistant claimed? Surely not. The changing color of the stone . . . a trick of some kind. The seeing of the Star-That-Never-Moves, a lucky guess. The fire from a stone . . . well, he could not deny that it had happened. Maybe the shiny charm that had been used in the one-eyed man's hand.

But even as he thought of all these things, Heron had no thought at all of turning back. In fact, he was all the more determined. It would never do to let a party of outsiders such as this to cause him to lose face.

Originally, he had only mildly opposed the capture of the woman and child by Otter and his brothers. It might even be amusing to have a beautiful woman from an entirely different people around the village. Otter or one of his brothers could take her as a wife, and adopt the boy, who seemed strong and fairly quick. Heron would have had no objections.

His feelings had changed after the arrival of the men who sought the woman and child. The newcomers were obviously quite different from anyone who had ever been here before. Heron had had an uneasy feeling about it, and had urged Otter to give up the woman and be done with it. That, he now knew, would have been best. But Otter was stubborn, and the woman had been *his* captive.

If they had been able to foresee the events that had happened since, the council might have forced Otter to give her up. But the party of outsiders, even with the strange powers of the white-hair, seemed to present little threat. After all, three men, one with only one eye and one appearing old and maybe blind . . .

It had become apparent before morning that he had been wrong about them. The strangers had apparently known all along that they had lied about the woman. They had freed her and the boy, killed seven people, burned one of the lodges, and actually escaped. He still could not believe it.

Heron tried to console himself with two thoughts: One, the outsiders had not escaped without injury. The warrior who had seemed most capable of the three was now dead, even though the man had managed to take Otter with him. His other consolation was more of an anticipation. When they caught up with the fugitives, vengeance would be sweet. He hoped they could capture all of them alive, and played out in his mind what indignities could be inflicted. Slowly . . . yes. They could take plenty of time for the torture and debasement. Let the woman see the destruction of her husband's manhood, and then let *him* watch while the warriors administered *her* punishment. Heron smiled, an expression that reflected no humor, only vengeful rage.

89

ach day now seemed a little brighter, more hopeful. It was three sleeps since they left the dying Snake behind with regret, and pushed on to save themselves. There would be time later to mourn, to sing for the friend who had given his life.

They avoided contact with any of the towns or groups of lodges that they passed. They could easily skirt around such dwellings. Sometimes they encountered other travelers on the trail and could not avoid a brief interchange in hand signs. There was always risk that those they met would later contact the Shaved-heads and tell of their whereabouts, but that could not be avoided.

It was not even certain that they were pursued. After the first day they took fewer pains to conceal their trail. Either they were followed or not, and there was nothing much to do about it. They even risked a fire each night, sheltered from view and well off the trail. This allowed them to cook what game they were able to take as they traveled. Rabbits, squirrels, once a turkey. The adults took turns at watch, to allow rest for each. They were falling into a pattern of travel, hunt, sleep, move on.

There was the gnawing doubt, though, about whether they were followed.

"We hurt them badly," Nils observed. "Would that not keep them from following?"

"I am made to think," said Dove, "that it might *make* them follow us. These Shaved-heads seem very proud. They would look for vengeance."

Odin nodded. "That is true, what little we saw. Dove saw more of their ways, and she is right. But maybe we need to be sure."

"How can we do that?"

"Well, how far back could they be?" Odin pondered. "A day's travel? I will go back and see." He glanced at the position of the sun. "It is a little past midday. I should reach where they would camp for the night by about dark, then travel back to you by morning."

"But you would have no sleep," Nils protested.

"It is only like a longer watch," Odin said. "We must be sure, Wolf."

He rose from where he had rested, waved a quick good-bye, and trotted away on the back trail. Dove shouldered her pack.

"Let us go," she said simply.

Nils was not comfortable with this, but realized that it must be. They had succeeded with their original escape, but it was essential for them to know whether they were hunted by vengeful Shaved-heads. It would make a great difference in their manner of travel, not to mention their possibility for survival.

They camped fairly early, near the trail and with no fire. Nils would take the first watch, and Dove the second, close enough to watch the trail and greet Odin some time near daylight. It had been agreed that if he did not overtake them by full daylight, they would travel on. Odin would rejoin them when he was able.

Or if he is able, thought Nils, and quickly thrust such an unpleasant idea from him. Odin was experienced, and had proved himself a survivor repeatedly. He shifted his position against the tree, and glanced back over his shoulder at the two sleeping forms behind him. His heart was heavy at the danger he had brought on his wife and son.

Both were holding up exceedingly well, it seemed. There was no complaint from Sky, who now seemed to regard this as an adventure like the river trip.

The larger of the still figures behind him, Dove . . . His heart was filled with love for her. He had been so fortunate to find such a woman, here in a strange world so far from his own. Was there ever another such woman, *anywhere?* And he had repaid her love and trust with this. They were fugitives, in danger of their very lives, and she did not seem to blame him. That made his guilty feelings lie all the heavier on his head.

Dove stirred, sat up, and glanced at the sky. The Seven Hunters, in their circle around the North Star, showed it to be about midnight. She stepped a little way from their cold camp, behind some bushes to relieve her bladder. She had drunk much water before retiring, Nils knew, to cause her bladder to awaken her for the second watch. It was a practice of the People, one he had used himself.

She returned to pick up her robe and moved toward him, snuggling beside him with a short greeting.

"How goes it?"

"Good. I have seen nothing."

"Our son sleeps well."

"Yes. He is a good son, Dove. Much like his mother."

He spread the edge of his robe and drew her into its warmth, holding her close and enfolding them both.

"Good! You are warm to hold," he said.

His wife chuckled. "You thought I would be cold?" she asked.

"No. But it is good that you are warm."

She laughed softly again, the musical sound that warmed his heart and sent him into flights of fantasy.

"And you," she said. "Stay with me a little while to warm *my* robe?"

"I am made to think, woman, that it is not robes you want me to warm," he said seriously. He kissed her lips, moist and warm and eager. . . .

"You must get some sleep," she said a little later. "I should not have kept you up."

"I did not complain," Nils reminded her. "I will sleep well."

"And I must stay awake," she sighed, teasing him.

"You want me to take your watch?"

"No, no. You know I only tease you. I have slept."

He gave her a last kiss and rose to spread his sleeping robe where Dove had been before.

It was still some time before dawn that Dove came alert, at the sound of someone or some *thing* approaching on the back trail. She rose quietly and readied her war club. In a few moments, though, she thought she recognized the lone figure that trotted easily toward her in the dim starlight.

"Odin?" she called softly.

The man paused in midstride and turned toward her.

"Dove?"

"Yes. Over here. Sit."

Both sank to a sitting position and Odin glanced over his shoulder at the sleeping forms on the ground a few steps away. His breathing was a bit labored from prolonged trotting.

"They come," he said simply.

"I thought so. We did not look for you until morning. They are close?"

"No, but close *enough*. A half day, maybe less."

"How many?"

"Ten, twelve."

"Should we wake White Wolf?" she asked.

"No, let him sleep." Odin looked at the sky. "Maybe I will sleep a little. Are you all right?"

"Of course. Wolf took the first watch."

"It is good. I sleep, now."

Odin spread his robe and rolled warmly for a very short night's rest.

At dawn's first light all four were awake and moving. It was no real surprise to find that they were followed. In a way, it was a relief, because now they had some sense of *what* they faced ahead. It is far better to meet a real danger than to approach the unknown.

"We will try to confuse the trail," Odin said, "but not all the time. Just sometimes. Then they must be careful, be sure of *everything*, because they will not know which is real."

They moved on, Odin pausing sometimes to suggest a strategically placed footprint. At one rest stop he seemed to be studying a fallen tree that was balanced precariously on the steep slope above the spring where they drank.

"What is it?" asked Nils.

"Do you remember," Odin mused thoughtfully, "that people where we stayed one winter, who used deadfalls so well?"

"Yes. What—"

"Look at the log, there. It is almost a deadfall big enough for a bear. Those rocks above—"

"Odin, we cannot stop to hunt bears."

"Not bears, Shaved-heads."

"You are *serious!*"

"Yes, maybe. Something to slow them up."

"But it would slow *us*, too."

"A little. But if there were fewer of them, it helps us."

"They would never stumble into such a trap!"

"True," Odin agreed. "It must not look like a trap. The bait must be somewhere else."

He rose, walking to look here and there from various angles.

"They will reach this place just before dark," he said, half to himself. "That is good . . . the light . . ."

Even as he moved around, he began to prepare the trap in his mind.

•　　•　　•

White Heron and his war party came down the trail a little before dark. He had been on this trail long ago, and seemed to remember that there was a spring, a clearing—a good place to spend the night.

It seemed now that the fugitives were aware that they were still followed. Ferret had painstakingly unraveled the misleading trail, but it was slow.

"They are very clever," the tracker protested, excusing himself from the wrath of his leader. He had just spent quite some time assuring himself that those they followed had gone straight ahead. Ferret thought so, but there was a broken twig and one incomplete footprint.

Now it drew near time to stop for the night. The tracker moved on ahead, making sure that the main party did not wipe out any significant tracks or signs that would have been useful. He was certain, too, that they were gaining on the fugitives. The tracks seemed fresher.

Ah, yes, there was the spring, ahead. That must be the one that White Heron remembered. This was, of course, a good place for an ambush. He had no real concern for that, because three adults and a child would not waste a half-day's escape time to attack the dozen well-armed men of a war party.

So he moved forward with some degree of confidence, ready to relax for the night. Heron was only a few steps behind him, and the rest of the party strung out by ones and twos behind. Ferret was well out in the clearing when he caught a glimpse of something beyond that did not belong there. Partially hidden behind a tree, the figure of a man . . .

"Look out!" Ferret cried, diving for cover. Behind him, the straggling file came alert and men rushed to the shelter of the bushes along the bluff. Too late, they struck the tightly strung thong. The trap sprung, and the rumble of the falling log seemed to shake the earth. Other logs, brush, boulders, all came crashing down in a cloud of dust and debris, as the warriors scattered.

Only two were trapped and crushed, but others sustained injuries. Heron, who was just behind the tracker, escaped unscathed. By the time the dust settled, Ferret had realized that the figure behind the tree was an effigy, made of an empty rawhide pack, sticks, and dry grass.

he days and nights now melded together in a meaningless blur. It seemed that something should have happened to end the suspense. At some point the Shaved-heads would turn back, would they not? But it had not happened. In fact, each time Odin backtracked to see where their pursuers were camped, they were a little closer.

"I am made to think," Odin said seriously on his latest return, "that they will *never* turn back."

"But are we still in their country?" Nils asked.

"I do not know, Wolf," Odin said, exhaustion plain in his tone. "This is not about a place, though. Not now. We have shamed them. Besides, the Shaved-heads may not think of one place or another. They think it is *all* theirs if they can take it."

Nils said nothing, but he felt vaguely uncomfortable over that theory. The last time he heard it voiced in those terms, it had been at Straumfjord, and . . . well, no matter now.

"How many are there now?" he asked, to change the subject.

"Ten, maybe. It is hard to tell, unless I get too close. I am made to think we killed two with the deadfall. I saw another who limped, and I do not see him now, so maybe he went home."

"But they are closer now?" asked Dove.

"Yes. It is easier for them to hunt than for us. We have to stop, and they can keep coming while one or two stop to hunt."

"Sometime," Dove said, "we have to fight them."

Both men were startled. Both had hesitated to accept this possibility, even to themselves. Now, to have it spoken by this gentle woman . . .

"Maybe not," said Nils hurriedly. "They may turn back." But he knew that it was a false hope. It was as Odin said. They will *never* turn back.

He tried to think of some way to even the odds. They *had* cut down the size of the pursuing party somewhat. But not enough. The deadfall trap had only been a lucky accident. They would not find another such opportunity. Besides, the Shaved-heads were alert to such traps now. It would not work again.

One good way to discourage a war party would be to kill their leader, he pondered. Odin had identified that one, the big man White Heron, with whom they had exchanged stories. Heron had given the impression of being a stubborn man. If he led this party, it was probably his strength and determination that fed the others. To kill him would surely be a help, but . . . No, it was too danger-ous. If Heron fell, the whole area would be swarming with warriors bent on vengeance.

The tracker . . . they did not know his name, but he was skillful. Tricks and deceptions that Odin had believed to be foolproof were reasoned out or untangled in an unbelievably short time. To kill the tracker . . . No, it was not practical. Even if they could identify him, the same dangers applied. They would have to kill both the leader and the tracker, and at the same time . . . No, too dangerous.

They moved on, weary, discouraged, and hungry. Dove was right. Some-time, they would have to turn and fight. The fugitives would have one advantage, no matter how small: They could pick the time and place.

That was small comfort.

Heron looked around the circle of sleeping forms. Ten! Ten, counting himself. They had been a war party of fourteen when they left the village. Each time he went through this process of counting numbers he became furious all over again. Seven, they had lost in the initial escape, before the war party even formed. Then the dying man on the hill . . . that one had earned respect, taking Otter with him . . . *eight.*

The trap set by the fugitives had been a complete surprise, and had claimed two more good men. *Ten.* High Hawk had been injured badly enough to turn back, and now there were only ten left in the war party. A couple of those still limped.

From time to time there was a dim warning in the deep recesses of his mind. Maybe the powers of this strange holy man . . . *No!* He would not admit such a thing. These were only people, who by trickery and luck had made *his* people look foolish. They must die. Moreover, they must die slowly, *pleading* to die. Only then would his vengeance be complete.

He tossed another stick on the fire, watched it smoke, catch fire, and begin to blaze. Two men approached and he glanced up, noting the look of concern on their faces.

"We would speak with you, Heron."

He was startled. Was there something that he did not know?

"Yes, what is it?" His tone was a bit tense, and came out somewhat more irritably than he intended. *Well, so be it,* he thought.

"My chief, we have been talking of this."

"Of what?"

"This war party. It is not as we thought."

Heron felt his temper rise.

"What do you mean?"

"We . . . it is this way: This looked to be a short and easy war party, Heron. Three men, a woman, and a child. A quick thing, maybe a day or two. Some honor, some fun, home to sing and dance and tell of the victory. But it was not so. Three have died, counting Otter. High Hawk was—"

"Stop!" Heron said through clenched teeth. "You are a coward!"

The young warrior reddened.

"That is not true, Heron. You know that I have counted honors. Elk, here, too. Our bravery has never been questioned. But this is different."

Heron had risen from his seat and now glared furiously at the other. "The difference is that you have never become a coward before. Are you afraid of these strangers?"

"I . . . no, my chief. But the powers of this white-hair . . . can you not see? *Ten are dead,* Heron! Three since the war party started. Is it not unwise to challenge such power?"

"You call me foolish?" Heron demanded. It seemed for a moment that he would strike the young man.

"No, Heron, I only question. How important is it to catch these people?"

"They have shamed us!" raged Heron. "They must suffer for that!"

"But it is we who suffer! How many more will the power of this holy man kill?"

"It is as I said," Heron blustered. "You are afraid!"

"Not of battle or of dying, Heron. Of the strange powers of the White Wolf, yes! He is not of this earth. I am made to think he could crush us all at any time he wishes."

Heron grunted contemptuously.

"Huh! He could not save his own helper, the one who died on the hill."

"The one who killed Otter," nodded the young man. "The holy man's power cannot always stop such things. If they are to happen, they do. But think of this, Heron: They have lost one. *How many have we lost?*"

Again, it appeared for a moment that White Heron would strike the young warrior. The others stared, fascinated and unbelieving. One of their most time-honored customs forbade such a blow. Heron actually raised his hand to strike, which would be a dishonor not to the other warrior, but to himself. A man does not strike one of his own.

At the last moment, Heron seemed to realize that his leadership was in question. He lowered his hand and tried to regain his composure. Yet when he spoke, his voice was high-pitched and tight.

"If you question my leadership, you are free to go home. *Any* of you!"

There was a long silence, and finally one of the other men spoke.

"Let us all sleep on it, Heron. We do not question your leadership."

The confrontation was over, but it was a quiet and uncomfortable evening. White Heron moved among the warriors, making small talk, trying to joke and pretend that there was no problem. Yet it lay there like a sleeping bear in winter, ready to waken with dreadful destruction. Some of the men, Heron knew, would stand by him to the death under any circumstances. He was confident in the support of six. Two, he felt, maybe three could not be trusted. He completely avoided contact with Blackbird, who had challenged him. There was no point in crossing trails with such a man. In fact it would be good if the cowards *did* leave. Two, three . . . even so, he would have a strong war party. Seven capable warriors. They would still outnumber the fugitive men by three to one. Even if the woman put up a fight, it was a clear victory.

Heron finally rolled into his robe, his temper cooling. Now that he was alone with his own thoughts, he found that he did have some doubts. There was no question that something about the white-hair was definitely different, and that he did have powers and gifts beyond understanding. Even allowing for the expected exaggeration by the one-eyed assistant, here was a powerful holy man. There had been some impressive tricks demonstrated by these outsiders. Could it be that the holy man could really turn himself into a wolf? Well, so be it. He, Heron, had killed wolves before. Actually, the pelt of a white wolf might be quite attractive on his bed.

There was a gnawing area of doubt, of course. Such a wolf might be supernatural, immortal. If so, it could not be killed. *Nonsense*, he told himself. *Anything can be killed. A wolf . . . But what if such a wolf is mad?* whispered the quiet voice of doubt. That would be another matter. The slightest scratch from the fangs of such a creature meant certain death.

He tried to thrust such worries aside, concentrating on the anger he felt toward the traitorous Blackbird and his cowardly friends. That was reassuring, but the anger kept him awake. It was nearly morning when he finally fell into a fitful slumber, to dream of a wolflike creature that stalked him in the dim light of the false dawn. The creature rushed at him, and he could almost feel its hot breath as he looked into its hairy face and blue eyes . . . *blue!*

Heron sat up, relieved to be back in the real world, but still shaken. It had been so real! It was really dawn now, and the others were rising, attending to nature's call, yawning and stretching. A man trotted over, one who had been on watch.

"Two are gone, Heron."

"Gone? What?"

"They have gone home, maybe. Blackbird and Smiling Elk."

Heron leaped to his feet, his temper flaring. Then he managed to control himself, at least partly. He finally answered, trying to speak casually through clenched teeth.

"It is good."

"*Good?*"

"Yes. There is no place in this war party for cowards."

Eight, he was thinking. *Only eight are left.*

91

erhaps White Heron was fortunate that he had any followers left at all. There were whispers that he had gone mad, and that this whole war party now had no purpose except revenge.

Heron would probably have conceded that point. Now he was determined to catch and punish the fugitives. He knew that there were some in his party who whispered about it, but he did not care, not really. There were loyal men in the party who would back him in anything he wanted to do. They would keep the others in line. Any who were questionable in their loyalty were gone now. Blackbird and the other one. Sniveling cowards, the party was better off without them anyway. He was *glad* they were gone. The seven who remained, eight counting himself, were the reliable ones anyway. They could be counted upon.

Why should there be a problem, anyway? His party outnumbered the fugitive warriors four to one. Even if the woman was a fighter, which seemed a good possibility, those three could not prevail against eight skilled warriors. He almost hoped that the woman *would* prove to have spirit. It would make the process of subduing her more interesting. And she *was* quite beautiful, of course. Heron had agreed with the unfortunate Otter on that point. Even muddy and exhausted, with her hands tied, her dignity of bearing had been apparent. There was a look of eagles in her eyes. This was too good a woman for the likes of Otter and his brothers anyway. Maybe that was why Heron had felt so strongly that she should have been released when her man came searching for her.

Now it was different. Her fate was secondary to the primary goal, the capture and death of the men who had shamed his warriors. Even so, he hoped that they could take the woman alive. Maybe he could claim her. Yes, that would be good.

"Come," he called to the sleepily moving warriors. "Let us get started. Maybe we catch them today. If not today, maybe tomorrow."

The little party of fugitives was already on the trail, knowing well the importance of distance. They were becoming discouraged. Food was scarce, and they had not been able to stop and hunt for several days. All of them suspected now that there must come a day when the pursuit would end in a battle to the death. Their goal would be to maintain as much control as they could over the circumstances of that final meeting.

Odin, in the lead, stopped and seemed to be studying the trail.

"What is it?" called Nils from the rear. He moved forward, and the four gathered at a point where the trail branched. It was not a plain division of the path. The smaller of the trails was vague and difficult to see, winding off through the bushes that grew in profusion here. It was exactly the sort of place that Odin often chose to plant a false trail.

"Break a few twigs?" asked Nils.

"No," said Odin thoughtfully. "We have done that, and it slowed them only a little. I am made to think, though . . . What if we lay a false trail, and then *follow* it?"

"Where does it go?" asked Dove.

"I do not know, my sister. Here, it goes that way, away from the river. They know we are following the river, and to leave it might mislead them. We can head west for a while, then turn back north after we lose them."

If we lose them, thought Nils. But there seemed no harm in trying. It would be hard to worsen their situation.

Odin now took several steps down the main trail, leaving a plain track or two. He then stepped to his left, a long stride to an outcrop of rock.

"Wolf, you follow me a step or two, then step back into your own tracks, and all three start down the little path. Break twigs, make it plain. I will cut across to meet you on that trail."

It was done in a short time and they moved on, away from the river, heading into rough country, hoping it would take their pursuers some time to figure out the ruse. With luck, maybe they could escape altogether. None of them really thought so, but it was a good feeling, a change from the day-after-day sameness.

Even better, Odin was able to shoot a deer that afternoon. It had appeared on the trail ahead, a fat yearling, its spike horns sticking up like pointing fingers. It turned to flee, but stopped for another look, its last. Odin's arrow struck just behind the left ribs and tore forward through heart and lungs. The animal dropped, almost in its tracks.

Hastily, they butchered out all of the choicest cuts that they could carry, pausing only to perform the ritual apology. Packs of meat wrapped in pieces of deerskin were prepared for all to carry. Even Bright Sky would bear his own small pack of meat. They moved on, feeling better about the world and everything in it now.

Behind them, a buzzard turned an extra circle and dropped a little lower to see what lay so still in the clearing on a dim game trail. It folded its wings partway and dropped to land in a dead pine not far from the carcass. Another bird, a tiny speck in the distance, saw the descent, and veered in that direction, followed by another, and yet another. From a distance that would be a day's travel for humans on foot, the great black creatures began to gather.

"What is it, Ferret?" asked White Heron. "Another trick?"

The tracker was standing, staring at a dim game trail that branched away from the main route.

"I am not sure. I am made to think that this trick is the real trail."

"What? That makes no sense!"

"No, stay back, everyone. This trick, the little path, it is too easy, maybe. Let me go down the main trail a little way."

Ferret walked down the trail, stepping carefully, trying not to obliterate the trail he sought. He was completely out of sight among the bushes, a bowshot away now. Heron was growing impatient. Ferret suddenly reappeared, trotting carelessly and pointing to the west.

"They did take the other trail," he said.

"*Away* from the river?" Heron demanded. "Why would they do that?"

"Maybe because we did not think so. This man is very clever, Heron. He overdid the *false* false trail only a little. I might have missed it."

They hurried on, Ferret in the lead.

The day was half gone when they stopped at the top of a rise. The tracker stood staring at the sky ahead.

"What is it this time, Ferret?"

"Buzzards. A big kill. See?"

At least six or eight of the giant birds circled on fixed wings, riding the rising currents of air.

"That is a long distance away," noted one of the warriors.

"Yes," agreed Ferret. "But it could have to do with those we seek. Maybe they have made a kill, maybe they *are* the kill." He turned to Heron. "I am made to think we can hurry now. This trail seems to lead there, and we can gain distance by moving fast."

"It is good," grunted Heron.

They moved on at a distance-eating trot.

On another rise, well beyond the circling column of scavengers, Odin paused to stare along the back trail.

"We have made a great mistake, Wolf," he said sadly.

"What?"

Odin pointed to the circling birds. "They will tell the Shaved-heads."

"What?"

"The buzzards, over our kill. The Shaved-heads will see them too, Wolf," Nils said.

"That is true. They see what we see. But they will know by now which way we went, and that the buzzards may have something to do with us. This lets them hurry. We already took much time to butcher the kill. This lets them get closer yet."

Nils was nodding agreement, seeing the situation before Odin finished his explanation. "So what is to be done?"

Odin gave his usual noncommittal gesture, then began to speak slowly. "I am made to think that it is meant for us to face them."

"Face them? Odin, that is madness. They would not talk. They hunt us like animals, to kill us." He glanced sideways at his wife and son, thinking but not speaking of other fates reserved for them.

"Yes, I know. We must fight for our lives." He paused and chuckled. "Wolf, we have faced worse!"

"But we did not have a woman and child with us. We had Sven-son."

"That is true. But, as before, we can choose the time and place. For a while, we can still stay ahead of them. Then, a plan will come. Maybe attack *them*, as they sleep."

"No, that is too dangerous. Too many—"

"Maybe not, Wolf. There are no more than nine or ten. Kill one or two at night. An arrow from the darkness . . . Soon there are only seven, maybe."

"But we would have to separate, or all four try such a thing. No, it is too dangerous," Nils protested.

"I could go back, find their night camp," Odin insisted.

"And if something happened to you?"

Odin smiled, amused. "That is true. You are helpless, no?"

Nils smiled. "No, but—"

"I understand, Wolf. But let me go back to see where they are. Then we keep going. A plan will happen."

It was well past dark in their cold dark camp when Odin rejoined the other three.

"How is it, my brother?" asked Calling Dove eagerly.

"One less," Odin said. "Their sentry. This will make them cautious, slow them some."

"How many now?" asked Nils.

"That, too, is something to speak of," Odin said, sounding a bit puzzled. "I counted only eight men. Seven, now. Some must have gone home."

"But why?" Nils asked.

"Who knows what a Shaved-head thinks? But maybe their leader is losing his power. I am made to think that this is good, Wolf."

"There are still seven," Dove reminded dryly.

"Yes, my sister. But remember, we will choose the time and place to fight. You can still use your war club?"

She started to retort, but realized that her brother was teasing her.

"Maybe," she said. "But only if you need help."

Still the situation was more serious than that, and they were all well aware of it. They quickened their pace the next morning, starting before it was fully light. They were well aware that their pursuers, too, would be sure to start as early as possible. The Shaved-heads would also have an additional motive for vengeance. Odin had furnished them that, with the arrow that had struck down the sentry.

But that could not be helped. One advantage the fugitives had this morning. It was no longer necessary to try to lay false trails, for the pursuers were too close.

This, of course, provided an advantage that was available to the Shaved-heads as well. This was no longer a contest of skill and wits, but one of speed.

No one mentioned, but all of the fugitives were well aware, that the war party was unencumbered by a woman and child.

92

The land was a little different now. The broad flat flood plain along the river had given way to rougher country. Rocky hills and ravines rose in seemingly endless array. The traveling was rougher, but to balance that disadvantage, there were more and better places to hide, or to elude pursuers.

The trail they followed had turned and twisted, branched, and joined others. It was practically impossible to decide which was the main trail, or if such a thing actually existed. All were probably game trails, used since the beginning of time and appropriated for use by whatever humans happened along. This would explain their wandering nature, the seeking for the easiest path in a general direction. Nils thought of an expression from home, "as crooked as a cow path." For the first time he fully understood it. True, the animals involved were deer and elk rather than the cattle and sheep of his homeland, but the principle was the same. The meandering, the search for the easiest way . . . not a bad way, really.

The network of these dim trails allowed the fugitives to maintain their general direction. Odin insisted that they maintain their northwesterly course, which would eventually bring them closer to the People. It was not a matter of great discussion. Direction was not particularly important anyway, compared to escape. The northwest direction did, however, take them out of the territory of the Shaved-heads. At least, they thought so. There was no way to know for sure.

Twice they had resorted to the sun-stone to reestablish that direction. When the sky had been overcast and fog lay heavy in the hollows, it was hard to maintain a sense of direction. It was at such times that Nils felt enclosed, entrapped by the trees and rocks around him. He longed for open skies and far horizons, the high seas, with a fast ship under his feet, responding to the wind in her sails.

Increasingly, however, their position seemed to become more hopeless. They had not discussed it, but it was apparent that they could not play cat and mouse in the rocky hills and glens indefinitely. Food was in short supply, and they could not pause for very long because the Shaved-heads dogged at their heels. Several times they had seen the war party behind them, perhaps crossing the bare knob of a hill that they themselves had crossed earlier in the day. It was hard for Nils to estimate distances, because much of the travel now was up and down the hills, rather than across the land.

They were tired, bone-tired, gaunt and drawn, and sometimes it seemed that they could not go on. They would stop to rest, and fall asleep for a few moments from sheer exhaustion. Only the fear of what lay behind would thrust them back on their feet to move on.

Each morning, after a fitful night's sleep, things seemed a little brighter. Enough so that they kept moving, at least. All of the adults knew, however, that the time was drawing near when they must choose the place to make the last stand. Probably sooner, rather than later, because each day they grew weaker.

The level, grassy valley was pleasant to see. They came upon it from the south, and it stretched for some distance northward. To their right, the valley was bordered by a ridge of hills like those they had been crossing for several days.

"Wait," said Odin. "Let us consider this."

"The travel will be easier in the open," Nils observed.

"True. But I am thinking, it places us in the open, where we can be seen."

"We could cross it at night," Dove said. "There should be good moon-light, too."

"Maybe," Odin agreed. "Maybe too good. But the thing is this . . . how close are those who follow us?"

There was silence for a little while, and then Odin spoke.

"I am made to think we must know. I will go back to see."

"But—" Nils protested.

Odin waved down his objection. "No. You go on, and I will catch up. Stay along the base of these hills to the right, follow them north. See the notch in the ridge, there? Wait for me below that."

He turned and was gone, and the other three plodded on.

Calling Dove was tired, and she knew that the others were, too. Just ahead of her, Bright Sky followed his father doggedly, step after step. The boy had never complained, though she knew this must be very hard for him. It had been hard for them all.

It was well past noon when White Wolf called a halt. They were near the notch in the ridge, and here they would wait for Odin. Then they could decide whether to head west across the valley, move on northward along the shoulder of the ridge, or try to seek refuge in its rolling hills.

They had not waited long before they saw Odin approaching along their back trail. He was running, and it was apparent that something was urgent. He trotted to where they waited, and stood for a moment, panting from exhaustion.

"They . . . come. . . ." he gasped, pointing.

Dove could not see the war party, but knew that it must be as Odin said. Once more, the Shaved-heads had gained on the fugitives. The final battle was ever closer. It was apparent that they could not cross the valley now, even by moonlight. Their pursuers were too near, and they would surely be seen. Likewise, to go north along the base of the hills would be too exposed. They must try to find refuge in the hills.

Odin, who was breathing more easily now, shifted his pack and started up the slope, following a dim path that angled back southeastward along the shoulder. Dove started to speak about the direction, but realized the situation quickly. The quickest *path* led that way, and direction had now lost all importance. The problem now was simply to find a place to try to hide. Preferably, one that would be defensible.

"Wait," said Odin suddenly. He turned aside and puttered around among the sassafras bushes.

"What is it?" called Nils.

"Maybe nothing. There is a canyon here."

The big, old trees had practically concealed that fact. Oaks, sycamores, nut trees, and the heavy underbrush effectively hid a deep and narrow cleft or rift in the hillside. The tops of the giant oaks that grew from the floor of the rift were *below* where they stood.

The trail they followed led over practically solid stone, a dark limestone that seemed to be a major part of the entire ridge. But it would not leave tracks!

"Maybe we can fool them one more time," Odin said.

He held aside a sassafras bush, and motioned the others down the steep face of the canyon wall. Nils led the way, turning to help his son.

It was a very dim trail that led downward. Odin followed Dove and tried to make sure that all traces behind them were hidden. They reached the bottom of the canyon, and Dove heard the murmur of water. She was hot and thirsty, and the sound was pleasant. The whole place was peaceful, sheltered, and quiet, with only a birdsong here and there. She felt protected, somehow, in the shelter of these massive gray walls and the canopy of leaves overhead. Even though it was late in the season, ferns and grasses were still green here in this sheltered place.

Dove looked around and gasped aloud. "Look!"

At the very head of the canyon, a massive ledge of stone lay across the rift, forming a cave. Its ceiling was high enough to stand upright, its floor several paces across. It would give comfort and shelter. The four weary travelers walked into its mouth and dropped their packs on the sandy floor.

"A fire?" asked Dove.

"Maybe later," Odin said. "Let us wait, for now. We can find water, rest, get some sleep, maybe."

There was a seep spring beside the cave, and a rivulet of water told of larger pools below. Dove picked up a waterskin and made her way down to the pool. She noted the rugged walls of the ravine. In many places, great slabs of stone like that which formed the roof of their cave had fallen away from the rim to slide toward the bottom of the rift. She saw one that must be three paces long, nearly as wide, and as thick as a man's arm is long. That one leaned almost upright against the canyon wall.

Her husband approached.

"It is a strange place," he said quietly.

"Yes. Its spirit is good, though."

He nodded, and they stood there looking around them, unsure what to say. In the power of the emotion that they felt here, anything that might be said seemed unnecessary.

Dove was unsure whether it was the depth of their own emotion or the powerful spirit of the place itself. But she knew that he felt it, too. It was fitting, she thought, to find such a place, on a day that might be their last. That thought itself seemed rather unimportant, somehow, though she knew it must be faced.

Even so, she was startled when her husband voiced a similar thought.

"This," he said calmly, "is not a bad place to make our last fight."

Dove looked at him sharply. She was thinking of the words of the death song, "today is a good day to die."

And a good *place*, maybe.

"Maybe they will not find us," she said.

He put his arm around her, and held her close for a moment. "Maybe not."

But they both knew.

•   •   •

It was late afternoon when the war party made its way along the path at the canyon's rim. Those below sat quietly, listening to the shuffle of feet and the words of conversation that they did not understand. Odin stood below, directly beneath the point where the rocky path led to the bottom. There was a moment when it seemed that the Shaved-heads had missed the trail and had gone on. Then, a one-word exclamation, and complete stillness.

The sassafras bush at the rim of the canyon was pulled cautiously aside, and a face peered down. There was an instant of recognition as the tracker looked into Odin's eye. Odin's bow twanged, and Ferret had no time to draw back, even. He toppled forward, tumbling and rolling through rocks and bushes, his limp form coming to rest against the trunk of a hickory halfway down the bluff.

Nils hurried quietly to Odin's side. Odin turned, a grim smile on his face. "That," he said, "would be their tracker."

By the hammer of Thor, thought Nils, *he still thinks we will escape!*

93

hey will attack in the morning," Odin said positively. "There is not time now, before dark. They will search for any other ways down, probably attack from different directions, if they can."

It was nearly dark, and the fugitives sat in the mouth of the cave, warming themselves at the fire. There was no reason not to enjoy a fire now. Those who sought them already knew their location and their status. They might as well be comfortable on the last night of their lives.

Even Odin seemed to have abandoned any other hope. The Shaved-heads could keep them in the canyon. It would be possible to survive there for a little while, with water and small game. Sooner or later there would come an arrow from ambush, or a knife in the dark, and the fugitives would be one less, then another.

But neither Odin nor Nils felt that it would be that way. It was not the manner in which the Shaved-heads did things. No, in all likelihood, they had explored the canyon rim quite well before dark. They would have noted any possible paths in or out of its depths, and would plan an attack to overwhelm the fugitives.

"Would they wait a day?" Nils asked.

"Maybe," Odin answered. "But we must be ready tomorrow morning. If they do not come then, surely the next day."

Nils nodded, deep in thought. He had been fasting for a day, not entirely of his own choice, but their food supply was nearly nonexistent. He had saved his share for the child. Now he found that he was past the hunger pangs of an early fast, and into the next phase. That, as he had experienced before, produced a sharpening of all the senses, a bright, crisp clarity of thought. He still saw no way to survive their present situation, but was able to assess it more objectively.

If they were to meet their pursuers in one last battle, let it be so. He could die with a weapon in hand, like a true Viking. His companions, too. Their ways were, after all, not so different. *But if a fight to the death is imminent, let it be on our terms,* he thought. The idea was quickly expressed.

"Odin, let us attack *them!*"

"*Attack?*"

"Of course. This gives an advantage. Not much, but we do not *have* much."

"That is true. Attack before *they* are ready."

"Yes! *Before* dawn, just before—"

"We can slip up and over the rim. They will have a campfire, will be sleepy, just getting up! It is good, Wolf."

Not good, thought Nils, *but better than waiting to be killed.*

They began to prepare themselves, though there was little to do. Their weapons had hardly left their hands for many days. Most of the preparation was emotional and personal. Calling Dove had indicated immediately that she, too, would go over the rim with them. The way she gripped her heavy war club left no room for argument.

"I do not intend to become a trophy for some Shaved-head's bed," she stated flatly.

She also took Bright Sky aside for a last lesson.

"I can go with you," he pleaded tearfully. "I can help."

"No, no, my son. But listen carefully now. You must stay here in the cave. If we come back for you, it is good. If the Shaved-heads come, do not try to fight them. Do as they say. But as you grow up, you must remember: No matter what you are taught, *you are a man of the People.* In this you must take pride, and remember our ways. When you can, go home to the People."

There was much about this that he might not understand, but she hoped that he would remember.

Odin was rebraiding his hair, making himself presentable for the crossing-over. Nils knew that Dove, too, would do so. He found himself wondering about what he should do to prepare for this final event.

He wished that he might send a message to his family. Well, they surely thought him dead anyway. They would have long since mourned for him, and recovered from their loss. Years had passed.

Still, he felt that he should leave some evidence of his passing. Maybe, sometime, another Norseman would come this way, and it might be of interest to note that one Nils Thorsson had been here. A bit of carving on a stone, perhaps. That slab down by the stream, maybe. It was so massive that no one could move it, yet smooth and flat on its face. He could stand to work on it, and sometime in the future someone could stand to read it easily.

A tool . . . all that he had was his short sword. Well, its point, finely tempered, would cut the limestone quite well. It would become dulled, but he could resharpen it. By sunrise it would matter little, anyway.

Now, *what* to carve? His name? Maybe, though pretty long. It should be something, though, to identify him. The colony at Straumfjord had known that he disappeared into the interior. Thorwald Erickson, too, had known. If he could establish an approximate date, and a way to guarantee its truth . . . In the clarity of his fasting condition, he now began to realize, the simplest way to convey that the message was genuine would be to make it in the form of a riddle. One that only another Norseman would understand. He could use the *old* runes, taught by his grandfather. How pleased Grandfather would be.

Nils returned to the idea of a date. The exact date? He would have to guess because Sven's bark calendar had been lost in the accident with the canoe. He counted days on his fingers. Early November, it must be, the Moon of Madness for the People. This struck him as an ironic joke, and he chuckled aloud. But did it matter?

"What is it, my husband?"

"It would be hard to explain, Dove. I was thinking of my grandfather. Thoughts that would please him."

"He is probably thinking of you, then."

"Grandfather is long dead, Dove."

"Of course. How else could he help you now?"

The hairs prickled on the back of his neck. The People were so straightforward, so understanding. No, not understanding. One can never *understand*, he had decided. Accepting. *Of course*, Dove had said, and she was right. He smiled. "Thank you, Grandfather," he murmured. Then he turned to the others.

"There is a thing I must do," he explained. "I would leave a message on the stone by the stream."

The others nodded. "I will stand watch," Odin said.

Nils approached the stone, stuck his torch in a crevice, and ran his hand over the smooth gray surface, planning the placement of the runic characters. Yes . . . nine in all, it would take. He placed the sword point on the rock and struck a gentle blow with a hammer stone he had chosen from the stream bed. A chip of limestone flew off, leaving a small linear pit. Another, and another . . . Each character would be a little taller than the length of a man's finger. Now a careful shaping of each letter in the old alphabet, not in the current one.

Nils could practically *feel* his grandfather's smiling approval from over his shoulder. In fact, he looked around. There was nothing of his grandfather, but the moon was rising, just past full. He felt a calm, yet at the same time an excitement and exhilaration.

He wondered what the Shaved-heads must be thinking about the clinking metallic sounds that he was making. They would undoubtedly think it a ritual of some sort. In addition, they had been liberally supplied by Odin with the story of the white wolf.

The entire situation now struck him as a great joke, one quite appropriate to the Moon of Madness. He paused in his stonecutting and raised his head to utter a long-drawn quavering wolf howl. *That* should give the Shaved-heads something to ponder!

Even as he did so, the entire scheme of the thing seemed to fall into place before him. It was still probable that they would all die in the morning. But was that not the entire purpose of the berserker, to go out with honor in a blaze of glory? And was that not also the purpose of the Death Song of the People? It was much the same, except for the frenzy generated in the Norse berserker. Maybe even that, he thought.

As if in answer, there came floating down the ravine the high-pitched, plaintive melody of the Death Song, sung by two voices a little way apart.

"The earth and the sky go on forever. . . ."

Nils raised his head and gave vent to another full-throated wolf howl. He could have sworn that there was an answer from somewhere beyond the next ridge.

• • •

"What are they doing?" demanded White Heron of his sentry.

The white of the young man's eyes showed plainly in the moonlight. He was very nervous.

"I do not know, Heron. A ceremony of some sort, maybe. That sound, like striking stones together, has gone on for a long time. I have seen nothing."

"Huh! They try to make powerful medicine, I suppose."

The young warrior nodded. It was plain that he would have preferred to be almost anywhere else this night.

Now a chanting song rose from another place in the canyon.

"How many are there?" the nervous sentry asked, as if to reassure himself.

Heron snorted indignantly. "You know there are only two men, a woman, and a child."

"I . . . I thought . . . maybe it sounds like more. Could anyone have joined them?"

"No one of this world," Heron snapped, and promptly wished that he had not said it. "Did you want to look over the edge to see?"

"No, no."

There had not been much incentive to stick one's head over the rim after what had befallen Ferret. His body was still lodged halfway down. At least, from what they had been able to determine from a quick look now and then. Now, with the chanting and the wolf howls, no one cared to take much risk.

"This is all a trick," Heron explained. "We will kill them in the morning, and they know this. They have no magic that can stop six warriors."

He thought he saw doubt in the young man's eyes, but decided to drop the thought.

"Blue Dog is across on the other side," Heron informed the sentry. "We do not know if there is a way out there, but we must watch. I do not want these to escape."

"We will attack them at dawn?" asked the nervous sentry.

"Yes, as soon as it is light," answered Heron, turning on his heel.

94

It was well before light, however, that Heron rose. He had not slept, and few of the others had. Soon, the sentry from the other side would join them, and they would be ready for the attack.

They had discovered no other satisfactory place to descend, so he planned to have bowmen on the rim to protect the first man or two into the canyon. All knew the general attack plan, and would gather as they rose.

The sounds below had ceased some time ago, and there had been nothing but silence from the canyon. He still wondered about the odd clinking sound that had taken place. It had ceased shortly after the chanting and the wolf howls. Those howls had certainly been disconcerting. A chill crept up his spine at the recollection.

There had been a while after that, when a continuous grinding or scraping sound had issued from the canyon, as if someone was rubbing something very hard against a stone. A bone or a flint, maybe. He could not imagine for what purpose. The ritual medicine of the strange, possibly mad, holy man, no doubt.

He still found it hard to think of that one as a serious threat, because of his white hair and blue eyes. Those marked him as old, and probably infirm. True, the skin of the holy man appeared young. The facial fur was white, too, and gave an odd appearance. Well, no matter. If the man was human, he would bleed and die like any other man. If he could actually change to a wolf, so be it. Wolves bled and died, too, did they not?

The moon was still giving quite a bit of light as Heron walked again to the sentry near the path's upper end.

"Anything?" he asked.

"No. Some slight sounds below. Nothing like last night."

"It is good. Are you ready for a fight?"

"Yes," came the answer.

At least the young man showed more confidence than he had earlier. "You can be a bowman here at the top," Heron said softly. "The others are rising. Soon, now!"

Heron turned to go, but caught a glimpse of motion at the sassafras bush that marked the head of the path. Something white, coming up and over the edge, a wolflike creature pulling itself up and over by its front legs. Then it *saw* him, and rose on hind legs to rush at him. Something—a weapon? was held in its right paw, and its white skin gleamed in the moonlight. The weapon caught the moon's rays and reflected them like the flash of a silvery minnow in a clear stream. Blue fire seemed to flicker along its edges, and the white wolf-man raised it to strike. Heron knew that he was doomed, even before the horrible screaming howl came from a half-human throat. He could feel the creature's hot breath, and looked for an instant into its hairy face. The eyes, wild and frightening— *blue* eyes.

Behind the wolf-creature, other dark forms were pouring over the rim, and he heard the chanting, as he had in the night. All of these things were happening at once, flashing through his senses. There was a sound of running feet from the campfire, the twang of a bowstring, and the sound of a falling body. From the corner of his eye he saw the sentry struck down by one of the dark forms.

Then the weapon in the naked wolf-man's hand descended. There was no pain for a moment, only a numbness that began where his neck joined his left shoulder. He could not raise the arm. The blue eyes glared into his for another moment and the creature leaped high over Heron as he fell, to attack another foe.

Heron's sight was dimming fast. He tried to count . . . who was left? Anyone? And in his ears, the strange wail of the chanting mingled with another unearthly howl. . . .

It was quiet now, the sun rising blood red behind the trees on the opposite rim of the canyon. Odin surveyed the scene, the dead bodies, and turned again to White Wolf.

That one sat on the ground, slowly coming out of the trancelike state that had occurred before, many years ago. Odin had doubted that they could survive, this time. Truly, the Norseman *must* have powerful medicine.

"We are not dead?" Nils asked, dazed. "Where is Dove?"

"Dove is safe. She went down to see about her son."

"It is good. The Shaved-heads?"

Odin looked around the area. "Dead, mostly. I am made to think there was a sentry across the canyon, but we did not see him. That is their chief, whom you struck down." He pointed to a still form a few paces away.

"Will they come back?" Nils asked dully.

"There is none to come back, Wolf. The sentry is maybe halfway home and still running. He will warn of your power."

Nils shook his head to clear it, and turned to see Dove climbing over the rim, leading Bright Sky by the hand. She smiled and came to kneel beside him.

"Are you feeling better?"

He nodded. "What now, then?" he asked.

Odin shrugged. "Whatever we want. I am made to think, though, that this is a sign. When we go away from the People, bad things happen, no?"

"Say more," Nils requested.

Odin hesitated a moment. "Well . . . do you want to go back through the country of the Shaved-heads to find our canoe?"

Nils thought about it for a little while, his head now beginning to clear. Somehow, it seemed vastly more important that his family was safe.

"We could start to travel," Odin mused, half to himself, "winter with somebody north of here. Anyone can use two extra hunters, and with your powers, Wolf . . . Then, on north in the spring."

Nils looked at his wife and son. Somehow, it did not seem so important now to learn where the Ericksons might be this season, or the next, or what might have transpired at Straumfjord. Or in Stadt. He placed an arm around the shoulders of Calling Dove as she knelt beside him, and the other around Sky.

"It is good," he said huskily. "Let us start home to the People."

Epilogue

I

Black Bear addressed his war party in the flickering light of their campfire. It was well away from the spot where the fugitives had entered the canyon.

"Let us consider now, my brothers. Shall we wait for these people to come out? Or should we attack in the morning?"

"It will be dangerous to attack," observed Sees All. "Their tracker is very skillful. He can be expected to have some more tricks."

"The woman, too," said another man. "The women of these plains people fight like men."

"Do you think this tracker is her husband?" said another.

"No," answered Sees All. "I am made to think we killed her husband, before. I have watched her. But the child is hers."

"Yes. But she is pretty, no? Maybe she would like a new husband tomorrow," said Spotted Cat with a leer.

There was a ripple of soft laughter around the circle.

"Do you think you are man enough for her, Cat?"

More laughter.

"We will see, come morning."

"Enough!" said Black Bear sternly. "There are decisions to make."

"I say we wait," said an older warrior. "There are only a few places where they can come out. We put a man or two at each—"

"How do you know of this?" demanded another warrior. "You have been in Madman's Canyon?"

"No, but what of that?" responded the other. "Some talk so boldly of going in to attack. Is it not dangerous to tempt such a spirit as this? Do you want to be the first to enter the canyon?"

"Those are tales to frighten children," snorted another warrior disdainfully. "I say we go in after them."

The answering silence told more than words. Brave warriors they might be, but to take chances with things of the spirit . . . There were few who would argue that it was worth the risk. There were many doubts, and not all were well informed about this powerful spirit-place.

One of the younger members of the party spoke.

"My chief, may we know more of the story of this place, and its name?"

Black Bear nodded, turning to one of the older warriors.

"Crane, you are a storyteller. Can you answer this?"

Crane rose, with the storyteller's instinctive feeling for visual effect. He placed himself at best advantage to use the firelight, shadow, and the thin light of the half moon. In the woods behind him, the listeners could hear the cries of night birds, and the hollow call of a hunting owl, like the cry of a lost soul. It was not reassuring.

"It was many lifetimes ago," the singsong chant of the storyteller began. "Many of the details are forgotten now, but the story lives.

"A people who lived here—maybe our ancestors—had captured some intruders. One was a very strange medicine man, with powerful gifts of the spirit. He was, maybe, a little bit mad. It was said that he could change the color of stones, merely by holding them in his hands. His party was spared by their captors, who feared these powers.

"But the captives escaped, led by this madman and his assistant, who had only one eye, in the center of his forehead. They were pursued, and took refuge here, in this canyon, as evening came on."

"As these have done?" asked the young warrior uneasily.

The storyteller looked at him sternly. It was partly the interruption of the story, but the similarity could not be missed. The storyteller decided to ignore it, and to go on with his tale.

"Just at dawn," he continued, "the war party was attacked by the madman, whose powers had caused him to change into a white wolf. Many warriors were killed before they managed to escape, leaving most of their supplies and belongings behind.

"Since that time, people have been afraid to go into the canyon very much. And that is why it is called Madman's Canyon. The power of his spirit is still there. It can be *felt*."

Crane sat down. The circle around the fire seemed to draw closer. No one spoke. Sees All tossed another stick on the blaze, and a shower of sparks flew upward. Despite this, the shadows that circled the firelight seemed to press forward, rather than retreating.

Black Bear started to speak, but his voice was tight and high-pitched. Embarrassed, he cleared his throat and tried again, with better success.

"Now, my brothers, let us decide what we will do."

II

Tracker rose sometime before dawn. He had felt it essential to sleep a little, but had drunk much water before retiring, so that his bladder would wake him early. He attended to that need, and glanced at the sleeping forms of the others in the dim light of the setting half moon.

There seemed little point in fleeing farther, but he wanted to get some idea of the enemy's strength, and how eager they were to attack. Possibly he could lead his little party up and out over the other wall of the canyon. The attack would not come before dawn, surely, but they would have watchers posted. Tracker had always felt confident in the dark. Maybe he could find and silently kill one or two of their scouts. That would slow the pursuit, because the war party would take more time to be cautious.

He had hardly departed when Elk Woman awoke and looked quickly around. Deer Mouse still slept, but Spirit Walker stirred, coming awake quickly. The yellow-gray of the false dawn was beginning to shed its ghostly sheen over objects in the canyon.

"Where is Tracker?" asked the holy man.

"I do not know, Uncle. I am made to think he is watching."

The old man coughed and spit, clearing the phlegm from his throat.

"Uncle," Elk Woman began hesitantly, "I have dreamed."

Instantly he was alert, attentive.

"What was the nature of your dream, daughter?"

Now she was hesitant. Would he think her crazy?

"I—I," she stammered. "It was probably nothing, Uncle. A strange dream of a warrior with white hair, though he did seem young, somehow. He . . . this is the strange part . . . it seemed that he changed into a wolf, and attacked the enemy. He ran howling up the path. . . ." She paused, confused. "*That* path, Uncle!"

She pointed to the rocky animal trail down which they had descended into the canyon.

The light was growing stronger, and she saw his eyes widen.

"What does it mean, Uncle?" Elk Woman asked in wonder.

The old holy man shook his head.

"I do not know, daughter," he said thoughtfully. "It may have been this man who carved the stone." He was silent for a few moments before he spoke again, and then his words came in hushed tones that were almost reverent. "My dream was much like yours."

Tracker reached the rim where the trail came over the edge, and spent a long time in watching and listening. There was nothing. He had already determined the best places for the Shaved-heads to post watchers, but these places seemed unoccupied. Puzzled, he reconnoitered each spot very carefully, then went looking for their camp. He had a good idea where that would be, a level area at the point where the grassy valley met the wooded hills.

He circled twice, still puzzling over the absence of the enemy. Finally, still fearing a trick, he approached the still-warm ashes of their fire. He could find no sign that anyone had even slept here. But he hurried back to the canyon, fearing that the campfire itself had been a deception. No, the graying light of dawn still showed no sign of their pursuit.

He climbed to a vantage point and watched in all directions until the long rays of the rising sun touched the valley and the hills beyond.

It was rising, too, he knew, on the distant Sacred Hills of the Tallgrass country. He left his post and hurried back toward the cave in the canyon. He glanced in the direction of the stone, whose spirit now seemed to him to dominate the area.

His heart was good, and for the first time in many days his thoughts hurried ahead of him. He was eager to rejoin those who waited below. It had been difficult for them, he knew, but they had not complained.

He was sure that the medicine of old Spirit Walker had helped to guide them. *Aiee*, what wisdom in the heart of that old man.

The child, tired though he might be, had never complained, and had done more than his part. Deer Mouse seemed much like his father, Shoots Far. Ah, it had been hard to lose his wife, family, and such friends as Shoots Far.

A lump rose in his throat as he moved toward the canyon. He thought of Elk Woman, widow of his friend. She had suffered the same grief as he, yet had managed to do her part. There had been no time to mourn yet. Now maybe theirs could be a shared mourning for what both had lost.

It would take time, but those who have shared much grief have closer ties. She had many fine qualities, was strong, sensible, enduring all the hardships they had suffered. And she was really quite beautiful. Well, time would tell. . . .

Tracker made his way down the path and saw the others waiting in the mouth of the little cave. He glanced aside at the stone with its strange carved characters as he passed. He could feel again the power of its spirit. He did not understand it, but must one always understand?

Aiee, Elk Woman looked tall and proud, there in the light of a new day! He strode up to the waiting trio.

"They are gone," he said simply.

"The Shaved-heads? *Gone?*" asked Spirit Walker.

"Yes, Uncle. They left last night."

The holy man nodded, as if somehow he had expected it all along.

"It is good," he said.

Tracker was looking at Elk Woman's face, and at the look of hope, though there were tears beneath her long lashes.

"Yes," said Tracker gently, "it is good. We are going home."

Afterword

R eaders may have wondered about the runestone. Is it a real place; does the stone exist? Yes, it rests in the setting described, just outside the town of Heavener, Oklahoma.

I had heard of this runestone, and finally took a few days to go and see it for myself. Frankly, I was prepared to be unimpressed. There are several runestones in various parts of North America, some known to be fraudulent, and I was suspicious. I came away completely convinced that regardless of any others, *this one is real.* The *feel* of the place, its spirit, as my Indian friends say, is very powerful. I decided to do a little more research, to verify or to refute my impressions.

This began a period of eight years of research and study (intermittently, of course) during which the manila file folder labeled "Vikings?" grew fatter and fatter. I learned that the Choctaws, when they came into the area shortly after 1800, knew of the runestone, and regarded it as ancient at that time.

Translation of the inscription, a date in the early eleventh century, was not accomplished until after World War II. Parts of it had been translated, but other runic characters seemed to be incorrect. Alf Monge, the Norwegian cryptographer who studied this mystery, theorized that it involved the use of both "old" and "new" runic alphabets. The new system came into use in the ninth century, so the date, November 11, 1012, *would* be appropriate for the lifetime of a person who knew both alphabets.

But what were the Norsemen doing at that time? It did not take long to learn that the Viking days of raiding the Isles were behind them, and they were turning to colonization and trade. Apparently the climate was somewhat milder then, and the longships crossed the north Atlantic regularly, colonizing on Greenland, Iceland, and Newfoundland. The colony at Straumfjord is historical fact. Archaeological excavations at L'Anse aux Meadows, Newfoundland, in the 1980s, are strongly suggestive of this colony. There is some evidence of trade along the east coast of North America, possibly as far south as the Carolinas.

But *Oklahoma?* I studied maps, and to my astonishment, discovered that I could put a Viking within a few miles of the runestone by water, by either of two routes. Now I was hopelessly hooked on the idea.

It was at about that time that I learned of one of the Norse epic poems entitled "The Death of Thorwald." Thorwald Erickson, brother of Leif, was killed by natives while attempting to explore the *"interior"* of the continent. The description of the locale is highly suggestive of the Gulf of St. Lawrence. The date was within a decade of that on the runestone. Further, the description of the round skin boats used by those natives is remarkably like the later "bull boats" used by the Mandans. But the Mandans were on the upper Missouri River, not the east coast, were they not?

I really did not want to consider Mandans in the novel that was beginning to shape itself in my mind. That nation has always been the subject of wild speculation, somehow. Mandans were considered "different." There have been theories that they were descendants of the Welsh explorer, Modoc, that they were one of the Lost Tribes of Israel, and everything between and since. I resisted joining such flights of fancy, but decided to spend a little time in the study of Mandans, anyway.

Again, I was in for a surprise. Mandan legends tell of a time when they lived far to the east, on a *salty* shore. Their creation story tells of men climbing from inside the earth by means of the roots of a giant grapevine. They came into the sunlight, saw the world covered with vines bearing grapes, and took some of the tasty fruit back down to show the others. Is it coincidence that the name that the Norsemen gave to the new continent in the same area was *Vinland,* because of the grapevines they saw? There are accounts of the wine-making activities of the colonists.

By now, I had abandoned the idea of having my fictional Norsemen sail around Florida and up the Mississippi, though this would be possible. Oceangoing ships do pass today within two days' walk of the Heavener runestone. The Port of Catoosa, near Tulsa, Oklahoma, is some hundred miles *upstream.* Norse longships could have navigated the Arkansas River.

But I thought it more likely that a lost Norseman might travel west with migrating tribes. It was quite common among native cultures until more recent times to "adopt" a visitor or even a captive. There was a distinct advantage to the acquisition of another hunter or fighting man. And yes, I learned, several of the Siouan tribes, probably including the groups who became Mandans, *did* migrate westward at about that time, A.D. 1000.

In the process of re-creating the overland trek, I attempted to learn what tribes and nations they might have encountered. Many connections are obscure, but it seems quite likely that they would have encountered the Cherokees in the northern Alleghenies, so this meeting is included in the story. I chose one of several variant spellings for that nation. Since written languages were rare or nonexistent, these names were handed down in oral tradition, and were completely phonetic. I chose Chalagee arbitrarily, with the advice and consent of Robert Conley, Cherokee author, who uses Chalakee. Other spellings include Tsallaghee. There is a theory that even Allegheny is a form of that nation's name, in the ancient Eastern Trade Language. That was a simplified mixture of tongues that would be analogous to the more modern Pidgin English.

Likewise, the Mandans and the Hidatsa seem to have become closely associated at about this time, possibly on the trek westward. It seemed logical to include this contact, but in a minor role. I had envisioned a meeting between the Mandan and Hidatsa at some point where both crossed the Mississippi. In my story, the Hidatsa have crossed, and the Mandans are building boats on the east bank to cross the following spring. There is some limited contact between the two.

Some time later I was startled when, in a reference book nearly a century old, I discovered a mention of the early association of these two tribes. The Mandan word for the Hidatsa was Minitari, "they who crossed the water." The Mandans' term for themselves however, was "the people on the bank." I had written it exactly that way several months earlier, in what I thought was a fictional account.

At any rate, this migration would put our lost Viking on the Mississippi watershed, still longing for a return to the sea, and home. Downstream, the tributaries that would lead him to the site of the runestone. An accident, capture, or pursuit might easily lead upstream on such a river as the Arkansas. Maybe even simply curiosity, and the explorer's classic mindset, "Because it's there."

There are very few Mandans left now. They were decimated by smallpox in the nineteenth century. But I talked to Indians of nations who were once their neighbors. All agreed that in their own various cultures, the Mandans were considered different. Light skins, different bone structure, some with curly hair

. . . "Just different." I had been talking to one man about this, and as I turned to go, he gave me another idea to ponder.

"Oh, yes," he said, "you know they had green eyes?"

I found myself uneasy about the possible Mandan connection. There have been many wildly speculative theories, including that espoused by Hjalmar Holand. Holand was convinced by the existence of the Kensington runestone in Minnesota that Vikings visited there in the 1300s. They moved on westward across the continent, he insisted, and remained with the Mandans in the Dakotas, thus accounting for some Mandan physical and cultural anomalies.

Holand wrote several books in defense of his theories. The Kensington stone has been largely discredited as a modern hoax, perpetrated by one Olaf Ohman and a couple of his fun-loving neighbors as a prank. The Minnesota Historical Society possesses a taped interview with relatives who knew of the fraud, but Holand remained unconvinced until his death in 1963.

It must be admitted that it is possible that the Mandan characteristics so often described are simply a genetic result of intermarriage. It is equally possible that there was some infusion of outside genetic material. It seems to me more likely, however, that such contact, if it occurred, was probably *before* or *with* the pre-Mandans' move westward at about A.D. 1000. The Norse are known to have been active in the area where the pre-Mandans lived. It was the appropriate time for an adopted Viking to accompany them on the westward migration. Actually, many of Holand's somewhat fanciful observations on the Mandans seem to fit this theory better than they fit his own.

By 1300, climatic changes had gripped northern Europe as well as America. Winters were colder and more forbidding and the north Atlantic crossing had become more dangerous. Seagoing powers were now the nations of southern Europe, where the crossing to America involved almost insurmountable distances. The continents were virtually isolated again, not by cultural change as much as by ever-changing world climate.

There was to be yet one more surprise in the production of this book. After the manuscript was finished, I learned of a new proposed translation of the cryptic message on the stone. To quote the brochure of the Oklahoma State Parks Board, ". . . research is never static . . . further discoveries or research could change the thinking on the history of the origin of the runestones."

Dr. Richard Nielsen rejects the Monge translation and believes that the actual message is a name: "Glome's Valley," and not a date. I have no quarrel with that, or with any other translation. That is not my area of expertise. My purpose is to tell a story, and that story is not about *what* the stone's inscription says, but *how* it came to be there.

What did Nils Thorsson carve on the stone in my story? We don't know. A date, a name? Was Glome the name of his honored Grandfather? Of Helge Landsverk's father?

Yes, it's all speculation. I'm sure that there are those who will be quick to criticize my premise. Of course, their criticism will be speculation, too. It, too, must be within the same historical framework and the factual geographic and cultural reality in which I have attempted to work. I only claim that within this framework of known fact, it *could* have happened this way.

Don Coldsmith
1995